Dear Arabesque Reader,

Thank you for choosing to celebrate ten years of award-winning romance with Arabesque. In recognition of our literary landmark, last year BET Books launched a special collector's series honoring the authors who pioneered African-American romance. With a unique three-books-in-one format, each anthology features the most beloved works of the Arabesque imprint.

Sensuous, intriguing and intense, this special collector's series was launched in 2004 with *First Touch,* which included three of Arabesque's first published novels written by Sandra Kitt, Francis Ray, and Eboni Snoe; it was followed by *Hideaway Saga,* three novels from award-winning author Rochelle Alers; and the third in the series, *Falcon Saga,* by Francis Ray. Last year's series concluded with Brenda Jackson's *Madaris Saga.*

This year we continue the series with Donna Hill's *Courageous Hearts* collector's series, and the book you are holding, *Seductive Hearts,* which includes three of bestselling author Felicia Mason's most popular romances—*For the Love of You, Body and Soul,* and *Seduction.* We invite you to read all of these exceptional works by our renowned authors and hope that you look for upcoming collector's series from Bette Ford, and Shirley Hailstock later this year.

In addition to recognizing these authors, we would also like to honor the succession of editors—Monica Harris, Karen Thomas, Chandra Taylor, and the current editor, Evette Porter—who have guided the artistic direction of Arabesque during our successful history.

We hope you enjoy these romances. Please give us your feedback at our website at www.bet.com/books.

Sincerely,

Linda Gill
VP and Publisher
BET Books

FELICIA MASON

SEDUCTIVE HEARTS

ARABESQUE

BET BOOKS™

BET Publications, LLC
http://www.bet.com
http://www.arabesquebooks.com

ARABESQUE BOOKS are published by

BET Publications, LLC
c/o BET BOOKS
One BET Plaza
1900 W Place NE
Washington, DC 20018-1211

ISBN 1-58314-659-8

First Printing: May 2005
10 9 8 7 6 5 4 3 2 1

Printed in the United States of America

Contents

For the Love of You

ACKNOWLEDGMENTS

I would like to extend a heartfelt thank you to the following people: Judith R. Hall and Tonawanda "Fondy" Korff for liking the original idea; Mary Anne Gleason for fixing the earrings and demanding more chapters to read; Lynette McLauren for laughing and crying in all the right places and giving me the term "goosehead"; Wendy Haley for introducing me to organized romance writing and for always having the best advice; the members of Chesapeake Romance Writers and the former Tidewater Romance Writers for constant encouragement; the organizers of the Virginia Romance Writers' Step Back in Time conference for putting together a dynamic and inspirational conference; Jesse E. Todd, Jr., for providing a retreat, a ready ear, and for always having his office open; the late-night crew at Kinko's—Cynthia, Chris, and Aldwin; Linda Hyatt for saying "yes"; and to The One who bestows gifts and makes all things possible.

CHAPTER 1

Kendra knew she was in trouble when she missed her second period in a row.

The nineteen-year-old college sophomore bit her lip and stared at her reflection in the bathroom mirror. *Pregnant.* The word sounded like a dread disease. So much for Oscar's assurances that he would pull out in time.

Having a baby might not be so bad, she thought, as her eyes dropped down to her stomach. She let her fingers flutter at the place where a small life might even then be forming. She and Oscar could make do. He was about to graduate. Even if he didn't find a job right away, they would have a few months to figure out the finances before the baby was born. She would probably be showing a little by the end of the semester, but at least the school year would be completed.

A quick calculation proved she probably wouldn't be able to enroll in classes for the fall semester. The baby would be born sometime in September. But with a little luck, some planning, and some sort of part-time job, maybe she'd only miss one or two semesters.

A baby! Kendra grinned despite her worries. Her café au lait complexion was smooth, her brown eyes bright with sudden anticipation. She'd been told often enough that she looked younger than her nineteen years. Sometimes she wasn't sure if that was good or bad. More than likely, proof of age would be required before they could get a marriage license. She ran her fingers through her loose, shoulder-length hair.

Oscar had a powerful physique. Their child, if it were a boy, would probably be tall and husky like his father. She stepped back from the full-length mirror to look at her figure.

"If you're a girl, I hope you aren't cursed with these hips," she said aloud while turning to the left and right.

Kendra was oblivious to the fact that she was put together well. It had never occurred to her that her curved hips, full breasts, and long legs were the topic of many male conversations on campus. She didn't view herself as one of the beauty queens who all seemed to belong to the same sorority. She just went to class, studied hard, and participated in a couple of the more academic organizations like the speech and debating clubs. The rest of her free time she spent in choir rehearsal.

Living at home, away from the hustle and bustle of dormitory life, limited her extracurricular activities somewhat. But being at home meant she had more time with Aunt Kat. Kendra and her aunt did many of the things a mother and daughter would do: they went to church and Bible study together, visited a senior citizen's home once a week, and spent time talking as they cooked their meals every day. Aunt Kat liked to bake; Kendra had learned to cook without recipes while working beside her day in and day out.

Sometimes Kendra wondered if it had been a mistake choosing to live at home rather than on campus. At times she felt cut off from the rest of the world, as if she were missing a great deal of what college was supposed to be about. But, she remembered with a smile, had she lived on campus, Oscar may never have noticed her.

They met late in September. Kendra had almost been late for class. Her car was getting a tune-up and wouldn't be ready until early in the afternoon, so she was taking a bus to school. She'd been standing at the corner stop for a good fifteen minutes. The book bag slung over her shoulder was heavy and the pile of plastic folders in her arms threatened to land in a heap at her feet. She decided to take a look at the bus schedule tucked in the back pocket of her jeans. Maybe she'd read it incorrectly and had already missed the bus to campus.

Concentrating on the maneuver that would yield the schedule without collapsing her burdens, Kendra didn't see or hear the low-slung convertible drive up to the light.

Oscar MacAfree watched the pretty girl's struggle. When a gust of wind blew her hair in her eyes, a smile curved his lips. She automatically lifted a hand to clear her vision. About twenty plastic report folders tumbled to the ground. Oscar shook his head. The light turned green and he had shifted the car's gear to go when the girl bent over to retrieve the folders. The way the tight denim of her pants stretched over her derriere immediately had him imagining them in bed together. The quick fullness in his own jeans told Oscar that there had to be some follow-up on this babe.

Kendra dropped the book bag off her shoulder and grabbed for the folders. It had taken several hours to get the workbooks for the speech club in order. And now the wind was going to blow it all away. She had retrieved about half of them when she noticed a man a few feet away picking up the others. As he reached for the last one Kendra heard the rumble and exhaust of the bus. Since she was no longer standing at the bus stop, the driver ignored her and kept on going, straight up the street.

"No! Wait!" she yelled, waving after the bus. But it was too late.

Kendra shifted the folders from her left arm to her right so she could glance at her watch. Her shoulders slumped. Even if she ran, there was no way she could get to her seat in Sociology 205 before the professor finished the morning lecture. Next to a political science course on constitutional law, it was her favorite class.

"Excuse me, I believe these belong to you."

The deep voice drew Kendra from her musing. She looked up, then up some more, until she saw the face attached to the massive body. Oscar MacAfree, all-star running back for the college football team. The scuttlebutt on campus and in the local newspapers was that he would be snatched up in the National Football League's first round of draft choices in the spring.

Close your mouth, girl, Kendra thought to herself. She tentatively reached out her left hand to accept the folders Oscar was offering.

"Thank you."

"Just missed your bus, huh?" Oscar said, indicating with his head the direction the bus had taken.

"Yes. Now I'm going to miss my class. I hope I can get the notes from someone," she said on a sigh while turning to walk back to the place where she'd dropped her book bag.

Oscar watched the sway of her hips and wondered how he'd missed her on campus. He was quite familiar with the residents of the female dorms. She must live off the yard, he guessed.

"You don't live on campus do you?" he asked as he helped settle the backpack on her shoulders after she'd stuffed as many folders as would fit into the bag.

"No. I live on Sycamore, a couple of blocks from here," she said before remembering her manners. "I'm sorry. My name is Kendra. Kendra Edwards."

She stuck out her right hand to shake his, but he just smiled at her.

"It's a pleasure meeting you, Kendra. I'm Oscar MacAfree. Look, let me give you a lift to class. I'm headed the same way but mine doesn't start for another fifty minutes."

Kendra looked doubtful. Even though she, like everyone else, knew who he was, he was still a stranger. Accepting rides from strangers was something she didn't do.

Oscar guessed why she hesitated and then smiled in assurance. "I don't bite," he told her, leading the way to the passenger door of his sleek, red convertible. "I'll even promise not to ask you out until we get to the building where your class is held."

Kendra laughed in delight and amazement. *The* Oscar MacAfree was flirting with her. Some things shouldn't be questioned, she thought as she let him assist her into the car.

Their first date was to the movies that weekend. Oscar pursued her for three months before she finally agreed to sleep with him.

That was a little more than two months ago, and now she was pregnant.

"Kendra, I'm home. Are you here, child?"

"Upstairs, Aunt Kat," she called in answer to her aunt's summons. Aunt Katherine, who had raised her since her parents were killed in a car accident, was the only family Kendra knew. She had been six when her parents died and had only pictures and fuzzy memories of them.

Katherine Edwards, a deaconess and head of the missionary board at Sixth Mount Zion Baptist Church, was just getting home from midweek prayer service. Kendra decided it might be best to wait a while to tell Aunt Kat about the pregnancy. First of all, she needed to make a doctor's appointment to make sure she was indeed in a family way, then she wanted Oscar to be the first to know. They would have so many plans to make.

Tomorrow was the day Kendra and Aunt Kat visited the senior citizens. They would spend the next few hours making and packing several dozen cookies to take to the senior center. She turned off the light in the bathroom and headed downstairs.

A week later, a telephone call from her family doctor confirmed that she was expecting. It was another three days before she was able to catch up with Oscar. His telephone line was always busy and every time she went to the athletic dorm to see him, she was told he wasn't in. An article in the campus newspaper reported some sort of problem about Oscar being two passing grades shy of graduation. They had had the academics versus athletics discussion one night after a game. Confident that he would have a long professional football career before settling into a coaching or cushy sports announcer's job, Oscar didn't share Kendra's concerns about having something else to fall back on. For her part, Kendra hadn't decided what she wanted to do, but graduation was another two years off, and she had plenty of time to make up her mind.

Standing in the athletic dormitory office, she amended her thought. With the baby coming, her own graduation would have to be postponed. The bluejean skirt she wore was short and showed quite a bit of leg. The school sweatshirt she had put on clearly outlined her breasts. Kendra's hair was pulled back and clasped in a ponytail. With the exception of a touch of lipstick, she wore no makeup. Yet the men in the room were obviously taking note.

"Would you please ring Oscar MacAfree's room?" she asked the young man at the desk. She smiled absently at the other three men in the office.

"Baby, why you wanna see him? Tell you what, I'm outta here in 'bout half an hour, let's you and me take a drive around the city," the desk attendant told her as he looked her up and down in male appreciation.

Before Kendra could decline his invitation, one of the guys popped the attendant on his head, knocking onto the floor the backward baseball cap he wore.

"Hey, man, why you do that?" he asked, bending over in his chair to retrieve the hat.

"You better cool out, my brother. That's one of Mac's women."

Kendra frowned at the description but noticed the immediate deference she seemed to get.

The attendant looked almost frightened. "Hey, no offense. I mean, I didn't know who you was and all. No offense, okay?" he said while punching in the access code to Oscar's room.

Kendra, still trying to assimilate the knowledge that she was "one of Mac's women," stared at him. Slowly she lifted her eyes to the student who had warned his buddy off. He shrugged, then went to pick up the remote control for the television. The others just grinned at her.

"You can go on up now," the desk attendant told her. As she turned to leave, he called back, "We're cool, right? Mac don't need to know about this. Okay?" Kendra's silence didn't assure him.

In the elevator headed to the seventh floor Kendra considered a couple of things. First, Oscar's attention seemed to be waning. If anything, after they shared sex a few times, he had virtually ignored her. He didn't call as often, the flowers stopped, and she could rarely, if ever, reach him on the phone.

Second, he had never offered her any true sign of commitment. She took a close look at the diamond and ruby bracelet on her right wrist. Oscar had presented it and matching earrings to her for her birthday in mid-November. She'd always remember what he told her as he clasped the bracelet on her delicate wrist.

"Kendra, I bought you rubies because I know when we come together, and it will be soon, you're gonna burn me up so hot that I won't be able to stand it. These rubies are a symbol of that fire."

She succumbed to the pressure and the pleasure less than two weeks later.

The elevator doors opened. A party was going on somewhere on the floor. The music was loud. She took a deep breath and headed to the suite of rooms where Oscar lived with some of his teammates. The resonant strains of a pop artist led to the open door of Oscar's suite. About a dozen jocks and as many women were standing, sitting, or dancing in the room. Oscar, flanked by two women who looked like cover models, was holding court on a sofa. One of the women was draped across his lap and seemed to be . . . No, it couldn't be, Kendra thought.

On a shuddering sigh, Oscar looked up, noticed Kendra standing in the doorway, and called out to her.

"Kendra, come on in and join the party. We're celebrating. Ahhhh," he moaned when one of the girls slipped her tongue in his ear.

Kendra recognized the team's quarterback as he walked up and handed her a beer. He wrapped an arm around her shoulder and drew her into the room.

"Glad you could make it, baby. What took you so long getting over here? Did you have to go to a prayer meeting or something first?" he asked. A few people, including Oscar, joined in his laughter.

Disoriented, confused, and on the verge of anger, Kendra shook free of the quarterback's embrace. Standing near the sofa where Oscar and the two women reclined, Kendra took a steadying breath and began.

"Oscar, I need to talk to you."

Laughter rippled across the room. One of Oscar's bookends buried her head in his shoulder and chuckled.

"She sounds like your Sunday school teacher, Mac. Who else calls you Oscar?" she cooed. Then imitating Kendra's indignant tone but adding a bit of sultry teasing, the woman added loud enough for everyone to hear, "Oscar, I need to talk to you, too." Running her hands over his chest, she whispered something in his ear. Oscar laughed, then kissed the woman on the mouth and pinched her behind.

Kendra's eyes widened. She noticed a sudden pounding in her temples. She pressed the icy beer can to her forehead for a moment, then set it on the end table before beginning again.

"Oscar, it's important. I need to speak with you. In private," she added when the two women settled even more comfortably in Oscar's lap and at his side.

"Hey Mac, Tony, check it out!" someone yelled from across the room while gesturing to the large-screen television that flickered without sound. Footage from the college's championship game was being aired.

"Turn it up, man," another answered.

In seconds, the newscaster's voice drowned out the music from the stereo. "Running back Oscar MacAfree has been cleared for graduation, college officials said today." Cheers and high fives filled the lounge area. Oscar had disengaged himself from the girls and was sitting on the edge of the sofa.

"Earlier this week," the announcer continued, "published reports said the senior, who is expected to make the first round of draft choices in April, would not graduate on time. The twenty-two-year-old MacAfree, who rushed for more than a thousand yards this past season, had said he would consider an NFL contract without a college degree."

The screen flicked to an interview Oscar had with the television sports reporter. Kendra bit her lip and tried to stop trembling. Everyone in the room had known about Oscar's academic crisis except her. She, who was supposed to be his girlfriend, had read about it in the newspaper and was now getting the good news after the fact, on television.

The announcer's voice filtered over her. ". . . athletic director said there had been a calculation error in the registrar's office. And in other sports news . . ." Cheers filled the room. Again the television's sound was muted. Rap music now pumped from the stereo speakers and Oscar was calling for a toast. He grabbed the beer Kendra had put aside, popped the top, and gestured for quiet as his friends gathered around with beer cans held at the ready.

"To fame, fortune, and football," Oscar declared before taking a huge swallow from the can. Amid more cheers and congratulatory slaps on his back, Oscar absorbed the adulation like a king among his loyal subjects. The music bounced off the walls, and Kendra's headache intensified.

Oscar danced over and grabbed Kendra about the waist. "Why the sad face, pretty girl? It's a party. We're celebrating my good fortune," he told her.

"Oscar, we have to talk. Let's go to your room."

"Yeah, let's go to my room. Talking's not what's on my mind though, baby. I've missed you."

As they headed in the direction of his bedroom, Kendra couldn't hold back her irritation.

"You didn't look too lonely to me."

Oscar laughed. "You jealous of those wenches? I can't even remember their names. They were down at the TV station earlier today and followed us back on the yard for the party. Don't you know you're my main thing?"

Kendra was doubtful but somewhat encouraged. If she was Oscar's "main thing" there would be no problem with them getting married. Their family was already started. And now with the graduation clearance, and with the draft coming up, it didn't look like they would have any financial difficulties. Maybe she'd be able to get back in school earlier than anticipated.

Oscar closed the door to the private room that was one of six off the main lounge in the suite. He pulled Kendra into his arms.

"Now, what was it you wanted to talk about, pretty girl?"

Kendra had come to cherish the endearment. Even if he'd never said he loved her, Kendra knew that Oscar was attracted to her. She wasn't sure why, particularly when the competition looked like the two women waiting for him on the sofa, but she felt secure in his approval of her and her ability to excite him. Tiny ripples of desire coursed through her when Oscar's mouth settled on her neck. She felt his hand unclasp her barrette and slide up to massage her scalp before descending again to stroke her breast.

He pulled her closer to him and she felt his hard arousal. It reminded her of what she came to discuss.

"Oscar, listen to me," she said, pushing against his chest.

"Baby, I am listening. I hear your body talking to mine in a serious way." He kissed her eyes, her nose, her lips. Kendra was melting before him, but she had a mission.

"Oscar, I'm pregnant."

He jumped back as if she'd slapped him. The desire in his eyes had vanished. He stared at her as if she'd grown two heads and a tail.

Very clearly and very slowly he asked for clarification. "What did you say?"

For a moment Kendra was frightened. Oscar looked as if he would hit her. She blinked back tears that had suddenly formed in the corners of her eyes. His murderous expression didn't bode well. She bit her bottom lip and looked up at him.

"We're going to have a baby. In September," she added tremulously.

Oscar whirled her around and slammed her against the door. Kendra cried out when her head and back hit the frame.

"I know I heard you wrong, bitch. I know you're not standing there trying to pass off some crumbsnatcher on me." His hand on her throat was cutting off her air.

"Oscar, you're hurting me," she managed to gasp. He let her go and she slumped against the door. He stomped away to stand near the bed.

"You expect me to believe that you all of a sudden got pregnant?" Oscar stalked back to her and Kendra braced herself. "Baby, I'm a star. I don't have the time or inclination to be saddled with a kid, particularly when I don't even know if it's mine."

"Oscar!" Kendra was outraged. "You know good and well you were the first and only person I've ever slept with. I thought you'd be happy about this. We can begin our lives together with the baby."

Oscar looked at her and laughed. "Begin our lives together. Have you lost your mind? I'm getting ready to begin *my* life and it doesn't include a kid." He looked at her closely. The tears that had started to trek down her cheeks softened him.

"Look, Kendra. I'm sorry about that. I know I was the first guy you were with. The brat must be mine. There are some alternatives here."

Hope flared within Kendra. After getting over the initial shock, she figured he had come to his senses. When he walked to his desk and opened a drawer she stepped away from the door. She ran the sleeve of her sweatshirt over her eyes to wipe away the tears. Everything was going to be okay. The hard part was over. All she had to do now was tell Aunt Kat.

Katherine wouldn't be pleased but she could be pacified with a wedding date.

"Do you want to set a date for before or after graduation?" she asked from where she was standing.

"Now," he answered. "As soon as possible." With his back to her, Kendra couldn't see what he was doing at the drawer. She smiled.

"Okay. That's kind of fast. Can we still have a traditional wedding? I've always wanted to walk down the aisle in a flowing white dress."

Oscar turned to her. He shook his head and with a snort came to stand before her. Kendra looked up at him and smiled.

"You just don't get it, do you Kendra?" he asked.

"What?"

He walked her toward the door.

"You were a good chase. It was fun. The sex was okay. I've had better. In time you'll probably develop a little more technique."

He was being so gentle that Kendra was sure she was imagining the ludicrous things coming out of his mouth. Oscar took her hands, which had been clasped together, and pressed something into them.

"What you don't seem to understand," he continued in the same tone, "is that I don't want you and I don't want the kid. Here's some money. Get rid of the problem."

She looked at him. He wasn't smiling. But surely he couldn't mean what he just said, Kendra thought. The small life growing inside her was their child. Could Oscar so callously consider it a problem that would simply go away with a wad of money? The deadly calm in his eyes told her he wasn't joking. Kendra opened the door and fled the suite.

She wasn't sure how she got home. As she pulled into the driveway behind Aunt Kat's car she wondered if she'd caused any accidents. Like a disaster video played over and over on television newscasts, the scene in the suite kept rolling through her head.

An abortion was something she had never contemplated. It had never really mattered. Until now. She glanced at the money balled up on the passenger seat. She left it there as she got out of the car. There were alternatives. She'd give Oscar the night to cool off. He'd see reason in the morning. Surely the scene at the dorm had been caused by too much alcohol and stress. Even if he didn't want to get married there were other things they could do.

Kendra let herself into the house and followed the soft gospel music to the kitchen where Aunt Kat was busy mixing cake batter.

"You're up late, Aunt Kat," she told the woman as she kissed her aunt on the cheek. Kendra then opened the refrigerator door and pulled out a container of milk. Maybe some warm milk would calm her nerves and get her over this next hurdle.

"The missionary society has its anniversary tomorrow afternoon. I promised to bake a couple of cakes. You were out late tonight. I thought you had some important exams coming up next week."

Kendra poured a cup of milk and put it in the microwave to warm. She'd forgotten about midterm exams.

"I'll pass with flying colors," she assured her aunt, who hummed along to "What a Friend We Have in Jesus" as she poured batter into the pans.

Kendra waited for her aunt to get the cakes in the oven before she approached her.

"Whew. Now I'm going to set the timer just in case I fall asleep on the sofa waiting for those to finish up. When are you going to bed, child? You know we have to be at the church for Sunday School by nine-thirty."

Kendra pulled out a chair at the kitchen table for her aunt and then one for herself.

"Aunt Kat, there's something I need to tell you," she began.

"What is it, child? You can talk to me. Now that I look at you, you do look kind of peaked. What's wrong, Kendra? You have a fever?" Katherine reached across to feel Kendra's forehead.

"No ma'am, I don't have a fever and I don't know how to tell you this." The microwave beeped that the milk was ready. Kendra sighed.

Katherine got up, got the mug from the appliance and set it before Kendra on the table. Kendra wrapped her hands around the warm cup as if it were her only anchor in life.

"Aunt Kat, I'm pregnant."

There was a stunned silence in the room. Only the music from the radio provided any relief. Afraid to look at her aunt, Kendra concentrated on the words of the hymn "Amazing Grace" now on the air.

At last, the agonizing silence was too much to bear. Kendra chanced a glance at her aunt. The woman, who was in her early fifties, looked like she had aged a decade in a matter of minutes. When finally she spoke, Katherine's voice was barely a whisper.

"When your Mama and Daddy died I took you into my home and raised you like the daughter I never had. I gave you food, shelter, and clothing and tried to teach you how to love God and how to be a lady," Katherine said. She looked beyond Kendra to a place in the past. She ignored the young woman's silent tears.

"Your Mama was a beauty. My brother, Charlie, fell in love with her the day they met. The night you were born I think I was prouder than they were. We had a little girl. You know your parents lived here in this house for a few years before they got a place of their own. After they died, I put you in the bedroom they had had so you might feel closer to them."

Kendra turned away from the censure blazing in her aunt's eyes. "Aunt Kat, it was an accident. I didn't mean—"

Katherine didn't let her finish. "You have disrespected and shamed me and the memory of your parents. You have disrespected yourself and most of all the church. I will not have a slut living under my roof." Kendra gasped at the insult and started crying even harder.

"Aunt Kat, I do love you and respect you. This was an accident. It was the first time I had ever—"

Katherine silenced her with a quick shake of her head. "I should have known something was going on when you started coming in later than usual. And I don't want to hear about how you let some snot-nosed boy violate your body."

Katherine stood up and issued the punishment.

"I want you out of my house before I get back from church service. I'm gonna pray for you, child, cause you're gonna need it. I don't want anything of yours in my house when I get back. I don't want to know that you were ever here. You've brought shame and disgrace on me and on this family. I'll never forgive you for that." She paused and closed her eyes. "I don't want to see you again."

Katherine turned and left the kitchen. She didn't see Kendra's head fall in her hands as she wept at the table.

It took Kendra most of the night to pack her belongings. She had no doubt that Aunt Kat meant every word she'd said. She had called Oscar's room, but there was no answer. Driving to his dormitory was her only option. Surely he would have calmed down by now.

Shortly after dawn, she stuffed the last bag into her car. She had backed out of the driveway when the carrier tossed the Sunday newspaper in front of her.

She put the car in park and went to retrieve the paper. She picked it up and rolled the rubber band off. Oscar's story was probably in the sports section. But she didn't get beyond the front page of the newspaper.

The big, bold headline screamed at her. MACAFREE KILLED IN CAR ACCIDENT.

Kendra fainted on her aunt's front lawn.

CHAPTER 2

Seven years later.

Malcolm Hightower eased the black Saab into what looked to be the last available parking space at the community college. He wondered again how he'd gotten himself roped into the role, albeit temporarily, of law professor. He knew a lot about the law but very little about teaching. Setting ground rules would be the first order of business, he thought, like no excuses for missing classes or turning assignments in late. He hadn't gotten any breaks in law school and he wasn't about to offer any to a group of paralegal students.

The roster of people enrolled in the course included sixteen women and five men. He'd already memorized every name. All that was left was attaching faces to the names on the computer printout he'd been given. Malcolm turned the car's ignition off but let the smooth and haunting melody of an alto saxophone drift over him. With a CD player, telephone, and portable computer, the console of his luxury car looked more like an airline pilot's cockpit than the front of a passenger vehicle.

Mentally running through the things he wanted to accomplish that night, Malcolm glanced at his watch. He was thirty minutes early. He'd wanted to arrive before his students, but by the looks of the parking lot, being early was late at this school. He checked his leather attaché case to make sure the course outlines, textbook, and assignments were there. Then he cut the power on the CD player, got out, and started walking toward the main entrance.

As a favor to the dean of the college, who was an old friend, Malcolm had agreed to teach the course when he'd gotten the panicked telephone call. A full-time professor had contracted malaria on a trip overseas and would not be available. At the time, Malcolm thought he'd get a kick out of teaching. Now he wasn't so sure. What if he was unable to explain things well? The law, a living and breathing thing to him, consumed his life. Would he be able to convey that passion to twenty-one would-be paralegals, or would they think him one-dimensional? He didn't care if they hated him. He'd despised Manfred Grafton, the arrogant son-of-a-bitch who turned out to be his best and most challenging law professor. But Malcolm liked challenges. So he'd given as much hell as he got in class and still managed to earn an A in the course. He viewed teaching as a new type of challenge.

As he walked down the hall, looking for his classroom, Malcolm noticed but did not acknowledge the admiring glances thrown his way by some of the women standing around waiting for the evening's classes to begin. The tailored steel gray double-breasted suit, the wing tip shoes, and confident stride spoke of power and authority. He was used to and generally ignored women's responses to him. Most of them just wanted one thing—to give him eternal grief—so he was oblivious to the sex appeal that he wore as easily as his clothes.

Malcolm located his assigned room and pushed the door open. Five students were already in attendance.

"Good evening. Are you here for courts and litigation?" he said in greeting, asking no one in particular.

A pretty blond woman who had been chatting with two women in the front of the classroom spoke up as they watched Malcolm comfortably settle a thigh on the edge of the instructor's desk.

"That's what we're here for, but who are you? Where's Professor Schaeffer?"

Malcolm looked the students over as he balanced his briefcase on his knee. "Dr. Schaeffer was doing some research in West Africa and caught malaria while in Cameroon. He's doing better now but won't be able to return to the United States for some time. I'm Malcolm Hightower, your substitute professor for the semester."

"Are you going to be hard?" another student piped up. Malcolm smiled as he looked at her sitting alone in the back of the classroom.

"Well, I don't know. Let's just say I hope you will feel academically challenged."

"There went my easy A," one of the blond student's friends groaned.

Malcolm and the others laughed at her comment. His rich baritone filled the room and washed over the women. He got up to inspect the various posters and informational fliers on a bulletin board and pretended he didn't hear the final comment from one in the group of three.

"It's gonna be a long semester if I have to sit here and look at that gorgeous piece of meat for three hours every week. Talk about a hard body."

By seven o'clock all but one seat in the front row was taken. By twenty minutes after the hour, Malcolm had gone through the roll list, had passed out and reviewed the course outlines, and was getting ready to give the class a brief overview of his background when the classroom door opened.

Kendra was mortified when all eyes turned to her. Being late on the first day of class was bad enough; not being able to slip in unobtrusively was downright embarrassing. And just my luck, she thought, the only available chair is right in front of the professor.

Not a word was spoken until she was settled and had taken a note pad and pen from her canvas satchel.

"Ms. Edwards, I presume?" Malcolm asked of her.

Kendra nodded. "I'm sorry I'm late. I was detained at work."

"Ms. Edwards, I and just about everyone else in this room work for a living. Yet we all managed to get here on time. This class begins promptly at seven. I'd suggest you take note of that and wear a watch next week."

Kendra mumbled "yes, sir," and bit her lower lip. She didn't dare look at any of her classmates. Only Malcolm saw the man in the back row wince at the tone he'd used with the late student. As Malcolm again picked up his introduction to the class, the man shook his head in disgust.

More than two hours later, the students filed out of the room with their assignments for the next week. Not a single one of them had expected the first night to last the entire scheduled time. Professor Hightower had definitely established the ground rules on tardiness and class length.

Kendra stood by her desk, waiting as the man who'd sat next to her questioned their professor on the assignment. Kendra felt it important that she let the teacher know she wasn't routinely late. The depositions had taken longer than she or her boss had anticipated. Late nights weren't the routine at the law firm where she worked as a legal secretary, but they weren't unheard of either. It had been a scramble to get a babysitter to fill in the few hours she was at work later than usual. Thank goodness for Nettie, her closest friend, who had come to the rescue.

Kendra had the opportunity to study the professor as the other student talked. She immediately noticed two things that she hadn't realized earlier: his gray eyes matched his suit, and the feeling she originally thought to be lingering embarrassment was something much more elemental. It had been a long, long time, but Kendra belatedly recognized it as the beginning of desire.

This man's skin reminded her of warm cocoa on cool nights. Using her own five-foot-seven-inch frame as a guide, Kendra guessed he was a few inches over six feet. While he wore the expensive suit like a badge of honor, and probably for the intimidating effect it imposed, she wondered what he looked like in casual clothing. After listening to him lecture, she imagined how easily he could sway juries. While he spoke with perfect diction, Kendra detected an oh-so-slight Southern inflection in his speech. The rich baritone was like honey meeting molasses on a biscuit hot from the oven.

Kendra laughed out loud at the image. She'd missed dinner and was thinking of Malcolm Hightower in terms of food. But she caught her breath on the thought of another type of hunger he could satisfy.

Malcolm raised an eyebrow. The sound of Kendra's low and husky laughter affected him like a feather caressing his body. He felt the telltale fullness that had plagued him since he first saw her. His body's involuntary reaction to the woman irritated him. She'd probably done it deliberately, knowing the effect her laughter had on men. And what was that last utterance, he wondered. It sounded like the type of half sigh, half gasp typically heard in bedrooms.

"Good night, Professor Hightower. Thanks," the other student said. "See you next week," he said including both Malcolm and Kendra in the farewell but leaving Kendra a long, lingering look that the professor missed.

Malcolm watched the student leave and vaguely wondered if he'd answered the man's questions. His brain was scrambled and he was none too pleased with the person who had caused the dysfunction. He clicked his briefcase closed and looked at Kendra.

When Kendra glanced up, Malcolm Hightower was staring at her with what could best be described as a frown on his face. She started forward.

"Professor Hightower, I wanted you to know I wasn't intentionally late. I work for a law firm and—"

"Ms. Edwards, save the excuses. Just get to my class on time, do the work, and we won't have any problems."

Kendra wasn't about to grovel. She straightened her shoulders, looked him in the eye, and said a firm "Good night."

Malcolm didn't realize he was holding his breath until the door closed behind her and he let out a weary sigh. He sat on the edge of the desk and tried to figure out what was so compelling about the woman and why he had been so rough on her. Maybe she deserved a lecture for being late. The jolt of sensual awareness he'd gotten when she stood framed in the doorway had taken him by surprise. With the elegant French roll hairstyle, conservative long-cut suit and low pumps she wore, he'd already pegged her as some sort of office professional. Her clear skin was enhanced by the touch of strawberry-colored lipstick she wore. There were more beautiful women in the world perhaps, but Kendra Edwards had the wholesome prettiness that Malcolm thought had long disappeared from womankind. It was probably an illusion she'd perfected, he decided, as he turned off the lights and departed the classroom.

"It took you long enough. What were you in there doing, meditating?"

Malcolm only grunted at his best friend and law partner Robinson Mayview III. Robinson represented the other active half of the firm Mayview, Jackson, Hightower and Associates and had sat in the class just to irritate Malcolm. He'd slipped in unnoticed with about ten students shortly before the class began. The scowl Malcolm had sent in Robinson's direction when he discovered his partner in the back row was interpreted by the students as an instructor who wasn't going to be much fun and would probably be a pain to deal with.

Used to Malcolm's moods, Robinson walked down the hall with his friend and continued in a scolding tone. "You were awfully hard on that Edwards woman, Malc. Didn't you say all of these people work full-time jobs?"

"Yeah, so what?"

"So maybe you've forgotten what it's like to go to school and juggle a job. Where's your sensitivity, man? Every woman you meet isn't like Monica."

Just the mention of his ex-wife's name set Malcolm's teeth on edge and added to the overall irritation he was feeling with regard to "that Edwards woman." He almost kicked open the door to the building but Robinson got there first and eased their exit.

"I have the court reserved for ten-thirty. Meet you there?" Robinson asked. Malcolm nodded curtly and turned toward the area of the lot where his car was parked.

Maybe a fast and furious hour on a racquetball court at the health club would ease some of the irrational frustration he was feeling.

Unlike Malcolm, who wanted to forget the encounter with his attractive student, Kendra used the drive home to analyze her reaction to the part-time professor.

First and foremost, it was unexpected. Hot on the heels of that thought was the fact that the man was her teacher and it was ethically wrong to get involved with a professor. "Getting involved" with a professor or any other man was so far from Kendra's reality that she didn't see any harm in the fantasy of what if. What if, for example, they were lovers? But Kendra's imagination refused to dwell on that most unlikely event. Probably married with seven children; besides that, the man didn't even like her. Maybe he was hostile with everyone. Being late to class the first evening was unfortunate but it wasn't fatal.

The class wasn't even required in her curriculum. She'd seen the ad for the community college's spring semester and thought it might be interesting. Working the elective class into the schedule of classes she was taking to complete her bachelor's degree was difficult but not impossible. She'd even worked out the child care dilemma so she could enroll in courts and litigation.

The lights of a convenience store caught Kendra's attention and she thought of her twin daughters who were probably still up and waiting for her. It had become something of a tradition with the family; just as Kendra quizzed Kayla and Karin on their days at school, the girls had fun turning the tables on their mother at the beginning of each semester.

Malcolm Hightower no longer on her mind, she pulled into the store's parking lot to get the girls a treat.

CHAPTER 3

After a bout of the flu that kept Kendra flat on her back for the better part of a week, she felt well enough to make it to her law class two weeks later. She didn't take any of the prescription medication she'd been given because she didn't want to chance falling asleep in class or having an accident on the road. She did, however, tuck a box of tissues and some throat lozenges in her bag along with the law textbook and assignment for the week. If she didn't push herself too much, she'd get through the night with just sneezes. She was grateful the girls hadn't picked up the bug since a quarter of the attorneys and staff at her offfice had.

When she realized she wouldn't be able to make it to class the previous week, she'd called Professor Hightower's office. The person who answered the telephone came through on the promise to send Kendra a copy of the assignment. She'd felt bad about missing the second session, but was prepared for the night to come.

She arrived fifteen minutes early and wasn't surprised to see him already there.

Malcolm almost swore out loud when he saw her enter the room. His reaction had been relief mixed with disappointment when Kendra Edwards failed to show the previous week. For a reason he was still unsure of, the woman had gotten to him. When he'd found himself daydreaming about Kendra, he'd made a date with a woman who owned an art gallery in town. They'd met at a reception and she seemed to understand and accept Malcolm's no strings, no rings approach toward relationships. If the gallery owner had been hoping for an energetic night in bed like they usually had, Malcolm disappointed her. A kiss on the cheek at her front door ended their night and it was all this Kendra Edwards' fault, Malcolm fumed. His body had been and still was begging for release. But not with just anyone.

Tonight she wore an oversized college sweatshirt and a pair of screaming tight jeans. Malcolm envisioned her long legs and full thighs wrapped around his hips. It was going to be another difficult evening, he thought. With her long hair pulled in a ponytail she looked a far cry from the cool professional woman she had appeared two weeks earlier. She looked about seventeen years old. At thirty-four, Malcolm felt like a lecherous old man.

Had Kendra guessed the direction of Malcolm's thoughts she never would have taken the seat in the front row. But she was determined to prove to this man that she wasn't cowed by his overbearing manner. Difficult professors were a fact of life. She probably would have made a better impression if her eyes weren't swollen and her nose not running. She'd barely had the energy to get dressed. Maybe coming tonight had been a mistake, Kendra thought as she pulled out the assignment and put it on her desk. Taking one of the cold pills seemed like the thing to do. She glanced at her watch. There was plenty of time to dash to a water fountain before class started. She grabbed her bag and got up.

"Leaving so soon, Ms. Edwards?" Malcolm asked. The four students in the room who had been quietly reviewing their notes looked up.

"I'm just going to—"

"I thought I made it clear the first night that my class is not one you should take lightly. You were a no-show last week, Ms. Edwards. You missed three hours of notes. I doubt that you're ready for the quiz we're having this evening."

It took Kendra less than ten seconds to make a decision. This man and his pompous attitude wasn't worth the aggravation; not when it was a course she was taking for the fun of it. Some fun. Not dignifying his baiting with a single word, and leveling a look at Malcolm that undoubtedly was reserved for things that crawled out from under rocks, Kendra walked out of the door and didn't look back.

Malcolm felt the first bit of trepidation when he collected assignments from his students. There, on the desk where Kendra had been sitting, was a neatly typed eight-page analysis of and answer to the discussion question. Maybe he'd been wrong about her. Maybe she had been headed to the ladies room when he shot his snide, not to mention uncalled for, remarks her way. He'd heard the other students' snickering after she'd left. He'd held her up to undue ridicule and felt less than the professional he knew himself to be.

But Malcolm was unprepared for the bombshell that came his way the next morning. He'd been at his desk for almost two hours when his private line rang a little before eight.

"Hightower," he answered.

"Morning Mr. H," a muffled and congested voice on the other end replied.

"Christine? Is that you? What's wrong?" he asked his secretary of five years as he took note of the time. Even though her workday officially began at eight-thirty, Christine Wright was usually in the office by seven.

"I must have the same thing your student had."

The sinking and sick feeling Malcolm himself had been having since the previous evening came back full force.

"What are you talking about, Christine?"

"Your student, last week," she managed around a sneeze and a moan. "She called, said she was ill, had missed almost a full week of work. She asked if she could get the homework assignment so I mailed it to her."

Malcolm closed his eyes and counted to ten. "Might this have been a Kendra Edwards?"

"Achoo! Ooh, sorry about that, Mr. H. Yes, Kendra. That was it. Pretty name. Sounds Celtic don't you think? Did you know she works over at Sullivan and O'Leary? Well, anyway, I put the message that she called on top of the Anderson file on your desk."

At Malcolm's request, one of the associates in the small firm had picked up the Anderson file and was handling the civil complaint. There was no telling what had happened to the telephone message slip.

"Thanks for calling, Chris. Hope you're feeling better soon. You know I can't manage without you."

"Don't forget you and Mr. Mayview have a two-thirty meeting with the representative from that welfare jobs program," she told him before ringing off.

Malcolm dropped the telephone receiver back in the cradle. Guilt was something he didn't wear well, but he was feeling it in spades.

"Damn."

Later that day, he was still brooding over how he had treated Kendra. After lunch with Robinson, he decided to walk back to the office. He had a little free time before the meeting with the woman from the Achieving Against All Adversities program. As he passed a florist's shop he thought about his secretary and entered the store. A large arrangement of mums and a fruit basket would be delivered to Christine. She'd enjoy the flowers while her husband munched on the fruit, Malcolm guessed as he collected the credit card receipt and turned to leave. But something stopped him.

He didn't question or analyze the impulse. Looking around the shop he spotted a vase of calla lilies. The softly elegant flowers reminded him of Kendra. Turning back to the surprised clerk he made a second order and asked for a plain card.

The Mont Blanc fountain pen he pulled from his inside pocket matched the wine-colored suit he wore. On the card he wrote: *Sorry I was such a heel. My behavior has been inexcusable.*

He signed the card Malcolm Hightower.

"I'd like these delivered this afternoon to Ms. Kendra Edwards at the law firm Sullivan and O'Leary."

He signed the second credit receipt and included a tip that had the counter clerk's eyes bulging. Malcolm hightailed it from the shop before he thought better of the impetuous purchase and how it might be received on the other side of town.

The meeting with Toinette Blue lasted less than thirty minutes. Drumming up support for a jobs program, the woman made the rounds of professional and blue-collar businesses in an attempt to get owners to provide employment to welfare mothers willing to work. Achieving Against All Adversities, commonly known as the Quad-A program, constantly fought uphill battles. Not only were employers skittish about an untried labor force in uncertain economic times, on many occasions the welfare queen stereotype reared its ugly head.

"All welfare mothers are not fat, black women who constantly have babies to get a bigger check," Toinette told the principal partners of Mayview, Jackson and Hightower.

"In fact," she continued when Robinson encouraged her with a smile and a nod, "sixty percent of the nation's families who receive Aid to Families with Dependent Children are white. And yes, there are people who find ways to abuse the system, that's true of just about every circumstance in life. But did you know that the average monthly grant for a family of three, a mother and two children, is just three hundred seventy-seven dollars? That's not going to finance a late-model Cadillac or too much of anything extravagant."

The success of the six-year-old program was evident in its alumnae, she told them with a smile. At forty-something, Toinette Blue was a striking woman, a fact Robinson took note of with pleasure. Her short natural haircut was streaked with silver. She told her friends that the gray had come in not as a result of a difficult or burdensome personal life. Each strand of gray, she said, represented a time when she had been told no since she started work with the Quad-A program. But she'd learned early in life that "No" could be turned to "Yes" with persistence and hard work. Toinette Blue wasn't afraid of hard work.

As she talked to the partners, she seemed amused with Malcolm. Despite his recalcitrant expression, she knew he was listening intently. With the partner, Robinson Mayview, she got the impression she was preaching to the choir.

Letting the young but attractive Mayview work on his partner seemed to be the most appropriate course of action. So the spiel that usually would have taken an hour was cut down to about twenty minutes. Toinette invited Malcolm and Robinson to a presentation the group planned for Chamber of Commerce members. When she left, Nettie Blue felt confident that both men would attend the presentation later that week.

Both did, but Malcolm arrived late. Robinson had saved a seat for him in the back of the conference room. About 150 people sat enthralled as Toinette told her story.

Robinson pressed a finger to his mouth to silence any comments Malcolm may have made as he slid into the chair. Malcolm shrugged and turned his attention to the woman at the podium. Dressed in a cream and white striped jacket and cream-colored skirt, Toinette looked the part of an executive director. Without amplification, her clear voice carried to the back of the room.

"I'd like each of you to take a close look at the person sitting on either side of you. Do you think that person was ever on welfare? Does he or she remind you of any of *these* people?"

When she stressed the word these, the lights dimmed and images filled the projection screen behind her. First, an obese black woman with pink curlers in her hair and a cigarette dangling from her mouth grinned at the camera. Next were a white man and woman standing before a beat-up car. The man held a beer can in salute. Two dirty, bedraggled and barefoot children sat on the hood of the car. The third image was of several Hispanic children ostensibly watching television while a man and woman nuzzled each other on a sofa; the couple seemed oblivious to the small eyes watching their increasing stages of undress.

The harsh, sometimes painful images continued through ten slides. When the last photograph faded away and the room lights brightened, Toinette began again.

"I was twenty-five and pregnant with my fifth child when my husband decided he'd had enough of the wife and family thing. Married at sixteen, I had no marketable skills. I knew how to have and raise children. Brought up to believe the husband provided for his family, it never crossed my mind to finish high school, to learn a trade, to know how to be more than a wife and mom. Reality was harsh. With no money coming in after my husband walked out, the bank wasn't real sympathetic to the pleas of a young mother who wasn't even sure how to spell mortgage let alone pay it."

Robinson glanced at Malcolm as Toinette Blue told the group her history. Malcolm's stony expression provided few clues to how he felt about what he was hearing. But he, like everyone else, was focused solely on the woman on the stage.

"To ensure that my children had food to eat and clothes to wear, I quickly learned about food stamps, Aid to Families with Dependent Children, poverty, and the projects," Toinette said as she left the podium and walked to the edge of the platform in an attempt to get closer to the audience.

"For more than ten years my children and I shared our apartment with roaches, mice, and bullets. I couldn't go to school because I didn't have child care. When I had someone to watch the kids, I didn't have the money for bus or taxi fare to get to the school. Every time I got a job, the food stamps and medical assistance would decrease. I was told I had a job so I could afford to pay health insurance—even though the job paid minimum wage and part of that had to go toward transportation to and from the job site.

"Don't let anyone fool you into believing that the majority of people on welfare are there because they are lazy, because they don't want to work, because they would rather mooch off of productive, tax-paying citizens rather than help themselves. A lot of the people on welfare are there because they have no other choice," she said as she walked the length of the platform.

"A few moments ago I asked you to take a look at the people sitting next to you. Do that again quickly."

When the audience complied she said, "Now, I'd like everyone who has ever been on welfare to stand."

About twenty people in the room stood. They then turned so everyone in the audience could see their faces. Mostly women, they were black, white, Hispanic, and Asian.

"Standing before you, ladies and gentlemen, are people who are no longer dependent on welfare assistance," Toinette said. Murmurs filled the room as several of the people standing were identified as colleagues or coworkers of people in the room.

"They are standing on their own two feet. They support their families, pay taxes, and give back to their communities," Toinette continued. "Each of the people standing before you is an alumnus of the Quad-A program. People like you took a chance on each one of us and gave us the opportunity to become self-sufficient through meaningful employment. Quad-A provides child care and transportation to program participants. We hold workshops on business etiquette and attire. Participants are encouraged to finish—or begin—their high school, GED, or college studies. We have the grants to provide those services, but we are dependent on you to provide the jobs."

A woman and man walked onto the platform and joined Toinette at the podium. Malcolm's entire body tensed when he saw her. He didn't need Toinette's introduction to recognize Kendra Edwards. He knew the man to be Bosworth Sullivan, the senior partner at Sullivan and O'Leary. Kendra looked the cool professional woman again. The black raw silk suit and soft white blouse with the overlaying collar didn't hint at the curves Malcolm knew were hiding under the business dress. Her hair was in the severe but elegant French roll style. He didn't realize he was sitting on the edge of his seat until Robinson touched his shoulder; he had been blocking the view. Malcolm tuned in again to Toinette's words.

"Sullivan and O'Leary was one of the first firms to provide employment opportunities to Quad-A program participants. Bosworth Sullivan is here this evening with Kendra Edwards to tell you more about how one law firm has benefited the community and its business environment."

After a few words of praise about the program, Sullivan turned the microphone over to Kendra. Like her best friend, Nettie, it didn't take long for Kendra to have the audience absorbed in her tale.

"I grew up with expectations that were no less than middle class. But at nineteen and after two years of college, I found myself very pregnant and very alone. The twins I eventually gave birth to needed more than their mother's fantasies of Prince Charming coming to rescue them. They needed formula, diapers, regular medical checkups including the expensive barrage of shots," Kendra said while scanning the audience. An accomplished public speaker, she made and held eye contact with many people while never losing track of her thoughts.

"Welfare had always been something those other people were on," she said. "You know, the shiftless ones who popped babies out so they could get an extra hundred dollars a month. Those women with boyfriends who were drug dealers. Those people with loose morals and no values.

"Well, one day I looked up and there I was living with those people. With one mistake, I turned into one of them. In the eyes of society, I was as they were. If I told you the name of the project where I lived, every one of you would recognize it as one of the ones always featured on the evening news or in the newspapers as the site of a shooting, a drug deal gone bad, a place where in the words of songwriters Rosamond and James Weldon Johnson 'Hope unborn had died.' "

Kendra didn't see Malcolm in the back of the room. As Malcolm watched Kendra, Robinson watched Malcolm. Kendra's husky voice held all of the emotion and fear a nineteen-year-old would have experienced when thrust into an unfamiliar world.

Kendra had no doubt that even the people who came to the presentation with a closed mind about the Quad-A program would at least leave thinking about how they could help.

It was with that confidence in herself and the program she represented that Kendra volunteered time to recruit for Quad-A. Even though she no longer lived in the projects and her daughters were well cared for, she passed by her old home every day on the way to work. With so many people still trapped in the vicious cycle of poverty, Kendra viewed it as her duty, her responsibility to help others out of the situation she'd found herself in.

"One day five years ago, while doing laundry, I read a flier that had been tacked onto the wall in the laundromat," she continued. "The flier promised child care, transportation, and a job with significant income just for calling a telephone number. I had no phone in my apartment so I used one of the quarters reserved for drying clothes to make the call from the pay phone in the laundry. The person who answered the phone was Toinette Blue. She told me to come in to their office and to bring the babies with me. My clothes didn't get dry that day but my life got turned around."

The audience laughed at the small joke and applauded when Kendra stepped back from the microphone. Bosworth Sullivan stepped forward.

"Kendra Edwards was the second person our firm accepted as a Quad-A program participant. In the program's six years, we've had almost twenty people referred to us. The success rate is ninety-seven percent. I'd like to say all of them still work for us. But unfortunately for Sullivan and O'Leary, some of them have been lured away to even higher paying jobs at other locations. We've managed to keep Kendra."

While Sullivan talked, Kendra scanned the audience. She recognized some of the faces. Half of the people at this presentation were from small businesses that might be able to accept one or maybe two people from Quad-A. The others represented mid- to large-sized law, accounting, and insurance firms able to absorb more manpower.

While used to being in the spotlight, Kendra couldn't shake the feeling that she was being watched more intensely than usual by someone in the crowd. Just when she assumed it merely her imagination her gaze landed on a man in the back of the room. She caught her breath and grabbed the edge of the podium for balance.

It was him. Why was he here? Kendra broke eye contact with Malcolm and turned her attention to Sullivan. Her knees felt weak and her heartbeat seemed dangerously accelerated.

Kendra willed herself to calm down. Even though he was standing beside her, it seemed that Sullivan was talking from a far-off distance. She vaguely heard him wrap up the pitch to accept Quad-A workers and plastered a dazzling smile on her face.

Nettie, who had watched Kendra from the edge of the stage, knew the moment her friend had spotted Malcolm. Kendra's reaction told Nettie all she needed to know about whether or not Kendra had an interest in the man. After seven long years, the frost around Kendra seemed to be melting. Walking back to the podium to conclude the program, Nettie decided she'd do her part to further assist the meltdown.

Information tables with fliers, brochures, and sign-up forms were on either side of the room. Malcolm got up to work his way through the crowd to get to the area where Kendra was talking one-on-one about the program.

"We need to do our part and work with these people," he said turning back to Robinson.

"Somehow I thought you might feel that way," Robinson answered him dryly. "I'll go do the sign up since I'm sure there's other business you'll want to attend to." Intent on his destination, Malcolm failed to hear the chuckles from Robinson that followed him.

Kendra didn't have to look up to know he was standing behind her. Even if her nose hadn't picked up the earthy scent of his cologne, the goose bumps that suddenly covered her body would have provided the clue. Stalling for the precious moments she needed to gain her composure before confronting Malcolm, she rashly told the woman she'd been talking with to call and set up an appointment. Kendra promised the woman that she herself would make the presentation to the director of human resources at the woman's insurance firm. When the woman shook her hand and walked away with an armload of papers on Quad-A, Kendra had to turn and face Malcolm.

"I didn't think you were a quitter, so why did you drop my class?" he asked without preamble.

With the high-heeled black pumps Kendra almost stood eye to eye with him. She was grateful that he didn't have the psychological advantage of height over her.

"Because I don't need to waste my time or energy with professors who think it's a privilege for me to be in their class, professors who think calla lilies can excuse abominable behavior."

Malcolm smiled at her straightforward response. "So, you think you have me summed up in a tidy little package?"

"That's where you're wrong, Mr. Hightower. I don't think of you at all. Excuse me, please." Kendra turned on her heel and left Malcolm standing there.

Please, God, let me get out of his sight before I fall down, she prayed. Kendra bit her lower lip and only nodded as she passed people. The brief encounter had left her shaken and disoriented. She begged God's forgiveness for the lie she'd told Malcolm. She did think of him—too often, that was the problem. And she vowed she'd eat the live salamanders the girls had brought home from school before she ever admitted to Malcolm Hightower that the calla lily was her favorite flower.

Malcolm watched the graceful sway of her hips as she made her way through the throng of people. He wondered if he stood a chance of getting in her good graces. Since he'd been doing uncharacteristic things since the moment he met her, he didn't question his firm resolve: Kendra Edwards was worth the challenge.

CHAPTER 4

Kendra's hair fanned the satin pillowcase. Malcolm had pulled all of the pins out and had spent long moments just gazing at her and running his hands through the thick tresses. Now, however, his attention was focused on her neck. The kisses he rained on her were practically unbearable. Kendra couldn't breathe but she felt she would die if he stopped. Pulling him closer, she ran her hands over his bare back and luxuriated in the feel of his curly chest hair on her chest and midsection. Her breasts were still hidden from his view by the lacy black bra she wore. Belatedly, she realized the whimper she heard in her bedroom had come from her.

When Malcolm's mouth left her neck, she moaned in protest. But before she could voice a complaint, his large hand covered one of her lace-covered breasts. The pad of his finger teased the nipple of one while his mouth found the other. Kendra cried out at the contrast of moist mouth meeting lacy fabric and hardened bud. In mild frustration at the obstruction, Malcolm pushed aside the brassiere cup. She enjoyed the feel of his body too much to use both of her hands to unsnap the front hook. With one hand Kendra fumbled with the clasp until Malcolm's mouth took the place of her hand. In a move that had her gasping, he unhooked the snap with his mouth, then turned his attention back to the luscious fruit revealed before him.

As Malcolm suckled like a newborn child, Kendra's hips arched off the bed. Her body ached for his touch in a deeper, more elemental way. The tingling that had started in the pit of her stomach was now focused lower.

The male hardness of him pressed against her. She wanted the torment to end. She wanted it to last forever. When Malcolm lifted his head to gaze into her eyes, she writhed beneath him. His weight was welcome, comforting. Slowly, seductively his gaze roamed down her body. He chuckled at the tentative hand inching its way to his maleness. Kendra's moans filled the room when he denied her access to what she sought. Malcolm put her hands on his shoulders and again lowered his head to her body. This time to lick her. Kendra cried out at the exquisite torture.

Two doors down the hall, Kayla sat up in bed.

"Karin," she whispered to her twin sister. "Karin, are you awake?"

"Yes, Kay. Do you hear Mommie?"

"Uh-huh, I think she's sick with the flu again." Kayla got out of bed and sat on the edge of her sister's bed. Her stuffed teddy bear, Ashanti, who was named after an ancient African kingdom, was clutched in her small arms. Both girls' concern and uncertainty showed on their faces.

"Maybe we should call Aunt Nettie," Karin suggested.

"It's awfully late," Kayla responded, looking at the big clock on the nightstand that separated their beds. In the dark, only the bright orange numbers flashing 2:30 were visible in the stomach of the teddy bear clock.

"I know what, let's get a wet washcloth for her head and a glass of orange juice. Mommie said that made her feel better the last time."

Kayla agreed with the plan and the two girls went to fetch the items. Ashanti the teddy bear and its twin, Askia, who held the namesake of an ancient African warrior king, traveled with the girls.

Kendra's entire body was hot and feverish. The soft cotton nightgown she wore was damp and clinging to her. She'd awakened a few moments ago and was still appalled at the unconscious but erotic dream she had had about Malcolm Hightower. She was sitting propped up in her bed trying to catch her breath when there was a soft knock on her open bedroom door.

"Mommie," both girls began. Kendra reached over and flicked the switch on her bedside lamp.

"Hey, what are you two sleepyheads doing up at this hour?" The girls approached her bed. Kayla took careful steps so the glass of juice she was holding wouldn't spill. Karin jumped up on her mom's bed and put the damp washcloth at Kendra's forehead.

"We heard you, Mommie, and thought you were sick again. Do you feel better now?"

"Here's some juice," Kayla said, handing Kendra the glass. "Should we call Aunt Nettie?"

Kendra was profoundly grateful that the room was too dim and her daughters too young to recognize the blush that she knew crept up her face. She took a sip of the juice, then put the glass on the bedside table.

Unfolding the washcloth, she buried her face in it and prayed that it would cool her embarrassment. She'd made so much noise during the dream about Malcolm that her daughters had been awakened. She felt guilty over that and decided to make amends even though Kayla and Karin couldn't guess her thoughts.

"I feel fine, ladies," she said hugging the two girls to her. "I just had a bad dream. Tell you what, I think I need the two of you as well as Ashanti and Askia to keep the bad dreams away for the rest of the night."

The girls instantly recognized the treat of sleeping in their mother's big bed. They scrambled down and claimed the two bears that had been dropped at the door.

After the evening's second round of goodnight hugs and kisses, Kendra smiled as she watched the twins settle on either side of her. Her world revolved around Kayla and Karin. They were secure in her love and she in theirs. The small family had been through many trials and tribulations, but Kendra had managed to shield her seven-year-old daughters from the worst of it.

In very little time, the twins were fast asleep. But it was another two hours before Kendra was able to relax enough to drift back to sleep. Neither her daughters nor the teddy bears were able to protect her from the lingering thoughts of what it would be like to make love with Malcolm Hightower.

Daylight arrived much faster than Kendra would have liked. The girls sensed that Mommie was still out of sorts so they let her sleep in an extra half hour. They left their teddy bears to protect Kendra and quietly went to the living room to watch cartoons. Saturday morning before breakfast was the only time Kendra allowed them to watch television without permission.

At seven-thirty, Kendra stumbled from bed and made her way to the apartment's single bathroom that separated her bedroom from the girls'. A quick shower chased the cobwebs from her brain but didn't diffuse the self-directed anger she felt over the night's wayward dream. But as she toweled herself dry, her nipples tightened and her thoughts turned to Malcolm.

Kendra swore to herself and stomped back to her bedroom to get dressed. By the time she got to the kitchen, she had determined that she wasn't going to take her surly mood out on the girls. Making a mental note to call Nettie for a sister-to-sister gripe session, Kendra called to the twins.

"Who wants pancakes?"

The affirmative cries of "I do, I do" helped Kendra put things into perspective. Her happiness wasn't important as long as Karin and Kayla were cared for, loved, and no longer subjected to the danger that lurked in the projects. She didn't give a thought to the fact that she had inadvertently linked Malcolm and the prospect of his love to her own happiness.

The Edwardses made it to the public library with just two minutes to spare before the start of story hour. They'd lost ten minutes of time when Karin announced that she couldn't find her library card. Only after frantic searching through pockets and drawers did the little girl remember she had used the library card as a bookmark and it was in the car in her book bag.

Every Saturday morning Kayla and Karin participated in Children's Story Hour at the library. While they listened to stories, made crafts, interacted with other children, and chose books to take home for the coming week, Kendra used the time to study in a quieter section of the library. After several years of squeezing in night classes whenever her work schedule allowed, Kendra had almost completed the coursework for her bachelor's degree.

There had been times when she didn't think she could do it. Only Nettie's encouragement and her own conviction that it was important to complete college got her through. Since her first paycheck from Sullivan and O'Leary she had been saving for the twins' college education. Her time in the projects tad taught her the value of money. She didn't spend frivolously and safeguarded every dime. Some people thought money was the root of all evil. But Kendra thought it, along with education, was the foundation of stability and safety. With the firm's policy of reimbursing employees who wanted to advance their education, Kendra only had to pay 20 percent of the cost for her classes and fees.

She had enrolled in the courts and litigation class at the local community college with the thought that law school would be an option after graduation in May. A paralegal course, she thought, would have given her a taste of law school. But Malcolm Hightower had managed to ruin that notion.

As if the mere thought of him had conjured him up, Hightower was standing in front of her when Kendra looked up.

"Hello, Kendra," Malcolm said as if they met in the library every day.

Her breath quickened and her cheeks became warm. Too taken aback to speak, Kendra just stared at him. He looked like a regular person. Gone were the power suits and ties. Faded Levi's and a knit shirt stretched over his muscles. Kendra looked down at his feet. The wing tips had been replaced by a pair of Nike running shoes.

Malcolm smiled at her perusal and tried to ignore the way his body responded to her scrutiny. He pulled out a chair and sat across from her before she was able to notice the effect she had on him.

"Wh-what are you doing here?" she finally managed.

"Last time I checked it was a free country and this is a public library. I'm the public."

"Look, you—" Kendra huffed. But Malcolm's quickly raised hand stopped her.

"I apologize for that. You seem to bring out the worst in me." Malcolm grimaced when he realized what he'd said. Another indignant huff from Kendra told him how he was faring in the small-talk department. He tried again.

"Kendra, let me start over, okay?" She folded her arms and rolled her eyes at him. Malcolm ignored that.

"My name is Malcolm Hightower and it's a pleasure meeting you," he said extending his right hand. At first Kendra just looked at him. Manners won out, however, and she extended her own arm for a handshake. But Malcolm held her hand longer than necessary. When Kendra had the presence of mind to snatch it back, she felt as if she'd been burned.

When she saw the quick as a flash fire in his eyes, she wondered if Malcolm had felt the same thing. But his gray eyes were shielded when he continued and she guessed it had been her imagination. "I understand, Ms. Edwards, that you are one of the recruiters for the Achieving Against All Adversities program. My law firm is considering taking on one or two of the people from your program."

"Is that a fact?"

"You're making this very difficult."

"Mr. Hightower—"

"Call me Malcolm."

"Mr. Hightower, I'm not sure why you're here today. But," Kendra said as she pulled out a business card and handed it to him, "here's the address and telephone number of the program office. I'm sure Toinette Blue or one of the volunteers will be able to assist you on Monday."

Despite her jumbled feelings about the man, Kendra had no intention of letting a prospective program job site slip through her fingers simply because this man made her uncomfortable in ways she'd forgotten even existed. Giving him one of Nettie's business cards and referring him to the Quad-A office was the least she could do.

"Mrs. Blue has already answered all the questions I had. We met earlier this week." Kendra took note of that and added it to the list of things she would talk with Nettie about.

"As a matter of fact," Malcolm continued, "I was here pulling up newspaper clips on the program."

"There were photocopies of articles in the information packets," Kendra pointed out.

"True, but you were drumming up support for the program. Had there been any negative publicity, I doubt those articles would be in a public relations package."

"You are a real skeptic aren't you?"

"I'm a realist, Kendra. I've represented enough clients who weren't straight up with me to put much trust in what people tell me."

Kendra knew without being told that he referred to more than just an attorney-client relationship. For the first time she wondered if he was married. Before she could clamp the notion, she'd voiced the thought in a question.

"Might I hope that you're asking for a purely personal reason," he responded. Kendra was mortified. The grin that grew broader on Malcolm's face told her that the blush was growing deeper. Not for the first time, she cursed her light brown skin that wouldn't hold her secret shame.

When she turned away, Malcolm had pity on her and simply answered the question.

"No, Kendra. I'm not married. I've been divorced several years now." Malcolm was gripped by an irrational panic when he realized he didn't know if Kendra herself was married. She wore no rings but definitely seemed to be the hearth and home type.

"Are you married?" he asked, then quickly added "or seeing someone?"

"Why do you ask?" she countered.

As the saying goes, it was time for Malcolm to fish or cut bait. If she was available, he was in for the long haul. There was something about this woman that answered an emptiness within him. For too many years he had relied on his instincts in the courtroom to win over hostile juries, to make the right judgment calls for his clients and for his law firm. Those same instincts were telling him right now that Kendra was worth whatever battle she put forth.

His silence almost frightened her. Kendra watched as his eyes changed from a pale to a smoky gray as he studied her. He seemed to have come to some sort of conclusion and Kendra wasn't sure she wanted to know what it was.

"I was asking, Kendra Edwards, because I'd like to take you out to dinner," he finally responded.

"I don't date, Mr. Hightower." With that she gathered her books and papers and went in search of her daughters.

Malcolm sat at the table for a moment after she departed. Kendra hadn't answered his question, but she had revealed more than she realized. She hadn't flatly refused him, she just declared that she didn't date. While some people might conclude that she didn't date because she was indeed married, Malcolm guessed that she was single and didn't date for some other compelling reason. He'd lay odds that it had to do with the watered down version of her life story that she'd presented to the Chamber of Commerce presentation the night before. The story, while compelling, had been too pat, too sanitized, to be the entire truth. If she was pregnant as a college student, why did she say she was all alone? What role did the father of her twins play in her life and where was the rest of her family?

There was passion in Kendra Edwards. It came through in her presentation and it radiated from her like the beacon from a lighthouse every time he was near her. Tapping into that passion would be as difficult as mining for diamonds. But like the precious gems that remain sheltered within the core of a mountain, Malcolm knew that Kendra, a diamond of the first water, was worth a few sleepless nights. Unfortunately for Malcolm, he'd had more than just a few sleepless nights since he'd met her.

Kendra and Nettie played telephone answering machine tag for the next two days. They met for lunch Tuesday. Nettie acted the innocent when Kendra questioned her about the meeting with Malcolm Hightower.

"Why didn't you tell me you had had a meeting with Hightower?"

Nettie speared a strawberry in her fruit salad and laughed. "You wanted me to miss the expression on your face when you saw him in the crowd? It was priceless, Kendra." She popped the slice of strawberry in her mouth, then rooted around for a piece of cantaloupe.

"This isn't funny, Toinette."

Nettie looked up at Kendra and her face softened. She put her fork down and reached across the table to grasp Kendra's hand, which was wrapped around a water goblet. Kendra hadn't touched the spinach quiche artfully arranged on a china plate.

"I'm sorry, Ken. I didn't realize it was that serious."

"What are you talking about?"

Nettie smiled ruefully. "You haven't called me Toinette since the day you walked into the Quad-A office five years ago. Tell me about it," she prodded gently as she squeezed her friend's hand.

Nettie was the only person who knew Kendra's entire story. Built on total honesty and common ground, their friendship started the day Kendra walked into Nettie's office. The bond between the two women grew stronger every year. To Kendra, Nettie was mother, sister, confidante, and best friend. To Nettie, Kendra was those things as well as strength and inspiration. They were both committed to the goals of the Quad-A program and both women knew the value and reward of hard work.

Nettie knew and understood why Kendra had not been with a man since the father of her children was killed. And despite overtures and offers from single as well as married men, Kendra didn't date. Not only did she not want to give Kayla and Karin the impression that a series of "uncles" traipsing through the house was the norm, Nettie knew that Kendra was afraid. Kendra was afraid of giving her heart and having it broken, but most all she was terrified of ever having to be dependent on government handouts to ensure the well-being of her daughters.

If Malcolm Hightower had managed to storm Kendra's defenses, the turmoil her friend now experienced was understandable.

Kendra looked away from the intensity of Nettie's gaze. She pulled her hand back, rubbed her eyes, and sighed.

"I had a dream about him, Nettie," she practically whispered. "It was unlike any dream I've ever had."

Nettie nodded her head for Kendra to continue.

"I felt, I don't know, I felt out of control. I felt wanton. When I woke up I was angry because it hadn't been real. Did I tell you I saw him Saturday? He was at the library checking up on the program. Said he was looking for negative publicity in newspaper articles."

Nettie smiled at Kendra's disbelieving tone but didn't interrupt.

"Nettie, I was so embarrassed. Of course, he didn't know why, but the idea of having a sexual dream about him . . ." Then on an oddly irritated note she added, "He probably couldn't or wouldn't even do in real life the things he did in my dream."

Toinette raised an elegantly arched eyebrow at that comment. If Kendra was able to respond to Malcolm in an unconscious erotic dream, there was hope for her in reality. The time had come for Kendra to rejoin womankind. But before Nettie could launch her plan, Kendra continued.

"And you know the worst of it?" she asked as she finally cut into the quiche. "I was making so much noise, I woke the girls up."

"You're kidding?"

"No. It was two-thirty in the morning and they thought I had the flu again. They brought me juice and a cold compress for my head and asked if they should call you to help care for me."

Nettie got a kick out of that. Her laughter drew appreciative glances from two men dining a few tables away. She smiled at them before turning her attention back to Kendra.

"What did you tell them?" she asked of the girls she had come to love like her own children and grandchildren.

Kendra swallowed a bite and took a sip of water before responding. "That Mommie had had a bad dream."

"Smart thinking."

"I thought so at the time. The next morning I still felt guilty about waking them up. So after the library, instead of just going to the zoo like we'd planned, we also went shopping. I let each one pick out something special. Kayla chose a purse and Karin picked out new hair ribbons."

"Sometimes you're too indulgent with them. What did you get for yourself?"

Kendra looked surprised. "What do you mean?"

"The three of you went shopping. The girls bought things. What did you buy for yourself?"

Kendra frowned at her. "You know I don't spend money on frivolous things."

Working on the quiche, Kendra missed her best friend's scowl. "So what should I do?"

"About what?"

"About Malcolm Hightower. He asked me to dinner, you know."

Nettie's fork stayed suspended in midair for a moment, then she placed it back on her plate. "When?"

"When what?"

"Sometimes I think we're playing Who's on First here, Kendra. When did he ask you to dinner and when are you going?"

"He asked me Saturday at the library and I'm not going anywhere with that man. I told you how he treated me in class."

Nettie signaled for their waiter who arrived with the check. She dabbed her mouth with the linen napkin and left enough cash to cover the meal and a tip.

"Come on."

"I'm not finished yet. Where are you going in such an all-fired hurry?" Kendra protested.

"We have about half an hour before you have to be back at work. That's plenty of time to find you a new dress. Something little, in black or maybe red."

Nettie was practically dragging Kendra from the bistro.

"Have you lost your mind, Nettie? I don't need a new dress. I have a closet full of clothes."

"Yes, I know. You're a wonderful seamstress and you have a closet full of those boring law offfice suits and skirts and a ton of ancient jeans and raggedy sweatshirts. You need a knock 'em off his feet number that shows off those long legs."

They were hurrying along the sidewalk now, moving with the flow of lunchtime office workers.

"Nettie, first of all I can't afford the type of dress I know you're talking about and secondly, I don't have anyplace to wear something like that."

"You can afford it. You're just so used to hoarding money for the girls' future that it's become second nature to you. But don't worry. This one is on me. And you're going to wear it when you go out on that dinner date with Malcolm Hightower."

Familiar with her girlfriend's whirlwind personality, Kendra didn't bother to reemphasize that she had no intention of going on a date with Malcolm. But right now, letting Nettie wind down seemed the best course of action.

CHAPTER 5

An auction, the proceeds of which would benefit several charities, was being held Saturday night. Since Quad-A was one of the intended beneficiaries, a representative had to be there. Nettie had, of course, planned to go. But when Malcolm Hightower called that Wednesday saying he would be at the auction and wanted to go over some details of the program while there, Nettie suggested that he escort her.

"I'd be the belle of the evening if I walked in on your arm, Mr. Hightower. This old lady would be the envy of every young girl in the place," she told him.

Malcolm laughed and gallantly said he'd have to have an eye exam the next day because he hadn't met an old lady named Nettie Blue.

After ringing off with Malcolm, Nettie called three of her kids and asked if they'd bring their children to her house Saturday night for a sleepover. As she'd expected, every one of them gladly agreed. A night alone with a spouse coupled with the added bonus of not paying a sitter was too good a deal to pass up. Knowing the twins hadn't seen their friends in a while, Nettie casually mentioned the sleepover to Kendra, Kayla, and Karin as the girls did school work at the kitchen table early Thursday evening.

"Please, Mom. Can we go?" Karin asked.

The reinforcement from her twin came quickly. "We'll get our weekend homework all done before we go. Right Karin?"

"Right."

"Pleeese," they both chimed. When Kendra nodded, they let out whoops of joy.

"What should we bring, Aunt Nettie?" Kayla asked.

"Let's see. Well, you'll need your sleeping bags, of course. You have play clothes at my house. Kendra, will you pack church clothes for them? I know these two angels are in Sunday School every week. I can't say the same for my grandkids so I try to make sure they get a little religion when they come to stay with me."

Kendra laughed, then bit off the thread she was using to hem a skirt. "It's a little bit, too. You never stay for the eleven o'clock service."

Nettie grunted. "Hmmph. Lasts too long for me. And it takes an hour to take up the collection. I don't think God wanted it done that way. Offering takes an hour and the sermon is delivered in less than fifteen minutes. Those folks have their priorities mixed up."

"I keep telling you you're going to the wrong church. You should come with us one Sunday."

"Will Carol and Jamal be there?" Karin asked.

Kayla giggled. "Karin likes Jamal. That's why she wants to know if he'll be coming. You gonna sit next to him in Sunday School, Karin?" Kayla teased.

"I do not like him," Karin protested.

"Do too."

"Do not."

Kendra put the skirt aside. "Ladies, that's enough."

Nettie laughed. "Yes, Miss Inquisitive. Carol and Jamal will be there. So will Lisa, Jessica, and Thad. Pack a couple of old shirts. We may have time to do some fingerpainting."

Kendra shook her head. Nettie loved these get-togethers with the children. She usually got dirtier than they did. Kendra was already planning the quiet evening she'd spend at home. First a bubble bath and some soft music. Then maybe a good romance novel and a cup of tea. It had been a while since she had done nothing but pamper herself for an evening.

But late Friday afternoon Kendra smelled a trap when Nettie called her at work. The note of panic in her friend's voice just didn't sound sincere.

"Can you do me a huge favor, Ken? I've found myself in an incredible bind."

"Sure, what's up?"

"You know all of the kids are coming over here for the weekend. Well, I forgot there was a charity auction I'm supposed to attend Saturday night."

Incredulous, Kendra dropped the file folder she was in the process of putting away. "You want me to entertain seven kids while you schmooze at an auction?"

"No, I hadn't thought of that but now that you mention it," Nettie added for effect.

"Don't even think about it."

"What I wondered is could you cover for me at the auction? The literacy council, the battered women's shelter, and Quad-A will split the proceeds. Someone needs to represent the program."

In lieu of looking at her friend, Kendra pulled the receiver from her ear and stared at it for a moment before putting it back to talk to Nettie.

"Are you trying to tell me you just happened to forget an event where the program was going to get some money?"

"It's been a long week, girl," Nettie offered as an excuse.

"Well, okay. How long is it supposed to last?"

"Probably a couple of hours. The usual. Eat, greet, smile, and make contacts. Thank the committee at the end. And you know what?"

"What?"

"You even have something to wear. That little white sheath we bought earlier this week will be perfect."

"Hmmmm. Nettie . . ." Kendra said, now wary.

"Gotta go, girlfriend. Thanks. I'll stop by the apartment to get the girls around six. I'll even drop you off at the hotel where the auction will take place. It starts at six-thirty. See ya."

Three things made Kendra very, very suspicious. First of all, Nettie never, ever "forgot" things that concerned the Quad-A program. Second, the reference to the dress was highly suspect. And third, just how did Nettie think Kendra would get home if Nettie drove her to the event?

The next night, Kayla and Karin sat on the edge of their mother's bed and watched her get dressed. They were clothed in jeans, sneakers, and matching tops. Their hair ribbons and shoelaces, Karin's red and Kayla's blue, differentiated them from each other.

Kendra put the finishing touches on her hair and makeup. She modified the French roll by allowing curly wisps to hang at her temples and nape. Then standing in only her hose and undergarments Kendra reached for the white dress. It didn't have enough to it to be called a dress, she thought derisively. Leave it to Nettie to pick out something totally uncharacteristic for Kendra to wear. The short sheath was covered in glimmering white sequins and looked like something only fashion models wore on runways. While her front was completely covered, the scoop neckline took a wild plunge in the rear. Most of Kendra's back would be exposed in the dress. Real people didn't go outside in things like this, she thought.

Careful not to mess her hair, she shimmied into the creation.

"Will one of you zip me up, please?" she asked, backing up to the bed. Kayla did the honors and Kendra stepped into a pair of white satin high-heeled pumps. She'd picked up the shoes on sale months ago with the intention of having them dyed to match a dress she'd planned to make. Since she hadn't gotten around to buying the fabric, the shoes had remained in the back of her closet. Tonight they were a perfect complement to the barely-there dress she wore.

Kendra walked to her jewelry box and pulled out a pair of pearl earrings. She put the posts in her ears then frowned at the image of herself in the dresser mirror. "Pearls go with everything but they look awfully plain in this get up," she said aloud.

"Wear the red, Mommie," Karin suggested. "You never wear the red."

Kendra turned around and contemplated her daughter. At seven, Karin had an unerring sense of style. The ruby and diamond earrings and bracelet would be perfect with the white dress. She rarely wore the set because she considered the jewelry her daughters' only legacy from their father. Kendra no longer had any emotional attachment to the items. They were pretty jewels that she rarely, if ever, wore.

She'd had the set appraised once and was shocked at its value. Many times during the lean years, she'd been tempted to sell or pawn one or the other. But each time she did, she thought of the babies who would grow up not knowing their father. By the time she'd gotten on her feet financially and emotionally, the bracelet and earrings were stuffed in the back of her jewelry box and usually forgotten.

"That's not a bad idea, little one," she answered as she dug through assorted costume jewelry. She pulled the little velvet bag from its corner and poured the stones in her hand. She replaced the pearls with the rubies, then managed to clasp on the bracelet.

Kendra twirled around to face her daughters.

"Ta-duh! What do you think?"

Both girls clapped and giggled. "Mommie, you look beautiful," Kayla cried.

"Like a fairy princess," Karin added.

From the bedroom doorway Nettie added her opinion. "Knock him off his feet."

"Aunt Nettie!" The girls bounded from the bed, hugged Nettie and ran to get their overnight bags.

"I didn't hear you come in," Kendra said.

"Ready?"

"I'm ready," she said picking up a slim white evening bag. "Knock who off his feet?"

Nettie had the grace to look slightly guilty as she turned and headed down the hallway toward the living room.

"Uh, I had an escort for the evening. He'll meet you there," she mumbled. "Let's go, girls," she called from the front door.

As Kendra locked the door to the first floor apartment and headed down the front steps, her friend's words registered.

"Escort? Who, Nettie?"

But Nettie was already in her car and had the engine running. The girls were strapped in the back seat. Kendra had little choice but to slip in the front seat. She pulled on her seat belt, then turned to glare at her best friend.

"Tell me this escort isn't who I think he is."

"Now, Kendra. He's seems like such a nice man. And you yourself said he'd asked you out. This auction just sort of came up and was the ideal situation."

"Came up my foot. You set this whole thing up, didn't you?" Kendra said, gesturing toward the back seat where Kayla and Karin listened avidly to what sounded like an argument between their mother and Aunt Nettie. "I knew I smelled a rat."

"Kendra, you're overreacting. All you have to do is walk around with him, make a little small talk, and you're outta there."

Nettie would bet the proceeds from the night's event that Malcolm wouldn't let Kendra out of his sight, quickly or otherwise, particularly after he got a look at the dress she was wearing.

She'd called Malcolm about an hour before she left to pick up Kendra and the girls, told him she had an unavoidable conflict, begged his forgiveness, and asked if it would be okay if Kendra came in her place. It had been a struggle not to laugh on the telephone. Nettie wished she had been able to see his expression.

Whereas Malcolm had been delighted at the switch, Kendra was downright angry. Nettie had no doubt that she'd get over it.

"Just remember, Nettie. Payback is sweet."

Kendra didn't utter another word the entire trip.

Malcolm saw her the moment she entered the grand ballroom. In an instant he understood how the Prince had felt when first he set eyes on Cinderella. Toinette Blue had done some fancy maneuvering. Not for even half a second did he believe her story about a sudden and unavoidable conflict. But if the woman was going to push Kendra into his arms, he had no objections. He excused himself from the cluster of people he had been chatting with and made his way to where she stood.

Kendra had pulled out the invitation Nettie gave her and had handed it to the person at the registration table when she felt him approach. She took a deep breath and braced herself. She didn't know that as she turned to him her face held such an overwhelming expression of anticipation that Malcolm couldn't speak. He could barely breathe.

His gaze dropped from her eyes to her shoulders then to her breasts. He watched her so intently that for a moment, Kendra thought she had her dress on backward. He looked as though he were photographing her for all time. Something intense flicked in his eyes as they again met hers.

"Cat got your tongue, Mr. Hightower?" Her husky voice held a challenge.

Malcolm's need, strong and pounding in his veins, felt overwhelming. When at last he found his voice, it came out a cross between a croak and a choke. "Our table is this way."

Tingles of awareness slithered down Kendra's arm as they made their way through the press of glamorously dressed people. Malcolm's right arm rode at the small of her bare back and her pulse skittered erratically. Dreaming about him touching her and the real thing were worlds apart.

So wrapped up in how they felt, neither Kendra nor Malcolm noticed the approving glances tossed their way. They made a striking pair: He tall, dark, and handsome in the black tuxedo, and she, slim and feminine in the stunning white dress with fire dripping from her ears.

The glittering jewels caught the attention of an older couple whom Malcolm and Kendra passed. The woman gripped her husband's arm. They stared long and hard as the younger couple passed by. The man then turned to inquire after the name of the statuesque beauty who was being escorted by one of the city's most eligible bachelors.

As it turned out, the evening included dinner and dancing before the auction. Kendra didn't think she could bear it if she had to be held by Malcolm. The power that radiated from him made her weak. She had barely been able to hold up her end of the conversation that ebbed and flowed around their table during dinner. But as the dessert dishes were cleared and the orchestra began a mellow Duke Ellington piece, Kendra knew there was but one place she wanted to be.

"May I have this dance, Ms. Edwards?" he asked formally.

Kendra nodded and placed her hand in his. He led her to the dance floor and did the one thing he'd wanted to do all evening: pull her into his arms.

She feels like heaven, he thought as he noticed how well they fit together.

I've died and gone to heaven, she thought. I'm going to send an angel down to shoot Nettie, but I've died and gone to heaven.

Kendra smiled at the thought about her friend and Malcolm's heart turned over.

"Kendra, I don't remember if I've told you this evening, but you look absolutely divine."

"Thank you. You're not looking so bad yourself."

Malcolm smiled and drew her closer as they slowly danced to the romantic tune. "I got the impression earlier that you weren't too pleased to be here, particularly seeing me here."

"Let's just say that I've come to a new awareness. I'm still plotting the demise of my best friend, though."

"Shhh, I'm a lawyer. You're not supposed to admit to opposing counsel that you committed the crime."

Kendra smiled and Malcolm fell deeper. "Put the handcuffs on then, counselor. I'm guilty as charged."

Malcolm turned serious. "Kendra, I apologize for the way I treated you when you were enrolled in the class. I'm still not sure what came over me."

Kendra nodded and rested her head on his shoulder as the last refrain from Ellington drifted away and the haunting melody of a saxophone drifted across the ballroom. She granted herself permission to live the fairy princess' life for one evening.

"Thank you for the flowers, Malcolm. Apology accepted."

"Does this détente mean that maybe we can be friends now?" he asked.

"Maybe so. I'll think about it."

Malcolm smiled and pulled her even closer. They danced until the orchestra picked up the beat with a big band number.

Before long, the master of ceremonies called a halt to the dancing so the business of the evening could get under way.

Items and services had been donated for the charity event. There was something for every taste, desire, and budget: twenty hours with a masseuse, a year's membership at a health club, dinner for two at assorted restaurants, season tickets for every conceivable professional sport as well as to the opera, the symphony, the ballet and even an amusement park, the services of an accountant during tax season, a year of tune-ups and oil changes for a vehicle, the service of a housekeeper once a week for six months, weekends at a ski resort, at a campground, and at a bed and breakfast. The bidding went fast and furious and got almost cutthroat a couple of times.

A dispute over who had made the highest offer for the masseuse was about to turn unpleasant when the owner of the salon stepped to the microphone and said that for the same nine-hundred-fifty-dollar bid he would donate another twenty hours of a masseuse or masseur's time. The conflict resolved itself with both sides happy, more money for the three charities, and the already jovial atmosphere increased tenfold.

"At the rate people are bidding, none of us will have to worry about fund-raisers the rest of the year," Kendra whispered to Malcolm as two airline tickets for anywhere in the continental United States were claimed for twenty eight hundred dollars.

"There's more to come," Malcolm told her from where they stood at the edge of the crowd. The program promised an exquisite sapphire and diamond ring, a trans-Atlantic cruise on a luxury ship, and a pair of his and hers Rolex watches. With the generosity of the attendees, Malcolm guessed that each of the big-ticket items would be auctioned for at least twice their retail values.

Malcolm, who had put in bids for a collection of compact discs, had been outbid by a big, blond man standing next to him.

"If I make a claim for that cruise are you going to give me a run for my money?" he asked the man.

"You bet," the man replied good-naturedly. "The wife is already picking out the wardrobe for the trip."

"Well, I'll just sit that round out," Malcolm said, laughing.

Kendra glanced at Malcolm. Had he been serious about bidding on the cruise? In Kendra's estimation, the retail price of the trip was itself staggering. Malcolm had that kind of money to burn? Kendra thought the man next to them had been joking, but when the trip on the luxury cruise ship came up, he was brutal in his bidding. Absolutely astounded, Kendra could only stare as the man held up his bidding card and the auctioneer took note of it.

"Calling once, calling twice. Sold! To bidder number eighty-seven."

Kendra introduced herself and thanked him personally.

"Shucks, honey. That was nothing. It's more fun than just writing out a good will check to an organization. The wife and I enjoy these little auctions. She's been on that damn boat three times already. I'd just as soon fly and get where we're going. But the wife likes the romance."

"I'll bet you enjoy it, too," Kendra told him with a smile.

The big man's booming laughter rang out, then he put his finger to his lips and said, "Shhh, don't let my secret out." He took a swallow from the drink he'd been holding. Malcolm excused himself to go refresh their drinks.

"You're from the Quaddra group, right? What is that?" the man asked. "We know about literacy and the battered women's shelter. Been helping them out for years."

"Quad-A," Kendra corrected. It wasn't the first time someone had mingled her name with the program's name. "It's an acronym of sorts for Achieving Against All Adversities."

"I like that," the man declared. "I achieved against some adversities myself before I built my business. Oh, shoot. Pardon the manners. The name's Trammer. Ben Trammer," he said extending a large, calloused hand.

Kendra instantly recognized the name of the founder and president of Trammer Engineering and Electronics. The company was based in Texas but had offices all over the country. The conglomerate built and manufactured everything from houses and shopping centers to computer games and gadgets.

"My girls drove me crazy until I got them that newest hand-held computer game of yours."

Ben laughed. "Shoot, my grandkids were the same way. I don't understand those little things. Hands too big," he said while holding up one of his. "My oldest boy runs that division of the company. Growing up, he always had wires and such all over the house. Got his degree in computer technology and told me that he had an idea for a new business for the family. He's been running it ever since. Me, I like to build things."

"Are you in town visiting?"

"Yeah. The goddaughter is getting married tomorrow. Have you ever heard of a wedding on Sunday? Craziest thing."

"Now, Ben," his wife said as she approached from the side and took his arm. "A Sunday wedding is unusual, but Paige is getting married and that's the important thing. Hi there," she told Kendra.

Just as bubbly as her husband, the older woman stuck out a hand and introduced herself as Maggie. Her blue eyes sparkled with laughter at her husband's dubious expression about the merits of a Sunday wedding.

"Pleased to meet you, Maggie. I'm Kendra Edwards."

"Kendra represents the Quad-A program, Mag. They help people get off welfare," Ben told his wife.

"Really. How interesting. That's one of the groups for this benefit." Then remembering something. "You *were* bidder number eighty-seven weren't you?"

"Yes, ma'am," Ben replied with mock meekness. He winked at Kendra. Kendra took delight in the give and play between the couple. They obviously loved each other and had spent many years cultivating the easy camaraderie.

"How do you get people off welfare?" Maggie asked.

Kendra needed no additional entree to talk about Quad-A. When Malcolm returned a few minutes later she and Ben Trammer were exchanging business cards.

"It was a pleasure meeting you, Kendra," Maggie told her while shaking hands.

"Enjoy the wedding tomorrow."

Ben rolled his eyes, then extended his hand to Malcolm. "Your wife's a jewel. Nice meetin' you." As they walked away, Kendra, flustered, turned to Malcolm.

"I'm sorry. He just assumed . . ."

"It happens at these types of affairs," Malcolm said. With no hint that his mind was mulling over the idea of Kendra as his wife, he enquired, "Did you make a new contact for the program?"

"Yes, I think so. They are a lot of fun. I'll pass his name and number on to Nettie."

So distracted at the notion of being mistaken for Malcolm's wife, Kendra didn't realize that she was being called to the podium. And she didn't notice the intense perusal she was getting from across the room.

Malcolm touched her bare arm and Kendra started.

"They're calling you for comments."

"Oh."

Kendra got her scrambled thoughts together and gave a gracious and heartfelt thank you to the people who organized the auction and to those who made donations through their bids.

From where they stood in the middle of the crush of people, the older couple who had taken note of Kendra and Malcolm earlier in the evening continued to intently watch Kendra.

With the festivities at a close Kendra was at a loss of what to do next. She needed a ride home but even with their newfound friendliness, she felt uncomfortable making the request of Malcolm. The very notion made her feel that she'd be dependent and indebted to him—the very last things she wanted to feel.

Malcolm solved the problem by making an offer.

"It's still early. Would you like to go for a drive? I'd suggest a walk along the waterfront, but it's probably chilly outside."

Kendra gathered her program and her handbag from their table. "A drive where?" she asked.

Her query confirmed for Malcolm that Kendra had been telling the truth when she'd told him she didn't date. Any other woman would have known immediately that a drive about ten o'clock on a Saturday evening would probably lead to one place, particularly when the participants were two single people who striked sparks off each other at every turn. Malcolm again shifted mental gears about Kendra. Take it slow and easy, he coached himself. You don't take dynamite to the entire mountain when mining those diamonds.

"Just around the city. When was the last time you did that?"

Kendra frowned. "Never."

"Well, you're overdue."

Clear and cool outside, the stars twinkled like tiny diamonds on black velvet. Staring out the passenger window Kendra sat next to Malcolm as he navigated the Saab through city traffic. The smooth leather seats and soft jazz coming from the CD player should have been comforting. But the confining intimacy of the car frightened Kendra. Tense and nervous, she sat clutching the small handbag with a near-death grip.

Aware of her tension and its cause, Malcolm aimed to put her at ease.

"Thank you for agreeing to let me escort you this evening. I realize you didn't have much cause to want to."

"It was a favor to Nettie. Someone had to be here and she had all of the kids for the evening."

"You have more than two children?"

Kendra took the question the wrong way. Defensive, she turned to face Malcolm. She didn't notice that the maneuver left even more of her thigh exposed than the short dress already allowed. Malcolm took a quick swallow and prayed for strength.

"So you think I'm like one of those women in the film presentation who has baby after baby?"

Surprised, Malcolm glanced at her. "I didn't say that at all. You said Nettie had *all* of the kids, implying there were more than two. I simply asked a natural follow-up question."

Conceding the point, Kendra looked down at her hands. She was financially removed from the projects, but even after the shelter of time,

Kendra felt twinges of unease—as if she didn't really fit in when around people like Malcolm Hightower and Ben and Maggie Trammer. The expensive dress and the dazzling jewelry could make her forget for a few hours, but usually it came down to something like this: Getting defensive at every little word.

"I'm sorry," she said. "I'm so accustomed to trying to shatter myths about welfare mothers, particularly black welfare mothers, that I forget malice isn't intended with every comment."

Kendra placed her handbag on the dash, unsnapped her seat belt, held her hips off the seat and tugged her dress down. Malcolm sighed as she rehooked the safety belt.

"I had hoped you wouldn't notice," he said with obvious regret.

When Kendra looked at him with the question in her eyes, Malcolm gestured toward her hemline. "That your dress had slithered up your legs. I was enjoying the view."

Kendra smiled at the compliment. "You're supposed to be watching the road. This isn't something I would normally buy, let alone wear outside. It was a gift from Nettie."

"I like that woman more every minute," Malcolm mumbled.

Kendra heard his comment and smiled again. "She's hard to dislike."

"Nettie's gift to you is pretty but it doesn't compare to the beauty that is your gift from God."

"Thank you," Kendra muttered, unsure how to respond to the kind words, let alone the husky timbre of Malcolm's voice.

At a red light, Malcolm reached a hand to Kendra. His fingers caressed the elegance at her ears. Four slim diamonds formed the top of the earring. At its center was a round cut ruby half the size of a dime. A trail of diamonds and smaller rubies dripped from the bottom of the earring.

"Enchanting," he said as his fingers hovered over the nape of her neck. He gave in and softly caressed her smooth skin before again placing his unsteady hand on the steering wheel.

Assuming he spoke of the earring Kendra gave an explanation. "They and this bracelet," she said holding out her right arm for him to see, "are the only real jewelry I own. Actually, they belong to my daughters. The bracelet and earrings are a gift from their father."

The light turned green and Malcolm hit the gas with unnecessary force at the mention of the man in Kendra's life. Kendra glanced at him sharply as she caught her breath from the sudden takeoff.

"Is there a problem?" she asked him. His steely profile told Kendra he was angry but she couldn't imagine the cause. About to ask him, Malcolm broke into her thoughts.

"Where is he?"

"Who?"

"The father of your twins."

Kendra looked at him and for a reason she couldn't explain, she longed to ease the tension lines that had formed at his mouth and eyes. His hands gripped the steering wheel so hard Kendra could see the outline of his bones through the brown skin.

"Why do you ask?" she said softly.

Malcolm pulled the car into a park that overlooked the twinkling lights of the city. Still relatively early in the evening, the park was practically deserted. About two hundred yards away, a couple sat on the hood of their vehicle and appeared to be quietly talking. Fighting back the irritation gnawing at him, Malcolm pressed a button and the sunroof opened to reveal a glass-enclosed view of the clear night sky. He turned off the ignition and unsnapped his seat belt before turning to Kendra.

"I want to know who the competition is, where he is, and why the hell you spent two years on welfare when he should have been supporting you and his children," Malcolm demanded angrily.

Kendra sighed. She recognized Malcolm's righteous indignation but didn't guess at the jealousy that propelled it.

"Oscar is dead," she told him quietly. "He died before Karin and Kayla were born." She didn't question the fact that she willingly gave Malcolm more information than she usually shared with people, information she regarded as intensely personal.

The breath swooshed out of Malcolm and he rested his forearms on the steering wheel. "I'm sorry."

"There's nothing to be sorry about. You didn't know me then. I was nineteen. I was scared and pregnant and alone. I did what I had to do to make sure my girls had food, clothing, and shelter."

"Where were your parents?"

"They were killed in a car accident." She didn't mention Aunt Katherine. After seven years, those memories still hurt. Kendra had been banished from the only family she had but she kept in touch in her own way. Each year on the girls' birthday she sent a photograph of the twins to Aunt Kat. She had the girls write a short letter to the relative they'd never met, then she mailed the package. There had never been a reply but the packages were never returned. Kendra still managed to hope for the best.

She continued. "Many times I was tempted to sell the jewelry. Lord knows I needed the money. But every time I walked into a pawn shop, I thought about Kayla and Karin. It wasn't their fault that they didn't have a father and I had no right to get rid of the one thing of material value he left."

"So he knew you were pregnant and gave you the jewelry for the girls?" Malcolm asked.

Kendra's bitter laugh had him turning to her. "Hardly. Look, it's a gorgeous night. I'd rather sit and enjoy it than talk about ancient history."

Malcolm realized there was no need to press Kendra. He'd found out more than he had expected he would. Now was the time to relax and take pleasure in the company of a beautiful woman.

The jazzy saxophone was soon replaced by mellow piano ballads—romantic ones that had both Kendra and Malcolm wondering what the other was thinking, feeling.

With Kendra reclining in the seat gazing at the stars Malcolm took the opportunity to study her. Captivated as much by her quiet strength as her physical attributes, Malcolm compared what he knew about Kendra to the women in his life. His older sister, Sandra, had been feeding him dates for more than five years. Concerned about Malcolm's continued lack of interest in developing a permanent relationship with anyone, Sandra finally stopped setting him up with her fellow physicians and introduced him to a more avant-garde type. Hence, the casual relationship he had with the gallery owner.

Malcolm frowned in the night. He couldn't remember the artist's name. He also couldn't remember the last time he truly enjoyed himself with a woman without sex coming between them. Holding Kendra close on the dance floor had been the closest thing to heaven he could imagine. She fit him the way no other woman had, including the woman who had shared his life and his name for four gruelingly miserable years. Marrying Monica had been a mistake. What he thought had been love was postadolescent lust. What Monica mistook as a cash cow was . . .

Malcolm shut out the thoughts of his ex-wife when his muscles tensed and he felt the telltale throbbing of an oncoming headache. Divorced for almost ten years, Monica's influence on Malcolm still manifest itself in headaches and irritability whenever he happened to think about her. His mother had tried to warn him. But at twenty years old Malcolm wasn't interested in Belle Hightower's opinion on his love life. He loved his mother dearly, but he figured it had been a long time since she had been in love. She just didn't understand how he felt. At twenty-one, Malcolm married Monica. He still wasn't' sure if his mother's tears at the wedding were of anguish or joy.

Malcolm didn't delude himself over his feelings about Kendra. He wanted her. Badly. But more than the physical release and pleasure of intercourse, he wanted to know what made her smile, what made her so fiercely loyal and protective of her daughters. What made her commitment to the Quad-A program so intense that she would agree to let him escort her to the auction when they'd had a less than auspicious beginning?

The tension slowly ebbed from Kendra and for the first time that night she truly let herself relax. She could no longer fool herself into believing Malcolm Hightower was just an insufferable professor. There was more to the man and Kendra longed to decipher the pieces of his puzzle. For now, she refused to analyze the what if's and what about's. Right here and now there was starlight above, city lights ahead, mellow music surrounding her, and the most gorgeous man she'd encountered in years sitting beside her. When she turned her head to look at him, their eyes met.

Surprisingly gentle, his lips covered hers in the barest of butterfly touches. Malcolm then pulled away, but Kendra raised a hand and stroked his cheek. She ran her fingers in a light caress across his lips. Malcolm kissed her fingertips. He gazed into her eyes. The affirmation he found there reassured him. Kendra felt his lips again touch hers like a whisper. But she wanted, needed more from him. The simple caress set her aflame. She returned the kiss with reckless abandon. Had she been aware of anything but the melting way she felt when he touched her, Kendra would have been shocked at her behavior. Malcolm intuitively realized that and fought with himself to end the sweetness that he willingly drank from her mouth.

Utilizing every ounce of control he possessed, Malcolm kissed her once, twice, then pulled away. He wasn't surprised that his breathing was ragged. Kendra didn't seem to be faring much better. She sat with her eyes closed. For long moments neither of them spoke. It was a time of quiet understanding and gentleness, a time to take stock of the situation and choose either the forward path or the one that held no tomorrows.

Kendra silently marveled at the racing of her heart. It had been so very long since she'd kissed a man. Kissing had never been like this. She couldn't remember ever feeling this light, this free. It was as if something dormant inside her opened and blossomed with the first touch of Malcolm's lips. Where would or could this first kiss lead?

Kendra eventually broke the silence.

"I only have the twins."

"Excuse me?"

"You asked earlier if I have more than two children. I only have Karin and Kayla. Nettie is having a sleepover at her house tonight with her five grandkids and the girls. This was my evening to pamper myself with a bubble bath, some peace and quiet and the house all to myself."

Malcolm didn't say anything.

After a moment Kendra sat up quickly and pressed her left hand to her chest in the age-old protective mannerism. "I didn't mean . . . That wasn't an invitation to . . ."

"I know," Malcolm told her as he took her hand. He pressed a gentle kiss into her palm before surrendering it back to her. He started the car and pulled out of the park.

CHAPTER 6

The calla lilies arrived on Kendra's desk at ten o'clock Monday morning. She glanced at the card. *Would you have lunch with me today? Callahan's. 12:30.* It was signed simply Malcolm.

"Are the ladies over at the Quad-A office going to enjoy these as well?" one of Kendra's coworkers asked, gesturing to the arrangement.

Kendra had thanked Malcolm for the first set of flowers he sent; she just didn't tell him that she'd rejected the gesture by having the delivery person take the flowers to the Quad-A office. She did have enough presence of mind to snatch the card from the greenery before he'd left. She had planned to throw the card away, but after reading Malcolm's apology, she couldn't quite bring herself to do it. Even now, as she held the invitation to lunch, Kendra thought of the other small card tucked in her wallet. Out of sight definitely did not equate with out of mind.

"No," she answered her colleague. "I think I'll keep these."

"Must be someone special. Those are rather expensive this time of year. Anyone I know?"

The secretary doing the inquiring was a known gossip in the office. After five years of employment Kendra still managed to keep her coworkers wondering about her social life. That she had two daughters and volunteered with the Quad-A program was common knowledge. But that's about as far as it went. She'd turned down so many dates and had deflected so many advances from men in the large law firm, a rumor had circulated about her sexual preference. When approached by a woman who thought she might accommodate her, Kendra very politely but unequivocally told the paralegal that she was not of that persuasion and didn't date anyone. Period. It got around that the attractive and thoroughly efficient Kendra Edwards wasn't interested in office politics or romance. She did her job, did it well, and went home.

Bosworth Sullivan wasn't senior partner in the fifty-lawyer firm because he kept his head in the sand. He knew more about the people he employed than many of them ever would have guessed. Word got to him that the junior secretary who had been hired through the Quad-A program was not only discreet but circumspect. Sullivan put a note in her file. She'd come into the firm as a receptionist. Six months later her talent and aptitude was rewarded with a promotion to junior secretary. When a position as pool secretary to two associates opened a year later, Sullivan knew just the person to fill the job. It was a significant promotion. After three years in the position, Kendra had received nothing but praise from her superiors. Her yearly evaluations were always glowing reports: "She's professional but personable, a hard worker, a fast learner. Would make a good paralegal or attorney with the proper training."

Kendra had no clue that her handling of the quagmire known as office relationships had had some bearing on her professional advancement. She did know that she wasn't about to give the woman standing before her any juicy tidbits to take to the cafeteria or the watercooler.

"I doubt it," she finally responded in answer to the woman's question about the identity of the flower sender. Kendra acknowledged to herself that even she would be curious about two arrangements of pink and white calla lilies arriving in as many weeks.

When Kendra slipped the card in her suit skirt pocket without offering any more details, the woman got the hint. As she walked away, Kendra shook her head.

"Janice pumping you for information?"

Kendra recognized the voice of one of her bosses. Eric Slater was in his late thirties, married with four children. He represented one-seventh of the firm's contract law division.

"Yes," she said as she traded the file folders he handed her with three more that she pulled from a pile on her desk.

"I must admit I was wondering, too," he said smiling.

"Is that a fact?"

Eric laughed. "You'd make a damn good poker player. You don't give anything away."

"Keeps me out of trouble." She glanced at the open appointment book on her desk. "You have a lunch meeting with the K team," she said, referring to the firm's contract division members. "And a four o'clock with representatives from the Waterbird Foundation. The brief is in the file."

Eric headed back into his office. But before closing the door he poked his head back out. "Not even a hint?"

With a mock regretful expression, Kendra shook her head no. Laughing, Eric shut his office door. Kendra chuckled as she studied the calla lilies. Malcolm Hightower was turning her world upside down.

Off the beaten path and known more for its afterwork crowds, Callahan's wasn't jammed with midday lunchers. The people dining there tended to be quieter, with the focus on serious conversation and good food instead of networking and being seen.

When Kendra arrived, Malcolm was already waiting at a secluded table. Kendra took note that any conversation they had would be private. Malcolm stood as she walked up with the hostess.

The smile Malcolm gave Kendra transformed his face. No evidence existed of the tension lines that had been present a few days before. The chocolate brown double-breasted suit he wore complemented his rich skin tone. The tie, with its bright green, yellow, and brown pattern, would have been a disaster on another man. On Malcolm the bold design was a mark of individual style and panache. He took her hands in his and leaned forward. The kiss on her cheek was short and friendly, as if they were two old friends who always met for lunch.

"Thank you for joining me. I wasn't sure if you'd come," Malcolm told her as he helped her into her chair.

"The flowers are beautiful. You're causing a stir at my office, though."

"How so?"

"Let's just say that, by now, there are probably odds on whether or not an engagement ring will be seen on my finger in the immediate future."

"That bad, huh?" he said, secretly pleased that Kendra's receiving flowers at work was outside the norm. "I'd forgotten how intense the gossip mill could be at large firms."

"You worked for one?"

Malcolm nodded. "It seems like a lifetime ago, though. It was right after I finished law school. I clerked for a judge, then worked at a big firm for two years."

Their waiter arrived. After they placed their orders Kendra picked up their conversation.

"How did you land at Mayview, Jackson, Hightower?"

"You did some homework?"

Kendra laughed. "You flatter yourself, Hightower. The Quad-A program application. Besides, you included the name of your firm on the course outline," she said.

"I'd forgotten about that."

"What? That I was a student of yours or that I volunteer with Quad-A?"

"Both."

Kendra didn't say anything, but she wondered if her welfare background bothered Malcolm. Maybe she was just a curiosity to this man, with his tailored suits and luxury car. Kendra also remembered that the bids he'd made at the auction weren't of a size to be ignored.

Unaware of her thoughts, Malcolm gave a quick rundown on his history. "I was married at twenty-one. Divorced at twenty-five. After the stint with the judge and the large firm I got an offer at Mayview, Jackson. A buddy from undergrad had gone on to law school and had joined his father's firm. When his dad started thinking about retirement, they started looking for me."

"Who is Jackson?"

"Marshall Jackson was an original partner, along with my buddy's father. He died many years ago. The terms of the estate make his widow a silent partner and ensures that the name stays. Robinson's mother has the same protection should anything ever happen to his father."

"It's all very familial."

"Part of the charm of a small operation. Robinson and I have four associates and a single paralegal. We probably need to expand a little. It would help the work load."

Their talking ceased as their waiter placed lunch before them. Malcolm attacked the pastrami and provolone with gusto. They ate in companionable silence for a few moments.

"You said you were married. Do you have children?" Kendra asked.

"No. Thank God!"

Kendra blanched. Well, so much for that, she thought. If the man hates kids, I can't get involved with him. Malcolm realized the course of her thoughts when Kendra took a sudden and intense interest in the turkey salad garnished with pineapple and raisins on her plate.

"I didn't mean that the way it came out. I love kids, but I thank God every day that my ex-wife and I didn't have any. The divorce was ugly enough without adding a custody battle into the mix. Had we had children I would have never seen the end of her."

"That bad, huh?"

Malcolm grimaced. "Let's talk about something else. Like you. Tell me, what do you do when you're not at work or doing presentations for Quad-A?"

Kendra dabbed her mouth with her napkin, then laughed. "Hate to disappoint you, but that's about it. I go to work, go to church, and chauffeur my girls around."

Malcolm smiled. "If they are half as pretty as you, you're going to have two heartbreakers on your hands."

The compliment came in the middle of what had been a no-pressure lunch. Flustered, Kendra took a sip of iced tea to gain her composure.

"Do you always blush when people say nice things about you?"

When Kendra looked up, Malcolm had his elbows propped on the edge of the table. With his chin resting in one hand, he contemplated her. There was no mistaking the sensual regard in his eyes.

"Do you know how embarrassing it is to be a black woman whose skin turns red? I thought I'd overcome the ailment."

Malcolm decided against asking her if she knew how hot she made him, if she had a clue that he wanted to whisk their lunch away and make love to her on the linen-covered table. He instead eased the pressure on her by leaning back in his chair. His quick smile was self-deprecating when he heard Kendra's audible sigh of relief.

"I have box seats at the symphony. Would you join me Saturday evening?"

Kendra thought about his invitation for a moment and was about to say yes when she remembered the school play. While the girls were at their piano lesson that night, she planned to finish the costumes they needed for the second-grade production of *Beauy and the Beast.* Karin had landed the role of a teacup while Kayla was one of the townspeople. With the exception of Wednesday, which was family night for Kendra and the girls, Monday was the only evening she had left to complete the costumes.

"I'm sorry. I'd love to, but the girls have a school play Saturday."

Hearing the genuine regret in her voice, Malcolm decided it was time to push. "What about Friday?"

"Friday? I thought you said the tickets were for Saturday."

"They are. But Friday night we could go to dinner. Dancing."

"Didn't we just do that this past Friday?"

Malcolm nodded. "And I loved every minute of it."

Kendra knew he was referring to what had happened in his car at the park. Her uncertainty was evident when she bit her lower lip. Malcolm swallowed and gripped the edge of the table. The image of her moist tongue softly kneading her lip was more than he thought he could bear. He ran his hand over his face and took a deep breath.

"How about it?"

When Kendra nodded, he exhaled a long sigh of contentment and gave her a smile that sent her pulse racing.

The date set, Malcolm picked up his fork to finish the red potato salad that accompanied his sandwich.

Kendra was glad she was sitting down. Had she been standing, she didn't think her knees would have supported her during the relentless line of questioning and its sensuous overtones. Malcolm probably operated that way in court, she thought. Wear 'em down until they confess.

After a few minutes of eating with just the noise of other diners in the background, Malcolm picked up where they'd left off.

"Has it been difficult being a single parent?"

"At times. Since Quad-A, Nettie has been there when I've needed guidance. Sometimes I've regretted that the girls don't have a father. I remember how special my dad was to me. I wish I had a brother or an uncle, someone they could see in their lives as a male role model. But I guess it's no use lamenting that fact. I think it could have been worse if I had had boys."

"Little girls need dads, too," Malcolm told her.

"Look, I spend time, lots of time, with my girls. They have piano lessons on Monday nights, ballet on Thursday. Every Wednesday we do something together at home. Saturday mornings we go to the library, then head to a museum or the zoo or something. If spending most of my weeknights and all day and evening Saturday with my children means I have no social life, so be it. When my daughters are my age, I want them to be able to look back at their childhood and say 'Hey, my mom did all right even though she was a single parent.' "

Malcolm absorbed all that she'd said and then some. Kendra had unknowingly answered more of the questions he had about her. He recognized the chip on her shoulder about some things. And he was absolutely certain there were no men in her life. He knew that she put her children's happiness way above her own. He also knew her schedule. The one thing Kendra needed more than anything else was the chance to live a little; she was still a young woman—she needed to *feel* young again.

Malcolm had a plan.

The week went by in a blur. Despite the fact that Malcolm's name was drawn in curlicues along the edges of her exam paper, Kendra aced a quiz in her sociology seminar, the last course she needed to graduate. The girls had a final fitting of their play costumes Wednesday evening. While Kayla and Karin attended their ballet lesson Thursday night, Kendra and Nettie had a heart-to-heart at the Quad-A office.

Kendra usually spent Thursdays volunteering for the program. Whenever possible, Nettie scheduled Kendra's presentations for Thursdays to avoid the big babysitter dilemma. But there were no presentations for the night and all the paperwork was complete. The two women sat cross-legged on the carpeted floor of the children's recreation room and sipped chocolate milk from paper cartons. They were supposed to be cutting out butterflies and flowers for a bulletin board that heralded the coming of spring. They had been on the floor for a good forty-five minutes and not a single flower or butterfly had emerged from the construction paper that still waited in colorful piles.

"Nettie, I'm frightened. What if he wants to have sex? What if he *expects* to have sex?"

"Ken, if the man was going to force the issue, it would have been done by now. Friday night was the perfect opportunity for him to make his move. From what I gather, he was every bit the gentleman. Who was it who called me at the crack of dawn Saturday saying all he did was kiss you on the forehead and tell you good night at the door?"

Kendra's shoulders slumped. "I know. It's just that I don't know what I want. He seems to be everything I thought I wanted in a man but now I don't know."

"What is it that you don't know?"

Kendra frowned and tried to put her feelings into words. "I don't know. It's like sometimes I pick up this undercurrent that he thinks I'm beneath him because I'm a secretary and he's a lawyer. Because I was on welfare and he wears thousand-dollar suits. Other times, I think it's just me and my hang-ups, my imagination."

"I think you're exaggerating on how much his clothes cost. But that's neither here nor there. Has he ever said or done anything to make you believe he thinks less of you because of your background and what you do?"

"Not really. And every time I call him on it he has a legitimate explanation on how I misunderstood or jumped to conclusions."

"You know what your problem is, girlfriend?" Nettie said. "You've let that no-good Oscar MacAfree and those lecherous old coots at Sullivan and O'Leary shape your opinion of all men. You need to loosen up. You're too young to be languishing away."

"I don't see you out in the streets kicking up your heels."

Nettie laughed. "I'm forty-seven with grandkids. You're twenty-six. There's a big difference. Besides, I don't think you even know how to flirt."

Kendra's snort at the idea reinforced Nettie's opinion. "If he told you he liked your dress, what would you tell him? And I'm talking about that hot little number we got for you to wear to the auction, not one of those puritan outfits you wrap yourself in."

"For your information, Miss Know-It-All," Kendra said, "he did and I told him he wasn't looking so bad himself." She stuck her tongue out at Nettie in a "so there" gesture.

"Not bad. Maybe there is hope for you. An even better response would have been, 'I bought it with you in mind,' or perhaps an innocent, 'Do you think it's too short?' "

Kendra laughed at the audacity of her friend. "You are incorrigible. I'd never say anything like that." She paused. "But I do know the hemline met with his approval."

Kendra quickly told Nettie about Malcolm's regret when she tugged her dress down in his car.

Nettie was incredulous. "You mean to tell me you sat alone in that car with that gorgeous man and all you did was talk?"

The unwelcome blush crept up Kendra's cheeks. Nettie noticed it before Kendra could hop up to throw their milk cartons away. "Praise God, hallelujah, there's hope. I thought the man had let me down," Nettie muttered under her breath.

"What about tomorrow night?" Kendra asked from across the room. When she returned, she grabbed a pair of scissors and a few sheets of construction paper before heading to a table. Sitting in one of the child-sized plastic chairs, she folded a sheet and began cutting out a butterfly from yellow construction paper.

"What about it?" Nettie said as she got up to join Kendra at the table.

Kendra gave her an exasperated huff.

"Ken, I'm a pretty good judge of character. I don't think this man is going to push you to do anything you don't want to do. Keep in mind that I said anything you *don't* want to do. Now, I can tell you're battling with this thing. You have to let it develop at its own pace. If a sexual relationship is where it's headed, it will come with time. If not, it won't happen."

"And the girls? I'm just supposed to say, 'Leave the house, Mom has a date she'll probably bring home for the night'?"

Nettie's smile was indulgent, like one bestowed upon a daughter just emerging into womanhood.

"I think you know the answer to that, Kendra. And I know you're a responsible parent. I would suggest that you talk with them about dating. If you haven't done that yet, maybe now's the time to tell them that Mom will be going out in the evenings occasionally."

"It'll be like I'm deserting them."

Nettie pulled the scissors from Kendra's hands and took the construction-paper butterfly that she had made. "No, Kendra. You're not deserting your girls by going out on a date for the first time in seven years. You're like the butterfly," she said, unfolding the paper. "It's time to emerge from the cocoon, test your beautiful wings and soar."

The two women hugged. Through Kendra's silent tears she realized that she had just closed a chapter of her life.

Nettie was the first to pull back, but she held Kendra's shoulders and gave her a stern look.

"Kendra, do you know anything about condoms?"

Heat stole up the younger woman's face.

Later that evening before tucking the girls in for the night, Kendra sat on the edge of Karin's bed. The twins faced their mom while hugging their twin teddy bears.

"Hey, I wanted to ask you guys something," Kendra began. "What would you think if Mom went out from time to time?"

"Out where?" Kayla asked.

But Karin was quicker on the uptake. "You mean like a date with somebody? Whoopee!" she shouted, tossing the teddy bear, Askia, in the air.

Kendra couldn't halt the frown that marred her face for a brief moment. "And what do you know about dates, young lady?"

"Well, Angie Simmons at school, her mom goes on dates all the time," Karin said.

"And stinky Myron, he said his father wanted to ask you on a date one time but you didn't seem to want to," Kayla added.

"But we were glad you didn't because if you went on a date with stinky Myron's dad, we might have to be nice to him at school."

Too overwhelmed by her daughters' response, Kendra didn't bother to correct them from their assessment of their classmate.

"So you're saying it wouldn't bother you if I went out on a date?"

"Just as long as it isn't stinky Myron's father," Kayla said.

"Yeah. We were thinking about asking Aunt Nettie to help us find someone to take you out on a date, but if you got one all by yourself that's really cool," Karin told her mother.

Kendra was positive that she'd just been insulted by her offspring, but there was little help for it. Her seven-year-old girls were sitting there telling her to get a life.

"Well, I'm glad you two are so happy about it. I have a date tomorrow night."

"Oooohhh," the girls said in unison before falling back on the bed and erupting in giggles.

Kendra slid off the edge of Karin's bed and pounced on the girls. The tickling frenzy was on. Laughter from all three echoed across the room. The twins had perfected their tickling technique. Wiggling from under Kendra, they managed to end up on top. With her stomach on the mattress, Kendra was at the mercy of the little fingers flittering at her sides. After several minutes of torment, she finally caught her breath enough to yell "Uncle!" amidst her laughter.

The girls let her up and she planted a big sloppy kiss on each of their noses. Before Kendra could get a word in, the twins hit her with a barrage of questions.

"Does your date work at your job?"

"Is he cute?"

"Is he tall?"

"Does he have kids?"

"What kind of car does he drive?"

With a girl on each knee, Kendra laughed. She fell back on the bed so Kayla could scramble under the covers. She then plopped Karin in the middle of her bed.

"Are you two sure you're just seven years old?"

"Mommmiiee," they both whined in mock severity.

"Okay, okay. Let's see. No. He doesn't work at my job. Yes, he's cute. Yes, he's tall. No, he doesn't have any kids and he drives a black Saab."

"What are you gonna do on your date?" Karin asked.

"They're gonna kiss, silly. That's what people do on dates, right Mom?" Kayla said.

Kendra had thought seven a bit young for a discussion on the birds and the bees but if they were harboring the notion that people only kissed on dates it was time to nip something in the bud before it became a problem.

She tucked Kayla in, then turned to Karin's bed. When she finished, she again sat on the edge of the bed, this time Kayla's.

"No, sweetie. That's not all people do on dates. They go to eat, they talk. Sometimes they go to the movies or to a concert. Most of all they get to know each other. People get to know each other by talking about their feelings."

"When does the kissing come?" Kayla wanted to know.

"Well, there are different kinds of kissing," she began. Karin interrupted.

"The kissing like Susie Kent's parents do when they think nobody's looking."

Mrs. Kent was vice president of the Parent-Teacher-Student Association. Kendra couldn't imagine when Kayla and Karin would have seen her kissing her husband. She didn't, however, pretend that she didn't know what the girls were talking about.

"Mommies and Daddies kiss to show how much they love each other. Sometimes people who go out on dates kiss to let the other person know that they care about them."

"Are you gonna kiss your date tomorrow, Mom?" Kayla asked.

"You're not supposed to ask that, goosehead," Karin responded to her twin. "Grown-ups don't kiss and tell, right Mom?"

"Right. I think it's lights out for you two."

Kendra gave each girl a kiss on the forehead and turned out the light as she left their room after wishing them pleasant dreams. She had no doubt that the discussion on kissing would continue without her.

Kendra pulled the door closed and collapsed against the frame. That had been the toughest twenty minutes she could remember in quite some time. Before she realized it, it was going to be time to have the real discussion on the birds and the bees with her daughters. Kendra wasn't sure if she was looking forward to it or if she was dreading the moment.

The one thing she was sure of was that she wasn't going to let her daughters grow up like the naive little chit she had been. She'd believed Oscar's assurances that he would pull out in time. That proof showed up nine months later. In all honesty, Kendra didn't regret that moment in time because it had created two of the most beautiful children on the planet. But she had no intention of reliving that experience with Malcolm Hightower or anyone else. She headed down the short hallway to her room and thought about the little box she'd purchased at a drug store on the way back from Nettie's office.

CHAPTER 7

The babysitter arrived twenty minutes early and gave Kendra the extra minutes she needed to calm her nerves. She had changed clothes twice.

She wanted to make a good impression with Malcolm, but she didn't want to give him the wrong idea. The white dress had been a deliciously sensual aberration in her wardrobe; and while she was assured that the dress looked good on her, with so much skin showing, she'd felt self-conscious all evening the night of the auction. Nettie constantly rode her about the so-called missionary outfits she wore to work and the scuffy jeans and T-shirts she put on the rest of the time.

The fact of the matter was that Kendra's afterwork wardrobe was, indeed, sorely lacking. After trying on and discarding a red and green print dress she decided made her look like a Christmas tree, and a snappy blue and white sailor-look suit, Kendra settled on a straight black skirt with a black peplum jacket. The jacket had elegant black and gold braid trimming. Kendra jazzed up a pair of plain black high-heeled pumps by clipping two bows in the same braid design onto the front of the shoes. Rooting around in her jewelry box, she found the matching earrings she'd made with the leftover material.

Kendra stepped back and took a look at the total effect in the full-length mirror in her bedroom. She was pleased. She looked graceful and refined without appearing pretentious or overeager to hop in bed. With that thought, she walked back to her closet and dug out the box of condoms she'd purchased the night before. She slipped two of the little packages into her handbag.

"Hmmm, better safe than sorry, girlfriend," she said aloud as she added another two to the purse.

Kendra jumped when the doorbell rang. Miss Bessie and the girls were making brownies in the kitchen. Even as she tried to decide whether or not to go to the door herself, she heard Kayla's and Karin's ruckus as they raced to take a look at their Mom's date.

"Young ladies do not run," she heard Miss Bessie call after them from the kitchen. Bessie Jones had been watching the girls for about two years. As babysitters went, she was reliable, honest, and scrupulously mannerly. Kendra had no fear that her daughters weren't well cared for when Miss Bessie was in charge.

Kendra flipped the switch for her bedroom light and walked the length of the short hallway. She stood just out of the line of sight from the front door. She wasn't really surprised to discover that Malcolm's rich baritone as he introduced himself to the girls sent little ripples of pleasure down her spine.

The spitting image of their mother, the two little girls took Malcolm's breath away. He wondered what it would be like to have children, daughters and sons in his own image. The unpleasant mental picture that had always come forth when he thought of having children with his ex-wife was vanquished in the space of a moment. Children he and Kendra created would be as beautiful as the two standing before him. Their expectant faces and childhood exuberance made him smile. While he'd spent time with his young nephew, B.J., Malcolm had not had much experience with little girls. He guessed that they were a lot like big girls, so he'd come prepared.

"Hi there. My name's Malcolm," he said in greeting to Kayla and Karin.

"You're our Mom's date, right?" Karin asked without preamble.

"That's right. But I wanted to make sure it was okay with the two of you."

"We talked about it and we think it's cool that Mom is going out. Are you two going to kiss?" Kayla inquired.

"That's enough, Kayla," Kendra said from the doorway. Her young daughter seemed to have developed a preoccupation with kissing.

The smile that played about Malcolm's mouth would have been a cause for dismay if Kendra herself hadn't been wondering the same thing as Kayla.

"Malcolm Hightower, I'd like you to meet my daughters, Kayla, with the pink ribbons, and Karin, with the green. Girls."

"It's a pleasure to meet you, Mr. Hightower," Kayla said.

"Good evening, sir," Karin said.

Malcolm pulled out the hand he'd been holding behind his back. "I've always been told that beautiful women should have beautiful flowers." He presented Kayla with two red and white carnations in green tissue paper. He then turned to her sister and gave her an identical arrangement. For Kendra he had a single pink calla lily.

Kendra's hand trembled as she accepted the delicate flower.

"Thank you," she murmured.

Kayla and Karin were more vocal in their thanks.

"Wow! Flowers for all of us. That's really cool," Kayla declared.

"Mine are better than yours," her sister said.

"Are not."

"Girls, please," Kendra gently scolded. "Your flowers are identical, just like you and just like Ashanti and Askia. What do you say to Mr. Hightower?"

"Thank you," they said in unison.

"We're gonna go show Miss Bessie, okay, Mom?"

"Okay. Have Miss Bessie put your flowers in a couple of vases."

"What about yours?" Kayla asked.

"I'll hold on to mine for a little while."

As the girls skipped out of the room, Malcolm and Kendra overheard Kayla's not-quite-sotto-voce remark, "I bet they're gonna kiss now."

Kendra fought the heat she knew was evident on her face. When she looked up at Malcolm she forgot how to breathe. He was so close. The moment before his lips covered hers, Kendra heard him say, "I'd like nothing better."

It started as a gentle caress, but the pent-up hunger they both felt was more than either of them could control. Malcolm's tender assault overwhelmed Kendra. She opened to his probing tongue as he pulled her closer to him. His moist, firm mouth demanded a response and Kendra answered the call. She drank in the sweetness and lost herself in the beauty of the moment.

At the same time, they remembered where they were, that the girls were just down the hall. Kendra was unsteady when she stepped away. She turned to a low table and picked up a vase for the calla lily she still held. Malcolm used the respite to bring himself under control. He burned for her. And given Kendra's response to him, she felt the same way he did. Sitting across from or next to her at dinner would be torture. Slow and easy, he coached himself. But that part of Malcolm that wanted Kendra most was screaming for a fast and hard release.

"I . . . I'll be ready in just a moment. I need to say goodbye to the girls," Kendra managed from where she stood a few feet away.

As she headed toward the kitchen, Kendra realized that never in her twenty-six years had she felt so alive, so energized. She felt as if she were on the front seat of a roller coaster. But the exhilaration that zipped through her was followed quickly by an uneasy trepidation. Was she falling for Malcolm Hightower or was she starved for male attention and simply falling for the affection he bestowed on her? Would she be a bad person if she gave in to the clamoring demand of her body? She'd been swayed by flowers and pretty words once before. Was this the same or was it, as she wanted to believe, special, sincere, for real?

Kendra kissed the girls and bid Miss Bessie good night. She still had no answers to her questions by the time she and Malcolm reached the rooftop restaurant. Throughout their meal, the restaurant slowly revolved, lending them a panoramic view of the city.

"Would you care for dessert?" their waiter asked as he displayed a cart of sumptuous sweets.

Malcolm raised an eyebrow at Kendra, who took a delicate sip from the glass of white wine she had nursed through the last portion of their dinner.

"I don't think I have room to spare," she said.

"The strawberries with fresh cream are excellent this evening. Not too heavy," the waiter cajoled with a smile. Kendra watched Malcolm's gray eyes darken and wondered if he shared the sensual image that had come to her mind with the dessert recommendation.

She'd spent the entire meal anxiously awaiting the next sensuous salvo from Malcolm. But he had been the perfect gentleman. There hadn't been a single subtle demand, no burning looks, not one stolen kiss, not even a double entendre. He hadn't tried to touch her in any way and had seemed unmoved when as they talked during dinner she briefly touched his hand as it rested on the table. Irrationally, Kendra was peeved. Had he been toying with her earlier?

Kendra didn't know how close Malcolm was to breaking. The back of his palm still felt singed where she'd gently touched him earlier. But Malcolm was a man of control and he'd decided when they left her apartment that Kendra would have to come to him. He didn't know the entire story about her past, but he sensed that Kendra had to come to grips with it as well as what she was feeling about him. He wanted, God how he wanted, to draw her into his arms. The dancing he'd planned wouldn't do. To dance, he'd have to hold her. And that would be torture.

He nixed the notion of decadent strawberries and cream for dessert and willingly guided Kendra out of the intimate setting after paying their bill.

"Where to now?" Kendra asked as Malcolm settled into the driver's seat of his luxurious Lincoln Town Car. He managed the big car with ease. He'd decided to drive what he called his "formal" car after noting Kendra's discomfiture in the smaller Saab. He wanted this to be a no-pressure date. But the possibilities of what could be accomplished with the seats reclined in the town car made Malcolm uncomfortable. He refused to dwell on it.

"It's a surprise," he told her. But since he'd privately ruled out dancing, Malcolm had no idea about what they would do next. They were both too dressed up for something as everyday as the movies. While considering a show at a comedy club, Malcolm spotted the inviting bright lights of a miniature golf course. Perfect!

When he turned into the establishment's crowded parking lot, Kendra looked at him questioningly.

"This is miniature golf," she said.

"Yep."

Malcolm parked the car, got out, and walked around to open her door for her.

"We're not exactly dressed for miniature golf."

Malcolm quickly scanned Kendra from the top of her head to the toes of her high-heeled shoes. He liked what he saw—a lot. "I didn't know they had a dress code," he said.

Kendra looked at him. Then she started to laugh. "You're on, buddy," she told him as he helped her out of the car.

They spent the next two hours with teenagers on dates and families taking an evening out. They were by far the best-dressed pair on the course. At the windmill round, Kendra kicked off her shoes, handed them to Malcolm, and settled in to make her putt. Her hole-in-one drew applause from the people waiting behind them. Laughing in her victory, she skipped to the place where Malcolm stood scowling and planted a quick, wet kiss on his lips.

"Better luck next time, baby," she playfully taunted as she snatched her shoes. "Loser buys the ice cream."

"Well, I like butter pecan, so you'd better get your money ready. I'm a wizard at the waterfall, and that's the next round. You're gonna eat my dust," he predicted.

"Promises, promises." Kendra slipped her shoes back on and held out her hand for Malcolm.

They strolled hand in hand to the next course, where Malcolm proceeded to embarrass himself. His ball ran so far afield of the channel leading to the waterfall that a little kid offered a pointer.

"Hey mister, you're supposed to try to make it go to the waterfall, not around it."

Everyone within hearing distance, and particularly the folks who were a stroke behind Malcolm and Kendra, joined in the good-natured laughter at Malcolm's expense.

"What's your name, son?" Malcolm asked the boy.

"Mike."

"Well, Mike. I missed that shot because I had interference."

"What interference? The wind wasn't blowin' or anything."

Kendra giggled at Malcolm's halfhearted attempt to redeem himself.

"See that lady over there, the pretty one with the long hair?" Malcolm asked the boy. When the child nodded, Malcolm continued. "She distracted me."

The boy wasn't buying it. "No, she didn't. She was just standing there. I saw her. Maybe you need to try this again. I can show you how."

At that, Kendra burst into all-out laughter. The boy's mother, also chuckling at the exchange, called to him. Malcolm sighed and made his way to Kendra. He couldn't quite manage the doleful expression he affected, and a hearty laugh escaped from him.

"Come on, mister," Kendra told him, as she linked her arm with his. "Last round. Let a pro show you how it's done. By the way, I like rocky road."

Less than twenty minutes later, Kendra the victorious sat on a bench licking two scoops of rocky road ice cream from a cone. Malcolm, legs stretched out and crossed at the ankles, sat beside her, working on two scoops of butter pecan.

"It was a lucky shot," he mumbled.

"Still pouting? Poor baby," the giggle ruined Kendra's attempt at sportsmanlike sympathy.

As they finished off their ice cream cones, Kendra leaned over and kissed Malcolm on the cheek.

"What was that for?"

"For giving me the most fun I've had in years," she told him.

Malcolm counted the evening a success.

It wasn't until the next morning as Kendra transferred her driver's license from the small evening bag to her everyday purse that she remembered the condoms. Other than the steamy kiss in her living room, Malcolm had made no demands on her. Her trust in him jumped several notches.

Less than an hour later, Kayla and Karin resumed their books at the library's main desk. Kendra walked with them to the children's section, where they pulled their name tags out of the pile and selected two plump pillows to sit on during story hour. Kendra saw them settled, shifted the backpack full of her own study materials, and turned to leave. Malcolm stood before her. The thing she noticed after observing how well his blue jeans fit was the small hand in his. It was attached to a boy about the same age as Kayla and Karin.

"Hi there," she told them.

"Hi yourself. Kendra, I'd like you to meet B.J. B.J., this is Miss Kendra Edwards."

"Hi, Miss Edwards," the child told her. To Malcolm he said, "You're right. She's really pretty."

Malcolm sighed. "You're blowing my cover, young man. Go check in and grab a pillow so you can hear the story."

Amused, Kendra stared after the boy's retreating back.

"I didn't quite see you as the Hansel and Gretel type," she said. She watched the boy have a name tag made and then, as if he were equipped with a radar device, hone in on Karin and Kayla and settled himself between the twins. "I also didn't know there was a rent-a-kid operation around here."

"I didn't rent him. I borrowed him from his parents for a few hours."

"Uh-huh."

Malcolm fell into step beside Kendra as she made her way to the area where she always did her schoolwork.

"I need to spend more quality time with my nephew."

"Uh-huh. How much did you have to pay him?"

Malcolm laughed. "Five bucks. But it was money well spent. It would have been ten, but I assured him that the best-looking babes hung out at the library."

"Best-looking babes, huh?"

"Definitely," Malcolm assured her.

Kendra had to give him credit in one regard: Malcolm had gone out of his way to share her company. She dropped her backpack on a table and looked up at him.

Her smile chased away every coherent thought in Malcolm's head.

"Well?" she asked him.

"Well?"

"Well, what are you going to do while I study?"

"Study?" he stupidly repeated. Malcolm had been a menace on the miniature golf course. Now he couldn't even form simple sentences. The T-shirt she wore distracted him. It promoted a long-defunct rhythm and blues band. But if Malcolm wasn't mistaken, and there was no way he could be in this instance, Kendra's ripe breasts would be a handful and then some.

Kendra took a book out of the bag and waved it before him. "You know, study. School. Grades. Term paper. Graduation."

"Oh." Get a grip, Hightower, he told himself. Malcolm forced his brain to function. "Is it a subject I can help you with? I'm a good tutor."

"I'll just bet you are," Kendra said as she sneaked a peek below his waist. Malcolm seemed to be having a few problems, but Kendra couldn't be too critical. She wasn't faring much better. She crossed her arms in a self-conscious gesture to shield from his view the suddenly puckered nipples of her breasts. But he'd already noticed.

Malcolm latched on to the one word that helped him focus on the present.

"You're going to be graduating from the paralegal program?"

For a moment Kendra was confused. "Paralegal? Oh," she said, pulling out a chair and sitting at the table. Malcolm sat in the heavy wooden chair next to hers. "No. I was just enrolled in your class to gauge my interest in law school. I'm getting my bachelor's degree in sociology in May. Just under three and a half more months and this odyssey will be complete. It's taken forever. But that's what happens when you can only take one or two courses at night every semester."

Malcolm gestured to the books and folders she pulled from her backpack. "Senior project?"

"Thesis. The outline and preliminary literature review are due this week. Malcolm, I don't mean to be rude. I am enjoying your company, but this is the only time I really have for absolute study. After story hour the kids make crafts, then pick out books for the coming week. I have less than two hours to get this done."

"I'm sorry. I wasn't thinking. I'll let you get to work and I'll do the same."

For the first time, Kendra noticed the slim leather attache case he carried. When he pulled a legal size file folder crammed with papers from the case, Kendra looked at him.

"The teaching part is fun. Grading papers leaves a lot to be desired," he told her.

Kendra smiled, then buried herself in her schoolwork.

They worked in companionable silence. Several times Kendra got up to consult a reference book or check a fact. Each time Malcolm's gaze followed her. After her third trip, he gave up all pretense of grading papers. Kendra had worked nonstop for well over an hour. He should have had at least a dozen of the assignments read and graded in that time period. He was barely into the second one and had no clue what score he'd given the first student's efforts.

As a man, Malcolm could appreciate Kendra's physical beauty. But what he felt about her went beyond the possibility of great sex. He admired her determination to complete her college education. Other women would have given up after the pregnancy; other women may never have committed themselves to finishing the coursework. He admired the relationship she had with her daughters. When he arrived at the house to pick Kendra up for their date the night before, Kayla had said they'd talked about Kendra going out with him. How many other women would discuss their relationships with their children? While inquisitive as young children should be, Kendra's daughters were mannerly. Obviously, Kendra raised them in the old-school methods, which included respect for one's elders.

And today she'd let him know that he was infringing on her valuable study time. But she'd done it with grace. She could have told him to buzz off in no uncertain terms. She also could have bagged her schoolwork and let the chips fall where they may in her class the next week. But not Kendra. A little flirting was not going to divert her from her goal. She was totally committed: to her children, to her schoolwork, to the Quad-A program. Kendra Edwards personified the strong African-American woman.

Malcolm realized he was in love with Kendra, and the thought left him reeling. His heart swelled with the headiness of the emotion. In love. So this is how it felt, Malcolm thought. He wanted to cherish her. Make babies with her. Be a father to her daughters. To grow old with Kendra at his side.

"Was it nineteen-eighty-five or nineteen-eighty-six when the space shuttle *Challenger* exploded?" she asked out of the blue.

With her hair in a ponytail, her brow knitted in concentration, and her lower lip captured in her mouth, Kendra was unaware of the captivating picture she made. Malcolm's mouth curled in a tender smile. He added her unconscious habit of biting her lip to the things he loved about her.

When he failed to answer, she looked up and was arrested by the intensity of his gaze. "What's wrong?"

"You are an incredibly beautiful woman," he told her. Still sorting through his new awareness, Malcolm didn't elaborate on the statement and realized Kendra probably thought he was referring to her physical attributes.

Kendra beamed under the compliment. "What brought that on?"

Malcolm just shook his head and smiled at her. "*Challenger* was in nineteen-eighty-six. I'm going to go check on the kids. They should be wrapping up soon."

"Okay. The girls know where to find me."

When Malcolm left, Kendra chewed on her pencil and wondered about the change she sensed in him.

Kendra wasn't at all surprised to see Malcolm and B.J. at the library the next Saturday. Kayla and Karin had talked nonstop about the boy during the week. B.J. drew their picture, B.J. had a puppy. B.J. thought it was cool to have a twin. When she finally despaired of hearing the boy's initials, she asked the girls what they stood for. The identical stricken looks told Kendra they hadn't thought to ask. Knowing her daughters, Kendra figured they'd have that bit of information before they were all seated.

She and Malcolm settled at the same table they'd shared the previous week. Malcolm actually managed to get some work done this time, but he confessed to himself that he'd spent half of their quiet time just watching Kendra.

The outing Kendra and the girls had planned for after story hour was a trip to the science museum. As the five of them stood in the library lobby, Kendra extended an invitation to Malcolm and B.J. to accompany them. In the ladies room, the girls had told her that B.J. stood for a lot of things. The boy was named after his father William Joseph Bliss, Sr., so B.J. was short for Billy Joe, Bliss Junior, and even Bill Junior.

Excited about spending more time with his newfound friends, B.J. pleaded with his uncle to let them go to the museum. When Kayla and Karin added their voices to the appeal, Malcolm conceded. "I need to call and make sure it's okay with your folks. They're expecting you."

"No, they aren't. They went to Washington today," B.J. told him. "You're supposed to take me to Gram Belle's house, remember?"

"I forgot about that. Well, let me give her a call so she won't worry about you."

"We'll meet you in the parking lot," Kendra told him.

Malcolm found the pay telephones near the restrooms and dialed his mother's house.

"Good day," she responded on the third ring. Malcolm smiled at the way his mom had always answered the telephone.

"Hi, Mama, it's Malc."

"Hello, baby. Did you enjoy story hour? What was today's selection, Goldilocks and the Three Bears?"

Malcolm laughed. "I don't have the foggiest. I spent the time grading papers."

"I'll wager you didn't get much done if your lady friend was there. I hear she's very pretty."

"It's obvious you've been pumping that poor, innocent child for information."

"Hah. All he can talk about is Kayla and Karin. What's with the K's in this woman's family?"

Malcolm chuckled. "I don't know, Mom. Want me to ask for you?"

"Don't you dare. Why are you calling? I would think you'd be trying to court your lady friend."

Malcolm didn't say anything but he liked the old-fashioned notion of courting Kendra. He smiled into the receiver.

"Hey, Mom?"

"Yes, baby."

"I'd like for you to meet her."

Malcolm could hear his mother's surprise. In the almost ten years since his divorce, Malcolm had dated but he'd never, ever brought anyone home to meet his mother.

"Okay, son," Miss Belle finally responded. "Why don't you invite her and her girls to Sunday dinner."

"I'll ask, but that's awfully short notice. If they can't come tomorrow, will next Sunday be okay?"

"You know it is. Now, why are you calling me?"

"We're all going to the Natural Science Museum. So I'll be bringing B.J. in a little later than planned.

"No problem."

"Did Sandra and Bill get off on time?"

"Of course not. There was some emergency at the hospital and they were both tied up in the emergency room. They caught a later flight. Luckily, the panel Sandy is on comes later this afternoon. They'll be able to get some rest before the main part of the conference starts. Malcolm?"

"Yes, ma'am?"

"Why are you gabbing on the phone with me? Don't you have three kids and your lady friend waiting on you?"

"You're right. I'm outta here. Love you."

Before he rang off, Malcolm heard his mother's soft entreaty.

"Malcolm?"

"Yes, Mom."

"I'm very happy for you, son."

"Thank you, Mom. Me too. I'll see you in a few hours, okay?"

"Have a good time."

When Malcolm put the telephone receiver back in its cradle he realized that one of his mother's traits that he respected the most was her quiet dignity and strength. It wasn't a news flash to him that Kendra shared the same character traits.

When he joined the small group impatiently waiting for him, Kendra suggested lunch before the museum. Malcolm suggested they take one car. Since his town car was bigger than her little Escort, they took his vehicle. When the children were settled and strapped into the back seat, Kendra pulled her own seat belt around her. When she snapped it in place, she looked up and gave Malcolm the thumbs up sign. But the smile in his eyes contained a sensuous flame and Kendra knew he remembered the kiss they'd shared when last sitting in his other car.

Malcolm made the mistake of asking where the group wanted to eat lunch. He got four different responses for his trouble but he chuckled at Kendra's "Callahan's." Malcolm tossed his vote in with Karin, who wanted pizza. It took another round of intensive voting to come up with which pizza place.

"Is it always this difficult?" Malcolm murmured to Kendra.

Her low husky laugh stirred him. "Difficult? You got off easy, my friend."

Malcolm simply shook his head.

And so it went. For the next few weeks, Malcolm and Kendra got to know each other better through lunch dates and shared Saturdays with the girls. Only one thing marred what Malcolm considered a perfect courtship: Kendra's stubborness when it came to him buying things for her or the girls. Kendra had refused to talk to him for three days after he bought B.J. and the twins in-line skates one Saturday. Kendra had gotten in a huff over the impulse purchase. Malcolm didn't understand what the big deal was; the skates were expensive but worth every penny. It was his treat and the kids had wanted them.

"You let the girls' father buy you diamonds and rubies, but you make a fuss about a couple of pairs of skates," he'd told her.

"It's different," Kendra hissed back at him, careful not to let the children hear their discussion.

"It's not. What's the problem? I thought you'd be pleased."

"Well, I'm not Malcolm. I make my own way."

Malcolm could only stare at her. "I thought the skates would make the girls happy. They wanted them."

"People don't always get what they want in life, Malcolm. And most times, they live to get over it."

Malcolm shook his head at the memory. Kendra had a tendency to overreact about some things. But that was her only fault and he could live with it.

He hadn't mentioned it to Kendra and probably never would, but he was pleased when her friend Nettie Blue gave a sort of blessing to their developing relationship. Nettie, with some assistance from Kendra, worked with the business manager at Mayview, Jackson, Hightower and had three Quad-A program participants lined up to start work at the firm. Malcolm was satisfied. His partner Robinson was amused, particularly over the change in Malcolm. The way he was acting, a person would think that Malcolm Hightower had invented love.

Intrigued by Nettie Blue, Robinson asked her to lunch one day and was surprised when she accepted. While they spent most of the time talking about Quad-A and Malcolm and Kendra, Robinson found himself enjoying Nettie's company.

Malcolm didn't give a thought to how much Kayla and Karin had come to look up to him until one Wednesday. The import of being invited to the Edwards' apartment to play Monopoly hadn't escaped his attention, particularly since the invitation was for a Wednesday evening: their family night.

Kayla had just soundly defeated them all. Kendra got up to make more microwave popcorn. Malcolm scooted backward on the floor until his back was supported by the edge of the sofa. He leaned his head on the cushion and heard the girls approach.

"You ask," Karin told Kayla.

"You said you were gonna do it," Kayla replied.

Before they could launch a round of "Did not, did too" Malcolm intervened. "What's up?"

When he heard them both take deep breaths, Malcolm sat up and opened his eyes. He got the distinct impression that whatever was coming was pretty important to them.

"Our dance recital is this Friday," Kayla started.

"And all the kids will have their moms and dads there to see them," Karin pitched in. With their backs to the door, the twins didn't see Kendra approach with the replenished popcorn bowl.

"Since our dad died a long time ago . . ." Kayla picked up.

"We were wondering if you would go to our recital. You don't have to pretend to be our father or anything," she added in a rush, when Malcolm understood that that's what they really wanted him to do. "We just wanted you to come."

"Please," they both added.

Overcome with emotion, Malcolm could only stare at the twins. He blinked back the tears that formed at the corners of his eyes. Kendra bit her lower lip and let her own tears fall. She hadn't realized how much the girls missed by not having a father. She watched as Malcolm opened his arms to her daughters.

"I'd be honored to come to your recital. Thank you for inviting me." He enveloped them in a hug. Malcolm had never experienced the joy he felt at that moment. If this was the stuff of fatherhood, bring it on, he thought.

After the girls had each kissed him on the cheek, he made a production of looking at his watch.

"I think it's bedtime for the ballerinas," he told them.

"Do we have to?" Karin whined.

"Yes," Kendra told them as she placed the bowl on the coffee table. "You got an extra half hour as it is. You have school tomorrow."

"Good night, Malcolm," Kayla said.

"Nighty night. Don't let the bed bugs bite," Karin told him.

Malcolm tossed a throw pillow at their giggling, retreating figures.

Kendra sat on the sofa near him. He placed his head in her lap as she gently stroked his cheek. "Thank you for that, Malcolm. You didn't have to promise them."

"I want to be there."

Kendra leaned down and softly kissed him. The embrace had little to do with sex and everything to do with gratitude and shared tenderness.

"I told you they'd be kissing," the triumph in Kayla's voice carried to the sofa.

"Go to bed, ladies!" Kendra scolded. Malcolm simply chuckled as the sound of two pairs of running feet faded and a door slammed shut. The door didn't mute the "Whoopees!" heard from the twins' bedroom. Kendra covered her face with her hands in dismay. Malcolm laughed out loud and pulled her into his lap for a kiss that meant business.

CHAPTER 8

For almost two weeks Malcolm fought for the future of a seventeen-year-old boy who along with his fifteen-year-old brother had been accused of robbing a liquor store. Two clerks had been killed in the ensuing gunfire and the brothers, both being tried as adults due to the viciousness of the attack, faced the electric chair if convicted of the crime. They maintained their innocence, saying they had been framed by local gang members. Malcolm hadn't believed them and had been reluctant to take the case until the brothers said the gang members didn't like them because they got good grades in school and wanted to go to college.

Robinson didn't doubt Malcolm's abilities as a defense attorney, but he did question the brothers' culpability. Robinson believed that the old Malcolm would have listened to the youths' story, maybe empathized with their plight, and then sent them on their way to another attorney. The new Malcolm, the Malcolm influenced by Kendra Edwards and three Quad-A employees at the law firm, had given the boys a chance.

Tied up with his own cases, Robinson had been unable to hear the hours of testimony presented at the trial. But he, like Malcolm, followed the accounts of the proceeding as reported by the local media. After deliberating for almost twelve hours, the jury came back with verdicts of not guilty. The boys' mother wept openly in the courtroom. It was her photograph on the front page of the newspaper that Robinson studied as he sipped a cup of coffee in his office Friday morning. Malcolm had won. While there had been much speculation in the press about how the mother had been able to afford Mayview, Jackson, and Hightower, Robinson was the only person other than the boys' attorney who knew that Malcolm had taken the case pro bono, without charge. Robinson had not questioned his partner's decision.

There was a knock at Robinson's office door. It was too early for his secretary to be in, so he wondered at the intrusion. When he called for the person to enter, one of the Quad-A program participants stuck her head in the office.

"Mr. Mayview, I'm sorry to bother you. I saw your car in the lot when I came in and thought I might ask you something."

"Sure, what's up? But why are you here," he glanced at his watch, "an hour before starting time?"

The woman stepped into the office but left the door open. "There was some filing I wanted to get done. I didn't do anything wrong, did I?"

"No, no. I was just wondering." As the Quad-A program employee explained that she'd wanted to get some feedback on her work thus far, Robinson's thoughts drifted to Kendra Edwards. She was good for Malcolm and her program was good for their firm. The Quad-A people worked harder than the employees they'd hired through regular channels. Even with the demands of the capital murder trial he'd just had, Robinson hoped Malcolm had had time to see Kendra. If he hadn't, Robinson didn't expect to see his partner until Monday.

As it turned out, Malcolm had not seen Kendra. She'd left a congratulatory message on his home answering machine after hearing about the outcome of the case on television. Since he had reason to celebrate, Malcolm contributed his surly mood to not seeing his lady. And forced celibacy wasn't helping matters a bit.

About four o'clock he called her office. He had to see her. Tonight. Prepared to beg his mother to babysit Kayla and Karin if need be, Malcolm waited while the switchboard operator connected him to Kendra's desk.

"Kendra Edwards. How may I help you?" she answered.

"By having dinner with me tonight."

"Malcolm!" He grinned at the change in her tone when she recognized his voice. "You did a great job defending those kids. Everyone was talking about it over here. The public jury is still out on whether they did it, though."

Malcolm was glad he'd won, but the case was over and done with. There was but one priority in his life now. "Will you have dinner with me tonight?"

"Of course I will. And guess what? You're in luck. Nettie has the girls for the weekend. Another of her big sleepover things with her grandkids."

Thank you, God, Malcolm silently mouthed.

"How's seven?" he asked.

"Sounds good to me."

"Casual. My place. I'll grill a couple of steaks, toss some salad."

Kendra paused. They'd never had dinner at his town house. Kendra had been there a couple of times, but only for brief moments. The three-story home was a well-paid decorator's dream. High-tech gadgets littered the third floor, from a high-definition big-screen television to a state-of-the-art sound system that only an audiophile could love. The first floor consisted of a library and three spare bedrooms while the middle floor was Malcolm's primary living space. The focal point of the great room—which was twice the size of Kendra's entire apartment—was the spectacular view of the waterfront from a wall of floor-to-ceiling windows. A gourmet kitchen and the master suite rounded out the second floor. Kendra felt overwhelmed by opulence every time she entered Malcolm's private domain.

He heard her hesitancy and cursed his impatience. "If you'd prefer, we can go out somewhere. I just wanted to get away from crowds."

"I can understand that. It looked like there was a microphone in your face every moment for the last two weeks. Your place sounds fine. I'll bring dessert."

The steak was tender, the salad crisp, the cheesecake divine. Kendra had run out of things to talk about. The case, the twins, and the Quad-A program could only take up so much time. Kendra turned down the offer of a glass of after-dinner wine and wandered over to the huge windows that overlooked the bay. Malcolm had set the scene for seduction, but he hadn't followed through. The lights that had been dimmed faded away completely, leaving the warm glow from the myriad candles in crystal holders scattered about the room.

The only sound came from the soft jazz piped in from hidden speakers. But when the last note faded away, neither Malcolm nor Kendra moved to put more CDs in the system. The tension in the room was palpable. Kendra stood at the windows, gazing into the night, her profile illuminated only by candlelight and the distant muted light from the kitchen. Malcolm sat on the sofa, quietly contemplating her. With one arm stretched across the sofa's black leather and a leg casually resting on the sofa cushion, he managed a calm façade. There was no hint of the inferno raging within him. But still he waited. He had learned to live, albeit painfully, with the hardness that pressed into his trousers every time he was near Kendra. He watched her and wondered at her thoughts.

Goosebumps suddenly covered Kendra. She wrapped her arms about her but the movement made her uncomfortable. Her sensitive breasts were full, the hardened nipples crying for his mouth. Kendra wanted Malcolm so badly she thought she might explode with the pain of it. But still he sat there. He'd not made an untoward move the entire evening, yet she'd seen the desire glowing in his eyes. She turned to face him and in the space of a moment, she realized with all clarity and understanding why he waited. He waited for her to decide if their relationship would take this next major turn.

What happened or didn't happen next would be her decision. She appreciated and respected his control, his willingness to wait. If she said no right now, it would be okay. But no was the farthest thing from Kendra's mind. She wanted him. She wanted him like she'd never wanted anything else. Kendra knew that Malcolm would be a gentle and caring lover—that's what she needed, because it had been so very long since she had been loved. She made her decision. It was time.

Kendra dropped her arms and walked to him. When she stood above him, their eyes met. Malcolm watched her but remained silent.

Kendra held out a hand, which he clasped within his own.

"Make love to me, Malcolm."

He softly kissed the back of her hand. Kendra gasped when his tongue flicked her skin. With just a gentle tug from him, she tumbled into his lap. Malcolm gazed into her brown eyes and lost himself. With one arm he cradled her. The other gently caressed the edge of her face. He unsnapped the bow that held her hair and ran his fingers through her thick tresses. He bent his head to nibble on her neck and Kendra arched toward him. Malcolm trembled with desire, but still he hesitated. He eased her onto the sofa, half covering her body with his own.

"Kendra, are you sure?"

In answer, Kendra framed his face with her hands and pulled him to her. The kiss was wet, deep, and urgent. Their tongues met in a frantic duel. Kendra ran her hands over his head, down to his shoulders, then across his back. His weight settled on her, pushing her into the softness of the sofa cushions. When at last their lips parted, Malcolm eased himself up. But Kendra halted the motion by reaching for one of his hands. She placed it over her left breast.

"Make love to me, Malcolm."

"Oh, my God," he moaned. He bent his head to hers while gently kneading the fullness of her breast. It was Kendra's turn to moan.

"Please . . ." she begged.

But Kendra was unable to articulate what she wanted. She tugged at her blouse and Malcolm understood. With one deft motion, he pulled the silk up her body and over her head. Her hair fanned the sofa cushion. Malcolm could only stare. Her breasts spilled from the lacy brassiere she wore. He vaguely noted that the soft lavender undergarment matched the rest of her outfit. He could hardly wait to see if her panties completed the ensemble. He unhooked the front clasp of her bra and drank in the sight of her.

"You are so beautiful," he told her. The tenderness he felt at that moment transcended sexual desire. For forever and always he wanted Kendra at his side.

But Kendra didn't guess at those thoughts. She only saw the flame burning within his gaze. She lifted her breasts in offering to him. Malcolm accepted the gift with greedy anticipation. He flicked his tongue over one erect nipple and Kendra cried out. The pleasure mixed with pain propelled her. She pulled his head until his mouth covered the entire top of her breast. As Malcolm suckled her, Kendra writhed beneath him. It was too much; it was not enough. Kendra wanted more. *More.* She thought the sparks shooting through her body would surely set them afire.

Her murmur of protest was quieted when Malcolm ceased ministrations of one breast and moved to its twin. Because it was a feast he'd thought would be forever denied to him, Malcolm dined with gusto as they stretched out on the sofa. With his mouth still taking delicious nips and bites at her breast, Malcolm's hand smoothed over her stomach and slipped under the waistband of the pants she wore. When his hand encountered more soft lace at the core of her, Malcolm smiled. He cupped her and Kendra arched into his hand. Her nails raked across his back. Through the fabric of her panties, he could feel the dampness that prepared her for him.

"Melt for me, sweet Kendra," he murmured as his mouth left her breasts and traveled up her neck. Kendra couldn't talk, couldn't think. All she was capable of doing was feeling the exquisite torture of Malcolm's touch. When she felt his hand slip beneath the barrier of her panties, she whimpered. The sound almost sent Malcolm over the edge.

"I want to feel you," she told him as she struggled with the shirt he still wore.

Malcolm reluctantly eased his hand from the hot core of her and used the moment to bring himself under control when she ripped the shirt from his back. From a distance he heard a button or two hit the marble coffee table a few feet away from them.

At last Kendra's fingers touched the warm skin of his chest; she luxuriated in the hard feel of him. Everything about Malcolm was hard. The strength of him pulsated beneath her fingertips and there was no way she could ignore the heavy fullness of the lower part of his body as it pressed into her.

"I want more of you," she told him insistently.

"Let's go to the bedroom," he said.

But when Malcolm lifted himself off of her and stood at the edge of the sofa, Kendra didn't move to get up. She wiggled out of the pants and kicked them away. She then tugged at the lacy panties. Malcolm was frozen at the spot. He didn't move. He didn't breathe. The sight before him was straight from a fantasy. Kendra dangled the tiny bit of lace from her finger before letting it drop to the floor. Malcolm's eyes followed its trail even as his hands worked at the belt of his trousers. Soon he stood before her, tall and majestic in his maleness. Kendra smiled up at him and lifted her arms toward him. She waited as he retrieved a small package from his pants pocket. She knew a moment's embarrassment when she realized she had been so caught up in the way he made her feel that she'd forgotten about protection. She dropped her arms and covered her face. Malcolm knelt before her.

"Kendra, you know I'll never hurt you."

It wasn't a question, but Kendra nodded. Malcolm gently removed her hands from her face and kissed his way up her arm. When he started nibbling at her nape, Kendra forgot any distress she may have been feeling.

"I'm a little cold," she told him.

"Let me warm you," he said as he covered her body with his. Malcolm's hand hovered just above her breast. The sensual teasing made her ache.

"Malcolm, please."

He smiled down at her. "Please what? Stop? Continue? Tell me what you want me to do, Kendra."

She pulled him to her. The kiss was long and satisfying but still she wanted more. She guided his hand to the place where it had been.

"Ahh, I'm beginning to understand your silent language," he told her. "Is this what you want?"

This time when Malcolm's hand cupped her, there was no material to shield his probing hand. He knew without a shadow of a doubt that Kendra was ready for him. But he knew it had been a long, long time since she'd been with a man. He wanted to take her on a solo trip to paradise before he found his own release.

He lowered his head to her body. Licking and nibbling the feast before him, he made his way to the triangle that was the entrance to her womanhood. When he went lower, Kendra's legs opened before him. Every nerve ending in her body was alive, tingling and focused on the place where Malcolm worshiped her. When Kendra arched to meet the gentle thrust of his tongue, Malcolm groaned. He replaced his mouth with his finger and watched her face. When he eased one finger into her, Kendra's pleasure was pure and explosive. Instinctively she clamped herself around his finger as he stroked her.

"Sweet Jesus," Malcolm groaned.

When he felt the first convulsive tremor of her release, Malcolm eased his finger from her and settled himself between her soft thighs. His manhood trembled and twitched in expectation. Just as Kendra tumbled over into ecstasy, he entered her with one thick thrust. She was sweet, so sweet, and tight as a virgin.

Kendra cried out and raked his back. Absently Malcolm wondered if he would bear the marks of her desire. But then Kendra met him and he forgot everything except the pleasure rippling through him. Kendra wrapped her legs around him and met the fury of his passion. He filled her to the core of her being. Each powerful thrust carried them higher, higher. The world spun off its axis when together they reached the summit. Wave after wave of rapture poured over them. Malcolm collapsed on top of her. Long moments later they'd both caught their breath enough to think coherently. Malcolm was still sheathed inside Kendra's heat.

Making love to Kendra was like he'd fantasized it would be: hot, explosive, addictive.

"Are you okay? I didn't hurt you, did I?"

The satisfied smile Kendra gave him reassured Malcolm. "You would have hurt me if you hadn't eased the torment you caused."

Malcolm chuckled and pulled her closer. Contentment and peace flowed between them. Malcolm settled her gently at his side. He kissed her hair.

The dormant sexuality of Kendra's body had been awakened. She marveled at the sensations and was stunned by the intensity of her desire. Never, ever had she felt so complete. When she stirred beneath him, she felt Malcolm again grow hard. She looked up at him.

"I can't get enough of you," he said, almost apologetically.

"Same here," she told him. "Your sofa feels heavenly, but I think I'd prefer a bed this time."

Malcolm kissed her. "As I recall, I was trying to go to the bedroom when you pulled a striptease on me. I'm just a man, Kendra. There's no way I was going to be able to walk away from that."

As her low, husky laugh washed over him, Malcolm growled hungrily.

Kendra smiled. "There's a tiger in here somewhere," she said. "I think I'd better tame the beast before he does any damage."

"I'll show you damage, woman," he said as his lips covered hers. He left her burning with fire when he pulled away and reached for another small packet. He ripped it open and was about to again protect them when Kendra's soft hands stopped him.

"Let me," she said.

As her fingers wrapped around his swollen maleness, Malcolm sucked in his breath.

"Uh, Kendra . . ."

"Shh, I can manage." Like soft rain on a slick window she ran her fingers up and down the length of him. Malcolm sat back on the sofa and endeavored to endure the exquisite torture.

"Kendra . . ."

Without taking her eyes from his, Kendra leaned down and kissed the velvet tip of him. His flesh leaped in her hands.

They never made it to his bedroom.

CHAPTER 9

More than one person paused to smile at the pretty lady who practically skipped down the street, swinging the small grocery bag at her side. Kendra's heart sang with delight. Surely anyone who saw her, she thought, would know that the warm glow radiating through her came from being well-loved and in love. In love! The realization literally stopped her in her tracks a block from her apartment. For the first time in her life, she understood the meaning of true love. She felt as if she were soaring on the wings of an eagle.

Over the past two days with Malcolm, she had been reborn, rejuvenated. Surely this feeling was unique. Did every person in love feel lighter than air? Did every tomorrow look brighter than the day before? When she'd given Malcolm Hightower her body, she'd given him her heart as well.

With the maturity of a grown woman, she recognized that what she'd felt for Oscar MacAfree so many years before had been purely physical. She'd thought herself in love then, but the feelings she now had could not compare to the ones she'd had as a naive nineteen-year-old. She started walking again, this time reflecting on her relationship with Malcolm.

With Malcolm she felt complete, a total woman. She'd opened herself to him and had burned in his arms. Her wantonness had come as a surprise to her. Half the time he made her so weak in the knees, she couldn't think straight. At other times she got such a kick out of being with him that she couldn't imagine not having him in her life. She thought of their zany date at the miniature golf course and smiled. Malcolm made her laugh. He also encouraged her to grow and respected her need and desire to complete her education. And the girls, oh, how they adored him. Kendra hadn't let on that she'd heard their conversation one evening as Karin and Kayla speculated on whether Malcolm and their mother would marry. While Kendra considered herself a modern woman, self-sufficient to the nth degree, she admitted to her secret self that she desired marriage as much as her daughters desired a father. She'd been raised to value two-parent households and family values even though her own parents had been killed when she was very young.

Was Malcolm Hightower the one? Kendra thought he was. There was but one small yet significant glitch: He didn't love her. Once before Kendra had made the dangerous mistake of assuming that passion equated with love. In that instance, instead of marriage and happily ever after she'd gotten a thousand dollars in rumpled bills and a terse directive to "get rid of the problem." After Oscar had been killed, the money he'd pressed into Kendra's hands that last night had come in handy; but not the way he'd intended. She'd used it for medical checkups and to get a starter supply of diapers and formula.

No way, no how would she assume that Malcolm wanted more from their relationship than already existed. That morning before he brought her home, they'd made tender love on a lounger on his deck. Yes, Malcolm desired her. But she had entered this relationship with her eyes wide open. There might be wishful thinking on her part, but she would entertain no erroneous assumptions regarding a gold band on her ring finger.

So lost in her thoughts was she that Kendra walked past the house where she and the girls rented their first-floor apartment.

"Hey Kendra, you live over here," a voice broke in to her reverie.

She turned around and laughed as her upstairs neighbor, Bob, bowed and pointed the way to her front door.

"Need some help?" she asked him as he pulled an overflowing box of papers from his car.

"I'm good. This is the last load. Layla just carried up a box."

"Long time no see," she told him as she ran up the steps and held the door for him.

"That's what happens when the folks upstairs are both accountants. I don't think we've actually been home longer than twelve hours since the first W-2s were sent out."

"I know you're not complaining. Where's the after-tax-season vacation this year?" she asked.

Bob laughed as he hoisted the box on his shoulder to climb the flight of steps leading to his apartment. "Three weeks on the sunny beaches of Bermuda."

"Send a postcard so we'll be able to properly envy you," she called up to his retreating figure.

"You got it. Give the twins a hug for us."

Kendra closed the door and pulled out the key to her apartment. Nettie would be bringing the girls home in a couple of hours. Kendra planned to surprise them with a cake; she'd walked to the corner store to get candy sprinkles for the icing. She let herself into the still apartment. Leaving the front door open, she latched the glass and screen storm door to let the spring breeze drift through the rooms.

She made short work of mixing the cake batter and putting the pans in the oven. The action reminded her of her last night at Aunt Katherine's house. Maybe thinking of Oscar earlier had her thoughts drifting to Aunt Kat. She wondered how the older woman fared. In the early days, Kendra had called, but Aunt Kat's anger had not diminished. Every time, she'd hung up as soon as she recognized Kendra's voice. Time had dulled Kendra's pain over the rebuff. Now she simply sent the photos of the girls every fall. Her address and telephone number were included in every mailing but she'd never heard from her only relative.

If she and Malcolm married, Kendra thought, Kayla and Karin wouldn't have Aunt Kat but they would have a wonderful grandmother in Miss Belle. Kendra set the oven timer, then opened the refrigerator and poured herself a glass of apple juice. She knew she should go over the last portion of her senior project, but her thoughts were too scattered to concentrate. She passed by her book bag, which rested on the hall table, and continued to her bedroom. She turned her bedside radio on and the Sunday afternoon jazz immediately had her thinking of Malcolm. The smile that curved her lips was purely feminine, unmistakenly sensual.

She took a sip from the glass, then put it aside on the nightstand. She kicked off her sneakers and drew her knees to her chest as she snuggled up against one of the many plump pillows that decorated her bed. She wondered if the same delicious tingling she felt every time she thought of him would ever fade. She hoped it wouldn't.

Malcolm marveled at the treasure he'd found in Kendra. He imagined himself married to her and father to her two beautiful daughters. While fairy tales were the stuff of little girls' dreams, he couldn't help anticipating a happily ever after. There was but one major flaw in the fantasy, he thought as he reclined in a lounger on the deck off his bedroom early Sunday evening. He didn't know if Kendra loved him. Yes, she enjoyed his company. Yes, her passion was a conflagration that burned hotter each time they came together. But what of her feelings? Did she desire a future with him, or was he simply the cathartic release she needed to heal the wounds of her past? The latter thought made him frown. Malcolm had no desire to compete with a dead man for Kendra's heart.

Malcolm left the lounger and walked to the railing of the deck to contemplate the horizon and his options. Forcing the issue might make her bolt. If she was comfortable with their current arrangement, he might never get to play a larger role in her life. He willed himself to have patience and bit back the urge to pick up the cordless telephone and call her.

They'd spent the remainder of Friday night alternately dozing and making love. At dawn they stood wrapped in each other's arms, watching the pink and gold streamers of daybreak across the sky. Malcolm wanted to spend every sunrise and every sunset in Kendra's embrace. He chided himself over the fanciful thought. Before he could forge any future out of what they now shared, Malcolm felt he had to be sure Kendra wasn't in love with a ghost. Fate had played a cruel trick on him, Malcolm thought. After the hellish purgatory of life with his ex-wife, Monica, he could glimpse heaven but was barred from entering its gates. As night closed around him, Malcolm wondered why he was being punished.

Malcolm acknowledged that he still wanted her. He'd been reluctant to let her go earlier that morning. Kendra needed to put the finishing touches on her project so she'd be able to graduate next month. While he wanted to ravish her on her sofa, he conceded the fact that in this case, maybe, academics were more important. After all, it wasn't as if they hadn't made love so many times over the weekend that they'd both lost count. In the great room, in the kitchen, on the deck, on one of the weight benches in his exercise room, in the shower, in the Jacuzzi. And they'd actually, eventually, managed to get to his big bed. They had only paused long enough to eat, for Kendra to check in with Nettie and the girls, and for them to take a short walk on the beach. The stroll had been cut short by their overwhelming urge to be in each other's arms again.

The remembered passion made him smile. But the curtain of nightfall that fell around him didn't give Malcolm the answers he so desperately sought.

The telephone on Kendra's desk rang early the next morning. Malcolm's voice on the other end promised an afternoon delight if she wanted to spend her lunch hour with him. Kendra's naughty laughter as she accepted the invitation washed over Malcolm and made him fervently wish that the morning would fly by.

When the phone rang again about eleven o'clock, Kendra thought it might be Malcolm calling to see if their lunch date could begin early. But the vaguely familiar voice on the other end belonged to a woman.

"Kendra, hi there. This is Lydia Anderson in Mr. Sullivan's office."

"Good morning, Lydia. I'm sorry, but Eric is in court and John is with a client right now," Kendra said, referring to the two attorneys she worked for.

"Oh, that's quite all right. I was calling to speak with you. Mr. Sullivan would like to see you at your earliest convenience."

Kendra had been working at Sullivan and O'Leary long enough to know that when the senior partner called, the wise employee's earliest convenience was immediately.

"I'll be right up."

Kendra replaced the receiver and quickly ran through the list of reasons Bosworth Sullivan would want to see her. With only one item she could think of, it was a short list. The summons had to be about the Quad-A program. Maybe the firm wanted to take on more program participants and Sullivan wanted a recommendation from her. Since her speaking engagements rarely, if ever, interfered with her workday, and her annual work appraisal had been favorable six months prior, Kendra didn't think the call to appear was about her job performance.

Kendra pulled a small pink compact from a desk drawer and quickly touched up her lipstick. She smoothed her already immaculate hair while peering into the tiny mirror. Snapping the case shut, she left her desk and headed for the appointment. Ignoring the elevator, Kendra walked the circular flight of stairs to the executive offices. As she pushed open the double glass doors that led to Bosworth Sullivan's and Grady O'Leary's offices, Kendra had a horrible thought. What if Sullivan wanted to cease the firm's involvement in the Quad-A program?

She approached Lydia Anderson's desk.

"That was fast," Lydia told her, smiling. "Come right this way." Lydia knocked on Sullivan's door but didn't wait for a reply as she pushed it open. "Kendra Edwards to see you," she announced as she stepped aside to let Kendra enter the inner sanctum of Sullivan and O'Leary.

She'd been in Bosworth Sullivan's office before. But never in the capacity of defending the Quad-A program's merits. Not a bit of the inner turmoil she felt or the strategy she planned to change his mind showed as she watched Sullivan approach with a smile and his hand extended in greeting.

"Kendra, come on in. I'm so glad you could make it," Sullivan said as he shook her hand in a firm but cordial greeting. "Have a seat."

Sullivan led her to a sitting area in his office. Sunlight streamed through the windows that overlooked the city. Several healthy green plants took the edge off the otherwise austere interior of the room. Kendra settled herself on the edge of a forest green wingback chair.

"What can I get you to drink? I have coffee, juice, some bottled water, and I'm sure I can have Lydia scare up some tea if you'd prefer that."

"Nothing, thank you."

"You sure?"

"Yes." Stop prolonging the torture, Kendra screamed to herself. Just drop the bomb and get it over with.

Sullivan poured himself a cup of coffee. Leaving it black, he joined Kendra in the sitting area and placed the cup and saucer on a table. He took a seat opposite her in a matching chair.

"I meant to tell you a while ago what a great job you did at the Chamber presentation. I understand the Quad-A program got several referrals that night."

"More than ten companies decided to participate. Most of them only placed one person, but every position counts."

"That's right," Sullivan agreed. He reached over and picked up his coffee cup, ostensibly to take a sip of the hot beverage. But he instead studied Kendra.

Cool as a cucumber, he thought. She hadn't flinched or fidgeted and he could detect not an ounce of nervousness in the woman even though he knew most of the firm's employees dreaded a summons to the executive floor. Sullivan knew he'd made the right decision.

"I know you must be wondering why I called you here this morning."

It had crossed my mind, she said to herself. To Sullivan she responded by slightly nodding her head.

"Well, you're about to graduate, right?"

"That's correct. I'll be earning my bachelor's degree next month. Graduation is scheduled for the fifteenth. I'd like you to be there, since you so graciously made it possible for me to attend school and remain employed."

Sullivan waved her comment away with one manicured hand. "It had nothing to do with graciousness and everything to do with selfishness."

"How so, may I ask?"

"On the few occasions when we make those Quad-A presentations together I'm not just talking out the side of my mouth about you being a valued employee here," he said, pausing for a brief moment to drink from his cup. "Your work has been exemplary since the first week you arrived. It's all documented, you know. Not just Quad-A employees. Everybody. I sign off on every performance appraisal and every raise. I like to keep tabs on my people. But more important than that, I like to make sure that I keep good people."'

Kendra wasn't sure where this was going, but it didn't seem to be headed down the path that she'd worked herself into a frenzy over.

"To that regard," Sullivan continued, "your graduation will mark a significant milestone for you and for Sullivan and O'Leary. As you may know, we recently completed an internal study of how resources are allocated within the firm. What we discovered is that there's a group of people out there who have for all intents and purposes been sort of wandering around without any direct and consistent supervision. So we developed an administrative position to deal with it."

Not sure what reaction Sullivan expected of her, Kendra just nodded and let him finish his explanation.

"The position requires knowledge of running a law office, a college degree, and familiarity with the politics and corporate environment of Sullivan and O'Leary."

Oh, my God, Kendra thought as she began to get a clue.

"With the exception of the degree, you fit the qualifications of the position from the moment we created it on paper. Kendra, what I'd like to offer you, effective after your graduation, of course, is the position of director of administrative services."

It wasn't possible for Kendra to mask her surprise. "Mr. Sullivan . . ."

"Hear me out before you say yea or nay," he interrupted. "If you decide to accept the position, there are a couple of provisions attached, strings, if you will."

Kendra sat back in the chair and willed her heartbeat to slow down. It seemed that the late hours and total dedication to the job had finally paid off. But what were the strings?

"While you're already quite proficient at what you do, there are some areas where you'd need some training. The best way to get that training, we've decided, is to provide it within the parameters, or as close as we can approximate it, to the workday. The hours for the first year would essentially be seven in the morning to three in the afternoon. It's an eight hour workday, but with enough time left in the afternoon to complete the training.

"Director of administrative services is more than just a fancy title. With the exception of Lydia and Grady O'Leary's executive assistant, you'd be responsible for all of the secretaries and administrative assistants who aren't attached to associates. You would manage the mail room, administer the Quad-A program, and hire and fire all administrative support staff such as couriers and clerks. That's both here and at our two satellite offices. Does any of that sound like something you'd be interested in?"

"Well, yes, but I've only been with the firm five years."

"Kendra, it doesn't take five years to recognize talent and potential. You are very organized, you're personable, and I believe you're capable of doing this job. Eric and John agree. Yes, it's a lot of work. But as I said, when we did the internal study, we noticed the glaring lack of a coordinator to make it all work. I feel you are our best internal candidate for the position."

"What is the training you mentioned?"

Sullivan smiled. He picked up his coffee cup and went to refresh it. "May I get you something this time?" he asked her from the wet bar.

"A glass of water with lemon will be fine."

"Evian, Perrier, or Calistoga?"

Kendra's brain was reeling. The man had just offered her the promotion of a lifetime and he was calmly asking her to choose a brand of water to drink. When she didn't immediately respond, he held up a light green bottle and looked at her. Kendra nodded.

Aha! Sullivan thought triumphantly. I've finally ruffled her. Kendra Edwards had the ability to make people feel as if what they were saying or doing was the most important thing in the world to her. But by the same token and practically a paradox, her cool professionalism and detachment surrounded her like a shield. It was the perfect combination.

Sullivan walked back to his chair, balancing Kendra's water goblet and his cup of coffee. She accepted the glass and was taking the first sip when Sullivan said, "The training I'd like you to take is the first year of law school, at the firm's expense of course."

To her credit and without knowing that she'd passed another of Sullivan's little tests, Kendra didn't spill, spit, splatter, or choke on the water. She swallowed it and very calmly placed the glass on the table between their chairs.

"What's the catch? My firstborn children aren't up for grabs."

Sullivan chuckled. "I told you at the outset. Purely selfish reasons. We don't want to lose you. If making you an offer you can't refuse, or what we hope is an offer you can't refuse, will make you stay with us, we're prepared to do what needs to be done. I realize that the demands of the job and the classes will leave you very little time to work with Quad-A. I know how important the recruiting for the program is to you."

"I'd like some time to think about this," Kendra heard herself say. Have you lost your mind, she screamed at herself. Quick, say yes, before the man comes to his senses and changes his mind.

"That's not a problem," Sullivan told her. "With your graduation coming up, I'm sure you're considering the options open to you. I just wanted to make sure that our offer was on the table as you considered the others. A note on the law school thing. While we'd foot the bill for the first year, if you decided you wanted to finish, we can come to some sort of agreement on your workday but I'm only prepared to pay forty percent."

"I understand," Kendra told him. But she didn't really understand. She felt as though she'd just slid down Alice's rabbit hole.

"Good. You can get back to me in a few weeks. Take your time deciding. There's one other thing we haven't discussed. Salary."

Sullivan then quoted an amount that was more than double her current income. Absolutely astounded, there was no way Kendra could control the tiny gasp that escaped her mouth. She masked the sound with a discreet cough behind her hand. She wanted to put her head between her knees to keep the blood flowing. She instead took another sip of water. She couldn't form any response to what Sullivan had just told her so she simply nodded her head as if the salary seemed reasonable but she'd have to give it some thought.

Sullivan misread the gesture and quickly amended the amount upward by ten thousand dollars. In a jerky movement, Kendra put the glass on the table and prayed that she would get out of Sullivan's office before she started hyperventilating.

"I'll get back to you with my decision," she managed to say.

"Excellent," he told her, standing as she did. Kendra turned to make her way to his door. "Oh, I just remembered something," he added. "I know I've given you a lot to think about, but I have a more immediate request that concerns the Quad-A program."

After the morning's surprises, Kendra wasn't about to speculate.

"I'm the special program chairman for our regional bar conference. It's in Atlanta in May. I was wondering if you or Mrs. Blue would like to make a presentation to the group. You'd have about two hundred or so captive lawyers. Maybe Mrs. Blue is thinking of expanding the Quad-A program to other cities. The conference will be a good way to spread the word. Since I'm heading up the special programs, I thought that might be a good one."

Kendra nodded. She hoped it wasn't too obvious that she was using the doorknob for support. "I'm sure she'd jump at the opportunity. Would you like me to give her a call?"

"No. I'll do it. We haven't chatted in a while."

Kendra extended her hand. "Thank you for the job offer, Mr. Sullivan. I'll give it strong consideration." Sullivan shook her hand, bid her a good day, then shut his office door.

Bosworth Sullivan was tickled with himself. The meeting had been a success. While he was pretty sure Kendra would take the job, he was more pleased that he had finally flapped the unflappable Kendra Edwards.

Across town at the Quad-A office, Nettie's hands shook as she replaced the telephone receiver in its cradle. The call had been short and to the point. She'd listened first in amazement and curiosity and then with growing fear. What the caller threatened would shatter the security and independence it had taken years to cultivate.

CHAPTER 10

Kendra didn't trust her legs to carry her down the circular stairwell, so she punched the button for the elevator. What Bosworth Sullivan offered was everything she'd ever wanted in life—with the exception of loving and marrying Malcolm Hightower. She'd be making not just decent but *good* money; she'd be in a position of authority, and she'd be in a position to make a difference at the firm. A practical woman who'd learned the hard way about naive dreams and making assumptions, Kendra had to take into consideration what was best for her and the girls if Malcolm wasn't in her future. She could finally buy a house. Not anything particularly fancy or expensive, just a place she could call home with trees and rose bushes. She'd grown up in a house and wanted Karin and Kayla to know the experience of coming home to *home,* not coming home to a small apartment.

The elevator arrived and she stepped in, joining two clerks and a mailroom attendant. She greeted each with a smile, struck by the notion that she could soon be managing them and their supervisors.

When the door whisked open seconds later Kendra walked to her desk and sat in her chair. Law school. With what seemed merely a minor detail to him, Sullivan had given her the solution she'd needed. Kendra had taken the law school entrance exam and had scored fairly well, but coming up with the finances to pay for the expensive training had been another matter entirely. Absolutely unwilling to dip into the twins' college fund, loans had been her only other option. The idea, while unpalatable, seemed the only recourse. Until Sullivan's offer.

She glanced at her watch. She had about half an hour before her lunch date with Malcolm. She made fast work of the things she needed to get done.

The plan was to meet at Callahan's, then slip away to one of the downtown hotels. Granted it was indulgent but Malcolm wanted Kendra so badly he thought he'd die from the pain of it. He'd spent a sleepless night tossing and turning in his big, empty bed. In the two days and nights they'd spent together, Malcolm had grown accustomed to sleeping and waking with Kendra's supple body in his arms, her scent and softness assuring him that it hadn't all been a dream.

But Kendra seemed reluctant to leave the restaurant. As a matter of fact, she didn't seem herself at all.

"Kendra, what's wrong? Are you feeling ill?" Malcolm asked. Suddenly contrite, he realized what was ailing her. While their time together had barely taken the edge off of his desire, it had probably taken a toll on Kendra's body.

"I-I'm feeling a little shell-shocked right now."

Malcolm was glad she felt shell-shocked. It was exactly the way he felt every time he saw her. But, in the spirit of compassion and genuine concern for her, he compromised.

"Listen, we don't have to go to the hotel," he told her. "Let's just stay here and enjoy a leisurely lunch together. How's that?" he asked while lifting her hand and pressing a kiss into her palm. When his tongue gently licked the tender pale skin, Kendra felt the warm rush that seemed to be a part of her whenever Malcolm was near.

"Hotel? Oh!" she said with the beginning of a blush creeping up her face. "The hotel. I'd forgotten."

Malcolm frowned. "I think my manhood has just been insulted. And I'm not sure that we've been talking about the same thing. You first."

"Oh, Malcolm. I'm not sure where to begin. It's just so amazing. And to think, he said he wanted to get his offer on the table while I considered the others. The others! As if I've had time to job hunt."

Malcolm signaled for a waiter, then took both of her hands in his. "Kendra, the best place to start is the beginning, because I have no idea what you're talking about."

Kendra giggled and Malcolm's gut clenched. Girlish laughter was rare from Kendra. He felt as if she'd bestowed a gift on him.

A waiter arrived. "We've changed our minds and will be having lunch," Malcolm told the man. "What are today's specials?"

The waiter quickly ran though the list of luncheon offerings and took their orders. When they were alone again, Malcolm encouraged Kendra to tell her tale.

"'Now, what is it that has you so wound up that my loving has been relegated to the back burner?" Malcolm said in jest.

Sitting in the middle of the crowded restaurant, there was little Kendra could do to physically express to Malcolm how he made her feel. She slipped off her gray pumps and meandered one stockinged foot up the hem of Malcolm's trousers. The other traveled up the inside of his other leg.

"Malcolm, let me assure you, your lovin' keeps me on a slow burn." His eyes smoldered with a fire that promised endless ecstasy when they again found themselves in a private place.

"You're tormenting me, woman."

"Good. Now you know what it feels like."

"Would it make you happy to know that I'm about this close," he said, holding his thumb and index finger about an inch apart, "to ruining a perfectly good suit."

The spark of eroticism in her smile was practically his undoing. He was saved by the waiter, who arrived to refill their glasses of iced tea. Kendra eased one foot off of his lap and the other out of his pants leg.

Malcolm's tortured expression made Kendra laugh. But the low, throaty sound did little to ease his discomfort.

"Okay, Kendra. Now that you have me all worked up with no hope of concentrating on anything except calculating when we'll be together again, tell me your story."

Kendra smiled at him. She reached for a packet of crackers the waiter had left on their table.

"Bosworth Sullivan offered me a terrific promotion today," she said, bubbling with energy.

"Congratulations. Did you take it?"

"I told him I'd think about it. He seemed to believe that I have a bevy of job offers to sort through and wanted to put his bid in."

Kendra tore open the packet of crackers and bit the end off of one of them.

"Do you?"

"Do I what?" she said after swallowing the morsel.

"Have a bevy of job offers in the wings?"

But before Kendra could respond, Malcolm continued. "Lots of firms are looking for good legal secretaries. If nothing else, your experience with Sullivan and O'Leary could parlay into a position that paid you more money. They are one of the largest firms around, so you can't really go to a larger one."

Kendra looked at Malcolm. Did he think that she had reached her aspirations when she was promoted to secretary at the firm? Maybe Malcolm thought that's all she could or would ever be, given her background. Kendra viewed her work at Sullivan and O'Leary as meaningful and furfilling, but Malcolm made it sound like money was the only thing that mattered and that she couldn't possibly want to do anything else.

"We're never really talked about this, have we?"

But Malcolm didn't meet her eyes. He kept his gaze at something or someone over her shoulder, as if he were embarrassed to look her in the eye.

"Talked about what?" he asked.

"My dreams and aspirations."

"Yes, we have. You've worked hard and you're about to earn a bachelor's degree. That's an aspiration that you've almost met."

Kendra thought about what he'd said. "That's true. This promotion will help me reach my next goal," she said. But Kendra wasn't sure if Malcolm even heard her. All of his attention was focused across the restaurant. When she turned around to look, nothing appeared out of the ordinary. Diners were eating and talking, a college-aged young man was bussing tables, waiters and waitresses were taking orders. It was a typical afternoon at Callahan's.

Maybe talk of her promotion bored him. Kendra had thought that Malcolm would have been happy for her. But that didn't seem to be the case. She was incredibly excited about the job offer from Sullivan, but Malcolm sat there unfazed. Kendra tried to hide her disappointment. His reaction wasn't at all what she'd expected. Maybe he didn't care. Maybe he'd gotten what he wanted from her in bed and now that the hunt was over, saw no reason to be careful of her feelings. He'd hurt her without realizing it.

Each time Kendra tried to start up a conversation, Malcolm gave short one- or two-word responses. He didn't try to hide the fact that he wasn't paying attention to Kendra; he just kept staring at something over her shoulder. When she turned again to see what was there, she saw nothing but other diners and the busboy cleaning off tables.

"Malcolm, what's wrong?"

"Huh? Oh, nothing," he said.

When their lunch arrived, they ate in strained silence. The sensual mood of their earlier exchange was gone. It wasn't until Kendra got back to her office that it dawned on her: Malcolm had not asked what job she'd been offered.

When Malcolm returned to his office, he placed a call to his accountant. He waved Robinson in when his partner knocked on the open door while Malcolm was on the telephone.

Robinson plopped onto the sofa that was arranged in a conversation grouping in the office. Malcolm had spared no expense when he'd had his office decorated. With the antique cherry furnishings and original oils, the room reeked of power and affluence. Both of their offices overlooked the private garden Robinson's father had meticulously groomed. When in full bloom, the roses and other flowers perfumed both rooms.

Robinson got up and went to the wet bar, where he poured himself a glass of juice. He unashamedly eavesdropped on Malcolm's side of the conversation.

"That's right. One is fifteen. The other one is seventeen. . . . No, I don't know if he's picked out a college. I just know that they both want to go. . . . Start a high-growth fund for the younger one. It should be able to earn some interest in the next three years. . . . Yes, that will be fine. Now, for the older one, what do you recommend? . . . Yes, a fourth of it will have to come out in less than a year. . . . I don't know. Just do it. Send me the paperwork. Thanks. Talk to you later."

Malcolm rang off and looked at Robinson, who was staring at him.

"Did you just do what I think you just did?" Robinson asked.

"What do you think I just did?"

"Set up college funds for those two kids you got off last week."

Malcolm nodded.

"Why?"

For a brief moment Malcolm looked embarrassed. Then his features changed and a look of contentment settled over him. "This afternoon I was at lunch at Callahan's with Kendra. Something I saw there made me realize how fleeting hopes and dreams can be without tangible backing." Malcolm shrugged. "I just want to make sure that those boys' dreams aren't deferred by the accident of their financial circumstances. And that when they get to college they can concentrate on their studies and not have to constantly worry about next semester's tuition."

"I'm almost afraid to tally up the total cost of that case. First, pro bono work. Now this. Are you turning into an old softie, Malc?"

Malcolm grinned at his best friend. "Don't let the word out."

Robinson stood and then took a seat in one of the leather-bound chairs in front of Malcolm's desk. "Hey, man. I wanna ask you something, brother to brother."

"Shoot."

"You know Toinette Blue, the woman who runs the Quad-A program?"

"Nice lady," Malcolm answered, thinking about the dress she'd bought for Kendra and the finagling she'd done to get them together for the benefit auction.

"Very much so."

Malcolm raised an eyebrow at Robinson's tone. "Do I detect more than professional interest here?"

"You would if I could get her to see me as something other than 'that nice young man.' We went to lunch a few weeks ago. I don't think it ever crossed her mind that I'd asked her simply because I wanted to be with her. She arrived, and I believe left, with the notion that I was only interested in what she had to say about Quad-A."

"Flowers worked for me," Malcolm mumbled.

"What was that?"

"Nothing. Lunch meetings have a tendency to do that. Why don't you ask her out to dinner? Someplace nice, cozy, intimate."

Robinson hopped up and paced Malcolm's office. "And give her what excuse for the invitation?"

"The truth is always a good idea."

"The truth? That I find her fascinating, that she turns me on? I don't think so, my brother."

"Why not?"

"She'd probably think it was incestuous. She looks at me as if I'm one of her sons."

"That could be a problem."

"It's a problem only if she makes it one. I think she'll make it one."

"How old is her oldest child?"

"Thirty."

Malcolm grimaced. Robinson caught the look.

"I know, I know. I'm just four years older than her eldest. What do you think I should do?" Robinson said as he again plopped into one of the chairs in front of Malcolm's desk.

"Did my ears just deceive me? I know I must have heard you incorrectly."

"Malcolm—"

"Stop the presses. The great Casanova is without a line. He's floundering in a sea of indecision in matters of the heart."

"This is not funny, man," Robinson told him.

"Never thought I'd see the day when Robinson Mayview was without a solid rap for the ladies."

Frustrated, Robinson rubbed his hands over his hair in a jerky motion. "Malcolm . . . Look, I knew I never should have brought it up," he said, hopping up and heading for the door.

Malcolm hurried from around his desk and caught up with his partner. With a hand on the door frame and Robinson halfway out of the office, Malcolm apologized.

"I'm sorry, Rob. I couldn't help a little baiting there."

Robinson's quick self-deprecating smile told Malcolm a lot about his friend's depth of feeling for Nettie Blue.

"Just ask her to dinner. Use Quad-A if it'll get you in the door, but after that let her know how you feel. When you lay your cards on the table you'll either have a straight flush or you'll go out."

"It's the second part that worries me."

"Just ask her out."

Robinson nodded. Malcolm slapped him on the back.

Later that night, Kendra told Nettie all about the job offer. She then told her about Malcolm's distracted and disinterested reaction.

"Nettie, it's like I was telling you before. The man has a hang-up about secretaries and welfare people."

"I think you're being ridiculous. If he had any sort of hang-up, he wouldn't have patiently wooed you."

"Men do all sorts of things to get women in bed with them, Nettie. I have some very expensive diamonds and rubies I can show you if you don't believe me."

At the mention of the jewelry, Nettie paled on the other end of the receiver. "Kendra, there's something I need to tell you."

The click of an incoming call on Kendra's telephone interrupted Nettie.

"Can you hold for a second while I see who that is?" Kendra asked.

"Sure." Granted a temporary reprieve, Nettie sighed.

Malcolm was on the other line for Kendra. She clicked back to Nettie and asked if they could continue their conversation later. At her house, Nettie closed her eyes and offered a prayer appealing to the Supreme Being for everything to turn out all right.

"Kendra, I owe you an apology for this afternoon," Malcolm began. "You were telling me about your promotion and I was off in in la-la land somewhere. I'm sorry. Will you tell me about it now?"

Kendra wanted to ask him where his mind had been, but she couldn't form the words. No matter how she tried to phrase the question, she knew she would come off sounding like a jealous nag or a whiny complainer. So she kept her silence and told Malcolm the entire promotion story, starting with the phone call summons.

"That is fantastic!" he exclaimed when she'd finished. "I'm so proud of you. Sullivan and O'Leary has a substantial support staff. So, when are you going to give him your answer?"

Kendra laughed. "Well, part of me wanted to say yes on the spot and grovel at his feet." After Malcolm's chuckle she continued in a playful nasal tone, "But the cool professional woman that I am said 'Let me get back to you on that, darling.' " Kendra dissolved in a fit of giggles.

"We have to celebrate," Malcolm told her.

"What did you have in mind?" Kendra said, stretching out on her bed. The unconscious, soft sound she made while doing so put Malcolm's body on alert.

"Well, I was originally thinking about something along the lines of champagne and balloons. But right now, I'm thinking about finishing what you started at lunch today."

"Mmmm, is that a fact?"

"Kendra, stop making that noise."

"What noise, Malcolm?"

Kendra's sultry purring had him tied in knots. "Those soft little moans in the back of your throat."

"Do you mean like this?" She mimicked the breathless panting that had come from both of them during the weekend.

"That's it. I'm on my way to your place."

"You can't, Malcolm. The girls are asleep."

The girls! He'd forgotten all about Karin and Kayla. For the second time that day, Malcolm had been thwarted. Since he didn't think Nettie Blue would take the girls every weekend, he would have to do some planning to arrange private time with Kendra.

"Let's celebrate by going to dinner tomorrow night, the four of us."

"Don't you have a class to teach tomorrow?"

Kendra laughed at the swear word that came from Malcolm. He'd obviously forgotten about his students.

"Tell you what," she said. "You come over for dinner Wednesday. I'll make something special."

"We're celebrating. You're not supposed to cook. You guys be ready. I'll bring dinner. What time?"

"Can you make it as early at six o'clock? Even then the girls will have you think they're near starvation."

"Okay. See you at six Wednesday. And Kendra, I . . ." Malcolm paused. He'd been about ready to say "I love you," but over the telephone just wasn't right. He wanted to tell her of his love when it was just the two of them and the mood was right, with candles, calla lilies, and wine.

He quickly amended his statement to "I miss you."

"I miss you, too," she told him.

But a few minutes later, as Kendra pulled the cool bedsheet up over her, she couldn't help but speculate about the short pause she'd detected. She was fairly certain that he was about to say something else. She went to sleep smiling.

For Malcolm, Wednesday seemed to take forever and a day to arrive. He'd placed a take-out order of Chinese food that was enough to feed eight people. But when he pulled up in front of Kendra's apartment, he frowned. Her car wasn't there. Surely she didn't forget about their date. Empty-handed, Malcolm bounded up the stairs. Kendra answered his knock.

Unable to resist, Malcolm hauled her into his arms without a care of who might see them. His lips slashed over hers in a fierce possession that made them both weak. No light or airy thing, the kiss was hot, hungry, and demanding. Crushed against him, Kendra felt every bone in her body melt. She wasn't sure she'd have been able to stand on her own two feet if Malcolm's strong arms had not been supporting her. As his mouth danced a rhythm that shattered her equilibrium, Malcolm's hands slid down her back, cupped her rounded bottom and drew her more intimately in contact with his need. Clasped in an embrace as close as two people could get without being physically joined, Kendra still tried to get closer. Her hands caressed his hair, his neck, his back, while their mouths sucked and pulled. His tongue explored her in ways Kendra found devastatingly erotic. She wanted him here and now and with such incredible need, she was incapable of thinking anything except how Malcolm made her feel. Electrified. Hot as ice, cool as fire.

His lips left hers to nibble at her earlobe before searing a path down her neck and shoulders. Kendra's breath came in pants and gasps as each kiss confirmed for her that she'd never grow old enough to tire of Malcolm's loving.

The sense of urgency that propelled Malcolm made his heart thunder. Long moments later, when his brain finally decided to reconnect itself to the rest of his body, he realized that the soft whimpering he'd heard coming from Kendra was a direct result of the not-so-gentle exploration of his hand at her breast. At some point he'd managed to slip a hand under her shirt and up her body. Through her brassiere, Malcolm could feel the puckered excitement of her breast. He couldn't resist one final caress before he reluctantly removed his hand and smoothed her blouse. His mouth, deprived of its treat, was suddenly dry.

"Jesus, Kendra. You make me crazy," he breathed while putting some distance between them and resting his hands on the relative safeness of her waist.

But Kendra didn't respond. She couldn't. Her body still tingled. Blood pounded in her brain and her emotions whirled. What spell had he cast to make her so eager for him? So willing to toss away caution and convention for just the touch of his hands?

Malcolm rested his forehead on hers while they both caught their breath. The passion that had so quickly flared between them took some time to recede. For almost five minutes they stood supporting each other, trying to come to grips with the frenzy of their ardor.

When finally Kendra thought she could speak, she lifted her head and offered Malcolm a trembling smile.

"Hi."

Malcolm chuckled and pulled her to him for a quick hug. "Hi, yourself."

"If that's how you normally say hello, I think you need to knock on my front door more often."

"Kendra, quite honestly, I don't think I'd survive the experience. You have no idea what you do to me."

"Well, I can feel one thing," she told him with a saucy smile.

"And if you don't let me cool down, there might have to be an awkward explanation if Karin or Kayla notice the odd bulge in my pants."

Kendra smiled. "With Kayla's preoccupation with kissing, she'd be the one to do the asking. So counselor, how long do you need to cool down?"

"Fifty years might do it."

Kendra gave him an odd look as she followed him down the steps and to his car. Was Malcolm implying that he wanted them to have a future?

He opened the back door of his town car and started pulling out boxes and bags.

"I hope you invited some people to help us eat all of this stuff," Kendra said, accepting her share of the load to carry.

"Well, I couldn't remember what everyone liked, so I got some of each."

Kendra shook her head at the extravagance and watched Malcolm shut and lock the car before maneuvering into his arms the things he'd placed on the hood of the vehicle.

"Malcolm, you really spent too much. It's just dinner."

"So you'll have some leftovers for lunch tomorrow. No big deal. Hey, where's your car?" he asked.

"I dropped it off earlier today for the mechanics to check on something. It's been making a strange noise. They didn't have time to get to it so I left it overnight and took the bus home."

"You should have called. If you'll drop me off tonight, I'll leave this car with you so you can get to work in the morning."

"No need," she told him. "The bus stop is right at the corner. Thanks, though."

Walking in front of him, Kendra didn't see Malcolm's hurt expression. It wasn't the first time Kendra had rebuffed one of his attempts to help her. She wanted to be independent and it drove him crazy. He had the wherewithal to make her life easier, yet she turned him down at every opportunity. When their television went on the fritz a week or so ago Malcolm offered to buy a new one, a nice twenty-seven-inch baby with stereo surround sound and dual remote. But Kendra had flatly refused.

The only time he'd been able to buy the twins something was the Saturday when B.J. had lured them all into a sporting goods store. Malcolm bought his nephew a pair of state-of-the-art in-line skates and had had Kayla and Karin sized and outfitted as well. Kendra had been livid. The skates had cost almost a month's rent. The next day she'd slapped the cash into his hands and didn't speak to him for three days. She never explained why his gesture had made her so angry. Malcolm didn't bother to tell her he bought the girls shares of stock in the sporting goods store with the money Kendra had so stubbornly given him.

And now, now she wouldn't even depend on him enough to ask for a ride home or accept a freely made offer of available and convenient transportation. Malcolm swallowed his frustration and managed to hook a finger around the screen door to open it for Kendra.

They were barely in the apartment when a crash and a thud came from the kitchen, and a scream rent the air.

CHAPTER 11

"Mom!! Mom! Come quick!" Kayla's terrified screams rang through the apartment. Kendra dropped every parcel she carried and tore through the living room and hall to the kitchen where the twins were. Malcolm was hot on her heels.

Karin lay crumpled on the floor while blood pooled around her. Broken pottery, dishes, and cookies littered the counter and the floor. A three-step ladder was overturned, with one of Kayla's legs tangled in it.

"She's dead, Mommie! She's dead! I didn't mean to kill her," Kayla cried hysterically while kicking at the ladder and scrambling through the shards to get to her sister's side. Kendra raced to do the same.

"Oh, my god! Karin! Karin? Can you hear me, baby?" Already on her knees cradling her daughter's head in her lap, Kendra frantically searched for a pulse in Karin's wrist. But the blood. There was so much blood she could barely concentrate. Kendra used her blouse to soak up some of the life fluid that Karin was losing.

Through the mist of her panic she yelled for the sobbing Kayla to call 911. But then Kendra heard another voice telling her daughter not to. Suddenly Karin's limp body was pulled from her arms.

"Don't take my baby! She's hurt. Don't hurt my baby."

"Kendra, she's going to be okay. Do you hear me? She's going to be okay."

The calm voice penetrated Kendra's alarm. Death couldn't steal Karin, she was just a little girl. She looked up at the man who held her daughter in his arms. It wasn't Death who had snatched Karin but

Malcolm. Malcolm. Kendra nodded and slowly rose to her feet. Don't panic, she told herself. Panicking won't help the situation. Take a deep breath.

Still looking disoriented and frightened, Kendra at least had a grip, a slight one, but a grip on her panic. She reached into a drawer of kitchen towels and grabbed several before gathering Kayla up and following Malcolm through the apartment. She had the presence of mind to grab her purse before closing the door.

In the few minutes it took to get Kendra, Karin, and Kayla in the back seat of the car, Malcolm prayed as he'd never prayed before. He'd never forgive himself if the little girl he'd come to love as a daughter suffered serious injury while he'd been on the front porch kissing Kendra.

He had assured Kendra that Karin would be all right, but he didn't know that for a fact. Blood covered the front of his shirt where he'd held the girl. Malcolm had never seen so much blood. That couldn't possibly be good.

Tires screeched as he whipped the big car onto the street and rushed toward City Hospital. Malcolm punched in 911 on his car telephone and told the dispatcher to alert the hospital. He then hit a single digit and let the automatic dial function of the phone call another number.

"Get me Dr. Sandra Bliss or Dr. William Bliss *now,*" he barked at the person who answered. The person's response didn't suit him. Malcolm had a few choice words to share until he heard his sister's voice on the other end. He quickly told her what had happened and they would be at the emergency room in about six minutes or so.

In the back seat of the car, Kendra rocked her unconscious daughter and softly sang the little girl's favorite song from Sunday school.

"This little light of mine, I'm gonna let it shine. This little light of mine, I'm gonna let it shine."

Kayla hadn't stopped crying, but the soothing melody helped calm her. Soon after they'd gotten into the car, Kendra had pressed Kayla's small hand to the weak but definite pulse at Karin's neck to prove to herself and Kayla that Karin was still alive. Now, Kayla held her sister's hand and slowly rocked back and forth with her mom.

Malcolm broke every existing speed limit and ran a red light, but he got them safely to the hospital in less than twelve minutes.

Emergency room attendants stood at the door with a stretcher. They efficiently whisked Karin from Kendra's arms and dashed the little girl into rooms where machines beeped and lives were saved . . . and lost.

After parking the car, Malcolm found Kendra and Kayla in the waiting room. Kendra had Kayla cuddled in her arms as she tried to fill out the forms the hospital required, but her hand trembled so much she couldn't write. When she saw Malcolm approach, she tried a little levity.

"It's a good thing I remembered to grab my purse. We must look a fright." But Kendra's wobbly smile collapsed, and hot, silent tears streamed down her face.

"You both look incredibly beautiful to me," Malcolm told her as he knelt before her chair. Not bothering to hide his emotions from Kayla or anyone else in the waiting room, he pulled Kendra's head to his and kissed her. The tender caress made Kendra cry even more.

"Is she going to be okay, Malcolm? I don't know what I'll do if she's not okay."

"She's being attended to by Sandy, who's the best doctor in the city, so don't you worry."

But Kendra's question served to further upset Kayla, whose pitiful whimpering grew again to full-blown sobs.

"I didn't mean to hurt her, Mommie."

"Oh, I know, sweetheart," Kendra told her as she kissed the top of her daughter's head. In a soothing, circular pattern, Malcolm rubbed his hand along the girl's back.

"Hey, what are all of these tears for?" he asked Kayla. "There's enough water here to fill a swimming pool."

Kayla gave him a trembly smile.

"We were trying to get some cookies from the top of the refrigerator. But, but . . . my foot slipped on the ladder and Karin, who was on top, fell down. She hit her head on the counter and, and . . ." The girl dissolved in tears again. "Is she going to bleed to death, Mommie?"

Kendra wiped the tears from her daughter's face and hugged her close.

"The doctors are stopping the bleeding right now," she said while trying to mask her own uncertainty. "And you know what?"

"What?" Kayla said, sitting up and regarding her mother between sniffles.

"B.J.'s mom is the doctor who's making Karin better."

"B.J.'s mom is a doctor?"

"Um-hmm. And so is his dad. They work here in the hospital."

That news seemed to comfort Kayla. She nodded her head once and for all the world reminded Malcolm of Kendra after Kendra came to a decision about something.

"Well, B.J.'s mom won't let anything bad happen to Karin," Kayla declared. And with that statement, she dried her eyes on her shirt and looked around the waiting room for the first time.

Malcolm smiled. "I remember the faith of being seven," he told Kendra.

Kendra leaned over and kissed him. "Thank you for being the voice of calm and reason back at the house. For a minute there, I thought I was going to lose my mind."

Malcolm patted her jean-clad thigh and got up to sit in the chair next to her.

"Come over here, Miss Kayla," he told the girl while transferring her from Kendra's lap to his. "Your mom needs to fill out some papers for the hospital."

A woman who had been standing near the nurse's station watched the tender scene across the waiting room. She couldn't hear the words the family spoke to each other but their love for each other was evident. The man had kissed his wife and tenderly stroked his daughter's back.

The woman, outfitted in a springtime Sunday-go-to-meeting dress and comfortable white shoes, wondered what sick relative they anxiously awaited news about. She had been visiting a friend in town, and held a prayer cloth, a Bible, and a handful of religious tracts. She and her friend had decided to pray with the sick and shut-in before going to Wednesday night prayer meeting.

She was about to go to the family and offer a few words of encouragement when the little girl sat up, dried her eyes, and looked around.

The woman gasped and clutched the prayer cloth to her bosom.

Concerned, a nurse looked up. It wouldn't have been the first time a person had had a heart attack while visiting someone else in the hospital.

"Ma'am? Are you all right?"

"Wha . . . what did you say?" The woman stammered. She had yet to take her eyes off the family. She couldn't see the wife because the man blocked her view. When he pulled the little girl into his lap, the woman bent her head and started filling out paperwork.

"Are you all right, ma'am? Are you feeling any distress?"

The woman turned to the nurse and replied with a sound that was part laugh and part sob. "Yes, I'm feeling distressed. But it's not what you think. I'm fine. Thank you for your concern, child," she said while absentmindedly handing the nurse a Bible tract.

The woman again looked at the family huddled together across the room. The mother was still writing. The man protectively held his daughter with one arm and had the other wrapped around his wife's shoulders. The woman didn't recognize him and still couldn't see the mother. But she knew the little girl.

With seven years' worth of photographs to prod her memory, Katherine Edwards had no diffficulty recognizing her great niece.

CHAPTER 12

Katherine took a tentative step toward the family, then lost her courage. As she whirled around and ran into the ladies room, she collided with her friend Hattie, who was on the way out.

"Katherine! What's wrong?" Hattie asked while steadying the other woman.

"It's her," Katherine whispered.

Hattie looked around. "Her who?"

Katherine pushed her friend back into the restroom so they could talk. She put her Bible, purse, and the religious tracts on the vanity but clutched the linen and lace prayer cloth.

"Kendra's out there," she told Hattie.

"Kendra your niece?" At Katherine's nod the other woman continued. "I thought you said she moved out of state years ago."

"Lord forgive me cause Jesus knows I wronged that child," Katherine said more in prayer than to her friend. With the prayer cloth bunched in her fist, she paced the small room. "Jesus, forgive me. She's a sweet girl, always has been. And she tried so hard to make up. But my pride, Lord, my sinful pride. I wouldn't let her in. And now she probably hates me. It's my own fault but I just couldn't countenance what she'd done."

Katherine suddenly remembered Hattie, who silently watched her. Katherine turned to her friend. "I'm gonna go to her right now and apologize. Maybe with her husband and little girl there she won't be too upset. Lord, Hattie, she was a pitiful thing that last night. If I hadn't been so angry I probably woulda seen how scared and how young she was. But

I didn't see nothing but the anger and wrath that that old Satan kept feeding me. I kicked her out, Hattie," Katherine said as two tracks of tears trickled down her face. "I kicked my own blood relation out of the house."

Hattie embraced Katherine and let the woman silently cry on her shoulder. "Katherine . . ."

But Katherine didn't hear her. She was still lost in the past.

"Mister Albert, Albert Walker, the next door neighbor, found her passed out on the grass. I told him to leave her there. I didn't care. I'd been on my knees all night and still couldn't find forgiveness in my heart. I listened to her pack, Hattie. And just like I told her, she took everything out of the house that was hers. She was always an obedient child. I never had any trouble with her. She was the spittin' image of her mama. But she got her daddy, Charlie's, height and coloring. Lord have mercy Jesus, I hope they forgive me for the way I treated their child."

"Katherine, Kat, can you hear me?"

Katherine pulled away from the embrace.

"Of course I can hear you, Hattie. I'm not deaf."

Hattie chuckled. Whatever had just transpired, the old Katherine was back.

"Kat, I'm not gonna pretend that I know what you're talkin' 'bout here. But that'll come with time. What I think we need to do before you go out there is have a word of prayer."

Katherine nodded. "You're right. The Lord will give me strength."

The two older women got on their knees on the tile floor in the restroom. With their heads bowed and hands clasped together, Katherine began to pray.

Outside in the waiting room, Kendra had completed the forms and the three of them sat awaiting word on Karin's condition. Kendra prayed for her daughter's well-being and unconsciously hummed the tune to "This Little Light of Mine."

Malcolm, resisting the urge to storm into the emergency room and find out what the holdup was, continued to gently rock Kayla in his arms. While she no longer cried, Malcolm could feel the tension in the little girl's body. But as Kendra hummed the song over and over, Malcolm felt Kayla relax. She eventually drifted into a light sleep.

Kendra got up and paced the area in front of Malcolm. Hugging her arms to herself, she anxiously glanced at the emergency room doors each time they opened.

"They've never really been sick," she told Malcolm. "Except for the time when they were twenty months old. Kayla caught pneumonia. God, was I terrified. Then, just when I thought the storm was over, Karin started developing symptoms. The next thing I knew she had a temperature of one hundred and four. I didn't have a telephone or a car but knew I had to get her to the hospital. I ran outside to call 911 from the pay phone at the corner, but it and the one two blocks over had been ripped out of the booths."

Kendra shook her head and shuddered. "I didn't know what to do. I'd left the babies in the apartment alone while I was trying to get an ambulance. I was running down the street back to the apartment, terrified out of my mind that Kayla, who was up and feeling better, may have set the place on fire. There were always stories on the news about mothers who went to the store for cigarettes or something and came back and all their kids were dead. I kept imagining that that would happen."

As he listened to Kendra, Malcolm clutched Kayla to him as if he would protect her from any future danger. The picture of Kendra's terror chilled him.

"I was almost to the apartment when this car drove up. The windows were all tinted really dark. But the driver had his window down. There were five or six of them in there. Drug dealers. They preyed on the little kids in the projects, had them run the drugs. I'd seen them out my front window every morning before the kids went to school. It was like an open-air market. I used to think that more cash exchanged hands in front of my window than on Wall Street every day."

The sound of a siren approaching made Kendra pause. She and Malcolm watched as the emergency medical technicians whisked a person on a gurney into the emergency room. When the hubbub ended, Kendra shuddered, sighed, then picked up her story.

"I'd learned early on that the easy way to get shot was to dis the dealers. But that night, I just didn't care. When one of the guys in the back rolled his window down and called to me, I ignored them all and kept running to the apartment. That apparently pissed them off. The driver cut the car up over the curb and blocked me. By that time I was hysterical. I was crying and babbling about the phone and the fire and the babies and pneumonia. They, of course, thought it was funny."

Kendra looked at Malcolm and sighed again. "Well, to make a long story short, I just narrowly escaped being raped that night. I think what saved me was that I reminded the main guy, one of the ones in the back seat, of his little sister. That didn't stop him from demanding that I pay him fifty dollars in food stamps to use his car phone. It was then that I knew that somehow, someway, I had to get out of those projects."

With a bittersweet smile she added, "About a month later I saw the flier advertising the Quad-A program on the bulletin board in the laundromat. Once I hooked up with Nettie, I knew I had to do what I could to help other women who were trapped in the projects. People who were victims of their circumstances."

Malcolm had no words for Kendra. While listening to her he'd felt rage, fear, and helplessness. No words to her would have expressed his fury. But he was impotent in his rage. There was nothing he could have done to protect Kendra so many years ago. Kendra had come through, she had survived and was a stronger woman for the experience. Maybe too strong to need the after-the-fact comfort he could offer.

He reached his free hand to her. When she clasped it, Malcolm softly kissed the back of her hand and then her palm. Kendra reciprocated the embrace, then gently stroked his cheek. The moisture she found there surprised her.

"Oh, Malcolm, it was a long time ago," she whispered as she bent a knee to get eye level with him.

About to respond to her, Malcolm paused and looked up at the woman who had approached them.

"Kendra?"

Kendra blinked. The voice. It was Aunt Kat, but it couldn't be. In a single fluid motion she rose, turned, and came face to face with the woman who had forced her to confront the harsh and bitter realities of being an adult and a single parent.

"Aunt Kat?"

Katherine flinched as if she'd been hit. The beautiful young woman standing before her was the same girl she'd thrown out of the house seven years ago. Kendra had grown up. Still pretty, she had the filled-out look of a mature woman instead of the child she had been. Incredibly disconcerting was the fact that Katherine's last image of Kendra's tear-ravaged face as she sat at their kitchen table was the same image she saw now. This time, though, Katherine hadn't caused her tears and Kendra's shirt was covered with what could only be dried blood.

Katherine took a look at the man who was holding the girl. They, too, had blood on their clothing.

Not knowing how to respond to either the situation or to her niece, Katherine just stood there. She nodded her head when Kendra again inquired, "Aunt Kat, is that you?"

"Yes, it's me, child," Katherine finally said.

Kendra swayed as if she might faint. Malcolm reached a steadying hand to the small of her back and Kayla stirred.

For years Kendra had practiced what she would say when she saw her aunt again. But the recriminations, the apologies, the begging for forgiveness all seemed to stick in her throat. She didn't know what to say. Not here, not now, when the only important thing was whether her daughter would live or die.

Kendra took the older woman's hands in hers and leaned forward. She kissed Aunt Kat on the cheek, surprising both herself and her aunt.

"Hello, Aunt Kat. Are you here visiting?"

"Uh, yes. I was in town, visiting with Hattie Williams. You remember her, don't you? She used to live down the street from us when you were little."

"Yes, I remember Miss Hattie," Kendra said. "Give her my regards."

Kendra felt as if she were standing outside her body watching the bizarre conversation unfold. By rights, Kendra thought, she should be raging at the person who had by rejecting her when Kendra had needed her most, sentenced her to life in hell. Could Aunt Kat know or begin to imagine what it had been like to be nineteen with two little babies to care for? Did she know that Kendra had needed her aunt's advice, support, and love on more occasions than Kendra could even remember? How different would her life be today had she had Aunt Kat's support through the years?

But none of those thoughts got articulated in the awkward tableau. Kendra looked dazed. Katherine looked frightened. And Malcolm wondered what the hell was going on.

"Kendra, honey? Are you okay?" he asked while stroking her back.

Kendra looked down at Malcolm. Manners kicked in and she by rote made the introductions.

"Katherine Edwards, Malcolm Hightower. Malcolm, this is my Aunt Katherine."

With his head, Malcolm gestured to Kayla, who was waking up and rubbing her eyes. "I apologize for not standing, ma'am. She needed the rest." He extended his free hand to Katherine, who shook it with timidity.

Katherine looked at the little girl and Malcolm, then turned her attention back to Kendra.

"Is he the one?"

"Aunt Kat," Kendra said in warning. But she was interrupted by a male nurse who approached.

"Mr. and Mrs. Hightower, I'm Dr. Bliss's scrub nurse. I wanted to tell you that your little girl is going to be okay. Dr. Bliss will be right out to speak with you," the nurse said.

"Thank you, sir. But we're not—" Kendra started.

"B.J.'s mom made Karin all better?" Kayla piped in.

The nurse squatted down and gently tugged on one of Kayla's thick braids. "Yeah, she's all better, sweetie. We heard a lot about the two of you in there."

"What they heard most was me saying 'If anything happens to this child, my brother is going to kill me,' " Sandra Hightower Bliss said as she joined the group.

No one noticed Katherine Edwards quietly slip away.

Kayla slid off Malcolm's lap and went to stand next to her mother while Malcolm stood and stretched his legs.

"You're B.J.'s mom?" Kayla asked under the protective wing of Kendra's arm.

"That's right, and you must be Kayla."

The girl nodded.

"Well, Kayla, Malcolm, and Kendra," she said with a smile to alleviate the worried look Kendra still wore. "Karin's going to be just fine. She's going to have a headache for a little while. All the blood made it look much worse than it was. She should be ready to go home in an hour or so. I just want to make sure she's stabilized and doesn't show signs of a concussion. I'd advise that she stay home from school for a day or two."

"Thank you. Thank you for saving my little girl," Kendra murmured in abject gratitude while pumping Sandra's hand. "And it's a pleasure to finally meet you."

"Don't thank me. She's the fighter. And I just wish we could have met someplace fun, like over a barbecue or something. But Malcolm always was one for grand entrances. You had the ER dispatcher in a huff after screaming at her on the telephone. Really, Malcolm," Sandy gently scolded.

"Can we see her?" Kendra and Malcolm asked at the same time.

"Sure," Sandy said. "But how about we find some cleaner clothes for you all? I don't want you to scare the girl when she sees you three looking like extras from a horror movie. Wait here, I'll see what I can do. Bill might have a shirt you can wear, Malc."

Sandy and the scrub nurse walked away. Kendra turned around to set the record straight with Aunt Kat about her marital status. But the older woman was nowhere to be seen.

"Where did Aunt Kat go?"

Malcolm looked around. "Don't know. She was here a minute ago."

Kendra shrugged. "Well, I always know where to find her. I think," she added in afterthought.

A few minutes later the three of them, donned in matching green hospital scrub shirts, entered the room where Karin lay in bed surrounded by white sheets, white pillows, and white bandages.

"Hey, how come I didn't get one of those shirts?" she demanded when she saw them.

Kendra laughed and ran to her daughter's bedside.

"Oh, baby. I was so worried about you. How do you feel?" Kendra said while examining all of her daughter's features.

"My head hurts, I'm thirsty and sleepy," she declared.

Kendra kissed her forehead, which was swathed in bandages, and then Karin's cheek. "Well, goosehead, that must mean you're feeling better."

Kayla let go of Malcolm's hand and tentatively approached the bed where her twin lay.

"Karin?" Karin turned to her sister on the other side of the bed.

"Karin, please don't hate me. I didn't mean to make you fall and get hurt. The ladder moved. I'm sorry." Kayla managed to get the last part of her apology out before she started crying again.

Karin tried to sit up but winced against the pain. "It wasn't your fault,

Kay," she told her sister. "We shoulda got the potato chips or the raisins on the counter."

"Yeah," Kayla sniffled. "You promise you're not mad at me?"

"Yeah."

"Are we still friends?" Kayla wanted to know.

Karin nodded.

"Friends, sisters, twins forever," the girls chanted, a pledge they had obviously made to each other before.

"Except now we don't even get to eat the Chinese food Malcolm was bringing over," Karin observed.

"I'll bring you all the Chinese food you want, sweetheart," Malcolm promised from where he stood at the door.

"With chopsticks?"

Kendra turned to Malcolm and smiled. The warmth in his answering smile echoed in his voice. "With chopsticks," he assured the girl.

"Hey, Mom, will you sing a song for us?" Karin asked.

"You bet, sweetness," and she launched into the song that had carried them through the night's ordeal.

Leaning against the wall, feeling somewhat like an outsider but wishing with everything he was worth that he wasn't, Malcolm watched Kendra and her daughters. What he shared with Kendra and the girls was too special to just toss away. Kendra wasn't in love with him, but lots of couples married for lesser reasons. More than anything, he wanted to marry Kendra. Malcolm had enough love to go around. Convincing Kendra was the trick. And if that wasn't enough to worry about, he had to figure out who the mysterious Aunt Katherine was, why she disappeared, and why she and Kendra acted as if they were virtual strangers.

By the time Kendra and Malcolm picked up Karin's prescription and got some food into Kayla, it was close to midnight. Both girls were fast asleep when they returned to the apartment. With Malcolm carrying the injured Karin, and Kendra holding Kayla, Kendra led the way to the bedroom the twins shared. She and Malcolm deposited their precious bundles in the girls' respective beds. Malcolm left the bedroom while Kendra tugged off their jeans and sneakers and got both girls tucked in. Since Sandy had suggested a mild sedative for both of them given Karin's injuries and Kayla's distress, they would sleep undisturbed until the late morning or early afternoon.

From the hospital, Kendra had called Eric Slater, her boss, and explained what had happened. He'd told her to take all the time she needed with her daughters.

Kendra sat on the edge of Karin's bed and gazed at her child. She ran her hands over the girl's thick braids and smoothed the child's forehead.

She did the same for Kayla, then bent and kissed each one. The prayer she offered up before leaving was one of thanksgiving that they hadn't been more seriously injured in the fall.

Turning out the light, she softly closed the door.

She found Malcolm cleaning up the food she'd dropped in the living room.

"You're probably going to have to get this specially treated," he said, indicating a reddish-orange stain on the carpet that most likely had been caused by sweet-and-sour sauce.

Kendra's wan smile concerned Malcolm. Except for the few and brief tears she'd shed at the hospital, Kendra hadn't really let go of the tension and fear she'd been experiencing. And the mysterious disappearing aunt probably had something to do with the faraway look he'd caught on her face several times during the evening. But right now, Kendra looked like she would collapse.

Malcolm dropped the sponge he'd found while straightening the kitchen, got off his knees, and led Kendra to the sofa. He sat next to her and patted her hands, her *cold* hands, he noted.

"I put some coffee on. It should be ready now and will warm you. Let me get you a cup, okay?" he asked while getting up.

Kendra's vacant silence frightened him. She sat clenching her hands together, looking lost and confused. Vulnerable. Childlike. Half afraid to leave her for the few moments it would take to pour the coffee, Malcolm stepped away from the sofa.

"Please don't leave me, Malcolm."

Her plea, a whispered entreaty, touched Malcolm in a place that had been cold for a long, long time; a place where flowers of the heart didn't need soil or rain to make them grow. Kendra's smile was their sunshine; her tears their sustenance.

When the dam broke, Malcolm knew that she cried for her daughters, for her own lost innocence. She cried for the past and the future, for yesterdays of pain and suffering and for the uncertainty of tomorrows to come. Malcolm held her and rocked her and encouraged her to let the anguish and fear flow from her body. She cried as if she hadn't ever done so, with great wracking sobs that tore at Malcolm even while he acknowledged that they were a necessary release for Kendra.

But as he held her, Malcolm felt his body respond to her nearness. He kissed her hair and breathed in her fresh scent. The comforting caresses along her back and up and down her arms subtly changed. Malcolm hardened in anticipation, yet chastised himself for his insensitivity. Now was not the time or the place to express those emotions. But as Kendra's weeping eventually subsided and she brought herself under control, she nuzzled his neck.

Malcolm tensed when her mouth opened and her tongue ran the length from his ear to the collar of the scrub shirt he wore.

"Kendra . . ." he warned even as his arms tightened around her.

"Shhh," she answered as she lifted her head and pressed her fingers to his lips. Her fingers were soon replaced with his lips when she bent forward and begged of him, "Make me whole, Malcolm. Love me and make the pain and fear go away."

Malcolm licked the last of her salty tears from her face, then merged his mouth with hers. While he felt the need to be tender and gentle, Kendra directed the wild kiss and drank greedily from his mouth. Her hands roamed his hair, his face, his chest. She pressed herself close to him and nudged her hips into his hardness. She wanted to lose herself in his embrace.

In a sudden move, she pulled away and left Malcolm bereft. But then she yanked the hospital shirt above her head and in one deft maneuver unfastened the black bra she wore and bared herself to him. Malcolm's heart beat triple time but Kendra didn't give him the opportunity to choose which fruit he would suckle. She pulled his head to her chest and his mouth latched onto the closest orb. She arched her back and urged him to pull and nip. Rough games weren't her style or preference, but tonight she wanted to be dominated, to know that she didn't always have to be in charge of her life and in control of her emotions. Instinctively Malcolm knew that for tonight Kendra needed this release like she needed oxygen to breathe. He gave one last, lingering swirl against her hardened nipple, then claimed her mouth in a fast but deep kiss and lifted her into his arms.

Without error he found her bedroom and bent a knee into the softness of her queen-sized bed. He put her in the middle of the bed amidst a mountain of lace and eyelet pillows. When he turned to close and lock her bedroom door, Kendra wiggled out of her slacks and panties and pushed the pillows to the floor. By the time Malcolm returned to her he wore nothing but the proud stance of ancient African kings and the rugged sensuality of a big man who was comfortable with his body, a man in his prime.

Kendra's eyes roamed the strength and power of his physique and lingered on that part of him that made him distinctly male, distinctly Malcolm. She lifted her arms and he came into them. Of tender words and whispered promises, there were none. Conversation would have been intrusive. Kendra wanted him now and hard and fast. Malcolm took the moment he needed to protect them and to ensure that Kendra was ready for him. When his hand came away from her core, he brought it to his mouth to lick her sweetness from his fingers. While highly erotic, the sight made Kendra cry out her frustration at his delay.

When at last he settled between her soft, brown thighs, she arched into his embrace. Malcolm would have prolonged the teasing but his body clamored to be sheathed inside Kendra. Her impatient wildness spurred him and her softness beckoned. He entered her with more force than would have been his norm. Kendra wasted no time establishing their rhythm. She squirmed beneath him and drove him mad. She gasped in sweet agony when he thrust again and again and filled her to her very womb. Passion pounded through her veins and Malcolm was there all the way.

In what seemed like no time and forever, Kendra shattered into a million glowing stars. Malcolm, less than a heartbeat behind her, groaned his satisfaction and collapsed in her arms.

Sated for the time being, they fell asleep wrapped in a tight embrace: Malcolm still inside her, Kendra's long legs wrapped around his hips.

Three times during the night they woke and loved again. Each time, they managed to slow their frantic coupling, until an hour or so before dawn, when they came together with such sweetness that Kendra cried from the beauty of it. The hysterical longing that had taken control of her had mellowed and softened to a thing to be savored. Throughout the night, Kendra had been a glowing image of fire and passion, Malcolm's fantasy come to life. Now as she cradled Malcolm's head at her breast and slipped into the gentle, peaceful sleep of the fulfilled, her last thought was of when and if she would ever tell him she loved him.

Despite her interrupted sleep, Kendra awakened at her usual hour. She slipped from Malcolm's embrace, checked on the girls, then went to the kitchen to make coffee. She smiled when she saw the pot Malcolm had brewed the night before still warming on its pad. She dumped it and made a fresh pot of the heady brew.

Malcolm woke to the smell of Colombian coffee, sugar, and cinnamon. He relieved himself in the tiny bathroom, then padded to the kitchen, where he found Kendra taking a batch of homemade cinnamon rolls from the oven.

"Good morning, beautiful."

She turned at the sound of his voice and her smile was his breakfast. Kendra placed the baking pan on a trivet and went into his arms. Malcolm's fingers trailed up her arms, leaving a path of fire in their wake. Their morning kiss quickly turned into more than a simple greeting. Malcolm pulled her against his fast-rising appreciation of her beauty.

"Hungry?" she murmured against his lips.

"For you, always."

Kendra smiled and swatted at the hand that tried to dip into the folds of her silk wrapper.

"Let me get you some coffee to help wake you up," she said, turning away and going to a cabinet for a mug.

"Kendra, trust me. Every part of me that needs to be awake already is."

She wasn't surprised when he came up behind her, circled her waist with his hands and nuzzled her neck. Kendra let herself luxuriate in the sweet sensation, but didn't let the embrace deter her. She turned in his arms and pressed a mug of steaming coffee into his hands. After refreshing her own cup and turning the oven off, she gestured for Malcolm, who hungrily watched her, to have a seat at the table.

When assured of his undivided attention, Kendra sat down, took a fortifying sip of the hot liquid, looked down at her hands, and then at Malcolm. It was time.

"I need to tell you about Oscar. And about Aunt Kat."

CHAPTER 13

Malcolm knew they had to have this conversation, but after their night of unbridled passion, he definitely could have gone without hearing about the man who from the grave held Kendra's heart captive.

Tell her now, his heart demanded even as his head told him that he didn't have a chance with her. Kendra had probably made some inane pledge to the man that she would never love again. Malcolm ached to his very soul. He was losing Kendra, and the only weapon with which he had to fight was his heart.

"I know I should have told you earlier, particularly about Aunt Kat," Kendra began.

Malcolm interrupted her. Her hands had been wrapped around her coffee mug but Malcolm disengaged her fingers and brought them to his lips. After kissing them, he was reluctant to let go. It was now or never. He had to tell her what he'd known for weeks. Kendra made him complete. He only regretted that he didn't have soft music and calla lilies at the ready.

"Kendra, before you begin you need to know how very much I love you."

Kendra gasped. She yanked her hands free and brought them to her mouth to help quell the trembling brought on by his confession.

"It's just physical," she said.

"Kendra, I love you."

But she shook her head. "It's just the sex, I know it is."

Malcolm's gray eyes darkened to slate and she knew she'd hurt him. She reached a tentative hand to his fists, which were now locked together on the table, but he rebuffed her by pulling his hands away and folding his arms across his broad chest. The rejection stung. Maybe she deserved it, she thought. But he couldn't really be telling the truth.

"I at first got the impression that maybe you hadn't been seeing anyone," Kendra said while staring at her coffee mug. Kendra had no wish to see the angry expression she knew he wore.

Had she actually looked at Malcolm, she would have known that he wasn't angry. His heart was breaking. Kendra didn't want him and the knowledge tore him apart. If anything, Malcolm looked like he would cry.

But Kendra, caught up in her own insecurities about herself and her ability to be truly loved by a man, didn't notice any of that. Seven years after the fact, Oscar's cruel words still haunted her, made her feel incompetent as a woman.

"So when we finally came together," Kendra continued softly, "I figured you just hadn't had sex in a long time. I hadn't. Not since Oscar. I apologize for last night . . ."

Malcolm's mouth dropped, but Kendra didn't see it. The one night he'd felt alive and whole and in love beyond reason and Kendra was sorry it had happened?

"Last night was beautiful for me," she told him. "I'll always cherish the memory. I'm sorry I acted like such a, a . . ." She floundered for a word, then waved it away. "I don't know. I'm sorry I was all over you like that. I know I don't have much technique. That was one of my shortcomings Oscar pointed out before he was killed. Before you came along, I just hadn't had much practice."

Malcolm felt like she had punched him. "Kendra . . ."

She looked at him then, but his face was closed. She couldn't tell what he was thinking or feeling. She felt as if she were dying inside.

"No, I know you're being kind. I guess I should thank you. Before you leave me, I want you to know about Oscar, about Aunt Kat. About how I found myself living in the projects. I'm sure it'll change the way you think you feel about me."

Kendra, wrapping herself in her memories, didn't hear Malcolm murmur, "Kendra, I'll never leave you."

"I didn't grow up there. I didn't think I had any prejudice about people who did. In my hometown, which is about an hour or so from here, I knew where the poor people lived. They lived in projects. But their problems, the guns, the drugs, the unsafe buildings, just didn't affect my world. I was Mommy and Daddy's little princess."

Kendra smiled at the memory of her parents, then took a sip from her cup. "They were coming home from a town council meeting one night—my dad believed in being involved in local government," she said, smiling.

"There was a storm and he lost control of the car in the heavy rain. Aunt Kat, my father's only sister, took me in and raised me. I admit, I was sheltered and naive. Aunt Kat didn't believe in dances and the movies so I never really got that part of a young person's socialization skills."

Kendra got up and cut two cinnamon rolls from the pan, which had cooled.

She placed the plate before him, then handed him a knife and fork.

"Thank you," Malcolm said.

She lifted one of the gooey buns onto a plate for herself and sat back at the table.

"When it was time to go to college, we decided to save the money that would have been used to house me in a dormitory on campus. I lived at home. I'd always worked during the summers, just to have something to do, and had bought a used car while in high school. The money saved by living at home wasn't eaten up in bus fare. Now, don't get me wrong. We weren't poor. . . . I don't think." Kendra paused for a moment to reflect on that.

"You know, I don't know. Maybe we were poor. If we were, it never seemed like it. I always had everything I wanted. Aunt Kat was strict but she was fair. She even knew that Deacon Thomas's son, Elias, liked me. She didn't know that he used to sneak a kiss in the choir loft after junior choir rehearsal," she said with a laugh at the memory. "God, I wonder what happened to him."

Malcolm, who was slowly eating as Kendra talked, smiled. This was a Kendra he didn't know. The Kendra who had been a young and impressionable girl. He thought briefly about his own youth, about how different a child's perception can be on his or her home life. He thought about his mother and his sister and how far each of them had come.

Kendra continued as she watched Malcolm eat.

"Well, to get to Oscar. I met him my sophomore year in school. I was a virgin. Oscar MacAfree was the campus all-star." Kendra paused when Malcolm's brow furrowed. "You recognize the name?" she asked.

"Vaguely. MacAfree? MacAfree." Malcolm slapped his fork on the table when he brought up the mental file. "Running back. Was headed to the pros. Then, he, what happened to him? Some sort of accident or something. It was all over the sports news."

Kendra shook her head at the memory of that last night.

"Yeah, it was an accident. For a long time I wondered if I had contributed to it. It took me a while to realize that Oscar was headed toward destruction and that I had had little to do with it."

Kendra played with the cinnamon bun, smashing her fork tines into the pastry. She could no longer meet Malcolm's eyes.

"There had been this big to do over him not graduating on time because he was short some credit hours. I'd found out I was pregnant and went to his dorm to tell him. There was a party going on. He'd gotten word that everything was straight. Quite a few of the guys from the team were there and lots of girls. All of them had been drinking heavily, mostly beer.

"Oscar and I went into his bedroom and I told him. He was pissed. He slammed me up against the door and asked if the kid was his." Kendra unconsciously rubbed her throat in the place where Oscar had grabbed her so many years before.

Malcolm's eyes darkened as he watched her slowly rub a place on her neck.

"He finally believed me. But with the directive to 'Get rid of the problem,' he pressed one thousand dollars in my hand. He wanted me to get an abortion."

"That damn bastard. I'd kill him."

Kendra's smile was bittersweet. "He's already dead, Malcolm. He wrapped his Corvette around a tree sometime after I'd left the party. The newspaper said his blood alcohol content was almost point two. I guess he and his friends had been drinking all day. The good thing is that he didn't take anyone with him."

"A thousand bucks in cash and a Corvette. Was he a drug dealer?"

"No. I don't think so. First of all, Oscar was an athlete, a superstar, so he got all of the on-the-sly goodies that colleges and recruiters feed them. And second, he never did say, but I got the impression his family was pretty well to do. He wore pretty fancy jewelry, a couple of diamond rings, and a thick chain. His suite at the dorm had one of the huge big-screen televisions. None of the other common areas in the suites had one. I asked somebody about that one day and was told that Mac's parents had had it delivered. And remember the ruby bracelet and earrings I wore to the benefit auction?"

Malcolm nodded.

"That was my nineteenth birthday present from Oscar. He told me he bought the set, so I assumed his family had money. In hindsight, I realized it was a bribe to get me in bed. It worked," she added derisively. "But the real payoff was Kayla and Karin, so I won on all accounts. Lord knows there were times when I had that jewelry in my bag and was headed into a pawn store. But something stopped me every time. I kept thinking that just because Oscar had been cruel to me, it was no reason to deny his daughters the only legacy he left. As far as I'm concerned, the pieces belong to the girls. Karin was the one who suggested I wear the set to the auction."

Kendra pushed her chair away from the table. "Let me check on them again. Help yourself to some more coffee or rolls."

Malcolm released a long sigh after Kendra left the kitchen. The conversation was something he hadn't bargained on. Kendra seemed to think that what she had to tell him would make him stop loving her. What she didn't realize was that with her every word Malcolm fell more in love with her than the previous moment. They had more in common than she knew. He felt off balance and disoriented, as if he had been searching all of his life for this one woman, the one who was alpha to his omega. And for some reason, she felt she wasn't worthy of his love.

He refilled his coffee cup and was leaning against the kitchen sink when Kendra returned.

"They're still sound asleep. They look so big, like they've grown up overnight. My little babies aren't babies anymore."

More than anything Kendra wanted a hug, the reassurance that another human being could give but mostly the comfort of Malcolm's arms around her. But he stood lounging against the counter watching her. She couldn't read his expression and didn't know if he would welcome her even though he had professed to love her. It's just the sex, she kept telling herself. There's no reason for him to be in love with you. For him, it's just the physical relationship. At least, unlike with Oscar, she knew Malcolm enjoyed their lovemaking. Malcolm didn't complain about her "technique." But then again, neither had Oscar until he was dumping her.

Kendra's insecurities blinded her to Malcolm's feelings and made her doubt her own. In muted frustration he watched the series of expressions that crossed her face as she stood there. While he could guess, he didn't really know what she was thinking. He watched her take a tentative step toward him, then shake her head and step back. She turned in another direction and reached for the telephone on the wall.

"I'm going to call the school office," she told him.

Malcolm listened as she told the attendance clerk that the girls would be absent for the day and possibly the following day. She sighed when she replaced the receiver.

"Don't you need to be getting to work?" she asked.

"I'm the boss. I go in when I feel like it and right now you need me more than any briefs I could be poring through. Sit down, Kendra," he softly commanded. "Tell me the rest."

"Ah, yes. The rest of the sordid tale," Kendra said as she wearily lowered herself into the padded chair. "Where was I?"

"Oscar was killed."

Kendra nodded. "I left his dorm and went back to the house. Naive fool that I was, I thought he was just in a temporary upset. When he came to his senses he would be all ready for the big wedding. I told Aunt Kat I was pregnant and she . . . she . . ." Here Kendra faltered.

She didn't notice or feel the tears that slowly fell from her eyes. With a napkin in hand, Malcolm came to her and dabbed the moisture away.

She balled the napkin in her hands and Malcolm covered her hands with his own.

"Oh, God. That's all I seem to be doing today," she told him with a sniffle.

"What did your aunt do to you?"

Kendra looked up at him. "She kicked me out of the house."

Malcolm sucked in his breath. "Oh, Kendra. I'm sorry."

"She did . . . she did what she thought was right, I suppose. Aunt Kat is a holy and God-fearing woman. She's a deaconess and chairwoman of the missionary board at Sixth Mount Zion. I guess the scandal of her niece being pregnant was more than she thought she could bear."

"That still didn't give her the right to throw you out. Where was her Christian compassion?"

Kendra shrugged. "She told me to get out and never come back. So, I spent all night packing my stuff. I got everything in the car and was pulling out of the driveway to go to Oscar when the delivery person tossed the Sunday paper in the yard. I don't know what made me get it. But I did. And there on the front page was the story about him being killed."

Malcolm gently smoothed the hair at Kendra's temple, then bent to kiss her hands. He wanted to ask her if she had been in love with Oscar. But he found he didn't have the courage to ask, not yet.

"The next thing I remember I was on Mister Albert and Miss Francine's sofa. They were our next door neighbors. Mister Albert said he found me passed out on Aunt Kat's lawn. I don't remember any of that. I do remember how kind they were. Miss Francine made me some breakfast, scrambled eggs and bacon, and her lighter-than-air biscuits with honey. Apparently, Mister Albert had talked to Aunt Kat. He was upset by what she said but they wouldn't tell me what it was. As I was leaving, they pressed a handkerchief in my hand. Miss Francine gave me a bag of biscuits and honey and the phone number of her sister on a sheet of paper. I thanked them and drove until I practically fell asleep on the road. I had been up all night packing and had already had a long day the day before.

"When I couldn't keep my eyes open any longer, I took the first city exit and found a motel where I slept for about twelve hours straight. When I woke up I remembered the handkerchief the Walkers had given me. You now what was in it?"

"What?"

Kendra smiled. "Two hundred forty eight dollars. They'd gotten together all of the cash they had in their house and gave it to me. It was the most beautiful and the saddest thing. I cried and cried. Reality set in on the second day at the motel when I realized I couldn't afford to be handing what little money I had over to a motel clerk every day. I tried the number for Miss Francine's sister but there was no answer. So I bought a newspaper and started searching for an apartment and a job. I didn't figure Aunt Kat would keep me on her insurance and I knew prenatal care was going to be a problem."

"How long did it take you to find a job?"

"I got one, as a waitress in this greasy bar and lounge place, the next day. I didn't need a college degree to take orders and pour drinks. I got fired when I started showing and the manager realized I was pregnant. Part of the job was supposed to entice the customers. Pregnant women weren't considered enticing."

"I'll bet you were beautiful pregnant."

"Hmmph," was Kendra's only reply.

"Where were you living?"

"In one of those run-down, by-the-week or the hour motels that hookers use as their headquarters. I'd quickly found that I didn't have the money for a decent apartment. I didn't know anybody in the city and had misplaced Miss Francine's sister's number. I kept in touch with them, by the way. I never let them know where I was living because I was ashamed of the places, but I'd touch base. They said Aunt Kat had told people I'd transferred to a college out of state. That hurt, but there wasn't anything I could do about it. The Walkers had figured out I was pregnant, though. When I got settled I gave them my address and they sent up boxes of baby clothes. I'd never said a word about it, so Aunt Kat must have . . .

"I named the girls after them, you know. Karin Alberta and Kayla Francine. They're both dead now. Mister Albert had a stroke and Miss Francine died of natural causes a couple of years ago."

At Malcolm's inquiring look, Kendra responded, "I subscribe by mail to the hometown paper. I read the obituaries and the church and society news."

Malcolm smiled.

"Even though Aunt Kat didn't want me, I wanted to know what was going on back at home."

"Was this evening the first time you'd seen her since that night?"

Kendra nodded. "Over the years, I would call, but she'd hang up when she recognized my voice. The girls and I have portraits taken every year at their birthday. I've sent pictures of the twins to Aunt Kat every year since they were born. She's never acknowledged receiving them."

"So tell me how you found your way to the projects?"

Kendra sighed and pulled her hands away from Malcolm's. She knew there was no way Malcolm could relate to her experiences. He had never wanted for anything. His mother lived in a huge house filled with expensive furniture and antiques. His sister and brother-in-law were both successful doctors. And Malcolm, Malcolm seemed to go through money like water. He'd thought nothing of dropping almost five hundred dollars on skates for Kayla and Karin. While paying him back didn't break her, it had put a small yet totally unnecessary dent in her savings. Malcolm just didn't understand that for Kendra, that much money at one time had represented the difference between having electricity, heat, and food and living on the streets.

Malcolm wouldn't understand, but she'd come this far. She figured there was no harm in telling him the rest. Maybe after he heard the whole story, he'd come to the conclusion that they were too different to be together.

"After I got fired from the restaurant, I needed to find another job. I was nursing a cup of coffee in a doughnut shop while I pored through the want-ads one day. I overheard these two women talking about getting their welfare checks. One of them was saying how she qualified for a bigger apartment because she had so many kids. I didn't know anything about welfare checks and rent-free apartments so I asked them. The rest, as they say, is history."

"How did you survive it?" Malcolm asked, referring to the culture shock of being middle class, then being on the public dole. Kendra, however, assumed he was putting down people with less privileged backgrounds.

"Malcolm, the projects are just a place to live. The people who are there are just regular people trying to survive," she said, surprised at the unexpected anger in her voice. "Yes, there's a bad element and more often than not, the bad ones overshadow everything else. Part of my problem was that I was in way over my head with two little kids. I had never had to care for myself, let alone be responsible for somebody else's well-being. It's funny though, the things you learn, the things you do to survive."

"What do you mean?"

Kendra shook her head and wouldn't answer him. How could she have been wrong about him! She felt a dull pain in her chest.

"Kendra, please don't shut me out."

She pushed her chair away from the table and put distance between them. She hugged one arm to her and pressed her other hand to her mouth as she stood in front of the sink. How could he love her, if he didn't respect her? All of his claims of love meant nothing. She bit her lower lip and shook her head.

"Nothing. It's nothing, all right?"

"No, it's not all right," Malcolm said, coming to stand before her. "I want to understand."

"There's nothing to understand. The only thing you need to realize is that you and I, we come from different worlds. You of the tailor-made clothes and expensive cars. You spend more money on gadgets and dodads, material things like your sound system, your watch, those blasted roller skates, than I might hope to make in a year. It just seems so frivolous when there are so many people out there with so little."

"Kendra, I didn't always—"

She didn't let him finish. "I apologize for that. I didn't mean to get on my high horse and offer down an indictment on your lifestyle. It's just so much different than mine. You know, even with this new job that I've been offered, I can't see that I'd change the way I do things. I want to buy a house one day. The girls need a backyard and space before they completely grow up. I want them to have their own bedrooms. And you know what I want for me? I want my own bathroom. That's all I want is the privacy of my own bathroom, one with lots of windows for plants. A Jacuzzi like yours wouldn't be bad either," she said with a smile.

But Kendra's smile turned sad, because mentioning the Jacuzzi at Malcolm's town house underscored the difference in their financial situations.

"We just come from different worlds," she murmured again before brushing past him to walk out of the kitchen.

Malcolm caught her and pulled her to him.

"Kendra, no matter where you've lived or what you've done, that doesn't stop me from loving you. My love is unconditional."

She stiffened in his arms. "I don't think you can love a thief."

"What are you talking about?"

"A thief, Malcolm. A shoplifter. I stole things from a store."

"Tell me about it."

"What are you, some kind of pervert? You sound like Freud, 'Tell me about it, my dear.' You like hearing about all of the bad things I've done, don't you? Does that make you feel more of a man?"

Kendra couldn't get in any more of her angry barbs because Malcolm's lips had covered hers. The only way to stop her attack was to close her mouth, and he knew just one way to do that. He took her lips with a savage intensity as his tongue plundered her mouth. Kendra at first fought him. She pushed at his chest with her fists, but he only tightened the cruel embrace. Before she knew it, her hands stopped pushing against him and crept up his masculine form to pull his head closer to hers. When Malcolm at last pulled away, they both breathed heavily.

Soft as a whisper so that he had to strain to hear, she started speaking.

"I hadn't learned how to budget the money and food stamps and found that I was broke. I didn't even have a dollar or two stashed somewhere. I was relatively new to the neighborhood and hadn't made any friends, no one I could borrow money from. One of the girls was running a slight fever and I didn't have a single can of formula. I went to the convenience store anyway. I don't know, maybe I planned to ask the manager to extend me some credit. I was in the formula aisle when there was a disturbance at the register. Some gang members were hassling the clerk. No one was watching so I took three cans of formula and a bottle of baby aspirin. I walked out of the store as if I didn't want to be a part of anything that might happen with the gang. No one saw me take the stuff."

Kendra swiped at the tears that were running down her face. "That thing ate at me for a long, long time. When I got the job at Sullivan and O'Leary I sent twenty-five dollars cash back to the store, attention to the manager, with no return address and no note. I was too embarrassed to admit what I'd done."

Malcolm pulled her into his arms. This time the embrace was tender.

"Kendra, I don't think there's a court in the land that would convict you for what you did. And to top it off, you made your own private restitution. You shouldn't let this bother you."

"And you won't let it bother you, knowing that you're dating someone who shoplifted?"

"Kendra, you did what you had to do and you did it without malice, for your daughters. You don't need to feel guilty about it and it doesn't change the way I feel about you."

"I can feel the way you feel about me," she said, rubbing herself against the fast-swelling lower part of his body. "And like I said before, it's just the sex. When you get enough, you'll walk away and I'll be alone again. I've learned to be alone."

With that, she gently extricated herself from his arms and went to check on the twins.

CHAPTER 14

Kendra tried to reach Aunt Kat later that day. But after there had been no answer on the two occasions she called, Kendra remembered that Aunt Kat was somewhere in the city with Miss Hattie. Her attempt to locate a Hattie Williams in the telephone directory proved unsuccessful.

As if reliving with Malcolm her life before Quad-A could bring up all the demons of the past, Nettie's news when she came to the apartment Thursday evening to see Karin shook the foundation of Kendra's existence.

Nettie delivered an armload full of stuffed animals and other goodies for the twins, then sat with them until they drifted to sleep. She closed the miniblinds in their room, turned off the light, and joined Kendra on the sofa.

Ostensibly Kendra was reading through the senior project she was about ready to turn in. In reality, she'd read the same paragraph introduction six times. Had she and Malcolm had a fight? Were they still a couple? Was he sincere about his professed love for her or was he just, as she suspected, confusing the physical with the profound? More importantly, was she doing the same thing? After reading them a story and visiting with the girls for a while, Malcolm had left about ten o'clock that morning. He'd kissed her on the cheek and said he'd call. Did that mean he'd call today? Tomorrow? Next week or next year? Was that a polite "Goodbye and have a nice life?"

"Hey, girl. Are you there?"

Kendra smiled up at Nettie. "My body is here. I just don't know about the rest of me. They asleep?"

"Knocked out," Nettie said, taking a seat next to Kendra. "Ken, baby, I know this is not the best of timing, that you're probably still worried about Karin and, I take it, something happened between you and Malcolm last night."

"It shows that much?"

"Partly. But he called me this morning and said you'd need some looking after more than Karin and Kayla. He didn't elaborate, but I got the message."

Kendra nodded. If nothing else, Malcolm was sensitive to her needs.

"This week has lasted forever," Kendra told her friend. "Whatever your dire news is I'm sure it'll fit right in. It's difficult to believe that it was just Monday when I was walking on clouds over the job offer." She took a deep breath. "Okay. Tell me."

Nettie thought about and discarded all of the ways she could sugarcoat what she had to tell Kendra. In the end she just spit it out.

"The MacAfrees want the girls."

Kendra's confusion was evident. "What are you talking about? The MacAfrees, as in Oscar?"

Nettie nodded. "I got a call Monday morning from John MacAfree, he's Oscar's father. He said he and his wife, Etta, saw you at the benefit auction. They apparently recognized you and tracked you down through the program."

"That's ridiculous. How could they recognize me? I've never even met them. And to my knowledge Oscar hadn't taken any pictures of us together . . . although he probably should have just to keep track of which woman was which."

The bitterness in Kendra's voice did not escape Nettie. Since she knew Kendra no longer had feelings for Oscar, she guessed that what she heard from her friend had something to do with Malcolm. That must've been a hell of a fight or whatever it was they'd had last night, Nettie mused.

What Nettie first said finally registered with Kendra. "They want the girls? What do you mean they want the girls?" The rising hysteria in her voice alarmed Nettie.

"I don't think it's legal or even possible, Kendra. So don't get yourself in a panic. I'm just telling you what the man said so you'll be prepared when they call."

Incredulous, Kendra asked, "You gave them my home phone number?"

"No, Ken. I told him they could reach you through the Quad-A office."

"Okay. What exactly did he say?"

"The conversation was really short. He identified himself as John MacAfree and asked for you. I told him you weren't at the Quad-A office. He said there was one of two things about you that he wanted to say: You were either a thief and had gotten hold of some very expensive jewelry that belonged to him or you were somehow connected to his dead son."

"Oh, my God."

"Kendra, they recognized the rubies from Oscar. Have you ever heard of J. Mac & Son Jewelers?"

"Who hasn't? It's one of the biggest jewelry store chains here in the . . ." Kendra's voice faded away with the significance of who Oscar's parents were. They were very rich, very powerful, and even if their claim on Kayla and Karin had no legal grounding, they could cause lots of trouble for Kendra.

Kendra sighed the sigh of the very old and very weary. She sank back into the sofa cushions.

"What makes them think the twins are Oscar's? How did they find out about the girls?" Kendra asked softly.

"He didn't say. I'm assuming they are just assuming, given the age of the girls. It's easy enough to find out about them. They could have gotten that information just by talking to the right people at the auction."

"So now what?"

"He called again today. I told him you were unavailable through the end of the week. They want a meeting."

"Okay. Set it up for next week. Not Monday though. Can it be at your office?"

"You got it."

"I'm going to need a lawyer."

Nettie looked at Kendra and smiled. "That's the one thing you have lots of, Kendra. And there's one in particular who has a vested interest."

When by Saturday night Kendra still had been unable to reach Aunt Kat, she decided to pack the girls up for the drive to the town where she grew up. Karin's injuries were healing so well, it was almost as if she'd never had the accident. Kendra's emotional injuries were another story. While she projected the cool persona of a professional woman when at work, and could sway even the most unwilling person to free up a job opening for a Quad-A participant, her personal life was in a shambles.

Kendra felt a need to return to the place where it all began. To put her life in perspective. Maybe visiting the places where she grew up would give her some grounding. And she wanted to take the girls to the church where she had once sung in the choir, presented Easter speeches, and portrayed Mary in the Christmas pageant.

Of Malcolm, Kendra didn't know what to do or what to think. Nothing had been resolved between the two of them. Flowers and other goodies had been delivered by courier for the girls. Kendra had been expecting a calla lily, but Malcolm disappointed her. There was nothing for her in the delivery. He called Saturday morning. When she'd mentioned that she was going to drive to her hometown, Malcolm asked if he could join them. Kendra hesitated.

"Malcolm, there's a lot I need to sort through right now. I just need time to think, to be with the girls and think."

It hurt, but Malcolm accepted the rejection.

"Okay, Kendra. Call me when you return no matter the hour, okay?"

"Malcolm, I—"

"Please, Kendra. Just call me when you get back."

"Okay," she said softly as she hung up the phone.

Malcolm felt helpless. He swirled his desk chair around and vacantly stared at the roses blooming in the garden outside his office. He was losing Kendra and it seemed there wasn't a damn thing he could do about it.

Angling his head a little, he looked at a photograph on the credenza. He, Sandra, and their mom grinned at the camera. The snapshot had been taken the day he graduated from law school. Malcolm thought about a similar photograph, one that had been taken many years before the one he now studied; one that he didn't proudly display in his office but was just as special to him.

Malcolm stopped pretending that he was going to get any work done. Because he usually spent Saturdays with Kendra and the girls, he was at a loss as to what to do. He wanted to be with Kendra, but she seemed to want no part of him, at least not right now. Malcolm prayed that she would call as she had promised.

At the Quad-A office, Nettie had finished explaining the program to a young couple. The wife was pregnant and soon wouldn't be able to work. The husband had been laid off and was in need of employment. Nettie gave them all the information they needed and told them to read it over and get back to her.

Now, sitting at her desk, she pondered Kendra's situation. Kendra probably hadn't told Malcolm about the MacAfrees, and he needed to know. Was it her place to get in the middle of their relationship? Nettie was in a quandary. She, of course, wanted to help, but how could she make things better without making more of a mess than already existed? For some reason, Malcolm's law partner, Robinson Mayview, came to mind. Nettie found herself dialing his home number before she even realized she was doing it.

He answered on the second ring.

"May I speak with Robinson Mayview, please."

Robinson immediately recognized her voice. Toinette Blue had called him! He didn't dwell too much on the euphoria he suddenly felt or how his heart had constricted. Toinette had called him.

"This is Robinson," he said as nonchalantly as he could manage.

"Hi there. This is Toinette Blue, from the Quad-A program. How are you today?"

"Wonderful since I'm hearing your voice, Mrs. Blue."

"Didn't I tell you to call me Toinette or Nettie? You make me feel like an old lady with that 'Mrs. Blue.' "

That was the last thing Robinson wanted her to feel like. "Okay Toinette. To what do I owe the pleasure?"

Nettie smiled on the other end. This man was a charmer through and through. It was a shame he was so young.

"Well, I'm in a bit of a jam and needed someone to talk to. You know all of the players and I could use your perspective."

"I take it some disaster has befallen the fairy-tale romance of Kendra and Malcolm."

He'd said it in jest, but Toinette's silence and then her sigh told him something was seriously wrong. Robinson gripped the receiver.

"Toinette? Are you still there?"

"I'm here. I'm sorry. I'm just at a loss as to how I can help them."

"Tell you what. Let's meet somewhere in about an hour. How about Memorial Park? It's quiet and we shouldn't be disturbed if we find a place away from the kids' area."

She agreed, and Robinson quickly made a call to a delicatessen that specialized in picnic baskets to go. Even though they were meeting to talk about Malcolm and Kendra, Robinson planned to make sure Toinette knew how he felt about her before they departed.

Robinson saw her before she spotted him. Wearing a yellow and white jumpsuit with matching full-length duster, Toinette was resplendently regal. The overjacket billowed and flowed behind her in the gentle breeze. Robinson's smile of appreciation was purely male, only for her. When Toinette saw him several yards ahead she lifted a hand and waved at him. At just that moment, a child's ball rolled in front of her. Toinette bent to capture it, then bent at the knees to wait for the toddler who chased it to catch his breath. She handed the ball to the child, murmured a few words Robinson couldn't hear, and tousled the child's curly hair. He watched Toinette straighten and the child head back to his game.

Could women in their late forties safely have children? The thought popped unbidden into Robinson's head. More than anything else, that thought made Robinson realize the ramifications of dating an older woman. If he and Toinette had a relationship, he would have to change the way he felt about some things—like having children. He was surprised to discover that that didn't disturb him as much as he thought it would.

"Good afternoon, Mr. Mayview," she told him with a bright smile when she reached him. This man is too attractive for his own good, Toinette thought to herself. Why does he have to be so young? I'm old enough to be his mother yet when he smiles like that I feel like I'm fifteen.

Robinson leaned forward and kissed her on the cheek. "Good afternoon, Mrs. Blue. Your beauty is that of queens."

Toinette laughed and tapped him on the arm. "Oh, I can tell we're gonna get along just fine."

"It's true," he told her as he guided her to an area sheltered by azaleas in bright red, white, and pink bloom.

From the wicker picnic basket he pulled a blanket and spread it on the cool grass.

"You think of everything, don't you?"

"I try my best," he told her, reaching up a hand to assist her down.

Robinson served her cheese and bits of cold turkey and chicken. He placed fresh fruit and chopped vegetables on a plate in the middle of the blanket. Chunky chocolate chip cookies went on another plate. After selecting morsels for himself, he got to the point of their meeting.

"So, what's up with Kendra and Malc?"

It took Toinette a few minutes to catch Robinson up on what had happened with the twins and why she felt her best friend and his best friend needed some friendly guidance.

When she finished, Robinson sat quietly for a moment. "You know, I know it hurts you to see Kendra in pain. I just now realized how close the two of you are. But in all honesty and fairness to them, I think you, we, need to let them solve their own problems. We could get into the mix and really mess things up. Kendra and Malcolm are both adults. They'll be able to come to an understanding."

Toinette sighed. "In my heart I know that. I just hate to see her unhappy."

Robinson reached over and gathered one of her so-soft hands in his. He gave it a gentle squeeze. "They'll work things out," he assured her.

Robinson then deftly turned the conversation away from Kendra and Malcolm and on to more general topics. Before long they were debating the style and ability of some of the great jazz artists, the lost past of the big band, and the plethora of up-and-coming jazz quartets.

Robinson wasn't about to let an opportunity slip away.

"There's a terrific jazz quartet playing at the amphitheater tomorrow afternoon. Would you like to go?"

Toinette's eyes narrowed speculatively and she cocked her head to the side. She nipped a piece of celery, chewed and swallowed it, then looked directly at Robinson. Both female awareness and amusement danced in her eyes when she asked him, "Are you asking me out on a date? And if so, don't you think I'm a little old for you?"

"Yes. And no."

Toinette's eyebrows rose and she made a small sound that made Robinson's insides clench in anticipation.

Suddenly feeling she was no match for the subtle challenge she recognized in Robinson, Toinette lowered her eyes and studied her fingernails. Their light flirting had gone a step further. He was so young! Thirteen years her junior.

"We need to talk about this," she murmured.

Well aware of what she meant, Robinson had no intention of letting her doubts work against him. So when he spoke, he deliberately misunderstood.

"What's there to talk about? We both like jazz quartets and it's going to be a beautiful day tomorrow." Robinson paused. "Oh, but you're right. We will have to talk some more, since we disagree on who's the greatest horn player of all time. You might be right on Dizzy and Satchmo, but Miles was a master."

Toinette looked at him and chuckled. "You're a smooth operator, Mayview. Smooth. I like that."

Robinson dipped his head in a small salute to the conversation they were really having. Toinette could have imagined the playful wink he gave her but she didn't. It had been real. Her delightful laughter rang through the park.

It had been seven years, but everything looked the same, as though time stood still in Kendra's absence from the town. She waved to passersby while Kayla and Karin, strapped in the backseat of Kendra's sporty white Escort, took in the sights and sounds of their Mom's hometown.

Kendra turned down Sycamore and drove past the house where she grew up. Aunt Kat's car wasn't in the drive but she wasn't surprised. If she'd finished her visit with Miss Hattie Williams, Katherine Edwards would be found in only one place on a Sunday morning. Kendra glanced at the digital clock on her dash: 10:30. If in town, Aunt Kat was probably finishing up a Sunday school class.

Toys cluttered the front yard of the house next door. Kendra wondered how long the new family had been living in Mister Albert and Miss Francine's home. She debated over whether or not to point out the houses to the girls, then decided they'd get around to asking eventually.

"That's the house where I grew up," she told them, stopping the car so the girls could get a good look. Amidst a profusion of azalea bushes and the shade of two sycamore trees, the two-story frame house looked cozy and inviting.

"Are we going to go in to meet Aunt Katherine?" Karin wanted to know.

Kendra eased off the brake and continued down the street. "I don't know, sweetheart. Maybe. I just don't know right now."

"Where are we going now?" Kayla asked.

"It's almost time for church, so we're going there."

"We missed Sunday School lesson today."

Kendra smiled at Kayla's observation. "Yes, you did. But I think God understands that you were on the way to his church here."

About fifteen minutes later they were being ushered to seats in the already crowded main sanctuary of Sixth Mount Zion Baptist Church.

Kendra accepted a visitors' envelope from the usher and asked why the church was packed.

"Today is our annual Homecoming service," the usher told her. "People from all over who used to be members here come back for a special program. You're in for a treat, too. The former youth choir director is here with his choir. They just recorded an album in Washington, D.C."

The irony that Kendra had chosen this day to visit the church didn't escape her. Maybe she would find the peace she sought in the comfort of the familiar.

She saw Aunt Kat file in with the other deacons and trustees of the church. Aunt Kat's white dress was crisp and sharp, but even from a distance Kendra could see the dark circles under her eyes. For the first time, Aunt Kat looked old, old and very tired.

Before long, Kendra, like the girls, was caught up in the spirit of the service. An a cappella rendition of "Amazing Grace" from the guest choir left not a dry eye in the sanctuary.

Kendra recognized Deacon Thomas when he came forward to pray. But instead of praying, the chestnut-complexioned man pulled a harmonica out of his suit pocket. The notes of the same song sprung from the tiny instrument and filled the sanctuary. When he finished, Deacon Thomas slipped the harmonica back in his pocket and bowed his head.

"Dear gracious heavenly Father, we come to You today with humble spirits and grateful hearts. We thank You, heavenly Father, for waking us up this morning and starting us on our way. You didn't have to do it, Lord. But we're glad You did.

"Thank You, Lord Jesus, for getting all of our visitors safely to us today. Many of them traveled the dangerous highways and byways to be in Your house this morning. Thank You, Lord, for bringing them all back home for this day. Lord, shower Your grace and Your love over each of them and all Your children assembled here today. Give them the strength to do the impossible, Lord. And give each one a measure of faith to believe that all things work together for Your good. If any of them are troubled, Lord, ease their spirits with Your loving kindness. If any are sick today, Lord, heal their bodies with the touch of Your hand. We know and believe that the Master's hand can heal all, save all, touch all. Lord, all these blessings we ask in Your son Jesus' name, Amen."

Murmured amens filled the air and the choir began a soft answering chant. Through the announcements and welcome of visitors Kendra sat, oddly touched by the deacon's prayer. She realized that she had probably been prayed for many times during the years, whether in name or spirit; the elders of the church always lifted up in prayer those who had passed through the doors of Sixth Mount Zion. She briefly wondered if any members of the church knew the real reason she'd suddenly disappeared. Maybe the Walkers had told people. Francine and Albert Walker didn't have any young children or grandchildren, yet they'd sent boxes and boxes of new and used clothes for the babies. Maybe they'd gotten them from members of the church.

When the fairly large congregation rose to bring their tithes and offerings, Kendra knew Aunt Kat would see them. She and the girls would walk right by Aunt Kat's front row seat. Kendra started to just send the girls, but the words of Deacon Thomas's prayer haunted her: the strength to do the impossible, the faith to believe that ail things work together for good. If all things worked together for good, then maybe the seven-year rift between her and Aunt Kat could be mended.

Kendra rose and followed the girls down the aisle. With a vague smile or distracted wave of a hand she responded to old friends and church members who recognized her.

Katherine had been singing and clapping to the upbeat song the choir sang during the collection. But she abruptly stopped in midclap when she saw Kayla and Karin. Her eyes flew up and came in direct contact with Kendra's. Katherine gave her niece a trembling smile, then stared after the retreating forms of her great nieces. They were dressed in matching red dresses with lace collars. Kendra paused before her aunt but didn't know what to say.

"Kendra, girl. You sure done growed up. Come here and give me a hug." At ninety-seven, Sister Lou Ida Roberts was the oldest member and official mother of the church. Age hadn't dulled her eyesight or her memory. Kendra obediently went to the woman, kissed her on the cheek, and hugged her.

The opportunity to do the same with Aunt Kat had passed. Kendra found comfort in knowing that there were people who were genuinely pleased to see her and she them. Minutes later she was back in her seat listening to the pastor's morning sermon. His deep, rich voice was that of an orator with Southern roots. Without a need for technological amplification, his voice filled the sanctuary; the singsong cadence adding power to his words.

"Oftentimes, we find it difficult to tell the very people that we love and cherish the most how we feel about them. Too many times in my years as pastor here, I have sadly, sadly officiated over funerals where family members fling themselves across the casket of their loved ones, crying 'I'm sorry, Mama.' 'I love you, Daddy.' 'I didn't mean to do it, sista.' 'Forgive me, brother.'

"But it's too late!" he boomed. Cries of "Amen" and "Preach, pastor" came from parts of the sanctuary.

In the front row, Katherine Edwards rocked and clenched her prayer cloth.

"The ears no longer hear and the heart no longer beats," the pastor continued. "The time for I love you and I'm sorry has passed. But right now, brothers and sisters. Today, on this homecoming day, when our friends and family are gathered back in the fold, today is the day when we need to put aside those petty grievances. Put aside the hurt you feel 'cause thirty years ago sister got a new dress and all you got was a pair of gloves. Put aside the jealousy you've been harboring 'cause your brother's family saved their money and bought a home and you still living in an apartment. Put aside the animosity you feel 'cause you didn't have a solo in the choir and sister so-and-so had two."

Laughter, "Amens," and intermittent applause filled the sanctuary at the minister's words.

"Pastor's stepping on some toes today!" The woman next to Kendra murmured.

Yes, he is, Kendra thought. And it's taken me seven years to put aside my own hurt and anger. What was the sense in being angry at Aunt Kat? Anger and hurt feelings hadn't changed anything. As the minister had said, maybe now it was time to put aside the unpleasant memories of the past and get on with the future. If she was to have a reconciliation with Aunt Kat, rehashing seven years' worth of heartache wasn't going to accomplish much.

Aunt Kat had done what she thought was right. And Kendra had survived the best way she knew how. Yelling and screaming and holding on to anger wouldn't change the past and was likely to have a negative impact on the future. Sitting in her seat letting the pastor's words minister to her, Kendra found within her heart the ability to forgive her Aunt Katherine.

The pastor ended the rousing sermon with a plea for estranged family members to come forward for prayer. Even as Kendra rose to go forward, she heard Aunt Kat's voice.

"Pastor? Pastor, may I have a moment?"

CHAPTER 15

When the minister nodded, Katherine walked to the center of the church. Slowly she turned and faced the congregation. Kendra stood where she was in her pew. A trustee handed Katherine a microphone. She took a deep breath and began.

"Pastor Leonard's words touched my heart and convinced me this morning," she told the people who looked at her with open curiosity. "Seven years ago I sinned against God and my family when I turned my back on my brother's child in her time of need. Many of you all remember my niece, Kendra. She lived with me after her parents got killed. She grew up in this church. She's here today with her two little girls. Before God and this congregation I want to apologize to her for what I did. I was wrong to force her out of my home. Kendra, I hope . . . I hope you can find it in your heart to forgive me."

Katherine broke down in tears, but Kendra was already beside her. Together the two women stood before the church, sobbing and supporting each other.

"Kendra, child, I'm sorry. I had no right to turn my back on you," Katherine said. "I know you've probably had some hard times."

"I did. And for a long time I was angry with you. But Pastor Leonard's words touched me today, too. Holding on to the bitterness won't change anything. So I'm letting it go. I'm just sorry that I let you down."

"You didn't let me down, child, I failed you."

"God commanded that we love one another," the pastor said as he came to stand by the two women. "I know and you know that Sister

Edwards and her niece, Kendra, aren't the only two people in here today who need to ask God and themselves for forgiveness. While an usher brings Sister Kendra's little girls here to the altar to join their mother and aunt, I want the rest of you who need to be set free from the shackles of hurt and anger and animosity to come to the altar in the spirit of love and forgiveness."

The usher who had seated them led Kayla and Karin to the front of the church. Eyes wide, the girls got their first look at the woman who never answered the letters they sent each year. As Katherine bent to apologize to them for that very thing, other people filled the altar area. Many were crying as they apologized to and made amends with their family members.

By the time the pastor gave the benediction, the church was alive with the babble of people who hadn't said a word to each other in years and had plenty of catching up to do.

Hours later, Kendra and the girls sat around Aunt Kat's dining room table eating chocolate cake and laughing about some of the things Kendra did as a girl.

"Mom, did you really catch a rabbit with your lunch box?"

Kendra and Katherine laughed at the memory.

"I sure did."

"But it took the poor thing weeks to stop jumping away every time you came near. Jumper thought you'd catch his ear again."

Kayla and Karin looked at each other and grinned. "Mom, can we get a rabbit?"

Kendra shook her head in wonder at the unified request. "Aunt Kat, this is what I was afraid of," she said, chuckling. "I'll think about it," she responded to the twins.

"Can we look at the picture album again, Aunt Katherine?" Karin asked.

"Yes, child. It's up in your mom's old room."

"Clear your plates, ladies," Kendra reminded them.

"Yes, ma'am," they responded as they took their dessert dishes to the kitchen and disappeared upstairs.

"You've done a good job with them, Kendra. I'm proud of you."

"Thank you, Aunt Kat. You gave me the proper guidance."

Katherine sipped from her tea and cut another piece of cake for herself.

"The man with you at the hospital, is he their father?"

Kendra sighed. It would take time before she and Aunt Kat were totally comfortable with each other. But she had no intention of letting the older woman make her feel guilty about her relationship with Malcolm.

"No, he's not their father," Kendra finally answered. "Their father was killed several years ago. Malcolm and I have been dating for a few months now."

"Kayla seemed very comfortable with him at the hospital."

Kendra tried desperately not to sound defensive in her response. "She is. So is Karin."

Something in Kendra's voice reached Katherine, who stretched a hand across the table to her niece.

"Kendra, child. I done spent the last seven years regretting what I did to you. I'm not about to make the same mistake twice. You understand what I'm telling you, child?"

Kendra nodded.

"Good." Katherine patted her hand and rose from the table. "I'm gonna go cut up some of this cake so you can take it back with you. I know those pretty little girls of yours have to go to school tomorrow and you probably got to get back to work. I don't want you driving at night. It's dangerous out there."

Kendra smiled at the familiar refrain. It looked and sounded like everything was going to be okay.

"Aunt Kat?"

From near the archway leading to the kitchen Katherine turned and regarded Kendra.

"I love you, Aunt Kat."

Katherine' smile was tender and thankful. "I love you, too, child."

Nettie scheduled Wednesday at six-thirty as the time Kendra would meet with the MacAfrees. She acquiesced to Kendra's adamant demand that Malcolm not be involved. Kendra wanted to meet and talk to Oscar's parents without the threat of lawyers and litigation in the air. If they could talk person to person, maybe things would not end up being as dire as Nettie had made them out to be. In Kendra's estimation, enough forces were at work without adding Malcolm to the mix. But before the meeting ended she would wish that he had been by her side to weather the ordeal.

From Nettie's office, Kendra watched the older couple alight from a silver Mercedes-Benz. Nettie met them at the door of the center. Kendra, dressed in the black suit and white silk blouse she at times wore to Quad-A presentations, took a deep breath, offered up a short prayer, and rose to her feet as John and Etta MacAfree swooped into the office. He was massive. He looked to be about six feet, six inches tall and on the top side of three hundred pounds. With just a glance, Kendra knew where Oscar had inherited his powerful physique. The wife, while not petite, was dwarfed by her husband's presence. But the diamonds that dripped from her fingers and her ears spoke volumes and seemed to add height and power to her.

Nettie made the introductions and asked if anyone wanted coffee. Etta MacAfree started to answer in the affirmative but her husband cut her off.

"Forget the pleasantries," he thundered, cutting straight to the chase. "Miss Edwards," he said, stressing the title *Miss.* "We know for a fact that you attended the same college as our son, Oscar. We also know that you and he dated for several months."

John's gaze flickered over Kendra, first in disdain but then in appreciation for his son's selection of a bed partner. The child from their union was probably exquisite, he thought.

"The third thing we know is that you were pregnant when our Oscar was killed. Oscar's best friend told us that Little Mac and his girlfriend had had a big fight the night he was killed. All Tony knew was that it concerned the girlfriend being pregnant. He said Little Mac stormed off without telling him anything else. I want to know if that child is our grandbaby."

The man's pompous and high-handed attitude irritated Kendra to no end. Some things, she realized, were hereditary. She fervently hoped that Kayla and Karin hadn't inherited the gene mutation.

"Mister MacAfree, I don't care for your tone or your attitude. If you came here thinking you would bully me, you'd better think again . . ."

"Kendra . . ." From where she stood near the desk, Nettie took in the growing scowl on John's face and the increasing nervousness of Etta MacAfree. Diamonds flashed and sparkled as the woman wrung and twisted her hands.

John took a threatening step toward Kendra. "Look here you little—"

"John! That's enough," Etta interjected, surprising Nettie and Kendra with the power and authority in her voice. With a light touch that barely seemed enough to restrain, Etta held her husband at bay.

"Miss Edwards, Mrs. Blue, I apologize for my husband's outburst. You must understand," she said, turning to face Kendra. "It's been very difficult for us to accept Little Mac's death. He was our only child, my only son. When it came to our attention a couple of years ago that he'd left a girlfriend, one who was pregnant, we became obsessed with finding her. With finding our grandchild. But every lead we had proved a dead end. Not only had you vanished, but that idiot, Tony, Little Mac's best friend, couldn't remember or didn't know your last name. We'd given up hope of ever finding you or the child who was our last link with our son. Then, we saw you at the benefit auction."

"The rubies you strutted about in were the giveaway, Miss Edwards. I designed the set almost ten years ago," John said. "Since I'm the one who gave the stones to my son as a too expensive gift for some girl who probably wasn't worthy of wearing them, I knew when I saw you at that auction that you'd either stolen the set or that you were the girl we'd been searching for."

Etta sighed. Whatever progress she'd made with the woman was now shot to hell after John's insulting remarks. After forty years of marriage, she'd been unable to get her husband to try catching flies with honey instead of his bitter vinegar.

"Mr. MacAfree, I do not like or appreciate your implication that I'm a thief."

"Then you are our son's former girlfriend!"

"I don't see how that is your business, sir. If I did date your son and if he did give me jewelry, it was a gift and belongs to me."

"I knew there was gonna be a price," he growled. "Money-hungry bitches from the projects always have a price. How much do you want?"

Outraged, Kendra lifted a hand to slap him. Nettie, anticipating the move, grabbed Kendra's arm and pulled her out of immediate proximity of the man. "Don't give him grounds for an assault charge," Nettie whispered in Kendra's ear.

"John, you've gone too far," Etta murmured, even as Kendra echoed her thought.

"You've gone too far, Mr. MacAfree. I agreed to this meeting thinking that maybe we'd be able to depart, if not friends, at least not enemies. I thought that surely Toinette had exaggerated when she told me about you. I can see now that her description fell far from the mark. We have nothing else to discuss. I suggest you leave."

John snorted derisively and flung a large hand out to encompass the office. "You suggest I leave? Do you think some little ghetto threat will frighten me? I can have this ragtag operation closed down in a day."

"John, that's enough."

"Damn straight, it's enough. We want the kid, Miss Edwards," John told Kendra. "You'll be hearing from our lawyer."

"I'll see you in court, Mr. MacAfree."

Arms folded across her chest, Kendra stood her ground until John stormed from the office. Etta gave Kendra a tight, apologetic smile before following her husband to their car. It wasn't until she saw their taillights disappear from sight that Kendra crumpled to the floor. Nettie ran to Kendra's side and assisted her friend up and into the desk chair.

On a great shuddering sigh, Kendra picked up the receiver on Nettie's desk and punched in Malcolm's office number as Nettie wiped the tears from Kendra's face with a paper tissue.

"Hightower."

"Malcolm. It's Kendra. I'm in trouble and I need your help."

"Where are you, baby?"

"At Nettie's office. On the edge of the projects."

"I'm on my way."

Nettie put the receiver back in its cradle and Kendra dropped her head on Nettie's desk.

"What am I going to do?" she cried. "Oh, God. What am I going to do?"

Nettie did what she could to comfort Kendra until Malcolm arrived.

* * *

It was the first time since her welfare days that Kendra had to depend on someone else for her family's well-being. The fact that Malcolm was her rock helped take the sting, but not all of it, out of the defeat of dependency. She'd confided in her boss that she could be having a personal legal problem on her hands. And after telling Eric Slater the nature of the problem, the next thing Kendra saw was Sullivan and O'Leary's top custody and domestic relations attorney standing in front of her desk. That had been a week ago.

Now, she sat in Malcolm's office surrounded by lawyers, her lawyers: Malcolm and Robinson, and Connie Woods from Sullivan and O'Leary.

"This is the most ridiculous claim I've ever read," Connie said, flinging the MacAfree's complaint against Kendra to the floor.

"But they filed a lawsuit against me."

"Honey, anybody can file a lawsuit," Malcolm told her.

"My guess is that this is some kind of bluff on their part," Robinson weighed in. "They were able to find out a little about Kendra's history, that's easy enough given the Quad-A presentations. Blinded by their obsession to find an heir, they probably figured that you'd be frightened, even intimidated by their wealth and power. They also probably assumed that you had no recourse or, at best, limited recourse."

"I am frightened," Kendra said in a small, quiet voice. "They said I'm an unfit mother." She sat stiffly in one of the leather chairs, her hands tightly clasped in her lap.

"And everybody in this room knows that that's not the truth," Malcolm told her. "If it came to it, and it won't, we could have so many character witnesses for you that it would make their heads spin."

Malcolm had seen Kendra like this once before and it both unnerved and frightened him. He could tell that she clung to her self-control with all she was worth, but she looked battle weary. The problem was, he didn't know if she would welcome any comfort he might offer.

"He said I stole the rubies."

"No, you and Mrs. Blue said he told you both that he gave the jewels to his son as a gift to the son's girlfriend. Because it's totally groundless, that isn't even included in this complaint," Connie assured her.

"So what you're telling me is that their claim for custody of the girls has grounds and merit?" Kendra reasoned.

Connie smiled in admiration. "You'd make a damn good cross-examiner, Kendra. No, what I'm saying is that they have the right to file a lawsuit. We have the right, given the law and the facts of the case, to win."

Kendra's eyes sought Malcolm's. He knew that she was thinking about her confession to him that she'd stolen the formula and baby aspirin.

"You're a good mom, Kendra. You have nothing to worry about."

Kendra tried to find courage in Malcolm's words. She needed as much as she could muster.

In the following week the MacAfrees, particularly John, were relentless in their efforts to see their grandchild.

Karin's innocent question one evening shook Kendra to the core of her being.

Remembering something she'd meant to ask, Karin looked up from her homework. "Hey Mom, we're not ever, ever supposed to get in a car with strangers, no matter what they say, right?"

Icy dread filled Kendra as goosebumps broke out all over her arms. Slowly she put aside the book she had been reading. Don't panic, she coached herself. Don't frighten them.

"What do you mean?"

Karin chewed on her pencil, looked at her twin, and frowned. "Well, it was kinda strange, the other day. It was after school. Kay went back inside cause she left her homework on her desk . . ."

"I didn't leave my homework, I left my book bag."

"It's okay, Kayla. Go on, Karin, tell me about the stranger."

"Well, while Kayla was gone, this big car drove up. A man got out and looked at me. Then he came up and asked me if I wanted to take a ride to see Grandma." At that, Karin crinkled her nose. "I told him I wasn't allowed to talk to strangers and that I didn't have a grandma."

"Except Miss Belle," Kayla interjected. "She's not reeeeaally our grandmother, but she said she can be our grandma in spirit and that we can call her Gran Belle like B.J. does."

Crestfallen, Karin looked at Kayla. "Do you think I hurt Gran Belle's feelings when I didn't tell the man I had her for a pretend grandma?"

"I don't know, Mom, what do you think?"

Too scared to think, Kendra sat at the kitchen table trying desperately not to tremble and show her fear to the twins. The MacAfrees were trying to kidnap the twins!

In the back of her mind it registered that Malcolm's mother, Belle Hightower, had been incredibly sensitive to the girls. But that wasn't important at the moment.

"Karin, sweetheart. Can you describe this man or the car?"

The little girl's eyes got big. "Yeah, he looked like a mountain! And the car was the color of a nickel."

John MacAfree looked like a mountain and he drove a silver Mercedes.

"You did the right thing, Karin. Never, ever, get in a car or go away with any stranger. Do you both understand that?"

The two girls nodded. Kendra relaxed.

"I knew. I just wanted to make sure," Karin assured her.

"Hey, Mom, since we're talking about weird stuff, you ever get the creepy crawlies?" Kayla wiggled her shoulders to demonstrate. Kendra tensed again.

"Yeah, we were talking about that the other night," Karin piped in.

"Creepy crawlies like what?"

"Like somebody's watching you. But when you turn around nobody's there."

This time Kendra couldn't control the tremors or the fear in her voice.

"Okay, ladies. You two go in the living room. I'll be there in just a second. There's something really important we need to talk about."

Something in Kendra's tone subdued the girls. They quietly left the kitchen and Kendra went to the wall telephone.

She wasn't sure whom to call first, the police, Malcolm, or Connie. In the end, she decided against the police but did summon Malcolm, Connie, and Nettie, her best friend.

She had argued with herself on whether or not to tell the girls about the MacAfrees. She'd been reluctant to get their hopes up about having grandparents when those very people were trying to legally steal them. What if everything worked out in the end? What would she have accomplished if what should have been a loving introduction to the twins' grandparents was precluded by ugly words and hurled accusations?

But now, it sounded like the MacAfrees were resorting to illegal methods. Did they think themselves above the law? Did they hope to buy from Kayla and Karin the love that probably would have come naturally if given the opportunity to grow?

The girls sat quietly on the sofa as they waited for their mom.

"Hey, Kay," Karin inquired while worrying her lower lip in unconscious imitation of Kendra. "Mommie looked real scared."

"Yeah. Do you think that man was bad? Maybe he was the one watching us and making us feel the creepy crawlies."

"You think so?"

"I dunno. Let's ask Mom when she comes."

"Ask me what?" Kendra said, walking into the living room. She settled herself on the sofa between the girls, then pulled Karin onto her lap. Kayla snuggled close.

The girls looked at each other.

"Well, we were wondering if maybe that man was a bad man. Maybe I shoulda found Officer Bob," Karin said.

"Who's Officer Bob?"

"He's the policeman who makes sure us kids are safe at school. He tells everybody to just say no to drugs."

Kendra nodded. The DARE officer was doing his job if the school children felt comfortable enough around him to talk to him about other things.

Kendra still wrestled with what to tell the girls about John and Etta MacAfree. It wasn't every day that a mother had to tell her children that the grandparents they'd never met were trying to steal them away.

"Girls, I want you to listen really close because this is important," Kendra began. "The man you saw at the school is, is . . ."

She started over again. "A little while ago, I found out that you have grandparents. Your father's parents live right here in the city but I didn't know that. They want to meet you but there's a little problem."

"What's the problem, Mom?" Kayla asked.

Here Kendra hesitated. "Well . . . well, just like you two shouldn't talk to strangers, Mom has to be careful, too."

Would a small lie hurt? Kendra wondered. Her next words could destroy any chance of trust the girls might develop toward the MacAfrees. In an instant, Kendra decided that stretching the truth was applicable in this situation.

"Just because they say they're your grandparents, doesn't mean they are. Mom needs to make sure. So I have some people checking."

"Why would someone say they were our grandparents if they weren't?" Karin wanted to know.

Kendra hugged the little girl to her breast.

"Well, sometimes people want children so badly that they'll do anything to get them. People don't always tell the truth like they are supposed to. Until I tell you, I don't want you to go near anyone you don't know. Okay?"

The girls nodded. The doorbell rang.

If she was surprised at seeing Nettie arrive with Malcolm's law partner, Robinson, Kendra didn't show it. Malcolm arrived about ten minutes later and Connie followed him by about five minutes.

Kendra introduced the girls to Robinson and Connie and explained that they were safe strangers, that it was okay to go with either Connie or Robinson if one of them showed up at the girls' school. Because the girls trusted Malcolm and Nettie as they did their mother, there was no need to go through with them the same drill of "Who am I?"

Kendra had the girls repeat the story about the man in the car and the creepy crawlies.

Reluctant to broach the topic but realizing it necessary, Connie asked Kendra to consider a bodyguard for the twins.

"A bodyguard? Do you think that's really necessary?"

"Kendra, he's approached Karin in person. And someone has been watching them. If they aren't going to fight fair . . ." Malcolm remembered the twins sitting there listening in wide-eyed fascination. "If this type of thing continues," he amended himself, "It's going to be necessary. We can't take chances."

"I agree with Malcolm, Kendra," Connie told her softly.

Kendra looked at Nettie, who nodded her head in concurrence.

"Okay."

"Okay? Mom, does that mean we get a bodyguard?" Kayla said.

Kendra bit her lower lip and nodded.

"Wow! I bet we'll be the only kids at school with a bodyguard," Kayla said. "Wait till we tell everybody!"

"You can't do that girls," Nettie told them. "If you tell everybody, you'll blow the bodyguard's cover."

"He's gonna be undercover? Wow!!"

"That's really cool," Karin said while grinning. "We get our own undercover bodyguard."

"Why don't you two go get ready for bed? I'll come tuck you in and read you a story," Nettie promised.

"Okay." The girls scrambled from the sofa and raced each other to the bathroom.

Malcolm came up behind Kendra and circled her waist with his arms. "You okay?"

Kendra nodded. "I can't afford a bodyguard, Malcolm."

He pulled her closer to him and kissed her hair. "For once, Kendra, please let me do something for you."

Too disturbed by all that had been transpiring in the last three weeks, Kendra nodded her okay.

"Good," he said.

"Our hearing date is the twentieth," Connie said. "That's a Friday. We're to meet in the judge's chambers first. I'd advise that the girls not be there. They should be shielded as much as possible."

"I'll take them for the day," Nettie volunteered.

"That's five days after my graduation," Kendra observed.

"Which is next week," Malcolm said.

"Where'd the time go?" Kendra murmured.

Despite the shambles of her personal life, Kendra hadn't forgotten about the promotion she'd been offered. She made an appointment to meet with Bosworth Sullivan. They'd hashed out the remaining details of the job, decided that Kendra's start date in the new position would be the first of June, and came to an agreement on where her office would be located.

Sullivan asked if Kendra would make a presentation at the lawyers' regional bar conference. Kendra agreed, even though she knew her attention would probably be on whatever the outcome of the court hearing would be. The hearing was scheduled for a Friday and she'd have to leave for Atlanta the following Sunday.

Their business concluded, Kendra rose.

"I hope to see you at commencement exercises next week."

"I wouldn't miss it for the world, Kendra. You've done us proud," Sullivan told her.

They shook hands and Kendra went back to her desk.

The week flew by. The girls identified the man who was their bodyguard but never got the chance to speak to him. Kendra, Malcolm, or Nettie dropped them off and picked them up at school every day.

John MacAfree's car had been spotted near the school but the man never made another attempt to talk to either of the girls. Kendra wasn't sure if the MacAfrees even realized that there were two children instead of one.

The couple's underhandedness seemed to have abated, so Kendra was shocked speechless one afternoon as she and Nettie ate lunch in one of the many downtown eateries. Kendra looked up to find Etta MacAfree standing at the edge of their table.

CHAPTER 16

As Kendra started up, Nettie raised an elegantly manicured hand to hail assistance.

"Please don't call the troops out on me," Etta said, twisting the gold braided chain on her alligator skin handbag. "Kendra, I just wanted to apologize for all of the grief my husband has caused you in the last few weeks."

Nettie harrumphed. Kendra sat back down and warily regarded Etta.

"Did you follow us here?"

"Yes. But it's not the way you think. Not the way my husband had your daughter watched. I was very, very angry with John when he told me what he'd done."

"Have a seat, Mrs. MacAfree," Kendra offered.

"Ken, I don't think that's a good idea. Malcolm or Connie should be here if you're going to talk to her."

Kendra went with her gut reaction. Etta MacAfree wasn't here for a trick or a diversion. Something bothered the woman. Kendra shook her head at Nettie and extended her hand in invitation for Etta to be seated.

A waiter placed a table setting for Etta but she waved him away and refused the offer of tea or coffee.

"Kendra, I want you to know that I am truly sorry that things have gotten to this point. It's my husband's fault, I know. John hasn't been the same since Little Mac died."

"That's no excuse for this frivolous lawsuit or for stalking the gir—"

"Why hasn't he been the same?" Kendra broke in to avoid having

Nettie tip the woman that there were two girls. "It's been seven years since Oscar was killed."

Etta looked from Nettie's unrelenting face to Kendra, who just seemed to want some answers. Etta worried the white linen napkin, fingered the condensation on her water goblet, then looked up at Kendra.

"I'm just as much to blame as Mac. I didn't want any more children after I had Little Mac. Maybe if there had been other children, our lives wouldn't seem so unfulfilled now that our son's gone. John, everything he did he did for Little Mac. I guess you know we own a couple of jewelry stores."

"That's an understatement," Nettie mumbled. Kendra only nodded.

Etta looked at Nettie and smiled sadly. She held out her hands so Kendra and Nettie could get a better look at the stunning jewels that covered her fingers and wrists.

"I feel like a walking billboard. I constantly worry that some hoodlum is going to hit me over the head to get one of these meaningless little baubles. Yes, I guess to say a couple of stores *is* an understatement. I'd give every single one of them away tomorrow if it meant I could live like a regular person again."

She sighed and took a sip of her water. "Little Mac, he was a spoiled thing. We always gave him everything he wanted. The car he was driving when he was killed, he'd seen it at an auto show. All he ever had to say was 'I want' and we got it for him. I realize now that that was a mistake. I don't think Little Mac understood the value and reward of hard work. He never had to. We made sure of that. I regretted it all of his life."

"Tell me something, Mrs. MacAfree," Kendra said. "What made you and your husband come after me?"

"We told you the other night. The rubies. John had designed the set. It was a show piece that we hoped would fetch quite a bit. But Little Mac begged for it. He said he had a really special girl he wanted us to meet and that he wanted to give the rubies to her for her birthday. Of course, we both thought it was far too expensive a gift for a girl who was probably the flavor of the week."

Kendra gasped, but she'd known all along that while she had been faithful to him, Oscar had no compunction about seeing other women. Etta's next words confirmed the fact.

"In that, Little Mac was just like his daddy. Always had an eye for the pretty ladies." Etta looked away in slight embarrassment. "John and I have always had an . . . an understanding, so to speak. He knows where home is."

Neither Kendra nor Nettie commented on that revelation.

"Why are you fighting me tooth and nail when all you had to do was say 'Hello, we're Oscar's parents, we'd like to get to know you,' " Kendra fumed.

Etta regarded the poised woman who, if things had been different, could possibly have been her daughter-in-law. "That was my suggestion. But John, after he found out who you were, wouldn't hear of it."

"What do you mean found out who she was?"

Etta looked at Nettie, then flushed. "Well, I mean, she was on . . . she was there representing a . . ." Etta quickly glanced around to make sure no one at nearby tables could hear. "She was representing a welfare program," Etta whispered, leaning toward Kendra and Nettie.

"No!" Nettie said theatrically. "Well, Lawd have mercy, call out the National Guard."

"Nettie, please," Kendra pleaded.

Nettie looked from Kendra to Etta, rolled her eyes, and announced that she was going to the powder room, where maybe the air was a little purer.

"I'm sorry," Kendra began after Nettie stomped off in a huff. But Etta cut her off by reaching a ringed finger to Kendra's hands, which rested together on the table.

"No. I probably deserved that. It was a bitter pill to swallow knowing that somewhere out in the city there was a child who was the only heir we'd ever have and that that child was living—had lived—in the squalor of welfare. I think that's what really sent John over the edge. Here he'd created what was supposed to be a black dynasty, only there wasn't anyone to take it over."

"Had your son had his way, Mrs. MacAfree, there wouldn't have been anyone period," Kendra said, tacitly acknowledging the fact that Oscar had been the father of her child.

"What do you mean?"

"He gave me a thousand dollars and told me to get an abortion."

Etta covered her mouth with her hand and shook her head as if to deny Kendra's words. "Little Mac wouldn't do anything like that."

"Believe what you will, Mrs. MacAfree. Apparently, Oscar didn't tell his friend Tony everything about that night. As far as I'm concerned, your claim is negligible. And given that we can prove what you and your husband have been doing over the last two weeks, I don't think the two of you have a prayer."

"Kendra, we just wanted to know our grandbaby. Is that so wrong?"

Kendra reached for her handbag and pulled enough money from her wallet to cover the lunches she and Nettie had only half eaten.

"No, Mrs. MacAfree," she said, dropping the money on the table and rising to go. "What's wrong is the way you went about it. I have to get back to work, so if you'll excuse me."

Etta nodded. Kendra left the woman there with her diamonds and her regrets.

* * *

The morning of Kendra's graduation dawned bright and beautiful but there was little joy in Kendra's heart. She'd worked so long and so very hard for this accomplishment, yet today, the day that should have been one of the happiest in her life, was eclipsed by the threat the MacAfree's presented. Then there was Malcolm. Without reservation or hesitation he'd come to her aid when she needed his legal expertise. But not once since the morning of their discussion had he spoken of love. She wasn't even sure if they were still supposed to be a couple.

Kendra tried to put things into perspective. She'd be starting a fairly high-powered job in just a few weeks. She may have lost Malcolm, but she and the girls had found Aunt Kat.

"Some consolation," she mumbled as she rolled out of bed and padded to the bathroom for a shower. "Like Aunt Kat or a job will hold me in the middle of the night."

By nine-thirty Kendra and the twins were dressed. Nettie was treating them all to brunch after the commencement exercises so they ate a light breakfast of toast and juice.

At the spot where she and Nettie had agreed to meet, Kendra was surprised to see Robinson and Malcolm standing with her best friend.

Malcolm wore a slate gray double-breasted suit. The suit along with the crisp white shirt and red and gray tie made him look formidable, but Kendra knew better. She tried to stop her heart from pounding just from the sight of him but it was no use. She loved him, and now he didn't care about her. She took in the lines of fatigue beneath his eyes and wondered what case was keeping him awake nights. Kendra longed to ease the tension from his face and his body but Malcolm no longer wanted her. She smiled a faint hello in his direction and extended her hand in greeting to Robinson.

Malcolm watched her and wanted to cry out his frustration. He hadn't slept a full night's sleep in the two and a half weeks since Kendra had declared that their relationship was based on sex and nothing more. A hundred times he'd picked up the telephone to call her; at least twenty times he'd driven by her apartment. He wanted her. God, yes, he wanted her. But what Malcolm wanted was the whole shebang: Kendra as his wife, best friend, and lover; the girls as his daughters.

She stood in a flowing white dress that had gold trim and gold buttons along the sleeves and pockets; her graduation robe casually draped over her arm. The twins were darling in identical short sleeve sailor-like dresses. Malcolm bent a knee and opened his arms to them. The twins ran forward for a hug but Malcolm had eyes for only Kendra.

"Malcolm, you look very handsome today," Kayla declared after she and Karin had been hugged and kissed.

"Why thank you, Miss Kayla. You two are looking very fetching yourself. As is your mother," he added under his breath.

"What does fetching mean?" Karin asked.

"It means very pretty. And I agree with him," a new voice added after approaching the group.

"Aunt Katherine!" the girls squealed and ran to the woman, who enveloped them in more hugs.

"That's how they should be with the MacAfrees," Kendra quietly observed.

"Life isn't perfect, Kendra," Nettie answered.

"I know. And there are no fairy-tale endings."

"The ending is how you make it, Ken," Nettie said, taking a glance in Robinson's direction.

Kendra's eyes followed Nettie's. She shrugged off the melancholy mood that haunted her and with a devilish grin regarded Nettie.

"Yes, girlfriend. We must talk about that."

"Uumph, umph, umph," was Nettie's only reply. Kendra laughed delightedly and put an arm around her best friend's shoulder as they walked to the place where Nettie had reserved several seats.

The sound of Kendra's laughter tore at Malcolm. With most of Kendra's attention on the upcoming battle with the MacAfrees, and considering the trip he had to make to Atlanta, Malcolm didn't see how or when he and Kendra would have any time alone in the next couple of weeks. Somehow, someway, he had to make her realize that his love ran deeper than their physical encounters. But he was at a loss as to how to do that. With any other woman, he would have bought jewels or maybe a fur coat even though it was summer. But he couldn't buy Kendra anything. She'd just reject whatever he bought and find some way to use the gesture against him.

He'd never been in love before, so he didn't know how to go about telling and showing Kendra that he loved everything about her, that he was in love with *her*, not just what they did together in bed. All he could offer her was time; maybe with time Kendra would sort out her feelings and realize that they were meant to be together.

The commencement exercises, which included as keynote speaker a state senator who exhorted the graduates to pay their taxes and vote for him in the next election, were a blur for Kendra. She only half listened to all of the remarks as she sat in her white cap and gown in the midst of a sea of similarly dressed classmates. Because she'd been going to college practically one class a semester for several years, she knew very few of the people in her graduating class. But she'd gotten excellent marks on her senior thesis and had chatted briefly with her department chairman.

Kendra thought about the job she'd be taking over in a few weeks. Bosworth Sullivan had given her the time between her graduation and the start of the new position as paid vacation. She had no doubt that he'd heard about the custody hearing, but she was grateful for his sensitivity.

She'd fly to Atlanta the following Sunday for two days of Quad-A presentations at the lawyers' convention. Kendra hoped she'd be able to concentrate on the presentations. The success of her meetings in Atlanta could determine whether or not the program could be expanded to other cities. But none of it would be important, she mused, if the MacAfrees prevailed in court.

Kendra jumped when a hand touched her shoulder.

"Hey, it's taken four long years for this. Don't you want to go get your degree?"

Kendra nodded and smiled at the happy grad who'd been sitting beside her and was now prodding her to get going. It was time to march to the stage and accept the degree from the college president. "It's taken me nine years," she told the young man.

"Wow! My folks woulda had a cow if it'd taken me nine years to finish."

Kendra only smiled and filed in line to receive her diploma.

After the official declaration and the celebratory tossing of tasseled caps, Kendra found her family and friends waiting for her.

"Mommie, you're graduated!" Kayla exclaimed.

"Can I see your degree?" Karin asked.

"Ooh, me too. I wanna see."

Kendra handed them the leather-bound folder with the directive, "Be careful. Don't tear it."

"Get it, girl," Nettie told Kendra while pulling her into a hug. "It's been a long road but you traveled it well. I'm so very proud of you."

"I never would have made it without you, Nettie. Thank you so much."

Kendra wiped at the tears that she and Nettie shared.

"We're like a couple of old leaky faucets," Nettie said while dabbing at her eyes.

Kendra accepted congratulations from Robinson and from Aunt Kat. When she looked up, Malcolm stood before her.

Kendra's eyes darted from his face and the mouth she wanted to cover with her own to his hands. Malcolm carried one pink calla lily.

He placed the flower in one of her hands and clasped the other in his.

"Kendra, some calla lilies grow best along the muddy shores of African rivers. Their beauty shines forth despite their surroundings. You remind me of the calla lily. You've been through a lot, yet you stand tall and beautiful like the calla. Congratulations, beautiful Kendra. I'm very happy for you."

He leaned forward and touched his lips not to her waiting ones but to her cheek.

When he pulled away, he paused. As if it were something beyond his control to stop, Malcolm reached a hand to Kendra's mouth. Gently he traced a finger along the contours of her lips. When Kendra's tongue brushed the pad of his finger he snatched his hand away as if he'd been burned.

It was the first indication since the night of the accident that Kendra still wanted him. Maybe there was hope, he thought. She'd somehow distanced herself from him, even as they'd worked together on the case against John and Etta MacAfree. Kendra had been polite but distant. Confused and unsure of how to bridge the gulf that had grown between them, Malcolm had done nothing. She had been adamant in her assessment of their relationship. Yet, what she'd just done with her tongue instantly made him hotter than hot. If he did anything except ignore it, he would be proving Kendra right: that it was just the sex he was after.

Kendra could have cried out her anguish when Malcolm yanked his hand away from her mouth. He was repulsed by her touch now. At least he was honest about his feelings, she thought. Telling him about her welfare days may have been a mistake, but at least she knew how he felt. He could be kind, and he could still impress her with tender gestures like the calla lily, but he no longer wanted her.

With not another word, Malcolm turned his back to her and went to the twins. Kendra didn't know that for Malcolm it was either walk away or haul her into his arms and love her on the grass with all the world watching.

Kendra didn't have time to dwell on the misery she felt over Malcolm's rejection. A contingent of attorneys from Sullivan and O'Leary was headed in her direction. Bosworth Sullivan and Grady O'Leary led the group that consisted of Connie, Kendra's immediate supervisors, Eric Slater and John Crashen, and two of the lawyers she'd worked for in her early days at the firm.

The law office group, along with Robinson, Malcolm, Nettie, and Aunt Kat made the sum total of Kendra's close friends and acquaintances.

"Kendra, congratulations," Sullivan said, speaking for the Sullivan and O'Leary group and shaking Kendra's hand.

"Mrs. Blue," he said turning to Nettie, "when we took a chance on the Quad-A program all those years ago, I never would have thought that the program would be such a success. Kendra's achievement is yours as well. On behalf of Sullivan and O'Leary, I'd like to thank you for bringing Kendra to us."

Nettie beamed.

Eric Slater stepped forward with a gaily wrapped package. "Kendra, this is from me and John. You have no idea how much we and all of the contract division are going to miss you."

Kendra thanked them all and was about to invite everyone to the brunch gathering when Karin cried out.

"That's the man, Mommie! That's the man who tried to make me get in his car," the girl exclaimed while pointing at John MacAfree, who was dragging Etta in his wake.

Kendra spun around to grab the twins but Malcolm and Nettie already had them and pulled them to her side. A man who had remained inconspicuous in his watch during the commencement exercises came forward. He made no attempt to conceal the large gun holstered in his jacket. With a shake of her head and a quickly lifted hand, Connie halted the bodyguard, who still watched over the girls.

The group of lawyers closed ranks around Kendra and the girls as John and Etta MacAfree came to a halt before them. The girls tilted their heads back and stared openmouthed at the big man.

"You're a stranger and you tried to make me get in your car," Karin accused.

Whatever words John MacAfree had been prepared to utter stuck in his throat as he took in the sight of the twins.

"Oh, my God," Etta whispered. "They're beautiful." She reached a hand out to caress the curls that flowed down Kayla's back. But the little girl pressed closer to her mother's side.

John finally lifted angry eyes to Kendra. "You thought you'd keep them hidden from me?"

"Mr. MacAfree, I hid nothing from you. As I explained to your wife last week, this is all your doing."

John turned on Etta. "You talked to her and didn't tell me!"

"Now, John . . ."

"State your business, Mr. MacAfree," Connie said.

With her command, John, for the first time, took in the other people standing around Kendra.

"Jesus," he said when he, as a longtime business owner and civic leader, recognized the senior partners from Sullivan and O'Leary.

He recognized Malcolm Hightower and Robinson Mayview from seeing their pictures on television and in the newspapers. He also knew Connie Woods. She was the best in the business. He knew that because he'd tried to hire her to represent them in the mess with the Edwards woman. Now he understood why she had been unavailable.

"Jesus," he said again as his eyes darted over the group. Kendra Edwards had more legal power standing in her corner than he'd ever want to tackle in a lifetime. His own attorney had advised that his case against the Edwards woman didn't stand a chance. They'd been unable to find a speck of dirt against her. She paid her bills on time, and from all indications, didn't have a life outside of her job.

Kendra Edwards wasn't at all what he'd expected. She didn't have a slew of boyfriends and worked diligently to get other women off welfare, according to the report he'd been given by the investigator he'd hired. She was a ripe piece of flesh, all right, but she didn't flaunt herself around. She was beautiful, poised, and educated. John had hated to admit it, but she was just the type of woman he would have wanted for a daughter-in-law.

Etta had tried to tell him, but he hadn't listened. Now, as he stood watching her boldly stare him down, John knew he'd lost. He'd built an empire that would crumble when he died. And he'd completely mangled any hope of getting to know his grandchildren. Little Mac had left him two beautiful granddaughters but John realized he'd blown any chance of ever getting to enjoy them.

Before fourteen pairs of eyes, the fight drained out of him. The big man's shoulders slumped and within seconds he seemed to have aged twenty years. John MacAfree had turned into a defeated man. He closed his eyes and bowed his head. "All I wanted was to see and know my grandbaby. Now there's two, but I still don't have any."

Etta circled his waist and offered her husband some of her strength. "It's gonna be all right, Mac. It's gonna be all right."

John sought Kendra's gaze. "Miss Edwards, I owe you and your family an apology. I got carried away and I didn't take time to think about your feelings. If I know my son, I know he was probably the same way with you."

While the victory obviously belonged to Kendra, John MacAfree met the unrepentant, even hostile eyes of each of the adults standing before him.

"I had hoped to intimidate you with my size and with my fancy attorney," he told Kendra. "I figured that you wouldn't be able to afford a decent lawyer and that by the time you figured out that our claim didn't have a whole lot of validity, you would have settled out of court with us getting the best part of the deal. Looks like you get the last laugh on all counts. I'm sorry for the pain I must have caused you in the process."

He took one last look at the twins, who weren't quite sure what was being played out around them. All the adults seemed on edge. Kayla spotted the bodyguard and nudged her twin. John followed their gaze.

His short bitter laugh had the twins looking at him again. "I should have taken the hint when the protection showed up. He's quality."

John put his arm around his wife's shoulder and together they turned to leave.

"I'll have my attorney withdraw the petition in the morning. We won't be bothering you anymore."

Kendra's voice halted them as they walked away. She handed the gift she was holding to Nettie. "Mr. and Mrs. MacAfree?"

The couple turned around. With Kayla holding her right hand and Karin holding her left, the three walked toward the MacAfrees.

With a heavy sigh, Kendra continued. "Mr. and Mrs. MacAfree, I'd like you to meet my daughters, Kayla and Karin. Girls, this is Mr. MacAfree and Mrs. MacAfree. They are your grandparents." She would do this in Oscar's memory, for the good of her daughters.

"Really?" Karin asked.

"They're the for real grandparents, not fake ones?"

"They're the real thing."

"Did you know our father? He got killed before we were born," Kayla said.

"How come you're so tall? If you're our grandfather are we gonna end up as big as you?" Karin asked.

John ran one of his large hands over his face at the girls' questions but not before Kendra saw the tears that glistened in the man's eyes.

Without a care for stains she could get on her yellow silk suit, Etta MacAfree fell to her knees on the grass and hugged the twins to her.

Malcolm watched Kendra shake John MacAfree's hand, then step aside as he, too, got on his knees to get closer to eye level with his granddaughters.

Malcolm felt sick. On one level he was delighted that all had ended well and that the twins would know their natural grandparents. But on the level where his heart resided he knew the union developing between Kendra and her old boyfriend's parents only spelled disaster for him. If, by some fluke, Kendra had been thinking that what they shared was special, the MacAfrees were there to remind her of all the reasons she'd loved their son. If Kendra decided to choose a memory over his flesh and blood, so be it, he decided. He'd let her go if it killed him.

Only Nettie and Robinson saw Malcolm quietly walk away.

CHAPTER 17

Nettie, Kendra, and Bosworth Sullivan had decided that the best course of action would be for Kendra, who had law office experience, to make the pitch for the Quad-A program at the attorneys' convention. At the law firm's expense Kendra would attend the gathering, make two large group presentations, and be available to answer questions about the program. Nettie would do the follow-up.

But it was with a sad heart and not much enthusiasm for the trip, that Kendra boarded the plane bound for Atlanta. She hadn't been gone all of ten minutes and she already missed the girls. She'd never been separated from them longer than a day. Three days seemed unbearable. They would be staying with Nettie, so she didn't worry about their care; she just felt guilty about leaving them behind.

As she settled in her first-class seat she wondered what Malcolm was doing. She missed him desperately. Now that she finally knew what true love felt like—an aching emptiness without Malcolm—she wondered how she could have pushed him away as she'd done. Maybe he'd been sincere when he'd said he loved her.

She hadn't needed anyone to send a telegram or flash a light bulb over her head to let her know how she felt about him. She loved him. It was just that simple . . . and that difficult. They came from two different worlds but now, in hindsight, that didn't seem like grounds to destroy a relationship. It was a foundation on which to build.

Malcolm wasn't perfect, yet she loved him. Maybe the same was true for Malcolm. He could love her despite her faults. Now, though, he might never know how she felt. She hadn't seen him or talked to him since the previous Sunday, her graduation day. Nowhere in sight when she finished introducing the girls to the MacAfrees, Kendra had assumed he would call. But he hadn't. And now the hauntingly beautiful words he'd whispered to her seemed more of a farewell than anything else.

You've been through a lot yet you stand tall and beautiful like the calla. Congratulations, beautiful Kendra. I'm very happy for you.

His words had offered no promises, no tomorrows. But Malcolm didn't have to be the person who made the first move toward salvaging their relationship. Sure, they had a couple of rough spots to smooth over and she wanted to know point blank how he felt about her past. Maybe they could overcome their differences. The only way to find out was to talk to him.

Kendra resolved to call Malcolm as soon as she reached the hotel in Atlanta. With thoughts of how she'd start the conversation with him, Kendra closed her eyes and leaned her head against the headrest.

At that moment, Malcolm boarded the plane and found his seat in the front row of the first-class section. He wanted to go on this trip about as much as he wanted a root canal. But he had promised to sit on a panel about defending juveniles charged with death penalty offenses. After seeing his briefcase tucked into an overhead compartment, Malcolm settled in his seat and thought about the two brothers he'd managed to win acquittals for.

Not only had he taken a chance on them in the courtroom, he'd staked a personal claim in their futures by providing the means for the brothers to go to college. Education was the ticket out of poverty. No one knew that as well as Malcolm. Seeing a college-aged kid busing tables in Callahan's had reminded him of that cold, hard fact.

Malcolm sighed, then declined the offer of a complimentary cocktail from a flight attendant. There was but one thing Malcolm Hightower wanted. Kendra Edwards. He wanted her love, her laughter, her body pressed against his. He tried to quell the last thought, since all it managed to do was make his own body's response all the more uncomfortable. Living without Kendra in his life had been like living without oxygen. He'd loved her practically from the first moment they met. She made him whole, and enabled him to put his life into perspective. Material possessions did not define success and happiness, he realized. Success was watching Kendra accept a hard-earned college degree. Happiness was seeing two little girls in pink tutu's swirl across a stage in a dance recital.

Malcolm tried to pinpoint exactly where things had started to fall apart with Kendra. He'd learned a lot about her the night Karin had been injured. And yet, she'd always seemed reserved around him—except when they made love, his straining body clarified. He tried to ignore the reminder.

It hadn't been until the night at the hospital and their conversation the following morning that he realized the depth of Kendra's conflict with their lifestyles, their financial situations. You should have been honest with her, Hightower, the voice of his conscience whispered. He tried to ignore the admonition.

The one thing Malcolm couldn't ignore was the miserable way he felt without Kendra. The airline wouldn't allow him to make a call on the cellular telephone he traveled with. But he couldn't wait until he got to Atlanta to call her. When the airplane reached cruising altitude he'd use one of the credit-card accessed telephones provided as a service to first-class passengers. Malcolm dropped his head back on the headrest and endeavored to clear his mind of everything except what he planned to tell Kendra.

Some time later, Malcolm smiled. With his eyes still closed and his senses fine-tuned, he'd been so successful at blocking his mind of everything except Kendra, he could actually hear her voice, smell her perfume.

"One of the reasons the program is so successful is because the participants want to be able to live a better quality of life. Quality of life is defined by each person. For me, it meant a safe neighborhood and good schools for my daughters."

Malcolm's smile broadened. His mind knew all of the reasons why the Quad-A program was important to Kendra. Maybe that's why when he imagined her talking, she spoke about the program. Malcolm shifted in his seat and adjusted the seat belt. Just the thought of Kendra made him partially erect. Imagining her sweet voice and honeyed lips caressing him as they made love had him tense, heavy, and ready.

"No, this trip is for the program. I'll be giving a couple of presentations."

Something wasn't jiving with the weird fantasy Malcolm was having. Kendra was talking but not really to him.

"Really! Well, tell you what, here's my card. Let's get together for coffee. I can give you some more information about the program. All of the paperwork was FedExed to the hotel. . . . I'm staying at the same hotel! Let's make a date to meet."

Malcolm's eyes popped open. This was no dream! Kendra's voice wasn't in his head. He was hearing it live and in person and she was making a date to meet some guy at a hotel. Before he even realized it, Malcolm had unsnapped his belt and was on his feet whirling around toward her voice.

"Kendra!"

The flight attendant came running and nine pairs of eyes looked up at Malcolm. The tenth pair, the brown ones that belonged to Kendra, widened in surprise, then dilated in desire.

Instant heat pooled in her lower body and her breathing, breathing that had been perfectly fine a moment ago, seemed ragged, uneven.

"Malcolm," she mouthed. But no sound came forth. All of her senses, all of her being focused on the man who stood in the aisle first glaring at her and then devouring her with his smoldering gaze. Malcolm showed not the first inkling of embarrassment, although Kendra could feel a blush inching up her cheeks, particularly when the woman she had been chatting with spoke up.

"Would you like to sit here, sir? Kendra and I were just talking about a wonderful program she works with. But we're going to meet up later today at our hotel." Even as she spoke, the woman gathered her handbag and unsnapped her seat belt.

"Mrs. Fitzmoore, that won't be . . ." Kendra started to demur. But then she glanced up at Malcolm. "If it won't be much of a problem."

"No problem at all. Here you are. I'll just take your seat." The woman brushed by Malcolm and claimed the seat he'd had. The flight attendant, realizing no disaster was at hand, returned to her duties. Malcolm slid into the seat next to Kendra.

Without a single word between them, Malcolm freed Kendra from the safety belt and hauled her into his arms. The kiss was everything a kiss should be: deep, demanding, and desire-driven. Kendra fell into it with a wild recklessness. Malcolm's lips set her aflame. The pit of her stomach went tizzying into a wild spin and the toes of her feet curled. This is what she'd wanted, what she had needed.

Malcolm drowned in her embrace and burned them both. His tongue traced the soft fullness of her lips. Kendra mimicked the move and Malcolm surged against her.

When it finally dawned on them that they were on a commercial flight with interested folks straining to see the action, Malcolm reluctantly pulled away from her.

"God, I've missed you." His ragged breathing matched Kendra's.

"Not half as much as I've missed you," she managed.

"I've got to have you, Kendra," he murmured.

"Just as soon as this plane lands, I'm yours."

The next thirty minutes were pure agony for Kendra and Malcolm. They didn't speak, they didn't look at each other. The result of even a smoldering glance could have been disastrous given that they sat trapped on an airplane with no privacy. But in the middle of the seat, their hands clasped in a near-death grip.

At the airport, Malcolm arranged to have their luggage sent to the hotel. They grabbed a cab and made fast work of checking in. The firm had reserved a suite for Kendra so it was to her rooms they went.

No sooner had the door closed, than Malcolm pulled Kendra into his arms. He buried his head in her neck and branded Kendra with tiny kisses. With an urgency on the far side of frantic, Kendra scrappled with the buttons on his shirt, trying to get her hands on his hot flesh. Malcolm shrugged out of his sport jacket without losing physical contact with Kendra. It had been so long. So long since he'd tasted her honey, so long since he'd been sheathed inside her warmth.

Kendra moaned and pressed closer to his hardness when she felt his hands in her hair pulling out the pins. Kendra's thick tresses tumbled over his arms in a luxuriant soft mass, its sweet-smelling softness Malcolm's undoing.

"Now, Kendra. I've got to have you now."

In response Kendra tugged down her hose and panties, kicked them away and hiked up her skirt. Malcolm's mouth closed over hers and he fumbled with the zipper of his slacks. Mindless with passion and want of her, he freed himself and backed Kendra up against the door.

"Wrap your legs around me and let me feel you come apart in my arms," he murmured in her ear.

"Oh, oh, aahhh," was all she managed when his tongue danced a waltz in her ear.

Even as she ran her hands over the muscled strength of his chest, Kendra remembered the one thing they'd forgotten.

"Protection, Malcolm. Do you have a condom?"

The words penetrated Malcolm's lust-filled head. Condom? Protection?

"Oh, God." His hands and mouth stilled. He tried to regulate his breathing. Nice and slow, slow and easy. Nice and slow, slow and easy. If he kept repeating the chant he'd be able to get himself under control. Against the door, Kendra squirmed. Malcolm tensed.

"Don't move. Don't even breathe," he said.

"Malcolm, I want you."

Malcolm trembled at her words. "Sweetheart, I, uh, I'm about to lose it here. I'm going to step away from you and I want you to go to the sofa and sit there."

"But—"

"No buts, Kendra. I want you so badly that I think I'll die or break. But you're not on the pill and I don't have a single condom with me. I wasn't expecting to see you so there was no reason to be prepared. Now, please, please, just go to the sofa and wait for me."

Incredibly touched by Malcolm's sense of responsibility at the expense of their mutual satisfaction, Kendra framed his head in her hands and kissed him full on the mouth. Malcolm tore his lips away as if he'd been burned.

Kendra smiled. Knowing that he'd meant every word, she did a quick sidestep, retrieved her hose, and backed up into the living area of the suite.

When he was sure that she was gone, he let his hands collapse onto the door. With just his palms supporting his weight, Malcolm dropped his head beneath his arms and counted to ten. Then counted to twenty.

"Nice rear view," she told him.

Malcolm's strangled chuckling wafted back to Kendra. He counted to ten again.

"Are you going to stay there all night? You make quite a sight with your pants bunched down at your ankles."

"You're going to make quite a sight when I get my hands on you again," he said as he pulled up his briefs and trousers and retrieved his jacket.

Malcolm joined her in the living area but wisely chose a chair rather than join Kendra on the soft-looking sofa. It looked as soft and inviting as he knew the woman to be. If he kept thinking about Kendra's well-being he could be a responsible adult. He could go without having her. Think about something else, he coached himself. Unfortunately, his manhood was in immediate and direct conflict with the part of him that knew he was doing the right thing.

With hooded eyes and a mouth suddenly drier than the Sahara, Malcolm watched Kendra repair her dishabille. Seemingly oblivious to his torment—or well aware of it and making him suffer all the more—Kendra made what Malcolm considered a production of smoothing her panty hose back in place. She then shook her head and finger-brushed her hair. After finishing, she sat quietly for a moment then lifted her eyes to his.

"Thank you, Malcolm."

"For what?"

"For giving me another reason to love you."

Malcolm's eyes darkened to slate and his heart clenched.

"What are you telling me?"

"I'm telling you that I love you. That you mean the world to me."

"Oh, Kendra." Malcolm got on his knees before her and rested his head in her lap.

"There are some things we still need to talk about, but I wanted you to know that I do love you . . . even if you no longer care for me." Stroking his head came naturally to Kendra.

"Will you be here when I get back?" he asked.

Out of all the possible reactions Kendra could have guessed would come from Malcolm after telling him she loved him, that wasn't one of them. The old insecurities leaped to the surface.

"You're leaving me?"

"Only as long as it takes me to find a big, big box of protection."

The smile in her eyes held a sensuous flame, a flame that needed little kindling to get it roaring to the intensity of a few moments past. Malcolm hadn't responded to the latter part of her statement, so that obviously meant he no longer cared. But he wanted her. Kendra willed herself to accept that fact and to enjoy the comfort of his body as long as it lasted.

"Tell you what. Let's both of us cool off before we . . ." Kendra got no further because Malcolm had risen. His big hands were kneading her breasts and his mouth was lowering to hers. If Kendra had been expecting a sensual onslaught Malcolm fooled her. The kiss was wet, sloppy, and playful.

He patted her thigh and hopped up. "I'm outta here before I can't leave."

"I'll come with you. I may as well register for the convention." As she stood tucking her blouse back into the waistband of her skirt, Kendra looked up at Malcolm, who was shrugging into his jacket.

"Malcolm, why are you in Atlanta?"

"I think we're here for the same conference. The regional bar association. I'm on a panel.'

"I'm giving a couple of Quad-A presentations."

Malcolm nodded.

"Where's Nettie?"

"Keeping the girls. She's going to follow up on leads and contacts I make here."

Malcolm nodded again. "Ready?"

Kendra reached out a hand to him and together they left the suite.

Almost two hours later they found themselves back in its entryway with Kendra's back again pressed to the door.

"Do you have a thing against beds?"

"No. You just make me so hot I forget they exist."

"How about we play Hansel and Gretel?" Kendra suggested.

"What do you mean?"

"I'll be Gretel and instead of bread crumbs you follow the trail of my clothes."

With that pronouncement, Kendra kicked off a high-heeled shoe, dangled it from her finger for a moment, then dropped it. Its twin followed a few steps later. Then came her skirt, her blouse, her half slip, a lacy camisole, her hose. By the time she got to the bedroom all that was left were her itty bitty lace panties.

Malcolm had dogged her steps and discarded his own clothing in concert with Kendra's. He stood before her in a pair of briefs that left no misunderstanding about his desire for her. In his hand were several small packages. He tossed all but one on the bedside table.

"If memory serves correctly, you said earlier that you liked my rear view." Malcolm kicked off the briefs. "How does the front view grab you?"

Kendra sucked in her breath at the sight of Malcolm. He was splendid in his nakedness and Kendra knew but one way to pay homage. Without a word, she sank to her knees before him.

Malcolm cried out and grabbed fistfuls of her hair. His fingers massaged her scalp while what she did with her mouth made him weak in the knees. When he could stand it not another second longer, he pulled her up and placed her in the middle of the bed they'd share. He inched her panties off. His lips on her fevered skin followed the descent of the cloth. He worked his way back up her body by starting with her toes. Kendra's back arched and she cried out his name as Malcolm slowly, agonizingly, deliciously sucked every one of them.

She'd barely recovered from that when she felt his hands caressing the inside of her thighs. Her legs parted and his fingers brushed the triangle of her femininity. Of their own volition Kendra's hips arched to meet him.

"Yes, sweet Kendra," he murmured, his warm breath tickling the place where she wanted him most. "Quid pro quo can be so beautiful."

With those words his mouth found her core and lapped her sweetness. With an enthusiasm that made Kendra wrap her thighs around his head and shoulders, Malcolm returned the sensual favor she'd given him. She fell apart and moaned her satisfaction when her body's convulsions slowed down to slight tremors.

Malcolm loved her through her climax, then brought his body to lie beside her. He stroked her breasts and toyed with the hard pebbles that were her nipples.

"Do you feel what you do to me?" he needlessly asked. The turgid length of him pressed against her. Kendra turned in his arms and Malcolm found himself on his back.

"It's past time I helped you with that," she said as her hand found and stroked his maleness.

"Ahhh, Kendra. What you do to me!"

"You like that, huh?" She reached over his head for one of the small foil packets. "Let's see how you like this."

Malcolm fought for control as Kendra's soft hands protected them. Then, before he could tell her to go slow, she sat astride him and lowered herself onto his hardness.

All of his thoughts scattered to the wind as Kendra established their pace. First fast, then slow, retreat then plunge. Faster. Harder. Deeper. Kendra worked him over and bled him dry. She shouted her release when her world shattered into a thousand glittering stars. Malcolm pumped into her and wished that he were spilling his seed into Kendra's womb, creating a child from their union.

Kendra's last words before she drifted into a well-satiated sleep were "I love you, Malcolm."

Malcolm smiled as he cradled her, spoon-fashion, in his arms. "You're my world, Kendra, my life."

He wasn't sure if she'd heard him. But it didn't matter. Weeks ago he'd professed his love to her. She knew how he felt.

They woke during the night and loved again.

When morning dawned, Kendra and Malcolm shared a breakfast of fresh strawberries, steaming muffins, and Colombian coffee.

"We missed the opening reception last night," Kendra observed.

"But we had more fun."

Her answering laugh had Malcolm wondering if maybe they could miss the morning sessions as well. Kendra recognized the gleam in his eyes and wagged her finger.

"Unh-uh, buddy. I have work to do." She paused, biting into a succulent strawberry. "But tonight . . ." she promised.

"Please God, make this day go fast."

CHAPTER 18

Together they sat through the opening plenary session on lawyer ethics. When it ended they walked to the lobby. Kendra headed to the concierge's office to make sure her box of Quad-A program materials had arrived; Malcolm thought to take a quick break before the concurrent panels began. His own panel discussion was scheduled for the next day.

"I'll see you at lunch?" she asked.

"How about if we skip the luncheon and meet in my room?"

"I like that suggestion, counselor, but I need that time to meet, greet, and talk shop. My first presentation is before lunch, the second one is in the late afternoon. And I need to find Bosworth Sullivan before the first one."

It was difficult for Malcolm to mask his disappointment.

"Cheer up, counselor," she told him, patting his cheek. "We have all night long."

Malcolm took her hand and pressed a kiss into her palm. "I only hope I can hold out that long."

"Still moonlighting as a janitor, Malcolm?"

Both Kendra and Malcolm turned toward the sweet-as-honey voice that had addressed Malcolm.

The petite woman was draped in a peach and cream ensemble that screamed designer original. From her hair, coiffed in a short, asymmetrical bob, to her feet, enclosed in high-heeled pumps an exact match to her outfit, the woman's bearing, manner, and looks said "I'm rich and I know it."

"It's a pleasure to see you're still the warm, gracious woman you always were," Malcolm told her.

The woman bared her teeth but the movement could hardly be called a smile. She flicked her gaze over Kendra and dismissed her as insignificant. Kendra's eyebrows rose at the silent snub but she remained silent.

"Malc, darling, aren't you going to introduce me to your, um, friend here?" the woman said, her Southern drawl pausing just long enough on the word *friend* to imply all manner of sordidness in the relationship between Malcolm and his companion.

Malcolm looked at the woman and shook his head in disgust. "Some things never change, do they Monica?"

"Whatever do you mean?"

Malcolm sighed.

Was that a note of wistfulness Kendra heard from him? Because she was at his side and studying the woman who stood before them, Kendra missed the scowl Malcolm leveled on the woman. All she saw was the woman's one-hundred-watt smile that transformed her face into a vision of delicate loveliness. And that winning smile was directed at Malcolm.

"Kendra Edwards, this Monica Davis Hightower Huntsworth. Monica is my ex-wife," he added for Kendra's benefit.

For a moment, Kendra's heart stopped. This was Malcolm's ex-wife? This high society, beautiful woman is the person who had shared Malcolm's name, his life, his bed? Even as she extended her hand in greeting to Monica, Kendra mentally compared herself with the woman. When she finished her tally, Kendra came away with more evidence that Malcolm was slumming when it came to their relationship. He obviously had more things in common with a woman of Monica's background.

Monica glanced at the hand Kendra offered and just briefly let her fingers touch Kendra's. She quickly moved her small hand and waved it as if she'd touched something unclean, letting a little half-laugh escape her lips.

"So nice to meet you, dear. What is it that you do?"

"I'm a . . ." Kendra started.

"Kendra's here representing her law firm," Malcolm interrupted.

At that news, Monica's bearing changed. She dropped the black Southern Belle affectation and offered Kendra a genuine smile as well as her hand in greeting.

"Oh, you're a lawyer. Why didn't you say so? How nice to meet you. Are you a partner at your firm? Have you met my husband, Judge Oswald T. Huntsworth? He's going to be on a panel about lawyers who transfer their judiciary skills to the bench. You don't want to miss that one."

With peculiar annoyance Kendra listened to Monica's prattle and witnessed the transformation in the woman.

"No. I am not a lawyer," she said with brittle iciness. "I'm here representing the law firm as a—"

"There's no real need to get into all of that, Kendra," Malcolm said taking her elbow and attempting to steer Kendra clear of Monica.

By this point, the annoyance Kendra had been feeling toward Malcolm's deliberate attempt to avoid having Monica know what she did for a living had blossomed into anger. She yanked her elbow free of his grip.

Monica watched the little power struggle with growing delight. "My, my, how interesting."

"Monica . . ."

So blinded by her anger, Kendra didn't hear the growl in Malcolm's voice.

"I am not a lawyer, Mrs. Huntsworth. I'm a secretary, and I'm here representing a welfare jobs program."

Monica frowned. "Welfare? Secretary? Good heavens!"

"Kendra, don't call yourself a secretary, you're not—"

Kendra turned on Malcolm with a fury that made him take a step backward. "I'm a secretary, Malcolm. I type letters, take dictation, sort files, and make sure that the attorneys I work for get to their appointments on time. Before I got this job I was on welfare, Malcolm. That's W-E-L-F-A-R-E. I know in your book that's worse than the plague. God, why did I ever get involved with you? I should have known better. But you know what, Malcolm Hightower? Mister highfalutin' Buppie attorney? You can just go straight to hell and take Miss Scarlett with you."

With that Kendra stormed away and left Malcolm standing in the lobby with Monica.

"A little trouble in paradise, Malc," she murmured. Monica's laughter was a knife in Malcolm's heart as he watched Kendra angrily punch the button for an elevator.

Kendra wasn't quite sure how she did it but she got through the rest of the day. She made both Quad-A presentations and got lots of positive feedback from attorneys who wanted to investigate the possibility of using the program to boost their staffs in their respective cities. Bosworth Sullivan seemed delighted with the response, so she assumed all had gone well.

With her mind on Malcolm's betrayal, she had no way of knowing if she even spoke in coherent sentences during the presentations. Twice Kendra had seen Malcolm and each time she turned away, hoping he hadn't caught the anguish in her eyes.

She skipped the banquet that evening. There was no way she'd be able to sit through three hours of inane chitchat with strangers when her heart was breaking in two. Malcolm had come and banged on her door for a good five minutes, but she merely sat on the sofa, listening to his pleading that she open the door. She willed the pain to go away but it seemed to have a life of its own. It consumed her and brought forth tears that ravaged her face.

Everything she'd suspected about Malcolm had turned out to be fact. His true colors showed around his ex-wife. His problem with her background was more than a problem. It was so deeply ingrained that he was embarrassed to admit to Monica that his girlfriend was a secretary. Ex-girlfriend, she amended. In her mind she'd known that it would come to this. She just had had no idea that it would hurt so badly, that Malcolm would be so cruel.

Kendra pulled her legs up and wrapped her arms around her knees. She'd already changed her flight and talked to both Bosworth and Nettie. Not only was there no need to stay an extra day, she knew she wouldn't be able to bear seeing Malcolm. While Kendra was on her way home early in the morning, Nettie would be on a corresponding flight to Atlanta. Miss Bessie, the babysitter, would watch the twins until Kendra got home.

The girls. Kendra sighed. How would she ever explain to them that in Mommie's book Malcolm was persona non grata?

Kendra had hoped to check out of the hotel the next day without seeing Malcolm, but she wasn't to be so lucky. He was laying in wait in the lobby even though it was six-thirty in the morning.

"Kendra, wait," he called to her.

Kendra paused in the act of tipping the bellboy. "A cab to the airport, please," she instructed while passing money to him. She ignored Malcolm.

"Kendra. Sweetheart. Let me explain."

At that, Kendra turned to him. "Explain? You want to explain? I heard you loud and clear yesterday, Malcolm. You almost had me believing that it was all my imagination. But it's not. You have this fundamental problem with who and what I am. But you know what? It's not going to change. You can't wave a magic wand over me and transform me into a little snobbish package of perfection like your ex-wife."

"Kendra, it's not what you think. Monica always—"

"Always what, Malcolm? Monica always puts your friends and acquaintances down? Monica always acts like that? I can understand her behavior, Malcolm. There are some black folk out there who have no clue how the other half lives. John MacAfree is one. Monica is another. I can understand that. What I can't understand or forgive is how you treated me. Did you think I have no feelings? That your deliberate attempt to sugarcoat what I do and what I am wouldn't cut me like a knife?"

Kendra wiped at the tears that fell and ruined the makeup she'd used to conceal the dark circles under her eyes. Circles that had been caused by a night spent crying without sleep.

"Kendra, I love you."

She jerked back as if he'd slapped her. "How can you say that? How can you stand there and say that after the way you treated me yesterday?"

"Kendra . . ." His voice was pleading. But she raised a hand to halt his speech.

"No. Just shut up. I don't want to hear any of your sorry explanations." Kendra shook her head and wiped at her eyes again. "You know what the saddest part is?"

Malcolm wisely held his tongue. Kendra needed to vent and was in no mood to hear his "sorry explanations" as she'd so aptly put it.

"The saddest part is that once again I fell for a lying sweet-talker. And even worse than that, I let you get close to Kayla and Karin. I'll get over you, Malcolm. I have a tendency to land on my feet even though I have to wallow in the mud for a little while before I find my footing."

Malcolm grimaced at the words she threw at him, a reference to what he'd told her the day she graduated.

"But what's really going to be difficult," she continued, "is helping the girls get over you. They loved you a whole lot." Like I did, she added to herself.

"Your cab's here, ma'am," the bell captain announced from his station.

"I'm coming."

Kendra took one last look at the man who had reintroduced life and love to her lonely existence. In his arms she'd found incredible joy. But now, now there was an empty place. In one respect, she had lied to him. Yes, she'd get over his betrayal. She just wondered if the healing process would take the next ninety-nine years.

With the picture of Malcolm standing before her etched in her memory for all time, Kendra turned on her heels and went to her cab.

She left without saying goodbye.

The cold war waged for several weeks. Kendra refused Malcolm's calls, his letters, his flowers. Especially his flowers. She couldn't look at a calla lily without getting depressed. This was worse than even Oscar up and getting himself killed. Worse because this time, she was in love—in love with a man who despised everything that she was.

Responding to Kendra's mood, the twins moped around the apartment. The one time they'd asked about Malcolm, Kendra had uncharacteristically snapped at them. Every night the girls listened to their mother's muffled crying. They finally told Nettie, but the older woman was at a loss as to how to explain to the girls that Malcolm and their mother had had a big fight and were no longer seeing each other.

Nettie had finally agreed to go on an official date with Robinson Mayview. The previous night, they'd gone to a dinner theater. Nettie had been shocked speechless when at the end of the delightful evening, Robinson pulled her into his arms.

The kiss was tender, sweet, and light as a summer breeze.

"I've wanted to do that for a very long time, Toinette Blue," he'd told her.

"You have? But I'm so much older than you, Robinson."

"If you think age has anything to do with how I feel about you, you need to think again."

This time when Robinson drew her into his arms, Nettie couldn't mistake his physical response to her. But he didn't press the advantage of her confusion. The second kiss had been slow and drugging. Though short, it had left her weak, confused, and desperately wanting more.

Nettie smiled and pressed her hands to her mouth, remembering the short encounter. She needed to talk to Kendra about her developing relationship with Robinson. But she knew Kendra was in no mindset for that type of discussion. During their date, Nettie and Robinson came to an agreement: Nettie would talk to Kendra and Robinson would talk to Malcolm. Maybe the two friends could help the couple get back on track.

But Nettie made no headway with Kendra, and at Malcolm's town house, Robinson was striking out with Malcolm.

"Economics shouldn't matter," Malcolm argued.

"Is that why you surround yourself with so many expensive toys that you look like the Buppie from hell?"

Malcolm flinched as he stared out the windows of his great room, remembering Kendra's similar words. But Robinson wasn't finished.

"Man, all your life you've been running from the demons of poverty," Robinson said. "You and Sandra have set Miss Belle up like a queen and she deserves every bit of it. But what you forget, the thing that both Sandra and Kendra know . . ."

Malcolm turned and raged at his friend. "Who the hell are you, trying to lecture me?"

For a moment Robinson looked just as frustrated and just as angry as Malcolm. Then he sighed and changed tactics. This time his voice held no accusatory bent.

"Look, homeboy. You love Kendra, right?"

Malcolm nodded.

"And you love her girls?"

Malcolm nodded again and folded his hands across his chest as he waited for Robinson's point. It came quickly.

"What makes you think Kendra isn't fighting the same or similar demons as you? Granted, she comes off with that cool 'I'm in control' persona but how do you know what she battles with every time she gives one of those Quad-A presentations."

Malcolm silently regarded his friend as Robinson continued.

"While you have enough money socked away to know you'll never again have to face a three-room shack in Carolina, Kendra has to face those projects every time she asks someone to lend a helping hand for the program. That has to be a sober reminder for her. If she lost her job tomorrow, how many months could she hang on before she was forced back to welfare, back to her own private nightmare?"

Malcolm took a seat in one of the leather chairs near the window. He chewed over the truth Robinson spoke.

"Think about it man," Robinson added. "You played right into the hands of that bitch Monica. While you have enough armor and scar tissue to deal with her venom, you let her hurt Kendra by seeming to enforce Monica's poison."

Malcolm sighed. "You've made your point, Mayview."

Robinson, knowing when to retreat, let himself out of his partner's town house.

With just his thoughts and his regrets as company, Malcolm sat alone in the quiet room for another hour.

The small package in the white corrugated cardboard box looked like a refund premium. Maybe it was the Kente cloth she'd ordered as a bonus for buying the African children's books for the girls, Kendra thought as she took the day's mail and sat on her living room sofa to go through it. But the object carefully wrapped in layers of tissue paper wasn't multicolored Kente cloth. It was a photograph.

The sterling silver frame was heavy and expensive. While beautiful, it wasn't the frame that took Kendra's breath away. In the aged photo was a much younger Malcolm. The snapshot had obviously been taken his high school graduation day. Flanked by Miss Belle and Sandra, Malcolm, in black cap and gown, grinned from ear to ear. So did Sandra, who was dressed in a simple cotton dress. Miss Belle stood tall and strong with a quiet, satisfied half-smile playing about her mouth.

Their home, the house the trio stood in front of, hadn't seen a coat of paint in twenty years. The weather-beaten wood looked as if a moderate wind would send the entire structure tumbling to the ground. The dilapidated shack was a far cry and a world away from the luxury waterfront town house Malcolm called home or the sprawling colonial where Miss Belle now lived.

Kendra didn't realize she was crying until a tear dropped onto a slip of paper that had been enclosed in the package. She instantly recognized Malcolm's bold handwriting.

Mama read about Hampton Institute and Howard University in Ebony magazine. She wanted her two kids to go to college. She did what she had to do to make sure we did.

Kendra brushed at the tears on her face and glanced at her watch. She had almost three hours before Nettie brought the girls back from the storytellers festival. She quickly changed clothes and grabbed her keys. She left the apartment with the precious photograph clutched protectively in her arms.

CHAPTER 19

The security guard sitting at the receptionist's desk recognized Kendra as the Quad-A lady and waved her through without question. The peacefulness of the law firm on a Saturday morning mocked the inner turmoil Kendra felt as she turned down the hall that would take her to Malcolm's office.

Malcolm sat at his big desk, staring into space and absently playing with a Slinky. Working one-hundred-hour weeks hadn't taken his mind off Kendra. He'd toyed with the idea of going to the African storytellers festival he'd seen advertised in the newspaper. It was just the sort of activity Kayla and Karin would enjoy with their mother. But he'd decided against it. If they were there and there was going to be a scene between himself and Kendra, he didn't want the girls—children he considered his own even though he didn't have the right to—witnessing it.

So instead of going to the festival, he'd come to the office. He glanced at his watch. It was eleven o'clock now. He'd been sitting at his desk for five hours. He couldn't remember if he'd gotten anything accomplished. That's just the way it was these days. His life was a shambles and it was his own making.

Malcolm swiveled his chair around and stared at the garden Robinson Mayview, Jr., had declared necessary to maintain his sanity. Malcolm now understood what the retired lawyer had meant. The flowers had a calming effect on him. Until he thought about the ones he'd sent Kendra. The florist called and said she'd refused every delivery. Malcolm sighed.

Sending Kendra the photograph had been a mistake, he thought. He wondered whether or not she'd even received it. He had purposely left his return address off the package. If she'd gotten it, would she know that it had been sent in love as both an explanation and an apology? He doubted it. She'd reject the photograph as easily as she'd rejected him.

Cursing his own ineptitude, Malcolm set the toy aside and turned his attention to the files on his desk.

The quiet knock on his door a few seconds later surprised him. Other than the security guard, he didn't think anyone else was in the building.

"Come in," he called.

Kendra took a deep breath and willed herself to relax as she pushed the door open. When she stepped into the office and saw Malcolm looking expectantly up at her, she forgot how to breathe. So did Malcolm. For a full minute neither one said anything.

Malcolm silently feasted on the beauty that was Kendra. Her brown skin was free of makeup. The jeans and cotton camp shirt, coupled with the ponytail she had her hair pulled in, made her look almost as young as her daughters. But there was nothing girlish about the curves that filled out the jeans. Malcolm's body quickened at the sight of her. Would he ever stop wanting this woman?

While his heart beat double time, he outwardly appeared as collected as she.

Malcolm's cool regard unnerved Kendra. For a brief, brief moment her spirits soared when she saw the love and desire shining in his eyes. But quickly, so fast as to make her think she'd imagined it, his eyes shuttered and his expression hardened. Kendra felt her heart break all over again.

"I'm sorry. I shouldn't have come," she said, turning to go back out the door.

But quick as a flash Malcolm was out of his chair and around his desk.

"Kendra! Don't go," he said while catching her arm. "Come in. Have a seat. I was just, uh, going over some briefs."

He ushered her to the large sofa strategically positioned to get the best view of the garden. Too keyed up to sit, Kendra wandered to the sliding glass doors and stared out at the rose bushes. For the first time, Malcolm noticed she carried his high school photograph. He hoped that was a good sign. But Kendra could just as easily hit him over the head with the heavy frame. It could do some damage, and he didn't doubt that he'd deserve it.

Why wasn't he saying anything, Kendra screamed to herself. Well, she decided, she'd come to him, so she would make the first move.

"Malcolm—"

"Kendra—"

They'd both started at the same time.

Nervous laughter filled the office. Malcolm yielded.

"I'm sorry. You were going to say?"

Kendra wiped a suddenly damp palm on her jeans. She gestured with the photograph. "I got this today," she began as she walked away from the windows and sat on the arm of the sofa.

"Malcolm, it's beautiful. I cried when I got it and came straight over here. But I can't keep this," she said, offering it back to him. "It's obvious this picture means a lot to you."

Malcolm took the proffered item, then sat on the opposite end of the sofa. He fingered the gilded edge of the frame as he began.

"Kendra, I sent it to you because I wanted you to have it. I wanted you to understand that, well, all of this," he said waving at his luxurious office, "all of this is just packaging. The real Malcolm is a dirt-poor boy from North Carolina. No matter how far I run, or how many degrees I can tack on the wall, the real me is in this picture."

Kendra didn't interrupt him as she slid onto the sofa cushion and tucked one long leg under the other to get more comfortable.

"Mama was a domestic. We never really knew our father. Mama said he'd been killed during a card game in a fight over a bottle of bourbon. Mama washed floors and cleaned toilets to keep food on the table. Then one day, while cleaning up for a black doctor, she came across an *Ebony* magazine that featured Hampton Institute in Virginia and Howard University in Washington, D.C. She asked Doc Pritchard's wife if she could have the magazine. Mama brought it home and told us she was going to send us to Hampton and Howard."

Malcolm put the photograph on the seat cushion between them, then sat forward and steepled his fingers. Kendra reached for the picture and hugged it to her breast.

"That night Sandra and I made a pact. If Mama got us to those fancy colleges, we'd get her out of that shack where, when it rained, it was drier outside than inside. Sandy said she wanted to be a doctor, so I decided I'd be a lawyer. We figured we'd make lots of money with those jobs.

"Mama took in ironing to help achieve her dream for us. You know that United Negro College Fund ad where the bus drives by the kid at the roadside?"

Kendra nodded.

"That kid was me one semester. Doc Pritchard had helped out a lot. Sandy got all sorts of academic scholarships but my grades weren't all that hot. By my sophomore year, I was working two jobs during the school year and whatever I could find during the summer. But by the end of the summer, before I was supposed to go back to school for my junior year, I didn't have enough. Sandy was in medical school by that time and was doing it on loans. She did what she could to help. So did Mama. But when August arrived we were about one thousand dollars short for my tuition. My grades weren't good enough to convince the school I'd be a good risk. Mama couldn't get a loan from any bank and Doc Pritchard had died."

Malcolm leaned back on the sofa and stared at the ceiling.

"The bus passed me by. It nearly broke Mama's heart."

Kendra reached a hand toward Malcolm but then pulled away. She wasn't sure if he'd accept her sympathy.

"That fall, I got a couple of jobs. I worked as a farm hand on the weekends. Every morning I caught a commuter bus with about thirty other guys and worked at the shipyard in Newport News. It was a bitter pill to swallow knowing that the college was in Hampton, the city right next to Newport News, but I couldn't go. By January I was a new person. I'd saved enough to get back in college and school took on a whole new meaning. I graduated two years later in the top ten percent of my class."

Malcolm got up and went to the bar in the corner.

"Juice or water?" he asked Kendra.

"Juice, please."

Malcolm poured a glass of apple juice, Kendra's favorite, and a glass of grapefruit juice for himself. He handed her the glass and sat in the overstuffed chair next to the corner where she was curled on the sofa.

"The rest you sort of know. Sandy graduated from medical school and did her residency. I did the law school thing. Just as soon as we could, we got Mama out of that shack and into a three-bedroom house with an upstairs and downstairs, a washer and dryer. The works. We bought her the house she's in now five years ago for her fiftieth birthday and told her we'd fill it with grandchildren."

Malcolm laughed. "She keeps pointing out that she and B.J. get awfully lonely knocking around by themselves."

Kendra smiled and Malcolm was again reminded of why he loved her. Her smile lit up the room and his heart. He put his glass on the coffee table, got up and sat next to her. He took her hands in his and caressed her fingers. Bringing her hand to his mouth, he kissed first the back, then her palm.

"Kendra, I'm sorry. I'm sorry I hurt you. I'm sorry I let Monica hurt you. Monica has never wanted for anything in her life. She's always been pampered. I found myself trying to pamper her after we got married even though I didn't have the endless bucks her daddy the doctor had.

"We got married after my first year in law school. I thought I was in love. But I'd mistaken lust for love. I guess I was so overwhelmed by the fact that a high-society co-ed wanted to be with a poor country boy that I was blinded to the truth about her. To this day I don't know why she agreed to marry me."

Malcolm gave a derisive snort. "That's not true. I do know why she married me. She thought I'd be a long-term bankroll. She didn't believe she should have to work. Her mother never worked, she'd always point out."

Kendra smoothed the rough lines that had gathered from his brow as he talked about his ex-wife. In a gesture meant to soothe, she lightly stroked his hands.

"You know the television comedy skit where everyone holds down fifty jobs?"

Kendra nodded.

"Well, that's how I was. I went to classes during the day, waited tables in the early evening, then worked from midnight to four in the morning as a janitor. I'd type papers for classmates when I could fit it in. Monica would get angry when I was too tired or too stressed for sex. Yet, I was supposed to keep her in two-hundred-dollar pumps. God, she really pissed me off!"

"Malcolm, that was a long time ago," Kendra said, continuing the soft caressing.

"Yeah, and seeing her at the convention brought it all crashing back. I know how petty and vicious she can be. In trying to protect you from her I inadvertently set you up for her insults. I apologize for that. Kendra, I wasn't trying to put you down. I was trying to remind you that you're no longer a secretary but whatever it is that new job makes you at Sullivan and O'Leary."

"It makes me director of administrative services."

Malcolm smiled. "Yes, Miss Director."

"Malcolm," she began softly. "I'm the one who should apologize. After five years, it still rankles to hear people demean my job. Secretaries play an important part in any business. If we all walked out of our offices Monday morning, commerce would come to a grinding halt."

"I know. I didn't mean to demean you."

"I know that now," she told him. "And there's something else I want you to know."

Malcolm couldn't control the tension that suddenly had him on alert. Something in Kendra's tone made him regard her with trepidation.

"You probably couldn't tell from my behavior the last few weeks, but I want you to know I love you very much. I realize that you don't necessarily feel the same way but I think it's important that you know."

"You love me? You don't still have feelings for Oscar MacAfree?"

Kendra frowned. "Where in the world did you get the idea I still had feelings for Oscar?"

"I don't know. Every time I tried to tell you how I felt, you'd start talking about him."

"I never loved Oscar, Malcolm. I know that now. I was in love with the idea of the campus all-star paying attention to me. From the bottom of my heart, I love you. I'm in love with you, Malcolm."

"Kendra, that's how I feel about you. My love runs deeper than sex, deeper than I ever thought it possible to love another human being. Will you have me?"

"Have you?"

"As your husband, lover, and best friend. As father to Kayla and Karin and all the other kids we'll fill my mother's house with." Malcolm took both of her hands in his and gazed into her luminous eyes. "Will you marry me, Kendra Edwards?"

Kendra, too shocked to speak, just stared at him. She finally realized she was crying when he brushed the wetness from her face.

"That's all I seem capable of doing these days. I rarely ever cry, you know."

Malcolm thought about all the occasions he'd given Kendra cause to cry and all that she'd lived through in the last seven years. He smiled.

"I know. Just tell me this. Do tears mean yes or no?"

Kendra flung her arms around his neck and they both tumbled into the sofa cushions. She covered his face with kisses.

"Tears mean yes, I'll marry you. But the girls have to agree to it."

"Then I better make sure you have reason to present them with a convincing argument," he said while putting a halt to Kendra's playful kisses by slanting his mouth over hers.

He eventually pulled at the cloth-covered band holding her hair and it spilled around his face in soft, fragrant waves.

"I love you, Kendra."

"Show me."

Malcolm did, and their love transformed his office and their future into their private paradise.

EPILOGUE

Kendra lay in bed gazing at Malcolm, who slept at her side. She loved this man so much, she wondered at her heart's ability to contain the love and the joy she felt each time she was near him, each time he touched her, each time they made love. She shifted a little to get more comfortable, to get closer to him. Even in his sleep Malcolm looked hard, unrelenting. But Kendra smiled. Sometimes Malcolm seemed more intense than he ever had before. She knew, however, that his intenseness, while awake or sleeping, came from worry about her.

Unable to resist, she reached out and gently caressed the man who snuggled next to her, his head tucked comfortably in the crook of her arm. With just a slight turn of his head, Malcolm's mouth would brush her breast. A heavy aching filled Kendra at just the thought. Her breasts were full and ripe, hungry for his touch.

Malcolm shifted, and as if just Kendra's thoughts could make him do her bidding, his mouth came in contact with the softness of her left breast. Kendra didn't know or care if the movement was a conscious thought of Malcolm's. She just needed him to ease the discomfort in her overly ripe bosom. She guided his head to the place where she wanted his mouth. In seconds, his tongue swirled around the tip of her breast and then his mouth closed over her, gently nipping and suckling.

Kendra let the fire race through her body. The heat built as Malcolm worked her over. She knew the exact moment when he woke. He turned on his side and one of his arms went under her back. He smoothed his other hand across her abdomen and found the waiting breast. He caressed the nipple, hard and ready for him, but he was careful not to hurt her. The gentle kneading motion of his hand on her breast became more of a massage than a caress.

"Feel better?"

Kendra shook her head no. "Make love to me, Malcolm. I want you."

He let her feel the fullness of him. "I know you do, honey. I want you too."

"Then why . . ."

"Because the doctor said we shouldn't."

"What does he know?" Kendra asked.

Malcolm moved his hand from her breast to her distended abdomen. He rubbed his hand over the mound and grinned when he felt the child growing there kick and squirm. He leaned over and kissed Kendra's stomach.

Then with one hand resting on her stomach, he looked into her eyes. "I love you Kendra Hightower."

She smiled. "I love you too, Malcolm Hightower." One last plea. "Make love to me?"

Malcolm chuckled. The quick, hard kiss on her lips wasn't what Kendra wanted.

"I think a foot massage will have to suffice," he told her.

Kendra sighed. There was just no tempting Malcolm these days. When she first began to show and pick up weight from the pregnancy, she thought Malcolm would turn away from her. But he'd become more gentle, more loving. He had marveled at each new change in her as her body grew heavy with their child. He followed the doctor's orders to the letter and sometimes drove her crazy with his thoroughness. He read books and more books about babies. He took Kayla and Karin to sibling classes. He showered Kendra with gifts and with calla lilies.

She didn't object to the things he bought for her. She now knew that Malcolm's generosity was borne of his love for her and the girls. There was no need to feel dependent or threatened by his actions. As a family, they shared equally. As partners, everything Malcolm owned he freely gave to Kendra. Without hesitation or reservation, Kendra freely gave him all the love she had for him. Through their marriage and the job Kendra held, the bouts of low self-confidence she at one time felt had disappeared. Today, she was a confident and self-assured woman.

Malcolm's hands began the soothing massage along her arches and heels. He rubbed away the soreness. But just as Kendra closed her eyes to give herself up to the tender ministration, Malcolm's mouth came down on her ankle. He nibbled on the sensitive flesh and Kendra's back arched off the pillow he'd tucked under her.

"Easy, Kendra."

"Malcolm, I love you."

Malcolm smiled as he continued to gently pleasure her.

Two weeks later, Calli Hightower was introduced to her sisters, Kayla and Karin; to her godmother, Nettie; her Aunt Katherine; her grandmother, Belle; and her adopted grandparents, John and Etta MacAfree.

Body and Soul

Thanks to good friends for patience and good times:
Adrien, Anne, Fondy, Judy, Net, Pam, and Roz

PROLOGUE

Robinson needed a plan. The way he figured it, the best way to woo the wily Toinette Blue would be to get in under her defenses. If he played his cards right, she'd be as wild about him as he was of her.

Robinson didn't spend a lot of time wondering why he was attracted to her. He just knew that Toinette was the woman he wanted to grow old with. Convincing her of that afforded him the challenge of his life. It would be better than arguing a case before the United States Supreme Court.

Robinson smiled, relishing the chase. He loved pursuing a beautiful woman. He always had. What made this pursuit different from the others was that he cared, he truly cared about the outcome. With all the other women, the prize, the goal had been simply a good time—in bed, dating, or just enjoying a lady's company. This time, however, the stakes were higher. Toinette Blue didn't know that yet. But she would soon. In the past, a physical release with a gorgeous woman was a worthy goal. Robinson definitely wanted the physical release he'd find in Toinette's arms, but he wanted more than sex.

He didn't pause to analyze the why of that either. It didn't matter. He'd established his goal.

The attorney glanced at his watch. He was twenty minutes early for their appointment. He'd met Toinette Blue in her capacity as director of a jobs program for welfare recipients. She thought this meeting was about the Quad-A program and his law firm's participation. Robinson had other ideas—at least about the subject of their meeting.

He decided to approach the seduction of Toinette Blue just as he approached the preparation and subsequent arguments of a particularly thorny case—with utmost concentration and just a touch of wicked cynicism.

He smiled to himself. Toinette Blue didn't stand a chance.

Toinette Blue put on the finishing touches of her makeup. Not for the first time she scowled at her reflection in the bureau mirror. Toinette was old enough, mature enough, and secure enough to recognize and accept that she was an attractive woman. Well, maybe not so much attractive as striking. Back in the days when she had a husband, that's what he had always called her: "a fine, striking woman."

Toinette's short-cropped hair was flecked with gray. She'd earned every strand while working with the Achieving Against All Adversities program. For six long years she had labored to get able-bodied men and women off the welfare rolls and into productive jobs.

Toinette smiled, then ran her fingers over her hair. She'd always kept her hair cut short. In the beginning, because it was cheaper: she couldn't afford weekly visits to a beauty salon. Over time, she'd come to love the carefree, natural style—that and the fact that people always called her "striking."

Some men preferred women with long, thick hair that they could run their fingers through. For just a second, Toinette wondered what Robinson Mayview III preferred. Then she shied away from that thought. Most likely, the young attorney with whom she was about to meet favored nubile young women with store-bought hair and body parts. No matter, she figured. Their meeting was about the Quad-A program, not hair preferences. And given that she was thirteen years older than Robinson Mayview, the point was irrelevant anyway.

Toinette shook her head. "But Lord have mercy, that brother is fine," she told her reflection, then laughed out loud. "Girlfriend, if you were twenty years younger, you'd give that boy a run for his money."

Still smiling, she picked out a tube of lipstick from the tray on her bureau top and carefully applied the color to her lips.

CHAPTER 1

"Robinson, how are we going to talk about the program in a dinner theater?" Toinette asked as Robinson escorted her into the hall.

"We'll have time to talk over dinner. I thought you'd enjoy this show, so I made reservations. Killing two birds with one stone," he told her.

More like counting chickens before they're hatched, he thought to himself as he watched expressions dash across her face. Her beauty arrested him. From her smooth-as-silk caramel skin to the smile that could make his heartbeat accelerate, Robinson liked everything physical about Toinette. The tall, slim woman was elegantly graceful.

Robinson smiled. He absolutely adored the vivid colors she wore. Toinette Blue obviously knew which styles and hues complemented her. Robinson wondered how she'd come out of the royal blue and gold jumpsuit she wore. Would it be slowly and sensuously or in a mad rush to feel his body next to hers?

"We'll have to talk all right, Mayview. You look like you're up to something," Toinette said.

Things were starting to perk up, all right, Robinson thought wryly. He knew how to run a seduction and rushing things was never part of the plan—particularly when a woman was already suspicious about his intentions.

Robinson thought about a meeting they'd had in Memorial Park about smoothing out a problem that had come up between his best friend Malcolm and her best friend Kendra. That day Robinson had deftly turned the conversation away from that couple and onto more general topics. He eventually parlayed that meeting into a quasi-date. He'd taken Toinette to hear a jazz quartet in the city's amphitheater. She'd looked at him then as she looked at him now—with quiet, somewhat amused, skepticism, as if she didn't quite have a handle on him but had no doubt that she would in very short order.

Robinson handed their tickets to the attendant and followed the young man and Toinette to their dinner table.

Toinette smiled up at the usher as he seated her. "Thanks so much, darling," she told the college-aged man. The usher beamed at her and cleared his throat before stepping aside.

"You're welcome, ma'am. If there's anything I can do for you, my name is Julian."

Toinette smiled at him. Robinson scowled. The boy was practically tripping over his feet as he ogled Toinette. Robinson all but glared at the usher until the boy went back to his duties. Robinson then took his seat and looked at Toinette.

Before he could say anything, Toinette put one slender elbow on the table, rested her chin on her hand, and looked Robinson dead in the eye. "Okay, Mayview," she said while giving him an amused and indulgent smile. "Why are we really here?"

Robinson cleared his throat. His number couldn't be up that quickly. Truth or dare? he thought quickly. Robinson always did like challenges.

"Well, first I wanted to thank you and all of the Quad-A staff members for providing our law office of Mayview, Jackson, Hightower with the very accomplished employees you sent."

"Thank *you*. We know that, if given the opportunity, all the people who come through our doors looking for a better life will find it. It's young people like you and Malcolm Hightower who make the program work. You give able-bodied and willing men and women the chance to make a better way in life."

Robinson winced at the phrase, "young people like you." As long as Toinette Blue felt he was too young for her, he would have problems. He didn't think she was too old for him.

"And what was the second reason?" she asked.

Trapped! Robinson decided that maybe, just maybe, he'd have to put a little more thought into developing a seduction plan.

"Second, I just wanted to spend some time with you." So much for that, he thought, while wondering where the truth had come from.

Toinette looked thoughtful for a moment, then simply nodded her head. She didn't acknowledge Robinson's statement, merely picking up her menu and studying the choices.

Robinson could have kicked himself. He knew he was a smooth operator with the ladies. Why did this particular woman make him feel so ill-equipped? He sighed and picked up his own menu.

Toinette hoped the slight, delicious trembling she felt didn't show. If she wasn't mistaken, Robinson Mayview had made a pass. Had that been a pass? She knew the man was a flirt and a born charmer. Her first meetings with him about the Quad-A program and later Malcolm and Kendra's problems had confirmed that. Weeks ago she'd agreed to go to an outdoor jazz concert with him simply because the offer had seemed to be a no-strings-attached invitation from a fellow jazz aficionado. Their light banter throughout the evening had been fun and flirtatious. They had even had a light-hearted, though spirited, disagreement on who constituted the greatest horn player of all time. At the end of the evening, Robinson took her home and said good night. That had been the end of it.

If Toinette had wondered since then what it would be like to be held in his arms, she chalked it up to her lonely existence. It had been nice to have an attractive man pay attention to her—if only for one night.

But now? What was this? Clearly this meeting had more of the trappings of a date than a business meeting. Was Robinson toying with her? He could have easily made an appointment at her office if he wanted to discuss the performance of his firm's Quad-A participants.

Toinette peeped over the top of her menu. Robinson's head was bowed as he read the various meal choices. Toinette liked to flirt, simply because innocent flirting made her feel young again. But this man, well, he was making her feel things that she hadn't felt in more than a decade.

She lowered her gaze back to the menu when Robinson looked up.

"I wonder if the flounder is good," he said in an attempt to make conversation. Where had all his smooth lines gone? He actually sat there talking about fish! Robinson was appalled. He wished he knew what she was thinking.

They were both saved the trouble of replying when the waiter appeared to take their orders.

Toinette, who hadn't read a single thing on her menu, ordered the chef's special. Robinson requested the same. As the waiter walked away, Toinette wondered what it was they had ordered to eat.

"What did he say was the special?" she asked.

"I was about to ask you the same question."

Toinette laughed and looked away, embarrassed at what they both seemed to be admitting.

Robinson settled back in his chair, a tiny smile playing at his mouth. Had he won a small victory?

Dinner went smoothly. They managed to find things to talk about. But little of their conversation had to do with the Quad-A program. Toinette had decided somewhere between the appetizer and the salad that this little tête-a-tête wasn't about business at all. But she was game. She'd go with the flow. After all, there wasn't anything wrong with spending time with a nice-looking man.

It wasn't until the dinner dishes were removed and the after-dinner coffee poured that Toinette got a copy of the playbill for the night. "Lovin' A Younger Man" was touted as the hit comedy play of the theater's season.

The spoon she had been using to stir sweetener in her coffee clattered against the china cup. With a hand that slightly trembled, Toinette put the spoon down and picked up the playbill.

Lovin' a Younger Man *is the hilarious story of what happens when a fifty-two-year-old woman meets the love of her life. Carolyn Tremont couldn't wait to introduce her new man, Marco Cane, to all her girlfriends. But what she didn't expect was the reaction they would have to the sexy twenty-seven-year-old video jockey. Love might be a many splendored thing, but what's a girl to do when "Yo MTV Raps" meets Lawrence Welk at the Dew Drop Inn?*

Toinette stifled a smile. "How'd you happen to choose this production?"

Undaunted by the challenge in her voice, Robinson poured creamer into his coffee, then remembered he drank it black. He looked at the cup, then shrugged his shoulders. "All the local critics have been raving. I thought it might be fun to see."

Toinette just nodded her head as the houselights dimmed.

By intermission, Toinette, right along with the rest of the audience, had laughed so much that her side ached. The curtains had closed with Carolyn's girlfriends, decked out and billed as Geri A. Trick, a hot new rap group, auditioning for a spot on Cane's video program.

Waiters and waitresses quickly served dessert while echoes of laughter and muted conversation filled the room.

Toinette flipped her arms up in a funky, fresh position and struck a pose. "Yo, yo, yo, Robinson, you think I should get a gold cap for my front tooth?"

"Yeah, the same day you get sized for combat boots to wear with your high-water bell bottoms."

Laughing, Toinette dropped her arms and turned her attention to the chocolate torte that had been placed before her.

"This is great," she said. "I'm really glad you brought me here tonight. I haven't laughed so much in ages."

"I'm glad you're enjoying yourself."

Robinson watched Toinette eat her dessert and was relieved that she appreciated the humor in the evening's performance. It could easily have backfired on him. The dangling earrings on her ears flashed and sparkled when she turned, laughing at a comment made by someone at the next table. Robinson watched Toinette's easy exchange with the strangers and smiled. Toinette Blue was a woman who had no problem adjusting to social circumstances. He liked that. She was confident, self-assured, and beautiful.

As he watched her, his thoughts took a slightly different turn. She could be every man's friend, a smiling, graceful woman. But did she have a lover?

Robinson knew Toinette was divorced. In one of the several Quad-A presentations he'd heard her make, she'd mentioned that her husband had left her when she was just twenty-five years old. Try as he might to believe it, Robinson knew it was inconceivable that a woman like Toinette would remain alone for long or by choice—not when even pimply-faced college boys got tongue-tied and puppy-eyed just by one of her smiles.

Toinette was tall and slim, but what she may have lacked in curves, she more than compensated in style and charisma. Half of the city's business population, male and female, had already caved in to her relentless and single-minded determination to provide job sites for men and women who wanted to work. In all the presentations she gave each year, in all the social functions she attended for the good of Quad-A, Robinson figured there had to be some man—or some *men*—who had captured her attention for more than business reasons.

Robinson didn't waste energy on petty jealousies. The men she may have dated in the past didn't matter. He planned to be the only man in her future.

The houselights blinked off and on, letting people know that intermission was coming to a conclusion. Robinson turned his attention back to the stage.

The second half of the production proved just as hilarious as the first. As Robinson pulled into the driveway at Toinette's house, she reflected on the evening's performance and wondered if there was supposed to have been a message for her in the storyline. In the end, the heroine got and loved her younger man.

Toinette chanced a glance at Robinson as he turned off the ignition of the car. No, she thought, the play had been fiction. This was real life. And the reality of the situation was that she was far too old to even speculate on the notion that Robinson might be interested in her as more than the Quad-A lady who liked jazz and live theater.

Besides, she figured as she watched Robinson walk around the car to open her door for her, she was a grandmother, for heaven's sakes. She had kids practically as old as Robinson Mayview. She should be introducing him to one of her daughters. It wouldn't do any good to fantasize about the man, even if he had the most delicious cinnamon-colored skin. She wondered what his large hands would feel like while caressing her body.

"Stop it," she said aloud just as Robinson opened the door for her.

"I'm sorry. What did you say?"

Toinette smiled. Robinson's blood pressure skyrocketed.

"Nothing. Was just thinking about some things," she said, taking his hand for assistance out of the car. For just a moment, so fast that she knew it was an accident, Robinson's body brushed against hers as he closed the car door and turned her toward her front porch.

She'd left the porch light on at her modest two-story frame house. Rosebushes in flagrant bloom scented the trellised archway. The porch swing, a favorite of Toinette's grandchildren, hung still and quiet in the soft summer night.

They climbed the few steps leading to the door. Toinette opened her small handbag and fished out her key.

"I'd like to thank you for a delightful evening, Robinson. The play was a riot."

"I'm glad you could join me. I'd like to get together again—soon."

In the quiet night, there was no mistaking Toinette's soft gasp of surprise. But she had to be mistaken about the look in his eyes, one of intensity, masculinity, and self-assurance. She watched his gaze drop to her mouth, and suddenly she felt insecure and vulnerable. She felt giddy . . . and young!

Robinson clasped her free hand in one of his even as his head lowered and his mouth covered hers. The kiss was tender, sweet and light as a summer breeze. He kissed her again. He exerted no pressure, made no demands. He simply staked a claim, then released her.

"I've wanted to do that for a very long time, Toinette Blue."

Dazed, confused, and wondering at the emotions that suddenly consumed her, Toinette stared at him. When she found her voice, it was a whisper. "You have? But I'm so much older than you are, Robinson."

"If you think age has anything to do with how I feel about you, you need to think again."

He drew Toinette into his arms, so close that there was no mistaking his physical response to her. But still Robinson remained gentle, letting her know how she affected him without taking advantage of her confusion or her uncertainty. He kissed her like a man who knew how to please a woman.

Toinette's knees grew weak, and she vaguely wondered how and when she'd fallen into this deliciously silken web. As Robinson's lips learned the contours of hers, she felt drugged and exhilarated at the same time.

He pulled away, then took the key from her hand and inserted it in the lock. When he opened the door, soft light from a lamp left on in the foyer spilled onto the porch.

Robinson placed the key in her palm and closed her fingers around it. He then raised her hand to his mouth and placed a soft kiss there. His intensity rooted Toinette to the spot; she was unable to think, unable to breathe.

"I'll call you."

With that he looked her in the eyes, then hopped down the steps and walked to his car. He didn't look back.

Toinette stared after him until his taillights disappeared from sight. Only then did she collapse against the doorframe.

"Lord have mercy."

CHAPTER 2

Toinette sat at her desk at the Quad-A office, the cup of coffee she'd poured for herself getting cold near her hand. She couldn't help replaying in her mind the date she'd had with Robinson Mayview. No way, no how could their evening be called anything except a date. And, as if she were some young thing, the man had kissed her. Kissed her! But it had been more like a brand, Toinette thought, because three days after the fact, she could still feel his hot kisses, so hot that Toinette wouldn't have been the least bit surprised to discover that the fire-engine red nail polish on her toes had curled away.

Robinson had said he would call. He'd sounded sincere at the time, but Toinette's phone had yet to ring with him on the line. The man probably came to his senses and realized she was almost old enough to be his mother. For just a fleeting moment, Toinette wondered what her life would have been like had she met Robinson when she was sixteen years old, or even when she was twenty-five years old. She'd married at sixteen and at twenty-five had been deserted, with four children and a newborn infant to care for. No, she thought, Robinson Mayview would not have been attracted to the woman she had been. No one would have. Not then.

But twenty-five was long gone and no magical clock could turn back time to make her a suitable age to date the dynamic young attorney. It was funny, she thought, how society deemed it okay for an older man to be seen with a younger woman, even a much younger woman. But when the tables were turned and the female had more birthdays to her credit than the man, the relationship was greeted with derision.

Life just wasn't fair. That, however, wasn't a news flash to Toinette Blue. Every day she worked with people to whom life had not been fair. Her priority now, today, was to get her mind off what might have been with Robinson, and on to what could be with Quad-A participants, if she located some more job sites.

Toinette picked up an accordion file which contained ten folders on prospective Quad-A employers. She selected one file and opened it. She smiled. This report had been completed in minute detail by her best friend Kendra, who occasionally did volunteer work for Quad-A. Only Kendra typed up her notes and ideas about the people she met while making Quad-A presentations. Most often, those notes provided Toinette with just the insight she needed to make a winning pitch for the program.

The file she'd opened was labeled *Ben and Maggie Trammer/Trammer Engineering and Electronics.* Toinette took a sip of lukewarm coffee, then settled back in her chair to read the file.

Met Ben and Maggie Trammer at benefit auction. Quad-A, literacy, and battered women's shelter to share proceeds from auction. Escorted by Malcolm Hightower of law firm Mayview Jackson Hightower and Associates.

Toinette grinned.

Kendra and Malcolm finally worked out their problems and then up and married each other in a quick and quiet ceremony. Thinking about the tempestuous two made Toinette's thoughts turn to Malcolm's partner, Robinson Mayview.

"Get back to work, girlfriend," she said out loud even as she turned her attention to the file.

Ben Trammer is founder, president, and CEO of Trammer Engineering and Electronics, one of the nation's leading—if not the largest—engineering and electronics businesses. Based in Texas. Several divisions of the company all over the country. They build everything from houses and shopping centers to computer games and gadgets.

Was standing next to me during auction. Bid a HUGE amount on a luxury cruise. Thanked him. He and wife like to give money through benefit auctions because "it's more fun than just writing out a good-will check." Got my name mixed up with Quad-A program. Called it the Quaddra group. Asked for info about program.

Oldest son runs computer games division. Trammer and wife in town for goddaughter's Sunday wedding. Goddaughter is Paige.

Exchanged biz cards. Very friendly, open couple; lots of laughter, sharing between them.

Ben Trammer's business card was stapled to the file folder. Kendra was so thorough. None of the other people who made frequent presentations for Quad-A provided the detail she did. But Kendra, a Quad-A alum, knew the importance of securing job sites for program participants. And Toinette was grateful for Kendra's meticulous notes. More often than not, Kendra's leads were the ones that led to long-standing partnerships with local businesses.

Toinette made a note. She'd do some research on Ben and Maggie Trammer's company and their philanthropic endeavors. She had been thinking lately that the Quad-A program could be expanded to other regions. The program had been operating for six years now. If there was a need in this city, there had to be one in other localities.

Toinette sat back in her chair, tapping her pen. So many people out there needed just an opportunity to better their lives. The Quad-A program and its benefits provided the opportunity. The majority of Quad-A alums had made the most of the program and no longer relied on welfare to provide for themselves and their families. Just the thought of reaching so many more people in other parts of the country made Toinette's head spin.

She'd mull the idea over some more. For now, she needed to go through the rest of the contact folders. She put the Trammer file to the side and went on to the next folder.

Robinson stared at the rosebushes that grew in profusion outside the sliding-glass doors in his office. His father, Robinson Mayview, Jr., had planted and cultivated the extensive garden, saying the rich red, pink, yellow, and even orange roses with their heady scents and dynamic colors always grounded him. "You've got to stop and smell the roses," his father had always told him. The elder Mayview had long since retired from the law firm. Robinson and Malcolm Hightower were the active partners now. A gardener maintained the flowers, but Robinson still paused now and then to let the blooms soothe him.

Robinson learned at an early age to appreciate natural beauty. His mother, Genevieve, was elegance and grace personified. She'd taught her son and daughter to appreciate art, music, fine wine, good food, stimulating conversation . . . and cultured roses. One result of that early training was that Robinson knew how to treat and respect women. Women, in turn, had a tendency to flock to him.

Would Toinette Blue find any of his interests stimulating? Or, he wondered, would she think his interests passé, even stereotypical of an affluent black man. Somehow, he thought not. Toinette Blue hobnobbed with the elite in her capacity as Quad-A director. She was probably just as comfortable at an upscale art gallery as she was tromping through the projects where her clients lived. Robinson frowned. He'd never really given it much thought until now, but the places Toinette frequented were downright dangerous. Her office, on the edge of one of the most notorious projects in the city, was bad enough. He wondered if she went into the community after dark.

He tried to dismiss his sudden and intense fear for her safety as ludicrous. Toinette Blue had been running the Quad-A program for years. If there had been some sort of problem, surely Malcolm would have discovered it back when he had researched the group so many months ago. Deciding that he was, indeed, overreacting, Robinson again focused on the courtship of Toinette Blue.

So far, he'd taken her to an outdoor jazz concert and to the dinner theater. They'd met a couple of times for lunch, but always with the jobs program as the focus and purpose of the meeting. The next time they were together it would be a full-fledged date, not a quasi one set up on the pretense of discussing business.

Robinson turned from the glass doors and glanced at the telephone on his desk. His fingers itched to call her. It had been three days since he'd held her in his arms for those brief, tantalizing moments. Three days since he'd seen her smile or heard her laughter or tasted her sweetness. He had told himself that he would wait seven whole days before calling her. A full week would give her enough time to think maybe she had been mistaken about his intentions, and therefore be that much more pleased to hear from him. A week would give him enough time to cool down before he saw her again.

Robinson wanted Toinette Blue. He wanted her badly. But he had to have a plan, and he couldn't rush things. The few stumbles and fumbles he'd made at the dinner theatre could not be repeated. But his mind remained a blank. In three days, the only realization he'd had was that he still burned for her. Just thinking of the way Toinette came alive in his arms while he kissed her on her doorstep made his body tighten.

"This is no way to live," he said aloud. A knock on his office door interrupted further thought.

"Come in."

His secretary, Zena Adams, popped her head in. "Delivery for you, Mr. Mayview. They won't let me sign for it."

Robinson scowled. It wasn't his birthday, and there was no pending case that required some sort of super-secret courier delivery. "All right."

He walked down the hallway and turned into the reception area. At the front desk, before clients and office staff, were three women dressed in skimpy harem dancer costumes. Every eye was glued to the trio. When Robinson approached and someone called out "Delivery for you, Mr. Mayview," one of the three turned on a tape of Middle Eastern music.

The music drew the other attorneys and secretaries from their offices.

The trio swayed and moved to the music, bells tingling as their voluptuous oiled bodies tantalized and enticed. Without a doubt, the dance was meant as a seduction.

Robinson ran his hands over his face and endured the teasing and the catcalls shouted above the display.

"You do manage to ensure that things stay lively around here," a deep voice remarked over his shoulder.

"I do my best," Robinson responded dryly to his law partner and best friend.

After what seemed to Robinson an agonizingly long time, the dancers completed their performance and turned off the tape. One of the women handed him a small envelope.

"If I don't see you tomorrow, I'll know you were, um, detained," Malcolm said while chuckling. Robinson had always had a way with the ladies. When they were in college together, Malcolm's attention had been on earning a degree. Robinson, however, had graduated summa cum laude in seduction.

"Show's over. Let's get back to work, folks," Malcolm called out as the dancers departed. Laughing and chatting, the law firm employees went back to their duties. Robinson opened the little envelope.

> A harem of one awaits you at 7:30 this evening. You know the place. See you then, sheik of my dreams.
>
> Marlena.

"Oh, God," Robinson groaned.

"Let's see," Malcolm said with great deliberation. "With that kind of performance and the cost to set it up, I'd say it was from either Marlena or Angelique. But it could have been that shy ambassador's daughter you met at that embassy party in Washington a few weeks ago. What was her name? Yasmin? Yanni?"

"Yeseni."

"That's right. Yeseni. But on second thought," Malcolm said, "this just reeks of Marlena. She's big on drama. Angelique is more subtle, don't you think? So, did I guess correctly, buddy old pal?"

"Go to hell, Malcolm."

CHAPTER 3

Later that afternoon, Robinson still hadn't decided what to do about Marlena. The woman was a handful and then some. They shared a casual relationship, all of their dates ending in the ever-resourceful and creative Marlena's large inviting bed. Much to his surprise, though, Robinson found that he wasn't all that excited about spending an evening with the woman. He had no doubt, however, that if he arrived at her apartment, she'd make him change his mind. Problem was, his heart just wasn't in it. That fact alone was out of character, but it wasn't the problem at hand, which was how to deal with Marlena.

Robinson took off his onyx and gold cuff links and rolled his sleeves up. Then, leaning back in his large chair, he kicked his feet up on the edge of his desk. He'd come to a solution the same way he argued a case.

"First," he said to the empty office, "Marlena went to some effort and expense to set up her little surprise. Second, nothing in our relationship would lead her to believe that it wouldn't be welcomed and appreciated. Third, I can't pretend I wasn't here to receive it because that would be dishonest and too many people were privy to both the performance and my presence."

Robinson closed his eyes and folded his arms behind his head. "Why don't you want to go, Robinson?" he asked himself aloud.

"Well," he answered himself, "because I'm trying to concentrate on Toinette Blue."

"Does spending the night with Marlena detract from a relationship that doesn't even exist?"

"You know, sometimes you don't serve me very well," he told his conscience. "But I know, I know. That's why I like arguing with you. But back to the case at bar. To answer the question, 'No.' It wouldn't detract from my relationship with Toinette since that relationship barely exists. It only exists in my head."

"So, what're you gonna do about Marlena, Rob?"

Robinson sighed and dropped his arms. The expensive mahogany furnishings and imported African carvings that adorned his office weren't providing any answers. He got up and went to the small wet bar in a corner of the office. He selected a bottle of Evian, then twisted off the top.

He glanced at his watch as he started to pace the room. "It's three-thirty. You could buy her a piece of jewelry and have it delivered with regrets."

He discarded that idea. The materialistic part of Marlena would like the bauble, but the woman in her would read the gesture for what it was, a buyoff.

"Okay. Jewelry is out. How about showing up at her door with flowers, then begging off, saying you have an early and important meeting?" He paused and took a swallow of water. "Hmmm," he said after a moment's reflection. "That has some merit to it."

Robinson went to the calendar on his desk but there were no late-night or early morning appointments. He buzzed his secretary.

"Yes, sir?"

"Zena, is there anything I've been putting off for some time now that can be scheduled for very early tomorrow morning?"

"Well, there is the Ferguson trust. But I understand the Fergusons are out of the country on holiday."

"Damn."

"I beg your pardon, sir?"

"Nothing," he said. "Anything else?"

"Not that I've made note of."

"Okay. Thanks."

Robinson left the water bottle on his desk and went to his partner's office. He greeted Malcolm's secretary and knocked twice before entering the office.

"Hey man, what's up?"

Malcolm looked up from the briefs he was reading and grinned at his partner. "That was some show out there earlier today. Not going to tell me who arranged it, huh?"

Robinson smiled and plopped into one of the leather-bound chairs in front of Malcolm's desk. "You know I don't kiss and tell, bro."

Malcolm just laughed out loud. "It *was* Marlena. Her fingerprints are all over that little performance. But since I know your evening is planned, what's up?"

"You have anything scheduled for *early* in the morning?" Robinson said.

"Like what?"

"Oh, anything. Meetings, depositions."

Malcolm cocked an eyebrow, then burst into laughter. "I don't believe it," he said when he got himself together.

"What?"

"You don't want to go."

"Whatcha talking about, man?"

"Marlena. Or whichever woman sent you that prelude to tonight. You don't want to go, do you?"

Robinson sat up in the chair. "What makes you think that?"

" 'Cause you used to pull this same line when we were in school. You'd get semiserious about a girl and all of a sudden you had to deal with the backlog of women at your doorstep. Man, I don't believe it. You know what your problem was then and now?"

"I'm sure you plan to enlighten me." Robinson leaned back in the chair and closed his eyes.

"Your problem, my brother," Malcolm said, "is that your mama raised you right. You can't bear to beg off and hurt the woman's feelings. So you try to come up with a legitimate excuse, backed up by the truth, for not going. As long as I've known you, you've never intentionally told a woman a lie. So here you are now trying to get me to be your alibi."

When Robinson didn't respond to Malcolm's baiting, Malcolm looked closely at his friend. Then, quietly: "What's her name?"

Robinson opened one eye and peered at Malcolm.

"What's her name, Rob?"

Robinson sighed. "Toinette Blue."

Malcolm leaned back in his chair and whistled. "Wow."

"Yeah, wow."

Malcolm thought about the beautiful older woman who had been responsible for getting him and his wife together. While he'd met Kendra in the brief time she was enrolled in the law class he taught, it was Toinette Blue who arranged, through friendly trickery, to have them go on their first "date." A smile curved Malcolm's mouth when he thought of the barely there and oh-so-sexy dress Kendra had worn to the function—at Toinette Blue's urging.

Toinette Blue was a striking woman. The silver in her hair coupled with that pretty smile made her so. She was also considerably older than both he and Robinson, who were the same age.

"You're talking about some baggage," he told Robinson.

"Hey look—"

"Don't jump defensive on me, Rob. I'm talking about emotional baggage. She has grown children. She's a grandmother. Her grandkids play with Kendra's girls."

"Age doesn't have anything to do with it," Robinson said, sitting up and regarding Malcolm. "Malc, she's everything I've been searching for. I could be happy with this woman. I know it."

"So what's the problem?"

"Well, for starters there's Marlena . . ."

"I knew I was right!" Malcolm said with a triumphant grin.

Robinson conceded with a nod. "Then there's the problem of getting her *not* to perceive that age is an issue."

"That sounds like a problem that's down the road. What's your immediate plan. For tonight?"

"You sure you don't have a deposition or something that I can sit in on?"

Malcolm's chuckles filled the office.

In the end Robinson had to call his regrets in to Marlena from a hospital pay phone. His sister, C.J., called, frantic because their mother had taken a pretty severe fall. As he dashed to the emergency room at City Hospital, horrid images filled Robinson's head: What if she ended up confined to a wheelchair for the rest of her life? What if she didn't recover from the fall? While still in a variety of civic and social groups, Genevieve Mayview was sixty-six years old. She met with a group of women her age who, just for exercise, walked through the empty corridors of a local mall three mornings a week. What if she was no longer able to do that?

The reception at the hospital wasn't what Robinson had anticipated. His father was there, so was C.J. They didn't look the least bit harried or worried. The elder Mayview absently flipped through a back issue of *Black Enterprise* magazine while C.J. was engaged in a conversation with a young couple. She had her notepad out and looked like she was in full journalist mode, working on a story.

"Dad?"

Robinson Mayview, Jr., looked up and smiled. He closed the magazine and stood to greet his son. "Rob. Glad you could make it, son," he said, clasping Robinson in a brief hug. "I tell you, after forty-four years of marriage you'd think I'd be used to your mother's antics. She sure gave me a scare this time, though."

Antics? His mother didn't participate in antics, Robinson thought, not the dignified Genevieve.

"How's Mom? What happened? Is she going to be okay?"

"She'll be good as new soon enough. Malcolm's sister Sandra is in there patching her up. It'll take her a while to get back on her feet, though. While she convalesces, I'll have time to pamper her like I did in the old days," the elder Mayview said with what to Robinson appeared to be a twinkle in his eyes.

Robinson ignored that. "Dad, what happened?"

Despite what was coming out of his father's mouth, Robinson wasn't all that sure that his father had a grip on the situation. Maybe he was in shock and was coping with the accident the best way he knew how. Robinson took a close look at his parent and, for the first time, realized that his father, like his mother, was getting old. The elder Mayviews had no concerns for money or creature comforts. The law practice had thrived under his father's care and continued to do so with Robinson and Malcolm at the helm. Once in a blue moon Robinson, Jr., would step out of retirement to represent an old or dear friend. But for the most part, he and his wife traveled and enjoyed their time together. Maybe the thought of her not being as active as she once was frightened him.

"She fell down at the mall," the elder Robinson offered as explanation. "I finally sent those caterwauling women friends of hers on home. They were frightening the nurses and all the patients."

Robinson was growing frustrated. What if she'd broken her hip? If his mother's girlfriends were so upset that they had to be sent home, the situation was probably worse than he'd even imagined. Maybe he could get some straight answers out of C.J. But as he turned to interrupt his sister's conversation, a doctor called out.

"Mr. Mayview, it's good to see you again," Sandra Bliss said while shaking the elder Robinson's hand.

"Good to see you, too, young lady. Are you taking care of that little boy of yours?"

"Indeed I am."

Robinson could have pulled his hair out in frustration. Malcolm's older sister was standing there chit-chatting instead of dealing with the issue. Then he had a terrible thought: His mother's condition was so bad that Sandy wanted to break it to Robinson and C.J. gently, without upsetting their father.

"Hi, Sandy."

"What's up, Rob?"

He couldn't stand it a moment longer. "How's my mother? Is her hip going to heal properly? Should I find a private nurse to stay at the house?"

Sandy and the elder Mayview gave Robinson curious looks. Before either of them could respond, though, an orderly wheeled Genevieve Mayview into the waiting room. Robinson knew it was his mother because he recognized her face. He didn't recognize—and couldn't believe—that she was wearing a bright purple and green warm-up suit. One leg of the outfit was rolled up over an ankle that was wrapped in bandages.

"Robinson, darling. You didn't have to come out here. It's just a little sprain."

Robinson leaned forward, kissed his mother on the cheek, then squatted down at her side. "Mom, what happened?"

"I fell at the mall."

"Dad told me that part. How did you fall?"

"Uh, well dear . . ."

"Hey Rob, I didn't see you come in," C.J. Mayview said as she approached the group. She also leaned forward and kissed her mother. "All better now, Moms?"

"Yes, dear, thank you."

"For God's sake, will someone please tell me what happened?"

"She fell at the mall," C.J. told her brother.

Robinson sighed. It was evident that his mother's condition wasn't debilitating. All he wanted to do now was find out how and why she'd fallen down.

"How? How did she fall at the mall?"

"Oh, good grief, Rob. Stop thinking about suing people. Sometimes you act like such a lawyer," C.J. scolded.

Robinson didn't dignify her comment with a response. But his father's chuckles, along with Sandy's, drew his attention.

Robinson Jr. patted his wife's hand, then quickly kissed her. "You may as well tell him, Jenny. He's going to find out sooner or later."

The younger Robinson looked at his mother. She was blushing! His mother sat in a wheelchair blushing.

"Rob, I don't want you to get upset or anything. It was just a little experiment."

Robinson braced himself for the worst, not realizing that he held his breath.

"I was trying out a pair of in-line skates," Genevieve Mayview confessed.

"I beg your pardon?"

C.J.'s giggles became laughter. "You heard right, big brother. Moms here was cruising down the mall corridor with the girls trying out in-line skates."

"Skates? You were on a pair of in-line skates inside the mall? Why?"

"It seemed like a fun idea at the time. And it was fun, until the stopping part," she replied calmly.

"I'll leave you all now," Sandy Bliss said by way of departure.

"See you later, Sandy," C.J. said.

"Thank you for everything, dear," Genevieve told the doctor.

With Sandy gone, Robinson turned his attention again to his mother. "Mom, you're in your late sixties. You could have been severely injured. Why were you wearing in-line skates?"

Genevieve latched on to the important part of her son's lecture. "What does age have to do with it? Age is a number. The store manager said lots of people wear those nifty skates these days. I wanted to try them out. Your father and I used to rollerskate together back in our day," she said with a soft look for her husband and the memories.

"Maybe when your sprained ankle heals we'll do that again," her husband responded.

The younger Mayview shook his head. His parents definitely were not acting their age.

Later that night, as Robinson readied himself for bed, his thoughts turned to Toinette Blue. He wondered if she'd like to go in-line skating with him.

It never crossed his mind that Toinette might think herself too old for the activity.

CHAPTER 4

Three weeks later Robinson was still at a loss as to how to convince Toinette Blue to take him seriously. As promised, he'd called her—exactly one week after their evening at the dinner theater. Their conversation, however, was brief. Toinette had been having some sort of crisis with one of her Quad-A clients and was dashing out the door. She'd essentially brushed him off with what to Robinson amounted to a distantly pleasant "How nice of you to call, young man."

Maybe giving her a full week to mull over the steamy kiss on her front porch was a bit much. She'd obviously come to some conclusions—conclusions that didn't bode well for Robinson.

In the time since last talking to Toinette, Robinson took Marlena to dinner to apologize for missing her harem production. He expected a scene, given that he was breaking off their somewhat casual dating. But he was pleasantly surprised. The flamboyant Marlena didn't bat an eyelid. Robinson suspected she assumed he'd either be back eventually or that the lovely three-carat diamond tennis bracelet he presented her with was a suitable replacement for his affections.

Right now, he was shoving a few things into his briefcase. He'd agreed to be a guest speaker for the Thurgood Marshall Club, a group of college students, mostly political science majors, who were considering law school. Whenever he had the chance, which wasn't often since summer classes usually met during the day, Robinson liked to talk with young people. It kept him in touch with what was happening a generation or so behind him. The pre-law club met in the evening, and he'd actually been looking forward to the exchange.

When he arrived at the Student Union building on campus, he was met by about thirty people eager for the discussion to begin. They started off generally enough with a few questions and counterarguments on the possibility of getting an impartial jury on some notoriously high-profile cases.

"But how can you know whether or not a prospective juror is lying?" asked a young man with round wire glasses similar to the ones Robinson wore for reading.

Robinson shrugged out of his double-breasted jacket, loosened his tie, and regarded the student. "That's why jury selection can take so long. There's a lot of questioning. People can be influenced by the slightest things and not think anything of it until something comes out during questioning at jury selection."

"Have you ever knowingly accepted a juror that you knew had a bias favorable to your client or a juror you knew to be lying?" a student asked.

Robinson smiled at the young man. "What's your name?"

"Aaron," the student responded.

"Have you been accepted into law school yet?"

"Yes. William and Mary, Georgetown, and Harvard."

"Made up your mind?" Robinson asked.

"I'm still thinking about it," Aaron said. "By the way, you haven't answered my question."

Robinson smiled again. "You're gonna do well."

Missing the byplay, another student piped up with a question about evidence and working with private investigators. Before long, the discussion had veered off to a heated debate on First Amendment rights of student journalists. Every now and then Robinson would catch Aaron's eye. The young man would smile politely, then offer up his opinion on whatever the current topic happened to be.

More than an hour later, Robinson pulled his suit jacket on while saying goodbye as the students filed out the room. The student named Aaron lingered, as Robinson expected he would.

"Wanna grab some coffee?" Robinson offered as he picked up his briefcase.

"Sure. There are a couple of coffeehouses within walking distance."

"They'll be kind of loud and crowded this time of night," Robinson said. "Mostly with people reading bad poetry and trying to relive and revive the sixties. Know anyplace more conducive to conversation?"

Aaron grinned. "My girlfriend loves coffeehouses, especially the bad poetry. But, yeah. I know a quiet place. It's a hike from here, though."

"We'll take my car."

It didn't take long to arrive at the place. It, too, was a coffeehouse, but the clientele proved a little older than the average college crowd.

"I play jazz here on Thursday nights with my group, Serenity," Aaron said after placing an order with a waitress.

Robinson ordered café au lait and almond biscotti. "Maybe that's why your girlfriend likes coffeehouses. You play in them."

"She's the vocalist for the group. That's how we met."

"Thinking about getting married?"

"We've talked about it. We may just live together for a while while I'm in law school. That should really freak my mother out. She's real big on the whole 'till death do us part' thing."

Robinson grinned. For some reason, he felt connected to this kid who reminded him of himself at that age: sure of himself and his place in the world. "Mothers are just like that."

"You ever been married?"

Robinson shook his head. "Came close a couple of times, though. Something always held me back. When I meet the right woman, I'll know it." He'd met the right woman, he thought briefly. But thoughts of Toinette scattered when the waitress brought their order and the conversation picked up where the group discussion had ended.

When they noticed the time, it was close to midnight.

"Aw, man. I have an eight o'clock class. I don't believe how fast the time has gone by."

Robinson looked at the empty dishes on their table. They'd turned appetizers into a meal. Robinson picked up the tab, left a generous tip for the waitress, and the two men went to Robinson's BMW in the parking lot. At Aaron's apartment building near the campus, Robinson pulled out a business card and handed it to the student.

"Give me a call if you ever need anything."

Aaron looked at the card, then at Robinson. "I'll take you up on that. It was a pleasure meeting you. Thanks for the coffee and for talking to our group."

"Same here. This was fun," Robinson said.

The two shook hands and Robinson pulled away from the curb as Aaron entered the building.

Talking with younger people interested in the law always made him feel good about what he did for a living. Robinson turned onto the expressway. Only then did it dawn on him he hadn't gotten Aaron's last name.

Toinette tried not to obsess over the fact that she seemed to have come down with a case of Mayview-itis. Every time she turned around something made her think of the attractive attorney.

Maybe she simply imagined the warmth and intensity of him. Robinson

Mayview was a nice man. He was probably just being polite. Robinson called, as he said he would, but it was a week after the play and she had been distracted by a young mother's problems. The girl's boyfriend had been caught dealing drugs out of her apartment and the girl was about to be evicted. Toinette tried to intervene with housing authority officials on the girl's behalf. But rules were rules, she'd been told; the tenant knew when she'd moved in that she could be evicted if she or anyone in the subsidized housing unit was arrested and convicted on drug distribution charges.

Along with a couple of Quad-A volunteers, Toinette had found the girl a new place to stay on the condition that she no longer associate with the man. Toinette knew the odds were against the girl. But the young mom needed a chance to prove herself. Toinette did what she could to help her.

Today, as she took a walk at lunchtime, her thoughts again turned to Robinson. A car that looked like his large blue BMW caught her attention. But the driver of the car wasn't Robinson; for starters, she didn't think Rob would drive around with gangsta rap blaring from the speakers; secondly the driver barely looked old enough to have a license let alone operate a vehicle. Toinette sighed.

The proliferation of drugs in black communities, particularly poor black communities, was the Number One cause of problems in Toinette's opinion. She'd come up with a way to get people who wanted to work off welfare and into productive jobs. But there seemed no way she could beat the insidiousness of crack and powder cocaine, the drugs of choice on the street.

Every day, Toinette thanked God that her children had escaped the lure of drugs. Had she been a different person she would say that her influence and guidance in their lives had been the determining factor. But she knew that wasn't the case. Drug addiction knew no economic or social or intellectual barriers. The only difference was that people with money were sometimes able to shield themselves or their loved ones from public display. The crack addicts she sometimes saw huddled together in alleyways and doorways were so like zombies—without hope or even the ability to care.

Quad-A participants had to be drug-free; and incorporated in the program was a Just Say No component that Toinette hoped worked. The one thing she'd come to realize in her six years of heading up the program was that she couldn't save the world. She'd started out with that misconception and had almost burned herself out trying to help people who didn't want to be helped. These days, she still did outreach, but she didn't force Quad-A down anyone's throat.

She greeted familiar faces as she turned the corner and headed back to the Quad-A office. On her desk there was a stack of mail to go through and more ideas on a proposal she had been thinking about presenting to Ben Trammer, the head of the engineering and electronics company.

The mail included an invitation to a reception given by the city's mayor for nonprofit outreach programs. "Bring a guest," the invitation read. Before she was even aware of her actions, Toinette had flipped her Rolodex to Robinson Mayview's name and had picked up the telephone.

She stared at the receiver in her hand. "This is business," she said aloud. "I'm inviting him because his firm is one of the newer Quad-A employers. I want to make sure he feels comfortable talking about the program in public."

As Toinette punched in the numbers, a smile curved her mouth. She was being only half honest with herself, and she knew it. What she wanted was to see Robinson Mayview again. If she saw him, maybe she'd get over the little obsession that seemed to be growing about the man. Goose bumps broke out on her arms when he answered the phone on the second ring.

"Mayview here."

For a moment, Toinette was at a loss for words. She'd expected to go through a secretary, giving her time to get detached. But hearing his voice brought memories of him holding her close, and fire shot through her body.

"This is Robinson Mayview. May I help you?"

"Hello Rob, uh, Robinson. This is Toinette Blue calling from Quad-A."

Robinson nearly shot out of his chair. She'd called! Toinette Blue had called *him.* Calm down, take it nice and easy, he coached himself.

"Hi there yourself. Call me Rob. No need to be formal."

Toinette smiled and settled back in her chair. There was no need to be nervous. He was, after all, just a man. But what a man! "Okay, Rob. Well, I was calling to invite you to a reception. The mayor is having one of his galas next Saturday to showcase all of the nonprofits in the city that work with at-risk populations. I got the invitation today and thought you'd like to join me."

Toinette held her breath.

"I'd love to," Robinson said with barely a moment's hesitation. "On one condition."

The surge of joy that suddenly filled Toinette was tempered. "What's the condition?"

"That you have dinner with me the night before."

Toinette grabbed the telephone receiver with two hands.

"Robinson . . ."

"You're supposed to be calling me Rob."

"Rob," she started again. "I'm not sure that—"

"Toinette, I'm asking you out on a date. A real date. Just the two of us, with no business function or agenda. Just you and me getting to know each other."

Toinette flashed hot and then cold. She so terribly wanted to say yes, but she was afraid. This was uncharted territory.

"Why?" she finally asked.

"Why what? Why do I want to have dinner with you? The answer is very simple, Toinette. I'm attracted to you."

If she hadn't been sitting down, she would have fallen. Robinson Mayview didn't pull any punches. She now knew where he stood. Did she have the guts to follow through on what he seemed to be proposing?

"Let me cook for you. My place, seven o'clock Friday night." Toinette's eyes got wide. Had she just said that? Had she just invited Rob Mayview to her home?

"Can you cook?" he asked lightheartedly.

Toinette took less than a second to get herself together. "So well that you won't want to leave."

Robinson's deep chuckle sent more heat through her. "In that case, I'll be there. Maybe I should bring a pillow."

Toinette's heart starting beating triple time. At a complete loss for words, she wimped out, ignoring his sexy comment and giving him directions to her house and a little more information about the Saturday evening reception. When Toinette rang off, she collapsed back in her chair, a deliciously feminine smile about her mouth.

In his own office, Robinson let out a whoop of joy that brought his secretary running.

CHAPTER 5

Toinette pored through the cookbooks that covered a shelf in her kitchen. She couldn't decide if she should try to impress Robinson with nouvelle cuisine or just make something simple. She thought about, then just as quickly discarded, the idea of fried chicken and mashed potatoes as too homey, too traditional. The impression she wanted Robinson to leave with was . . . well, she wasn't sure what kind of impression she wanted him to have. That seemed to be the problem.

After coming up with several menus, Toinette finally settled on a filling but easily prepared meal of asparagus salad, Cornish hen, couscous with diced carrots and celery, fresh French-cut green beans with almonds, and a light pan bread. A fresh fruit salad would round out the meal.

With a quick trip to the grocery store during lunch break, Toinette got all the items she'd need. Now as she moved about her kitchen to soft jazz on the radio, she wondered how she would react if Robinson made a move.

"Probably the same way you'd react if any man made a move. Laugh it off while making sure he gets the message that the advances aren't welcome." But they would be welcome from Robinson, that small voice answered. With all of the children grown and out of the house, there was nothing to interrupt an intimate evening.

Telling herself that the heat she suddenly felt radiated from the oven, Toinette fanned herself with an oven mitt as she checked on the baking

Cornish hens. Assured that all was well there, she started cutting and arranging the fruit so that the salad could chill in the refrigerator. She'd wait a little longer to add the vegetables to the couscous. The green beans she'd blanch and prepare after Robinson arrived.

A quick look at a wall clock showed she had forty minutes to spare before he arrived, just enough time to shower and dress. The dining-room table was set for two with her best china and stemware. Critically eyeing the low arrangement of cut flowers she'd bought as a centerpiece, Toinette fiddled with the flowers for a minute before the room and the table met with her approval. Untying her apron and draping it over a chair, she headed for the stairs and her bath.

The telephone rang.

Toinette ran up the stairs and grabbed the receiver in her bedroom.

"Hello?" she said while stripping off her slacks.

"Hi, Mom."

"Ba' Sis. Sweetie, how are you?"

Toinette's youngest daughter, Angela, sighed on the other end of the line. Toinette smiled. She knew Angie didn't care for the nickname Ba' Sis, but old habits died hard. Toinette's oldest child, Russell, was to blame for the nickname Angie couldn't shake within her family. He'd taken one look at Angela in her cradle and pronounced her "Ba' Sis."

But when Angie sighed again, Toinette paused in the process of wiggling out of her pantyhose.

"What's wrong, honey? Do you need money?"

"No, Mom. I'm fine. I hadn't seen you all week and wondered if you wanted to get together tonight for a movie and maybe a bite to eat."

"Tonight?" Toinette squeaked. "Uh, I don't think . . . No, honey. Tonight isn't a good night."

Angie laughed. "You and that Quad-A program. I tell you, Mom, you let those folks take too much of your time."

Toinette didn't correct her daughter's assumption. "What about next weekend? Or sometime during the week? I have a function at City Hall tomorrow night."

"I have a lot of appointments next week," Angela said. "So maybe the weekend would be better. I'll call you during the week, okay?"

"That sounds good, honey. Now are you sure you're okay?"

"I'm fine, Mom. Really. Talk to you later."

Toinette rang off, then finished pulling off her pantyhose. Angela always made her worry. Her youngest daughter didn't eat properly, never got enough sleep, and was always working late at her accounting job. Toinette was actually surprised that Angie had a free Friday night.

Unbuttoning her blouse, Toinette padded barefoot to the bathroom. She started to turn on the shower, but the idea of a luxurious bubble bath suddenly appealed to her. Stoppering the tub, she ran water and pulled out a tin of foaming bath oil beads. She dropped one, then two in the water.

"What the heck. Live dangerously," she pronounced before adding a third bead to the water.

She finished undressing and was about to step into the tub when the phone rang again.

"Well, good grief. What now?"

Toinette grabbed a towel and went back into the bedroom. Distracted, she picked up the phone, her attention more on the clothes she'd laid out that morning for her dinner date with Robinson.

"Hello?"

"Hey, Mom. What's up?"

This time Toinette sighed. Was every one of her children destined to call tonight? They never called on Friday nights.

"I don't like the sound of that 'What's up?' young man. Did you flunk a test?"

"You wound me, Mother," Toinette's baby boy said in his most stricken voice.

Toinette laughed. "Yeah, yeah. So get a Band-Aid, homeboy."

The laughter on the other end of the line made Toinette smile. She had good relationships with all of her children.

"Straight-A student here," Aaron Blue said.

"Then whose grades were those that arrived here last term? The report cards must have been switched at the registrar's office."

"That was just a temporary thing. I got distracted."

Toinette wrapped the towel around her. "Mmm-hmm. Hot music and fast women."

"Mom!"

"I speak the truth and you know it. Just don't forget the protection. It's a dangerous world. Now what's up, young man? A bubble bath awaits me."

"I was thinking about swinging through this weekend."

Toinette's eyes widened, and she grabbed the towel. "This weekend?"

Her son laughed. "Well, honestly, Mom. It's not like I'll be disturbing a big intimate weekend or anything."

"Uh . . ."

Silence answered Toinette. "Mom? Mom? You still there? Are you okay?"

"Yes, sweetheart. I'm here. It's just I have, uh, some plans for the weekend. I have a mayor's reception tomorrow night."

Toinette closed her eyes and crossed her fingers, praying that that would be enough excuse for her youngest, the most intuitive of her five children.

Not so lucky.

"Is there something you're not telling me, Mom?"

The normally fast-on-the-draw Toinette was having difficulty. "Well, to tell you the truth, I'll be having a relatively new Quad-A employer over. We have some details to work out." That was as close to the truth as she dared. Would he buy it?

"Mom, the mayor ought to name you Citizen of the Year. You never have any free time for yourself. The program is a worthwhile cause, but you need a life of your own. You should be out dancing, having a good time."

Toinette smiled. This child, her baby, was the one most attuned to her feelings and needs. It didn't upset him that she went out on the occasional date—unlike her oldest boy, who went ballistic with just the thought of his mother dating. Of all her children, Toinette thought, this one would likely have the least problem with the notion of her dating Robinson Mayview.

Her gaze darted to the digital clock radio on her nightstand. She'd lost almost twenty minutes just on the phone. She'd have to hurry or Robinson would catch her wearing nothing but a peach-colored bath towel. Toinette's thoughts involuntarily drifted to what Robinson's response might be if she answered the door wearing nothing but a towel. Now there was an interesting thought. . . .

"Mom? Are you there?"

"Huh? Oh! I'm sorry, baby. My mind was on something else. What were you saying?"

"Never mind. You never listen to me anyway. Sherri and I will probably stay up here this weekend. Maybe we'll drive down next weekend."

"That'll work. Ba' Sis will probably drop in next weekend, too," she said.

"All right, Mom. Go get in the tub. Your water is getting cold."

"I love you, baby."

"Love you, too, Mom. Later."

Toinette rang off the line and went to complete her toilette.

The doorbell rang as she was fastening one multicolored dangling earring in her ear. She glanced at the clock.

"Punctual, aren't you, Mayview."

She spritzed herself with a light perfume and took one last look at herself in the cheval mirror that stood in a corner of the room.

"It's showtime."

Robinson stood on Toinette's front porch wondering why he, a thirty-four-year-old man, felt like he was eighteen. Toinette was forty-seven, but he was standing at her door nervous, as if they were both teenagers going out for the first time.

He'd finagled this date out of Toinette and all he could think about was the moment when he'd be able to pull her into his arms. Just the memory of the last kiss could inflame him, and he'd deliberately kept that kiss brief. He'd had no other choice. It was either cut it short or lose all control.

He'd debated with himself on what to bring her tonight. In the end he had decided that traditional was best. As he held the half-dozen red roses and bottle of expensive white wine, he couldn't shake the image of a nervous kid anxiously awaiting his prom date.

This idea was dispelled when Toinette finally answered the door. She took his breath away. Clothed in a simple royal blue tank and skirt set, the only jewelry she wore were large beaded earrings. Her arms, bare where the tank top ended, were graceful, one casually placed across her stomach. The Indian design of the top with its multicolored embroidered edges matched the long wraparound skirt, accentuating her tall, slender body. With his eye for detail and quality, Robinson could appreciate the handwork and time that went into the design and creation of the set. More than the clothing, though, he appreciated the way the woman filled out the outfit. Toinette was slim, but she had curves in all the right places.

With a slow, downward perusal, Robinson noted that her legs were bare and that the polish on her toenails matched the polish on her fingernails. His gaze began the leisurely trek back up her body. When he again reached her face, an amused half-smile played about her mouth.

"Like what you see?" she dared.

"Infinitely."

Toinette just smiled before gently waving him into the house. As he passed her, she took the time to study his backside. Clad in a black double-breasted suit, Robinson looked the part of a successful attorney. Toinette smiled in appreciation for the way the slacks fit the man.

"These are for you," Robinson said, turning and handing her the roses.

She accepted the gift and bent her head to inhale deeply the scent of the flowers. "Thank you."

Just watching Toinette's sensual enjoyment of the fragrant blooms made him ache. It was gonna be a long, torturous night, Robinson thought. But not without its rewards.

"This is for dinner," he said, holding up the bottle of wine and stepping closer to her. "And this is for me," he said as he bent his head to hers and lifted her chin with a gentle hand.

Toinette's surprise was evident. Her mouth, in an O of exclamation, was ready for the tender assault. But before she could truly appreciate the embrace, Robinson pulled away.

He'd needed a taste, just a little something to fortify him for the evening. As he watched the speculation in Toinette's eyes grow to something that looked a hell of a lot like desire, he wondered if kissing her had been wise. But before he could wonder more about that, Toinette's expressive face became closed and set.

"We're going to have to set some ground rules, Mayview."

"Like what?"

"Like no hanky-panky."

The corners of Robinson's mouth edged up, as if he were trying—unsuccessfully—to hold in a smile. "Does a gentle kiss of greeting constitute hanky-panky?"

He was right, she reluctantly admitted to herself. Just because she melted at the first touch of his mouth didn't mean he shared the feeling. The quick kiss was no more than a tame salutation between friends. If she felt weak in the knees or read more into it, that was her problem, not Robinson's.

"You're right," she finally answered him. "I'm sorry. I was jumping to conclusions and well . . ." Her voice faded away. She always seemed to have this problem around Rob. Toinette was a woman for whom words and the gift of gab came easily. Except now, when Robinson Mayview looked for all the world like he wanted to ravish her on the floor. And she rather liked the idea.

Every nerve ending in Toinette's body was alive and aware of the sensual perusal that Robinson was giving her. But she had to be mistaken! No man could be that intense. His eyes never left her face, yet she felt as if she stood before him stripped naked. Keenly aware of his scrutiny, she stared back. His expression was a smooth blend of eagerness and tenderness . . . and something else—anticipation.

Her body responded before her mind did, and she swayed toward him. In one motion, he placed the wine bottle on the hall table and his mouth covered hers. Toinette wrapped her arms around Robinson's neck and gave herself up to sensation. His lips, more persuasive than she cared to admit, danced a gentle waltz along her mouth. Her fingers found the edge of his hairline and slowly combed through the close-cropped waves in his hair. She unknowingly pulled him closer to her inflamed body.

Robinson was sure that he'd died and gone to heaven. He'd fantasized about this moment for so long he almost couldn't believe that it was actually happening. But the feel of Toinette's warm lithe body in his arms reminded him that it was all too real. He tried, desperately, to keep it gentle, to keep it soft and easy. But when he felt her hands in his hair, her body's attempt to draw closer to his and her breasts crushed against his chest, he gave up all pretense of a mild-mannered gentleman. He wanted this woman—had wanted her for weeks, months even.

His mouth slanted and forced her lips open with his thrusting tongue. He took her with an intensity that made him shake. The kiss was like the smoldering heat that forged metal.

Toinette's entire body was on fire. Never in her life had she kissed a man and completely lost herself in a vortex of emotion. She felt as if she'd come home, as if she'd finally found the missing piece of her that made her whole. In Robinson's arms she found the passion that had eluded her for so many years. She felt his hand wander down her back and cup her derriere. Toinette moaned and threw her head back, giving him access to her neck. He rained nibbling kisses from her ear to her shoulders and back, lingering in every place where he felt her lower body surge into his. She felt his erection and responded to it in a movement as old as time.

"Toinette . . ."

"I want to touch you," she told him.

"Wherever you want."

Her fingers edged to the burgundy and blue silk necktie tied in a crisp knot at his throat. He unbuttoned his suit jacket to give her better access. Then, again, his lips found hers. Toinette forgot what she was trying to do when his firm mouth demanded a response. She gave it to him even as one hand caressed the smooth texture of his shirt and the undershirt beneath it, the barriers that stood between her and the skin she wanted to savor.

Sure that her breathing had all but stopped, Toinette kissed him back, then moaned her displeasure when his mouth left hers. But mere seconds later, she felt his hot tongue edging away the shoulder straps of her top. His mouth moved lower, and she let out an involuntary cry when she felt one of his large hands close over one breast even as his mouth inched toward the other.

The telephone rang.

"Rob . . ."

"Hmm?"

"I, I think the phone . . . The telephone is ringing."

"I thought that was the fire truck coming to put out the six-alarm fire raging in me."

Toinette smiled even as she tried to catch her breath. Without taking her eyes from Robinson's, she reached behind her for the telephone receiver on the hall table. She fumbled for a moment but eventually got the receiver to her ear. When Robinson stepped back, giving her some breathing room, she gave him a trembly smile of gratitude.

"H-Hello?"

"Hi, Mom. It's Judi."

Robinson reached out a hand and, with one gentle finger, traced the outline of Toinette's lips.

"Ahhh . . ."

"Mom? Are you okay? You don't sound so hot."

"I'm fine, sweetheart. How are you?"

Robinson took Toinette's free hand. Without losing eye contact with her, he drew one slim finger to his mouth. With his hand guiding hers, he ran her finger along the contours of his own lips, then guided the tip of her finger into his waiting mouth. Toinette's knees buckled. He took a step closer and wrapped a steady arm around her in support.

"I, I'm doing well," she managed.

"Well, you don't sound very well. Have you been working too hard?"

At her daughter's innocent words, Toinette's gaze fell below Rob's waist. Seeing where she stared, Robinson waited for her response.

"Uh, I've been . . . No. I haven't been working too, uh, hard."

He smiled, and Toinette was sure that he knew where her thoughts lay.

"Are you sure you're okay, Mom? You sound kind of breathless. Do you want me to stop by on my way to the airport?"

"No, sweetie. That won't be necessary. I was just, uh, doing some, uh, exploration."

"Well, don't overdo it. Everything in that house has been there for years. There's no need in trying to clean out ten years' worth of accumulation in one night."

Robinson nuzzled Toinette's neck, and the receiver she held clattered to the tabletop and then to the floor. Toinette dived for the receiver, then held Robinson at bay with one outstretched arm.

"Sweetie, are you still there? Sorry about that. I dropped the phone."

"I just dropped Lisa off at Leah's," Judi said. "I have a flight out in about forty minutes. I'll be gone for a week. Just wanted to say hi and bye."

Toinette tried to ignore the feathery caresses Robinson sprinkled along the arm she held between them. "Leah doesn't always have to keep Lisa when you're out of town. She can stay here."

"I know, Mom. But Leah has everything set up. It's practically Lisa's second home. She has her own room there and Leah's kids give her company."

"Stop it," Toinette whispered to Robinson when he easily lifted her arm and planted nibbling kisses from her wrist to her shoulder.

"What was that, Mom?"

"Oh, I was saying that you can stop it anytime you want to give you and Lisa as well as Leah's family a change of pace."

"Okay, Mom. I'll think about it. I just didn't want to put you out or to any trouble."

"Since when is it trouble to have my grandchildren over?"

Judi laughed. "Okay, Mom. I get the message. Listen, I'm going to run. Even though we're not seeing each other anymore, I want to give Victor a ring before I leave. You sure you're okay?"

"I'm fine, darling. Really I am. And Judi, forget about Victor. He is and always has been bad news."

"Mom, we've had this discussion before. Victor is a nice man who just happens to have strange things happen to him. We don't really date anymore. Lisa didn't care for him and I like to consider her feelings. But since her father and I split up and with my work schedule, I don't exactly have men lining up at my door to wine and dine me."

"Judith, that so-called nice man has been indicted three times, twice by federal grand juries. I tell you, where there's smoke, there's fire."

"Mom . . ."

"All right, all right. But I have to tell you, if it came down to choosing between Victor and that ex-husband of yours I'd rather you were with your ex."

"Mom."

"Okay. I've said my bit on the Victor issue. You have a good flight and I'll see you whenever you get back."

"Okay. And Mom?"

"Yes, dear."

"Get some rest," Judi advised. "You sound really worn out. I swear, those Quad-A people certainly get their pound of flesh."

Toinette shivered as Robinson licked her earlobe. She unconsciously pulled the earring from her ear.

Now thoughtful, she rang off with her daughter. It had taken her divorced-and-looking daughter to remind her that the ideal man for a girl like Judi was standing in her foyer. Robinson would make the perfect son-in-law. It didn't make sense and it just wasn't right what they had been doing—even though it felt so good. Ridiculous as it seemed, she almost felt as if she were betraying her daughter, or at least lessening the opportunity for women like her daughters Angie and Judi to meet and date eligible men.

Toinette stepped out of Robinson's embrace.

"I think you should leave, Robinson."

That stopped him. "Leave? I came over for dinner."

Toinette folded her arms and stared him down. "I'm not the main course. This is what I meant by hanky-panky. I cannot believe what we were doing. And right here, in the hallway!"

He'd pushed her too far. But her hot response had inflamed him practically beyond reason. Robinson wondered if he could salvage the evening.

"Toinette, I apologize for getting carried away. It's just that, well, for so long I've thought about how you would feel in my arms. It's been weeks since we've seen each other. I was just overcome by your beauty."

Toinette looked at him, then clasped her hand to her chest and let out an amused laugh. At Robinson's bewildered stare, she laughed some more. "Overcome by my beauty? What have you been doing, Mayview, reading bad paperback romances?"

Robinson looked at her and chuckled. "You think that's a bad line? How about 'Your beauty blinded me to all reason.' "

"Well, that's a little better, but it's still kind of hokey," she said.

"I don't believe I'm having this conversation."

"Look, I'm sorry for leading you on. I normally don't just fling myself into a man's arms. Let's just sit down, have some dinner, talk a little, and then you can leave. We'll just chalk this up," she said, waving a hand, "to experimenting. We've had a taste and gotten it out of our systems."

She was serious, Robinson thought. She actually believed that they could write off the fire they'd found in each other's arms as an experiment. He still burned for her. But he'd play by her rules—for now. She may have thought it a bad come-on line, but he really had been overcome by her and blinded to everything except the way she felt in his arms. That had never, ever happened to him before. In all his years of wooing and seducing women, he had never, ever lost control. But one kiss from Toinette and he'd been transformed into an overeager package of hormones. If she hadn't said no, he'd be making love to her on the foyer floor right now. Robinson sighed. If he wasn't still so aroused, he knew he'd be disgusted with himself.

"How about I pour us a couple of glasses of the wine I brought?" he suggested.

Toinette took his suggestion as acquiescence to her analysis. She turned and headed toward the kitchen, confident that the hanky-panky was over. Robinson followed, enjoying the gentle sway of her hips as she walked before him.

"I'll get a glass for you," she said over her shoulder. "No wine for me. I can tell I'll need all of my faculties with you around."

Robinson cataloged that bit of information but endeavored to be on his best behavior for the rest of the evening.

CHAPTER 6

He tried. He really tried. Only once did he slip. Throughout dinner they discovered they had the same eclectic tastes in music from jazz and hip-hop to classic and blues. Robinson collected African art and artifacts. Toinette collected strays: people and projects. They'd eaten dinner and were sitting on her living-room sofa talking when she got up to refill their coffee cups. His hand stayed hers when she started to add cream to his coffee.

"I drink it black," he told her. Robinson couldn't ignore the fine trembling he felt in her and gently caressed the back of her hand. He heard her soft gasp and watched her brown eyes dilate. She snatched her hand back, almost spilling the hot liquid in his lap. He placed the cup and saucer on the coffee table and watched her not-quite-steady hands add cream and two packets of sugar substitute to her own cup. So, he thought, all of her earlier talk about experimenting had been just that: talk. Her reaction to just a simple touch spoke more of passion than anything else.

When she sat again, it was across from him in a Louis XV-style chair that she'd said had been a gift from Russell, her oldest child. Robinson made note of the distance and smiled to himself. Despite her initial ground rules and protestations, he decided to turn up the heat just a little. "I don't bite."

"So you say," she murmured before taking a sip of the beverage.

"Are you afraid of me?"

"Should I be?"

Robinson smiled. That was one of the things he liked about Toinette Blue. She could dish it out as well as she could take it. "Only if you don't trust your feelings around me," he said.

"You have an unfair advantage."

"How so?"

Toinette put her cup and saucer on the coffee table before she responded. She crossed her legs. His gaze followed the action, then returned to her face.

"First," she said, "you're an attorney. You get paid to argue and think quickly on your feet. You know how to use words and subtle nuances to your advantage."

She raised her hand before he could counter with a statement to the contrary. "For example . . ."

"Yes?"

"That so-called simple kiss earlier this evening was anything but. There's no use in either of us trying to deny it."

"I know how I felt when I kissed you. I'd like to do it again." And again and again and again, he thought to himself. But he trod on dangerous ground. One false move and he could be doomed.

"That's another reason why you have unfair advantage. You know what you're after. I'm not sure I even want to play the game."

He sat on the edge of the sofa. "This isn't a game, Toinette."

"Then what's going on? I'm a lot older than you, a whole lot older. I'm a grandmother. You're a young, successful, single black man. A rare breed, according to my single daughters. I was talking to one of them while you were getting acquainted with my bosom before dinner. Why are you here having semantic duels with me instead of out dating one of my daughters, or any number of the other African-American women looking for a good man?"

"I'm where I want to be." Although, he thought, he rather liked the memory of getting acquainted with her bosom.

"Why?"

"Why am I here or why is this where I want to be?"

Toinette eyed him and nodded her head. "See, that's what I mean about semantic games. And look at you . . ."

At the exasperated tone in her voice, Robinson looked down to see if he'd accidentally spilled something on his tie or shirt.

"You sit there looking all sexy and intense. Men didn't look like you when I was coming along."

Robinson smiled at the compliment but decided he'd better not alert her to the fact that she'd consciously acknowledged she found him attractive.

"You sweet-talked your way into a date. Granted, I invited you here for dinner. But then you tried to seduce me in my hallway. You stared at my breasts, small as they are, all through dinner, and now you're sitting there smiling like the cat who ate the canary. I think I have a right to know what you're up to."

Used to listening to the sometimes rambling and usually defensive testimony of witnesses in the courtroom and accustomed to ferreting out the important stuff, Robinson was quickly able to cut to the heart of Toinette's complaint. She was attracted to him and was appalled by that fact. She was hung up on the age difference. In a matter of seconds, he thought of and discarded the ways he could approach the situation. He opted for head-on and only addressed the essential dilemma.

"Toinette, you're right. There is an age difference between us. I don't see that as a problem. I'd like to get to know you better. I don't want to date your daughters. I want to date you."

"But . . ."

He got up and walked to the side of the chair where she sat. "Before you cut me off, let me finish. I find lots of things attractive about you. Your smile. Your dedication to the Quad-A program. I like your jazzy attitude toward life. I've been attracted to you since you made the presentation about Quad-A to me and Malcolm all those months ago at the firm. I find you very physically attractive, and I don't mind telling you that."

Robinson put a hand on her shoulder. Toinette turned and looked up at him. He squatted down so he'd be eye level with her.

"I haven't said or done anything about it until now because I was afraid of your reaction," he said while lightly skimming a finger along her bare skin. "I was afraid that you might respond just this way. I don't know what I can say or do to make you believe that what I want is to get to know you better. And I mean all of you. I can't deny that I want you. You felt what you do to my body."

He took her hands in his and looked in the brown eyes that so captivated him. "You say you're too old for me. Maybe you're right. Every time I'm near you, I feel like a teenager who can't control his physical reaction. But I'm not a teenager, Toinette. I'm a grown man. I'm thirty-four years old and can handle rejection. If you say leave and don't come back, I'll do it. But before I go, I want to be sure you know I find you very appealing."

"I . . ." Her mouth suddenly dry, Toinette tried again. "I . . ." So many thoughts tumbled through her head, she wasn't sure how or what to say first. She hadn't been expecting his candor and therefore was at a loss as to how to deal with it.

There were rules that were supposed to be followed. Steps along the way. That much she remembered about dating. There was supposed to be a sort of parry and thrust, tease and flirt, before a man and woman got to this kind of discussion. But Robinson Mayview had cut through all of those elements of the chase.

She was confused but knew one thing for certain: What he seemed to be offering was something she wanted. She'd tried to fool herself, to make believe that she'd only imagined the intensity and heat she felt every time he was near. But it was real. So was her desire for him—despite the fact that half of her kids would have a fit, despite the fact that somehow it seemed wrong. She wanted him, too, and she was beyond the point in her life where she kidded herself about certain things.

But it had been so long, so very long since she'd had someone to hold, someone who cared about her as a woman, not as "Mom," "Grandma," "Aunt Nettie," and "that lady who can get you a job." Robinson Mayview was offering TLC, and the woman in her yearned for that care. But Robinson was so young!

"I have a son who is thirty," she blurted out. Then Toinette sighed. That hadn't been at all what she wanted to say. She'd wanted to tell him how he made her hot and cold, and how for this dinner engagement she'd bought and was wearing a very naughty, very skimpy little silk teddy. But the age thing was out in the open now.

"I'll look forward to meeting him," Robinson said.

Toinette grimaced. Russell, her oldest, was the one most likely to have a conniption if she started dating Robinson Mayview. But then she remembered something. It was her life. Her choice. If Russell didn't like it, that was his problem.

"I . . ." She faltered when Robinson lifted her hands to his mouth and pressed a gentle kiss there.

"Toinette, I didn't mean to rush you or to make you nervous. I apologize." Robinson stood up and Toinette followed. "I'll understand if you'd prefer I not go to the mayor's reception with you tomorrow night."

"Rob, no. I'd like for you to escort me. I . . . Things have just happened a bit too fast for me tonight. You didn't make me nervous; you made me wary. I question . . . I questioned your motives. I'm not rich, so you couldn't be after my money. If anything, it might be the other way around. The last thing on my mind is that you just want me for me."

Robinson smiled as he walked with her to her front door. "I have no hidden agenda, Toinette. And I don't mind saying that it's you I want, body and soul. That may be too much to ask, but at least you know where I'm coming from."

Toinette nodded as he opened the front door.

"What time should I pick you up tomorrow?" he asked.

"How about six-fifteen? It starts at seven, and it will take a little while to get downtown."

The warmth in his smile was echoed in his voice. "Then I'll see you at six-fifteen tomorrow." He paused for just a moment. "Toinette, may I kiss you good-night?"

Patiently he waited for her decision. After a moment she nodded and closed her eyes in anticipation of the hot embrace.

Robinson gently kissed her on the cheek, whispered, "Good night," and closed the door.

"Ophelia, just look at her. You'd think that boy was her date the way she's hanging all over him."

"I tell you, Pearline, it's just a shame the way these women flaunt themselves. I know for a fact that she's no spring chicken. He probably *is* her date, and I'll just bet he's young enough to be her son!"

Robinson scowled in the direction of the women standing a few feet from him and Toinette. Toinette was busy talking. The two old biddies caught his look and twittered away toward the hors d'oeuvres table set up in the museum's lobby.

The main hall in the contemporary art museum was the perfect backdrop for Mayor Griffin's gala. Guests wandered through galleries as they conversed and nibbled. Robinson hoped that Toinette had been so engaged in her conversation with the mayor's wife and the director of the battered women's shelter that she'd missed the poison aimed her way by the two nosy observers.

Holding his hand for all of five seconds didn't constitute "hanging all over him." Personally, Robinson didn't mind public displays of affection. Since he and Toinette hadn't engaged in any to date, he didn't know what her thinking was on the matter. The previous night he'd gotten an earful on her reservations about entering a relationship with him, even a casual one. Yet, she still wanted him to accompany her to this function.

Robinson had told her most of the truth last night. The fact of the matter was that he'd taken one look at her and known she was the woman for him. Yes, he'd dated other women in the time since he'd met Toinette, but nothing and no one made him think in terms of permanence the way she did. Phrases like "to have and to hold" and "from this day forward" came to mind when he was with Toinette, and even when he just thought of her during the day. Then there was the celibacy thing. That part might kill him. Robinson had had his share of women, all shapes, sizes, and colors. But he'd always been safe and responsible about it, even before safe sex was in vogue and literally a matter of life and death.

He looked at Toinette in her black on black jumpsuit and beaded jacket. She was fully covered, even conservatively dressed compared to the dazzling colors and jewelry she normally wore. Her signature long, dangling earrings, a perfect match to the beadwork in the jacket, represented the only extravagant part of her outfit. Robinson just wanted to know one thing: how she'd come out of it. It had been six long, dry weeks, and he didn't know if he'd survive. It wasn't conceit on his part when he acknowledged that any one of several simple phone calls would land him a bed partner for the night. Problem was, there was only one that he wanted and she was as skittish as a virgin.

The mayor's wife turned to him, and Robinson hoped she hadn't asked him a direct question.

"Mrs. Griffin was saying how your firm represents the new breed of corporate involvement in civic affairs," Toinette said.

Had he been holding her hand, he would have squeezed it for bailing him out of what could have been an awkward silence.

"One of the things that both my partner and I are committed to is giving back to the community," he answered without a pause. "In today's society, too many negative images and events are portrayed as representative of the entire population of people of color. I disagree. There are people out there striving, working hard, and doing the best jobs they can with what they have. If our participation in the Quad-A program helps somebody along the way, I'm for it and any other program like it."

As Robinson continued the conversation with the two women, Toinette took the opportunity to study him—really study him. It had been painfully obvious to her that the man wasn't paying the least bit of attention to the conversation before she had deliberately steered him into it. She wondered what had had his thoughts so far away.

Her own thoughts had a tendency to stray. Of late, the favorite random thought was what it would be like to make love to Robinson Mayview. He'd all but told her he wanted her that way the night before. Toinette wasn't an innocent. She'd been married nine years before her husband walked out on her and their five children. In the intervening years, she hadn't had a lot of time for anything except raising her family the best way she could. And somewhere in the back of her mind, she kept wishing and hoping and waiting for her husband Woody to come back.

She had lived the last twenty-two years as a single parent. She kept up with the times, though. Raising two boys and three girls and working with the young men and women she counseled through Quad-A guaranteed that. She'd given each of her kids straight-up talks about sex and was grateful that she had open and honest relationships with her children, so much so that when they were younger, her kids brought their friends over to get the questions answered that some of their parents found difficult to deal with.

Her own sexuality, though, well, that was a different matter. Mostly one she didn't think about. Until recently. Until a certain cinnamon-colored man kept her thoughts adrift on a sensuous wave. She'd barely slept the night before, wondering what might have happened if the telephone hadn't interrupted the foreplay in the hall. She'd been sexually attracted to men before, but not so mindlessly lost in sensation that she would have led a man straight to her bed or, in the case with Robinson last night, straight to the floor.

Would sex on the floor be uncomfortable?

"Mrs. Blue?"

Robinson touched Toinette's elbow to guide her attention back to the conversation.

"I'm sorry," she apologized. "I was thinking about the possibility of something."

"That's just what we were wondering about," chirped Mrs. Griffin, the mayor's wife.

"Given that the auction we held a while back was so successful, I've been giving some thought to having a bachelor auction this year," the women's shelter director elaborated. "An auction could be the annual fundraiser for Quad-A, the shelter, and the literacy foundation. One year we could get companies to donate products and services like last time, and on the alternating year we could do a bachelor or celebrity auction. What do you think?"

Toinette looked at Robinson and smiled. "Well, I think it would depend on whether or not Mr. Mayview and some of his friends would be willing to put themselves up on the block for a good cause."

The two other women eyed Robinson speculatively. "I think you're right, Mrs. Blue. But of course he'd do it," the mayor's wife declared to Robinson. "You just said you're in favor of programs to help the disadvantaged." She tapped Robinson on the arm with a small fan she held. "You'd probably fetch a thousand or two."

"I'd bid ten thousand myself," Toinette mumbled under her breath.

"Let's find Doris. She's in charge of the literacy program," the shelter director added for Robinson's benefit. "We'll all sit down next week to talk about this. We could probably pull it off in a couple of months if we wanted to."

With an action plan in place, the two women waved as they walked away, still discussing the possibilities inherent in a bachelor auction.

"Did I just get volunteered to be auctioned off to the highest bidder for a night with a stranger?"

Toinette laughed. "Yep. Once Mrs. Griffin gets an idea in her head, there's no stopping the steamroller."

With his hand at the small of her back, Robinson led Toinette to a pedestal display of modern art. They both leaned forward to get a better look at the twisted wire and nails that constituted the work.

Robinson moved closer and said quietly, "And did I hear correctly that you'd bid ten thousand for the opportunity?"

Toinette found out that forty-seven-year-old women could still blush.

CHAPTER 7

The next day at work Toinette composed and sent out letters about the Quad-A program to several people. She labored over the preparation of the packet to Ben and Maggie Trammer. After going through all of the most recent files on program contacts, she discovered that she had a short list of very influential individuals who, if approached the right way, might be open to the idea of providing the financial support to branch out Quad-A to other cities.

In addition to Ben and Maggie Trammer, who were based in Dallas, one other couple on the list represented an unparalleled opportunity: John and Etta MacAfree. The local couple owned a chain of very successful jewelry stores. The one person who might know if the MacAfrees would be open to the idea was Kendra: John and Etta MacAfree were her twin daughters' natural grandparents.

Toinette picked up the telephone and called her best friend at the law office where she worked. "What's up, girlfriend?"

"Nettie! I was just thinking about you. We haven't done lunch in a while. Want to get together this afternoon? Malcolm's in court most of this week, so I'm on my own."

Toinette glanced at her watch. "Meet you at the Sidewalk Café at twelve-thirty?"

"Sounds like a plan. And Nettie?"

"Um-hmm?"

"I want to hear all about this Robinson Mayview thing."

Toinette laughed a bit then shook her head. "Yeah. We need to talk about that Robinson thang."

"See you soon."

Toinette and Kendra's favorite place for lunch together was a restaurant and cafe. On warm summer days like today, they ate outside and people-watched as they chatted. Toinette arrived first and was led to a table that would give them both privacy and a good view. With so many new and wonderful things going on in Kendra's life, the two friends hadn't had as much time to sit and just talk the way they usually did.

"Hey girl. Sorry I'm late," Kendra said, sliding into the chair across from Toinette.

"I just got here myself."

A waiter arrived and took their orders. Kendra sat back and smiled. "Okay. Spill it. You look too radiant, too happy."

"I always look radiant and happy," Toinette replied laughing.

"Um-hmmm."

Toinette laughed, sipped from her glass of ice water with lemon, then took a fortifying breath. "He's wonderful. Me? I'm confused and horny."

"Nettie!" Kendra scolded while taking a quick look around to make sure no one had overheard Toinette's comment.

"I swear, Kendra. Sometimes you'd think I was the twenty-seven-year-old and you were almost fifty. Besides, it's the truth."

"Well, have you two . . . you know . . . ?"

"No. But it's always on my mind. I've gone all these years without sex but all of a sudden my body is on fire for this one man. It doesn't make sense."

"What do you mean it doesn't make sense? You're a woman. He's a man. You're attracted to him. He's attracted to you, isn't he?"

Toinette raised her eyebrows and cocked her head to one side. "Of that I have no doubt," she said dryly. "The part I don't get is why he's attracted to me in the first place. Ken, I'm almost old enough to be the man's mother, for God's sake!"

Kendra sat back in her chair and regarded her friend. "You're forgetting one thing."

"What's that?"

"You're not his mother."

Toinette sighed. "You make it sound so simple."

"It is simple. I don't understand your conflict here. If the two of you—"

"The conflict," Toinette interrupted, "is that I think I'd feel guilty as hell if we did something."

"Guilty? Guilty of what?"

Toinette slumped back in her chair. She said slowly, "I feel like, like I'm taking away from the market a man who should be with Judi or

Angie. They're your age. They are both young, attractive, stable women successful in what they do. And they're both out there wondering if all the men in the world are married, gay, in jail, or soon to be in jail like that no-good Victor that Judi sees from time to time. As their mother I sit and listen to them complain about not being able to find a good man. I commiserate with them. I give them ideas about where to find single, intelligent partners, and then what do I up and do? Hog the best one for myself."

Kendra's mouth dropped open. "You are really tripping."

Toinette leaned forward and sighed again. She ran her fingers against the condensation on the water glass, then looked at her friend. "Robinson makes me feel young and sexy and beautiful. My body picks up and responds to those feelings. My head won't let go of the other stuff."

Kendra took her friend's hand. "Nettie. You *are* young and sexy and beautiful. I can see it. Rob Mayview sees it. You need to allow yourself to see that. Get over the age thing. It's only an issue if you make it one. Judi and Angie aren't going to begrudge you finding a person who makes you happy. How many times have you told me they're always telling you to go out more, to date and have fun? You're sitting there talking as though if Robinson weren't interested in you, he'd automatically be interested in one of them. That's not true, and you know it. It sounds like he's attracted to the woman who is Toinette, and that means all of you."

"God, did you talk to him before you came over here? That sounds like what he told me."

"Then why aren't you listening to both of us?"

Toinette was saved from answering by the arrival of the waiter with their food.

"Thank you, darling," Toinette told him.

"Can I get you ladies anything else?"

"I think we're straight for now," Toinette answered, smiling. "Long day for you?"

"I'm just getting started. But if everyone is as nice as you, the day will breeze by."

Toinette smiled and laughed. "You're a darling."

The waiter left them to their meal. Toinette sipped some of her lemon water, then picked up a fork to start on her Caesar salad.

"You don't even realize it, do you?" Kendra asked.

"Realize what?"

"You exude sex appeal like the sun sends out warmth. Good grief, Nettie. If you turned it on like that with Robinson, no wonder the man is head over heels."

"What are you talking about? And, for the record, Robinson Mayview isn't head over heels about anything. This is a lust thing, some sort of deviated sexuality. Maybe he's always preferred elderly women."

"Elderly? Have you been taking some bad medication or something lately?"

Toinette winked. "I just said that to get your goat." She popped lettuce in her mouth and chuckled at Kendra's expression.

Kendra shook her head and started in on her chicken salad. Then, after a few moments: "What I was talking about is your flirting."

"I don't flirt. Well, not really."

"Uh-huh. Your 'not really' is enough to send a man in search of a cold shower. Like that waiter. The poor guy is probably in the kitchen patting himself down with chilled towels. Most likely you just looked at Robinson Mayview and brought the man to his knees."

Toinette laughed out loud. "Girl, you're the one who's tripping now."

Kendra grinned. "Seriously, Nettie. I think you're worrying about issues that don't need to be worried over. You are a grown woman with a woman's needs and desires. Your children are adults, and if they can't deal with that, then it's their loss, not yours."

Toinette shook her head. "When did you get so wise?"

"I've been hanging around a sister named Toinette Blue. Maybe you know her. Tall, gorgeous woman. She's somewhat of a flirt, but that's why the men are like kittens at her feet."

Amused, Toinette shook her head. The two women ate lunch in silence for several minutes.

"He came over to the house for dinner Friday night. Then on Saturday we went to the mayor's reception."

"When are you going to see him again?"

"I don't know. The time before this past weekend, he took me to a play called *Lovin' a Younger Man* and then he didn't call for a week."

Kendra put her fork down and stared at Toinette. "Nettie, the man took you to a play called *Lovin' a Younger Man* and you doubt his sincerity about wanting to get to know you better?"

"I don't doubt his sincerity. I question his motives."

"Motives? What about mutual attraction? Things in common? You two have things in common, right?"

Toinette simply nodded.

"Why are you viewing this as a crime? Motives are for crimes. There's nothing criminal about attraction between a man and a woman. Granted, Nettie, if the man was thirty years younger than you, I'd be worried. *That* would be criminal. But there's not enough age difference between the two of you to show, let alone worry about. You know what they say. You're as young as you feel."

"Well, sometimes I feel like I'm about eighty-two."

"That's because you work too hard. You worry about your kids too much. Not just your own kids, but every one of the folks who walks through the Quad-A office door you take on as a personal project. You don't take time out for you. When Malcolm and I were just getting to know each other, you were the person who told me to live with my heart, not my head. You were the person who told me that life goes on, that I was letting things from the past inhibit my today and my tomorrow. I think you need to take your own advice."

"I really hate it when you're right."

Kendra smiled but didn't answer.

"Well, don't just sit there. Tell me what to do!"

Kendra looked puzzled. "What do you mean tell you what to do?"

"What happens next? What am I supposed to do now?"

"Are you sure you're the same woman who had candid and frank talks about sex and relationships with your children? Judi once told me about your no-nonsense, straight-up chats."

"I'm not talking about sex here. I mean, what happens next? Do I call him? Do I wait for him to call me?"

"I don't know. Why don't you ask him out on a date?"

Toinette looked surprised and then intrigued. "You know, that wouldn't be a bad idea. Maybe something nonthreatening."

"Malcolm took me to play miniature golf one night."

"Maybe Jazz in the Park," Toinette mused. "That series of outdoor concerts is still going on."

"That sounds rather romantic. You could pack a picnic basket for two."

Toinette's face creased into a sudden and unmistakable sensual smile.

"Uh, Nettie, it's a public park. You need to keep that stuff in the bedroom."

"I was just thinking back to when we did have a picnic in the park."

"Picnic in the park? When were all these dates with this man going on? Where was I?"

Toinette waved her hand. "Oh, you and Malcolm were in the middle of some great crisis. I called Rob thinking maybe he might have an idea of how to get Malcolm back on the right track."

"I don't believe this."

"We met at a park to talk, and he brought a basket of food and chocolate chip cookies. He turned it into something like a date."

"Well, if you keep smiling like that, I'm going to believe that more than just talk was going on."

"No, we just talked." Then, after a pause, "And flirted a little."

"You're a mess," Kendra said, laughing. "And a flirt. So, are you going to ask him out on a date to the outdoor jazz series?"

"No. You're right. Jazz is too romantic. Sharing a blanket and listening to mellow music as the sun goes down would send the wrong message. I'm going to ask the man out, all right. And I know just the place to go."

* * *

Across town a business transaction was being made.

"I have a long stretch coming up. Are you sure this is going to be enough?"

"Look, babe. I told you I will never, ever let you down. Besides, if you need more, you know where to find me. You got my pager number, right?"

The woman nodded.

"Then we're square. You need me anytime, 24-7, you just page me and I'll get you what you need."

"Is there anything else you need right now?" she asked, seductively leaning into him.

"Well, now that you mention it."

Two days later Toinette called Robinson.

"I've been thinking about what you said last weekend," she told him. "And I've come to a conclusion."

"That conclusion being?"

"I should ask you out on a date."

"So are you going to act on this conclusion you've come to or are you just telling me about it to make me suffer?"

Toinette smiled easily. That was one of the things she liked about Rob. He took the directly subtle approach. She didn't view that as a misnomer, but as one of the unique things about Robinson Mayview that made her willing to step out on the very limb by which she could just as easily hang herself.

"Would you like to go out on a date with me?"

"I'd love to, Toinette. And thank you for not letting me suffer too long. Where are you taking me?"

"Someplace I haven't been in a long time."

"Well, that sounds intriguing. Tell me more."

"You don't have to wear a lot of clothes."

"Can you hold on for a sec? I think I need to turn the air conditioning on in here."

Toinette laughed. "You have a one-track mind."

"No. I'm just a man who knows what he wants out of life. I go after what I want."

"Careful, now. They tell me that skittish mares are the toughest to train."

"Warning heeded. Now where are you taking me?" he asked.

"When was the last time you rode a roller coaster?"

"Probably about ten years ago. Why?"

"Maybe you're overdue for a few wild dips and turns. Remember the sensation of slowly climbing the roller coaster mountain, then joyfully plunging over the edge in a wild frenzy that just made you scream?"

"I definitely need to check the AC," he replied quickly.

Toinette laughed delightedly. "Meet me at my house about ten Saturday morning. Dress casually."

"And how will you be dressed?"

"Oh, I'll be in something . . . comfortable."

"Ah, Toinette. You do know how to make a man suffer."

"See you Saturday?"

"I won't be late."

Toinette hung up the phone and dropped her head into her hands. "Oh, my God. I don't believe I just did that."

Saturday came faster than Toinette would have believed. Clothes were strewn all over her bed and spilling out of the drawers as she searched for just the right outfit to wear. She discarded jeans and split skirts and palazzo pants sets. Frowning at her reflection in a green-and-white sundress, she whipped the garment over her head, dropped it on the floor, and stood in bra and panties, in the middle of the mess.

"Shorts and sandals make you look like you're trying to look young," she complained aloud. "The sundress looks like something Aunt Matilda's grandbaby's niece wouldn't wear." Toinette wanted something that would serve a dual purpose: be fun and comfortable while being sleek and sexy.

She went back to the overflowing closet for another critical stare-down. A Kente cloth scarf caught her eye. Thoughtful, she pulled the scarf from the hook where it lay and ran the cloth through her hands.

She left the closet and went to the cheval mirror in her bedroom. She stood before the mirror for several minutes trying out variations with the scarf, tying it first around her head, then around her neck. She draped the scarf over one shoulder. Then she tied it in an elaborate knot at her bare waist.

"That'll work," she said, coming to a decision. She untied the scarf, tossed it on the dresser, then kicked through the clothes on the floor and back to the closet. Reaching back to a far rack, she pulled out a golden-colored cotton top. From another hanger she selected a pair of gold stirrup pants. From a shoe rack, she pulled out flats, then went to a giant hook on the closet door and selected a small square shoulder bag that could be draped across her body. She dumped the armful of clothes on a chaise longue in her bedroom, then went about the process of straightening up the room and hanging up clothes.

When she finished, she took a shower, powdered and perfumed herself, then walked to her lingerie drawer. Without pause she pulled out a very skimpy, champagne-colored teddy and slipped into the garment.

"Funny how you knew exactly what to wear underneath it all," she observed to herself.

By the time Robinson rang her doorbell at nine-fifty-five, Toinette was dressed. Her one concession to the nature of their date was to forgo long, dangling earrings in favor of dainty gold ones of Nefertiti's profile.

"Good morning," Robinson said when Toinette opened the door.

This time, it was Toinette who gawked. Robinson was, indeed, dressed casually. The cuffed khaki shorts and the tan linen shirt made him look both elegantly cool and ready for fun. A thin gold bracelet dangled from the wrist where he wore his watch. Toinette recognized his flat pecan brown sandals as one of the latest styles she'd seen in a men's fashion magazine. She tried not to dwell too much on the way the clothes fit the man.

"Like what you see?" he mischievously asked.

Remembering their similar conversation standing in her doorway just a week ago, Toinette had her answer ready. "Infinitely."

Robinson broke into a leisurely smile. "May I kiss you hello?"

"Not if it's the same way you kissed me good-night last weekend."

Robinson took one step forward and curled an arm around Toinette's slim waist. He touched one of her earrings. "You're just as beautiful as the ancient queens of Africa."

The gentle touch of his hand sent a warming shiver through Toinette, and she arched into his embrace. She raised her head even as he lowered his. With tantalizing persuasion his lips captured hers, demanding a response. Toinette wrapped her arms around his neck and kissed him back, reveling in the freedom she gave herself to indulge in and enjoy this passion.

Eventually, Robinson released her and started to take a step back, but Toinette stayed him. "Let's pretend this date is over so you can kiss me good-night."

"Be careful what you ask for, Toinette. You just might get it."

That's what I think I'm hoping for, she thought to herself as she locked the door, then followed him to the Jeep parked in front of her house.

CHAPTER 8

"Since I'm driving, do I now get to find out where we're going?"

"To Paramount's Kings Dominion to ride the roller coasters."

"That's in Virginia"

"It doesn't take long to get there from here," Toinette said while strapping herself into the Jeep, Robinson's second car.

He pulled out and headed toward the interstate. "Do they have a tunnel of love?"

Toinette laughed, then turned toward him. "I came to a few more conclusions while I was thinking about last weekend."

Robinson remained silent as he negotiated the Saturday-morning traffic.

"I'm not sure where you're headed, where we're headed, but I'd like to spend more time with you," she confessed.

"What made you have a change of heart?" he asked.

"Seeing you in shorts did it for me."

Robinson chuckled, accepting the answer for what it was. "Then I'll have to remember to always wear shorts around you. So, tell me about your kids."

"Well," she began, "my oldest, Russell, is a real estate agent. Russell is thirty. He's named for his daddy, Russell Woodrow. But he was always Russell and my husband was known as Woody."

"What happened to him?" Robinson asked cautiously.

"To Woody? He just left one day. I think the notion of being responsible for another mouth to feed was more than he could bear. We got married real young. I was sixteen. He was seventeen. But we were in love, so we got married. I dropped out of school after I got pregnant with Russell. Then, before we knew it, Leah was born the next year. Two years later there was Judi. Woody was working at a plant and had been promoted to supervisor, so we were doing just fine. Angela and my baby boy were surprises. I was five months pregnant when Woody said he was going out for some cigarettes. He never came back."

"When did you finally get a divorce? And did Woody send child support?"

"Divorce? Robinson, I might have newfangled ideas about open communication, but I believe that when God puts a man and a woman together they are together until death parts them. Woody left us. I always sort of figured he'd come back when he was ready."

"And when he didn't?" Robinson turned to look at her before again giving his attention to the road and the traffic. "It's been more than twenty years."

Toinette shrugged. "As for child support, no. That wasn't something I even thought about way back then. The bank eventually foreclosed on the house, and we moved into public housing. You know, when I think back to those years, I wonder how I ever got through it all. But it's true what they say: 'Whatever doesn't kill you makes you stronger.'

"My youngest is in college. The other ones all work outside the home, except for Leah. She's a housewife with two little ones. I'd show you the pictures of my grandkids," she said, holding up the tiny handbag, "except I have this little 'be cute' purse instead of my big bag. Remind me to show you when we get back."

"Okay."

"What about you? Do you have sisters and brothers? Children?" she asked.

"No children. In this day and age, I suppose that's something of an anomaly. Maybe it's just the way I grew up and was raised. My father was the head of the household, and he took care of the family, which was me, my mother, and my sister C.J. In my book, if a man has kids he's supposed to be responsible for them. So many young brothers today are just into the sex. They don't think about the life that can be created by the passion that burns hot one minute and cold the next."

She nodded in agreement. "Are you and your sister close?"

"So-so. Our jobs keep us both pretty tied up. She's a newspaper reporter and stays busy chasing stories. We're four years apart, so growing up I got to play the big brother and protector role, but she's pretty tough. She's good at what she does, too."

Toinette remained silent for a moment, curious but not sure if she should ask the question that had been on her mind these last few days.

But when she thought about it, she had nothing to lose and information to gain by posing the question.

"Robinson?"

He turned to look at her, then smiled. "Hmm?"

"Have you always dated older women?"

Robinson took one of her hands, brought it to his mouth, and pressed a kiss there. The simple touch made Toinette tingle from head to toe. She turned her hand and softly caressed his cheek.

"I've always dated beautiful women. Beauty for me is not the outside package, the height, the weight, the age, the race, or hair color. All of those things are accidents. Beauty comes from within. The sparkle in a woman's eyes, the way she treats herself and the people around her, the way she embraces life and living are the things I find important, the things I find beautiful. Does that answer your question?"

Toinette nodded. When she pulled her hand away, Robinson held on, entwining her fingers with his and resting their joined hands on his right thigh.

He'd answered the question in a way Toinette had not anticipated. Instead of a straight yes or no, he'd told her so much more, so much more that made her begin to question why she'd ever doubted him.

Robinson Mayview was all the things she wanted in a man. But, she was forced to admit, she had not given much thought to admirable qualities in a boyfriend or lover simply because she'd never viewed herself as available to have one. But Robinson was everything she wanted and everything she didn't know she was missing until he walked into her life.

He was articulate and gorgeous. He had a way of arching his left brow in a way that made her wonder if it was a deliberate or unconscious action. Whichever the case, it made him look sexier than ever. She could feel the firmness of his thigh beneath the shorts. Her gaze wandered down his bare legs, and she wondered what his legs would feel like next to her smooth ones.

Robinson was gentle but passionate. Just the thought of the action in her foyer the previous week made Toinette hot and achy with unfulfilled need. Lord have mercy, just looking at the man made her want to tell him to take the nearest interstate exit and find a motel. It had been a long, long time since she'd allowed herself the pleasure of a man's touch. Lunches and the occasional cocktail party with Quad-A employees didn't make her feel this way, hot and needy.

Robinson had told her on several different occasions and in several different ways that he was patient, very much so. If the action at her house was any indication, Robinson was a man with a slow hand.

"Lord have mercy." Toinette fanned herself with her free hand.

"You okay?"

"Um-hmm," she managed to him. Mmm, mmm, mmm.

They spent the remainder of the drive talking about roller coasters and water rides and favorite junk food to eat at theme parks. Once there, Robinson found a place to park the Jeep, and together they queued up for entrance to the park. When they got to the ticket booth, Toinette opened her handbag.

"Two adults, please," she told the cashier.

Robinson, standing close to her, took the money Toinette held out and put it back in the purse. He opened his own billfold and handed the cashier their entrance fee.

"But this is my date. I asked you out," Toinette protested.

He lifted her chin and kissed her quickly and firmly on the mouth. "But I'm an old-fashioned kind of guy."

Reeling from the taste and touch and smell of him, and wanting more, Toinette simply snapped the clasp on the bag and followed Robinson into the park.

Their first stop was a roller coaster. They waited in line for almost forty minutes, laughing and chatting with the people near them. When they arrived at the turnstile, Toinette turned to Robinson.

"Front-row seat?" The twinkle in her eye was a direct and mischievous challenge.

"Like to live dangerously, huh?" Robinson chuckled as he led her to the roller coaster's first box. "I'm game if you are."

Robinson handed Toinette into the seat, then followed her. He strapped himself into the contraption, then checked to see if Toinette was secure in her seat. The train began to pull out of the station.

"Uh, Rob? I think I want off."

Rob chuckled as the train slowly began its ascent, up and up, higher and higher.

"Rob. Oh, my God. We're going to die. What is this made of? Is this thing sturdy? Oh, my God. We're gonna die."

"Close your eyes and scream," he replied calmly.

"I don't want to close my eyes. If I'm going to plummet to my death, I want to see it."

"Don't look now, but here we go-o-o!!" Robinson yelled.

Toinette threw her hands up in the air and screamed as they went over the top. At the bottom of the hill, they whipped around a corner and she snatched her hands down and grabbed Robinson's. Before she could catch her breath, the coaster whipped around another bend and sent them spiraling through a tunnel, then up another steep incline only to be plummeted through the process again. In a matter of minutes, the thrill ride had ended and the train pulled into the station.

Breathless and laughing, Toinette followed Robinson out of the car. "Let's do it again!"

"I thought you said you were going to die?"

"I did. My life flashed before my eyes on that last spin. It was great."

They stood in line again and rode the same roller coaster. Then like two children discovering Christmas morning for the first time, they frolicked through the park, riding gentle as well as adventurous rides. Toinette didn't miss the fact that Rob took advantage of every opportunity to touch her, but without coming on incredibly strong. She responded to his affection like a flower blooming in the spring sunshine, at first slowly but then with more assurance.

After a while of walking through the park, Toinette suggested junk food.

"I'll treat you to some cotton candy," she told him as they walked hand-in-hand to one of the many food stands.

"Do I get to lick the sticky parts off your hands and mouth?"

Toinette regarded him with a sly look and a quick kiss. "Only if you're very, very good," she whispered in his ear.

"You really know how to torture a man, don't you?"

Something in his tone alarmed her. She'd just been teasing. Was he serious? Had she taken the flirting a step too far? She felt at a loss as to how to properly play the game. "Rob, I didn't mean to . . . I mean I'm sorry if you . . ."

Robinson pulled her to him, gently took her chin in his palm, and lowered his mouth to hers. The kiss was devastatingly sensual, and she was powerless to resist. Toinette reveled in it, oblivious to the fact that they were in a public place. This was too good, felt too right for any doubts or fears. Robinson covered every part of her mouth, then slowly, reluctantly released her. He circled an arm around her waist, and she rested her head on his shoulder.

"You make me feel so, so wanted," she said softly.

"I do want you, Toinette. But I'm not going to rush you into anything. If we have a physical relationship, we will. If we don't, we won't. Right now, I'm content holding you . . . and riding the crazy rides out here."

Toinette smiled. "You're a very special man, Robinson Mayview. If I'm not careful, I'll find myself falling for you."

"Don't be careful," he said staring in her eyes. "I'm here for the long haul."

They moved forward to get the cotton candy.

"How many, folks?" the vendor asked.

"One please," Toinette answered. Then, with eyes only for Robinson, "We'll share."

The sensuous smile that curved Robinson's lips made Toinette wonder what he was thinking.

With the spool of pink cotton candy in hand, they strolled to a park bench to eat the sugary confection. They watched passersby as they sat.

Toinette pulled a bit of fluff from the paper cone and fed it to

Robinson. He licked her fingers and made her giggle and blush. “Robinson!”

“Hmmm?”

“What are you doing?” she said, giggling.

“Making sure I don’t miss any. Wouldn’t want to waste good food, now would we?”

Toinette reclaimed her fingers for a moment, then pulled off some more candy, took a bite, and fed the rest to him. “No, that would be just terrible.”

“Oh, look. I think you missed a bit.” Robinson leaned forward to steal a kiss.

“Mom? Is that you?”

CHAPTER 9

Toinette jumped up and away from Robinson, the cotton candy and sensuous play instantly forgotten. Aghast, she stared at the young man and woman standing before her.

"Oh, my God," she replied.

"Mom. I thought that was you," Aaron Blue said. "And Mr. Mayview! Wow. We sure didn't expect to run into you two today."

"You know him?" Toinette asked her son.

"Toinette's your mother?" Robinson asked Aaron.

"Hi, Mrs. Blue," Aaron's girlfriend cheerily greeted Toinette.

"Oh, my God," was all Toinette could manage.

Aaron took control of the cross introductions. "Mom, you know Sherri already. Mr. Mayview, this is my girlfriend, Sherri Fields. I told you about her the night we met. She's the vocalist for Serenity. Sherri, this is Mr. Robinson Mayview. He's a lawyer and partner at Mayview, Jackson, Hightower."

Robinson shook Aaron's hand first and then Sherri's. "I never did get your last name the night we had coffee." And then, turning to Toinette, Robinson filled in the information gaps.

Toinette prayed that Aaron wouldn't make a scene. So far, her youngest son only seemed surprised to find her at an amusement park with someone he knew. Aaron hadn't expressed any outward dismay at the notion of his mother dating a younger man, a much younger man.

"We were going to drive home after leaving the park. But since you guys are here, maybe I'll just come home another weekend. Will that be okay, Mom?" Aaron looked at his mother for confirmation and then glanced at Robinson.

"Oh, that's right," Toinette answered. "You and Sherri were going to stop by this weekend. I'd forgotten. Oh, Lord! Angie is probably at the house now. She was gonna come over this weekend, too."

"Mom, don't go dashing home just to let Ba' Sis in. If she shows up, and you know how erratic her schedule is, she'll realize you aren't home and will go somewhere else." Then, turning to Robinson, Aaron asked, "How long have you guys been here today?"

"A few hours. We'd stopped for a quick snack but," he said, looking at the cotton candy Toinette had dropped on the ground in her haste to get away from him, "looks like we'll have to get some more."

Robinson closely watched Toinette. If she recovered from the shock of having her son see her kissing a man on a park bench, maybe he actually had a chance with her. Of all the times for one of her kids to show up. He'd been making progress. But Aaron's appearance could prove a major setback.

"I . . ." Toinette started. "We were just . . ." She sighed. "Sherri, Robinson, will you excuse us for a moment?" Toinette took Aaron's hand and led him a few steps out of earshot from Robinson and Sherri.

"Aaron, I, well . . ." Toinette took a deep breath. "Robinson and I have been sort of seeing each other for a few weeks now. He's younger than I am, but I really enjoy his company. He makes me happy. He makes me smile. And we have fun together."

"Mom, stop stressing yourself. I think it's cool. I've been telling you that you need to go out sometime and stop letting those Quad-A people suck up all your time. Mr. Mayview is all right. We talked for a long time about law. I'd even been meaning to tell you about his firm. I thought they might make a good Quad-A referral for you."

Aaron stopped, cocked his head like his mother, and peered closely at her. A small smile quirked his mouth. "Ah, man. I'm sorry, Mom. I didn't mean to disturb you guys last weekend when I called."

Toinette blushed. "You didn't disturb anything. He hadn't even gotten to the house yet." Then, realizing what her comment implied, she said quickly, "I mean, we weren't doing anything."

"Mom, calm down." Aaron hugged Toinette. "You couldn't have found a better guy. Mr. Mayview is really sharp." He glanced over Toinette's shoulder. "Drives a bumpin' BMW. And he's not bad-looking either. I better go get Sherri before she starts getting ideas."

"Aaron, this is really okay with you?"

Aaron kissed Toinette on the cheek. "You've always told us you just wanted us to be happy. I want the same thing for you. You deserve someone who makes you happy, someone who makes you smile. And I swear to God, Mom, I don't think I've ever seen you blush before. That's really cool."

Toinette blushed again and then laughed out loud. She pulled Aaron to her for a hug. "You're really cool, kid."

Together they walked back to the bench where Robinson and Sherri waited.

"We got some cotton candy," Sherri announced, holding up two cones.

"We just got here," Aaron said. "So we're gonna go walk around a bit, then ride some rides."

"It was a pleasure seeing you, Mrs. Blue, and meeting you, Mr. Mayview," Sherri said.

Aaron kissed his mother again, then winked at her, saying very softly, "Don't forget to be safe, Mom." He shook Robinson's hand. "It was nice seeing you again, sir."

"Call me Robinson, or Rob."

Aaron nodded. "See you 'round." He took Sherri's hand, and the young couple headed in the direction of the roller coasters.

Toinette collapsed onto the bench. "Oh, my God."

Robinson sat down beside her. "Toinette, I think your son just illustrated that there's absolutely nothing wrong with us being together."

Toinette shook her head. "My son just illustrated that what goes around comes around."

"What do you mean?"

"Do you know what he whispered to me as he was leaving?"

"What?"

" 'Don't forget to be safe.' Since they were old enough to know why boys and girls were made differently, I've preached safe and responsible sex to my kids. And now one of them is telling *me* that. I don't believe this."

Robinson smiled to himself but caught the grin before it reached his mouth. Aaron was on his side! One down, four to go. "Aaron has a good head on his shoulders. He can recognize a good thing for you when he sees it."

Toinette, momentarily distracted from her embarrassment, laughed out loud. "And you, I suppose, are what's good for me?"

"One of these nights you'll let me show you how good."

Toinette met the unfailing intensity and desire in his gaze. She managed a tremulous smile. "I'm starting to think that needs to be soon."

With that, she got up and held her hand out to Robinson. "Let's go find the water rides."

They spent the rest of the day at the park riding the amusements. They ate lunch at a pavilion and took a photo together. Each got a print as a memento. As night fell and the park lit up with bright multicolored lights, Robinson won a big red-and-white teddy bear at the Midway and presented it to Toinette.

"I'm gonna call him Bandit," Toinette told him as she looked first at the stuffed toy, then at the man.

"Why Bandit?"

Toinette hugged the bear to her bosom. "Because he's likely to steal my heart just like you're doing."

Robinson lifted her chin, bent down, and kissed her. The mere touch of his hand sent another warming shiver through her. She put the bear down and stepped closer into Robinson's embrace.

"You make me feel very special."

"That's because you are special. And you're beautiful. If you're not careful, I will make like a bandit and steal your heart. But it won't be a one-way affair. You already have mine, Toinette."

"Rob, I—"

"Shhh." He silenced her with a kiss. "You don't have to respond or explain. I just wanted you to know."

By unspoken agreement, they headed toward the parking lot.

Less than twenty feet away, Aaron and Sherri stood watching. "That brother has it going on," Sherri commented. "I think I'm jealous of your mom. Even from here you can tell they are in love with each other. That's really nice."

Aaron nodded and smiled as he observed the retreating couple walking arm in arm, a teddy bear dangling from his mother's hand.

"Why haven't you ever kissed me the romantic way that Mr. Mayview kissed your mother?"

"You mean like this?" Aaron tipped Sherri's chin up and teased her mouth until she whimpered in frustration. Then his lips settled over hers, and she wrapped her arms around his neck.

A little while later they came up for air. "If Mr. Mayview kisses your mother like that, I can see why she looks so radiant and happy."

Robinson and Toinette drove back to the city in companionable silence. At one point, Toinette drifted to sleep with Bandit clutched to her. Robinson's attention was split between watching the road and watching Toinette. A soft smile played at her mouth, and he wondered if she dreamt of him.

He hadn't meant to reveal his true feelings to her for fear that she would balk. But it had come out. He didn't regret the revelation, since he hadn't yet told her that he was head over heels in love with her and would gladly spend the rest of his natural days just looking at her. He got the feeling that she was starting to get the picture, though.

The scene with her son could have been awkward, but they'd all managed to come out of it with dignity intact. Robinson wondered how much, if any, trouble Toinette's other children would have with their relationship. Aaron hadn't proved a problem. With luck, the other four would be just as levelheaded as the young college student. As far as Robinson was concerned, age wasn't an issue, even though Toinette seemed to think it was. Good thing she finally seemed to be getting over it.

Robinson glanced at her again. Toinette's skin was smooth and wrinkle-free. Her arched eyebrows shadowed the brown eyes he couldn't see. He longed to taste her lips again. She was tall and graceful, elegant and self-assured. Except for the gray hair that added character to her classic features, Robinson thought she didn't look a day over thirty-five. It was difficult to believe that the dazzling woman he'd come to love was not only the mother of five grown children but a grandmother to boot. You couldn't tell it by looking at her.

Toinette stirred, and Robinson put his attention back on the road.

"Hey," she murmured sleepily.

"Hey to you, too."

"We there yet?"

"Almost. Another ten minutes."

Toinette rubbed her eyes and sat up. "Rob, thank you for today. I had a ball."

"It was your idea, remember?"

"Oh, yeah. I'm brilliant, aren't I?"

Robinson chuckled. "Brilliant and beautiful."

"Rob? What you said back at the park . . ."

He didn't pretend to misunderstand. He lifted her hand from Bandit and brought it to his mouth for a kiss. "I meant it, Toinette. You mean a lot to me, more than you know. I'm willing to take this at any pace you want. Just please don't tell me to get out of your life. I'm in too deep."

"I think I want to open the door a little wider."

Robinson looked at her, then negotiated the interstate exit that would lead to her house. "No pressure, Toinette."

"I'm not feeling any pressure. I'm feeling . . . Well, to be honest, I'm feeling very tuned in right now. Tuned in to the way you make me feel, tuned in to the way it might be between us."

"You're going to make me have an accident."

"Hmm. What kind?"

Robinson chuckled. "I meant a car accident."

"Oh."

"Don't sound so disappointed. The other kind probably isn't too far removed from the realm of possibility."

Toinette digested that bit of information. "Robinson, it's been a long time for me."

"For me, too."

Toinette got the distinct feeling that her idea of a long time without sex was a lot different from Robinson's, but she didn't pursue the line of thought or conversation.

Robinson pulled the Jeep into the space in front of Toinette's house, and he went around the car to help her out. He watched her lithe body stretch for her items in the back seat, and he prayed for strength. He wanted this woman, had been wanting her for some time now. He wasn't sure how much longer he would be able to hold out until he lost control. While his body registered impatience, his mind recognized the necessity not only for patience but perseverance. Passion could come and go. He wanted that and more from Toinette. She had all but acknowledged that she was ready and willing to take their relationship to a physical level.

"I think I have everything," she finally said.

They climbed the steps to Toinette's front porch. She reached in the mailbox and got the day's mail as Robinson opened the screen door.

"Well, Angela didn't come. She usually leaves a note on the door if she stops by and I'm not home."

Good, Robinson thought to himself. One less thing to distract you.

Toinette unlocked the door, and they walked into the dark house. She flipped a switch that bathed the foyer in light. Absently, she placed the mail and her small purse on the hall table.

Robinson put Bandit on top of the letters.

"Would you like some coffee? Maybe a glass of wine?"

"No, Toinette," Robinson said. "I want you."

CHAPTER 10

Toinette backed up. "Robinson, I—"

"I'm sorry," he quickly said. "I didn't mean to come on so strong. Just a few minutes ago I was telling you that we'll take this at your pace, and now here I am acting like a horny teenager. Forgive me?"

Toinette nodded hesitantly. "I'm the one who should apologize. I've probably been sending you all manner of mixed messages. This is all so new to me, and at the same time it isn't. Do you understand what I mean?"

"I think I do. Is the invitation for a glass of wine still open?"

"I'll go get a bottle of white and a couple of glasses. Meet me in the living room."

"Okay."

"Powder room is to your left if you need to go."

Robinson watched her walk to the kitchen; then he turned toward the living room. You idiot, he railed to himself. You get around the woman and all of a sudden you can't think straight. Get your act together, brother man, before she changes her mind completely or you scare her away for good.

He went to the front picture window and stared, unseeing, at the draperies. What a difference a few minutes could make. Less than half an hour ago, she was mellow and ready as they quietly talked in the Jeep. Now, she was skittish and uncertain again. Robinson ran his hands over his face in frustration. He was more frustrated with himself than anything else.

"I had a couple of bottles of Piesporter, 1979," Toinette said. She put a bottle, glasses, and corkscrew on the coffee table. Sitting on the edge of the sofa, she opened the bottle and poured two glasses.

"Are you going to join me or are you going to stare out that window all night long?"

Robinson turned with a smile, then caught his breath. She was so beautiful. He left the window and took a seat on the soft sofa cushions near Toinette. She'd taken off her shoes and sat with her back propped against a pillow in the corner of the couch. She had one leg tucked under the other with one arm resting on the sofa back, the other holding her glass.

He picked up his glass from the table, then sat back. "A toast."

Toinette smiled. "To what?"

"To good times, good friends, and fun."

Toinette nodded, then clinked glasses with him and took a sip of the slightly sweet white wine. "You're a paradox, Mayview."

"What do you mean?"

"I would have expected, oh, something else in a toast from you."

"Like what?"

"I don't know. Just something else." She drank from her glass and watched him. "What are you thinking?"

Robinson chuckled, then turned to her. "Do you want an honest answer or a comfortable one?"

Her eyebrows rose at that. "Sounds like a challenge. I'll choose honesty even though comfort is probably the safer course."

"You're sitting there looking soft and sexy. We've been up walking around all day and I was wondering if your feet hurt."

A smile ruffled her mouth. Toinette drank from her glass again, then uncurled her left leg and put both feet in his lap.

Robinson didn't need any additional encouragement. He drained half the wine from his glass, then put the delicate stemware on the coffee table. He settled himself more comfortably on the sofa and slowly caressed one foot from toe to ankle. He slipped the stirrups from her heels and began a soft kneading.

"Tell me how you decided to become a lawyer," she said.

"I didn't really think about it. My father was a lawyer. His father was a lawyer. People came to my grandfather for advice about their legal problems. He eventually studied for the bar, passed it, and became one of the first recognized Negro lawyers in the country. I never met him, but I've read his papers, studied his opinions. My father and Marshall Jackson opened the firm together. For a long time, it was just the two of them. I went to law school, came home, and joined their firm. Mr. Jackson started slowing down and eventually left active practice. He died quite a few years ago. Malcolm joined the firm about the time my dad decided he wanted to retire. Malc and I did undergrad together."

"Is your mother a lawyer?"

Robinson smiled. "No. My mother came out of Spelman in Atlanta. She taught school for a few years before she met my dad. She became a full-time wife and mother soon after they adopted me."

"You're adopted?"

Robinson nodded as he continued the slow ministration to Toinette's feet. She shifted her weight, getting more comfortable, and accidentally pressed a heel into the hardness he'd hoped to conceal from her.

Her gaze met his.

Robinson lifted her foot and lowered his head, his eyes never leaving hers. He ran one finger along the sole of her left foot and felt her tremble. His mouth rimmed the top of her toes, and Toinette involuntarily moaned.

"Are you frightened?" he asked softly.

She shook her head, then finished the wine left in her glass.

Robinson planted a kiss on her big toe, then leaned forward for the Piesporter bottle on the coffee table. He filled her glass and topped off his own.

He dipped a finger into his wineglass and proceeded to trace a moist trail along the sole of her other foot. He lowered his head, and his tongue followed the trail. Toinette cried out.

Robinson ran a hand along her leg even as his mouth further explored her toes. He nibbled and bit, and Toinette moaned.

"I never, um, never would have thought someone sucking my toes would be arousing."

Robinson lifted his head and looked at her. The slow smile transformed his face. "Are you aroused?"

"God, yes." It was a definite turn-on. She was on fire for him. Never in her wildest dreams would she have believed that a man could make her feel this way, achy and needy and wanting so much more.

He smiled again as his hands began a slow exploration up her legs. He leaned forward, her feet momentarily forgotten. He took the glass from her unsteady hand and placed it on the coffee table. Toinette watched him dip a finger into her glass. She held her breath, wondering where that finger would land.

He brought it to her mouth, where he traced the contours of her lips. Toinette licked up the sweet wine, then drew his finger into her mouth.

"You make me burn, Toinette Blue," Robinson said as he settled his body over hers, pressing her into the sofa cushions. "Do you feel what you do to me?"

Toinette slowly nodded even as she ran her tongue along the pad of his finger.

"I want you, Toinette. I can't lie about that. But I'll leave now. You just say the word."

Toinette took his finger from her mouth, wrapped her arm around him, and ran her fingers over the hair at his nape. "Stay."

Robinson's mouth came down on hers. Toinette gave herself up to feeling. She felt wrapped in a sensuous cocoon that enveloped her body and soul. In Robinson's arms she'd come home. His demanding lips caressed hers even as she felt his hand exploring other parts of her body.

"Let's go upstairs," she suggested.

Robinson again traced her mouth with his hand. Then he lifted himself off her and helped her up from the sofa. Toinette led him to the stairwell. Robinson locked the front door and turned the deadbolt lock. She held out her hand, and he followed her up the stairs to her bedroom.

Toinette turned a lamp on, then quickly glanced about her bedroom. Thank God she'd straightened up after the battle trying to decide what to wear that morning. The bedlinens were fresh because she changed them earlier in the day, not, she told herself, in anticipation of this, but because it was Saturday and Saturday was linen day. She went to her dresser and stared down at the perfume bottles lined up. Should she dab on more?

Robinson stood in the doorway watching Toinette. Now that they were actually in her bedroom, he could tell she was having second thoughts. She walked about the immaculate bedroom, straightening things that didn't need to be straightened, looking at everything except him. He followed her to the dresser where she stood alternately sneaking glances at him in the mirror and looking at the bottles.

He wrapped one arm about her waist and met her gaze in the mirror's reflection. "Which one?"

At her questioning look, he elaborated by taking her hand. "Which scent are you wearing here?" he said, trailing his other hand along her neck. Toinette leaned back into his shoulder and gave herself to him.

"And here?" he asked, raising her wrist and placing a soft kiss there. "And here?" he asked as he raised their joined hands and brought them to her breasts.

Toinette sucked in her breath as she watched him in the mirror place her hand and his over her breast. The dual pressure of their hands at her breast and his finger trailing delicious little curlicues along her neck made Toinette moan. She couldn't think, let alone answer a question. Robinson made her forget everything except the fire that burned in her for him.

Robinson leaned forward and pressed a kiss behind her ear. "Which one is it?"

Toinette tried to ignore the image of herself in Robinson's arms as she looked down at the dresser top. With her free hand, she found and pointed out the bottle of scent she'd worn that day. Robinson's smile was hungry, intense, male. Toinette couldn't stand it a moment longer. She turned in his arms, facing him, so she didn't have to withstand the extrasensuous torture of watching Robinson make love to her in the mirror.

He took her face in his hands and slanted his mouth across hers. The kiss was greedy and impatient, demanding and drugging. He finally stepped back half a space. Toinette raised dazed eyes to his. He smiled.

"You're very beautiful." He gave her a slow perusal from head to toe. On the trip back up her slender form, he paused at the Kente scarf tied at her waist. "This is pretty," he said, fingering the elaborate knot. "Is it a belt?"

Toinette shook her head, then reached behind her to untie the ends of the scarf. She untangled the knot and draped the long scarf around Robinson's neck.

"You're a very sensuous woman. Did you know that?"

Toinette shook her head.

"You are. Everything you do, from the way you walk—and that just drives me wild—to the way you talk and laugh. You get sensual pleasure from those things whether you know it or not. Why did you drape the scarf around me?"

"Because I like the texture of the material." Toinette's mouth curved in a quick teasing smile. "And I also briefly wished I had a fourposter bed."

"Ah, Toinette. You do know how to make me sweat."

Toinette ran a hand over his brow. "You don't seem too feverish to me."

He took her hand and ran it slowly, slowly down his body. "That's because the fever is centered in another place."

Toinette sucked in her breath, and her eyes dilated.

"Take off your top."

She obeyed the whispered command, then shimmied out of the stirrup pants.

"Sweet Jesus! Have you been wearing that all day?"

"I like lingerie."

Robinson fingered the lacy scalloped edge of the champagne-colored teddy. "There's not enough of it here to be called lingerie. I love it. Tell me something, Toinette. Each time we've gone out, have you been wearing little things like this under your clothes?"

She nodded. Robinson groaned. "Lord, give me strength."

"Why am I the only one who is half-dressed?"

Robinson looked at her and smiled. "I didn't want to rush or frighten you by tearing out of my clothes."

"Rob, I'm far from frightened, and if you go any slower, I'm going to implode."

"Well, we can't have that," he said, as he unbuckled the leather belt at his waist. He unzipped the khaki shorts and left the edges hanging open.

Before she realized she'd done it, Toinette's hands were at his shirt undoing the few buttons there. Robinson kicked out of his sandals, then took his watch off and placed it on the dresser top. He left the slim gold bracelet on his wrist.

He gently brushed her hands away and lifted the shirt over his head. Toinette's hands immediately found his bare skin. She rubbed her hands over his chest and toyed with one male nipple until it became a hard nub like her own.

Robinson's hands crept up her arms. He brought her hands together and kissed them. "It's not too late, Toinette."

"I want this, Robinson. I want you."

She led him to her bed, where she pulled the comforter and sheets back and got in. Robinson stood at the side of the big bed watching Toinette. His shorts hung open, and she could see the top of the black briefs he wore. There was no mistaking that he was aroused. All of a sudden Toinette wondered if she were doing the right thing. She wanted Robinson, of that she had no doubt. But making love was so, so personal. So intimate. He would see all of her. She knew she was falling in love, not just with the man but with the attention she was being given. But what about his feelings? He was in lust and in like, that she knew.

Robinson watched the fleeting expressions cross her face: desire and worry and uncertainty and finally this last look of confusion.

"This isn't something I take lightly, Robinson," she told him since he didn't seem inclined to join her in bed. "I haven't done this in a long, long time."

Robinson reached in his pocket, took something from it that he placed on the nightstand, then pulled his shorts down. Still wearing the black bikini briefs, he climbed into bed next to Toinette. He sat with his back to the headboard and pulled the sheet up to his waist.

"They tell me it's like riding a bike," he said. "Once you learn, you never forget."

Toinette laughed, then punched him with a small pillow. "You're incorrigible. But I'm serious, Robinson. I don't know if I'm ready for this."

Robinson pulled her into his arms. She snuggled against him, and his fingers began the slow exploration of her breasts. "Toinette, we'll take this at your pace. But I should tell you, your mouth is telling me one thing and your body is telling me another," he said, as one large hand surrounded her breast. He lowered his head and nibbled along her neck.

Toinette drew in her breath and willed her erratic pulse to slow down. "I, I can't control how my body responds to you, but I can control what I do with my body."

Robinson took her hand and covered it with his own. He pressed a gentle kiss into her palm. "Maybe I should leave now. If I don't, we might end up regretting what happens here tonight."

Toinette took his hand and, in like manner, kissed the palm. Her tongue gently licked his tender flesh, and she felt Robinson's body spasm. She studied his hands. They were large and well-formed; his nails were clipped short. She brought one finger to her mouth and kissed the tip before licking it from palm to fingertip.

"Toinette . . ."

"I don't want you to leave, Robinson. I just, well, I just want you to hold me for a little while. And I want you to be aware of the fact that my body isn't like the ones you're used to seeing. I'm not a young, nubile thing with legs that go on forever, perfect skin, and a tight rear end."

"Could've fooled me," he said, sliding down in the bed and bringing Toinette with him. "I think you need to get new mirrors here because what you see and what I see are two totally different things."

Robinson gently pulled the thin straps of the teddy off Toinette's shoulders. His hands caressed her body in a way that made her arch into him. His hands sought the snaps that held the bit of lingerie together between her legs, and she allowed him access.

"Robinson, I don't want you to be disappointed in me."

"That would never happen, Toinette. You're the most beautiful woman I've ever met. I've been anticipating this moment for months. It seems like years. You're trying to dissuade me, but I know what I want. You."

He took her hand and lightly brushed it over his straining erection. "That's my body's response to you, Toinette. Only to you. Do you feel what you do to me?"

Toinette nodded as her hand stroked him.

Robinson moaned, then he undid the snaps of her teddy and parted the material. He pulled the barely-there garment up and over her head and dropped it on the floor. He then took off his briefs. Robinson touched Toinette and knew she was ready for him. He kissed her slowly, then reached for the packet he'd taken from his pocket and drew the condom on. He shifted his body so that he lay atop her.

"Robinson?"

"Um-hmm?" he mumbled as his fingers began a slow dance and his mouth continued to feather kiss along her jaw, her neck, her shoulders.

"I haven't had sex since 1982."

That brought him up short. "What?"

"I haven't been with a man since 1982."

"Nine—nineteen-eighty-two?" Robinson couldn't keep the incredulousness out of his voice. "You haven't had sex for thirteen years?"

Toinette nodded. She wasn't sure how he would respond, but now she was afraid that telling him hadn't been the right thing to do.

"Jesus."

Toinette blinked back tears that had suddenly formed and made as if she would leave the bed. But Robinson wouldn't let her go.

Now he understood her hesitancy, the uncertainty that had been mixed with her obvious desire. Not only was she concerned about being older than he was, she hadn't had intercourse in more than a decade. Robinson couldn't even fathom the notion.

He wrapped his arms around her and held her in a gentle and loving embrace. He kissed her tenderly, lovingly, and with more than a bit of wonder. Then he flashed one of the smiles that had a tendency to make Toinette's heart flip.

He grinned down at her. "I don't know whether to be flattered or intimidated by that revelation."

Toinette grabbed a feather pillow and hit him over the head with it. "What arrogance. And now that you mention it, you should be both flattered *and* intimidated."

"Oh, really?"

"Yes, really."

"Well, let's just see how this makes you feel after those long years of abstinence."

Very slowly, very gently, he stoked the fire that had been burning between them. He eased into her, all the while whispering in her ear that she was beautiful, telling her with words and with action how much she meant to him.

Robinson loved her gently, reverently, all over her body until she begged for mercy and demanded an end to the exquisite torture. Toinette cried out her release, and Robinson soon followed.

Their sweat-drenched bodies clung to each other. She'd never, ever, felt so loved and cherished as she did in Robinson's arms. Toinette marveled at how buoyant she felt, how utterly rejuvenated.

"Lord have mercy, Robinson. Let's do that again."

CHAPTER 11

Less than three blocks from Toinette's house a woman was in trouble. "You know I'm good for the money, Victor. I promise you. I'll get it to you by next Friday. That's my payday."

"I'm tired of yo' weak promises, Miss Thing. You been telling me that same tired crap for three weeks now. You in my face always needin' something, but I don't ever see no cash."

"I just got a little behind. You know I'm good."

The man nodded. "Yeah. I gotta admit. You good at some things. That mouth of yours ought to be insured. You know that's the only reason I been letting you slide."

The woman nodded slowly, then for a brief moment, she looked like a child. She wondered how things had gotten to this state. She used to be proud and independent. Now, now she was . . . She didn't want to think about what she'd allowed herself to become. Slowly, she sank to her knees and unzipped his fly.

Robinson held Toinette through the night. They snuggled together and slept in her big bed. As morning sunshine brightened the room, they loved again. Afterward, they lay spent in each other's arms.

Toinette fingered the stubbly whiskers of Robinson's overnight beard. "I like the way this feels against my skin," she told him.

"Then you're a strange woman, Toinette Blue. You probably have whisker burns all over your body."

"I like all of you all over my body."

Robinson smiled, then pressed a quick kiss to her forehead. He sat up in bed, and undid the clasp on the thin gold bracelet at his wrist. Ducking under the sheet, he smoothed his hands down her legs.

"Wh-what are you doing?" Toinette managed to ask even as her body again prepared to welcome him.

"Leaving you something to remember me by," he responded. Robinson meandered his way to her ankle, where he attached the chain. He kissed her instep, then slowly made his way back up her body.

"Would you like to take a shower together?" Toinette suggested a bit breathlessly. "I've always wanted to do that."

Robinson untangled himself from the sheets and got out of bed. "No, I'm going to head home. There's some reading I need to do in preparation for a trial that starts this week."

A quick search near the foot of the bed yielded his briefs. With his back toward Toinette, he pulled on the underwear and then retrieved his shorts from the floor and stepped into the clothing.

From the bed Toinette watched him dress. Suddenly self-conscious, she tugged the sheet up and wrapped it around her body. Robinson sure seemed in a hurry to leave. She wondered if now, in the light of day, he regretted having made love to her.

"Robinson?"

"Hmm?" he said while stepping into his sandals.

She watched him quickly glance in the mirror and run a hand over his stubble. He wouldn't even look at her.

Toinette frowned. This was not how she expected the morning after to be. But, then again, she reasoned, she hadn't really thought in terms of a morning after. She'd never let herself get this involved with a man. Involvement, in Toinette's thinking, meant commitment. Commitment meant time for discovery, growth, and resolving issues from the past. Last night, she'd discovered that Robinson could do things to her and make her feel things that she'd long since forgotten even existed. In Rob's arms she'd felt loved and cherished and beautiful. Maybe that was his purpose for being in her life at this time. Maybe she didn't need a relationship so much as she needed a release from her self-imposed emotional exile.

"Did you want something, Toinette?"

She looked at him and noticed again that his gaze wouldn't meet hers. If that was the way it was, Toinette was mature enough to accept the night for what it had been—a pleasure. Robinson's tender words were just the love talk he'd needed to mumble to get her in bed. She didn't begrudge him that. She just wondered what would happen now.

"Thank you for last night," was all she told him.

"I had fun, too," he said. "I'll call you, okay?"

Toinette nodded.

"I'll let myself out," he said.

She watched him leave. At the bedroom door, he turned to her and smiled briefly. "See you later."

Toinette sat up in bed listening to his soft retreat. A few moments later she heard the front door open and close. Thoughtful, she slipped from under the sheets and went to the window to watch him leave. His Jeep was still at the curb but she didn't see Robinson. Then he was there, walking away from her, away from the glorious night they'd spent together.

Toinette made her way back to the bed and mentally reviewed the night. A slow smile spread across her face. Talk about good love. She stretched in the big bed then thought about the slim gold chain Robinson had attached to her ankle. Even though she would have preferred for him to stay a little while this morning, the man probably did have work to do. The drive to the amusement park had actually taken a while. He probably hadn't expected to be gone so long.

She'd been right about one thing though: Robinson Mayview was a man with a slow hand. Toinette smiled and hugged herself. Then she turned over and dozed off.

Robinson Mayview III was running scared. He let himself out of Toinette's house and stood on her front porch for a moment. He felt like he'd been hit with a steel wrecking ball. In his thirty-four years he had thought himself in love at least a time or two. Now he realized he hadn't even known the meaning of the word. Until now. Until Toinette.

She had been glorious in his arms, filling him with all the warmth and joy a man could ever wish for. If he never made love to her again, their night together would remain with him until he drew his last breath. Problem was, the only thing he wanted to do was stay in her arms. He knew he'd been abrupt with her as he dressed to leave. He just could not believe how much he still wanted her. More and more. Forever. If he'd taken one good look at her soft and sexy body, still radiating with the afterglow of their morning lovemaking, Robinson knew he would have crawled back in her bed and stayed. Forever.

Robinson took a deep breath of the morning air, then stretched. He glanced back at the door, wondering if he'd be welcome in her arms if he rang the doorbell and went back to her. Instead, he walked to his car and reluctantly drove away.

Up the street, Russell Blue stared after the man who'd left his mother's house. The frown on his face grew deeper as he watched the man leisurely stroll down his mother's walkway to the Jeep parked in front of the house.

Thankfully, his children, Carol and Jamal, had been arguing in the back of the van and didn't see the man. Russell had just turned the corner from a stop sign and was about to drive down the street when he saw the man walk out his mother's front door. He was able to make out part of the plates and jotted the license number down on the mobile clipboard attached to his dash.

Russell gunned the minivan down the street and came to a screeching halt in front of the house as the Jeep disappeared around the far corner.

"You two stay in here for a minute. I'll be right back."

"But we wanna see Grandma," Carol whined. "I want to show her my new dress."

"Yeah, Dad. You said if we got dressed early we could see Grandma before Sunday School."

"Just hold on for a minute. I'll be back." He locked the minivan doors and dashed up the walk and steps and banged on the front door. He didn't want to admit the fear he felt as visions of his mother's violated and bloody body filled his head. He'd tried time and again to get her to move to a safer neighborhood, but she'd insisted on staying near the people she served in the Quad-A program. Now some hoodlum had come and attacked her. At least he had a good description of the man, Russell thought. He ran through the information so he would be ready to give the attacker's description to the police: black man, tan shirt and shorts, short cropped hair, late twenties, early thirties. From the distance of a half-block, Russell couldn't be sure of the man's height, but he appeared tall and husky. Probably some drug addict that his mother had tried to help.

He banged on the door again and was about to smash his hand through the pane of glass next to the frame when the door creaked open.

"Russell Blue, what is your problem?" Toinette scolded. She'd taken a look through the peephole and had seen her oldest son's scowling face. Well, actually, now that she'd opened the door and taken a good look at him, Russell looked more like he was in a rage. "Why are you banging my door down so early in the morning?"

Russell quickly glanced over his mother. Other than looking sleepy, she was all in one piece. There was no blood. There were no visible wounds. She didn't seem any worse for wear. Russell grabbed her to him and hugged her. "Thank God you're all right."

Toinette hugged him back, then led him into the house. "Of course I'm all right, Russell. Why wouldn't I be?"

Russell Blue shut the front door and followed his mother into the living room, where she opened the blinds and drapes to let the morning sunshine into the room. Russell glanced about and his eyes landed on the wine bottle on the coffee table. Two half-full glasses of white wine were on the table. He looked up at his mother, a question on his lips. But before he could voice it, he noticed that the sofa cushions looked squashed in.

Russell took a critical look at his mother. She was wearing a long flannel muumuu. He recognized the floral-designed garment as the lounger his kids had given her the previous Christmas.

"What's up, Russ?" Toinette asked as she yawned and went to the sofa to plump up the cushions. She tried not to think about what had transpired there, but she couldn't help it. She felt herself flush as the memory of Robinson's mouth and hands almost overwhelmed her. She smiled secretly, then turned to her son.

"I, uh, brought the kids over. They wanted you to see their new outfits."

"Well, where are they?"

"In the van."

"You left Carol and Jamal in the van? Russell, what were you thinking?" Toinette went to the front door and left the house to get her grandchildren.

Russell picked up one of the wineglasses and stared at it. Lipstick rimmed a portion of the glass. He looked at the near-empty bottle of wine, then at the sofa. Thunder formed at his brow. She didn't greet him screaming and yelling for help. She seemed her regular old self, except for the hint of a smile at her mouth.

And he hadn't missed the gold chain his mother was wearing at her ankle. Toinette Blue was avant-garde in a lot of respects, but he'd never known his mother to wear ankle bracelets. She'd had male company last night. Male company that hadn't left until the early morning. Russell didn't realize he still held the wineglass until the delicate stem snapped in his hands. Liquid and glass fell to the carpeted floor.

The next day at work, Toinette called Kendra to get the information she needed about John and Etta MacAfree.

"Do you think they would be amiable toward the idea of providing the financial backing for a Quad-A Foundation?"

"I really can't say," Kendra told her. "Etta would probably like the idea. Selling John might be difficult. Then again, you know he's a changed man since he's gotten to know the twins. He's really opened up and isn't the overbearing monster he was back when he thought he could fight for custody of the girls."

"So what approach do you think would work? A phone call first and then a follow-up or a packet of information and the preliminary proposal?"

"I'd go the official route. Send the package first, then follow up with a call."

"That's what I was thinking, too. I sent the proposal off to Ben and Maggie Trammer. I'm going to call them today. Is there anything else you can recall about meeting them?"

"They were just a really fun couple. And they have a lot of money that they like to spread around to worthwhile causes."

Toinette smiled to herself. Thoughts of Robinson came unbidden when Kendra said "fun couple."

"Nettie? Are you still there?"

"Oh, sorry about that. What were you saying?"

"Um-hmm. I was saying that now that you got the Quad-A business out of the way, tell me about the real business. I'll just bet that's where you had wandered off to for a minute there. So, where did you take Mr. Mayview this weekend?"

"To an amusement park," Toinette replied. But he took me to paradise, she added to herself.

"Did you ride the roller coasters?"

"Every single one in the park. And, girl, you are not going to believe what happened."

"What?" Kendra asked eagerly.

"Aaron and Sherri were there and they saw me kissing Robinson."

"Oh, my God."

"That was my response, too."

"What happened?"

Toinette laughed. "Well, it wasn't actually as bad as I thought it might be. Aaron and Rob know each other. They met at a law club meeting on campus. Anyway, Aaron just seemed surprised and kind of amused to see us there."

"Did he say anything?"

Toinette smiled as she thought of her youngest child. "Yeah. He told me to have fun and be happy. Then he kissed me, and he and Sherri went on. We didn't see them the rest of the day."

"See?"

"See what?"

"See? I told you there was no big thing about you and Robinson dating each other."

"Then why did you first say 'Oh, my God!'?"

Kendra huffed. "Because your paranoia about all of this had me doubting my own good advice to you."

"Well, I'm not paranoid anymore. I've decided just to go with the flow."

"Oh? And what, may I ask, changed your mind?"

Toinette was still sorting through her feelings about Robinson. Their time together was still too new, too special to share right now. If she had launched herself into a meaningless affair, she meant to have a good time. If what she and Robinson had had was simply a one-night stand, the night had been one to cherish forever.

"Spending a little time with Rob made me change my mind," she finally answered Kendra.

"And is this flow you're just going to go with headed to a waterfall or a peaceful, babbling brook?"

"Girlfriend, as you well know, I'll take the more exciting ride any day. Bring on the whitewater rapids."

Kendra laughed. "You're a mess, Nettie. Look, I need to dash. I have a meeting in about five minutes. Do you want to get together for lunch this week?"

"How about Wednesday?" Toinette suggested.

"See you then at our place."

Toinette rang off and sat back in her chair. She twirled a pencil in her fingers for a few moments as she thought about Robinson. She spun her chair around and stretched out her legs. The multicolored high-heeled pumps were an exact match to the paisley suit she wore. Underneath her hose, at her ankle, glistened the gold chain that Robinson had given her. She wondered if there was some significance to it or if Robinson just made it a practice to give women jewelry. Whatever the case, she'd keep it on. For now.

A knock at her open office door drew Toinette's attention back to work. She looked up and invited the Quad-A aide in.

"Mrs. Blue, there's a young woman here to see you. She won't give her name. She just says that she heard about you and needs to talk to you."

Toinette put to the side the file folders piled in the middle of her desk. She smiled up at the aide as she pulled out a clean legal pad to write on. "Send her in."

Toinette made a practice of starting each new interview at her desk. If the situation warranted it or if the person seemed uncomfortable talking to someone behind a desk, Toinette would move the interview to the arrangement on the other side of the office. The sofa and chair were old but comfortable.

The aide showed a young girl into the office, then shut the door. Toinette got up and met the girl halfway to her desk. The young woman looked both frightened and sad.

Toinette offered a smile. "Hi there. My name's Toinette Blue. Dawn told me you had been asking for me."

The girl nodded hesitantly. She clutched a small handbag to her chest and her eyes darted about the room. She wore a pair of blue slacks that had seen better days, a stained shirt, and scuffed white pumps. On her shoulders was a backpack. Toinette noticed two incongruities: the girl's nails were clean and her hair was neatly pressed and combed.

"Would you like to sit down?" Toinette offered.

The girl nodded and moved to one of the chairs in front of Toinette's desk. Toinette sat in the other one and crossed her legs.

"What can I do for you?"

The girl looked around the office again and then took a quick glance at the door.

"There's no one else here," Toinette assured her. "It's just you and me. Whatever is said in here stays in here unless you want it differently. Okay?"

The girl nodded, then looked down at the purse in her lap.

"What's your name?" Toinette asked.

The girl jerked her head up as if she'd been slapped. "Uh, call me Hazel."

"Is that your real name?"

The girl's gaze darted about the office again. Then she looked down. For several moments she sat staring at her hands without saying anything. When she looked up at Toinette, tears streamed down her face.

"I'm so afraid," she whispered.

CHAPTER 12

Toinette got up and got a box of tissue. She placed it within the girl's reach on the edge of her desk. She then poured a glass of water for the girl from a pitcher on the credenza and handed it to the young woman.

"Thank you," the girl murmured. "I'm sorry."

"There's nothing for you to apologize for," Toinette said. She had been working with Quad-A too many years not to recognize some of the signals the girl was sending out. If she were to guess, Toinette figured there was an abusive boyfriend who probably was a drug dealer—that would explain the furtiveness and the fear. The hair and hands were inconclusive. The girl could just as easily be a beautician as she could be a runaway who'd discovered the streets were worse than home. Being generous, Toinette put the girl's age at about nineteen. But one thing Quad-A had taught Toinette was not to jump to conclusions and not to make snap judgments based on appearances. She waited for the girl to get herself together.

"Do you have to know my real name?"

"Not right now, if you don't want me to. If you want help from the Quad-A program, though, you'll eventually have to tell me."

The girl nodded, accepting the rule. Toinette waited.

"I, uh, I need a place to stay. They told me you could get me an apartment and a better job."

Toinette didn't bother to ask who "they" might be. She'd been working on the street long enough for people to send folks to her with no more recommendation than what the girl had just stated.

"Where have you been staying?"

"Uh, around. Sometimes I pack down with some friends. Sometimes I stay at Hope House. Other times I go to the Waters Motel."

Toinette nodded. If the girl who called herself Hazel had been at Hope House, there was a substance abuse problem. The Waters Motel didn't bode well. The place was frequented by prostitutes and addicts. Toinette tried not to sigh. This was likely to be a tough one.

"Are you clean?"

The girl looked down. Toinette rubbed her eyes and wished, not for the first time, that she could get her hands on the person who had formulated crack cocaine and then introduced it to the black community.

The girl started crying again. "I'm sorry. I couldn't, I couldn't find a place to take a shower today. I didn't mean to offend you, ma'am. I tried to wash up in the rest room at the gas station, but the attendant chased me out."

Toinette swallowed hard and bunched her hands together. She'd made an erroneous assumption about Hazel. There was more going on here than it seemed. And it would take longer to deal with than a standard referral to a drug rehab center.

"When I asked if you were clean, I meant have you taken any drugs in the last week?"

"No, ma'am. I don't take drugs."

On this Toinette had to be firm. "If you're not being honest with me, I can't help you. Quad-A participants have to be drug-free. Hazel?"

The girl didn't look up or respond.

Toinette leaned forward in her chair and touched the girl's hand. "Hazel?"

The girl finally met Toinette's gaze. "Is Hazel your mother's name?" Toinette asked softly.

The girl nodded.

"When was the last time you ate a hot meal?"

The girl wiped her eyes on her sleeve, then reached for a tissue from the box on the desk. She blew her nose, then apologized.

"On Friday. The Salvation Army truck came through. I got a sandwich, some soup, and an apple. And the man gave me a couple packages of cookies. I have one package left," the girl said, indicating the backpack.

Toinette wanted to cry. "How old are you?"

"Nineteen," the girl promptly responded.

"How old are you, Hazel?"

The girl looked down at the glass of water she still held. "I'll be seventeen next week."

* * *

Toinette took the girl to the Quad-A office kitchen and made sure she got a meal. The lunch that day for kids in the day-care center was spaghetti and meatballs with a green salad, garlic bread, and cake for dessert. Toinette told one of the kitchen workers to let the girl eat all she could and to fill a bag with peanut butter, dry soup, crackers, cookies, raisins, and fresh fruit to give to her.

While the teen ate, Toinette went to a supply closet and pulled out a female kit. She guessed the girl had some of the things in her backpack already, but Toinette wasn't going to take any chances. Each kit contained soap, a towel and washcloth, toothpaste and toothbrush, feminine hygiene products, condoms, deodorant, lotion, a pair of socks, a comb, a small mirror, and some lipstick and perfume samples.

Toinette took the kit and went back to her office to place a call.

"Yvette? Toinette Blue. I have a juvie here at the center. I don't know any particulars yet. I'm just letting you know. She may fly, but if she doesn't, I'll try to get her to you."

Toinette nodded as she listened to the Social Services caseworker run down a list of mandatory questions.

"Yvette. I just told you I don't have any details yet. You know I know this drill. I'm playing by the rules and letting you know right now." Toinette listened to the woman for a moment. "No, I don't have her real name."

Toinette listened to Yvette sigh, then she sighed herself as she rang off. She glanced at her watch and wondered if she had time to put the call in to Ben Trammer. She decided to wait. If the girl who called herself Hazel wanted to talk, she didn't want to have to put either the girl or Ben Trammer on hold.

Toinette sat back in her chair at her desk and thought about Hazel. The girl obviously was afraid, very afraid of something. Toinette wondered how long the sixteen-year-old had been living on the street.

A few minutes later, Dawn, the Quad-A aide, knocked on Toinette's open office door, then walked into the room. "She ran, Mrs. Blue. Some cop cars came tearing down the street with lights and sirens on. The girl looked up, grabbed the cake off her plate and the bag Eli had left next to her, and took off out the back door. I think she thinks we called the cops on her."

Toinette sighed. The Hazels made her job all the more difficult—and all the more challenging. For every Hazel she was able to save, Toinette felt like she paid a debt to society. She nodded slowly and smiled sadly.

"She'll be back, Mrs. Blue."

"Let's hope so," Toinette said. She pulled a black marker from her desk drawer and wrote *Hazel* in block letters on the kit. "Leave this outside the door tonight. If she comes back, she'll find it."

Dawn nodded and took the kit. The practice was a familiar one. If the right person got it, he or she would eventually come back for help. If someone stole the kit, hopefully the products inside would be of benefit to someone.

Toinette went to the Quad-A kitchen and poured herself a cup of coffee. "How much did she eat before she bolted?" she asked the cook.

"She was on the second helping of spaghetti," Eli told her. "She was packing it away, too."

"Good. That's good. She needed to eat."

With coffee cup in hand, Toinette went to the nursery and checked on the babies and toddlers. It was naptime, and the aides were straightening up the room while the children slept in cribs or on pallets on the floor. Quad-A provided childcare for participants who needed the service so they could work. Eighteen children were at the center today. The number fluctuated from day to day, but they could usually count on about fifteen daytime regulars. After school more children would come to the center until their mothers or fathers picked them up after work.

"Hi, Miss Nettie," a little voice said.

Toinette turned to the boy. She put her coffee cup on a bookshelf ledge and went to him. The child sat up on his pallet and grinned at Toinette.

Heedless of her suit, Toinette took off her shoes and got down on the floor. "Aren't you supposed to be sleeping?"

"I'm not sleepy."

"Would you like me to tell you a story?"

The three-year-old grinned, then climbed up into Nettie's lap. She cradled him in her arms and rocked gently as she started the story in a low, soft voice. "Once upon a time, there were three little pigs . . ."

The child was asleep before Toinette got to the second pig's fate. She kissed the child's forehead, then laid him out on his pallet and pulled the blanket over him.

As Toinette got up, one of the aides came up and smiled at her. "You spoil these kids rotten."

"Everybody needs to be spoiled a little now and then." She put her shoes on and picked up her mug. "I'm going to get a refill on coffee, then I'll be in my office if anyone needs me."

As Toinette walked back to her office from the kitchen, she wondered if the girl who called herself Hazel had had the opportunity to be spoiled a little before the cruel world had taken its bite out of her.

In her office again, she pulled out the Trammer file and reacquainted herself with the information. She reread the letter of introduction she'd sent the engineering and electronics magnate, then picked up the telephone receiver.

After being passed through two receptionists, she heard a big booming voice on the other end of the line.

"Mrs. Blue, Ben Trammer here. So glad you called. You know, the wife and I had just been talking about that nice associate of yours and her husband that we met at that little auction a while back. Then we up and turned around and your package was here. Talk about coincidence. Listen, I'm gonna be up in Washington the end of this week for a meeting with my people there. Can we get together then? Maggie and I are real intrigued about what you proposed."

Toinette was floored. This had been too easy. The man had said all of that practically in one breath and seemed eager to sit down and talk about setting up a Quad-A Foundation. "Of course. What day and time is good for you and where would you like me to meet you?"

"Hold on a sec. Let me look at this here calendar. How 'bout Friday. Let's make it lunch. My chef in D.C. likes to show off when I'm in town, so it'll be good. I'll send a car to your office round 'bout eleven or so."

"Well, I look forward to meeting you, Mr. Trammer."

"Shoot, ma'am. Call me Ben. No need for formalities. Now I'll see you on Friday."

Toinette rang off and plopped back in her chair. She kicked her feet up on the desk and crossed her legs at her ankles. The Texan with the cash sounded promising. Maybe her dream of extending the Quad-A program to other cities where more people could get off welfare was about to come true. Riding the crest of enthusiasm generated by the call to Ben Trammer, Toinette spent the next two hours putting together a packet and drafting a letter to John and Etta MacAfree. If the MacAfrees came on board, they would represent local backing for the project while Ben and Maggie Trammer would add the national perspective.

When she finished the proposal to the MacAfrees, she made up a dream list of the board of directors. With some effort and the right team in place, she could really pull this off.

Later that night, Toinette soaked away the day's victories and failures in a bubble bath. She counted the conversation with Trammer and getting the MacAfree package in the mail as victories. The failure had been with the girl who called herself Hazel.

Toinette wondered if the teenager had found a decent place to sleep for the night. Just the sound of police sirens sent her running. Toinette could only pray that the trouble the girl was in wouldn't get her killed before she got back to the Quad-A office.

As the soothing water worked its miracles on Toinette's tired body, her thoughts turned to Robinson. He hadn't liked the suggestion of taking a shower together. Oh, well. Win some, lose some.

She got up out of the tub and took a good, critical look at herself in the full-length mirror on the back of the door.

She was forty-seven. Being honest with herself, she figured she might be able to pass for forty if it weren't for all the gray in her hair. She ran a hand over the short, natural cut, then smiled at herself in the mirror. For the first time, she seriously thought about a little color, just enough to wash out the gray. She took a step closer to the mirror and changed the smile to an inspection of her mouth. She had all her natural teeth and, except for a cavity or two, was in good shape with the dentist.

She stepped back and turned in profile. Flat front. That had always been a source of personal complaint. But she hadn't been blessed that way. Leah and Judi had taken from their father's side of the family and were full-busted. Angie had taken after Toinette.

Toinette looked over her shoulder at the mirror. Her rear was nicely rounded. That was good, even if her front sagged a little. Giving birth to five children had done that. Her legs were long, but not model length. Overall, she gave the package a score of six and a half. Not bad, not good. Just average. She thought her best features were her eyes and her hands.

She looked down at her toes. Robinson obviously had a foot fetish or something. He'd spent a lot of time playing with her feet, something she was surprised to discover was highly erotic.

Toinette reached for a towel and dried herself. In her bedroom, she selected a blue silk teddy from her lingerie drawer and pulled it on. It was almost eleven o'clock. Robinson hadn't called like he said he would. But then again, it took him a week to call her back after he took her to the play. She climbed in bed. She'd wait one week. The man had seven days to prove whether or not his whispered words of love had been sincere. If she didn't hear from him in a week's time, she'd write the whole thing off as pleasant interlude.

Well, maybe not. Maybe if he didn't call, she'd . . . Toinette frowned. Had she been making a fool of herself? Was Robinson off somewhere right now laughing about their time together?

For some reason, she just couldn't accept that. He was probably just busy. Robinson had been too loving, too gentle, too devastatingly thorough for their time to be just one night.

Toinette turned off the light and lay her head on her pillow. She made up her mind. If he didn't call her in one week's time, she'd call him—and ask him out on a date.

Across the street, Robinson sat in his BMW where he'd been parked for the last two hours. When her bedroom light went out, he started the car and drove home.

CHAPTER 13

Robinson had been thinking about Toinette all day. He couldn't get her off of his mind or out of his system. So he'd driven by her house and then embarrassed himself by not having the nerve to knock on her door. There was so much he wanted to tell her and ask her, he wasn't sure he would even know where to begin. By the time he'd gotten his thoughts together, the light in her bedroom went out and she'd obviously turned in for the night. But still he wondered.

Why, after so many years of celibacy, did she allow him into her life? There had to be a reason, because Toinette was too attractive a woman for men, young and old, not to notice. Robinson thought of the young dinner theater usher's reaction to Toinette the night they saw *Lovin' A Younger Man.*

A smile curved his mouth as he drove home. Toinette had flirted with the young guy, yet she'd given herself to him. And what a woman! Robinson's body responded to the memory of Toinette in his arms, soft and gentle, demanding and giving. She gave totally, unconditionally, and, probably without knowing it, she wrapped him up so tight and secure that he never wanted to be free again.

When he left her abruptly yesterday morning, it had been because he knew he wanted to stay in her arms. Now, with the distance time afforded, Robinson conceded that it hadn't been a momentary thing. He still wanted to be by her side forever. But he sensed a reservation in Toinette, a holding back that transcended their physical relationship.

Robinson wondered about Toinette's husband. They had only briefly talked about her former married life. Woody, the bum, had walked out on a great woman. But Robinson was glad, so glad that he wasn't in the picture. Robinson knew a little of Toinette's background, most of it from what she willingly told people as a part of the public presentation for the Quad-A program. What he didn't know was why she hadn't married again.

And who was the man she'd slept with thirteen years ago? Even though he knew it to be ridiculous, Robinson was jealous. Who and where was that guy?

One other niggling thought escaped him as he pulled into his driveway and activated the garage door. It wasn't until he got in the house that it dawned on him. Did Toinette say she'd never gotten a divorce from Woody Blue? They'd been talking as he drove to the amusement park, and he had wanted to ask her about it, but their conversation had moved on to other things.

Robinson thought about it for a moment as he went to the kitchen. Toinette had been adamant about one thing: when God puts a man and a woman together, they are together until death parted them. That made sense. It even jived with what Aaron Blue had said before Robinson knew that Toinette was the college student's mother. Aaron had told him that his mother wouldn't take too kindly to the idea of him living with his girlfriend because his mother was "real big on the till death do us part thing."

He grabbed an apple from a pile in a bowl on the counter and checked his telephone messages. There were three. He absently listened to them as he looked through the day's mail left on the counter by his housekeeper.

"Mr. Mayview, this is Nancy Griffin. We chatted briefly the other night at the reception downtown. I would like to sit down with you sometime this week to talk about the bachelor auction we proposed. I've already left a message with your secretary. I'm just covering all the bases. Please call at your earliest convenience."

Robinson reached for a pen and jotted down the telephone number the mayor's wife left.

"What if I'm no longer a bachelor by the time your little fundraiser happens?" Robinson told the machine. Then he wondered where that thought had come from.

A couple of bills, three magazines, and a sweepstakes offer constituted the bulk of the mail. The one letter that caught Robinson's eye had the return address for the Claremont Home for Children. Robinson reached for a letter opener as the answering machine moved to the next message. He scowled and paused as the sultry voice began.

"Hi, Robinson. I haven't heard from you in awhile. I'm lonely. I miss you. Call me. Or better yet, come over. You know the way. The invitation is always open. Ciao, darling."

Robinson frowned. He thought he'd gotten rid of Marlena. Maybe his earlier brush-off had been too subtle. If nothing else, Marlena was persistent. If he ignored her, maybe she would go away. He wasn't even remotely interested in what she had to offer. He'd have to deal with Marlena soon, but not tonight.

Using the sterling-silver letter opener, he opened the envelope from the children's home as the third message began.

"Hey, Rob. This is Malc. Kendra and I wondered if you'd like to get together for dinner later this week. It would be a foursome. A babysitter will have the girls. Of course, Mrs. Blue would be accompanying you." Malcolm's chuckles made Rob shake his head.

Robinson took a bite of the apple and glanced at his watch. It was almost eleven. Toinette was already in bed but at least the dinner invitation gave him another reason to call her.

He pulled the letter from the children's home out of the envelope as the tape rewound and erased itself. A quick scan through the letter confirmed it to be a solicitation. He started to toss the missive in the trash, but one line caught his eye: "Children of color constitute the greatest population waiting for loving homes."

Genevieve and Robinson Mayview had adopted him thirty-two years ago. They were the only parents he'd ever known. Unlike some adopted children, Robinson had never been obsessed with finding his natural parents. He'd been mildly curious from time to time but not enough to go to any effort to locate the people. As far as he was concerned, his parents were a quietly elegant woman and a tough but loving father. Robinson himself had given quite a bit of thought to the idea of having children of his own. He had always wanted a big family. Growing up, it had been just him and C.J. While two was a nice even number, Robinson wanted a houseful of kids. And even though it wasn't an issue with him, he didn't want his own children to have to wonder from whence they'd come.

He put the letter to the side, grabbed another apple as he finished off the first one, then headed to his bedroom.

Still thinking about children, he stripped off his suit and shirt and pulled on a pair of sweatpants. He'd always known he'd have lots of children. That was one of the reasons he'd built such a big house with lots of land around it—kids needed a place to play and to roam. C.J., who preferred her condo in the heart of the city, had told him it was crazy for a single man to have such a huge house in the middle of what she called "the woods." To his sister, any lot with more than three trees on it constituted the woods. But Robinson had ignored her because he'd had a reason: the house would be perfect down the line. It was something that would come with time and when he found the right woman.

That thought brought him up short.

He'd found the right woman. She was forty-seven. She had five children and five grandchildren. Could a forty-seven-year-old woman safely bear children? It was a thought he'd never had reason to think until now.

With the remote control, Robinson turned the television on, then padded barefoot back to the dining room, where he'd dropped his briefcase on the way in the house. He glanced at his watch again. As much as he wanted to hear her voice, it really was too late to call Toinette. He'd call first thing in the morning.

In her own bed, Toinette stared at the ceiling in her dark bedroom. She wondered and worried if Hazel had found a safe place for the night. As a juvenile, there wasn't much Toinette could do to help the girl through the Quad-A program. She could refer Hazel to other programs and services, but that was about it. By law, she had to report contact with juveniles to Social Services. But she knew enough people to be able to get the girl some help—if she ever came back.

Toinette turned over and thought about the man who was turning her world upside down. Robinson had said he would call and he hadn't. Try as she might, and even though she had resolved to give him seven days, she couldn't get the man or their lovemaking off her mind. Restless, Toinette turned over again, trying to get comfortable. She pulled a pillow to her, then tossed it across the bed.

"Okay. So you miss him. Is that a crime?" she asked out loud. Yes, a little voice in her head answered. No, the other voice told her. Toinette sighed. She got up and in the dark walked to the dresser. She turned on a small vanity light and opened her jewelry box. She picked up a small gold band and stared at it for several minutes.

She slipped the wedding ring on her ring finger and looked at her hand.

"I promised you forever, Woody. But you broke the promise you made to me. You didn't even say goodbye. I loved you with everything I had in me to give, and you left me. You abandoned me and our children. I'm waiting. I've waited for you to come home. But now," she said, taking the ring off her finger and putting it back in the jewelry compartment, "now, I'm not so sure I want you back."

She was troubled by that thought. While not an overly religious woman, Toinette believed that vows made in a church before God were to be taken seriously. She and Woodrow Blue had been young when they married. But they were in love and had promised to have and to hold until death parted them. There was nothing in their wedding vows about when one party got tired of the other and walked away.

The one time thirteen years ago when she'd been unfaithful to Woody and had an affair with a man she'd met, she'd felt so guilty that she called a halt to the brief relationship. Now there was Robinson. And while she didn't exactly feel guilt, she felt something. Maybe confusion, maybe a lingering sense of wrongness.

Toinette sighed. "You're real anal about this, Blue," she told herself. Kendra told her time and again that she was wasting the best part of her life waiting around for a man who didn't deserve her. A secret part of Toinette was starting to agree.

She went to the chaise longue and picked up Bandit, the red-and-white teddy bear Robinson won for her at the amusement park. Carrying the bear, Toinette got in bed and held the stuffed toy to her. Her last thought before she drifted to sleep was of Robinson kissing her as they shared cotton candy.

The next morning Toinette's telephone was ringing as she walked into the office. With briefcase and purse slung across her shoulder and a cup of coffee in one hand, she reached for the receiver.

"Achieving Against All Adversities, this is Toinette Blue. How may I help you?"

"I've thought of nothing but you since I left you Sunday morning."

Toinette smiled as she placed the coffee cup on her desk and shrugged the two bags off her shoulder. "Will it go to your head if I confess the same thing?"

"Not if you promise to go out with me Friday night."

"Well, since I hardly want to be the cause of an overinflated ego, I'll have to say yes."

"May I be greedy and ask to see you sometime before then? Say, Thursday night, dinner with Kendra and Malcolm?" Robinson asked.

Toinette flipped through the daybook that rested open on her desk. Her regret was genuine. "I'm booked through the week. I have a couple of Quad-A lunchtime presentations and then a Thursday night workshop here at the center. I have a meeting in Washington Friday and that will take up most of the day. I have a proposal to take Quad-A national and branch out into other cities. There are several large public housing projects across the country where Quad-A could be an effective program."

"So you'd hire administrators for those cities?"

"Eventually. If this proposal floats, and my meeting in D.C. Friday afternoon is with a potential financial backer, I would go in and set up the program in places like Dallas, Chicago, and Atlanta."

"Toinette, some of those places are notoriously dangerous."

Toinette laughed off Robinson's concern. "I've been hanging tough here for almost seven years and nothing bad has happened. The center is right here on the perimeter of one of the toughest neighborhoods in the city. I think I know how to handle myself."

"Hmm," was all Robinson said before changing the subject. "Well, good luck with your meeting. What time should I pick you up Friday night?"

"Where are we going?"

"Well, I have had one place on my mind since I last saw you."

Toinette smiled. "I thought this was a date."

"Oh. Well, I know a really nice jazz club. They serve dinner and there's dancing."

"I love to dance."

"Do you like to slow dance?"

"I like that kind best of all," Toinette teased.

"You're going to be the death of me yet, Ms. Blue. I'll pick you up at your house at seven."

"I'll see you then."

"Oh, Toinette?"

"Yes, Robinson?"

"Are you going to be wearing one of those skimpy little satin and lace teddies under your clothing?"

"I don't know. I'll give it some thought."

"Toinette?"

"Yes, Robinson?"

"I'm partial to black."

Toinette's laughter rang through the office as she replaced the receiver.

CHAPTER 14

Before she realized it, the week had zipped by. Toinette took one last look at the material tucked in her briefcase. She had documents and case studies, budget and spending plans, news clips, and even the architectural floor plan for the Quad-A center. She wanted to have at the ready anything Ben Trammer might ask about. This meeting could very well determine if her vision for Quad-A would ever come to fruition.

She had hoped that Kendra would be able to join her for the meeting. But Kendra already had another commitment at the law firm where she worked. Toinette would be flying solo.

Toinette went to the center's rest room to take one last look at herself in the full-length mirror there. The cream-colored suit with its double-breasted jacket and long pleated skirt was the most conservative outfit she owned. It was also one of the most professional looking. Her hose matched the suit and her shoes matched the hose. She'd even substituted her trademark long dangling earrings for a pair of large but sedate pearls. She looked like the corporate executive she was going to meet.

Toinette pirouetted in front of the mirror, then took a deep breath and pushed the rest-room door open. The car from Ben Trammer would be arriving soon.

She checked in on the nursery and the older children's playroom. "Miss Nettie, you goin' out with a rock man?"

"No, Rasheed. Why would you ask something like that?"

" 'Cause there a big white car outside and Shaniqua said he waiting for you."

"I'm going to Washington, D.C. to see if I can get some more money for the Quad-A program so you and Shaniqua can continue to have a place to stay while your mom is at work. I want to set up some more centers for other children."

The child nodded and seemed satisfied with the answer. "I'm gonna tell Shaniqua. I told her you wouldn't be going to see no rock man."

The child skipped away and left Toinette in the middle of the floor looking puzzled. She went to her office, picked up her briefcase, then checked out with the center's assistant director before heading to Ben Trammer's car and driver. It wasn't until she was comfortably settled in the back seat of the late-model white limousine that she realized what the six-year-old had been asking. Other than maybe movie stars or athletes on television, the only people the child had ever seen in a limousine were drug dealers. Rock man. Crack cocaine was known as rock. Toinette sighed. There was so much to be done politically, socially, and educationally for young people.

As the big white car pulled away from the curb in front of the Quad-A center, a person who had been watching from across the street stepped out of the shadows of a bus shelter. The person watched the white car disappear down the street, then walked to a pay telephone on the corner and made a call.

"Mrs. Blue, I must tell you I'm very impressed with your presentation and with the Quad-A program. Maggie and I had a good ol' time talking with your associate Kendra Edwards and Mr. Hightower at that auction."

Toinette didn't bother to tell Trammer that Kendra Edwards was now Kendra Hightower.

"For a long time now we've been looking for a way to channel a little financial help into communities that could use it. You and your idea for a Quad-A Foundation came along at the right moment."

Even as Toinette wondered what Trammer's idea of "a little financial help" might be, the man named an initial grant and subsequent pledge that in actuality would eliminate the need for other financial backing.

"Does that sound like something you could work with? I know you'd need some staff. I can supply that, lend you a few people for the first year. Now I really like the idea of Quad-A centers in Dallas and in Atlanta. I can set you up with some office space in those cities 'cause my company has a presence, mostly in Southern cities. Don't know too much about Chicago. We don't have any offices there. Our Midwest plant and office is in Minneapolis, and, to tell you the truth, I can't remember the last time I was up there."

"Mr. Trammer, your generosity is overwhelming."

"I thought we dispensed with those formalities earlier. Call me Ben."

The big man looked at his watch, then punched a button on the communication console on the conference table where he and Toinette sat. "Ginger, tell Raphael that we're about to starve in here." He winked and smiled at Toinette. "The man has been raving about this 'divine' meal he's cooked up, and all we've seen so far are some grapes and some funny-looking cheese. When's the real food coming?"

Toinette could hear the stifled laughter in his secretary's voice. "Raphael said lunch would be served when you wished, sir. The dining room is ready for you."

"Find Maggie and have her join us. Thanks, Ginger."

Ben got up and stretched. Toinette rose along with him.

"Mrs. Blue . . ."

"Toinette, if you'd like," she interjected. "I thought we weren't being formal."

Ben grinned and nodded his head. "This has been a damn productive hour and a half. We've been talking business the whole time, though. Tell me a little more about yourself."

Toinette and Ben Trammer chatted as they made their way to the executive dining room at Trammer Engineering and Electronics.

Later that evening Toinette arrived home. With her head down glancing through the day's mail, she noticed a piece of white peeking out from the back edge of the hall table. She dropped her bags, put the new mail on the table, and got on her knees.

"Wonder how I missed you," she said, as she reached for the envelope. "I hope this isn't something important."

As she stood, she groaned when she recognized the seal of the college where Aaron was enrolled. "Well, at least this is the last year I have to worry about this," she said. The bill for the next semester had arrived. Toinette opened the envelope, spied the balance, and looked for the due date. She sighed. "That boy is going to have to pay for law school himself." She grabbed the other mail from the table, picked her bags up, and headed upstairs.

Deciding what to wear for the evening was easy. She and Robinson were going dancing. From her overflowing closet she chose a glittery gold dress with deep flounces at the hemline. A pair of high-heeled gold shoes that criss-crossed at the foot and ankle completed the ensemble. She showered and perfumed herself, then went to her lingerie drawer.

"So, you like black, Mr. Mayview," she said as she rooted for just the right garments. "Let's see how you like this little number." She pulled out a two-piece black lace set, then found the matching garter belt. Robinson would be in for a treat—if they got that far later tonight.

At the jazz club they ate a light supper, talked, and danced. Toinette couldn't keep her eyes off Robinson. The man looked good enough to eat. She couldn't help notice the envious glances thrown her way by a few women—and even a couple of men—in the club. Robinson seemed oblivious to everything, though. The man definitely knew how to wear clothes. The dark blue double-breasted suit in worsted-wool fit him like it was made for him. It probably was, Toinette thought.

And as if they'd planned what to wear out that night, Robinson's tie, a silk blue-and-gold geometric design, highlighted the shimmering gold in her dress.

During a break between sets, they talked. Their table was situated so that conversation would be relatively private. Robinson couldn't believe that they'd worn complementary outfits. But more than that, he couldn't believe how good Toinette felt in his arms as they moved across the floor.

"You're a terrific dancer," he told her.

"Thank you. I love to dance," she told him. "At one time I wanted to be a professional dancer. I grew up inspired by black dancers like Alvin Ailey, Katherine Dunham, and Janet Collins. I remember the first time I saw Janet Collins dance. She was a prima ballerina, the first black woman to perform on stage at the Metropolitan Opera House in New York. I saw her dance on a tour one year and decided that's what I wanted to do."

"Did you?"

Toinette smiled and shook her head. "No. Dancing is a dream that was deferred. I met Woody, and before long we were married and I was having babies. Dancing was relegated to something I watched on television or occasionally saw at a show. I'd dance around the house, though, with one of the kids in my arms. They thought it was fun."

A waitress came and took reorders on drinks for them. When she left, Robinson broached the topic he had been wondering about. "Tell me about Woody, Toinette."

Toinette picked up a chip and nibbled on it to buy herself a little time. What a question. So, Robinson wanted to know about Woody. Should she start by telling him that Woody had been the love of her life, the one and only man she'd once thought she'd grow old with? Or should she tell Robinson the other truth: that after years and years of being faithful to a memory, Woody was . . . what? The bottom line was he was still her husband even if he was absent. He was the father of her children. She loved him, didn't she?

And then there was the third truth to contend with. Did she dare risk her heart again with Robinson?

Toinette looked at Robinson who was patiently awaiting her answer. Toinette shook her head. "That ancient history? There's not much to it," she told him. "We got married when I was sixteen. I had four kids and then, when I was pregnant with Aaron, Woody walked out one day and never came back." And that, she thought, was the truth that still hurt the most.

"Did you try to find him?"

"Of course. I was frantic. I thought he'd been killed or kidnapped or something equally as dramatic. As time went on though, I realized that he'd just left. I've been told it happens that way sometimes. He didn't love me or the kids anymore. Maybe he thought it was too much responsibility for him to handle, having a wife and five children. We were awfully young. But I thought we were happy."

"When did you finally get a divorce?"

Toinette looked puzzled for a moment. People always assumed she was divorced. The truth of the matter was she'd never even considered it. There had been no reason to. Until now.

"I didn't," she told Robinson. "I've always figured he would come back when he was ready."

Robinson digested that bit of information. Then, with a steady gaze into Toinette's eyes, he quietly asked an important question. "Do you still love him?"

The blare of bass guitar, saxophone, trumpet, and drums drowned out any response Toinette may have given Robinson. The opening refrain to "Birdland" filled the club. Up and swinging her hips to the jazzy tune, Toinette stretched a hand out to Robinson.

He sighed to himself and let the music and Toinette erase any other thought from his head. They did the swing and the foxtrot and the rumba, dancing the night away. The final set of spicy Latin music had Robinson so worked up he wanted to take Toinette right on the dance floor.

When they got to Toinette's house, Robinson cut the ignition on his car and pulled Toinette into his arms. "I didn't know dancing could be so sexy," he said.

"When you dance you get in touch with your inner self. You can express yourself in ways that otherwise might never come out. The beat just sort of gets in your pores and comes out in ways that are elemental, earthy, true. I close my eyes and let the music take me," she said, smiling.

"Close your eyes."

Toinette did. Robinson's mouth covered hers in a kiss that was as bold as the hot dancing they'd done at the club. His tongue parried with hers, and she pulled him to her, closer, closer.

Robinson ran one hand along Toinette's thigh, then tugged at the low collar on her dress.

"Am I going to like what I see under here?"

Toinette's throaty laughter washed over him.

"That depends on if you're partial to black."

"Oh, God," he groaned. Then he slipped his hand between the folds of her dress and fondled the ripe fruit he found there. Toinette arched into his embrace and cried out.

A sharp bump to the side of Robinson's car had them jumping apart. "What the hell is going on here?!" an angry male voice shouted.

"Oh, my God. It's Russell," Toinette said as she frantically pulled her dress up.

"Why is he kicking my car? Who is Russell? Is this guy nuts?" Robinson flung his car door open and confronted the man who was alternately kicking the door and banging on the window with a fist that was bound to break the windshield.

Toinette hopped out of the passenger door and ran around the car to confront her oldest son.

"Russell, have you lost your mind? Stop it!"

But Russell Blue pushed Robinson against the side of the car and pulled back his balled-up fist. In an instant Toinette jumped between the two men.

Robinson saw the punch coming and was ready for it. What he wasn't prepared for was Toinette stepping between him and this nut who was obviously one of her children. Before he could push her out of the way, the man's right fist, aimed at Robinson's jaw, connected with Toinette's cheek and glanced off her shoulder.

CHAPTER 15

The force of the blow sent Toinette slamming into the side of the car, and she crumpled to the ground. Robinson went ballistic.

"Mom! Oh, my God. I didn't mean to—"

A fist crashed into Russell Blue's solar plexus and cut off any further words. The man doubled over trying to catch his breath. Russell took a hail of blows to his head and side before he recovered enough to respond to the attack.

He stood up and charged Robinson. An upper right hook connected with Russell's left eye as the two men hit the pavement with a thud.

Robinson, on the bottom and at a disadvantage, struggled to fight off the man. He took a few blows but had the advantage of rage and adrenaline pumping through him. This crazy person had hit Toinette! With that thought he flipped over and delivered a fresh volley of punches. The two men tussled and growled, with Russell cussing and threatening to kill Robinson every time he could take a breath.

Dazed and confused, Toinette shook her head and tried to figure out what had happened to her. For a moment she drew a complete blank. Then she remembered. She and Robinson had been making out in the car. Russell was banging on the window. Robinson got out to confront Russell. Toinette stepped between them. And her son hit her.

Russell hit her!

Toinette shook her head again, trying to get her bearings. Her shoulder was throbbing and her face felt on fire. She tried to stand up but found she didn't have the energy. She sat back again and closed her eyes for a moment. Then she heard the angry male voices and the sounds of a fight. She opened her eyes and took in the scene before her: her son and her lover locked in mortal combat. Robinson was crashing Russell's head into the pavement of the street. Then Russell got the upper hand and put a choke hold on Robinson's throat.

"Oh, my God," she moaned. "Stop it. Stop it!"

She realized that the two men didn't hear her. She pushed herself up using the side of Robinson's BMW as leverage. Her shoulder was pounding, but still she moved until finally she was able to stand.

"Russell, stop it! You're going to kill him!"

Riding the force of outrage now, Toinette confronted the two men. She pounded on Russell's back but to no avail. Kicking him in the side, she said, "Damnit, Russell Blue. I said stop!"

The two men rolled over and scrambled to their feet. Like two lions in warfare over territory, they circled each other and growled. Toinette stepped between them. For a moment she didn't know which one to confront.

Russell made the choice for her with a menacing fist in Robinson's direction. "Don't you ever, *ever* lay a hand on my mother."

"You're the one who *hit* her . . ."

Toinette cut Robinson off. "Shut up. Both of you. Just shut up. I do not believe that you two are out here fighting in the street like ten-year-olds. Russell, go home. I don't even want to talk about this or see you."

"Toinette, are you okay?" Robinson asked. "Let me check your cheek."

"I'm fine, Robinson. I'm just fine. You go home, too."

Neither man made a move to leave.

Toinette looked at one and then the other. "That's the way you want it? Fine. Stay out here. Put on a show for the neighbors. You already have an audience," she said, turning and waving a hand toward porch lights that were starting to flick on. "If one of the neighbors has called the police, tell the officers you want to kill each other."

With that, Toinette gave one last disgusted look at Russell, whose left eye was swelling. Blood dripped from a cut on his lip. Robinson's suit was ripped and torn, but he didn't look much worse for wear.

Toinette shook her head, then made her way around Robinson's car. She pulled her handbag from the seat and walked to her front door.

Robinson and Russell stared after her, then warily regarded each other.

"I don't know who the hell you are, but I want you to leave my mother alone," Russell said hotly.

"Your mother's relationship with me is none of your business. I'd suggest you go on and take yourself home like she told you."

"Look you—"

The slamming of Toinette's front door halted what Russell had been about to say. The two men turned toward the house and watched lights come on in the front room.

Robinson adjusted his suit and tie, then went to inspect his car. Surprised to discover the vehicle had not sustained any damage from Russell's assault, Robinson locked the car and dashed up the walkway to Toinette's door.

"Where the hell do you think you're going?" Russell bellowed from the street. He wiped his mouth on the sleeve of his sweatshirt and glared at Robinson's back.

Robinson ignored the man and rang Toinette's doorbell. He then knocked on the door. No response. He tried the doorknob. She'd slammed the door but had left it unlocked.

Robinson stepped inside. "Toinette?"

"Robinson, just go home please."

He followed her voice to the powder room.

Toinette stood in front of the mirror, pressing a damp cloth to her cheek. Robinson stepped into the small room and stood behind her. He put a hand to her shoulder, and she winced.

"I'm sorry, Toinette. Let me see."

Gently, he tugged at the collar of her dress and took a look at the bruise on her shoulder. Already it was turning an angry shade of red and dark blue. Robinson pressed a soft kiss to the spot. "I'm sorry, sweetheart."

"It wasn't your fault, Rob. I could kill Russell. Lord only knows what's gotten into that boy."

Robinson took a hand towel from the rack in the powder room and wet it. He then placed the compress on Toinette's shoulder. "This is going to hurt tomorrow," he told her.

"It hurts now."

"Let me see your cheek."

Toinette turned into Robinson's arms, and he took away the cloth she held at her face.

She flinched at the expletive that came from Robinson. "I swear to God, Toinette. If that man wasn't your son, he'd be dead right now."

"There's been enough violence for one night, Rob. I'm okay. It looks worse than it is."

Robinson tilted her head toward the light to better inspect the damage. He ran a gentle finger around the edge of the bruise. Then he lightly kissed Toinette's lips.

"Didn't I tell you to keep your filthy hands off my mother?"

Renewed anger flared in Robinson's eyes. A sudden thin chill hung on the edge of his clipped words. "You owe your mother an apology," he said, as he released Toinette and stepped into the foyer to confront Russell.

"You don't tell me what to do," Russell Blue countered.

Wearily, Toinette stepped from the powder room, the wet cloths in her hand forgotten as she looked at her oldest son. "Russell, didn't I tell you to go home?"

Russell turned in anger toward his mother. "Here I am worried to hell about you, thinking some hoodlum is stalking you, and you have this bastard pawing all over you."

Bristling with sudden indignation, Toinette rounded on Russell. "Now just wait a minute here, Russell Woodrow Blue, Jr. I brought you into this world and I will take you out if you ever, ever raise your voice in that manner to me again. By what authority and what right do you stand as judge before me?"

With one finger in his chest, Toinette backed her son down the hallway. "I raised the five of you by myself. Alone when your daddy turned his back on us and walked out the door. It was me, you hear me, *me,* who wiped your behind and cleaned up your bloody noses and made you feel better when the other kids called you poor and made fun of your second-hand clothes. It was *me* who raised you, and I did the best I could with what I had."

"What do you mean Dad turned his back on us and walked out the door?" Russell asked. "Just because his trips home from his job got canceled doesn't mean he turned his back on us."

But Toinette was too far gone in anger to hear.

"For twenty-two years, twenty-two years, Russell, I have spent my nights alone, wondering what I did wrong. Wondering why your father didn't love me and you kids enough to stay and be a responsible husband and father.

"I have earned the right, deserve the right, to a little love and happiness in my life. I think I've found it in Robinson. And if you don't like it, Russell, you can go the way your daddy did. Walk out the door and don't look back."

Russell paled at his mother's words. "What do you mean he walked out on us?"

"That's right, Russell. Your father left. He deserted us when I was still pregnant with Aaron. He said he was going to get a pack of cigarettes. I never saw him again. He never sent a dime of support for you all. Everything you ever got, I supplied. To this day, I don't know if the man is dead or alive."

"But you always said . . ."

Toinette sighed a weary sigh and her shoulders slumped as the fight drained from her. For so long she had tried to maintain a fiction with her children. She thought she'd covered all the bases: fake letters, birthday cards sent on time, sad explanations that planned visits home had to be canceled at the last minute—all done to preserve her pride and her children's memory of a loving father.

"Yes, I know," she told Russell. "I always told you all that he was working in another state. Maybe that was a mistake. I just didn't want you all to grow up with the hurt and anger and bitterness I felt toward your father. He was still my husband. And right or wrong, I loved him."

Robinson, listening to the exchange from the powder-room doorway, finally understood Toinette's reluctance to get romantically involved with him: she still loved her husband and believed in her marriage vows. The whole "till death do us part" thing, as Aaron Blue had told him, meant a lot to her.

Russell raised a hand to the bruise on his mother's cheek. "I'm sorry I accidentally hit you, Mom."

Toinette sighed and nodded. "Just go home, Russell. Get some sleep."

Russell's broad face softened, and he again quietly apologized to his mother. Then he lifted his head to glare at Robinson. "I'll deal with you later," he promised before turning and stomping out of the house.

Toinette locked the door and rested her head on the frame. A moment later the screeching of tires could be heard from the street. She gulped hard, hot tears slipping down her cheeks. Robinson came to her and wrapped his arms about her waist. He led her to the living room, where they sat on the sofa. Toinette turned into his embrace and cried in his arms. Robinson held her and rocked her and whispered soothing words to the woman he wanted to be his wife.

Eventually her crying subsided to a few sniffles. Before long, Toinette was asleep in Robinson's arms. Still, he held her and rocked her. Eventually he, too, drifted to sleep on the sofa.

When Toinette woke in the morning, she felt disoriented, confused, and sore. She also felt what could only be the stiffness of a man's erection pressing into her stomach. She opened her eyes and turned her head up.

"Good morning," Robinson told her.

Toinette groaned.

Robinson smiled as he levered himself and Toinette up, careful not to exert any pressure on her shoulder. When she relaxed into the soft cushions, Robinson leaned over and unstrapped the high-heeled sandals from her feet. "I couldn't get these off last night without disturbing you. I figured a night in clothes and shoes wouldn't do too much damage."

Toinette took a good look at Robinson. "Unlike the damage you and Russell tried to do to each other last night."

"Other than a knot on my head, I'm all right. It's you I'm worried about. Let me see."

Robinson inspected the now black-and-blue area on the side of Toinette's cheek. Anger flared in his eyes.

"Let it go, Rob. Russell is gone. It's over."

"I cannot believe what he did. Has he always been so irrational?"

Toinette soothed the lines at Robinson's brow. "He's always been hot-tempered and stubborn. Once Russell makes up his mind about something there's no going back even if there's evidence to the contrary."

Robinson opened his mouth to say something.

"Let it go, Rob."

Robinson drew her finger into his mouth and licked it. He then replaced her finger with her lips. Toinette relaxed, sinking into the healing embrace. She kissed him back with a tenderness and warmth that seemed new, a tenderness that made her heart swell even as she wondered at the emotion.

Robinson loved her gently and with reverence. Then he slowly pulled away, putting just enough distance between them so he could look at her. "I love you, Toinette."

Her eyes dilated in surprise. "Robinson, you're mistaking—"

"Hear me out before you discount what I have to say," he said. Turning so he sat on the edge of the sofa, he picked up her hands and gazed into her eyes. "I love you, Toinette. Yes, you're older than I am. There's nothing either of us can do about that. It doesn't matter to me. Yes, you have five grandkids and five children, one of whom is an imbecile . . ."

"Robinson . . ."

"I can deal with that. I wish my introduction to your son Russell had been similar to the one I had with Aaron, but life is not perfect. We can use what happened last night as an experience to learn and grow from or we can second-guess and cast doubt on what to me has been the most marvelous relationship of my life. You're the woman I want, Toinette. Always. And let me clarify something to remove all ambiguity. When I say that I love you, I mean I'm in love with you, body and soul. You have brought joy to my life in ways I never thought possible."

Toinette could only stare at him. He was serious. They weren't in bed, so he couldn't be mistaking passion for love. And while the man was definitely aroused, he hadn't made a single move toward a physical expression of desire.

"You're serious, aren't you?" she said incredulously.

"I've never been more serious about anything in my life. Nothing has ever mattered as much as loving you."

Toinette didn't know what to say or how to respond. She was falling for Rob, that much she could acknowledge within herself without any second-guessing. But love? Love in Toinette's book meant commitment and forever. She didn't have forever to promise him. Not while she was still married to Woody. Not when even after hearing his words, she still had doubts about the plausibility of a relationship with a man who was practically the same age as the son he'd fought with the night before. "Robinson, I—"

He stopped the hesitant flow of her words with a finger pressed across her lips. "You don't have to say anything, Toinette. You don't have to respond. I wasn't telling you how I feel to put you on the spot. I realized last night as you talked to Russell that there are some things that you and he, together and separately, need to work out. But as you think about all of those things, I want you to know that I love you and that I cherish you."

Robinson raised her hands to his mouth and pressed a kiss to her closed palms. "You are such a sweet man," Toinette said. Robinson lightly ran a finger over the bruise on her cheek.

"And you are a beautiful woman." Then, after a pause: "I never got to find out if there was a black surprise awaiting me under this." He fingered the glistening gold material of her dress.

Toinette smiled and turned her back to him, a clear invitation for him to undo the zipper of her dress.

Robinson pressed a kiss to the hollow of her neck, then slowly, tantalizingly, unzipped her dress. He trailed a path of kisses along the smooth brown skin of her back as it was revealed to him. The zipper ran to the small of her back. Toinette shrugged, and the soft material fell around her waist. Robinson unhooked the black brassiere and smoothed the undergarment off her shoulders and down her arms.

Snaking his arms about her, he captured the breasts that anxiously awaited his touch. Toinette gasped and leaned back into his embrace. As his hands fondled her breasts and nipples, Robinson buried his head in her neck.

His magnetism was so strong that Toinette wondered at her inability to resist. Then she acknowledged that she had no desire to resist. This was where she wanted to be—in Robinson's arms, being loved by him, being reborn and rejuvenated in his arms. At the base of her throat, a pulse beat and swelled as though her heart had risen from its usual place. Toinette smiled as one of his hands inched lower.

She stood up and turned toward him. The dress slithered down her body and pooled at her feet. She stood before him wearing nothing but a pair of lacy black panties, a matching garter belt, and a pair of sheer stockings.

Robinson took off his jacket and unbuttoned his shirt. The jacket, shirt, and undershirt joined Toinette's dress in a heap on the floor. He guided her to him, wrapped an arm about her hips, and buried his head in her stomach to lick her navel.

Toinette's giggles rang through the room. "That tickles!"

"Do tell. How does this feel?"

He tumbled her to the sofa and slowly ran a hand up her thigh. He stopped at the juncture where Toinette wanted him most and teased her. He slipped a hand under the band of her panties and Toinette arched into him. She cried out, and he smiled a purely male, one-hundred-percent seduction smile.

"Let's go upstairs," he said.

Toinette shook her head even as she guided his hand. "Takes too long," she managed to mumble. "I want you now."

Robinson leaned forward and kissed her. Then he removed his hand, picked her up, and settled her on the floor, clear of the coffee table. He came out of his slacks, shoes, and socks.

"Now," Toinette demanded.

He fumbled with a condom and joined her on the carpeted floor. Toinette had wiggled out of the panties. With a lingering look at Toinette's stockinged legs, he said, "It's a pity I'm not in the slow-hand mood to enjoy these."

Yet he lingered a bit as he unhooked the hose from the sexy black garment. Robinson placed a kiss at every point where hose and hook had been. Toinette squirmed beneath him, driving him mad.

"Robinson, you're making me crazy."

"Now you know how it feels."

In the next instant he thrust into her, and Toinette bucked up beneath him. They loved fast and hard, and when they were through, they both lay on their backs, staring at the ceiling.

"Toinette," Robinson said, "what was that all about?"

She sat up on one elbow and regarded him. "I don't know." She reached her free hand out and lazily drew curlicues along his chest. She smiled when Robinson took a shuddering breath and closed his eyes. "One minute I was trying to take in everything you were telling me and the next minute I wanted you like I've never wanted anything else in my life."

Robinson opened his eyes and stared into hers. "That's how I want you all the time. With every fiber of my being, until I can't think or breathe."

Toinette lowered her head. Her body's instinctive response to him was practically overwhelming. She kissed him with a hunger that was reciprocated. Before she knew what was happening she was on her back again. Robinson seared a trail of kisses from her neck and shoulders to the tips of her feet. She quivered at the sweet tenderness and gave herself up to sensation.

"The last time we were together, you offered a shower for two. Would you like to do that now?"

"If memory serves correctly," she said, "I made the offer and you bolted out the door."

Recalling the overwhelming feelings of love he'd had toward Toinette after their first night together and how he'd needed some time to sort through his thoughts, Robinson grinned sheepishly. "I, uh, needed a little time to think through some things," he said.

"And now that you've indulged yourself with this reflective period?"

"I'd like to take a shower with you."

Toinette's answering smile was the only response Robinson needed.

CHAPTER 16

They shared a shower and then ate a breakfast of waffles and fresh-squeezed orange juice.

"Spend the day with me?" Robinson asked.

Toinette sipped from her cup of coffee and regarded him from over the rim. "What did you have in mind?"

The seductive bent of her voice didn't escape Robinson. "Well, I'd meant doing something together outside. But I can be persuaded otherwise."

Toinette simply smiled. Then the telephone rang.

She got up to answer the phone, but not before walking behind Robinson and trailing a leisurely finger along the contours of his face.

"Hello?"

"Mom, hi. This is Leah."

"Hi, darling. Aren't you supposed to be at baseball practice or ballet class this time of day on a Saturday?"

"Well, I'm supposed to be, but Russell has had me on the phone for the last hour screaming about you and someone or other that he had a confrontation with last night."

Toinette sighed and Robinson looked up from the table. The expression on her face didn't bode well.

"Leah, I'm seeing someone and your brother doesn't like it." Toinette held out a hand to Robinson. He got up, took her hand, and squeezed it, offering to her the strength that he could.

"You're dating someone? Mom, that's wonderful! Judi and I had been saying how we hoped you would find someone to spend time with."

Toinette's mouth dropped open. "You're happy?"

"Of course I am. Mom, I want you to be happy. Russell just has these weird notions. Don't let him get to you. Did he really get in a fight with your man—I mean, your gentleman friend?"

Toinette looked at Robinson. She'd never really thought of him as "her man." The concept was rather jarring. Robinson was just Robinson. Then she smiled with a new realization. He was her man.

"Mom, you still there?"

"I'm here, sweetheart. Something just crossed my mind. Leah, you should know that one of the things I believe has upset your brother so much is that the man I'm dating is younger than I am."

"What's age got to do with it?"

Was it really that simple? Toinette thought.

Robinson frowned. Russell Blue hadn't said anything about age. Russell Blue hadn't said much of anything, period. He did a lot of growling and cussing though.

"I think you're right, Leah. What's age got to do with it?" Toinette looked at Robinson, then drew him closer to her. He circled his arms around her waist.

"Well, Mom, I can't talk long. I do have to get the kids to their practices. I just wanted to make sure you're okay. Russell can be given to theatrics and you know that temper of his. But in his own way he just wants what's best for you."

"Yes," Toinette agreed with her daughter. "Well, I'm fine. Really. Russell has some things he needs to work out."

"I'll call you sometime tomorrow after church, okay?"

"That sounds fine. Give Jessica and Thad a hug and kiss from me."

Toinette rang off and replaced the receiver. When she turned back to Robinson, his lips slowly descended to hers. His mouth, wet and warm, was a comforting shelter.

"I take it that was one of your children," he murmured.

"Um-hmm. Leah, my oldest daughter. Russell was bending her ear this morning about you and me."

"And who won?"

She smiled easily. "We did. We're two for one right now. Two more daughters to go."

Robinson rolled his eyes. "I can hardly wait."

With a pat on her rear end, Robinson let Toinette go and went back to the kitchen table. She cleared their breakfast dishes and put them in the sink to wash later. Then she wiped down the counters.

"I'm serious, Toinette. I'd like to spend the day with you."

"Okay," she agreed. "But I have a little work to do, some paperwork that I need to catch up on."

"How about I go home, get changed, and pick you up here in a couple of hours. Is two hours enough time?" he asked.

"Give me three."

Robinson's long-suffering sigh made Toinette laugh. "You'll need that much time to, uh, recharge your batteries."

Robinson got up and took the dishtowel from Toinette's hands. He backed her up against the counter, trapping her with the muscular length of his body and an arm on either side of her. His lower body pressed into hers, and she had no doubt that his batteries were fully charged.

"With you I'm always ready," he said.

She put her arms around his neck. Parting her lips, she raised herself to meet his kiss. It was slow and drugging and devastatingly thorough. A warm glow flowed through Toinette's veins as she lost herself in her man's embrace.

He left her mouth and brushed a gentle kiss across her forehead.

"Let me get out of here before I can't leave."

"See you in a few hours."

Robinson let himself out of the house. Toinette, smiling to herself, went in search of the paperwork she needed to do.

"Now's as good a time as any to pay bills, girlfriend," she said aloud. She thought of the college tuition bill that was due, and she lost a bit of the joy she'd been feeling. She hadn't wanted Aaron to have a lot of college loans over his head when he graduated so she had covered a part of his bill. As it turned out, Aaron had taken out a couple of loans, and still the money was short.

He wanted to go to law school. Toinette had already told her youngest son that she would help as much as she could, but she couldn't afford to pay for law school. Her moderate salary as director of the Achieving Against All Adversities program could only stretch so far.

Toinette grabbed a small wicker basket on the counter that held bills payable. Then she rooted in a drawer for a book of stamps. She carried the basket and the stamps and put them on the dining-room table, then went in search of her briefcase and her bank book.

With everything she needed on the dining-room table, Toinette couldn't put off the inevitable for another moment. Toinette was a people person. She liked to meet and talk to people. She liked to help folks who needed a hand. She liked to interact with others, play with kids, and do Quad-A presentations. Paper didn't exactly push her buttons. Except for pressing Quad-A work, she generally let paperwork, particularly bills and personal correspondence, slide until the very last moment.

"Coffee. I'll get some coffee."

She hopped up and went to the kitchen to pour a cup of the brew left over from breakfast.

Today was the very last moment for some of the household bills that were due or about to be overdue.

Carrying a ceramic mug, Toinette made her way to the dining room table. "It's awfully quiet in here."

She headed back to the kitchen to turn on a radio. She lingered a bit, turning the dial until she found a station playing a tune she liked. That bought her another couple of minutes.

"All right. All right," she said aloud to the conscience that was telling her to get to work.

Pulling out the first few envelopes in the basket, Toinette made quick work of writing checks to pay her electricity, telephone, gas, and cable television bills. She then moved to the credit card bills and wrote checks to pay for those.

Humming along with the female vocalist on the oldies station, she stuffed the checks in the corresponding envelopes and stamped them. She then pulled out the college tuition bill. The balance, in Toinette's opinion, was astounding.

"That boy is definitely getting a world-class education." She looked at the balance in her bank book and frowned. She thought she'd made a deposit, but there was no record of it—not surprising since she routinely neglected to record the amount of money in that savings account. Toinette had always figured it was safer if she didn't know how much disposable income she had.

Angela, her daughter who was an accountant, had been appalled when she first discovered Toinette's record-keeping habits. Toinette smiled, remembering the scolding she'd gotten.

"Mom, this is a disgrace. How do you know what's what? How do you know how much money you have or don't have?"

"Angie, baby, it's just money. The bills get paid on time for the most part, and the rest just sort of falls into place."

"Falls into place? Oh, my God. I don't believe this. Look, Mom, if you just keep all your deposit and withdrawal slips, I'll keep your accounts up to date. I cannot believe that you live like this. I know to the penny the amount in every one of my accounts: savings, checking, retirement account, certificates of deposit. Mom, how can you live like this?"

Angie, as Aaron would say, was kind of anal about that sort of thing. But that's what she did for a living. Angela had taken over the upkeep of her mother's accounts so Toinette didn't worry about pennies here and there. She just wrote the checks and kept moving.

As for the tuition balance, she figured Angela would have let her know if there was a problem. Toinette wrote her credit card number on the form to the college and made a mental note to have Angela transfer funds so she could write a check to the credit card company.

With the bills out of the way, she moved to the Quad-A paperwork in her briefcase. At least this was work, something Toinette could sink her teeth into. She went through the notes in her appointment book, checking off things that had been done and things she needed to do.

Next to the entry "Hazel," she put a question mark. No one at the center had heard from the girl in the days since she'd run out the back door. Maybe the girl had found some help. Toinette hoped so. There were so many Hazels out there—and so little that could be done for them if they didn't put a little trust in the people who could actually help. Toinette sighed. Living on the streets, it would be difficult for Hazel and kids like her to know whom to trust. Toinette underlined the girl's name, then made a notation to call a friend who operated a runaway hotline to see what kind of assistance might be available for the girl.

Toinette pushed the appointment book out of the way, then read through the proposal she'd written to Ben Trammer. Toinette marveled at the ease with which he'd approved the plan. During their lunch meeting, Trammer had even given the go-ahead for Toinette to make some site visits in the target cities. And according to Kendra, the MacAfrees were enthusiastic about the program. All systems were go.

Toinette grinned at the wonder of it all. Her dream was about to come true.

She glanced at her watch. "Okay, girlfriend. Let's get this last thing done."

From her briefcase she pulled some file folders with Quad-A spending data for the month and a calculator with adding tape. "Where's the ledger?"

She searched her briefcase again, this time dumping all the contents on the table. She frowned. The ledger with the program documentation wasn't there. Toinette got up, checked the foyer table. She went upstairs to look in the leather tote bag she sometimes carried to work. Then she remembered.

"You left it at the office on the credenza with the rest of the Trammer material. Okay, it's not the end of the world. You can still get this stuff done today."

Toinette went to the spare bedroom down the hall and pulled a box from the closet. Finally spotting what she was looking for, she pulled out the brown record book left over from Angie's supplies from a college accounting class. "I knew that holding onto this junk would come in handy one day."

Toinette put the box back in the closet and carried the notebook downstairs. Since she'd have to transfer the information from the temporary book to the real one, she used a pencil for all of the notations. She made fast work of the books.

Robinson left Toinette's house and drove to his office instead of to his own home. With three hours to kill before seeing Toinette again, there was something he realized he needed to do.

Russell Blue was a jerk, but Robinson was glad he'd had the confrontation with the man. There had been no time to reason with him, not that people like Russell Blue could be reasoned with. But Toinette's argument with Russell had shed light on something Robinson had been wondering about: why she willingly gave him her body but seemed guarded about declaring any feelings toward him. In some sense, Toinette still felt obligated to her husband.

Robinson parked his car, then let himself into the law firm. At his desk he flipped through his Rolodex until he found the name and number he was looking for. He dialed the number, fully expecting to leave a message with an answering service.

"Leo Stonehouse and Associates."

"Stonehouse? That you? I was ready to leave a message with your service."

"Hey, Rob. I was in for a couple of hours today. What's up? It's been a while since I've heard from you. Don't tell me you've up and contracted with another investigative service."

"No, nothing like that. But I could use your help on something. It's personal."

"I got your back, Brother. What do you need?"

"Can we talk somewhere?" Robinson asked.

"Okay. Let's see. I can finish this up in the next few minutes. Meet me at Callahan's Restaurant in thirty minutes."

"Sounds good. I'll be there."

Robinson rang off, flipped the Rolodex file to a blank card, and sat back in his chair.

He loved Toinette, and he'd told her so this morning. She tried to deny his words, but he hadn't let her finish her thought. She didn't even believe that he was serious about it. The player had finally met the one woman who meant everything to him, and she didn't even believe him; she'd called him "a sweet man." Robinson frowned. That was just one step beyond the banal compliment of being "a nice young man."

Maybe he hadn't been treating her the right way. Wine and roses he'd bought. They'd had plenty of sex, well, maybe not plenty, Robinson corrected. But their times together had been terrific. Toinette was some kind of woman. Had he known all along that older women were so attuned to every part of the lovemaking process, he may have dated older women exclusively in the past. Instead he'd found himself with women like Marlena and the ambassador's daughter who were superficially beautiful and good in bed but who lacked anything upstairs or in the heart where it counted. He attributed Toinette's appeal to her maturity, her outlook on life, the way she'd turned a bad personal experience into a program to help other people. He acknowledged that every older woman wasn't like Toinette. Every younger woman wasn't like Toinette. Toinette embraced life. Laughter and joy were just a part of her.

What about kids? the voice of his subconscious asked.

"Shut up. It's not an issue," he answered.

But it was an issue. Robinson thought about the letter from the children's home and reminded himself to go back and read it again. Maybe he'd talk to his mother about adoption. Genevieve and Robinson Mayview had adopted him. That was different, he argued to himself. If Toinette agreed to marry him, maybe she'd agree to have another child. Surely she was young enough to bear more children.

He swiveled the chair around, then got up and stared out at the rose garden. "Mayview, you have lost your mind. You don't even know if the woman loves you and you've jumped to the wedding and children."

Robinson glanced at his watch. He was supposed to meet Stonehouse in thirty minutes. Ten of those minutes had already passed. If he hurried, he'd be able to get to Callahan's without being late. He took one last look at the roses and made a mental note to buy some for Toinette. He then left his office.

In front of the restaurant, the two men shook hands. Stonehouse made a move to enter the door, but Robinson stopped him.

"Let's walk and talk," Robinson suggested.

Stonehouse gave him an odd look but nodded and fell in step next to his friend. The street, already bustling with Saturday morning shoppers, provided just the anonymous atmosphere Robinson wanted.

They walked several yards in silence. Stonehouse knew Robinson would begin when he was ready.

"I want you to find someone," Robinson began.

Stonehouse reached into his inner jacket pocket for a slim burgundy notebook.

"No notes, Stone. Just listen. I want you to find a guy named Russell Woodrow Blue, Sr."

Stonehouse tucked the notebook back in his pocket. "Bad debt or missing person?"

Robinson smirked. "I guess you could call him a missing person. He's been gone twenty-two years."

"What can you tell me about him?" Stonehouse asked.

"He was married and had four kids with another one on the way when he disappeared from the city."

"What's the case, Rob?"

Robinson, who had come to a jeweler's shop, paused and looked at the displays in the window. A diamond wedding set caught his eye. "I told you. It's not a case. It's personal. Send the bill to me at home. This isn't connected with the firm."

Robinson turned to look at the private detective he'd known for fifteen years. "I want to know everything there is to know about the man. Where he is, what he's been doing for the last twenty-two years, whether he's dead or alive."

"What else can you tell me? Do you have a photo or a last known address? Any family members around here that you know of?"

"He goes by the name of Woody. And he'd be about forty-eight. I don't have a photo. And I'd rather not say any more."

Stonehouse sighed. "You're not making this easy, Rob."

"Just find him, Stone." Robinson looked at the bleak expression on his old friend's face. "Look, man. I need your utmost discretion on this."

"You know you've got it."

"His wife's name was Toinette Blue," Robinson said. "She runs the Achieving Against All Adversities program here in town."

Stonehouse nodded. So it was personal. He'd seen a photograph of Robinson and Toinette Blue attending some charity event in the society section of the newspaper. He had one Quad-A employee working for his investigations firm. He didn't know what Robinson Mayview was up to, but he sensed how important the information was to the lawyer.

"And Stone?"

The investigator looked up from his feigned perusal of the jewelry.

"No one else on this investigation. Just you. If you can't do it, let me know now."

"It'll just be me, Rob. When do you want the report?"

"Last week."

Stonehouse nodded. He got the message.

Robinson reached out and shook Leo Stonehouse's hand, then walked into the jewelry shop. Stonehouse watched Robinson enter the building, then turned and walked in the opposite direction.

Inside the jeweler's, Robinson, a regular and discriminating customer, was immediately recognized and greeted by a smiling store manager.

"Mr. Mayview. What a wonderful surprise. Is there something I can do for you today?"

"Earrings," Robinson answered. "Show me some dazzling, dangling earrings."

"Right this way, sir."

Less than twenty minutes later, Robinson left the store with a small package. Toinette would look fabulous with the gemstone earrings he'd purchased for her. A quick glance at his watch told him he had about an hour and a half to kill before he was to meet her again.

Robinson walked the few blocks to where he'd parked his car, then drove home to shower and shave.

* * *

Across town, a nondescript blue sedan pulled up to a street corner. The young woman standing there looked to her left and then to her right before quickly stepping into the car's passenger seat. The vehicle sped away from the corner before she had time to shut the door.

"Your time is up, Miss Thing. Where's the cash?"

"I'm a little short."

"I don't want to hear it. You been stalling for weeks now. Your hot mouth is good, but it ain't that good."

The woman swallowed with a suddenly dry mouth, then unzipped the backpack she held. She pulled out a crinkled brown paper bag and placed it on the seat space between her and the man.

With one hand steering, the man dug into the bag and pulled out the cash, some of it crumpled bills. He threw a disgusted look at the woman, who cringed against the door of the car. He quickly counted the money.

"Maybe you need some incentive to get your act together. You're one hundred-fifty short."

"I promise you, next week. If you could just give me a little to get me by."

"No more freebies, baby. Get out."

The car came to a screeching halt in the middle of the street. The woman, too frightened to move, just sat there.

The man reached under his seat and pulled out a 9mm semi-automatic pistol. His cold eyes bored into the woman's as the cool steel of the weapon pressed against her temple. "Twenty-four hours, Miss Thing. I don't have my money in twenty-four hours, you better start making some arrangements with an undertaker man."

The woman nodded frantically and fumbled with the door handle. She finally managed to open the door and got a nudge from the man that sent her out the door and onto the pavement. The car sped away, leaving her crying in the street.

Toinette took more time than usual applying her makeup. She didn't like the extra layer of foundation, but it better concealed the bruise on her face. Her shoulder was still sore, so she rubbed ointment into it, then pulled on a loose top and a pair of blue pleated slacks.

Robinson hadn't said where they were going, but she figured casual was good. A pair of flat blue-and-green sandals completed the outfit.

Robinson had said he loved her, that he was in love with her. She'd tried not to think about it, because it was all so foreign to her. Toinette had been trying to digest that information while not dwelling on it in the time since he'd left the house. He seemed serious about it. In love. She hadn't been in love since the day Woody had walked out on her and their kids. She wasn't even sure if she knew what being in love felt like anymore.

Robinson made her feel special and young and beautiful. But those things didn't equate with being in love, did they?

Toinette opened the jewelry box on her dresser and looked at the wedding band Woody had placed on her finger so many years ago. Closing the jewelry case, she went to her closet and pulled out a box stuck way in the back.

Pushing and pulling, she maneuvered the heavy box to the chaise longue in her bedroom. She sat on the chaise and pulled a thick photo album from the box. She blew dust off the top.

Opening the old volume, she looked at the first photo enshrined in plastic: she and Woody mugging for the camera from a '67 Chevy. That car had been Woody's pride and joy. She turned the page and smiled at the images: she and Woody at a football game, at his junior prom. And then, their wedding pictures. Toinette looked long and hard at the photographs. She remembered the moment when she'd pledged her love to Woodrow Blue.

CHAPTER 17

The white dress belonged to her mother's sister and had been taken in on the sides. Nettie Anderson was tall but tiny. Pincurls plastered around the front of her head made a good headrest for her veil, a flowing creation of white taffeta and pearls that had been painstakingly and lovingly made by Nettie's best friend Sarah Cane.

"Ooh, chile. Woody Blue gon' drop on the floor when he see you coming down the aisle," Sarah cooed.

Nettie turned from side to side in the mirror. "Do you think I look all right, Sarah? I mean, this isn't really a wedding gown. It's just a long white dress."

"You getting married in it, ain't you?"

Nettie nodded.

"Then it's a wedding gown," Sarah reasoned.

Nettie stood facing the mirror and looked at her best friend standing at her shoulder. She and Sarah were more like sisters than best friends. A sudden and dazzling smile lit up Nettie's face. She whirled around and hugged Sarah.

"Thank you, Sarah. You're too good to me. And this veil. It's gorgeous. I'm going to keep it forever."

The two friends hugged. A knock at the door drew them apart. Sarah picked up a hankie from the dresser and dabbed Nettie's eyes.

"Now you can't be marching down the aisle with black streaks running down your face."

Nettie peered at the touch of pinkish-red rouge on her cheeks and the heavy black mascara that made her eyelashes feel funny. "I don't know about this makeup, Sarah. I've never worn all this stuff before. Just a little lipstick."

"You look beautiful. Shoot, I just wish it was me."

"Monk gonna be popping that question anytime now, Sarah. You just wait and see," Nettie assured her friend.

"Hmmph. He need to take some action like Woody doing."

"Nettie! Sarah! What ya'll doing in there. You gonna be late for yo' own wedding."

"Coming!" both girls yelled before looking at each other and erupting in giggles.

Nettie turned to leave the mirror.

"Wait a minute. You forgot something blue," Sarah reminded her. The dress was borrowed and old, the veil was new, and Sarah pressed a small pale blue handkerchief with lacy white edges in Nettie's hand.

"If you find yo'self up there crying, use this."

The two girls smiled at each other and then made their way to the church's front door.

In the vestibule, Nettie heard the "Wedding March" from the pipe organ in the sanctuary. Sarah went down the aisle before her and then Nettie slowly walked to the altar and Woody's arms.

She vaguely noticed how pretty her aunt had decorated the church. She and Woody stood under an arch of flowers. And then Reverend Johnson started the ceremony. When the preacher asked Nettie if she promised to love, honor, and obey Russell Woodrow Blue until death parted them, Nettie turned away from the preacher and looked up at Woody.

"I do because I love you," she had answered.

Woody grinned and bent low to drop a kiss on Nettie's cheek.

"We haven't gotten to that part yet, son," the preacher said.

The doorbell rang and Toinette's memories stopped. She clasped her chest with one hand and blinked back tears. Her wedding veil was hanging in the back of a closet. Her oldest daughter, Leah, had worn that same veil for her own wedding. And Angie, her youngest daughter, had already asked if she could wear it whenever she got around to getting married. Toinette closed the dusty photo album, put it back in the cardboard box and got up. She resolved to call Sarah tonight. The two old friends hadn't talked in years.

Toinette took one last critical look at her face. At worst, she figured it looked like she was trying to cover up a bruise. At best, she looked like a woman who wore too much makeup. She spritzed herself with a light cologne, then strapped a fanny pack about her waist. The doorbell rang again. Toinette dashed downstairs to greet Robinson.

"You look great," he said.

Toinette tenderly touched the bruise on her cheek. "I tried to cover it up."

"It'll fade away in a few days. Still hurt?"

Toinette nodded.

"Would you rather stay home?"

Toinette thought about the box of precious memories and broken promises waiting in her bedroom.

"No. I want to spend the day with you."

Robinson grinned. "Good."

"Where are we going?" she asked.

"The zoo."

"The zoo?"

"It'll be fun," he told her.

Toinette locked the front door and followed Robinson to the Jeep parked at her curb.

Together they strolled through the zoo. They threw peanuts to the elephants and watched the apes and chimps scamper through trees. Toinette stared at the big cats for a long time, absorbing their graceful beauty.

Robinson couldn't miss her pensive mood. "You've been awfully quiet today," he observed.

They walked hand in hand toward the aquatics building.

Toinette gave him a short, vaguely sad smile. "I've been thinking about things." Maybe pulling up all the old memories hadn't been a good idea. But it was too late now, she thought. Pandora's box was open.

"About what I told you this morning?"

Toinette stopped walking and turned to look at Robinson. "To some degree that. But mostly other things."

"Toinette . . ."

She motioned to an unoccupied park bench. "Let's sit over there."

They walked to the bench. Toinette sat and crossed her legs. Robinson sat down beside her. With one hand trailing along her neck, he encouraged her to speak—even though he had the feeling he didn't want to hear what she had to say.

"Talk to me, my beautiful Toinette."

"Rob, I'm having second thoughts about our, well, our seeing each other."

"You mean our relationship?"

"Do we have a relationship or are we just two people who enjoy spending time with each other? I think our definitions of the word *relationship* vary."

"Tell me what's on your mind, Toinette," Robinson said softly.

She smiled at him and tenderly caressed his cheek. "You're a very sweet man."

"Every time you say that I feel like a five-year-old."

Toinette brought her hand down and turned away. "I'm sorry," she said quietly. "I think of that as a compliment."

"Toinette, look at me."

She stared unseeing at two mallards crossing the walkway in front of the bench where they sat.

"Toinette?"

Slowly she turned to him.

"Talk to me, baby. If what I said this morning frightened you, just tell me. I need to know what's going through your head."

"Confusion. Confusion is what's going through my head, Rob. I thought I'd finally worked some things out. I was getting used to the fact that I'm almost old enough to be your mother . . ."

"Toinette, we've been through this age thing before."

"No, Rob. You've been through it. You worked it all out in your own head and then told me how it was going to be. Well, I'm several steps behind you in the reasoning and rationalizing process. Russell made me realize that I can choose to live my life the way I want to. I also care about you."

"But?"

"But what we're doing is wrong," she said. It had to be wrong, she thought to herself. She couldn't be in love with two men at the same time. Woody was gone, but he was still her husband and she loved him. Maybe.

"What's wrong about me loving you?" Robinson asked.

Toinette sighed. "You're making this so complicated. It's morally wrong." She quickly held her hand up to stop him from interrupting. "I know I try to come off as a nineties kind of woman. But, Rob, the honest-to-God truth is that I'm old-fashioned. Deep down where it counts, I believe there are lines that shouldn't be crossed."

"Help me understand, Toinette. What lines do you feel have been crossed?"

"Being with you. Sleeping with you. I shouldn't have done that."

Robinson brushed the side of her face with his hand. "But didn't it feel good?"

Toinette smiled sadly. "That's your age talking, Robinson. Everything that feels good isn't necessarily good for you. You learn that over time and by raising five children."

"So what are you telling me, Toinette?"

"I don't know. I honestly don't know, Rob. I like you. We have fun together. But things are just moving too fast for me. I know you probably think this 'relationship' is traveling at a snail's pace. Maybe if I were a younger woman, a different woman, I'd see things differently, maybe even see things the way you do. But I'm not somebody else. It's going to take me a while to reconcile these things."

Robinson didn't say anything. He didn't know what to say. This afternoon hadn't exactly turned out the way he'd planned. It sounded like she wanted a little breathing room. The fight he'd had with her son had probably brought all of this doubt on. Robinson didn't know how to—and didn't want to—make her choose him over her flesh and blood. Even though she'd done essentially that, he didn't think that the dispute and the ultimatum she'd given Russell looked the same to her in the light of day. It was one thing to tell your son to walk out the door and not look back and another to realize that he might do just that.

Then there was the husband. Robinson figured he didn't need a crystal ball to figure out what moral hang-up Toinette was suddenly having. Leo Stonehouse would get to the bottom of that mystery. In the meantime, he couldn't afford to lose Toinette after he'd spent what seemed like his entire life searching for her.

Robinson picked up her hand and brought it to his mouth for a gentle kiss. "Please don't banish me from your life. No more sex, no more fights with your son. Let's just slowly get to know each other better."

"I don't think patience is your strong suit," she told him.

"Try me. You'll see."

Robinson helped her from the bench, and they continued their stroll through the zoo. Their relationship had taken a new turn. Robinson couldn't say if it was a turn for the better or for the worse, but he had to deal with it, nonetheless.

They ate a lunch of hot dogs with sauerkraut from a vendor at the zoo. Then Robinson drove her home. He pulled the Jeep to the curb in front of Toinette's house and turned off the ignition.

Unsnapping his seat belt, he turned to her. "Toinette, I know you're having some doubts right now about where we may be headed. I promise to give you all the space and the time you need, if you'll promise me one thing."

Toinette looked at him. "What?"

"That you'll continue to let me see you. We can go out and spend time together as friends."

Toinette thought about that for a moment. She didn't see anything wrong with seeing the man. "Not like dates, right?"

Robinson couldn't lie to her. He could play by her rules and still woo her. With luck, he'd win her heart. "Like friends."

Toinette finally nodded her acquiescence.

Robinson smiled. "Good." He accepted the fact that they had just agreed to two different things. Toinette might claim chronological years and maturity on him, but Robinson knew that the couple with a solid foundation based on friendship stood the best chance of an enduring and loving relationship.

He got out of the Jeep and walked around to her side. But before Toinette could step out, he moved into the open space, blocking her in. "I have something for you."

Toinette smiled. "What?"

Robinson leaned over her and opened the glove compartment. He pulled out a small wrapped package and put it in Toinette's hands.

"What is it?"

"Open it and see."

Toinette ripped the bow from the top of the package and tore the paper off. Robinson grinned at her enthusiasm.

She opened the velvet box. "Oh, my God. Rob, these are beautiful!" She pulled one of the earrings from the box and held it up. "Lord have mercy, you shouldn't have. These are gorgeous." The stained-glass design of the doorknocker earrings took her breath away. Reds, greens, blues, and purples twinkled at her from the gold inlay.

Toinette's eyes widened. She looked at the jeweler's mark on the box. The colorful stones weren't glass but rubies, emeralds, sapphires, and amethysts. "Lord, have mercy, Robinson. These are real. I can't take this."

Robinson, unable to resist, lowered his head and captured her mouth. The kiss fed him and soothed him.

Toinette came up breathless. "Rob, I thought we were friends."

"We are. And that was a friendly little kiss."

"And these earrings?"

"A friendly gift for a beautiful woman."

Toinette looked dubious.

"I saw the earrings and thought of you. Please accept them as a token of my affection."

Toinette looked from the man to the jewelry in her hands. She placed the one earring back in the box and closed the top. "Thank you, Robinson."

He tried to contain his sigh of relief. "I'll walk you to your door."

At the door, he bent and kissed her on her cheek. "I'm glad we spent the day together. Thank you for giving that to me."

Toinette smiled, then raised a hand to caress his cheek. She opened her mouth to speak, then decided against it. She smiled up at him, lowered her eyes, and ducked in the door.

Robinson looked at the closed portal. Steepling his hands, he bent his head and offered a quick prayer to a higher power before heading back to his Jeep.

Inside the house, Toinette sat on the first step of the stairwell. She opened the box and looked at the earrings.

"Lord have mercy. What have I gotten myself into?"

CHAPTER 18

Later that evening Toinette fixed herself a cup of coffee, carried it to her bedroom, then settled on the chaise. She hadn't talked to Sarah in a while, but she still remembered her friend's Detroit telephone number.

As she waited for the number to connect and ring, Toinette fingered the photo album with her wedding pictures. She decided against reopening the album. Each image was still burned in her mind; she'd thought of little else while out with Robinson that afternoon.

"Monk residence," a woman's voice said over the telephone.

Toinette smiled when she recognized her friend's voice. She tucked her feet under her and leaned back. "Sarah. It's Nettie."

"Nettie! Girl, I was just thinking about you. Just the other day I told Monk I hadn't talked to you in a while. How's it going?"

"Sarah . . ."

"Oh, Lord. I hear it in your voice. Hold on a second."

Toinette smiled at Sarah's uncanny ability to determine her moods with just a word.

Before long, Sarah was back on the line. "Okay. I'm in the den. I told Monk I was on the phone with you and shouldn't be disturbed. He said, 'Well, I guess I'll see you sometime tomorrow. You and Blue don't know how to have a short talk.' "

"Tell that old scoundrel I said hi."

"I'll tell him tomorrow."

The two women laughed. Then Sarah jumped in. "I would ask about the kids, but we'll get to that later. What's wrong?"

"I got man troubles, Sarah."

"Hmm, that sounds like the best kind of trouble to me."

"Sarah, I think I'm in love."

"That's wonderful!" Then Sarah paused. "What do you mean you *think* you're in love? You're old enough to know if it's the real thing or not."

"Funny you should mention old," Toinette said.

Toinette then caught Sarah up on all that had transpired with Robinson, from their first innocent meetings and the play *Lovin' A Younger Man* to the fight he'd had with Russell and the earrings he'd given her that afternoon. The only part she omitted was their sexual relationship.

But Sarah heard the gap in the story. "So, have you and this man, you know, been together?"

Toinette sighed.

"Okay," Sarah said, interpreting the sigh. "So he's not that great in bed. He sounds perfect in every other respect."

"Sarah, he is a master blaster in bed. If I had known sex could be so good, I wouldn't have spent the last decade of my life without a man."

"Obviously not just any man, Nettie. This one. And a master blaster you say? Hmm. Can't say I've heard that one before, but it sounds good to me."

Toinette smiled, then shook her head. "That part of the relationship is irrelevant . . ."

"Speak for yourself, girlfriend," Sarah cut in.

"I'm just so confused right now."

"Confused about what? You just spent the last twenty minutes describing your soul mate to me, and now you tell me you're confused?"

"Well, what about Russell? They're practically the same age, and Russell obviously hates Rob. Then there's Woody."

"Look, I know Russell is your child and whatnot. I'm the boy's godmother, but, Nettie, you know that boy has always been stubborn."

"Sarah."

"I'm serious. You know I speak the truth. And he's never really accepted the fact that his father just left and made him the man in the house. I wouldn't cotton much to what Russell thinks about your relationship with Robinson. If he can't deal with it, that's his problem, not yours."

Well, there you have it, Toinette thought. Sarah had come to the same conclusion as herself. But the words she'd told her son had been spoken in anger, not in a rational manner.

"And as for Woody," Sarah continued. "Nettie, we have talked about this at least a thousand times in the last twenty years. The man is gone.

Gone for good. I think it's a blessing that you met this Robinson guy. He's been able to remind you that you're still a woman through and through."

"I don't know that much about him."

"So ask him. If you're gonna insist on this whole friendship thing, do like the man said and get to know each other better."

"I really hate it when you're so practical."

Sarah laughed. "That's why you love me, sister. Now, tell me what's been going on with your four other children."

The women spent another two hours catching up on their lives. They rang off, promising to stay in touch. Toinette felt much better after talking to her friend. She picked up and opened the jeweler's box to gaze again at the earrings Robinson had given her. Getting up from the chaise, she went to the mirror and put them on.

The set was beautiful. The brilliant hues of the gemstones sparkled as she turned her head first to the left, then to the right.

"What am I going to do with you, Robinson Mayview?"

The doorbell rang. Toinette went to the front window in the bedroom. Russell's minivan sat at the curb. She sighed. "Now what?"

She went downstairs and opened the door. "Russell, what do you want? I thought you said your peace the other night."

Standing in the door, looking contrite, Russell said, "I didn't mean to go off on your, your uh . . ."

"Friend," Toinette supplied.

"Yes, ma'am. Your friend. He just made me so goddamned—"

"Russell, you can take your foul language and go home."

"Mom, I'm sorry. Really I am. I just, well, I guess I overreacted."

"You guess?"

Russell sighed. "May I come in? Please."

With a semidisgusted look, Toinette stepped back to allow him in, then shut the door and followed him to the living room. She settled into her favorite chair, the Louis XV-style piece that had been a housewarming gift from Russell. She motioned for him to be seated.

Russell perched on the edge of the sofa and regarded his mother. "Mom, I am sorry that you had to witness that." Peering at her cheek, he looked at the camouflaged bruise he'd inflicted. "And I'm sorry I hit you. It was an accident, Mom. Really it was."

"If you weren't so prone to anger, none of this would have happened."

Russell sighed before settling back on the sofa cushions. "Mom, try to understand this from my perspective. The first time I saw that guy was early one Sunday morning. I was coming down the street with the kids, and I see some man tipping out your front door and then speeding away. You work around those criminal types all day. What was I supposed to think?

"Then I come over to just see how you're doing and find you sitting in a car making out like a horny teenager with the same god—"

"Watch your mouth, Russell. And if I've told you once, I've told you a thousand times, being poor doesn't mean one is a criminal. When are you going to get that through your head?"

Russell sighed and sat forward, perched again on the edge of the sofa. "Mom, this is very difficult for me."

"That's rather obvious," Toinette said drolly.

"Mom, I want you to be happy. I guess I just didn't want to have to see any evidence of it."

"That's a contradiction, Russell."

"I know. But it's how I feel. I mean, you are still married to Dad. He might be gone, but you still love him. That's what you've always said."

Funny how Russell managed to zero in on the very issue she had been wrestling with. Toinette watched the expectant, even hopeful expression on her son's face and realized she'd made a mistake in lying to him and her other children for so many years. In keeping their hope up and love for their father flourishing, she'd laid the emotional groundwork that had her tied in fits right now. Russell was thirty years old and deserved to know the whole truth.

Toinette crossed her legs and shifted in her chair. "Russell, there's something I need to explain to you."

"I hope it's in regards to what you said about Dad walking out on us. I've been thinking about that."

She nodded, then tried to pull her thoughts together.

"I think . . . no, I know, that I've done a disservice to you, your sisters, and brother. Your father and I, well, you know we got married very young. We were in love and saw no reason to wait until we were older. We'd been in love as long as we could remember. Maybe that was the first mistake. We'd only known each other, had never really dated anyone else. I was sixteen, your father was seventeen. Neither of us really got the opportunity to find out about other people or other experiences because we were so wrapped up in each other. You were born a year after we got married. Then before you know it, we had Leah and Judi and Angie."

Raptly listening, Russell settled again into the sofa cushions.

"We'd been having some money problems, as all young couples do. But Woody had a good job and we'd bought a house. You were eight. Do you remember the house on Johnson Street?"

Russell nodded. "Yeah. Leah and I had to share a room with Judi. Boy, was she a brat."

Toinette smiled at the memory. "The house was small. But it was ours, and we were proud of it. Or, at least I was. Well, anyway, we had a lot of mouths to feed and the house payments were large. Then I found out I was pregnant again with Aaron. Things started changing after I told your father I was expecting again. He started staying out later and later. I just figured he was working more overtime to get some extra money. One night when I was five months along with Aaron, your dad said he was going out to get some cigarettes. I never saw him or heard from him again."

"What do you mean you never heard from him again? You showed us the letters he sent each month. I still have some of them. You had us draw him pictures that we put in the letters we wrote to him."

Toinette looked down and then away. She swallowed back the tears forming.

"Mom?"

Toinette shook her head and then swiped a hand at a tear that managed to escape.

"Mom? You said he was working in another state and that he'd been injured and was in a veteran's hospital . . . a hospital that didn't allow visitors." Russell paused. Then he swore out loud. "There was no injury. No hospital. How could he even be a veteran if he married you at seventeen and went straight to work? You lied to me! You lied to all of us."

"I'm sorry, Russell. I—it seemed like the right thing to do at the time." Toinette got up, pulled a tissue from a box on an end table, then paced the area in front of the sofa. "It seemed like the right thing to do. Try to understand my viewpoint."

Russell hopped up to confront her. "Your viewpoint? You had us all living some sort of stupid fantasy."

"I didn't want you to hate your father! I was hurt and angry and confused and afraid. I didn't know what had happened to him. The police couldn't tell me anything. I didn't even have a job. I was a pregnant lady with four kids depending on me. If living a fantasy, as you call it, helped me cope with everything I had to deal with, I'd probably do it the same way again. At least you grew up with the fiction of a father's love. When we moved into the projects, your little friends didn't have that. Half of them didn't even know who their fathers were. At least you had good memories."

"I had false hope."

With her arms clinched around herself, Toinette balled up the tissue in her hand and turned away.

"So what are you trying to do with this young punk you're hanging out with? Are you trying to relive your wasted years?"

Toinette flinched as if she'd been hit. "Russell, you don't understand . . ."

"Is he taking the place of Dad or is he just taking advantage of a good thing that's being thrown at him? I'll bet he and his real girlfriends get a kick out of talking about the old broad he's messing with on the side. Are those fancy earrings from him? Payment for favors rendered?"

The cruel words, delivered like physical blows, cut Toinette to the quick. Too upset to speak, she shuddered at the waves of animosity pouring from her son. She only knew he'd left when she heard the front door slam.

As the tears fell, Toinette covered her mouth with her hand to hold in the scream that threatened to erupt from the core of her. Then, trembling, she made her way to the chair, where she collapsed and gave in to the racking sobs of regret.

Almost an hour later, Toinette still sat slumped in the chair. The tears had dried, but the regret and heartache remained. In one day she'd managed to lose both Russell and Robinson. She thought about calling Kendra, but it was late, and besides, there was no need to upset Kendra about an issue that had no solution.

Toinette got up and slowly made her way upstairs. She stripped off her clothes and left them in a heap on the floor. Emotionally spent, she fell into the bed. But sleep was elusive. When she finally drifted away, her rest was fitful. She dreamed she wore a wedding gown and that an angry, barking dog was chasing her as she ran down a street while clutching a teddy bear in her arms.

By Monday Toinette was still out of sorts. She arrived at the Quad-A center looking haggard and worn. The center employees knew something was wrong when she went straight to her office and shut the door. Mrs. Blue always started the day with coffee and a pep talk to the aides and then a trip to the nursery to visit with the children.

About midmorning, Dawn, the head aide, knocked on Toinette's door.

"Come in."

A huge arrangement of cut flowers preceded Dawn into the office. "These just arrived for you. Aren't they beautiful?"

Toinette looked at the flowers, then smiled for the first time that day.

"Here's the card," Dawn said, plucking the small envelope from the arrangement and handing it to Toinette.

"Thank you."

Not sure what else to say or do, Dawn turned around and left. If she noticed the circles under Mrs. Blue's eyes or the unusual amount of makeup her boss had on, she didn't mention it.

Toinette opened the envelope.

Like the fragrant blossoms of these flowers, you bring joy and sunshine to my life.

Robinson.

She started crying again. From memory she dialed Robinson's office number. His secretary put her through without delay.

She tried to get herself together and sound normal when she heard his voice, but she couldn't quite pull it off. "Thank you for the flowers," she said in a trembling voice.

"Toinette, what's wrong? They were supposed to make you smile, not cry."

"Oh, Rob. Everything is just . . . It's just a mess. Russell and I had a fight Saturday night."

"Why didn't you call me?"

Toinette shrugged, but Robinson, of course, couldn't see that.

"Toinette?"

"Yes?"

"Where are you?"

"At work," she mumbled.

"I'll be there in twenty minutes."

Fifteen minutes later Robinson's BMW came to a screeching halt in front of the Quad-A center. He dashed in the building and went straight to her office, followed by Dawn, who'd come to check on the commotion.

Robinson took one look at the listless Toinette, then picked up her handbag and helped her from the chair. "Mrs. Blue is taking the rest of the day off," he informed Dawn as he hustled Toinette out of the office and to his car.

Across the street, an observer took in the comings and goings at the Quad-A center. Watching the flurry of activity, the observer smirked, saying quietly: "My, how the mighty have fallen."

CHAPTER 19

Robinson drove straight to his home. Toinette didn't say a word the entire time but stared vacantly out the window. Activating one of the garage's three doors, he parked the BMW next to the Jeep. As the garage door lowered behind them, Robinson helped Toinette from the car. He led her through the utility room and across the dining room to his bedroom.

"Wait right here. I'm going to put some water on for some tea." He dropped her purse in an overstuffed chair that matched the cream-colored platform of his huge bed.

A few minutes later, Robinson returned and Toinette was standing in the same place he'd left her. He went to her. "Toinette, talk to me. What's wrong?"

She'd gone over this a hundred times the day before, and each time she'd come to the same bottom line. "Russell called me a whore."

Robinson's response tinged the room blue. "I swear to God, Toinette, the man might be your son, but I'm going to kill him when I see him again."

"It's unlikely that you or I will see him again. My daughter-in-law called me Sunday upset and crying. She said Russell forbade her or their children to see or talk to me again."

"Toinette, why didn't you call me? You didn't have to go through this alone. And you don't have to be a victim to his emotional blackmail."

"There's nothing I can do," she whispered, trying to hold back the tears that threatened to fall again.

Robinson folded her into his arms and hugged her. "Yes, there is. You have rights as a grandparent and can sue him."

"I'm not going to sue my son."

"You need to have him committed to a mental institution."

"This isn't funny, Robinson."

"I wasn't joking," he said. "Turn around." He turned her, then pulled off the multicolored Afrocentric duster that topped her matching dress. Tossing the duster onto a chair, he worked on the top button of her dress.

"I don't want to make love, Robinson."

"Neither do I. You're going to sleep."

"I'm not tired."

"Um-hmm." He stripped her to a bra, half-slip, and hose. Robinson swallowed and mentally steeled his resolve not to make love to her. It was a struggle, but he didn't touch her. Instead, he moved to the king-size platform bed and pushed aside the five overstuffed pillows and pulled back the brown ribbed comforter. Toinette sank into one of the chairs and watched him.

Going to the big walk-in closet, Robinson emerged a few minutes later with what was obviously one of his shirts. "You can put this on. I'll go check on your tea."

When he returned with a cup and saucer, Toinette was curled up in the chair, fast asleep. Robinson smiled. He placed the herbal tea on a small table, then gathered Toinette in his arms. She felt heavenly, all woman, soft and warm . . . and his.

Carrying her to the bed, Robinson placed her on the bed. He pulled off the mules she wore and tugged at the half-slip. Toinette was a vision of loveliness. Rob had to admit, he liked the way she looked in his bed: like she belonged there—forever.

He took a deep breath, then got her out of the pantyhose. Looking at the bra with its front hook, he decided he didn't have enough strength to remove that bit of cloth. As he pulled the sheet up and over her, he leaned over and kissed her on the mouth. "Peace to you, Toinette. I love you."

Robinson turned the ringer off the phone by the bed and lowered the custom blinds. He kissed Toinette's forehead, then quietly left the room.

Downtown, newspaper reporter C.J. Mayview was going through her mail. From an interoffice memo envelope she pulled a letter to the editor. "Copy to City Desk" was scrawled across the top with an FYI note attached. "Thought I'd pass this to you," the first note read. Underneath it, C.J. recognized her editor's handwriting: "C.J.: This could be something—or not. For your files."

She frowned. Hundreds of these things came in each year. So far, few of them had ever resulted in actual stories. She read the chicken-scratch handwriting.

"Deer Sirs: You always trying to do a investigation. You need to be looking into what be going on in these projects. Its bad and don't make no sense how some people always trying to adversity there problems and stepping on the rest of us who can't do as good."

C.J. read the semiliterate letter again. The last part didn't make any sense—few of the letters like this ever did. She stuck the letter in a file labeled *Projects—complaints* and went on to the next envelope. Twenty minutes later, she'd finished the mail, her coffee, and was on the phone checking out a news tip about an elderly man with Alzheimer's who was about to be evicted from his apartment.

In his kitchen, Robinson checked in with his secretary. "I'll be out for the rest of the day, Zena. If there's an emergency, I can be reached at home."

"You've had several calls since you left."

He reached for a pen and a piece of paper. "Give them to me."

"Marlena called. She didn't leave a last name or number. Said you'd know who it was."

Robinson rolled his eyes. "Next."

"Your mother called and wanted to schedule lunch with you this week. She said Wednesday at noon unless she hears from you otherwise," the secretary reported.

"Okay," he said, making a note on the sheet to call his mother to confirm. "Anything else?"

"Two more. A would-be client called. I made a preliminary appointment for a week from Thursday. It's a trust. And Mrs. Griffin, the mayor's wife, called. She said you volunteered to participate in a charity event and she has some good news for you."

"Volunteered, my foot. More like commandeered. What's her number?"

Robinson scribbled the number Zena gave him. "Anything else?"

"No, sir. That was all of the telephone messages."

"Okay. Tell Malc I'm at home if he needs me for anything."

"I believe he's in court most of the day."

Robinson rang off with his secretary, then called the ever-forceful social maven, Mrs. Griffin.

"Oh, Mr. Mayview. How good of you to get back with me so soon. I have wonderful news about the auction. I've talked with several people, and our committee has decided to accelerate this benefit. By pooling our resources and working around the clock, we know we can pull this together. The auction will be held a month from today. Can we still count on your support to be one of our celebrity bachelors?"

"I'm not a celebrity, Mrs. Griffin."

"Oh, you're too modest. It's just too bad your partner up and got himself married. That Malcolm Hightower would have been another excellent candidate."

Robinson rolled his eyes.

"I can count on you, Mr. Mayview, right? We have already secured commitments from a couple of professional football players, one of the television newscasters, and the owner of Callahan's Restaurant."

Robinson grinned. He wondered what favors had been called in to get the popular restauranteur out of his kitchen and on the stage for a bachelor auction. He then looked toward his bedroom where Toinette was sleeping. The way things were going now, it was highly unlikely that they would be married in a month's time. And Toinette had been present the night this harebrained idea was cooked up. Then, as a sensual smile curved his lips, he remembered that she'd said she would bid ten grand for a night with him. But they had not yet slept together then. Would she be willing to bid more now? Thoughts of Russell Blue intruded. The way things had been going the last few days, Toinette probably wouldn't bid a quarter to spend any time with him. Robinson sighed.

"Does that sigh of resignation mean yes?"

He'd forgotten about Mrs. Griffin on the line. "Yes, Mrs. Griffin. I'll do the auction. What's the time and place? And what do I have to do?"

"Oh, wonderful! I'm so glad you'll be participating. All you have to do is plan the actual date. It can be a night or a weekend, it's up to you. Maybe dinner and dancing. Maybe a weekend in Atlantic City or the Poconos . . ."

I don't think so, Robinson thought to himself.

". . . I've checked with some other groups that have done this in other cities. The date could be a limo ride with a show, or tickets to a sold-out concert. Camping if you're so inclined. You get the idea. Some people just leave it up to the bidder and make themselves available for whatever the bidder wants to do."

"I'll come up with something."

"Wonderful. Now here's the day and time." Robinson jotted down the information. "It's black-tie," she told him. "This should bring in quite a bit of money for the three groups. I know your firm has an interest in the Quad-A program. I've left a message at Mrs. Blue's office. I've talked with reporters at the television stations and with the society editor at the newspaper. This will be big, really big. And with the support of bachelors like you, Mr. Mayview, this fundraiser will be quite a success."

Robinson listened to more effusiveness from the mayor's wife, then finally got the woman off the line.

He went to check on Toinette and found her still fast asleep. Smiling down at her, he shrugged out of his suit jacket and tugged off his shoes. He picked up her dress and duster, then gathered his shoes and hers and padded to his closet. The space was almost as big as one of the spare bedrooms in his home, and it was full. One wall of the well-organized closet held nothing but suits. Slots filled with shoes from wingtips to running shoes lined the back wall. Robinson pulled spare hangers from the area where shirts hung and placed Toinette's dress on one and the duster on another. He lined her shoes up on the floor under her clothes. Then he put his own shoes next to hers and looked at them.

Rob smiled. He liked the symbolism.

He tugged off his tie and went to a slim turnstile built into one wall that held his collection of more than two hundred of the cravats. He found the appropriate color-coordinated spot for the mauve tie he'd worn to work that day and placed it on the rack.

Selecting jeans and a white oxford shirt to wear, he hung up his suit, took off the shirt he was wearing, and tossed it in a laundry bag of things to be dry-cleaned. Robinson quickly dressed. Then, standing at the door of the closet, he made a critical assessment of the space. From what he'd seen of her clothes, Toinette had as many or more different outfits than he. When they married, he'd have to expand the closet space.

Robinson walked through his dressing area and eyed likely spaces for another huge closet. He loved the solarium off the jacuzzi too much to mess with that space and figured Toinette would think the same thing once she saw it. Robinson settled on a spot in the bedroom where an addition could be built.

"Don't you think you're jumping the gun a bit, my man?" he mumbled to himself. He looked at Toinette's sleeping form. "No," he replied. He was just being optimistic. With one last look at Toinette, Robinson padded to the kitchen to prepare some lunch.

A while later, Toinette woke up refreshed. The bed felt so good she never wanted to leave it. And there was a faint but definitely pleasing scent that reminded her of the cologne Robinson wore. Toinette's eyes widened as she remembered exactly where she was. She sat up with a start and looked around.

She was in Robinson's bed! In his house. She'd never been to his home. Suddenly curious, she took a closer look at the room. It was decorated in rich creams and warm browns, earthy and soothing tones. This was definitely a room to relax in. A wall console undoubtedly held a television. An arrangement of cut flowers adorned a table next to a love seat in the room. Toinette pulled the sheet off and swung her legs over the bed. Her bare toes connected with deep pile carpeting that was to die for.

"Good god. The carpeting and padding for this one room probably cost as much as the carpeting for my whole house."

She then realized she wore only a bra and panties. "Thank goodness you wore the good stuff, girlfriend," she muttered. She looked around but didn't see her clothes. One of Rob's shirts was draped over a chair. She picked it up and put it on.

Feeling sufficiently covered, she took another look around the room. A fireplace! The man had a fireplace in his bedroom. Unbidden, thoughts of being with Robinson on the floor in front of that spot came to her and rattled her equilibrium. Toinette turned her back to the fireplace. A series of four watercolors hung above the bed. An African sculpture rested on a ledge nearby. Toinette leaned over, peering at the ledge and the matching end tables. She ran a finger over the textured marble of the top. "Nice."

Toinette's gaze wandered back to the flowers. It was nice to find a man who could appreciate natural beauty and didn't feel intimidated by so-called feminine things.

She didn't see her shoes anywhere and decided it was time to go in search of Robinson.

It took a while, but she found him in his home office. Standing in the doorway, she quietly watched him for a few moments. Every now and then he'd make a quick notation on a pad, then stick his head back in the volume he was reading. He looked totally absorbed in the task, and Toinette loathed disturbing him. But she couldn't walk around in his shirt for the rest of the day.

"Rob?"

He glanced up from the book and smiled at her. Marking his place with a Kente cloth bookmark, Robinson closed the volume and went to her.

God, did she ever look sexy wearing just his shirt and a smile. Robinson knew what delights the cotton covered, and his body responded. He tried not to stare. "Did you get a good nap?"

Toinette nodded, then crossed her arms over her chest. Robinson looked like he would eat her alive right on the spot. She had to admit, that didn't sound like such a bad idea. But they were supposed to be friends, not lovers.

"Hungry?"

Suddenly not trusting her voice, she simply nodded again.

"I made quiche while you were asleep." He took her hand and guided her to the kitchen. On a table in a nook off the kitchen, he'd prepared a place setting for two.

"You cook?"

"I have to be able to impress you with some domestic skills. Quiche is my favorite. I know how to make four types."

"A black man who makes quiche. Interesting concept," Toinette muttered.

"What was that?" Robinson said from the kitchen where he was pulling something from the refrigerator.

"Oh, nothing. You have a beautiful home, Rob."

"Thanks. I built this place several years ago. My sister and my parents thought I was nuts."

"Why?"

"Mostly because it's so big and so far out of the city. But I like space and figured I'd need the room. After you eat, I'll show you around."

A thought suddenly struck Toinette. "Were you married before?"

"Nope. Came close a few times, but it just wasn't right." He turned to stare at her. "I knew I'd know the right woman when I met her."

Toinette looked away, unable to bear the message in his eyes.

Robinson let the moment pass. He cut the cheese quiche and placed it in the microwave to warm. When the appliance beeped, he took the platter out and garnished two white china plates with green grapes, slices of thinly cut cantaloupe and melon, and a sprig of fresh parsley. He placed a plate before Toinette.

"Where'd you learn to do this?" she asked suspiciously.

"We bachelors have to go through survival training," he answered with a smile. "We learn how to make do for ourselves."

He headed back to the kitchen for two iced glasses and a pitcher of fresh-squeezed raspberry lemonade. He wasn't about to tell her that one of the women he'd dated had been a chef. The relationship didn't last, but he learned a lot about cooking and food presentation while dating her.

"I talked to Mrs. Griffin while you were asleep," he said. "She's steamrolling her little benefit auction through."

"If Nancy Griffin is heading up a project, you can rest assured there'll be nothing little about it."

"She's going to have it in a month," Robinson said, joining Toinette at the table.

"That's fast. She must have a cruise or something planned and wants to get this out of the way."

"Now why wouldn't she just be doing it out of the kindness of her heart and a sincere desire to push the plan through?"

Toinette plucked a grape and smirked. She popped the fruit in her mouth and watched Robinson regarding her.

"Don't do that."

"Do what?" he asked.

"Look at me like that."

"How am I looking at you?"

"Like you want to ravish me on the kitchen floor."

Robinson turned to look down at the tiled floor. Then he regarded Toinette with a sensual smile. "Actually, I was thinking about the dining-room table."

CHAPTER 20

"Robinson!"

"I'm just being honest with you," he said before taking a bite of the quiche.

"Well, I'm starting to think I could do with a little less honesty these days."

From the sad tone of her voice, Robinson knew she was talking about Russell. "Let's eat. Then we'll talk."

They shared a pleasant meal together chatting about general things like projects the mayor's wife spearheaded and how successful her husband might be in the next election. As they ate, Robinson got up to start a pot of coffee.

When they finished, Robinson showed her around the house. As they wandered from room to room, Toinette picked up on the melding of Afrocentric and contemporary themes throughout the residence.

"This is really beautiful, Rob," she said in the formal living room where glass-enclosed cases held African artifacts.

Rob came up behind her, and with one hand at the small of her back, he explained the pieces. "The drummer is from Nigeria. Actually, many of the pieces I own are Nigerian. My sister C.J. and I spent a month there one year. My parents said we needed a little culture, so they bought plane tickets for both of us."

"You two went alone?"

Rob rested his chin on her shoulder. "Um-hmm. It was a summer break when we were both in college, so we were old enough to wander the world by ourselves. I've been back twice since then."

Toinette eyed a figure on the second shelf. "Fertility doll, huh?"

Robinson smiled and snaked his hands around her stomach. The figurine had been a gift from C.J. one year. They'd had a long talk about families and children. His sister knew how badly he wanted a large family and had given him the wooden symbol of fertility to represent inspiration and hope.

"A gift from C.J.," he simply told Toinette.

He explained the provenance of some of the other pieces and then took her hand. "My pride and joy is in the study."

There he showed her a huge ceremonial mask mounted on a wall that was hidden from view when she had come in earlier.

"Lord have mercy, that's ferocious," she exclaimed. "But it's exquisite," she said, peering at the piece but not touching it. "I wonder how long it took to carve those details."

"Three years. There's a museum curator who has been trying to buy that from me for years. The answer's always no, though. Frustrates him to no end," Robinson said while grinning.

Toinette smiled and glanced around Robinson's work domain. She spied the volumes on his desk. "I'm disturbing you from your work."

"No, you're not. I'm just checking a case history on something." Actually, he'd probably be up half the night doing the research that he wouldn't pass off to a paralegal. But spending this time with Toinette was more important right now.

He pulled her to him and wrapped his arms about her waist. "Would you like something sweet?"

Toinette looked up into the face of the man who'd taught her to live and love again.

"I'd love something sweet."

Robinson's mouth found hers.

His kiss was slow and thoughtful. Her hunger for him grew with each passing second. Maybe she'd rethink the friends business. There was something about the way she melted in his arms that was more powerful than anything she could deny. His mouth, more persuasive than she cared to admit, made her rethink her resolve. Then she couldn't think at all. She could only feel . . . and love.

When Robinson at last pulled away, Toinette whimpered before she could stop herself.

"I made dessert," he said while still nuzzling her lips.

"I thought *that* was dessert."

Robinson smiled. "Woman, you do tempt me." He took her hand and led her from his office. "Come on before I get some ideas on the creative use of the furniture in here."

With a backward glance at some of the chairs, Toinette followed Robinson to the family room. She settled on one of the two matching love seats while Robinson went to the kitchen. He came back with a plate of pretty petit fours, then poured coffee.

Toinette eyed the small cakes. "Don't tell me you made these, too."

Rob grinned. "Well, I could tell you I slaved all afternoon while you were getting your beauty sleep. But I'll 'fess up. These are from the bakery down the street from the firm. I love 'em. My mother used to make them for her garden club ladies when I was growing up. I always liked to be around the house on garden club day."

"You and C.J. had fun growing up."

Robinson nodded. He picked up a pink petit four and fed it to Toinette. She bit the cake and licked a crumb from his finger.

Distracted, Robinson forgot what they were talking about.

"Thanks for coming to get me today," she said. "I'm not sure how much longer I could have held on."

Robinson selected a cake for himself, then moved a bit away from her so he could concentrate on the right thing. "What happened with Russell?"

Toinette's sigh was weary. She crossed her legs and her arms. "He came over to the house supposedly to apologize, but instead we ended up screaming at each other. Rob, he called me terrible things. I couldn't believe the man standing in front of me was my own flesh and blood. Yes, I know he was angry and I know he was upset but, but . . ."

Toinette covered her mouth with her hand as her eyes filled with tears. Robinson gathered her in his arms and let her cry.

After a few minutes, he softly asked, "What did he say exactly?"

Toinette pushed away from him and wiped her eyes with the back of her hands. "I'm sorry. I don't mean to be a weepy female. I just . . . I just don't know how to deal with this. It's like a nightmare that won't end."

Robinson calmly stroked her arm and waited for her to gather her thoughts.

"The earrings you gave me, they're beautiful. I love them."

Robinson smiled. "I'm glad you like them. But the glitter of those stones don't match your beauty."

"Russell asked me if they were payment for services rendered."

Robinson was off the love seat in a flash. "Toinette, the man has gone too far! I have had it up to here with him."

"He isn't going to allow me to see my grandchildren any more. That's my punishment for not telling him the truth about his father."

"Has Russell always been so hot-tempered, so quick to fly off the handle? The difference between Russell and Aaron is remarkable."

Toinette nodded. "Russ has always been like that. He grew up as the man of the house so to speak. As the oldest, he viewed himself as the protector and defender. Aaron, the baby, was always sheltered. He grew up not knowing his father at all so he didn't have the same type of emotional attachment as Russ. Russell's fiercely loyal about family. And I, well, here I am at this late date shattering everything that he's ever held dear."

Toinette shook her head sadly. "I wasn't honest with him or my other kids about what happened to their father. Russell came over to explain why he attacked you. I ended up telling him about his dad. And, well, he just freaked out. He's always had a hot temper but never anything like this." Toinette got up and paced around the love seat. "I don't think I handled it very well."

Robinson wondered if now was the right time to ask the questions he'd been wondering about. But before he could pose the first one, Toinette was talking again.

"I'd always told my kids that their father had gotten a job in another state. Then, when they started asking why he never came home for a visit, I told them he'd had an accident at work and was in a hospital that didn't allow visitors. They were all little kids and that seemed to satisfy them. I don't know, Rob," she said, coming to a stop behind the place where he sat. "Maybe the fiction was more to keep me from falling to pieces than to help the kids."

Robinson turned from his seat to look up at her. He took her hand and pressed a kiss in her palm. "You handled the situation the best way you could at the time."

"You know, if any of them know the truth, it would probably be Aaron. That boy got more love and more attention from me. I probably smothered him with it. He was my closest tie to Woody. When Aaron was a baby, I'd think about the night Woody and I conceived him. It was an accident, but we sure had fun. But I'd think about that and I'd pick him up and just cry. It's amazing that Aaron turned out an okay kid the way I babied him. The girls all seemed well-adjusted. But Russell. I don't know."

Toinette wandered around the room absently fingering a vase here, a figurine there. She pulled a cut flower from an arrangement on a piecrust table.

"The flowers you sent me at the office were beautiful, Rob. Thank you."

"Do you know why I love you, Toinette?"

She turned to face him, then went to the love seat opposite where he sat. Robinson allowed her the space.

"I love you because you're the type of woman who would give her children the gift of their father's love even if it wasn't deserved. You're the type of woman who took a bad situation and turned it around into a program that not only empowered you, but empowers other women to stand and choose their destiny instead of allowing circumstances and poverty to defeat them."

"Why has that never been a problem for you?"

"What?" he asked.

"My background, the poverty and welfare. Your pal Malcolm seemed to have some hang-ups about Kendra's background, and she spent just a couple of years on welfare. I was there for years and years before I got so fed up that I started Quad-A."

"Malc and I are two different people, Toinette. His upbringing was very different from mine. I was raised by a very well-to-do couple. They didn't have money like the Rockefellers or the Kennedys, but they lived well. They also taught me and C.J. the value and reward of hard work. We learned the lessons of the past, and we were raised to remember that we had the advantages we did because someone somewhere along the way paved the road that we traveled. So just as easily as they'd send us to Nigeria for a summer vacation, they'd send us to a program where we built houses for the indigent. My father was against it, but my Mom insisted C.J. and I go to public schools so we wouldn't turn into what she called uppity black folks."

Toinette smiled. "They did a good job."

Robinson tipped his head to her. "I'd like you to meet my parents."

"That'd be nice. As long as you introduced me as just an *old* friend," she said.

"Toinette . . ."

"Just messing with you," she grinned.

"So, what are you going to do about Russell?"

Her smile faded. "I don't know. His wife is all to pieces about what he told her. I can't even say that he'll come to his senses and get over it. He and Leah were always close. Maybe he'll talk to her and she'll get him to see reason."

Robinson leaned forward, picked up the plate of petit fours, and offered it to Toinette. She selected one with white and green icing.

"Toinette, where does this leave us? I know you said you want to be friends. I can deal with that." I hope, he added to himself as she crossed her legs and a smooth brown thigh tantalized him. Robinson felt himself grow hard. He took a deep breath and tried, unsuccessfully, to think of something else.

"It leaves us as friends," she said. Toinette wasn't about to admit she was already regretting her stand and was having a difficult time thinking of Robinson as just a friend. Not when she wanted him to hold her and love her and make the pain of her problems with Russell go away.

"Let me go find your clothes." Robinson hopped up and headed toward his bedroom.

Bemused at his quick change of subject, Toinette sat there for a moment and then got up and followed him. She found him in the closet.

"Lord have mercy. This is heaven," Toinette said, stepping into the room and looking around. "You have enough clothes to open a men's shop." Toinette went to stand before a three-way mirror in the closet. "This is awesome. I would kill for this closet."

"I had it custom designed when the house was built. The builder thought I was insane, but I knew what I wanted." Robinson pulled her dress from its hanger and turned to hand it to her.

Toinette was standing in front of the three-way mirror striking poses and making faces in the mirror. Then she found the tie rack and fingered the smooth silk. "Hmm, nice," she said. Spotting the tie he'd worn that day, she pulled it off the rack and draped it around her neck. She kicked one leg up on a shoe stand and gave him a come-hither look. "Why don't you come up and see me sometime, big boy?" she cooed.

Robinson dropped the dress and went to her.

Toinette's "Oh!" of surprise was drowned in his mouth. Her senses leapt to life as the urgent and demanding kiss swept her deeper into Robinson's world. When her knees grew weak, she clung to him. Robinson deepened the kiss and explored her backside with one hand. She writhed and Robinson groaned.

His mouth left hers long enough for him to unbutton the shirt she wore. Toinette took the silk tie from around her neck, draped it over his, and pulled him closer. With one unsteady finger, Robinson outlined the nipple through her bra and felt it grow round and erect. He lowered his mouth to her breast and suckled her through the lace. Toinette cried out. Letting the edges of the tie drop, she unhooked her bra while Robinson came out of his jeans.

Robinson lowered her to the floor. His tormented groan was a heady invitation that Toinette couldn't ignore. With the thick carpeting supporting her back, Robinson licked and kissed his way up Toinette's legs. Then he inched the panties from her.

"Love me, Robinson."

"I do, Toinette. I do love you."

He kissed her deeply.

"Mr. Mayview? Mr. Mayview, are you home, sir?" A voice from somewhere in the house intruded.

"Oh, God, not now," Robinson groaned.

Toinette's eyes widened. "Somebody's here!"

"It's Monday. It's my housekeeper. She probably saw the dishes and food in the kitchen."

Toinette squirmed under him.

"Don't do that, Toinette. I'm struggling here. Help me out."

"We have to get up," she whispered.

"I was hoping if we're very quiet she'll go away."

"Robinson!"

"Okay, okay." Reluctantly he stood and helped her up from the closet floor. He lingered though, for one last, deep kiss. His hands roamed over her and Toinette sighed into his embrace.

"Mr. Mayview?" the voice said, closer now.

Robinson ended the kiss, then bent to pull on his jeans and shirt. "I'll distract her. You can get dressed." He caressed her bare, rounded derrière, then stole one last kiss before leaving.

Toinette picked her dress and underthings from the floor and clutched them to her chest. "Lord have mercy, what a man!"

CHAPTER 21

By the time Toinette got back to her office, it was late. She had a Quad-A presentation that night, and she packed her materials. She and Kendra were going to pitch the program to the local board of Realtors.

A pile of messages was stacked on her desk. Toinette flipped through them to see if there was anything urgent. She pulled out the one from Ben Trammer, one from John MacAfree, and the one from Kendra. Nancy Griffin, the mayor's wife, could wait until the next day. A note from Dawn said that Hazel had come back to the center but left when she found out Toinette wasn't there.

Toinette sighed. Maybe Hazel would come back the next day. She hoped Dawn and Eli the cook made sure the girl got a hot meal before she left.

Toinette glanced at her watch, then dialed Kendra's office number.

"Hey, girl," Toinette said when she got her friend.

"Hi, yourself. We still on for tonight?"

"Yep. I'll meet you at their office." They confirmed the address and time. "Hey, Ken?"

"What's wrong, Nettie?"

"I was wondering. Are you free after the program tonight? Could we get together for a little while? I need to talk to you about something."

"Sure, Nettie. Malcolm can handle the girls. He's great at it."

The presentation went off without a hitch. Toinette's compelling talk about getting welfare mothers to be self-sufficient rarely failed to move audiences. Several people signed up on the spot for more information about getting Quad-A workers in their real estate offices. After the program, Toinette and Kendra drove to a coffeehouse.

At a back table they ordered latte and biscotti.

"Okay, Nettie. Out with it. What's wrong?"

"I'm in love."

Kendra grinned. "Rob Mayview."

"Is it that obvious?"

"Only to me. And Malcolm. He said Robinson is a trip to watch around the office these days. The man is apparently head over heels, and you have him going through some changes."

"What changes? He's always the smooth, intense one with me. Nothing rattles him." Toinette paused. "Nothing except Russell."

Kendra rolled her eyes. "What did Russell do now? Make Robinson declare his intentions while swearing an oath on a Bible?"

"I only wish it were that simple." Toinette lightly touched the bruise on her cheek. "See this?"

"Yes. I was going to ask you about that." Kendra peered at her friend's face. "It looks like someone hit you." Her eyes widened. "Robinson hit you?! Oh, my God. Nettie, why didn't you call me? We can go to the police station and file charges right now. I cannot believe he hit you!"

Toinette took Kendra's hand. "Ken, Robinson didn't hit me. He'd never do anything like that. He was defending my honor." Toinette stopped and looked away for a moment. She'd never quite thought of it in that light. No one had ever fought for her honor before. Rob was such a sweet man.

"If Robinson didn't hit you, who did?" Kendra demanded.

"Russell."

"Russell? Russell? That's even worse. Nettie, why didn't you call me?"

Toinette shrugged. "I don't know. It was late. I had a really rough weekend."

"What happened?"

"Russell hit me. It was an accident," she added quickly. "He was aiming for Robinson and then Robinson nearly killed him in the middle of the street."

Kendra's mouth dropped open. "Oh, my God."

"They put on quite a show for the neighbors."

Toinette caught Kendra up on what else had transpired over the weekend.

Kendra listened, open-mouthed. "Well, I'm glad Robinson had sense enough to take you somewhere where you could get some rest today," Kendra said after Toinette finished.

"Have you ever been to his house? That place is spectacular."

"Malcolm took me to a party there one night. Robinson is a great entertainer. And the man is apparently a dynamo in the kitchen. He had these great appetizers made from flaked tuna and grape leaves. I remember because everyone raved, and he said it was a recipe handed down to him from his mother."

So the man wasn't lying about being able to cook, Toinette thought. Not that she doubted his sincerity. It was just, well, odd. Woody never cooked. Woody could barely warm the baby bottles in a pan of water without burning the house down. Rob made quiche and hors d'oeuvres without effort. Toinette's thoughts then drifted to something else Robinson did like no other man. He could set her body and her soul on fire. Like in the closet that afternoon. Lord have mercy! They had been on the floor in the closet!

Toinette blushed from head to toe.

Kendra couldn't help notice her friend's reaction. "Ummm. You go, girl," she told Toinette with a saucy grin. "The man cooks, owns a successful law firm and a fabulous home. And to top it all off, he's gorgeous. Well, not as gorgeous as Malcolm, but that's okay. And best of all, he is yours." Kendra snapped her fingers. "You go, girl."

Toinette laughed delightedly. "You're a trip."

"You're in love with him. He's in love with you. Except for Russell, who I, personally, wouldn't worry about, everything sounds perfect to me." Kendra looked at Toinette. "But you're not happy. What's wrong?"

"Well, aside from Russell, there's the small but significant fact that I'm still married."

"Married? Oh, you mean to Woody. Nettie, that man has been gone for years. Get a divorce and be happy with Robinson."

"*And* he's younger than I am. I'm still not entirely comfortable with that, particularly when I look at Russ and know that he's just four years younger than Rob. When I think about it that way, I feel like a cradle robber."

"Well, I guess I can see your point on that. But does Robinson make you happy?"

"Deliriously so."

Kendra raised an eyebrow.

"Don't give me that look," Toinette said. "It's not that simple."

"Only because you insist on making it complicated. Look, you want my advice? If you love Robinson, hang on to him. Ride that wave as long as it lasts. You, more than anyone else I know, deserve to be happy."

Toinette smiled and squeezed her friend's hand. Their conversation then drifted to Quad-A program business.

"I'll be making the first site visit in a week," Toinette reported. "Ben Trammer wants to get rolling on this project. Oh, I got a call from John MacAfree today. Well, I got the message that he called."

Kendra nodded. "They're really excited about the Quad-A Foundation. He and Etta, particularly Etta, have been looking for something to channel their energy in."

"You mean besides the twins?"

Kendra grinned. "I tell you, Nettie. It's like he's a changed man. It's difficult to believe that John MacAfree put me through so much grief. Kayla and Karin adore him. I'm glad it turned out well, that the girls know their natural grandparents."

"All's well that ends well, huh?"

Kendra lifted her second cup of latte in mock salute. "I'll drink to that." She licked some of the foam from the specialty coffee. "John, or his secretary, was probably calling about an idea he had. He's thinking of tying in some sort of promotion with the jewelry stores. Maybe Trammer will do the same thing with his electronics division."

"Now there's an idea. I'll think on that. I'll be making some trips in the next few weeks. Will you keep an eye out on things at the center?"

"Not a problem. It seems like half the folks at the law office are on vacation."

"I'll check the calendar. There are a few presentations that need to be done. And one big one if I recall correctly."

"Nettie, I have you covered. All you need to worry about is getting these other cities to buy into the idea. I'm so proud of you. You've talked about this for years, and now it's all falling into place."

"Thanks to you. You met Ben and Maggie Trammer at that auction."

The two women finished their coffee and chatted for a few more minutes before settling their bill and leaving the coffeehouse. Across the street, a car that a parking valet was getting into caught Toinette's eye. For a moment it looked like Robinson's BMW. There were lots of BMWs in the Baltimore area, though. As the valet drove away, she looked up at the front door of the chic restaurant and saw a couple headed in. All she could make of the woman was lots of figure and lots of hair. Just when she was about to turn to give Kendra a hug, the man turned in profile.

Toinette's eyes widened. It couldn't be!

"Nettie, do you want to stop by the house for a bit? The girls should all be in bed, but Malcolm is still up."

"Huh?" Her gaze fell on her friend for a moment, then returned to the door of Chez Jolé, but the couple was gone. "No. No way," she mumbled.

"Okay. Well, he'll see you another time then," Kendra said.

Toinette shook her head and regarded Kendra. "What were you saying, Ken?"

"You can catch up with Malcolm some other time." Kendra hugged Toinette. "You take care. I'm very happy for you," she whispered before going to her car.

Toinette stood on the sidewalk, staring at the restaurant across the street. It had to have been just someone who looked like Robinson. Distracted and wondering, she went to her car and drove home.

Dropping her handbag and briefcase near the foyer table, she went to the kitchen and dialed Robinson's home. When she got his answering machine, she hung up. Then she called his office.

"Mayview, Jackson, Hightower and Associates. May I help you?"

Toinette looked at the clock on her kitchen wall. It was after ten at night. "Uh, Robinson Mayview, please."

"Ma'am, I'm sorry. The office is closed. You've reached the answering service. Would you like to leave a message for Mr. Mayview?"

"No. No message. Thank you." Toinette replaced the receiver. Thoughtful, she turned out the kitchen lights, then went upstairs to bed.

At Chez Jolé, Robinson was having a difficult time with Marlena. The woman didn't understand the word *no.* Bringing her here had been a mistake. He needed to be at home doing the research on the case that was coming up. But instead, he'd let Marlena talk him into this dinner.

He had tried to be subtle. He tried to be nice. He was too much of a gentleman to be rude. So here he sat, stuck with this woman, when he should have been at home or, better yet, with Toinette.

Robinson looked at the expensive bracelet he'd given Marlena. The diamonds flashed and sparkled when she flipped her wrist, an aggravating little habit that Marlena seemed to do quite frequently. It was a wonder the woman didn't get a crook in her wrist the way she kept flinging it around. Why wouldn't she take his lovely parting gift and part?

"Robinson, darling, you've been ignoring me," she pouted.

Robinson took a critical look at Marlena. She was a diva through and through, beautiful and flashy and she knew it. More than one man had paused to stare at her as they made their way to their table. She'd smiled at every one of them while clinging to his arm with the strength of an octopus. Marlena was just too much, too much everything: too much hair, too cloying. As Robinson studied her, he wondered when his tastes had shifted to women who were gently rounded, instead of overly ripe like Marlena. Part of the reason so many men stared at her was that they were anxiously awaiting the moment when she'd pop out of her low-cut dress. Robinson had to admit to himself that he'd been wondering the same thing, if for no other reason than sheer curiosity.

"Marlena, I told you on the phone. I'm seeing someone else exclusively."

She smiled a smile that on another day would have had them heading straight to her bed. "I know, Rob. You've said that before, yet you've always come back to what's good for you." She leaned over and gave him the full view of her cleavage.

He tried to resist, but his gaze lowered and his mouth went dry. He took a deep breath and tried to ignore what she was so blatantly offering. Marlena was a handful and then some. He well remembered getting lost in her ripe lushness. His head started pounding. Coming here had been a mistake, a big mistake.

"This divine bracelet is what let me know how you really felt," she cooed.

As she held her wrist before him, the subtle scent of her exotic perfume washed over Robinson. Oh, God, he mumbled as he felt himself respond to her sensual onslaught. He closed his eyes and counted to ten.

Marlena ran one long nail against the palm of his hand. "Are you thinking of how it used to be between us? My gallery is just around the corner. No one's there." She leaned closer, pressing herself against him. With one finger, she traced the sensitive spot behind his ear. "You make me burn, Robinson. I know you want me, too."

Robinson shuddered. "Let's go."

Marlena grabbed her small clutch and followed Robinson from the restaurant.

CHAPTER 22

The next day Toinette met with John and Etta MacAfree, then had a conference call with Ben Trammer's people. Her first site visits, Atlanta and Chicago, were scheduled for the following week. Ben Trammer had already assigned a support staff of five people to work with Toinette, and they had completed a lot of the groundwork.

From a file in her office, she pulled out detailed notes from a lawyers' conference Kendra had attended as a representative of Quad-A. Atlanta would be the easier of the two trips because of the visit Kendra had made and because Trammer's company was well-known there. In her experience working with Quad-A, Toinette had found that law firms were usually receptive to Quad-A employees, and larger firms could absorb more manpower. Toinette read Kendra's meticulous notes and made a list of people to call later that afternoon. If she could get people on board with a commitment to the program quickly, it would make the subsequent setup that much easier.

She then put a call in to Bosworth Sullivan, the senior partner at the law firm where Kendra worked.

"Mrs. Blue, what a delight and a surprise to hear from you," Sullivan said. "How are things going with you?"

"Just fine, Mr. Sullivan . . ."

"After all the time we've known each other, call me Boz."

Toinette raised an elegant eyebrow at that. She could understand the nickname, but she couldn't quite see herself actually calling the man

Boz. Sullivan's large law firm had been one of the first in the city to participate in Quad-A. Sullivan had hired Kendra from the program, and she'd worked her way up to an executive position at the law firm. Sullivan had been the one who had suggested Quad-A put on program presentations at the Atlanta conference. His support of and commitment to the program had been unflagging through the years. He even did presentations when his schedule allowed.

"As you know, one of my goals has been to branch Quad-A out to other cities. Well, it's finally going to happen," Toinette replied.

"That's excellent news. I'm very happy for you. I hope that regional conference helped. That's why I suggested it."

"As a matter of fact, it did. And that's why I'm calling. A Quad-A Foundation is being set up with grants from J. Mac & Son Jewelers and Trammer Engineering and Electronics."

Sullivan whistled. "You do know how to get the big guns in your corner, Mrs. Blue. That's one of the reasons I've always admired you."

Toinette smiled but didn't comment on the compliment. "Next week I'll be going to Atlanta and Chicago. I have a list of people Kendra met and talked to at the conference, and I wondered if you might have any other suggestions. It would be a fast turnaround, but I thought I'd check."

"Tell you what, are you free for lunch today? I can go through the Rolodex and bring you some names."

Toinette glanced at her day book. If she had lunch with Sullivan, she could dash to a store afterward and pick up anything she might need for the two trips.

"That sounds fine. Where shall I meet you?"

"How about Chez Jolé?" Sullivan suggested. "That's pretty central to both of us."

Toinette agreed, then rang off with Sullivan.

The intimate French restaurant wasn't exactly the type of place for a lunch meeting. But knowing Sullivan, he probably owned it, Toinette thought with a smile. The easy smile disappeared as she thought of Robinson. It *had* been him going into the place. She was sure of it. He was all spiffed up and so was the dazzling woman on his arm. How could he profess to love her one minute and be with another woman the next?

Then another thought occurred to her. Maybe Russell, with all his bitter and biting anger, had been right. Maybe Robinson did have "real" girlfriends. He knew all of her background, but when she thought about it, Toinette realized she knew very little about him. Robinson Mayview was thirty-four years old, successful, a partner at the law firm established by his father. His sister was a journalist. He could cook and his wardrobe rivaled anything she'd ever seen in men's fashion magazines. That didn't tell her anything about the man. Every one of those things was superficial. What, she wondered, did he think about children? Did he believe in God? Would he cheat on his taxes?

A man of his age, looks, and means wouldn't just be sitting around waiting for her to waltz into his life. What of current and former relationships? What about the young professional women who were bound to run in his social circle? Robinson was too sensitive and caring a lover, too in tune with her needs as a woman to be even remotely considered a novice at seduction. He'd been doing a number on her.

Toinette sat at her desk, her work forgotten. Maybe Russell was right. Maybe to Robinson she was just a dalliance in order to get a taste of a mature vintage before resuming the bubbly champagne offered by young beauties like the one at the restaurant.

Suddenly in a bad mood, Toinette looked at the flower arrangement still on her desk. She got up, dumped the flowers sent by Robinson into a trash can, and, as much as she was able to, put him out of her mind as she went back to work.

She met Sullivan at the restaurant. Try as she might, she couldn't help wonder which cozy little table Robinson had been nestled in with that woman. Chez Jolé had a reputation for two things: excellent food and intimate assignations. She'd been there once before with a state senator who ended up wanting more than a discussion on legislation that could impact the Quad-A program.

But as Toinette and Sullivan enjoyed a delightful lunch together, she realized something. She and Bosworth Sullivan had known each other for years. He had worked with her on the Quad-A program practically since its inception, and they were just here sharing a meal and talking business. Maybe jumping to conclusions about Robinson had been a mistake. For all she knew, the woman he had been with could have been a client.

Toinette smiled, unaware that Sullivan took the 100-watt smile as encouragement.

A discreet waiter served them dessert and coffee.

"Mrs. Blue, may I call you Toinette? We've known each other so long now. It seems the time for formality has passed."

"Of course," Toinette told him. But she just couldn't seem to call him Boz. For some reason the nickname made her think of the clown Bozo. What would Sullivan look like with a big red nose? Toinette tried, unsuccessfully, to stifle a giggly grin.

Enchanted, Sullivan rested both elbows on the table and smiled at her. "Share the humor?"

"Oh, I was just thinking that Toinette sounds so formal. Most of my friends call me Nettie."

"Well, I'd like to be counted in that number . . . Nettie."

Toinette's eyes widened a bit. Was that a husky tone coming from the erudite and dignified Bosworth Sullivan? Nah, she must have been mistaken.

"What I'm about to say, Toinette, I mean Nettie, may come as somewhat of a surprise to you. But hear me out, please."

Toinette nodded.

"As senior partner at Sullivan and O'Leary, I find myself wondering sometimes what I've worked so hard for all these years. If I walked away right now, the firm would continue to grow and flourish."

Toinette cut into the raspberry crepes and took a small bite of the heavenly sweet.

"What's missing from my life is love and laughter," Sullivan said.

"Um-hmm," Toinette said. She put her fork down and listened to him. Lord have mercy, if it were any other man, she'd swear he was putting a move on her.

"For many years now I've watched and listened to you. You're dynamite with the Quad-A program. I'm proud to say that my law firm had the vision, the foresight if you will, to get on board early. You and I have made what I think to be a significant contribution to our community."

"I'm glad you feel that way. Isn't it funny how the years just slip away. It almost seems like yesterday that I came to you with my proposal."

Sullivan smiled. "It was written on white notebook paper, and you were wearing a green dress with black buttons."

Toinette clasped her chest and laughed. "Lord have mercy. You remember that?" Toinette shook her head at the memory. "The program has come a long way."

"I remember everything about you," Sullivan said softly. He cleared his throat. "I guess what I'm not articulating very well here is that, Mrs. Blue . . . Nettie, I'd like to get to know you better. On a personal level. I find myself very attracted to your grace, your charm."

Toinette's mouth dropped open. She reached for her coffee to cover the reaction. "I-I . . ."

"Hear me out, please. I know I'm older than you. I'll be sixty next month. But age is irrelevant between two people who enjoy each other's company. You're a very beautiful woman, Nettie. I hope you don't mind me saying so."

"Thank you," Toinette mumbled. "But . . ."

"And race is also irrelevant," Sullivan continued. "In this day and age, mutual interests and shared joy are much more important than black or white, or any other color of skin. I guess what I'm asking is would you be averse to having dinner with me or going to the theater from time to time?"

Lord have mercy! Toinette thought. When it rains it pours. Sullivan was an attractive man in his own right. He looked like just what he was: a conservative white power broker. When she first met him, she'd wondered about him, but then her attention was so consumed by the Quad-A program that in her head he'd become simply Sullivan of Sullivan and O'Leary, one of Quad-A's major benefactors.

"Mr. Sullivan . . .

"Boz," he gently chided.

"Uh, Boz." The clown image popped up and Toinette cleared her throat in an attempt not to grin. "Bosworth, I don't know what to say. I . . . This is all so sudden. I never thought you felt this way. I, well, I'm seeing someone."

Sullivan patted her hand. "I can understand that. We all need and want companionship. I simply ask that you think about it. You have to eat and dinner is just a meal. May I call you sometime?"

Why me, Lord? Toinette wondered. Couldn't you just send me someone my own age? One is thirteen years younger and the other one is thirteen years older.

"Toinette?"

Toinette looked at Sullivan and smiled weakly.

He patted her hand again. "Just think about it."

Later that afternoon, Toinette was poring over a street map of Atlanta when she was interrupted by a knock on her office door. She looked up, surprised to see the door shut.

"Come in."

Dawn came into the office carrying a tray. "Mrs. Blue, you have been holed up in here all day. Here's some coffee and some cookies."

"It's awfully quiet out there. Lord have mercy, what time is it?"

Dawn settled the tray on Toinette's desk, then sat down. "Late. Almost seven-thirty."

Toinette looked at her watch. "Good grief. So it is. Well, I got a lot accomplished today. I'm going to be out of the office most of next week."

Toinette then filled Dawn in on what the Quad-A Foundation was going to do. "I'll be counting on you to take on a little more responsibility in terms of the day-to-day operation while I'm not here," she told the senior aide. "Once everything is up and running in the other cities, I'll be able to spend more time here."

At Dawn's somewhat worried expression, Toinette added, "I have every confidence in you, Dawn. Look at how you handle the childcare assistants, and you already supervise Eli and the kitchen staff."

"But what about all those phone calls and meetings? I don't know anything about that. And I sure can't stand in front of a bunch a people and talk up the program like you do."

"No need to worry about that. Kendra's going to pick up some of that slack. And besides, it's not like I'm going to be gone, never to be seen or heard from again. I'll be back."

Reassured, Dawn nodded. Then, "Uh, Mrs. Blue. Can I ask you one other thing?"

"Sure. What is it?"

Dawn sat on the edge of her seat, put both palms on Toinette's desk, and shook her head. "Who was that fine, *fine* brother in here yesterday? That man looked good!"

Toinette stifled a smile. "He's a close fr—" She then remembered she was irritated with Robinson. "He's one of the Quad-A employers," she amended.

"Ummph, ummph, ummph. Well, you keep on getting folks who look like him. We'll have women lined up for blocks trying to get in the program." Dawn stood up, ready to leave. "And Mrs. Blue?"

Toinette looked up at Dawn.

"If you ever don't need me here at the office, I'll be happy to go work at his business." Dawn left Toinette's office mumbling, "Brother has it going on."

Toinette sat back in her chair, reflective. If that was Dawn's response to Robinson, and Dawn was closer to his age than Toinette would ever be, what made her think she had what it would take to keep his eyes from straying? She ran a hand through her salt-and-pepper hair. Bosworth Sullivan was a more appropriate and suitable partner for her. Her vitality and his conservativeness would balance out. Sullivan was an older man, widowed and attractive in an elegant, old-world way. With him, she'd be the spring chicken.

But Bosworth Sullivan didn't make her knees weak or her heart flip. And he didn't make her smile for no reason. Just one man was capable of all that.

Toinette folded up the street map, stacked up the work that needed to be done the next day, then flipped through her appointment book to see what was scheduled for later in the week. Her days were booked solid, but she smiled at the Friday night notation: "PJ Party." Toinette always got a kick out of the sleepovers she had at her house with her grandkids and Kendra and Malcolm's twins. She and the kids did fingerpainting the last time. As she packed up her briefcase to head home, she thought about suitably messy activities for her and the kids to engage in.

But as she drove home, Toinette found herself comparing Bosworth Sullivan to Robinson Mayview. No matter how she tried to rationalize it, no matter which way she sliced, diced, or dissected it, Sullivan was a very nice man but he came up short every time. Her heart belonged to Robinson.

CHAPTER 23

Robinson met his mother for lunch the next day. Genevieve Mayview was smartly turned out in a cream brocade suit and pearls. Robinson leaned down and kissed her on the cheek.

"I was beginning to think you were going to stand me up," she scolded.

"I'm sorry. I got tied up at work and then the traffic was heavy."

Genevieve took a close, critical look at her son as he sat in the chair across from her. "You haven't been getting enough rest."

Robinson sighed. "It's been kind of rough going."

"Do you and Malcolm need more help at the firm? I'm sure your father would be willing to step in for a little while."

Robinson shook his head. "We're fine. As a matter of fact, we're going to start interviewing applicants for another associate's position next week. Everything at work is just fine."

"Then what's wrong, son?"

A waiter materialized. After placing their orders, Robinson answered his mother's question with a question.

"Mom, when did you know that Dad was the man you wanted to spend the rest of your life with?"

Genevieve smiled. "The first time I laid eyes on him. But I didn't let him know that. I gave him a good chase just so his victory would seem all the more sweeter."

Robinson chuckled. Then, serious, he asked, "What would you have done if despite your orchestrated chase, he still had reservations?"

She considered her answer. "I would have switched to the direct approach."

"And if that didn't work?"

Genevieve contemplated the small crystal vase that held a single yellow rose before answering her son. "What are you asking me, Robinson?"

"What if you've tried every way you know how to convince someone that, well, that you love them, but they still don't believe you? And just when you think you've overcome that hurdle, another obstacle is slammed in your face?"

"I think you ought to let her know how you feel," Genevieve said quietly.

Robinson looked up.

"If the obstacles are within your power to control, act on that power and do something about them," she continued. "But keep in mind that not everything is within your control and care. Sometimes you have to deal with the cards you're dealt. Sometimes, Rob, you have to fight for what you love."

Robinson sighed and shook his head. "Seems like I've been fighting an uphill battle since day one," he muttered.

"Then your victory, when it comes, will be all the more sweet because of the struggle."

Robinson grinned at his mother. "You're good for what ails me."

"That's what mothers are for."

The rest of their lunch was spent in casual conversation. Before long it was time for Robinson to return to the office for an afternoon appointment.

In her office, Toinette worked on the Quad-A books, getting everything prepared so Kendra wouldn't have a lot to do in her absence. She hurried through the work, glancing now and then at the slim watch on her wrist. She had to get to the bank to deposit a grant check so it would be posted that day. The staff payroll for the next week as well as other program expenses depended on that check. Not wasting the time it would take to dig out the bound accounting books, Toinette worked in pencil, using the temporary book she'd used once before. With so much going on, she still hadn't found the time to transfer all the data to the permanent record book.

A knock on her open office door distracted her. "Call for you on line two, Mrs. Blue."

Toinette frowned at the interruption. "Thanks."

No one ever called her on this line. She picked up the receiver and punched the flashing number with one hand and kept scribbling notes and figures in the record book with the other. "Achieving Against All Adversities, this is Toinette Blue. How may I help you?"

"Mom?"

Her son's voice got her attention. Aaron never called her at work. "Hi, baby. What's up?"

"I'm, uh, sorry to bother you at work and whatnot, Mom. But I'm in a kind of a bind and I need your help."

Toinette shook her head and sat back in her chair, crossing her legs. "No, Aaron. You cannot borrow my car for the weekend. The last time you did that, I got it back with a major dent in the left door and an empty gas tank to boot."

Aaron chuckled. "Come on, Mom. Forgive and forget."

"Um-hmm. Easy for you to say. That little accident of yours cost a pretty penny to repair. Well, if it's not the car, what do you need?"

"It's funny you mention money, Mom."

"Not to fear. I've already sent your tuition off. I'm glad this is your last semester."

"Uh, Mom. Do you think you could loan me some money? Something's sort of come up."

"No problem. I can put a check for fifty dollars in the mail to you today. Is that enough?" Toinette heard Aaron take a deep breath. She sat up in her chair.

"Not exactly," he said.

She grabbed the receiver more tightly. "What exactly then? Lord have mercy, Aaron. Are you in jail?"

"No! Mom, I'm not in jail. Yet," he added.

"What do you mean 'yet'? Aaron, what kind of trouble are you in?"

"I'm late on the rent for the apartment."

Toinette let go of the breath she hadn't been aware she was holding. "Thank God. You had me worried there. How did you fall behind a month? I told you it would be better if you lived in the dorms on campus. But no. Mr. Independence had to have his own place."

"Mom . . ."

"Don't 'Mom' me, Aaron Blue. Didn't Angela sit you down and explain about budgeting?"

"Yes, ma'am."

"And how many times have I told you to pay the rent first, everything else second?"

"At least a hundred," Aaron mumbled under his breath.

"I heard that, young man. Don't get smart with me. I'm having enough problems with your brother."

"What's wrong with Russ?"

"He's taken exception to my relationship with Robinson."

"Don't mind whatever Russell says, Mom. He's still bent out of shape about Dad leaving. He probably needs to go to counseling or something."

Toinette sat up straighter and held her breath. "You know about your father?"

"Sure, Leah and Judi told me all about it. I was just a baby, so I don't remember anything about him. But they showed me his picture and told me and Angie about how they would write pretend letters to him so you wouldn't cry."

Toinette's eyes widened, then she blinked back tears. "I didn't know they knew."

"Sure. Russell kept believing though. Leah and Judi always told him to wake up and smell the trash. Mom, do you think you'll be able to get me the money for the rent?"

Toinette forced herself to focus on the issue at hand. "Sure, sweetheart. I'll send a check today. I should have a spare few hundred dollars just resting about in my checking account."

Her sarcasm didn't escape Aaron.

"I'm sorry, Mom. I'll get it back to you as soon as I can."

"How much is a month's rent?"

Silence greeted her on the other end.

"Aaron, are you still there?"

"I'm here."

"Well, how much is the rent? Tell your rental office manager it'll be there by Monday."

"Mom, I'm going to be evicted tomorrow."

Toinette nearly shot out of the chair. "Evicted? What do you mean evicted? Nobody throws anyone out because they are a month behind."

"Mom, I'm three months behind on the rent."

Toinette dropped the receiver.

Dazed, she leaned down and picked it up again. "Aaron," she said quietly, "what did you say?"

"I'm three months behind. Tomorrow will be four. They let me go this long because I've been paying a little here and there when I had it. But now they said no more excuses."

"Aaron, I want a straight answer. What happened to the money?"

The young man was fast with the explanation. "See, Mom, it was like this. The group, well, we needed a new synthesizer and then there was this electric keyboard that Derek saw. We figured we'd put it on layaway at the music store. But then we got this gig in Pennsylvania. We'd heard there was gonna be a scout there from BET, and we wanted to be pumping for the show. So, Sherri made some costumes. And then, well, we had to have the synthesizer, and since the keyboard was there, we went ahead and got it because it would give us a better sound . . ."

"Aaron."

He continued talking over her. "Oh, Mom. I wish you could have heard us. It was sweet. We were so tight there were people crying in the audience. Then on the way back from the gig in Pennsylvania, the muffler blew out on Derek's car and we had to get that fixed 'cause we had to be in class Monday. I ended up missing part of my Constitutional Law class."

Finally out of steam and explanation, Aaron ceased talking.

"Aaron." The chill in Toinette's voice didn't bode well for her youngest child.

"Yes, ma'am?"

"Let me get this straight," she said slowly, enunciating each word. "You spent four months of rent money on a synthesizer, a keyboard, and a muffler?"

"It was important, Mom. Serenity is really going places. We got a call from—"

"Aaron, I don't want to hear about your calls. I sent you to college to get an education, not to be spending all your time and my money on some jazz group. Your grades took a dive when you got hooked up with this music thing. Now, I like music as much as the next person, but your priorities are screwed up. Do you hear me, young man?"

"Yes, ma'am."

Toinette thought of something. "If you're behind on your rent, how is it you still have phone service?"

Silence greeted her.

"Aaron?"

"The phone was turned off last week. I'm calling from a friend's house."

Toinette closed her eyes and rubbed the back of her neck. "Boy, let me tell you something. You better be glad you're up at that college and not standing here in front of me. Do you hear me?"

"Yes, ma'am."

"How much do you owe on the rent and how much is the overdue phone bill?"

Aaron cited a figure. Toinette clutched the telephone receiver and bit her lip. It was all she could do not to swear at her child. "Aaron, so help me God . . ."

"Mom, I'm sorry. I know I shouldn't have done it. But it seemed like we could pull it out. Serenity is really hot."

"Uh-huh. Tell me, Aaron. What are these so-called friends and fellow musicians of yours doing to help you out?"

"Well, Sherri lives in the dorms. She doesn't have any money except the allowance she gets from her folks," Aaron replied. "Ricky stays at home and has a couple of kids to feed. And Derek, well, he, uh, he sort of lives with me."

"What do you mean he sort of lives with you?"

"He got evicted from his place two months ago. He's been sleeping on the sofa here."

Toinette counted to ten before she spoke to her son again. "Aaron, I don't have that kind of money just lying around. I just paid your tuition and I paid the mortgage on the house."

"Mom, I'm sorry. I just didn't know where else to turn."

"You said sorry already. Sorry isn't going to pay your rent. Aaron, why did you wait so long?"

"Well, I thought . . . We all thought we could get enough to hold on for another month."

"You disappoint me, Aaron."

"I'm sorry, Mom." Then, after a pause: "Well, getting evicted won't be so bad, I guess. We're gonna put all the equipment in Sherri's dorm room."

"Tell me something, Aaron. What was your plan if you couldn't get the money?"

"There's a homeless shelter down the street from the coffeehouse where we play. Derek and I figured we'd stay there if we had to."

Toinette dropped her head into her hands. "Give me the name and the address of your rental company."

"But, Mom, you just said you didn't have—"

"Be quiet, Aaron. Give me the information and the exact amount you owe in back rent."

She picked up the pencil and jotted the information down. "And the phone bill?" She shook her head at the astronomical amount.

"We've been talking to an agent and promoter in New York," Aaron said by way of explanation.

"Save it, Aaron. I don't want to hear it."

"Mom, what are you gonna do?"

"I don't know, Aaron. I don't know. Is there a number where you can be reached?"

"Sherri can take a message at her dorm-room number."

"What is it?"

Toinette wrote it down. She then rang off with her youngest son before her anger got the best of her.

She sat back in her chair, closed her eyes, and took a deep breath. "These boys are going to be the death of me yet."

She glanced at her watch, then looked at the dollar amount her son owed for his apartment. Sighing didn't make her feel better, but it was all she was capable of doing.

She made a quick telephone call. As she concluded the conversation, her glance landed on the Quad-A program grant check. She picked it up and stared at it.

She tidied up her desk, put the check in her handbag, and left the office to do what she had to do.

Later that night, as she got into bed, Toinette wondered if she'd done the right thing. She felt badly about it, but there was no way she was going to allow her son to live in a homeless shelter if she could prevent it. Sherri had been ecstatic with the news and promised to let Aaron know that both his rent money and his phone bill had been paid. Toinette had wired the money directly to the rental office and the telephone company. She'd even wired an extra one hundred dollars to Aaron with the directive to buy groceries and nothing else. Lord only knew what he and Derek had been eating during the crisis.

She pulled Bandit, the stuffed bear, to her. Not for the first time that day she felt both depressed and anxious. She'd sacrificed her principles. Doing it for Aaron didn't make her feel any better. She hugged the bear to her and wondered if she'd be able to look herself in the mirror the next day.

CHAPTER 24

The young woman considered herself lucky. Timing was everything. She had been able to settle with Victor and even had enough left over to establish a little credit to her account. She kicked off her shoes and perched on the edge of the sofa. Just as soon as she got herself straight for the night she'd think about tomorrow.

Normally she didn't do this on weeknights. She tried to limit it to the weekends when she didn't have to work. That's how it all started. The recreational pharmaceuticals, as Victor first called the new treat, had been for a party buzz, just something to do on the weekends. But now her body couldn't wait another minute let alone another night.

She prepared everything then brought the crack pipe to her mouth. The telephone rang but she ignored it. There wasn't anything more important in her world than the sweet release she knew would come from the pipe.

By Friday, Toinette had put Aaron's troubles behind her. She'd talked to Angie who had agreed to sit down with her brother and come up with a budget and spending plan. As Angie pointed out, Aaron was going to have to get his act together if he was going to get through law school on a budget.

Toinette was packed and ready for her first trip. She would spend Tuesday and Wednesday in Atlanta. She'd have a one-day turnaround before she was back in the air, headed to the next city. Fresh clothes and prepared packets on the program would get her through the Chicago trip. That flight left early Thursday morning. With luck she'd be home Saturday. As she straightened up her office late Friday afternoon, she focused on only one thing: the fun she'd have with her grandkids and Kendra and Malcolm's girls.

She'd gotten a furtive call from her daughter-in-law. Russell had been called out of town for a Realtors' meeting. Paulette was going to bring the kids over even though she'd promised Russell she wouldn't. Paulette thought her husband was being unreasonable and childish. Toinette agreed and was secretly glad that her daughter-in-law had good sense even if Russell had been absent when God was distributing that gift.

A few hours later, dressed in snug, faded jeans, an old button down baseball shirt and white athletic socks, she opened the front door to Malcolm Hightower.

"Aunt Nettie!" twin voices yelled before hugging her hard. As usual, Kayla and Karin Hightower were dressed identically. But like their mother, Toinette never had any difficulty determining which identical twin was which.

"Is Jamal here yet?" Kayla asked. "Karin likes Jamal."

"Do not," her twin responded.

"Do too."

Toinette laughed and tugged on Karin's ponytail. "You guys are the last to arrive. Everybody's in the den."

"Bye, Dad," Kayla said giving her father a hug.

"Bye, Dad," Karin echoed.

The girls dashed to the den to join the other children.

Malcolm stood in the doorway shaking his head. "I don't know how you do it, Nettie."

"Keeping up with the kids keeps me young," she said with a saucy grin. "You gonna come in for a while?"

Malcolm shook his head. "Kendra and I are taking advantage of your largess and will be catching a movie. She was getting dressed when I left to bring the girls here."

"Well, you guys have a good time."

"Will do," he said. "Oh, I almost forgot." Malcolm handed Toinette a brown paper grocery bag. "Kendra sent pudding. Chocolate, vanilla, and something else."

Toinette accepted the bag and grinned. "I love pudding."

Malcolm laughed. "That's what Kendra said." He turned to leave, then he paused and turned back to Toinette who was about to shut the front door.

"Hey, Nettie?"

Toinette looked up at him.

"I just wanted you to know, I really like the change you've brought out in Robinson. He has a focus now, a grounding he never had before. It's good to see him enjoying life. You make him happy."

Toinette wasn't sure what to say to that. She gave Malcolm a half-smile, then raised her hand in a small wave.

"Night," he called back to her as he headed down the steps.

Toinette shut the door and leaned back on it. "And what about the change he's brought out in me? I've never been so confused in my life."

She could claim unsure feelings about Robinson while talking to her girlfriends. But she couldn't lie to her heart of hearts. She was in love with Robinson Mayview. Despite the problems—that she was now estranged from her son; that Robinson might be seeing at least one other woman; that she herself was married, the fact remained she was in love with Robinson.

Toinette sighed. Love wasn't supposed to be like this: unsure, contentious. Love was supposed to be joyous and beautiful. That's how she felt in Robinson's arms. Why couldn't those feelings translate to the other parts of her life when he wasn't around?

A dispute from the den over the remote control drew her attention away from Robinson and to the houseful of children. With the bag of pudding in hand she headed down the hall.

"Who's hungry?"

"I am! I am!" came the shouted responses when she skipped into the den.

Toinette's grandchildren, Carol, Jamal, Jessica, Thad and Lisa, along with Kayla and Karin, were sprawled over various pieces of furniture in the room. The kids had the television on loud and someone had tuned the stereo radio to a rap station. Music poured from the speakers.

She dropped the bag near the door, turned the music down and plopped on the sofa. Her lap was immediately filled by Lisa and Kayla.

"Did you guys eat dinner before you left home?" Toinette asked Kayla.

The girl shook her head. "Mom said we'd get plenty of junk food at your house so she told us to wait."

Toinette laughed. "Good for your mom. Who wants pizza?"

"I do! I do!" filled the room.

"Thad, sweetie, grab the phone book out of the kitchen. We'll order some pizzas."

Lisa wrapped her small arms around Toinette's shoulders. "Grandma, are we gonna fingerpaint tonight? I liked it when we did that last time."

Toinette kissed the girl on the nose. "No, darling. Tonight is the night for adventure."

"Like the Power Rangers?" Thad asked.

"Not quite. More like pirates hunting for hidden treasure," Toinette told him.

Eyes got wide around the room. In the chair they shared Jamal and Karin looked at each other and grinned.

"I'm gonna be Captain Hook," the boy told her.

"Okay. What do you want on your pizza?" Toinette called out.

"Extra cheese!"

"Pepperoni."

"Hot dogs."

"Eeewwh. Who eats hot dogs on pizza? That's nasty."

"No, it's not. I want peanut butter on my pizza."

"Peanut butter? If she gets peanut butter I want frogs legs on my pizza."

A collective round of "Eeewwhs" greeted that selection.

"What about marshmallows?" one giggly voice offered up.

"Aunt Nettie, they're being silly," Kayla said seriously from Toinette's lap.

Toinette nodded and dialed the pizza shop number. "I'd like four medium pizzas. Each one will be different," she told the order person. "One with everything. One with pepperoni. One with sausage, green pepper . . ."

"Don't forget the mushrooms," Jessica called out.

". . . and mushrooms," Toinette added with a wink to her granddaughter. "And for the last one, a cheese pizza with a generous helping of snails and puppy-dog tails."

"Grandma!"

"Aunt Nettie!"

The kids erupted in laughter and giggling and Toinette, laughing, fell over on the sofa with Lisa and Kayla clutched in her arms.

"What do you mean you're fresh out of snails and puppy-dog tails?" she asked the pizza order person. "Well, do you have any eye of newt or bat's wings?"

"Grandmaaa!"

"Okay, okay. I guess you'll have to make the last one just extra cheese. How long will it be?" Toinette gave her address, last name and telephone number and rang off.

"Grandma, they're gonna think you're crazy," Jamal said shaking his head.

"Maybe I am, laddie boy, maybe I am. Gather around, mates for the tale of crazy pirates who sailed the seven seas."

From a table next to the sofa, Toinette pulled a story book. With a wide-eyed audience gathered around her she started reading a pirate adventure story to the children.

By the time the pizza arrived, the seven children were engrossed in the tale. Toinette paid and tipped the driver then carried the boxes to the kitchen table. As Jamal and Thad dragged extra chairs into the kitchen,

Toinette pulled paper plates, cups, and napkins from a bag on the counter.

"So where'd the pirates bury the gold, Grandma?" Lisa asked.

"Yeah, Aunt Nettie, did they go back and get the bounty?" Karin said.

"Booty, the stolen stuff is booty," Kayla corrected.

"Whatever," Karin said dismissing her twin with a wave of her hand. "Did the pirates get the gold, Aunt Nettie?"

"Yeah, Grandma, did they?" Carol asked.

Toinette put a plate and napkin in front of each child. "You know, that's the intriguing part," Toinette said.

She opened the four pizza boxes and let the kids have at it. She snagged a slice of pepperoni pizza for herself, took a bite out of it and placed the remaining portion on a paper plate. She poured soft drinks and gave each child a cup.

"The pirate ship went down in rough seas and they never got back to find the gold and the jewels," she said.

"It's still there," Carol said with a hushed awe.

Toinette nodded. "It's still there. And you know what?"

"What?" seven eager voices replied as they munched on pizza and sipped soda.

Toinette moved around the chairs to a drawer. With a flourish she pulled out a piece of paper that looked old and ragged from wear and tear. "They left a map," she whispered.

"Wow!"

"A treasure map. That's really cool."

"And look," Toinette said coming to the edge of the table so all the children could see. "Do you see this X?"

Seven heads nodded.

"X marks the spot where the treasure is hidden."

"Aunt Nettie, that looks like your house!" exclaimed Kayla who was sitting closest to where Toinette stood with the map.

"There's treasure in the house," Thad cried out, pushing his chair back to commence a search.

"Hold it, hold it," Toinette said. With wide eyes the six-year-old looked up at his grandmother.

"Everybody finish eating then we'll go on a treasure hunt in the house."

Thad turned around and snatched another piece of pizza from one of the boxes and stuffed it in his mouth.

"Slow down, Thad, sweetie. The treasure isn't going anywhere."

"Okay, Grandma," the boy said around a mouthful of pizza.

Toinette and the children made inroads on the pizzas but there was still a lot left over. Toinette decided to leave it out on the table in case anyone decided they wanted more. She told all the kids to go sit in the den to hear the rules for the treasure hunt. She folded up the big treasure map and tucked it back in the drawer. She picked up all the cups from around the table, dumped the remaining contents and tossed the trash away. Then she grabbed another bag from the kitchen counter and joined the kids.

"Okay," she said. "This is what's known as a scavenger hunt. There's treasure hidden all over the house. Just inside the house. Not outside. And there are three places that are off limits. Grandma's bedroom, the basement and the attic. Does everybody understand? There's no treasure in those three places."

The children nodded their understanding of the rules.

"Okay." From the bag she held Toinette pulled out foam rubber scabbards, paper bags to hold the booty and miniature treasure maps. She gave one of each to each child, then settled a foam rubber parrot on her shoulder and a black construction paper patch over her eye. "On the back of your map, each of you has a list of the hidden treasure. The person who finds the most gets this," she said, whipping out a large gold-colored key from the bag.

"What is it?" Jamal asked.

"It's the key to the pirates' greatest treasure," she said dramatically.

"What's the pirate's greatest treasure," Jessica asked.

"The secret is in the treasure you find," Toinette answered with a smile.

"When can we start the hunt?" Karin asked.

Toinette looked at her watch. It was seven-thirty. "You have one hour. Start. . . . now!"

The children took off like lightning, laughing and yelling and scrambling over each other.

Toinette laughed and shook her head then went to the kitchen. She popped microwave popcorn and put two bowls of it on the kitchen table, dumped a bag of miniature marshmallows in another bowl and lined them up. Anybody who got the munchies and found his or her way to the kitchen could grab a bite. She retrieved the paper bag of pudding and popped the small containers out of the packaging. She put plastic spoons for the pudding in a paper cup on the table. Toinette grinned. Kendra was right, junk food reigned at Nettie's sleepovers.

"Hey, Grandma. What does this say?" Lisa asked.

Toinette bent down and looked at the word on the back of the treasure map. "Can you sound it out?"

"That's an F," Lisa said, pointing to the first letter of the word that stumped her. "And that's a L like my name Lisa." The girl tried several combinations of sounding the word out. "The picture is a towel but I don't know what this F-L is."

"Fluffy," Toinette supplied.

"Fluffy towel!" Lisa said. Then she slapped her hand over her mouth to keep her fellow pirates from discovering the clue. "There's treasure hidden in the fluffy towels, Grandma?"

Toinette smiled and shrugged.

"I'm gonna look in the bathroom!"

"Hey, Lisa," Toinette said.

The little girl turned around and looked at her grandmother.

"The bathroom's not the only place you find fluffy towels." Toinette nodded toward the kitchen sink.

For a moment Lisa looked confused. Then her eyes widened when they landed on the damp cloth draped over the sink. "Dish towels. Fluffy dish towels."

The girl ran to the drawer where Toinette kept dish cloths and place mats. She whipped the drawer open and rummaged through the neatly folded towels.

"Grandma! There's treasure here!" Lisa yanked out a container of blow bubbles. "I found a treasure!"

"Put it in your bag. There's more hidden treasure to be found."

"Thanks, Grandma," Lisa said as she consulted her map for the next clue. The girl grabbed a handful of popcorn then scampered off.

Toinette ripped the cellophane off another package of microwave popcorn and popped it into the appliance. "She's only five," Toinette rationalized.

"She needed a little help. The other kids are bigger than she is," she told the foam rubber parrot on her shoulder. The parrot just looked at her with accusing eyes.

Toinette laughed out loud at herself. When the popcorn finished popping, she took the bag and went to the den. Then she plopped on the sofa, picked up the remote control to the television and channel surfed with the sound down while the kids hollered and ran through the house. Every now and then victory cries could be heard when someone discovered one of the twenty-five hidden treasures she'd placed around the house.

Throughout the hour, a couple of kids asked for assistance with words. The tag team of Jamal and Karin discovered a stash of coloring books and crayons. Carol found the glow-in-the-dark pencils in the living room. Lisa cried foul when her cousin Thad beat her to a Slinky that was masquerading as a pencil holder. Toinette surreptitiously pointed out to Lisa that one of the pencils was a treasure: when sharpened, the fat pencil would write in three colors all at the same time.

When Toinette finally called "Time!" the children were reluctant to end the treasure hunt.

"Rules are rules, me buckos. Let's see how well you did," Toinette called.

With hands on hips Toinette looked down at the assembled youngsters and grinned. "You pirates are good but I know of one treasure you didn't find."

"What Grandma?"

"Yeah, Aunt Nettie. Which one did we miss?"

Toinette smiled. "Let's just go down the clue list and see if anyone figures it out."

They went over the list of clues on the back of the treasure map. Two clues had stumped all the little treasure seekers.

"Read number six again?" Jamal asked. He and Karin had found four of the treasures. Right now they were tied for second place.

"I can be a pirate's best friend sticking to him until the end," Jessica read aloud. So far, at five treasures, Jessica had found the most. "There's no picture clue with this one."

The children mulled the clue over and over. Then, all of a sudden, Lisa, who had been staring at her grandmother and mumbling the clue, cried out. "Grandma! I know it. I know what it is."

Toinette smiled at the girl. "Well, if you know what it is, go get it."

"Yeah, Lisa. If you're so smart, what is a pirate's best friend sticking to him until the end?" Thad asked his cousin. He was kind of disgruntled because he'd only found two treasures, just as many as Lisa had. If she'd figured out the clue, she'd be one up on him.

Lisa scrambled from the sofa and went to her grandmother. "Scoot down," she requested.

Toinette squatted so she was eye level with Lisa. "Aren't you going to go find the treasure?"

Lisa giggled. "You're so silly, Grandma. You are the treasure." Lisa plucked the foam rubber parrot from Toinette's shoulder and turned to face her cousins and friends. She held the parrot up for them to see. "A pirate's friend who sticks to him until the end."

She pulled the Velcro tabs from the parrot's feet and attached the bird to her shoulder.

Collective groans and boos from her fellow pirates filled the den. Then Thad started a round of applause for Lisa's ingenuity.

"Nice job, Lisa," Toinette congratulated the girl. She flipped the eye patch up so she could see better. "Well, well my little scavengers. That leaves one more clue. The clue of the key to the pirates' greatest treasure."

"We didn't find a key. We all looked, too," Carol said.

"Yeah," Jamal concurred. "We looked in the doors and in all the locks but there was no key."

"Give us a hint, Aunt Nettie," Karin said.

"Yeah, a hint," Thad said.

Toinette tapped her chin with a finger. "A hint, huh? Well, since you did so well with all the other clues, here's a hint. The kitchen."

"The kitchen? What kind of clue is that?" Thad complained. But when he looked up, he was the only child still in the den with Toinette. He jumped up from his spot on the floor and ran to join the gang in a search of the kitchen.

Toinette watched as the kids did a systematic search of the kitchen, as systematic a search as could be done while munching on popcorn and grabbing for marshmallows. Lisa, content with her parrot, had given up the chase for the key and was sitting at the table working the top off a package of pudding. Toinette looked at the bird on the girl's shoulder.

"I swear to God, I didn't help her with that one," she mumbled to herself.

Above the ruckus the children made, Toinette heard the doorbell ring. "Thad, don't throw popcorn at your sister," she admonished the boy as she went to answer the door.

Toinette looked through the peephole.

She opened the door to a very sexy-looking Robinson Mayview leaning against the jamb with a foot propping the screen door open. Even if she was convinced she'd seen him out with another woman she had to admit, the man looked good.

"Hi," he said.

"Hi, yourself."

"I was, uh, just driving through the area and saw all your house lights on. I figured you were up."

Toinette stood in the door not bothering to hide the fact that she was liking what she was seeing. Robinson was wearing a double-breasted rust brown suit with a cream and brown polka dot silk tie. He'd obviously forgotten that he had his wire-rimmed reading glasses on. Toinette thought they made him look even sexier, like he'd been in the middle of reading something important, thought of her and dropped everything to get there.

"Just driving through on a little trip out of your way, huh?"

He smiled a slow sensual smile. "Something like that."

Robinson studied her with the same wicked scrutiny she'd given him.

Toinette's mouth went dry.

"I've never seen you in jeans," he said.

Toinette ran a hand over a hip. "These are one of my favorite pair, old and comfortable. Why don't you come on in."

Robinson followed her in the house, his eyes never leaving her backside. "I think they're my favorite pair, too."

Toinette turned to him and he folded her into his arms. "I've missed you, Toinette."

Just as his mouth was about to lower over hers, a racket from the kitchen reminded Toinette of the kids.

"Oh, Lord. The treasure hunt. Come in and shut the door." She dashed off to the kitchen to check on the children.

She was greeted by a hail of popcorn.

"Hey, you're supposed to eat it not throw it," she scolded.

"Food fight!" a young voice yelled.

Before Toinette could say or do anything else, popcorn and marshmallows flew across the room as the seven children got caught up in the frenzy. Lisa took a plastic spoon, poked it through a fresh container of pudding, armed the spoon and aimed the missile at one of her cousins. The device quickly caught on. Chocolate, vanilla and tapioca went flying.

"Somebody's gonna get hurt," Toinette could be heard over the din.

Robinson stepped into the room. "What's going on in . . ." He didn't get any further with his question. A slice of pepperoni pizza landed square on his face at the same moment he felt a volley of something soft hit him.

A collective gasp of horror filled the kitchen, then the room grew deathly quiet.

Lisa lowered her pudding spoon. "Uh oh."

CHAPTER 25

For a heartbeat, nobody moved, nobody even breathed.

Robinson looked down at his very expensive tailor-made suit. But he couldn't see much because pizza sauce and a piece of pepperoni on his glasses obstructed his view. The only sound in the room came from the pizza slice as it plopped to the floor.

Robinson took the glasses off and wiped his face with one hand. He then got a look at the damage to his suit. His chest was spotted with white, and brown goo. Rob-inson plucked the pepperoni from his glasses and leveled a menacing look at all of the children, his gaze finally landing on Lisa. The little girl's lower lip started to tremble and he could see tears gathering in her eyes.

Toinette dashed to Lisa and scooped the girl up in her arms. "Robinson, she didn't mean . . ."

Robinson cut her off. "You guys are gonna get it now."

Before anyone knew what had happened, Robinson bent down and grabbed the slice of pizza from the floor and aimed it at a kid. He threw the pepperoni in the direction of Toinette and Lisa and then ducked down. In a crouch-run, he made his way to the table.

The battle had been joined.

Squeals of laughter filled the room. Lisa squirmed out of Toinette's arms and aimed her pudding projectile at Robinson.

"Oh, no you don't," he said reaching for a handful of popcorn. Even as he threw it at the girl, something soft landed near his mouth.

Robinson reached a finger up and tasted the stuff. "Umm, chocolate, my favorite."

"Look out, Mr. Robinson!" a voice yelled.

Too late. A bowl of marshmallows was dumped over his head. Robinson decided the floor was the safest place to be. He sat down but grabbed a kid on his way down.

"I tried to warn you, Mr. Robinson," the girl said laughing and squiggling in his arms.

"Oh, you think this is funny, Miss Hightower. Well, just for that, instead of protecting you. . . ." Robinson stood the girl up so she became a shield.

"No fair hiding behind a little girl, Rob," a soft voice said from behind him.

Robinson let Kayla go and turned around to see a devilish grin on Toinette's face. The woman was armed. Before he could shield himself, Toinette let go a spoonful of vanilla pudding.

Delighted laughter cascaded over Robinson. "Payback is sweet, they tell me," he told her.

"As sweet as that pudding?" she asked as she jumped out of his reach.

Toinette, Robinson and the children continued the food fight for another few minutes. It finally came to a halt when Thad remembered about the pirates' greatest treasure.

"Look at this kitchen," Toinette said. "I think the treasure will have to remain buried. No one will ever find it in this mess."

"We'll clean it up right now, right guys?" Jamal prodded.

A chorus "We'll clean it up" went through the kitchen as the children realized Toinette was serious. Little hands went about picking up pizza and scooping up marshmallows and popcorn.

While Robinson got up to inspect the real damage to his clothes, Toinette rinsed off her hands, dried them on a cloth then got on her hands and knees to search for extra sponges in the storage space under the sink.

Robinson pulled off his suit jacket and shook his head. This was going to pose a challenge to his dry cleaner. He draped the jacket over a doorknob and loosened his tie. Then he took the cuff links out of his shirt, dropped them in his pants pocket and rolled up his sleeves. When he turned around, his attention was riveted on Toinette's shapely derriere wiggling underneath the sink.

Robinson's own body responded to the sight. He'd been so long without Toinette. The comfortable old jeans she wore fit her like a glove, just the way he knew she fit him.

He took a deep breath and wiped his hands over his face. Now was not the time.

"Hey, mister. You gonna help us clean up?" a small voice asked.

Robinson looked down at the boy and smiled. "What's your name, son?"

"Thaddeus," the child replied.

"Well, Thaddeus, tell me what to do."

The child put his small hand in Robinson's and they went to clean pizza off the door of the microwave oven.

Across the room, Karin was sweeping popcorn into a dustpan Jamal held steady on the floor. "You guys know him?" he asked the girl, nodding in the direction of Robinson.

"That's Mr. Robinson. He's my Daddy's law partner. He's really nice, too. He and Aunt Nettie are dating, I think."

"Wow," Jamal said. He looked at Robinson with new eyes. He thought he'd heard his mom and dad arguing about somebody named Robinson. But he wasn't sure. If this Mr. Robinson didn't get mad when he got pummeled with pudding and if Karin liked him, he was okay in Jamal's book.

When the kitchen had some semblance of order again, the kids gathered around the table and asked about the treasure.

"We solved all the clues except one," Kayla said for Robinson's benefit.

"The person who gets the most clues solved wins the golden key that will lead us to the greatest treasure," Carol said. "I found three treasures. Jessica's winning right now. But Karin and Jamal are close."

Robinson lifted his gaze to Toinette who sat in a chair at the table. The woman was not only beautiful and sexy she was creative as well. She smiled at him and stole another piece of Robinson's heart. He wondered if she realized that she owned all of his heart.

"Well," he said to the children, "pirates usually leave maps to get them back to the treasure they bury."

"We know that," Thad said. He pulled a piece of paper from the back pocket of his jeans. "See, this is the treasure map."

"Number eighteen is the one we can't get," Jamal said from his place at the table where he studied his own map.

"When X marks the spot, you'll know I'm not a box," Robinson read. "What does that mean?"

A collective sigh of groans and moans filled the room. Toinette laughed and twirled the big golden key in her hands.

"If we knew that, Mr. Robinson," Karin said, "we'd know the answer."

Lisa's eyes widened. "Grandma!" The little girl turned in her chair so she could face Toinette.

"Don't tell me you figured out another one," Thad complained.

"What is it, Lisa?"

The girl grinned. "I think I know."

"Well, go get it."

"What did you do with it?" the girl asked.

"Do with what?"

"Grandmaaa!" Lisa scrambled from her chair and went to where Toinette sat. Toinette put the key on the table and held out her hands to show Lisa she wasn't concealing anything. Then she pointed toward a drawer.

Lisa went over and opened the drawer, pulling out the map. "X marks the spot," she said grinning.

Toinette started clapping. "Good for you, Lisa. That gives you four treasures." Toinette smiled as she handed Jessica the golden key. "Jessie found the most so she gets the key."

"But what's the pirate's greatest treasure?" Kayla asked.

"What does it say on the other side of the treasure map, Lisa?" Toinette prompted.

Lisa turned the paper over and with Robinson's help with the difficult words she read the clue: "X marks the spot but riches untold are yours to be found when you look in the breadbox and unfasten the locks."

For a moment the room was silent then there was a mad dash to the breadbox on the kitchen counter. Jessica got there first and rolled up the top.

"Wow!"

Jessica reached in the breadbox and pulled out the treasure chest. Colorful pictures of jewels and gold doubloons covered the cardboard box designed like a treasure chest.

"Does your key open the treasure?" Jamal asked his cousin.

Jessica carried the treasure chest to the kitchen table. The children gathered around as she stuck the big key in the lock. The lid popped open.

"Wow! It's gold. It's the pirates' gold!" Thad exclaimed.

Jessica reached in the box and pulled out one of the small, plastic mesh bags. Each one was tied with a string and had a tag on it. "This says Lisa," she said reading the first one.

Jessica pulled out more bags and passed them out until each child had a small mesh bag filled with gold coins. Lisa was the first to discover that chocolate lurked under the gold wrapping of each coin.

"Grandma, this was fun!" Jessica declared.

A chorus of agreement filled the room. The kids all applauded the adventure.

"Now, how about if we get this pudding and pizza cleaned up off everyone. Boys in the hall bathroom. Girls can go to my bathroom."

The kids dashed to the den to put their golden treasures in their booty bags then raced each other upstairs for baths.

Robinson, who had been quiet during the uproar, came to Toinette and wrapped his arms around her waist.

"That was really cool," he told her. "You're a fun grandma."

"I try," Toinette said. Any other comment she was about to make was drowned in Robinson's mouth. The kiss was sweet and urgent and delicious.

Robinson left her mouth and nibbled on her neck and earlobe. "I'd like to take you on an adventure."

"I'll think about it," she told him.

"Let me give you some incentive," he said, as his hand slipped under the baseball shirt she wore and captured a breast. Toinette arched into his embrace.

A voice from the other room intruded. "Aunt Nettie, we can't get in your room. The door is locked," Karin called.

"Coming, sweetie."

"Are you?" Robinson asked.

"Am I what?" When Toinette caught his meaning, her eyes dilated and she reached a hand down to stroke him.

Robinson sucked in his breath.

"We'll see who takes whom on an adventure," she said with a naughty smile as she left his arms and went to help the kids.

When all the children were bathed and in their night clothes they gathered in the den to watch videos. Toinette sat on the stairs combing Lisa's hair when Robinson walked up.

"Oh, you're still a mess," Toinette said looking at what was left of his once immaculate suit.

"I'm sorry I threw pudding at you, Mister," Lisa said.

Robinson bent down to the girl's eye level and tugged on one of the braids Toinette had finished. "That's okay. It was fun, wasn't it?"

The girl smiled shyly and nodded. Robinson leaned over and kissed her on the cheek. "Well, I'm glad you had fun playing the game. You found a lot of treasures didn't you?"

Lisa grinned and nodded her head.

"All done, sweetness. Why don't you go join the others in the den."

"Okay, Grandma. Bye, Mister."

"Call me Robinson."

"Bye, Mr. Robinson." Lisa waved and then skipped down the hall.

Robinson helped Toinette up.

"I'll pay for your dry cleaning," she said.

"No need. I had fun, too. But on second thought," he said remembering the gob of vanilla pudding she'd lobbed at him, "maybe you should be responsible."

Toinette wrapped her arms around his neck and laid a sizzling kiss on his lips.

"Then again, maybe not," he said when he caught his breath. "You sure are a sexy granny."

"And you're a messy attorney. Do you want to take a shower or something?"

"I like the 'or something' part but unfortunately we're not alone. I have a bag of clean clothes I keep in the car just in case I go to the gym. I'll change into those."

"You can use the hall bath. There are clean towels in the linen closet behind the door. Holler if the kids didn't leave any in there."

More than two hours later after an animated movie that each of the children had already seen at least a dozen times, every one of the little people was fast asleep. Lisa was curled up in Robinson's arms in an easy chair. Without disturbing Jessica, Toinette edged the girl's head from her lap then pulled an afghan over the sleeping child. She motioned for Robinson to do the same with Lisa then she turned off the television and the VCR.

"Meet you in the kitchen," she whispered to Robinson.

Toinette measured out ground coffee and poured it into a filter. She flicked the switch on the coffeemaker just as Robinson approached from the den.

Dressed in sweat pants, a Tuskegee University sweatshirt and athletic socks, he came to her. Toinette leaned up against the counter. "Bet you've never spent a Friday night in a food fight and then watching cartoons," she said with a smile.

But her smile faded as she watched Robinson stalk her. She braced herself against the counter and felt her body respond to the irresistibly devastating look in Robinson's eyes.

He stood in front of her, so close that Toinette wasn't sure where either of their bodies began. There was just one thing she knew she wanted right now.

Robinson looked in her eyes, certain that he had her complete and undivided attention.

"What?" she breathed.

"I love you, Toinette Blue. Will you marry me?"

CHAPTER 26

Robinson regretted the words as soon as he heard them come from his mouth. In the space of a moment he could feel Toinette go from tender and soft to tension-filled and nervous. Damn! He hadn't meant to propose to her this way, standing in a kitchen, dressed like a college kid. And definitely not with a roomful of little kids three steps away.

Toinette just did something to his brain—as well as the other parts of his body. But what he was feeling right now wasn't about sex; it was about forever and always. Seeing Toinette interact with the children made him realize all the more just how special a woman she was. He loved her smile, her zest, her inner beauty as well as the physical attributes that made him run hot with just the thought of her.

But now he'd messed up by blurting out a marriage proposal before she was ready. Stupid, stupid, stupid, he chastised himself.

Toinette pushed at his chest. Robinson dropped his arms and stepped back.

"Robinson, I don't know what to say. I, you . . ."

Robinson put one finger to her lips, silencing her. "Shh, I know you're not ready for that. I just got so caught up in how you make me feel that I jumped the gun. I do love you, Toinette. And I want to marry you. But I'm not going to rush you."

She shook her head. "Robinson, I can't marry you." She began to pace the area, careful not to get too close to him. "I mean, I care for you a lot. But I can't marry you."

The anguish in her voice didn't escape Robinson. Nevertheless, he was more than a little frustrated about this topsy-turvy relationship. Sooner or later they were going to have to decide what it was going to be, a relationship or not. The stakes were high, much higher than Robinson ever would have imagined them to be. His life felt like it was on the line.

"Can't or won't?" he caustically asked.

Toinette turned pain-filled eyes to him. How could she explain something to him that she herself was trying to figure out? If he'd just be content to keep things at a nonthreatening level for a while, she'd be able to sort out her feelings and figure out what to do. But instead he was standing there exerting pressure that she didn't feel comfortable dealing with, pressure that she didn't know *how* to deal with.

"Robinson, you ask for too much."

He ran a hand through his hair. "Toinette, I have tried to be patient. I have tried to understand and help you realize that whatever fears or doubts you have, we can work them out together. Together as two people striving for the same thing. You said you wanted to be friends. Okay. We're friends. Then you nearly burn me alive in the closet at my house."

Toinette blushed at the memory of being on the floor in his closet. If the housekeeper hadn't intruded, they would have made hot love right there amidst his suits and shoes. "I didn't mean to be a tease," she said quietly.

Robinson took a deep breath, then rubbed his eyes. "Toinette," he said, coming up behind her and placing his hands on her shoulders. He could feel the tension radiating through her. "You are not a tease. You are a warm, gracious, beautiful, and passionate woman. I love all of those things about you."

"I can't marry you, Robinson. Not now, not ever."

He turned her around to face him and was surprised to see tears on her face. "Toinette." With his thumb, he wiped at one of the wet tracks.

Robinson bent his head and gently kissed her. Then he released her and stepped back.

"Listen," he said. "It's been a long day. I'm sure the kids wore you out. Why don't you get some rest. I'll call you tomorrow." He looked at his watch, then amended himself. "I'll call you later today."

Toinette didn't say anything.

Robinson picked up his suit jacket from the doorknob, then let himself out of the house. Toinette eased into one of the chairs at the kitchen table and stared at her hands. As the clock struck one, she wondered why her life seemed such a mess.

She got up and poured herself a cup of coffee, then, with a dejected sigh, sat at the table again. The coffee got cold in her hands and still she sat there. She loved Robinson. He said he loved her. And he'd proposed.

"Lord have mercy, the man proposed to me right here in the kitchen."

Maybe domesticity turned him on. She looked down at her clothes.

There wasn't anything particularly appealing about how she looked at the moment, nothing that would set a man's heart aflutter—if men could even experience that uniquely female sensation. Toinette had to admit, her heart went aflutter whenever Robinson was near and even when he wasn't near. He made her feel like a woman, a natural woman. With a grin she realized she finally understood the words to the old soul song.

She thought about the kindness he'd shown to her earlier that week. Robinson hadn't hesitated when she needed him most, coming to her rescue.

Toinette sighed. "You didn't even thank the man for being your rock," she groaned aloud.

She heard the grandfather clock in the living room strike two. Surprised to find it so late, she got up, dumped the contents of her mug down the sink, and pulled the coffeemaker cord out of the wall socket. She glanced in on the kids, then turned the kitchen light out and padded upstairs to bed.

The artificial high had worn off and, like always, the woman lapsed into a deep, dark depression. How had her life gotten so off track? How could she continue to do this to her body? At times like this, she would swear and promise and commit to quit, to get help. But then, before long, the monkey would come back, taunting, promising, whispering sweet nothings until she could no longer resist. What had started as something to have a little fun with had turned into an obsession.

The woman got up from where she sprawled on the couch and made her way to a bed. Fully dressed, she fell face forward on the bare mattress and cried herself to sleep.

The next morning Toinette stayed busy in the kitchen while the children dressed. She made pancakes and fried apples for breakfast. After everyone had eaten, she piled the kids up in her car for a morning at the park. The children ran and jumped and played while Toinette sat on a park bench reading a book. Except she didn't get much reading done. Her thoughts kept turning to Robinson. She loved him. Why couldn't she just marry the man?

Then she remembered the reason.

Toinette slammed the book down on the bench and folded her arms, the beauty of the day spoiled with thoughts of Woody and Russell. She'd managed to go the whole evening last night without thinking of either of them. The light of day sure cast a pall over things.

A child ran up to her. "Grandma, my shoe came untied," Lisa said, holding her foot up for Toinette to see.

Toinette smiled at the child. "I thought your mom cheated and bought you Velcro snap shoes," she said, as she laced the child's tennis shoe.

"Those are my other shoes," Lisa said proudly.

"Oh, well, excuse me," Toinette said. She kissed the girl's head and watched her skip away to join the rest of the children who were tumbling through a large wooden fort.

Toinette placed a hand over her flat stomach. Robinson had taken an instant liking to all the kids last night. If she and Robinson got together, would he want her to have babies? Toinette frowned. Babies at her age. Lord have mercy.

"I'd rather have two root canals on the same day," she muttered.

But as she turned the idea over in her head, having Robinson's child would be nice. Special. These days, women had children well into their fifties. And there was that case of the older woman who had been a surrogate mother for her daughter and gave birth to her own grandchild. She and Rob had never talked about children. Maybe that's what he'd meant about building a big house. Did he hope to fill it with children? If so, then surely he needed a much younger woman.

Robinson would be a terrific father, she thought. He had been great with the kids the night before. Any other man would have hit the roof and maybe one of the children if his suit had been ruined like that. But Rob, well, he just took it in stride and joined the fray.

Toinette closed her eyes and smiled at the memory. That's how Robinson saw her as he walked up to the bench.

"Grandma, look who we found!" an excited Jessica said.

Toinette opened her eyes. Robinson, in a running suit and athletic shoes, stood before her holding Jessica's hand on one side and Carol's on the other.

He smiled down at her. "Good morning."

"Good morning."

The girls sat on either side of Toinette, leaving Robinson little choice but to stand before her.

"We saw Mr. Robinson jogging when we were on the tower," Carol said. "And he came over and helped Lisa and Thad build a sand fort."

Toinette smiled up at him and then, inexplicably shy, glanced away. The man had been playing in the sand with the children. How sweet, she thought.

Robinson watched her and was enchanted.

"We're gonna go now. Okay, Grandma?" Jessica said.

"Okay, darling. Be careful on the fort."

"We will," Carol said.

The two girls gave Toinette a hug and a kiss before waving to Robinson and running back to the play area.

Robinson settled himself next to Toinette. He picked up the book she had been reading and glanced at the title.

"Is it good?" he asked.

Toinette nodded. In truth, she didn't know if the book was a good read. Every time she started, thoughts of a certain man pulled her attention away from the story line.

"About last night, Toinette," he said.

"I'm sorry," she apologized.

"Sorry? For what? I had a blast." Until the end, he added silently.

"For being so, so indecisive."

Robinson squelched the frown that almost marred his features. Toinette had been anything but indecisive. He'd thought of nothing else in the time he'd been away from her. She'd said she wouldn't marry him. "Not now, not ever." Her words still hurt the heart she had stolen from him, stolen and then stomped all over.

"Toinette, I just want to know this. Tell me, what is it about me that you don't like? What have I said or done that makes the idea of being my wife so distasteful to you?"

Toinette could hear the anger under his words and searched within herself for the right way to respond. The picture of him entering the restaurant with that other woman flashed in her mind. From what Toinette had been able to see, that woman had been young, quite shapely, and had the long, thick hair that so many brothers were preoccupied with.

She looked at Robinson, opening her mouth to form the question. But as she began, she backed down. If the thrill ride with Robinson was over, it was over. There was no need to end on a bitter, accusing note.

"What?" he asked. "What were you about to say?"

Toinette shook her head. "I was just wondering," she lied, "how you'd feel if you had a son who hated you because of something you did in the past." But even as Toinette said the words, she wondered about Russell and their estrangement. She wasn't sure which part her oldest son was more angry about: her lying to him so many years ago or her seeing Robinson.

All of a sudden she remembered what Aaron had said that week. Aaron knew all about her fabrication! All of her children knew. Aaron said the older girls had told him that they wrote letters to an absent father to keep her from crying. Toinette bit her lip and swallowed. She refused to cry. Not now. She swiped a hand at the corner of her eye.

"Toinette, what's wrong? Don't cry," Robinson said. "Oh, for goodness' sake. I didn't mean to make you upset."

Robinson was torn between holding her and crying himself. What a mess he'd created. He searched in his pockets but didn't find a handkerchief.

Toinette unzipped the fanny pack at her waist and pulled out a tissue from a packet. "I'm sorry," she said, dabbing at her eyes. "This might be the last time I get to see Carol and Jamal," she explained. "They're Russell's kids. His wife brought them over last night because he was called out of town for a meeting."

"Toinette, I can help you with that."

"I don't want your help," she sniffed.

She could have slapped him across the face; her words had the same impact to Robinson. He got up. "Fine, Toinette. If that's the way you want it."

Toinette reached for his hand. "No. That's not what I meant, Rob."

He sighed and turned back to her. "Well, what did you mean? That sure sounded like a kiss-off to me."

"Rob, I just have a lot on my mind. First Russell, then Aaron and his problems at school. I had to put together the adventure for the kids and get everything ready for Atlanta and Chicago next week. I leave for Atlanta on Tuesday," she said.

Robinson interrupted. "I don't think it's a good idea for you to go traipsing through those projects. No one knows you there." Atlanta, and especially Chicago, had some of the nation's most notoriously dangerous public housing projects. Toinette would go in all sunshine and helpfulness and get attacked or killed just for being in the wrong place at the wrong time.

"I'm old enough to take care of myself, Robinson."

"Yeah, and old enough to know better," he shot back.

Toinette glared at him, then sighed. "I haven't really gotten a good night's sleep in the last couple of weeks. It's like everything is coming down on me at the same time. And then, then here you come talking about impossible things."

Robinson knelt before her and took her hands in his. "What's impossible about loving you and wanting to get married?"

Toinette shook her head. "I can't marry you, Robinson. I'm already married," she said quietly with a look of resignation.

Robinson misinterpreted her expression. He let go of her hands and stood up. With his arms folded across his chest and his expression stony, he stared down at her.

"You're still in love with him, aren't you?"

Toinette looked at him with anguish in her eyes. "Don't do this, Robinson. Don't do this."

Angry beyond reason, Robinson glared at her. "Fine, Toinette," he said, pointing a finger at her. "That's the way you want it? Fine. I'm out of here."

Robinson stormed away, leaving Toinette on the park bench with tears streaming down her face.

CHAPTER 27

Robinson drove around the city for hours trying to cool down. Toinette was impossible, completely impossible to deal with.

"Maybe that's why Woody left you. You were driving him stark raving mad."

Robinson thought about what he'd just said. Stopped at a red light, he pounded on the steering wheel and cussed at himself loud and long.

"Well, I never," a woman huffed.

Robinson looked to his left and realized his windows were down. He didn't even bother to apologize to the blue-haired little lady. When the light turned green, he floored the Jeep. He decided to go to the gym where he and Malcolm worked out. An hour or so in the pool or on the racquetball court would channel some of his pent-up anger.

As it turned out, the exercise didn't help. After swimming twenty laps and exhausting every sucker who agreed to go into the closed court with him, Robinson was still pissed off. Part of his anger was self-directed. The rest was leveled entirely at Toinette. She was the most stubborn, old-fashioned woman he'd ever met.

Robinson tossed his gym bag in the back of the Jeep and drove to the law firm. Maybe he could lose himself in some work. Lord knows he'd let enough things slide fooling around with Toinette.

As he entered his office, he caught a ringing telephone. He snatched up the receiver. "Mayview."

"Rob? That you? Hey man. I was all ready to leave you a message. I got the machine at your house and thought I'd try the office."

Robinson punched the speaker-phone button and went to the small refrigerator in the wet bar for a bottle of water.

"What's up, Leo? You have some information for me?" he asked the private detective.

"Ah, man. You put me on speaker phone, didn't you? I hate that crap. It sounds like I'm talking to Antarctica."

Robinson rolled his eyes and stomped over to his desk. He plopped down in his chair, picked up the receiver, and swiveled the chair around so he could see the rose garden.

"What's up, Stonehouse?"

"Oh. Hey, thanks, man."

"Do you have any information for me or not?"

"Well, what bee got in your bonnet today?"

"Stonehouse, if you just called to chat, I'm not in the mood, all right?" Robinson took a swig of the water.

"I think I've tracked down your man," the detective said. "To a little town about thirty miles outside the city."

"What's he do?"

"Don't know. I'm not even sure I have the right guy. I'm gonna go to the town first thing Monday and see what I can find. I'll let you know about it. Hey, Rob?"

Robinson continued staring at the rose bushes and swigging down water. "Hmm?"

"It's been a while since we got together, you know, did the circuit. I got a date tonight and she has a friend. They're both flight attendants."

"Yeah, so?"

"Is this Rob Mayview I'm talking to?"

"Leo, what are you babbling about?"

"So, they're flight attendants—friendly skies; coffee, tea, or me. Brenda swears her friend has it going on."

"Um-hmm. Probably looks like something the ASPCA rejected."

"Negative, my brother. This sister is hot with a capital H. I saw a picture."

"Then why are you pawning her off on me?"

"Brenda and I are kind of new. Don't want to spring any three-way surprises on her too early in the game."

"You are sick, you know that, Stonehouse?"

"And you're sounding like a brother who could use some company."

Robinson thought about that. A willing woman to take his mind off his problems actually sounded like a good idea. He definitely wasn't being taken care of at home. He frowned. He couldn't even claim to have a woman at home to take care of him. Toinette obviously didn't want him.

The only reason he was letting the detective finish the case was to solve the mystery of Toinette's missing husband. For his own sake, Robinson wanted to know what had happened to the man. The way he was feeling right now, he wasn't going to tell Toinette what Stonehouse found out about the guy.

He swung the chair around and put the water bottle on his desk. "What'd you say this woman looked like?"

Stonehouse chuckled. "Built like a Mack truck. Divorced. Mid-to-late twenties. H-O-T, my brother. And ready."

Robinson made up his mind. "Where are we going?"

He and Stonehouse made plans to meet at a club and then take the women for a late dinner. Robinson would meet them at the night club.

Robinson replaced the receiver and grabbed his keys from his desk. He put Toinette and her aggravating ways out of his mind and actually felt good about his plans for the night.

The only telephone message at his house was one from Marlena. In retrospect, he thought, it had probably been premature to dump her the way he did after their late-night dinner at Chez Jolé. Marlena had thought they were headed to an intimate rendezvous at the gallery she owned. Robinson had instead put her in a cab and sent her home. Maybe he'd been hasty. Depending on how the night turned out with the blind date, maybe he'd call Marlena when he got home.

Robinson felt the first twinge of guilt as he got dressed later that night. But he ignored it as he slapped on some cologne and shrugged into a loose-fitting amber-colored jacket. The baggy pants and soft Italian loafers gave him a carefully orchestrated look of casual elegance. He stood in his large closet and put his reading glasses on. He peered at himself in the three-way mirror and decided against the glasses. He tucked them in his pocket just in case Brenda's friend seemed to like the intellectual look. Robinson left before he changed his mind about this date.

He was not only pleasantly surprised but downright pleased with the blind date. Judi Christian turned out to be a very attractive woman. As he looked at her across the small table in the club, he smiled inwardly, for she was, indeed, built like a brick house. She wasn't an airhead either like Stonehouse's date, Brenda. Between the band's sets, the conversation turned to real estate. Judi said she was getting tired of coming home to a sterile apartment after her flights, particularly the overseas ones. She wanted a home.

Robinson had pulled out his glasses, put them on, and mentioned the ever-climbing interest rates and points.

Brenda had giggled and said her interest rate was climbing, and if Leo was lucky, he'd score some points. Robinson caught Judi as she rolled her eyes. He winked at her and she smiled.

For a moment, the way Judi cocked her head as she smiled reminded him of Toinette. Robinson banished the thought.

The music picked up again. "Would you like to dance?" he asked her.

Judi raised her hand and put it in Robinson's. Together they made their way to the crowded dance floor. Brenda waved energetically from where she and Leo were a few feet away.

Judi and Robinson gyrated to the beat. Conversation was impossible, so Robinson took the time to study her. From experience he knew a man could tell a lot about a woman by the way she moved on the dance floor. Leo had been right about one thing: Judi Christian was hot with a capital H.

After a few fast numbers and some house music, the band slowed the tempo down and Robinson looked at Judi with a question in his eyes. Not all women would slow dance with a stranger. She looked up at him and then stepped in his arms.

Robinson bit back a smile. She might slow dance with him, but she was being careful. She stayed a respectable distance away, not so much that it would be construed as prudish, but far enough for him not to get any ideas.

"So are those glasses real or just for effect?" she asked.

Robinson laughed out loud as he negotiated turns on the dance floor.

"What's so funny?" she asked with a smile.

"That's the kind of question a friend of mine would ask. In some ways you remind me of her."

"Is this a *good* friend?" Judi asked.

Robinson looked down at her. Brenda and Leo moved by. Brenda grinned and waved. Robinson smiled back at the couple. "The glasses are real," he told Judi.

She nodded and shifted in his arms. "Forewarned," she said.

Robinson chuckled to himself. Yeah, this woman wasn't stupid. He liked that. "What type of house are you looking for?" he asked.

"I don't know. Something small, manageable. I have a daughter, and she needs something that's really home for her. I'm away so much, sometimes I wonder if she remembers I'm her mother."

"How long have you been a flight attendant?"

"Three years. It's fun. I started soon after my divorce. I wanted a stable job that could provide for me and my child. What about you? Leo said you're a lawyer."

Robinson nodded. "That's what I've always done."

"Are you an ambulance chaser or a real lawyer?"

"And what would you say if I were an ambulance chaser?"

Judi looked up at him. "You don't look the type," she said simply.

He smiled. "I take that as high praise. I'm a partner in a medium-sized firm. My partner does criminal defense. I do a lot of corporate and trust work." He held her a little closer. "That meet with your approval?"

She didn't resist the embrace. "Sorry if I sounded a little critical. I've had some bad experiences."

"Haven't we all," Robinson muttered under his breath.

They were so close that Judi heard the words. The beat picked up. Robinson looked at Judi and she shook her head. He led her back to their table.

Robinson seated her and ordered another round of drinks from a passing waitress. His eyes followed the sensual movement as Judi crossed her legs. He swallowed and looked up. Judi was studying him with quiet laughter in her eyes. Her smile was part invitation, part wariness.

"Are you married, Rob?"

"Never married. No kids," he said.

Judi smiled and relaxed.

They spent the rest of the time at the club dancing and exchanging small talk. Robinson made sure he got her telephone number. For dinner the two couples went in separate cars. After the meal, she gave him directions to her apartment complex.

At her door, Judi paused. Robinson, catching the uncertainty in her despite their evening of good food, good fun, and conversation, didn't press. He took the key from her hand and unlocked her door.

"Good night, Judi. Thank you for a wonderful evening," he said.

"I had a good time, too. This wasn't bad for a blind date."

Robinson took the opening. "The next time we go out, it won't be a blind date." He posed the question as a statement.

Judi smiled. "That's right."

Robinson leaned down and kissed her on the cheek. "Night." He pressed her key back in her hand and walked down the hall to the elevator.

From her door, Judi watched him until he turned the corner that led to the bank of elevators. She went in her apartment, flicked on a light switch, and kicked off her high-heeled pumps.

"What a man! Awwahh!" she yelled and hugged herself. She dropped her small bag on the coffee table and sat on the white sofa.

She'd go down and check on the mail later. Right now, she just had to tell her sister about this date. Judi picked up the cordless phone and punched a single digit. She waited for a few moments while the speed dial function did its thing.

"Hello?"

"Leah? Hey girl. This is Judi. I'm home. Girl, I just had a date. This brother is something, too."

"I've heard that before, Judi. Remember Victor?"

"You're worse than Mom on Victor. Look, I know he's bad news. This guy, though, is genuine."

Judi filled her older sister in on the salient details. Then, "Is my little princess still up?"

"She's out. But she's excited about seeing you. Mom had another of her grand sleepovers. The kids have been talking about nothing else all day."

"I'll swing by tomorrow and pick Lisa up."

"See you then."

Judi pushed the antenna down on the telephone and placed it on the coffee table. She hugged herself again, then got up and prepared for bed.

Toinette had tried calling Robinson twice throughout the day. At eleven o'clock that night, she tried his house again. When the machine picked up, she hung up. She ran a bath and soaked until the water was too cold to stand. She got out, dried herself off, then put on a long cotton nightgown that closed with a bow at her neck.

She caught a glimpse of herself in the cheval mirror as she pulled the comforter off her bed. Between the gray hair, the makeupless face, and the nightgown, she looked like the old lady she felt she was.

Robinson had said as much. He thought she was too old to be starting the Quad-A Foundation program, too old for anything. Russell had been right all along. But she'd show Rob. She'd make a success out of the Foundation despite being almost fifty. There was nothing wrong with her age. It wasn't until Robinson Mayview entered the picture that she'd even thought about age.

Toinette thought about her oldest son. "You owe that boy an apology," she said aloud to her reflection. A part of her was still upset about what Russell had said, but she didn't want to lose her son. She was willing to offer the olive branch.

She got in bed and picked up the telephone on her nightstand. She called Russell, and, with apologies on both sides, they made amends. He promised to take her, his wife, and children to breakfast in the morning.

Toinette replaced the receiver and got comfortable in bed. Sunday breakfast with Russell would be nice. Sunday breakfast with Robinson would be nicer, but that obviously wasn't going to happen. She wiped at the tears that sprang out of nowhere and closed her eyes tightly. Eventually she slept.

Across town, the young woman with the drug problem made a decision. She was tired of living like this. From a street-corner telephone she called one number. The line rang and rang. She sighed, retrieved her quarter, and tried another number. Busy signal.

She slammed the receiver down and swore. She looked at the cheap watch on her wrist. She thought about the pretty, expensive one she used to own, but that was before its value became an asset she couldn't ignore. The woman wiped her nose and slung the small white handbag over her shoulder.

She started walking down the street that was busy with Saturday night revelers.

"Hey, Miss Thing."

She turned and looked at the expensive car she knew so well. The man calling to her was a friend, as friends go. But he was the type of influence she'd decided to get rid of.

"You looking awfully good tonight, Miss Thing."

She ignored him and kept walking.

"You a long way from home. Let me give you a ride."

That stopped her. She *was* a long way from home. She'd taken a taxi to get to the club district, then realized, too late, that she didn't have enough money to get home. She was hoping that buses were still running this late at night.

"You'll take me home and nowhere else?" she asked him.

"You wound me, Miss Thing. Of course, I'll take you straight home."

He'd been good to her—for the most part. She got in the car.

"You in the mood to party?" he asked her.

"Victor, I really want to go home."

He smiled. Then he reached over to the glove compartment and pulled out a small parcel. Her eyes widened when she recognized the contents. She reached for the bag of vials.

He chuckled and pressed a control that moved the front seat back a bit. "I'll make you happy, if you make me happy."

The young woman licked her lips and smiled at him. He put both hands on the steering wheel, dangling the bag as enticement.

"You always make me happy, Victor," she purred.

She inched closer to him. As he slowly drove the big car, she leaned down until her face was in his lap. She could feel his erection. She turned her head a bit and looked up at the drugs he so willingly offered for this small bit of pleasure.

"Come on, Miss Thing. Do what you do best."

The woman blinked back sudden tears. This wasn't what she did best. She couldn't imagine how and why she'd allowed herself to sink to this depth of desperation and depravation. She hadn't been raised this way. She thought of her family, of all the people who at one time had been so proud of her. By allowing herself to become a skeleton of the person she used to be, she'd let all of her family down. But most of all, she'd let herself down. She couldn't do this, she just couldn't!

She sat up and bumped her head on the steering wheel. Victor dropped the bag he had been loosely holding.

"Bitch, what you doing?"

"Let me out," she said while righting herself and scrambling to the passenger door.

He stopped at a red light, and she pulled on the door handle.

"Let me out, Victor. I don't want to do this anymore." She fought with the door but to no avail.

He laughed out loud. "You don't want to do this anymore," he said, mimicking her voice. "You a piece of trash, you know that?"

He pressed the electric control, and the door that she battled with opened. She jumped from the car and stood on the street corner, trembling. She watched as the car's tinted window rolled down.

He dangled the bag at her. "You'll be back, Miss Thing. You stinking crackheads always come back." He sped away.

Tears left heavy black streaks on her face as her mascara ran. The young woman wiped her face and her eyes with her sleeves and made her way to another pay telephone. This time a person answered on the first ring.

She couldn't stop the tears. Her words were choked. "Help me, please. I'm a drug addict and I need some help."

She listened to the voice on the other end and nodded. She looked up at the street sign and gave the person her location. The young woman hung the phone up and made her way to a bus-stop bench a few feet away. She wiped at her eyes again and waited for help to come.

CHAPTER 28

Monday was hectic for Toinette. She would be out most of the week, and all of a sudden there were a hundred little fires to put out before she could leave. John MacAfree called for an update on the Foundation plans. She met with the mayor's wife and gave her a list of Quad-A alums and benefactors who should receive special invitations to the gala benefit auction. Mrs. Griffin assured her that general invites had already gone out.

John and Etta MacAfree, Kendra and Malcolm Hightower, and the partners at the law firm Sullivan and O'Leary headed Toinette's list of about fifteen names. The event was two weeks away. She hadn't even had time to think about what she'd wear.

"You can worry about that later, girlfriend," she mumbled to herself as she checked off yet another item on her too-long list of things to do.

Bosworth Sullivan called and asked if she'd join him for a symphony performance that Friday night. Toinette was glad she had an excuse. She had yet to figure out how to let the man down gently, but as she grabbed her briefcase and purse to head out for a job-site visit, her last task of the day, she paused and looked at the telephone on her desk.

There was no real reason to put Sullivan off. It looked like Robinson was out of the picture. Unfortunately, he wasn't out of her system.

Toinette sighed and shut her office door.

"Dawn, I'm leaving now."

"Okay, Mrs. Blue," the senior aide said from her desk as she filled out a purchase order for food.

"If anybody needs me or if anything should come up, I've left the numbers of both hotels on my desk. All the flight information is there as well. And if, for some reason, you need to reach Ben Trammer of Trammer Engineering and Electronics, the corporate office number is there. I'll be at their Atlanta headquarters part of the day tomorrow. This should be a pretty typical week, though, so you don't have to worry about anything."

"And Kendra will be coming in for a few hours one day this week," Dawn pointed out.

Toinette smiled. "See, you're all set. You have her home and office numbers in your file, right?"

Dawn nodded and tapped the small telephone book on her desk.

"I know this place is in safe hands with you in charge," Toinette told her assistant director.

Dawn still looked dubious but got up to see Toinette out. A stop was made by the children's playroom.

"You leaving again, Miss Nettie?" the little boy Rasheed asked.

Toinette bent down and hugged the child. "That's right, sweetness. I'll be back, though."

"Where you going, Miss Nettie?" another child asked.

"To Atlanta to see if I can put together a Quad-A program there. Didn't you say you had some cousins in Atlanta, Shauna?"

The girl nodded. "Well, maybe I'll be able to help them have a place to stay after school while their mom works."

"That'd be nice," the girl said.

"It must cost a lot of money to start a Quad-A center like this one," another child observed.

Toinette nodded.

"You got a lot of money in that bag, Miss Nettie?" Rasheed asked.

Toinette laughed. "No, darling. The money hasn't come yet. But it'll come soon."

She stood up and looked at Dawn. The aide shook her head as she walked Toinette to the door. "That boy's gonna end up working on Wall Street one of these days."

"You're probably right. Well, my site visit is at two so I better hurry. See you next week."

At the newspaper office downtown, C.J. Mayview had just gotten back from lunch and was listening to her voicemail. The first call was a man complimenting her on that morning's story about a welfare mother who had beaten the system and was making a name and a life for herself. C.J. smiled as she listened to the message. The second message was a man angry about the same story. He ranted about the liberal media always in the laps of some crying person with their hands held out. C.J. shook her head and chuckled.

As the third message started, she took a sip of coffee and created a new file on her computer screen to start the story she was to file that afternoon. The third message was another ranter.

"Well, every day can't be wine and roses," she said, as she half-listened to the yeller. But something he said caught her attention. She let the message play through and then listened to it again.

"You're such a hot-shot reporter. Seems like you'd be interested in how money can become missing from one of those so-called do-gooder organizations. If you think only welfare queens achieve against all adversity, you'd better take a closer look at how and why the one in charge can live so flamboyantly. They strut about in their fancy cars and fancy clothes while us working-class stiffs have to sweat for every dime we earn. Report that, why don't you?"

The call ended when the man slammed his phone down. C.J. listened to the message again, jotting down notes as the man talked. When it ended, she saved the message in the voicemail system, hung up the phone, and looked down at the notepad she'd been writing on.

Mid-to-late 40s/50s. Angry. White? Traffic background noise.

Her impressions about the caller didn't tell her a lot. Of course, he'd left no name or number.

"That would make it too easy," she mumbled.

C.J. picked up a copy of that morning's paper and looked at the Page One story about the former welfare recipient. There was something about the call that didn't ring right. She picked up the phone and listened to the message again while she stared at the newspaper article. When the message ended, she had the missing link and something else. The reporter leaned over and pulled up the file folder which contained the complaints about and from the city's housing projects. She pulled out the semiliterate letter that had been passed to her earlier and read it again.

"Hmm."

C.J. picked up the telephone and called the newspaper's library. She requested hard copies of every story written in the last year about the Achieving Against All Adversities program. She knew that she'd get a lot of her own work in that bunch. Toinette Blue, the director of the welfare jobs program, had been a source for some time. In C.J.'s estimation, Mrs. Blue was honest and fair. But by the same token, there was something about the letter and the call that got her reporter antenna up.

She hadn't mentioned Quad-A in today's story. The woman featured in the article hadn't gone through that program. Yet the letter and the third caller had specifically mentioned adversity. The word was common, but not the type most people used in regular conversation.

While she waited for the clips, C.J. made a couple of calls and asked a few discreet questions.

In his office Robinson Mayview took a deep breath and dialed Toinette's office. Guilt had kicked in. He'd probably just missed her early that morning, and so he'd left a message at her house. Meetings kept him tied up most of the day, and now he had a moment to relax.

"Achieving Against All Adversities, this is Dawn. How may I help you?"

Robinson frowned. He thought he'd dialed Toinette's direct line. "Mrs. Toinette Blue, please."

"I'm sorry, sir. Mrs. Blue is out of the office. May I assist you?"

"What time will she be back today?" Robinson asked.

"She's out for the week, sir. Would you like to leave a message? If it's important, I can reach her."

"No, no message." Robinson hung up the phone. "Damn."

He'd forgotten that she said she had business trips to Atlanta and Chicago. She could be anywhere. He sat there for a minute moping before he turned his attention back to his work.

Later that evening, Robinson remembered something. At the park Toinette had said her trips started on Tuesday. Maybe he could still catch her at home.

He straddled a stool at the breakfast bar in his kitchen and called Toinette on the portable.

"Hello?"

Robinson grinned when he heard her voice. It seemed like ages since he'd last talked to her, even though it had just been over the weekend. God, how he loved this woman, even if she did frustrate him to no end. He had to make it right between them.

"Hello, is anyone there?"

"Hi, Toinette. It's Robinson."

Propped against pillows in bed, Toinette clutched her chest and caught her breath.

"Hi. Uh, can you hold on a sec? Let me get off this other line."

"Okay," he said.

Toinette clicked the line over. "Sweetheart?"

"Yes, Mom?"

"That's a call I need to take."

"Okay. I just wanted you to know I was back in town. Lisa tells me the pirate adventure was fabulous. She has her parrot on the headboard of her bed and the treasure map tacked to her wall."

Toinette smiled. "I'm glad she had fun."

"And she just raved about Mr. Robinson. I can't wait to meet this mystery man of yours. According to Lisa, he's very nice. I know you have to go, Mom, but I bet I know what he looks like. He's tall, with salt-and-pepper hair. Right?"

"Uh . . ." Judi obviously hadn't been talking to any of her brothers or sisters lately. Everyone else knew Robinson was younger than she was.

"And I'll bet he's a ringer for Harry Belafonte or Sidney Poitier," Judi added.

Maybe one of their sons or grandsons, Toinette thought with a shake of her head. But she didn't have time to get into this right now.

"Judi, I have to dash. I have a call waiting."

"Okay, Mom. Love you. I still have to tell you about this too-terrific guy I went out with. I'll call you when you get back."

"Good night, sweetheart."

Toinette clicked the phone to the other line.

"Rob?"

Dead air greeted her.

"Rob?"

Toinette stared at the phone. She'd taken so long with Judi that he'd hung up. She replaced the receiver and stared dejectedly at the telephone. She picked it up to call him and then changed her mind. He was already angry. The message she'd retrieved on her answering machine when she'd gotten in was more of the same on why she was too old for this foolishness and how it was unsafe for someone like her to go to those cities alone. If he was going to maintain that attitude, he could just forget it.

"Someone like me, indeed," she huffed.

She doubted that his anger had subsided; and then to put him on hold like that. Call waiting had its advantages. Tonight, though, the feature hadn't served her very well. But she missed him. Oh, how she missed him. This should have been a time of celebration, not a time of division.

Toinette got out of bed, went to the chaise, and got the stuffed bear Bandit.

"You know, Toinette," she told herself as she climbed back in bed. "A grown woman should not be sleeping with a teddy bear."

Bandit didn't reply. Toinette thought of Robinson and hugged the bear closer to her. Then she remembered something.

She hopped out of bed and went to her jewelry box, pulling out the slim gold chain Robinson had placed on her ankle the morning after they first made love. She held the bracelet in her hand for a moment and smiled.

She went to the chaise longue, lifted one slim leg, and attached the gold chain to the ankle where Robinson had first placed it. He'd told her it was something to remember him by. She remembered. Too well did she remember.

At his house, Robinson stared at the phone. He couldn't believe it. "She hung up on me! She hung up on me!" he said incredulously.

Robinson shook his head. "I don't believe this. I just don't believe this."

Toinette had put him on hold and then nothing. Malcolm had called on his other line, but Robinson had gotten off fast. Yet, when he'd clicked back, she was gone. He hadn't been on the line with Malc for a full thirty seconds. Toinette had hung up on him.

"Fine. That's the way you want it, Toinette. There are other women out there."

Judi Christian came to mind. So did Marlena.

Rob slammed the telephone on the counter and stomped off to his bedroom. Problem with those other women was he just didn't want them. He wanted Toinette Blue and she obviously didn't want him.

The next day, Dawn called Kendra at work.

"What's wrong, Dawn?"

"Well, I don't know. The dairy said it couldn't deliver any milk or juice or anything to the center. I mean, we have enough for the week, but this is supposed to be our regular delivery day. I called them when the truck didn't come."

"Was the center changed to another delivery day?" Kendra asked.

"No, that's the first thing I checked. They told me to talk to the accounting department."

"And what did they say?"

"That's what's strange," Dawn said. "The person I talked to got real smart with me and said if we wanted dairy products on time we ought to pay our bills on time."

"What?"

"That's what I said," the aide told Kendra. "I looked it up in our contractor books, and they were paid the same day as always."

Kendra sighed. Nettie wasn't gone a good day and things were already falling apart. "Okay, Dawn. You said you have enough milk, juice, and whatnot to get the kids through the week."

"Yeah, but next Monday is gonna be tight if we don't get a delivery before the end of the week."

"Not to worry," Kendra promised. "Give me the number and the name of the contractor. I'll see if I can find out what's up."

"Thanks, Kendra. I didn't mean to bother you at work."

"Not a problem. That's why I'm on call for you."

Kendra took the information and assured Dawn she'd take care of everything. She handled some pressing issues at the law firm where she worked, then called the dairy company. When she didn't get anywhere with the accounts receivable clerk, she asked to speak with the general manager.

"Ma'am, I've been trying to work with the Quad-A people," the manager told Kendra. "They do good work and all, but I got a business to run here. I can't afford to float charity cases."

"What are you talking about? I spoke with the assistant director today, and she says you were paid the same day and same amount as you've always been paid. We have lots of little kids depending on these dairy products every day."

"Miz Hightower, I got lots of employees depending on their paychecks. I can't pay them if I don't get paid from people like you."

Kendra shook her head. It was as though they were having two separate conversations. "Quad-A accounts are up-to-date. That's why I don't understand what the problem is."

"Ma'am, according to my records here, you all are overdue more than a month. Now normally, that wouldn't be a problem with my regulars. I know people fall behind from time to time. But this is a right regular occurrence with Quad-A."

"What?"

"I said—"

"I heard what you said. Listen, could you give me a little time? I'm not at the Quad-A office right now. I need to get there and check our records. I'm sure there's just some sort of accounting or data-entry error."

"If you say so, ma'am. I'll be here until about four-thirty."

Kendra looked at the clock on her desk. It was three-thirty now. Four-thirty didn't give her enough time to finish up her work, drive to the Quad-A center, and check Dawn's records. "That won't give me enough time today. When will you be available in the morning?"

They planned to talk the next morning. Kendra hung up the phone and added a notation in her appointment book. She shook her head. "Nettie promised me this would be an easy week."

Later in the evening, Kendra and Dawn sat in Toinette's office poring over the vendor accounts. "Something's not adding up, Dawn," Kendra said with a sigh.

"Maybe we missed something," Dawn suggested.

Kendra loosened the pins that held her hair up and massaged her head. "This is why I wasn't an accounting major. This gives me a headache."

Dawn laughed. "Yeah, well, neither was I. Ready to go through it again?"

Kendra nodded, and the two women went back through the ledgers of

Quad-A bills payable and money received. An hour later they were back where they started.

"This is crazy. Look, did Nettie leave enough petty cash here to cover the dairy bill?"

"She left what she called if-the-center-burns-down-and-the Red-Cross-has-run-out-of-aid-money cash," Dawn reported.

Kendra laughed. "Knowing Nettie, that should be enough to handle the national debt. Who else knows about it?"

"Just me." Dawn waved her hand to encompass the neighborhood where the center was located. "It wouldn't be a good idea to advertise that there's cash just lying around."

"Okay. Use that money to pay the dairy," Kendra said. "I don't know what the problem is. All the checks that were sent out are canceled, returned, and noted here. We'll let Nettie figure this out when she gets back. Just get what you need to see you through next week. I'll let the dairy general manager know what we're going to do. It shouldn't be a problem. Give me a call tomorrow if you need me for anything."

C.J. Mayview spent all Tuesday morning making calls and doing research. She pored over files and then left the office to talk to people who lived near the Achieving Against All Adversities center. A few of the things she heard made her curious. So she asked more questions.

By early evening, she didn't have anything concrete, not enough to justify a story. But she had enough to put a call in to Toinette Blue and see what was up. The center was located on the edge of the projects, so some of the stuff she'd heard on the street was undoubtedly a by-product of the neighborhood, not the center. However, by the time she made the call, the only person at the center was a van driver who happened to pick up a ringing telephone. She didn't bother to leave a message.

Robinson fiddled with the piece of paper that had Judi Christian's telephone number on it. Judi was an attractive, educated, and intelligent black woman. He could spend an enjoyable evening with a beautiful woman, or he could go home, sit around his house, and worry if Toinette was getting herself killed as she went smiling through dangerous neighborhoods handing out Quad-A business cards as if they were Bible tracts.

He decided on the former.

"Judi? Hi, this is Rob," he said when he got her on the line. "I know it's short notice, but I wondered if you'd be free for dinner tonight?"

Robinson smiled when he heard her response.

"That's great," he said. "Would you like to go to Chez Jolé'? The food is wonderful there. We can talk and get to know each other a little better."

She was waiting in the atrium lobby of her apartment building. By the time they got to the restaurant, Rob was antsy. He felt like he was cheating on his wife—and he didn't even have a wife.

Judi looked at him over a glass of white wine. "She must have been very special."

"Who?"

"The woman you're trying to get over."

CHAPTER 29

Robinson's gaze pierced hers. "Why do you say that?"

Judi put her glass down and ran one red fingernail against the rim. "You just have all the signs," she told him.

"What signs?"

She looked at him, then shook her head. "Never mind. Forget I even brought it up. Tell me about what you do when you don't do law."

Their conversation drifted on to general topics. At the end of the evening, Robinson took her home. They talked in the elevator to Judi's floor.

"I have a flight out tomorrow with a layover. I won't be back in town until Saturday."

"Where does your daughter stay when you're away?" Robinson asked.

"With my sister. She's there now."

"That's nice of her."

Judi nodded. "It makes it convenient. I don't have to worry about her when I'm gone."

The elevator opened, and they stepped out of the car. "Maybe I'll see you Saturday," Robinson said.

Judi turned as they walked down the hallway. "Sure. If you want. I usually crash when I first get in, though."

When they reached her door, Judi put the key in the lock, opened the door, and looked up at him. She caught her breath. This man was gorgeous! And he looked like he was going to kiss her. Off and on during the evening, she'd gotten the distinct impression that his mind was on something, or probably *someone,* else. It was nothing he said or did so much as what he didn't say or do. He hadn't tried any moves, and Judi knew from experience that that in itself was unusual in a brother. Now, for the first time all night, he seemed completely tuned in to her.

Robinson lifted a hand and gently caressed her face. "Thanks for a terrific evening," he murmured.

"Would you like to come inside?"

Robinson looked over her shoulder into the dark apartment. Judi's daughter was with her sister. The timing was right. The setting was perfect. The woman was willing.

An image of Toinette curled up sleeping in his bed hit Robinson. It was followed by mental pictures of her laughing on a roller coaster, throwing a spoonful of pudding at him, hugging a child, making love to him in the shower.

Robinson jumped back from Judi as if he'd been burned by her touch. Then he remembered his manners and tried to salvage the moment. He shook his head in answer to her question. "No. I'd better leave. I have an early day tomorrow."

Judi nodded, disappointed but understanding. "Well, maybe I'll hear from you Saturday."

Distracted, Robinson nodded. "Good night."

"Good night, Rob."

Judi slipped into her apartment and shut the door. She shook her head and went to the sofa. So much for that, she thought as she sat down. She dialed her sister's number.

"Hey, girl. Remember that brother I was telling you about? Well, scratch that. He's got it bad, but it's not for me. The woman he's in love with sure is lucky."

Robinson stood in the hallway staring at Judi's door. He rubbed his eyes and then slowly walked to the elevator. This night had been a disaster from start to finish as far as he was concerned. Judi probably thought he was married or gay. He wasn't either. He was simply in love with a woman who didn't want him, a married woman who was still in love with a husband who'd been gone for more than twenty years. Leo Stonehouse would have some answers about that soon.

He pushed the button for the elevator. As he waited, he rested his head on the wall and wondered why love was so damn complicated.

Late the next day, Toinette blew into the Quad-A office bubbling with excitement. Only Dawn was still there. Toinette poured a cup of coffee and gave Dawn the highlights of her trip.

"It was wonderful, absolutely wonderful. Everything was perfect, Dawn. Perfect!"

Caught up in Toinette's excitement, Dawn urged Toinette to share the details. Toinette sat in a chair next to Dawn's desk and crossed her legs. The thin gold chain sparkled at her ankle under her hose.

"First I met with the Trammer team at their office building. Dawn, it's fabulous. All glass and plants and mirrors. They showed me to my office there. Can you believe it? They set me up with my own office. Then we all met with city officials. I did a presentation for city leaders and the Chamber of Commerce. The second day, earlier today, we all went on a guided van tour of the housing projects in the city that could best benefit from the program. I even got to talk to a few of the women and got some of their ideas for what they'd like to see. It's gonna happen, Dawn. It's really going to happen."

Dawn grinned. "I'm happy for you, Mrs. Blue. You've worked real hard for this. Just think, a national Quad-A program."

Toinette smiled and clapped her hands together. "I can't believe it's finally happening. Trammer's people are big on focus groups. The Quad-A staff in Atlanta will set a couple of them up, and I'll fly back down for those in a few weeks."

Toinette took a sip of her coffee and got up. "Well, I see the world didn't fall apart in just a day and a half. I told you not to worry about anything."

"There was one problem," Dawn said.

Toinette turned to her. "What happened?"

Dawn explained about the dairy bill. "Did I do the right thing in using the emergency money?"

"Yes. That was fine. I'm just trying to figure out what may have happened. One check to them came back as insufficient funds a while ago, but that was just a matter of a deposit clearing the bank. It went through without a problem. I'll spend some time checking on that when I get back from Chicago."

"The girl named Hazel came by today. You missed her by about an hour," Dawn reported.

Toinette sighed and came to sit in the chair again. "I'm sorry I keep missing her. Did she say anything? Did she get something to eat?"

Dawn nodded. "But you don't have to worry about her anymore, Mrs. Blue. She didn't have that scared, haunted look. She said to tell you that she's gotten her life back on track. She called home and is working things out with her parents. She was cleaned up and had on a nice, pressed dress."

Toinette smiled. "Well, that's good to hear. That's great news. Lord only knows who or what she had been running from."

"She said to tell you thank you for the food and for the package you left for her."

"So she got it! Good for her," Toinette said. "Good for her. Anything else I should know about?"

"Nope. That's it."

"Well, let's call it a night. I have an early flight to Chicago in the morning, and you need to get home."

Toinette closed up the center, made sure Dawn got to her car safely, then drove home.

Thursday was uneventful. The milk delivery arrived, and Kendra did a Quad-A presentation to the local ministers coalition.

The next morning, Dawn had just finished overseeing the children's midmorning snack when a telephone call came in.

"It's somebody asking for Mrs. Blue," one of the nursery aides said.

Dawn took the telephone. "Achieving Against All Adversities. This is Dawn."

"Hi, Dawn. My name is C.J. Mayview and I'm a reporter. May I speak with Mrs. Blue, please."

"She's out of the office for the rest of the week, Ms. Mayview. Can I take a message for her? Or maybe I can help you."

"It's kind of important. I'm working on a story for tomorrow's paper. Maybe you can help me."

The reporter started asking questions about accounts and suspicious activity near and around the center.

Dawn's eyes widened as she listened to the journalist. Mrs. Blue didn't say anything about any newspaper reporters calling. Dawn wasn't sure how to handle this call. She definitely wasn't about to answer any questions.

"Uh, Ms. Mayview, let me get your number and I'll have someone get back to you. It'll probably be Kendra Hightower. She's in charge in Mrs. Blue's absence."

Dawn got off the line and quickly called Kendra.

"Kendra, sorry to bother you again, but there's a reporter who's asking a lot of questions."

"That shouldn't be a problem, Dawn. Nettie always handles media inquiries. It's probably someone who wants to do a feature story on someone in the program."

"I don't think so. This reporter was talking about drug activity at the center and misappropriation of funds."

Kendra sighed. What now? she wondered. "Okay, Dawn. What's the reporter's name and number?"

Kendra took the information and got off the phone. She looked at the journalist's name. "That's Robinson's sister. She's done stories about Quad-A before."

Relieved, Kendra put through the call. "C.J., it's been a while since we talked."

"That's right. I understand congratulations are in order. I heard you got married."

"Yes, thank you. That was a while back. Right now, I'm really happy for Robinson and Nettie."

"What?" the reporter asked.

"You know. Your brother and Toinette Blue. They've been seeing each other for over a month now. It's pretty serious. I'm glad Toinette has found someone she can be happy with. But I know that's not why you called. What can I do for you?"

For a moment there was nothing but silence on the other end of the line.

"C.J., are you there?"

"I'm here," the reporter said. Then she got down to business.

The more C.J. talked, the more Kendra sat up. This was a problem. A big problem.

"C.J., listen. I'm not at the Quad-A office right now. Let me finish up some things here and I'll meet you there later today."

Kendra scheduled the appointment for late afternoon. She was going to need a few hours to reach Nettie and figure out what was going on.

But catching up with Toinette proved fruitless. Kendra left messages at the hotel but Toinette had yet to check in.

"Knowing Nettie, she probably walked off the plane and straight into meetings," Kendra said. She bit her lower lip and resolved to deal with C.J. the best way she could.

Kendra drove to the Quad-A center, holed herself up in Nettie's office, and started poring through all of the center's books. What she found didn't make her happy. Money seemed to be missing. Lots of it. No wonder the dairy manager was adamant about not extending credit. The odd thing was that even though money looked like it was missing at points, it all added up in the end—as if it had been replaced later.

"Nettie," Kendra whispered. "What's going on here?"

But that wasn't the worst of it. The most incriminating thing Kendra came across was a slim volume that looked like a college-exam book. She recognized her friend's handwriting in the columns and notes.

Kendra closed her eyes and took a deep breath. When she opened her eyes, the ledger was still there. "Nettie, why are you keeping two sets of books? That's illegal."

She tried to reach Nettie in Chicago one more time but to no avail. As she replaced the receiver, the phone rang.

Kendra picked up the line. "Ms. Mayview is here to see you," Dawn said.

Kendra straightened up all the paperwork on the desk and shoved the ledgers in a desk drawer. "Send her in."

C.J. Mayview was best described as unconventional. She was a pretty woman but didn't bother to do anything about it. Kendra took in the camp shirt, the straight blue jean skirt, and the rugged backpack the reporter used as a briefcase. C.J. shrugged the pack off one shoulder as she walked into the office.

Kendra stood to meet her and shook hands with C.J.

"Have a seat. Can I get you some coffee?"

"No, thanks. I've had my six-cup limit for the day," C.J. said, smiling as she settled in the chair before the desk. "Kendra, I'm here just to check a couple of things out." She pulled a notebook and a pencil from her bag. "I got a strange letter and a strange phone call. Both seemed to be about the Quad-A program. I've talked to some people who report odd comings and goings here at the center. I believe in checking things out. Sometimes where there's smoke, there's fire."

None of the anxiousness Kendra felt showed on the surface. She smiled calmly at the reporter. "You've done Quad-A stories before, C.J. Of course, people come and go all the time. That's what we do. There are workshops for participants, mothers drop their children off before going to work. Volunteers and employees are in and out all day."

"Some of the residents in the area and across the street say there's drug activity or at least the type of behavior that goes along with drug activity."

Kendra shook her head. "That's one of the sad facts of life in this neighborhood. All we at Quad-A try to do is show people that there is an alternative to that, that they can make an honest living and care for their families without resorting to drug use or trade."

Kendra watched C.J. Suddenly a thought hit her. The reporter was fishing! She didn't really have a story. If she had hard and fast facts, she wouldn't be sitting there asking softball questions. If C.J. Mayview was known for anything, it was getting to the point and doing good journalism. Kendra relaxed in her chair, but not too much. There was still the matter Dawn had mentioned. Somewhere in her notebook, the reporter had a question about misappropriation of funds.

C.J. tapped her pencil on her notebook and looked at Kendra. "Look, I'm going to be straight up with you, Kendra. There are people in the area who believe Mrs. Blue focuses more on her . . ." C.J. paused and flipped through her notebook. "Here's the exact quote: 'That woman spends more time tipping out in her Saks Fifth Avenue designer clothes and stepping in that limousine than she does trying to help poor people. She never helped me, and I been over there lots of times.' I can tell you," C.J. said, "that's from a woman who lives across the street."

Kendra nodded and stood up. She walked to the one shaded window in Toinette's office, stared out of it for a moment, then turned to C.J. "I believe it. And I'll bet she's an addict. For some people, the hardest and the coldest fact about the Quad-A program is that you have to be drug-free to enter it. And that doesn't mean drug-free for this week. Toinette fought long and hard with this issue when coming up with the parameters of the program. In the end, she realized that she couldn't run a drug rehab center *and* a jobs program. It had to be one or the other. We can't send someone to a job site who might turn around and steal from the company or other employees to feed a drug habit. So, yes, some people are turned down. Repeatedly. And they probably resent that—particularly when they can see how well other people are doing with Quad-A."

C.J. closed her notebook and stood up. "Maybe that's my story, a comparison and contrast. I can work on that next week."

Kendra smiled at the reporter, but it was more to herself. C.J. didn't know! Thank God! She had time to sit down with Nettie and figure out what was going on with the books and the program funds. Now to get C.J. Mayview out of there . . .

"Kendra, would you leave a message for Mrs. Blue that I'd like to set up an appointment to talk to her about the program applicants and how many are turned down and for what reasons," C.J. asked.

"I will."

C.J. tucked the pencil and notebook into the back pack, then stood up to shake Kendra's hand.

A commotion outside the office spilled into the room.

"She's with somebody now, Eli. You can see her when she's done."

"I'm gonna see her right now. I got rent to pay and kids to feed."

Eli, the center's cook, burst into Toinette's office, followed by Dawn, who was trying to hold six other center employees back.

"Dawn, this ain't funny. Is the center closing down?" one woman called out.

Kendra cast a worried eye at the reporter. "Dawn, Eli, let me see Ms. Mayview out and then we'll discuss this." She tried to steer C.J. to the crowded doorway.

Kendra watched Dawn nervously look from the reporter to Eli and the group of women who were still trying to push into the office.

"Well, I can see you have your hands full," C.J. said.

"Mayview?" Eli said, turning to look at the woman. "Aren't you that newspaper reporter who did the story on us a while back?"

C.J. nodded while she reached in her backpack and pulled out her notebook.

"Well, here's a story for you," the big man boomed.

"Eli, we can talk about this in a staff meeting," Dawn said.

"Staff meeting, my foot. I want this out in the open," he said. Murmurs of concurrence came from the other employees. Eli turned his full attention to C.J. "Do a story on why our paychecks bounced today. The bank said they aren't honoring any of them."

C.J. started and taking notes and asking questions.

CHAPTER 30

Later that night, C.J. Mayview stood on the balcony of her condo. The lights of the city sparkled below her, but she didn't enjoy the view as she usually did. She felt as if she'd been put through a wringer. The bad part was she knew the worst was yet to come. She took a deep breath and then walked through the sliding glass doors to her living room. She wanted to make this telephone call about as much as she wanted to drive a knife through her heart.

After the pandemonium at the Quad-A center, she left and made a flurry of telephone calls from the newspaper office. The disgruntled Quad-A employees had given her all the leads she needed. Television didn't know about the story, so her Page One piece was an exclusive. She'd done good work.

The argument with her editor had been loud and long, but it was pro forma more than anything else. The conflict of interest was there, slapping her in the face. She was lucky her editor let her do the story. It was a good story, too. Talk about being at the right place at the right time.

"So why do you feel like you just got run over by a truck?" she said aloud. Her well-decorated condo didn't offer up any answers.

C.J. went to the bar and mixed herself a stiff drink. She took a swallow and then walked to the telephone. Taking a deep breath and another sip of the potent beverage, she dialed a familiar number.

When she heard her brother's voice on the other end, C.J. pinched the area between her eyes and took another deep breath. "It's C.J., Rob."

"What's this about a story on money missing from the Quad-A program, C.J.?"

So much for pleasantries, C.J. thought. Kendra Hightower had obviously talked to him. C.J. had wanted to tell Rob herself. But obviously she had waited too long.

"Rob, I didn't know. How was I supposed to know you were dating the woman? You know half the women in the city and have gone out with the other half."

"What exactly does this story of yours say?"

C.J. sighed. "That contractors for the Quad-A program don't get paid on time. When they do get paid, sometimes the checks are delayed. That the center couldn't meet its payroll this week and twenty people aren't getting paid. That residents and employees say the head of the program has a wardrobe that far exceeds that of a welfare jobs program director. That Toinette Blue, director of the Quad-A program, has been unavailable and out of town this week."

Robinson swore a blue streak. C.J. cringed and took another sip from her drink. When summarized so dispassionately, the story sounded worse than it was. She didn't have all the questions that she or her editors wanted answered. Only Toinette Blue could provide those answers, and she wasn't going to be in town until tomorrow. And Toinette Blue, the seeming culprit in all of this, was her brother's lover.

"C.J., Toinette needs a chance to respond to all of those charges. You have to be fair and allow her that. Can't this story wait a day or two, just until Toinette gets back and has a chance to give her side? Holding your story a day is not going to make a difference."

C.J. pinched the bridge of her nose again. She'd had this same argument with her editor and almost got thrown off the story for her efforts. She'd disclosed that her brother was dating the center's director. Her editor pitched a fit and then pulled the newspaper's managing editor in on the discussion. The bottom line was that Mrs. Blue was out of town but Kendra Hightower was and had in the past been the program's spokeswoman when Toinette Blue was unavailable. C.J. was going in to the office Saturday to follow up on the story. The rest of the media would be all over it, too, just as soon as the newspaper and her story hit the streets.

"Rob, I can't do that. We talked about it at work. I even suggested holding the story a day, but it was decided that it needed to run immediately."

"We talked about it? It was decided? What are you people—robots or humans? Don't you have any compassion? Jesus, C.J., I would have expected more from you than this. Do you know what Toinette's doing in Chicago this week? What she was doing in Atlanta earlier this week?" Robinson didn't give C.J. a chance to respond. "She's out there trying to put together Quad-A programs in other cities. Programs to help people get off welfare and into productive jobs and lives for themselves and their families. She has major corporate dollars behind her. Major money, C.J. And you're going to blow it all for one stinking byline."

C.J. got angry then. "Look, Rob. This is what I do. You've always known that. If you weren't sleeping with the woman, this wouldn't even be an issue. I can't keep up with every skirt you chase. Why don't you give me a list of all the women you're involved with so I can just disqualify myself from doing any stories that might be about them. I was giving you a courtesy call, going against the rules and letting you know what was going to be on people's doorsteps tomorrow. I thought maybe you could reach Mrs. Blue and let her know, since no one else seems to know where she is." She paused, silence greeting her. "Rob, are you there?"

"Thanks for nothing, C.J."

He hung up, and C.J.'s shoulders slumped. She tossed back the rest of the drink and wondered when journalism had stopped being fun.

At his house, Robinson kicked the sofa and slammed the telephone down. What a mess. And where the hell was Toinette? He left a message at her hotel soon after Kendra had called him. Kendra told him she'd left several messages, but no one had heard from her.

Robinson picked up the remote control to the large-screen television in his family room. The eleven o'clock news was just coming on. He adjusted the volume on the set. The familiar face of a female news anchor filled the screen. Robinson swore out loud. C.J.'s words came back to him and cut him: he'd briefly dated the television newscaster a few years back.

Robinson switched to a local network affiliate with a male anchor.

"In today's top national news, a shootout at a South Side Chicago housing project left a six-year-old dead and two other children wounded. An unidentified woman, who witnesses said was visiting the city, was also shot in the crossfire. Police have no suspects but believe the shooting was drug related."

Robinson dropped the remote and stared at the television.

Distraught mothers wailed on the news video. Neighbors reacted to the shooting, pointing at the spot where blood was visible on the ground. A woman's shoe and the contents of a handbag lay a few feet away.

"Oh, God. Please, no."

A cold darkness clutched Robinson's heart, and fear enveloped him. He bent down, picked up the remote, and switched to another channel. Similar videotape was playing out on that station. He listened to the report.

"An unidentified woman whom police believe was in Chicago for the first time was also wounded in the crossfire. Police believe the shooting stemmed from an earlier confrontation between rival drug gangs."

Robinson switched the channel to CNN and willed his heartbeat to slow down.

"It's not Toinette. It's not Toinette." If he said it and believed it, it would be true. But Robinson knew he was being irrational.

He realized then that the disagreements he and Toinette had were insignificant. Nothing else mattered but her love . . . and her safety.

"It's not Toinette. It's not Toinette." Lots of unidentified women went to Chicago every day.

But how many of them would be walking through a public housing complex in high-heeled pumps? Robinson realized he didn't even know her schedule; he didn't know how her trip was set up. She couldn't just walk off an airplane and into a community. There had to be a contact person, people she'd work with in the city. Kendra might know who those people were.

Robinson stood quietly for a moment doing a deep breathing exercise he'd learned. It cleared his head and let him think rationally. He would try the hotel one more time. He went to the telephone and dialed the number Kendra had given him earlier in the day. It was after eleven. Surely Toinette would be back from whatever business she had to do. He refused to believe she was in a hospital with a bullet wound, but still an icy fear gripped him.

He asked for her room and then listened as the line rang and rang. Then it switched back to the main desk.

"There's no answer in that room, sir. May I take a message?"

"When did she check in?"

"One moment, sir."

Robinson listened to the click of a computer keyboard.

"This afternoon, sir."

Robinson closed his eyes and prayed. "By any chance have you seen her?"

"Sir, there are lots of guests at this hotel. I—"

Robinson cut her off and gave a description of Toinette. "She's in town with a program called Quad-A, Achieving Against All Adversities," he said hopefully.

"Oh! The Quad-A lady. She's so nice. We talked for a few minutes before she left for dinner."

Robinson seized on that information. "You saw her? You talked to her? What time did she leave for dinner?"

"That was about an hour ago. She and about five people."

Robinson fell on his knees. Thank you, Jesus. Thank you.

"Thank you so much," he told the front-desk clerk. "You don't know how much that means to me." It had been daylight in the video of the shooting. Even though Chicago was an hour ahead, it would still have been night when the desk clerk last saw Toinette.

"Would you like to leave a message, sir?"

Robinson thought about all the messages he could leave for Toinette, all the things he wanted to express to her right now, his fear, his regret. But there was only one message that mattered. "Tell her Robinson said 'I love you.' "

"Okay, sir. I'll leave that message."

Robinson smiled and hung up the phone. He collapsed in a chair, propping his elbows on his knees. He rubbed his face with both hands and thanked God again for keeping Toinette safe. He loved her to distraction even though they were on the outs right now.

He leaned back in the chair and folded his arms behind his head. Toinette was safe and was coming home tomorrow. He'd get the flight information from Kendra and meet Toinette at the airport. He would apologize to her for getting angry. They would talk about their problems and come to a compromise that suited them both.

All of a sudden he remembered. He sat up and swore. C.J.'s article about the Quad-A program was going to be in tomorrow's newspaper. The story, as C.J. described it, was brutal. It would devastate Toinette. Quad-A meant everything to her. Robinson had no doubt that there was an explanation for every one of C.J.'s yellow journalism charges. If only she could have held her damn story for a day until Toinette got back. Toinette was a woman of integrity and honor. She wouldn't do anything to compromise herself or the Quad-A program.

He looked at the telephone and debated whether he should call the hotel again. Deciding against that, he called Kendra and got Toinette's flight information.

Russell Blue met his mother at the airport the next day. Toinette hugged him as he took her briefcase and garment bag.

"I'm glad I caught you," she said, returning his embrace. "When I saw there was an earlier flight, I took it. There was no need to hang around the airport all day. Lord have mercy, O'Hare is huge. But Russ, the trip was great. Just great. People there are excited about Quad-A."

Toinette took a good look at Russell. She wanted to make sure they were okay now. The call she'd made to him to mend fences had worked wonders. He'd apologized for the hateful things he'd said in anger. And today, when he'd agreed to pick her up at the airport, Toinette knew things were going to be okay. But right now, Russell looked terrible.

"Russell, what's wrong? You look like somebody died. Oh, my God! What's happened to Carol and Jamal?"

"The kids are fine. So is Paulette. Mom, there's something you need to know."

Toinette searched her son's face and tried not to panic. "What's wrong, Russell? What happened?"

"Mom, I wish I could . . . I don't know how to tell you this."

"What, Russell? What?"

Russell sighed and handed her the front section of that day's newspaper.

Toinette scanned the lead story and looked at Russell. "It's a story about congressional overspending. What's the big deal?"

Russell pointed to the bottom half of Page One.

Toinette looked down at the page and read the headline. She swayed as if she might faint. "Oh, my God. Oh, my God."

Russell steadied her with a hand at her elbow. "Mom?"

"Take me to the Quad-A office." Toinette pulled free from him, and, with purposeful strides, headed to the exit. Russell ran to catch up with her.

In Russell's minivan Toinette read the entire news article twice. "She makes it seem like I took the money and ran off with it. Why didn't C.J. Mayview just call me?" Toinette leaned her head back on the headrest. "This is what Kendra must have been calling about. We played phone tag most of the day. By the time I got back from a dinner meeting last night, I figured it was too late to call. And Robinson, he left messages, too."

Toinette thought about the second message she'd gotten from Robinson and smiled. It seemed he wasn't going to give up without a fight.

"Mom, I thought you said you weren't seeing that guy anymore. He's bad news. You know that reporter is his sister, don't you? He's probably the one who gave her the story just to get back at you for breaking up with him."

Toinette turned to Russell. "That's not fair, Russell. Robinson would never do anything like that."

"You told me and Paulette over breakfast that he left very, very angry. I think Mayview would do something like that. He's one of those cutthroat types."

Toinette faced front again in her seat. She turned Russell's words over in her head. Robinson wasn't a cutthroat type, but he had been angry, angrier than she'd ever seen him before. Then there was the aborted telephone conversation they'd had before her trip. Was he angry enough to plant a story like this with his sister? She didn't think so. But if he had done it, what was the second message at her Chicago hotel all about?

Toinette read the story headline again and then looked out the window. The damage from this article was going to be great. It had taken her years to build Quad-A up. One negative story would make all of her hard work crumble at her feet.

"Hurry up, Russell."

Russell looked at her, then floored the minivan.

A few minutes later, as Russell came to a screeching stop across the street from the Quad-A office, Toinette got a good look at the pandemonium. A horde of reporters gathered outside the center. Television satellite trucks blocked the street.

Toinette grabbed her briefcase from the floor and got out of the van. "Bye, Russell," she said.

"Good luck, Mom," he replied worriedly.

"There she is! There she is!"

Toinette crossed the street and walked into the frenzy of reporters that surrounded her. Microphones were stuck in her face and the barrage of questions came from all sides.

"Mrs. Blue, have you seen today's paper?"

"Did you steal the money?"

"How are your employees going to get paid?"

"Is the Quad-A center closing?"

"What is your response to the fact that police are investigating?"

Toinette had been working with the media long enough to know that the best defense was acting as if everything was under control.

She held her hands up to silence the pack. "Ladies, gentlemen. I've just returned from a business trip. Yes, I've seen today's paper. Let me meet with my staff, and then I'll come answer your questions."

"What about the contractors, Mrs. Blue?" a voice called out. "How long have they not been paid?"

Toinette held her hand up again. "The sooner you guys let me in my office, the sooner I'll be able to get you some real answers. Okay?"

She pushed through the crowd and pulled out her keys to get in the center. Inside, she found Dawn and Kendra.

"Nettie!"

"Mrs. Blue. Am I ever glad to see you," Dawn said. "It's a madhouse out there."

"Did you two have to run the gantlet?" Toinette asked.

"No. We went through the back door. They didn't see us," Dawn said.

Toinette put things on a chair, then went to a cart and poured herself a cup of coffee. A box of unopened doughnuts sat next to the sugar and creamer. Toinette took a sip of coffee, then turned to Kendra and her senior aide. "Tell me what's going on."

"Nettie, where have you been? I tried to reach you all day yesterday. I got the messages that you phoned, but every time I called back you were gone."

"I was in and out all day, Kendra," Toinette said. "By the time I returned from a dinner meeting last night, I figured it was too late to bother you at home." Taking the newspaper from under her arm, she tossed it to Kendra. "I know your message said it was urgent. I just figured whatever emergency it was you were calling about early in the day had either been resolved or could wait until Monday. That's what I get for assuming things."

"Nettie, I tried—"

Toinette cut her off. "I'm not blaming you, Ken. I'm blaming myself for riding so high on this whole Quad-A Foundation thing. The bubble was bound to pop sooner or later."

Toinette leaned against the edge of the desk and looked at the two grim-faced women. "Okay, start at the beginning."

At the airport, Robinson argued with a ticket agent.

"I'm telling you she was supposed to be on that flight. Toinette Blue. Check your records again. She was scheduled to be on Flight 1438 out of Chicago."

The exasperated customer service representative took a deep breath. "Sir, I've checked the passenger list twice already. Toinette Blue was not on that flight."

"Well, where is she?"

"Sir, I don't know where she is. Did you check with her contacts in Chicago? Maybe she decided to take a later flight."

Robinson ran a hand through his hair. "When's the next plane in from Chicago?"

"One-fifteen."

It was possible she'd gotten delayed or had changed her flight schedule. Robinson turned away from the ticket agent and headed to a bank of telephones to call Kendra Hightower. A television in a snack bar caught his eye, and there was Toinette talking to reporters. She was already in town!

Robinson dashed to the television and caught the tail end of the news report in which Toinette said she'd get back to the reporters after talking to her staff. Robinson made for the exit at a dead run.

CHAPTER 31

Robinson arrived at the Quad-A office at the same time as Leo Stonehouse. C.J. Mayview saw her brother get out of his BMW and groaned. "Jesus, Rob, the least you could do was stay at home," she mumbled under her breath.

She and other reporters had been milling about in front of the Quad-A center for more than an hour now. Toinette Blue had promised a statement, and no one was willing to leave and miss the chance for an interview.

C.J. recognized Stonehouse, who hailed Robinson. She wondered what was up with that. A few months back, the newspaper did a feature on private investigators. Stonehouse had been included in the article. What, she wondered, did the P.I.'s presence have to do with the problems the Quad-A program was having?

"Hey, C.J.," one of the television reporters called out. "Isn't that your brother?"

The question caught the attention of all the journalists and photographers who had been killing time chatting with each other.

Robinson turned his back to the media throng and pushed Stonehouse to the door. Dawn, who had fortunately been passing by the front door, let them in.

"Hey, man. I saw the news and thought you might be here when I couldn't reach you at home or at your office," Stonehouse said when they were safely inside the center.

Toinette and Kendra looked up at the new arrivals. "Robinson, what are you doing here?" Toinette said as she got up and headed to the door where the two men stood.

"It was easier than I would have expected," the man said. "The information was right on target. I knew you'd want this as soon as possible," he said, handing Robinson a portfolio.

"Want what as soon as possible?" Toinette asked. "And who are you?"

The man cast a quick glance at Robinson, who surreptitiously shook his head.

"Sorry, man, I know the timing is all wrong." The man patted Robinson on the back. He turned to Dawn. "Where's the back door?" She pointed him in the right direction.

"Who was that?" Toinette asked.

"He's someone I know."

"Well, what's that?" she said, nodding at the portfolio Robinson was unable to conceal.

Even as one part of her thrilled at the notion of seeing Robinson, another, stronger, part was mulling over what Russell had said earlier. Toinette looked at Robinson shift the portfolio to his other hand and then place it behind his back. Was this man she loved capable of the cruelty Russell had suggested?

Toinette had to admit that after hearing Kendra and Dawn explain the series of events that led to C.J. Mayview's article, it was possible that the reporter had gotten the material from any number of sources. But it was also possible that in a fit of spite, Robinson had planted it with his sister. Is that what the hotel message had been all about? The note from the hotel operator read, "Tell her Robinson said I love you." Had he gotten a bad case of the regrets and was trying to make amends for what he'd done? Was it all some sort of mind game on his part? He'd made it no secret that he was opposed to her making the Quad-A trips. Was this his way of assuring that the national program didn't get launched?

Toinette crossed her arms and stared him down. "Why are you here, Robinson?"

"Toinette, I lo—"

Robinson watched her tense and changed direction. "I looked for you at the airport. I went to meet your flight. I tried to reach you last night, but the desk clerk said you were at dinner."

"Have you seen your sister's article?"

"Toinette, I can explain." Right now, the only thing Robinson wanted to do was fold Toinette in his arms and never let her go. C.J.'s article was a nightmare, an abomination. He'd run outside before dawn and snatched the newspaper from the lawn. Standing outside, barefoot in the grass, he'd read the story by the light of his motion detectors. He wanted to explain to Toinette how he'd argued with his sister last night about the story. But he watched Toinette's eyes widen, and he knew he'd said something wrong.

"Toinette, I *can* explain. C.J. called me last—"

Toinette slapped a hand over her mouth. "Oh, my God. It's true. You admit it." She started backing away from him.

"Nettie?" Kendra came up and steadied Toinette. "Hi, Robinson."

His entire attention on Toinette, Robinson barely nodded toward Kendra. Something was terribly wrong here. He didn't know what it was, but he had no intention of leaving the center until he knew exactly what was wrong with Toinette.

"Toinette, C.J. called me last night to tell me about her story. I tried to reach you at the hotel, but you were out."

"What was the point in calling me, Robinson? Your damage had already been done."

Robinson shook his head. "Damage? I don't consider being in love with you as damage."

"How can you stand there and say that!" Toinette rounded on him. "You knew about this. You knew about this and yet you blithely call my hotel and leave an 'I love you' message. What was that supposed to translate into? 'I'm sorry for messing your life up. I'm sorry I got angry and did something I regret?' Well, it just doesn't cut it, Rob. It just doesn't cut it." Toinette spread her hands to encompass the center. "This is my life we're talking about. This is what I do, and you've deliberately sabotaged it."

Robinson ignored a wide-eyed Dawn and came to stand within a foot of Toinette. "What do you mean sabotage? I know how important this is to you. Why do you think I tried to reach you? Kendra tried to reach you, too."

"Robinson, don't play dumb. It doesn't suit you. You've made your position very clear on the Quad-A Foundation. You don't approve of it. Well, that's just too bad. If I can, I plan to salvage what I can of this mess and still go forward."

"What do you mean I don't approve of the program? I think it's great that you want to branch out into other cities. My concern has been for your safety, nothing else. I almost died last night watching the news. An unidentified woman visiting the city had been shot in a housing project, and I thought it was you."

Toinette took a good look at him. He looked and sounded sincere, but she still had an amount of doubt that couldn't be appeased by his words. "What's in the folder, Rob, and who was that man?"

"Toinette, it's not important. He was someone who knew I might be here and wanted to drop this off to me."

"If it's not important, tell me what it is."

"Toinette, for God's sake, you're being unreasonable. I told you it's not important."

"What is important," Kendra interjected, "is that group of reporters waiting for you outside. Nettie, you have to prepare a statement."

Toinette turned away from Robinson. "God, what a mess. How am I ever going to explain all of this?"

A commotion at the door drew Toinette's attention. Dawn, Robinson, Kendra and Toinette watched Eli burst into the center.

"Miz Blue, I saw you on television. Does this mean I'm gonna get paid today?"

A telephone rang. Dawn stepped away to answer it.

"Eli, I'm trying to get to the bottom of this right now. I'm sorry about the inconvenience to you. I know you have bills to pay." Toinette went to her purse and pulled out her wallet. She handed the big man some currency. "It's not a lot, and it doesn't cover your check, but please take this. Hopefully, I'll have everything straight by Monday and you'll be able to cash your paycheck."

Eli looked at the money she had pressed into his hand. The seventy-five dollars was enough to get his wife and kid some food and some formula and diapers for the baby.

"Mrs. Blue, Ben Trammer on line two for you," Dawn said.

Toinette's shoulders slumped. "This is the beginning of the end. I'll take it in my office, Dawn."

Eli watched his employer walk to her office. He'd never seen her look so sad. It wasn't like her at all. Miz Blue was always the person who cheered everybody up. She was the person who told him he could make something out of his life. She'd given him a job when no one else would. Miz Blue was the one who had convinced him to get his GED. She'd cared about him and his family when no one else did. Maybe it had been a mistake to go blabbing to that reporter. Maybe, like Dawn said, he should have waited until the reporter was gone to talk to Miz Kendra.

Eli looked at Dawn. She crossed her arms and scowled at him.

"I'm sorry," Eli mumbled. "I just panicked when that bank man said my paycheck wasn't no good. My family depends on me. This job doesn't pay a whole lot, but we get by. Dawn, don't look at me like that," he pleaded with the senior aide.

Dawn shook her head and turned away from him. Eli appealed to Kendra. "You understand don't you, Miz Kendra? I'm sorry."

"Eli, it's done now, so all we can do is deal with it," Kendra said softly.

Eli nodded. He looked at the money in his hand and then placed it on top of Toinette's purse. "I ain't gonna be talking to no more reporters." With one last look at an unbending Dawn, Eli left the center.

Toinette came out from her office a few minutes later. "Trammer was in town for a golf weekend and saw the noon news at the clubhouse."

"Has he pulled his funding?" Kendra asked.

"He wants to talk. He's on his way here. I've called John MacAfree. I'm going to tell the reporters we'll have a press conference at five-thirty. Maybe that way at least they won't continue to hang around outside the door."

"Toinette, we need to talk," Robinson said.

"You're still here?"

"Jesus, Toinette. Why am I getting the cold shoulder? I'm here to support you." Robinson looked at Kendra and Dawn. This was not the place or the time to be having this conversation. He went to Toinette.

"I know we have had our differences," he said, reaching out to rub her arm. "But we can work through those problems, just like we'll work through this crisis."

Toinette shrugged his hand away and crossed her arms. "Okay, let's start with why you told your sister to launch the investigation of Quad-A."

"What?!" Robinson yelled, so shocked that he dropped the detective's report.

"Nettie, how do you know that?" Kendra asked from where she sat.

Robinson looked to Kendra and then turned back to Toinette. "You think *I* had something to do with this? I don't believe this. This is incredible," he said, shaking his head. "You have a lot of nerve, Toinette Blue. I swear to God I don't know how or why I ever managed to fall in love with you. You are a living, breathing paradox. One minute you run hot in my arms and the next minute you're cold as ice. Well, I'm sick of it. Sick of it, you hear!"

Robinson bent down and retrieved the report from the floor. "Here," he said, slamming it on the desk. "You want to know what this is so badly. Take it. I tried to help you, tried to help us. And the thanks I get is your suspicion and filthy accusations. I'm finished, Toinette. I have had enough of your foolishness." Robinson stormed toward the door.

Toinette flinched at his anger, then got mad herself. "You've had no commitment to me," she yelled after him. "You say you love me, then I see you out in the street with another woman. How is that supposed to make me feel?"

Robinson turned around and waited for Toinette to reach him. He looked down at her. "You don't have to feel anything. You've told me time and again that you don't want to marry me, that you don't feel anything for me. Why should you start feeling anything at this late date?"

Robinson pushed the front door open and Toinette followed him. "Robinson, that's not true."

Cameras started clicking and whirring the minute they stepped outside. A microphone was stuck in Toinette's face.

"Mrs. Blue, is it true that the man who came outside a few minutes ago has been fired?"

"Mrs. Blue, what is your answer to the charges that money for the Achieving Against All Adversities program was misappropriated?"

Toinette had forgotten about the reporters. "I . . . No, Eli has not been fired. And I'll answer all of your questions in a press conference at five-thirty."

"Mr. Mayview," a reporter said, "it's my understanding that you are romantically involved with Mrs. Blue. Can you tell me, please, did you publicly court Mrs. Blue in order to feed your sister C.J. Mayview information about the embezzlement case against the Quad-A program?"

A hush fell over the crowd. Robinson found his sister in the crush and their gazes locked. C.J. looked stunned, then she started to shake her head.

He turned to face a stony Toinette. This was the ugliness that she believed about him? How little she truly knew him. He had been a fool to think that he'd finally found the perfect woman for him. Toinette was one of the worst kinds. She stood there dispassionately watching him.

Robinson turned cold, dull eyes back to the reporter. "No comment," he said. He pushed his way through the throng.

Cameras zoomed in on Toinette, then reporters dogged Robinson to his car. They fired questions at him but Robinson ignored every one. As he opened his car door, he turned back for one last look. Near the front of the center, standing just yards apart were two women he used to love: Toinette Blue and C.J. Mayview.

CHAPTER 32

Robinson didn't like to admit that he'd made an error in judgment. "You fall in love with the one woman who is immune to your charm," he said, as he drove with no destination in mind. "You fall in love with the one woman who brings more emotional baggage to a relationship than a team of skycaps could handle. You get hooked up with the one woman in the city who offered something new, something exciting, something unique, and she turns out to be the worst of the bunch."

Robinson passed a city bus that had an advertisement for the newspaper C.J. worked for on its side. "And you have a sister who is a piranha," Robinson said aloud.

He slapped a CD in the player in his car as he drove. When he looked up, he was in front of Judi Christian's apartment complex. Robinson raised an eyebrow. "Now there's an idea. A woman who can appreciate a man."

He pulled into the parking lot, then made his way to her apartment. Judi had told him she went to bed after coming home from a flight. With any luck, she'd let him join her there.

He rang her doorbell.

A few moments later, Judi opened the door a bit. "Rob?"

"Hi. I hope I didn't disturb you. I was in the neighborhood."

"Just a sec." Judi shut the door and Robinson heard her take the security chain off. "Hi, yourself," she said when she fully opened the portal to him.

Robinson smiled. He liked what he saw. Judi stood before him barefoot wearing a pair of blue leggings and an oversized Disneyland T-shirt.

"I was just getting ready to take a nap," she told him.

"May I join you?"

Judi raised an eyebrow and smiled. "Now there's a thought."

"I meant, may I come inside?"

Judi cocked her head for him to follow.

"Have a seat. Can I get you something to drink?"

Robinson felt like he could use a double of some hard liquor, but he didn't think that would be a good idea. "Whatever you have that's cold," he told Judi.

She went to the kitchen and a few moments later brought back two cold beers. She handed one to him, then sat on the sofa a cushion away from him. She tucked one leg under the other and faced him.

Robinson looked at the bottle and nodded. "Nice taste."

"I only like the best," she responded.

Robinson smiled. They clicked bottle tops and drank a bit of the brew.

"So when did you get back in town?"

"About two hours ago. I unpacked, read the mail, showered and washed my hair. I was just about to head to bed when you knocked."

Judi's comment about her hair drew Robinson's gaze there. Soft curls bobbed at her neck. He wondered if she'd yanked hair rollers out of her hair after spying him in the peephole. Robinson looked at her compact body curled on the sofa and wondered why he'd never had a physical reaction to this woman. She looked soft and inviting. She'd made it pretty clear that she was available and willing, even if she remained cautious. He, on the other hand, suddenly couldn't remember why he'd come there.

Judi watched him. She took a swallow of beer and tried to figure him out. He was definitely interested, but he always looked so guilty. Like just now. He'd been scoping her out and then his expression changed—as if he suddenly remembered the wife he had waiting for him at home.

"Tell me, Rob," she said, "is she very beautiful?"

Robinson lowered the bottle of beer from him mouth and placed it on the end table. "Who?"

"The woman you're in love with."

"Why do you say that? You mentioned something like that once before. What makes you think I'm in love with someone?"

"Look, you said you weren't married. I was willing to believe you on that. You brought me home the night we went out to dinner. I just knew you were going to kiss me. Then all of a sudden you jumped back like I had the plague or something. You looked then just like you look now—like a guilty husband."

Robinson leaned over and reached out to touch her. He pulled back at the last moment, crossed his legs, and repositioned a throw pillow to cover up for the move. "Are you always so forthright?"

"Always," she said. "My mother taught me that it's best to be straight-up and honest about things all the time. It saves the difficulty of trying to explain away polite lies."

"Sounds like you have a wise mother."

"You haven't answered my question."

Robinson sighed and dropped his head back on the sofa. "Yes, she's very beautiful. I think I fell in love with her the moment she walked into my office. It was a long time before I started to pursue her. She's a little older than I am, and she had to work that out in her head. The age difference has never been an issue with me. She has children. With the exception of one of them, everything's smooth there." Robinson turned to look at Judi, who had settled herself more comfortably on the sofa. She had her chin propped up on a plump pillow.

"In some ways you remind me of her," he said. "I think it's your smile. I've always liked women with beautiful smiles."

"So what happened to your relationship?"

"That's what I'm trying to figure out. I don't know, Judi. She's just so . . . I don't know. I think she's still in love with her former husband. That drives me nuts since I love her beyond reason. That bum doesn't deserve a moment's consideration from her after the way he treated her. But I'm the one who gets to suffer because of his negligence."

"Are you going to fight for her love?"

Robinson turned his head and regarded Judi. "I did. I lost. And it hurts like hell."

She offered him a small smile.

Robinson reached out a hand and touched Judi's. "I haven't been fair to you. I led you on. After dinner this week, I figured you'd come to the conclusion I was gay or married."

"Gay hadn't crossed my mind. Married was the disease I'd chosen."

He chuckled.

"Hey, you hungry?" she asked.

Robinson realized then that all he'd had to eat that day was a bagel he'd wolfed down early that morning. To emphasize the point, his stomach growled. "I think so," he said with a laugh.

Judi got up. "I'll make you a sandwich."

"Don't go to any trouble on my account."

"No trouble at all," she said. "I stopped at the grocery store on my way home from the airport. Be back in a jiffy."

Judi went to the kitchen and Robinson got up to look around her living room. The space was cheery and inviting. The combination living room-dining area was furnished in pickled oak pieces. Lots of green plants added color to the room.

Robinson went to a wall unit to look at Judi's collection of CDs. One shelf was crammed with framed pictures. One in particular caught his eye. Robinson pulled the brass-framed photograph out and stared at the smiling children.

Carol, Jamal, Jessica, Thad . . . and Lisa.

He knew every one of them. Jessica had won the pirate's golden key. He'd helped her brother Thad clean the microwave. Carol and Jamal were Russell's kids. That left just one child. Judi's child. Pretty, smiling, pudding-throwing little Lisa.

"Oh, God."

There could be no other explanation for the photograph. Robinson looked toward the kitchen, then the front door, wanting to bolt. But even as he thought about it, he knew that sooner or later Judi would find out the truth.

Still holding the photograph, Robinson scrutinized the other pictures. Sure enough, in one he recognized Aaron Blue. In another, a family portrait, stood Aaron, that psycho Russell, Judi with a gentle hand on her mother's shoulder, and Toinette smiling as she sat in a chair with her children around her. In yet another photograph, one that would have brought a smile to his face at another time, there was Toinette, holding a baby and grinning at the camera.

"How do I get myself in these messes?" he asked himself shakily.

"What was that, Rob?" Judi said, coming out of the kitchen with a tray of sandwiches and a bowl of chips.

Robinson took a look at Judi, a good, hard, critical look. "Oh, God."

If he had really looked at her before, he would have seen it. Whereas Toinette was tall and slim, Judi was average height and had a more filled out figure than her mother. But it was there in the face that he saw Toinette. No wonder Judi's smile reminded him of Toinette: every time he saw it he was looking at a version of Toinette.

Judi placed the tray on the coffee table. She looked over her shoulder to see if there was something or someone else in the apartment. "Rob, what's wrong? You're looking at me as if I just grew two heads."

Robinson held the photo of the children out to her. "When was this taken?"

Judi smiled. Robinson took a stumbling step back as if he'd been hit in the gut. Jesus! Why hadn't he seen it before? Here he had been thinking it was some sort of undeserved repressed guilt he had about Toinette every time the moment arose to get intimate with Judi. Had he listened to the still, small voice inside him, he would have known. Talk about guilt. How in the world was he going to explain this to Judi? In a moment he was going to have a hysterical woman on his hands. Toinette had massive hangups about age. What would her daughter think about dating her mother's boyfriend?

Judi scowled at his retreat but took the photo and went to the sofa. "We had this portrait done about a month ago. My mother complained that she didn't have a professional photograph of all her grandchildren, so the ones of us with kids dressed them up. We all met at the studio. My mother hasn't seen it yet. We're going to surprise her with a big framed version for her birthday."

Robinson looked at Judi, wondering again if he should just make a run for it. He'd never in his life been a coward about facing difficult situations. He'd had plenty, but nothing like this.

"Why don't you sit down and have something to eat." Judi, settled on the sofa, reached for a couple of potato chips.

"Judi, there's something I need to tell you. Something that you're not . . . well, it's important."

"You lied and you are married?"

"If only it were that simple."

"What then?"

He tried to figure out the best way to ease into this. If he approached it the right way, he could mitigate the damage. He looked at the photograph she'd placed on the sofa cushion. Robinson took one breath in and one breath out.

"Judi, I know all of the children in that photograph. Jessica, Thad, Carol, Jamal, your daughter Lisa. Toinette and I were dating for some time."

He waited for the explosion.

"Lord have mercy," she said.

Robinson winced. She even said it the same way her mother did.

Robinson watched her stare at him. She was looking at him as if *he'd* suddenly grown two heads.

Judi got up and went to where he stood. She looked him in the eye. Then she walked around him as if she were inspecting a side of beef at a butcher market.

"What's your name?" she asked.

Robinson wanted to edge away from her scrutiny, but he stood his ground. He'd made this mess; he'd see it through. "Robinson Mayview the third."

"Robinson? I thought Rob was short for Robert. Since we were just getting to know each other, I didn't think it important to ask."

"With your last name being Christian, I didn't think . . ."

"Because of Lisa I kept my married name after my divorce." Judi walked around him and went to the sofa. She picked up the photograph.

Robinson braced himself. He'd dive for the door if she hauled off and threw that thing at him.

"Lisa just raved about Mr. Robinson. Mr. Robinson this, and Mr. Robinson that. 'He didn't get mad about his clothes getting messed up.

He watched videos with us.' I, of course, assumed that my mother's gentleman friend was an older man. And I thought Robinson was his last name. But all the kids know that if they don't know an adult's last name, they have to put Mister or Miss in front of the first name." She looked up at Robinson. "My mother raised us old school, and we're doing the same with our kids."

Judi looked at him again and a slow smile peeked from the corner of her mouth. Then laughter bubbled out. Before long she was doubled over, laughing so hard she fell on the sofa.

Robinson, unsure, didn't move.

"Lord have mercy, what a comedy of errors," Judi said between guffaws. She caught her breath, looked up at Robinson, and fell out again.

"I'm not sure I see the humor in this," he said dryly.

Judi sat up and wiped her eyes. She'd laughed so hard that tears had come. She looked at Robinson again, and the chuckles revved up. She reached up and pulled at Robinson's hand until he sat on the sofa.

She scooted back until she braced the opposite corner. "This is wild. This is really wild. Wait until I tell Leah. Boy, is she gonna love this one."

"Judi . . ."

Judi, still chuckling off and on, looked at him. "Calm down, Robinson. No wonder you were looking as if you'd been hit upside the head. I guess you figured I'd do just that when I found out." She eyed him again. "Lord have mercy, this is rich."

"You say that just like your mother."

"What? 'Lord have mercy'?"

Robinson nodded.

Judi shook her head. "Robinson."

"Yes?"

She started laughing again. "No wonder you were terrified when you got a look at that picture. I mean, what are the odds of this happening? We met on a blind date, for goodness' sake."

"Judi, Mrs. Christian, I'm really having a difficult time with this."

"Don't jump all formal on me now. It's a bit late for that." Judi pushed the tray on the coffee table toward him. "Here, eat. I'll grab you another beer."

She came back a few moments later with two bottles of beer. "Well, I'll say one thing for you. Mom has good taste."

Robinson, tense and still not sure if this was the calm before the storm, didn't acknowledge the compliment. This situation was weird enough as it was.

Judi handed him a bottle and sat cross-legged in a chair across from him. "Robinson, calm yourself. I'm not going to fly off the handle. I'm not going to scream or holler or do anything psycho. This is just too funny."

"You'll pardon me if I don't see the humor," he said.

Judi uncrossed her legs and sat forward in the chair. "Robinson, from my perspective there's lots to laugh at here. And besides, you just gave me a wonderful, wonderful gift."

She got up and sat next to him on the sofa. She took his hand and squeezed it. "You've made my mother very, very happy."

Judi obviously didn't know anything about the Quad-A story, Robinson thought.

"For so many years my mom has been alone." She released his hand but still looked him in the eye as she talked. "She raised the five of us when my dad walked out. There's been no one there to make her happy, to make her smile. My mother is young. She gives all her time, all her energy to that Quad-A program she started. She always gives of herself without anyone there for her."

Judi got up and returned to the chair. "I mean, look at this from my perspective. I'd have reason to be pissed off if we'd slept together. But you haven't so much as even kissed me. Every time I thought the moment was, right, you jumped away."

"I kept getting mental pictures of your mother."

Judi smiled. "And look, before you even knew who I was, you told me about her, about your love for her. I mean, what daughter can be upset with a man who declares unconditional love for her mother? Don't you see the humor in this?"

For the first time, Robinson relaxed. He sat back on the sofa and nodded. "Maybe a little."

"You said you fought for her love and you lost. What did you mean by that?"

Robinson sat up. "You haven't seen the news today or the paper, have you?"

"No. Why?"

Robinson sighed. Then he told Judi all about the article his sister had written, the confrontation with Toinette at the Quad-A center, and how he'd wound up at Judi's apartment.

Judi was silent for a long, long time.

"Are you going to throw something at me now?" he asked.

"My mother didn't take that money. She'd give someone the clothes off her back if it would somehow help. How could your sister write something like that?"

Robinson got up and took a bite from the sandwich as he paced Judi's living room. "I don't know."

Robinson shook his head. He was still trying to come to grips with what C.J. had done. Maybe she was bucking for a Pulitzer in destroying lives. Robinson brought the sandwich to his mouth again and then sighed. If he could calm down enough to have a rational conversation with C.J. maybe he'd understand her point of view a little better.

He turned to face Judi. "I don't know," he said again.

He finished off the sandwich and got another one.

"Robinson, I think I know what happened to the money."

"What? Tell me. We can go and get this mess cleared up. Your mother doesn't want me anymore, but at least it can clear her name. I'm man enough to take rejection. I must admit, it's a unique feeling, but I can handle it. I love Toinette too much to have to see her go through this."

Judi shook her head. "No. I can handle this. I don't know for sure. I need to check something out."

"Judi, if you tell me, I'll see what I can do to get that newspaper to write a Page One retraction and apology."

"There's nothing for them to retract, Robinson. If what you told me is true, everything in the story is fact. My mother's employees didn't get paid and she was unavailable for comment."

"So tell me what you know. If necessary, I can get a private detective on it in five minutes."

"No, Robinson. I'll handle this my way." Judi got a napkin from the tray and wrapped two sandwich halves in it. "Here, take this. Go home and get some rest. You look like you need it."

"Judi."

"No, Rob. I'll do this my way. If I'm wrong about my suspicions, there's no need to cause unnecessary trouble."

She shepherded him to the door. Robinson's shoulders slumped. "She doesn't love me, so I guess in the end it won't really matter who clears her name or how it's done," he said, as Judi opened the door.

"Go home. Get some rest," she said stoutly.

Robinson stood in the hallway. "Thanks for not flying off the handle, for understanding about . . . Well, you know."

Judi smiled. "Anytime."

She shut the door as Robinson headed to the elevator.

In her apartment, Judi stood at the door. "You're wrong, Robinson Mayview. If Lisa and Leah are right, my mother is crazy in love with you. That's what's making her so crazy."

CHAPTER 33

At the Quad-A center, Toinette packed her briefcase. The reporters were all gone. Ben Trammer, his public relations man, and John MacAfree had long since left. The reporters had gone wild when the two influential business executives arrived at the center and then later stood by her side during the press conference. Toinette answered as many questions as she could until Trammer's public relations man called a halt to the media inquiry.

Trammer, MacAfree, Kendra, and Dawn had all offered to see her home but Toinette refused. She wanted to spend some quiet time in the center. Trammer promised to send the car back for her.

It sure looked like she was guilty. Toinette wasn't entirely convinced that Trammer believed her. If the circumstances had been reversed, she wasn't sure she'd believe him. But Trammer was willing to go out on a limb for her, for now. Quad-A received city funding, so the council or the city manager was bound to call for an investigation. Years of hard work down the drain.

"That part about the clothes was a cheap shot, C.J. Mayview," Toinette said aloud to the empty center. "Wearing stylish clothes does not make me a criminal. I thought you were one of the good guys."

Toinette sighed and went to the door. She locked up the center and walked to the car waiting at the curb. A liveried chauffeur opened the door for her. She looked across the street. People over there, the anonymous sources in C.J. Mayview's story, had painted the picture of her stepping into a chauffeured limousine as something illegal, something bad.

Toinette settled in the backseat. Funny, she thought, the last time she'd been in this car, she'd been headed to an appointment that would positively change her day, an appointment that brought happiness. Now she felt like she was headed to the electric chair.

Robinson got home and called Toinette. There was no answer at her house. She had probably turned off all the ringers, he figured. He'd have done the same thing. He wasn't even sure what he'd say if he got her on the line.

Robinson activated his answering machine. There were a ton of calls: the mayor's wife about the auction, four calls from C.J., one from Malcolm asking if Toinette needed legal representation, one from Leo Stonehouse apologizing for coming at a bad time, and the last one from his mother.

"Robinson Mayview the third, I just saw the six o'clock news. What in God's name is going on?"

"I wish I knew, Mom," he said, as he picked up the telephone and dialed his parents' number.

"Mom, it's Rob."

"Robinson, oh, my God. I saw the news. Are you all right?"

"I'm fine, Mom. I'm just fine," he said dolefully.

"Well, you don't sound fine. You sound worse than C.J. She's been on the telephone crying. What are you doing?"

Robinson looked around his empty kitchen. "Nothing."

"Robinson?"

"Yes, ma'am?"

"Why don't you come over here? We can talk."

"Look, Mom. If C.J. is there, I don't see any purpose in it."

"Your sister isn't here. She's at work," his mother replied.

"That figures. She's probably busy seeing how many more lives she can wreck."

"Sarcasm doesn't become you, Robinson," she responded crisply. Silent for a moment, she then asked, "Robinson, is this the woman you were talking to me about? Is she the one you are in love with?"

Robinson sighed.

"Darling, I'm sorry. Come over here, Rob, and we'll talk. Your father's out. It will just be the two of us."

"Are you sure your daughter isn't there?" he asked.

"Robinson."

Resigned, Robinson agreed.

About half an hour later, he let himself into his parents' home and went straight to the great room where his mother and father usually relaxed. Robinson found his mother seated on one of the room's three sofas working needlepoint. He'd grown up in this huge house. This room had always represented warmth and nurturing and home. Right now he felt so adrift, so alone. He had come to his mother's because he needed an anchor.

"Hey."

Genevieve looked up. "Hey, yourself."

Robinson went to his mother and kissed her on the cheek. "Another of your original designs?" he asked, indicating the needlepoint.

"Yes. I've undertaken a rather ambitious project, a tapestry."

"I'm sure it will be beautiful like all the others," Robinson said, plopping onto the sofa near his mother.

Genevieve put the needlework aside. "You look tired, son, almost as if you've been in a fight."

"I am. I was. I lost." Robinson leaned his head back on the sofa and closed his eyes. "Where's Dad?"

"He's been at the club all day. I left a message for him after I saw the news. They were out on the fairway without a telephone."

Genevieve Mayview soothed her son's weary brow. Robinson turned into the embrace and sighed. "I'm so upset with C.J. I could scream."

"This day hasn't been easy for her either, Robinson."

"Did you read that story she wrote?" he asked, indignation creeping into his voice.

"Yes, I saw it. I must admit, however, that I didn't read it until after she first called today. And I didn't understand the complete ramifications until after I saw you on the news. Tell me, Robinson, what has you so upset, the fact that the things in C.J.'s story are true or the fact that her story has hurt someone you love?"

She always knew how to get to the heart of the matter, Robinson thought. "I don't love Toinette anymore. C.J. either."

Genevieve chuckled at his petulant tone. "Then why are you here looking and acting like someone took all the toys in the sandbox and won't share with you?"

Robinson sighed and sat up with his hands dropped between his legs. He turned his head and offered his mother a boyish grin. "Maybe because when I was a kid and something hurt you kissed it and made it all better."

"I can understand and appreciate the boy inside of you wanting to be comforted, Rob, but the man you are now has to deal with this situation."

"You don't know the half of it."

Genevieve settled back on the cushions and crossed her legs. Robinson was ready to talk now. She'd be silent and let it come out of him in his own way.

Robinson rubbed his face and stood up. "I've been dating her daughter and didn't even know it. Toinette, my lov—uh, my girl . . ." Robinson paused. All this time had passed and he didn't have a single clarifying description of what Toinette was to him. "Lover" was too crude. "Girlfriend" seemed too flippant. He looked down at his mother and decided to err on the side of conservativeness for her sensibilities.

"Toinette Blue is my sweetheart," he said. "We had a falling out. She went her own way. I went out on a blind date and I found out today that the woman I went out with is one of Toinette's daughters."

"How old is this woman?"

"Judi? I don't know. In her late twenties."

"No, I meant your girlfriend," Genevieve clarified.

Robinson rolled his eyes and shook his head. "She's forty-seven and acts like the difference in our ages is a big deal."

"For a woman, thirteen years can be a big deal."

Robinson sat back on the sofa. "Then there's her husband who deserted her, her son who hates me, and the fact that she thinks I put C.J. up to that newspaper article today."

"I don't know about the husband part, Robinson. If she's married . . ."

Robinson waved a hand and slumped down in the cushions. "Only in her head."

"And what of her heart?" Genevieve asked.

"I think it belongs to him."

"You think? Robinson, I had hoped that I taught you better. It sounds like what you and Toinette need to do is sit down and talk. I mean really communicate. I would think that now, more than ever, she'd need you by her side. Right now, to her you probably look like a member of the enemy's camp, although Lord knows I'm not calling my own daughter the enemy. You know what I mean."

Robinson nodded, and Genevieve wrapped an arm around his shoulder. She then said, "If she loves you, and I think she does, what she needs most right now is you by her side. Work out your differences. Sometimes you have to fight for what you love. I don't just mean verbal altercations. Sometimes you have to put everything on the line. If you don't come out the victor, at least you know you gave a good fight and you loved well and deeply for a time."

Robinson seized on one thing she'd said. "You've never even met her. What makes you think she loves me?"

"The camera doesn't lie, darling. I and everybody else in the city but you saw the way she looked at you before that reporter asked his question."

Robinson left his mother's a while later. He had every intention of going home. Instead, he found himself in front of Toinette's house. Her car was in the driveway. He went to the front door. He got no response for his repeated efforts of knocking and ringing the bell. He tried to peer through the window, but the shades were drawn. Robinson backed down the steps and looked up at her bedroom window. She'd probably peeped out the curtains, spied his car, and was pretending to not be home. But the curtains were still. Robinson tried the door again, and then, resigned, drove home.

At a little seafood place near the water, Toinette sat with Bosworth Sullivan. She poked at the fresh oysters and fried clams on her plate. Sullivan watched her and smiled. Toinette was beautiful even when she was depressed. There was none of the usual flash and dash, however. Even her smile had dimmed.

He'd called her and had caught her at home. He was surprised she'd agreed to have dinner with him, but she insisted on a place where no one would recognize her. He brought her here, an out-of-the-way little place where the food was good and the view soothing. They'd spent the last twenty minutes talking about the day.

"Why do you believe me?" she asked.

"Because I know about and believe in your integrity, your honor. Besides that, I'm crazy about you. You affect me like no other woman has in a long time."

"Bosworth, our relationship can't take this turn," she said quietly. "I only agreed to come with you tonight because . . ."

Sullivan patted her hand. "I know why you came. You needed to get away. I understand that. It's the racial difference, isn't it? That's why you won't take this a step further."

Toinette shook her head and pushed her plate aside. She watched a gull dive for a tidbit of food on the decking. "No. That's not an issue. My heart, right or wrong, belongs to someone else."

Sullivan thought about the evening news he'd watched before calling her. "It's that man you were on television with, Robinson Mayview. The attorney."

The surprised and quizzical expression on her face made him smile sadly. "I saw you. I've often wished you would look at me that way. But I can see that that won't be the case." He patted her hand again. "He's a lucky man."

Sullivan looked out at the marina, then closed his eyes. When he opened them again and looked at Toinette, he was transformed from suitor and friend back to senior partner of one of the city's largest law firms. "Depending on how this blows, you may need a lawyer. I recuse myself because, well . . . suffice it to say a personal conflict. But I put at your disposal any legal resources you need, one person or a team. Sullivan and O'Leary is yours."

"Bosworth, you don't have to . . ."

He interrupted by taking both of her hands in his. He squeezed them gently. "From one old *friend* to another," he said.

Toinette looked at him, weighing his words. After a moment, she nodded.

* * *

If Toinette had had her way, she'd have spent Sunday alone in her house with the windows drawn feeling sorry for herself. Leah, Russell, Judi, and Angie, along with Kendra and Malcolm, made sure that wasn't the case. When she looked up, her house was full of people. Her daughters and Kendra shepherded her into the shower and saw that she got dressed. The big group went to church service and then to dinner. Someone suggested a movie, and they packed into cars to go to the theater. The comedy lifted her spirits.

By the time Monday rolled around, Toinette was feeling optimistic. After the initial shock and numbness, she now felt she could actually overcome the obstacles that stood before her. She tried not to think of Robinson, but she couldn't help it. He hadn't called. He hadn't tried to see her. But then, she hadn't given him any reason to want to. Russell reiterated his negative opinion and had been loudly argued down by Leah and Judi. Angie repeatedly said she just wanted her mother to be happy.

Judi and Leah had been acting odd, smiling at Toinette at strange times and whispering together like they used to do when they were children. Toinette sat at her desk and smiled. Her girls were really something. Neither one had ever met Robinson, yet they defended him like a champion. Russell had eventually stormed away.

She looked at the telephone and wondered what Robinson was doing. The Quad-A telephones had been ringing nonstop most of the day. Toinette endeavored to get her mind off Robinson. Her problems with him seemed to pale when compared to everything else that was wrong with her life.

"Then why can't you think of anything else?" she said aloud.

A knock on her open office door got her attention.

"Mrs. Blue?"

Toinette looked up at a worried-looking Dawn. Two police officers and another man stood in the door. Toinette stood up. "How may I help you, officers?"

The man with them spoke up. "Mrs. Blue, I'm from the city manager's office. I'm sorry to have to do this."

Toinette was served with a search warrant. She read the document, then nodded. "Dawn, would you get a couple of boxes, please."

She watched the officers pull ledgers and files from her office. Bosworth had told her to expect this. She just wasn't prepared for it to happen so soon. As her hopes and dreams were boxed up and labeled, she called Sullivan. With him still on the line, she asked a question.

"Officer, am I under arrest?"

"No, ma'am. We're just executing a search warrant."

She relayed that information to Sullivan and listened to his instructions.

"Can the center remain open and operating?" she asked.

The man from the city answered. "Mrs. Blue, after review of media reports, the city manager felt it in the city's best financial interest to audit the program's books and launch an immediate investigation. He wants to get this cleared up and taken care of as soon as possible."

"Can the center remain open?" she repeated. "I have children and working mothers who depend on Quad-A. If the center closes, they won't have a place for childcare."

"To my knowledge, Mrs. Blue, you can operate as normal. We're just here for documents."

Toinette told Sullivan that information and then listened to him. She rang off as the officers were carrying the boxes from her office. When they all left, she sat in one of the chairs in front of her desk. Dawn came in with a cup of hot coffee and pressed it into her hands.

"It's all gonna work out, Mrs. Blue. You'll see."

Toinette wrapped both hands around the mug, brought it to her mouth, but didn't drink.

"Look at it this way, Mrs. Blue," Dawn reasoned. "The immediate problem has been taken care of. I think the staff meeting this morning went well. You and Mr. Trammer assured everybody that things would be business as usual."

Toinette thought about the tense meeting she'd had with Quad-A staff members that morning. To her surprise, just as she was about to start the meeting, Ben Trammer walked in the front door. She'd thought he was back in Dallas. They talked briefly in her office before meeting with all of Toinette's employees. Trammer, in a gesture of faith, offered to meet the center's payroll. As they talked, Toinette thought about Aaron's tuition and his money problems. At one point, she couldn't look Trammer in the eye.

"Mrs. Blue, you even told everybody that the police might come," Dawn continued. "The aides were able to let the kids know in a way that didn't panic them when the cops did show. It's all gonna work out, you'll see."

Toinette gave Dawn a small, tight smile and finally sipped from her coffee. "Why don't you head on home."

"You need to do the same, Mrs. Blue."

As Dawn got up, Toinette placed the coffee cup on her desk. "I may as well."

Toinette picked up her things and left her office. Dawn shrugged into her blazer and pulled her own handbag from her desk drawer. She plopped the bag on the desk and rummaged for her car keys.

"All ready?" Toinette asked.

"Oh, I forgot about this, Mrs. Blue," Dawn said, handing Toinette a folder that was under her purse. "That man, Mr. Mayview, left this for you the other day."

Toinette looked at the folder as if it were poisonous. She stuffed it in the outside pocket of her leather case and forgot about it.

CHAPTER 34

Over the next two days, it was, for the most part, business as usual at the Quad-A center. Children arrived each day and afternoon; people came in for counseling and their workshops.

Toinette was surprised at the outpouring of love and support she got from the community. A steady stream of cards, notes, flowers, and telephone calls flooded the center from friends, program employers and participants, and even strangers. But silent was the one voice she wanted to hear; missing was the one note that would have made the ordeal seem bearable.

Toinette reached for the telephone to call Robinson. But as she picked up the receiver, she replaced it.

"You haven't given him any reason to call and lots of reasons not to. Take a hint, Toinette. You're old enough to get the picture here."

She'd had much time to think about Robinson in the last few days. All of the plans for the Quad-A Foundation had been put on hold until the investigation was completed. When she really stopped and analyzed the situation, Toinette took it as high praise that the mayor's office wanted the investigation wrapped up as soon as possible. And the mayor's wife was proceeding with plans for the bachelor auction. Toinette wasn't surprised, however, when Mrs. Griffin intimated that Quad-A may not end up as a charity benefactor.

"Wouldn't want me to dash off to the Caribbean with the cash, I suppose," Toinette said.

"Line one for you, Mrs. Blue," Dawn called into the office.

"Achieving Against All Adversities. How may I help you?"

"Mrs. Blue?"

"Speaking."

"Mrs. Blue, this is Captain Thriven of the police department. This is a courtesy call, ma'am. I'm calling to advise you that we may ask you to come in for questioning. We would like you to remain in the greater metropolitan area."

The lawyers Sullivan had made available to her had warned Toinette this call was coming. Still, hearing the words was like a slap in the face. Toinette gripped the receiver. "Captain Thriven, this is my home. I'm not going anywhere. I will fully cooperate with city authorities."

"Thank you, ma'am. Feel free to bring an attorney with you."

"Don't worry. I will," Toinette said dryly.

Toinette hung up the telephone and covered her face with her hands. She didn't know what she'd do if they asked for a polygraph test. She looked at her hands and wondered what it would feel like to be arrested, booked, and fingerprinted. "Lord have mercy. How am I going to get out of this?"

She reached for a tissue, but the box on her desk was empty. Toinette turned around and opened the outside flap on her briefcase where she kept a small pack of tissues. The report Robinson unsuccessfully tried to keep from her peeked out of the pocket. Toinette pulled it out.

"This is what started it all," she said. "May as well see how far-reaching his wrath was." Toinette had no doubt that Robinson regretted launching the initial investigation. She'd come to the conclusion that it started simply enough: he wanted to prove to her that the Quad-A Foundation work, particularly the groundwork, was best left to a younger person. He'd talked the talk of being concerned about her safety, but there was no cause for concern. Every step of the way the trips to Atlanta and Chicago were guided, with back-to-back meetings and presentations with civic and city leaders.

The shooting that occurred in Chicago while she was there had been tragic. She heard about it on the news in the airport the day after it happened. She wasn't anywhere near that complex the day of the shooting.

Toinette placed the report on her desk and turned to the first page. Then the second and the third and the fourth.

"Lord have mercy!"

Toinette flipped to the back of the report and read the last paragraph, then quickly scanned the whole thing, picking out a paragraph here and a statement there. Stunned, she stared at the pages. In the middle were photographs and copies of documents. "Oh, my God."

Her hands trembling, Toinette turned back to the beginning and read the private investigator's statement of conclusions.

* * *

Subject Russell Woodrow Blue, aka "Woody," deserted his wife, the former Toinette Anderson, and their four children, in 1973 and took up residence in a town thirty miles from the city. At the time of his departure, his wife was pregnant and soon to deliver a son. The subject changed his name—there are no court documents to support this—to Woodrow B. Russell and began a life separate and apart from his family. In 1975, subject married the former Rosa Parish. (See marriage license in the Index of exhibits. There is no Circuit Court record of divorce from Toinette Anderson Blue.) Subject and Rosa Parish Russell had two children together, Rosita and Phillip. Phillip Russell was killed in a bicycle accident at the age of five. Subject worked as a laborer for Regency Construction Co. and eventually purchased a quarter interest in the company. Subject was killed in a construction accident in 1989. (See attached newspaper clips, obituary, and death certificate.) Rosa Parish Russell remarried in 1992 and moved with her daughter to Phoenix, Arizona. Subject buried in Shady Pine Cemetery, Lot 14, Area 3.

By the time she finished reading, Toinette could barely hold the document, her hands were shaking so badly. A gamut of perplexing and confusing emotions washed over her.

"Why, Woody? Why did you do this to me? I loved you." She searched the cold, stark words for some explanation of why Woody had tired of her and their children. But the private investigator's report didn't offer up any clues. Holding raw emotion in check, Toinette turned to the pages of reproduced photographs.

A pretty, dark-skinned woman with Hispanic features smiled back at her in one photo. A studio portrait of two young children was in another. Toinette was willing to believe it was all a mistake until she turned the page. There, in an eight-by-ten color photocopy was a picture of Woody with the woman and the two children. Toinette touched the face of the child who died young, then she stared long and hard at the image of her husband.

"How could you do this? What did we ever do to make you abandon us?"

Toinette wiped at the tears. A terrible sense of wrongness, a sense of being cheated, stole through her. She looked through the Index at the other documentation the investigator had attached to the thorough report. There was even a copy of Woody's will! But there was no mention, not even a vague reference, to the other family he'd had.

"You just wiped us out of your mind like we never existed."

A knock on her open office door drew Toinette's attention.

"Mrs. Blue, are you all right? What happened?" Dawn asked, the worry in her voice evident.

Toinette shook her head. "Nothing. I'm fine. I'm fine."

It was clear from Dawn's expression that she didn't believe her. "Really, Dawn. I'm fine. I just got some startling news. What's up?"

"C.J. Mayview called. She wanted to talk to you. She said she's on her way over."

"Then I'm on my way out. I don't have anything else to say to her." Toinette grabbed her purse and clutched the private detective's report to her breast. "Dawn, can you handle things here? I'll be back. I have someplace to go. There's something I need to do."

"Uh, sure, Mrs. Blue. I'll be here. What time should I expect you back?"

Toinette, already halfway out the office door, shook her head. "I don't know how long this will take."

Toinette had one destination: Lot 14, Area 3, of Shady Pine Cemetery.

As she drove, she thought about the life she and Woody had shared together. But now Woody was dead. She was a widow. Her children had a half-sister somewhere out there. Toinette debated with herself on whether she should tell her children the truth.

"There have been too many lies already," she said, coming to a conclusion. She'd give her kids an overview. If any of them wanted to read the private eye's report, she wouldn't stop them. They all had a right to know what really happened to their father.

That thought brought her to Robinson.

"What a fool you've been, Toinette Blue," she said. She steered with one hand as she swiped at tears in her eyes. "You held out for the love of a man who didn't want you and you've lost the love of a lifetime."

She owed Robinson an apology, a big apology. She'd jumped to all manner of erroneous conclusions. Robinson had seemed genuinely stunned when she accused him of being in cahoots with his sister.

"You let your anger feed on a flawed assumption and look at the trouble it brought you. I'm sorry, Robinson. I'm so sorry."

As her car ate up the miles, taking her closer and closer to Woody's final resting place, the reason why Robinson would have hired a private investigator to find Woody became crystal clear. Toinette nearly ran off the side of the interstate when it finally sunk in. He loved her! Robinson Mayview loved her. Why else would he go to the trouble of trying to locate Woody?

"Oh, Robinson, I'm so sorry I doubted you."

A little while later, Toinette arrived in the town. At a gas station she asked for directions to the cemetery. From the cemetery office, she located the place where Woody was buried.

Toinette slipped her keys in her pants pocket and walked through the grass to Woody's grave. Large pine trees dotted the area. A marble headstone marked the place: *Woodrow B. Russell: father, husband, friend.* 1946-1989.

For a long time she stared down at the plot. Then she bent down and pulled a weed growing near the headstone. "All those years, Woody. All those years I waited for you and loved you. And a little part of me died each year you didn't come back. I kept telling myself that next year would be the year. Next year you'd walk in the door and say, 'Nettie, baby, I'm back.' But you never did. I lied to our children for you. I did what I thought was right at the time, and I've lived to regret it."

Toinette began to slowly pace the length of his grave. "Did you live to regret what you did? Probably not. You looked happy in that picture. As happy as we once were. Did you ever tell your other wife about me, Woody? Did you slip up and call her Nettie as you held her at night? I cried myself to sleep many nights wondering and worrying about you."

She kicked the ground as her emotions got the best of her. "You didn't deserve my love."

She looked up at the sky and then down at his grave, trying to compose herself. "I had a boy, Woody. The baby you walked out on was a boy. I named him Aaron after your favorite baseball player. He's a good kid, for the most part. He's in college now and wants to be a lawyer. But you don't care about that now. You didn't care then. How were you able to sleep at night knowing you'd walked out on me, on our children, on your responsibilities as a husband and father?"

Toinette wiped at the falling tears, angry at herself for giving Woody so much time to steal her life. Standing at the foot of the grave, she raged at his headstone. "I loved you. I waited for you, and you were off living some other life. I hope you were happy, Russell Woodrow Blue. I hope you were happy because you made my life a living hell."

Toinette hugged herself and rocked back and forth. She let the tears fall and the anger pour through her. "You made my life miserable, and now because of you I've lost a love that was truly special, truly mine."

Robinson stepped from behind a pine tree. He had finally given in to his need and love for Toinette and went to her. He'd missed her at the center by about ten minutes. Dawn told him she didn't know where Mrs. Blue was going, simply that she was upset and was clutching the folder he'd left at the center. A quick call to Leo Stonehouse gave Robinson all the information he needed. He knew Toinette and he knew she'd come here.

What he didn't know was if he'd be welcome. He had stayed far enough away to give Toinette privacy. After more than twenty years, Toinette deserved time alone with her husband. But now, after watching her, Robinson wasn't sure if tracking down Woodrow Blue had been the right thing to do. He'd heard little of what Toinette told her husband, but loud and clear he heard her scream, "I loved you!"

That admission on Toinette's part left Robinson little to be hopeful for. But it was done now. Stonehouse had, as always, done a meticulously thorough job. He'd even located Woody Blue's second wife and daughter in Arizona and awaited instructions on what to do with the information. No matter what happened now, Robinson thought, at least he had, as his mother said, loved well and deeply.

Robinson slowly moved toward her, his wingtips making little noise on the well-maintained lawn, until he stood within three feet of where she rocked and held herself.

"What am I going to do now?" Toinette asked Woody's silent headstone. "I'm back where I started. Mad at you and alone. Because of some stupid moral obligation I felt to you, I've lost Robinson."

"I'm here if you want me."

Toinette whirled around and stared at Robinson. Then her face crumpled. Robinson closed the distance between them and folded her in his arms. Toinette cried. She yielded to the compulsive sobs that shook her body, and Robinson held her, offering to her all his strength and all his love.

For a long time they stood together, standing at Woody's grave. When Toinette's tears subsided, Robinson pulled a handkerchief from his breast pocket and wiped her face. The silk lingered near the corner of her mouth, and he finally gave in to the temptation. His mouth slowly descended to hers. He gave her enough time to understand his intention and pull away, but Toinette wrapped her arms around his waist and met him halfway.

His kiss started gently, an exploratory balm that soothed and healed her. Then it grew demanding and urgent, an embrace of need and desire and hope. Toinette melted in his arms. His lips were warm and sweet on hers. And it had been too long since she'd fully given of her heart.

Robinson left her mouth and feathered kisses along her jaw, her neck. He framed her face in his hands. "I love you, Toinette Blue."

Toinette opened her mouth to speak, but Robinson silenced her with a finger across her lips. "Let me say what I came to say."

When she nodded, he continued. "I love you, Toinette. I'd never do anything to hurt you. The hardest thing in the world for me to do was stay away from you these past few days. I came here today knowing I don't have a right to be here, and I'll certainly understand if you're upset that I hired the investigator to find your husband. I kept feeling that the only thing standing between us was him," he said, nodding toward Woody's grave. "Well, there's also Russell, who for some reason believes I'm the spawn of Satan. But that's neither here nor there."

"No, Robinson," Toinette said as she raised a hand to caress his brow. "It's exactly on point. For too long now, I've let other people's actions have too much of an impact on my own life. I was listening to Russell when I should have been listening to my heart. I was thinking of what people might say about the difference in our ages instead of celebrating the beauty and the joy I found with you. I owe you an apology, Robinson."

Toinette stepped out of his embrace and walked a few steps away. She looked down at the ground, then out over the cemetery lawn before facing him again. "Robinson, I'm sorry for accusing you of being responsible for the article your sister wrote. I picked up the investigator's report thinking it was some information you supplied to her to get back at me for proceeding with the plans for the Quad-A Foundation. I know you're opposed to it."

Robinson traced her steps. "Toinette, I'm not opposed to the Foundation. I think it's a super idea. It will help lots of people. My concern all along has been for your safety. We never really talked about what you'd be doing in the cities. I had visions of you walking off a plane and straight into the projects. I almost had a heart attack when I heard the news about the shooting the other night. When I finally found a person who'd actually seen you alive and safe, I was so relieved that I just left the one short message."

"'Robinson said I love you,' " Toinette said, quoting the message she'd received at the hotel. "When I got back and Russell showed me the newspaper, I interpreted your message to be a form of apology and regret for what I thought you'd done. Robinson, can you ever forgive me?"

Robinson took her two hands and raised them to his mouth. He pressed a gentle kiss in each of her palms. "Only if you can find it in your heart to forgive me."

Toinette smiled. "You haven't done anything wrong."

It was Robinson's turn to step away. "Toinette, I don't know how to tell you this except to come right out and say it. The odds of it happening are one in a million, but after you dumped me I went out on a couple of dates with your daughter Judi. I didn't know she was your daughter at the time. I found that out when I saw a photograph of your grandkids at her apartment. Toinette, I swear to God nothing happened between us."

Robinson wasn't expecting to hear laughter, but Toinette's face lit up for the first time that day. She clapped her hands together once. "Lord have mercy! That's what those two were whispering and smiling about."

"What are you talking about?"

"On Sunday, Leah, Judi, Angie and Russell took me to dinner. All day long the girls, especially Leah and Judi, had been acting like they were fifteen again. Judi even told me that I could scratch any ideas I might have developed about her and the man she told me she'd been out with." Toinette looked at Robinson and grinned. "She said he was in love with another woman and that woman deserved his love."

Robinson smiled. "I'm glad you two see the humor in this."

"But Rob, I do want to know something else," Toinette said quietly.

"Anything, Toinette. My life is an open book for you."

"Was it you I saw with another woman going into Chez Jolé?"

He nodded. "Her name is Marlena, and she doesn't seem to understand the meaning of the word *no*. Toinette, there's nothing between me and Marlena. It would be dishonest of me to say that it's always been that way. For a while before you and I started dating, Marlena and I were pretty steady. It's apparently taken her a while to realize that it's over between us. She was starting to act rather possessive, almost as if the next thing she'd want from me would be gold bands and forever."

"You don't want that?"

"Yes, I do, Toinette. But only with you. I love you body and soul, Toinette Blue. No other woman compares with you."

Robinson held out his hand. Toinette clasped hers in his. "Standing in my kitchen you asked if I'd marry you. Is the offer still open?"

"There's no expiration date on my love," Robinson said.

"Then, yes. I'll marry you, Robinson Mayview."

Robinson's smile was brighter than the sunshine. He bent his head and kissed her full on the mouth.

"Do you suppose there's something kinky about kissing in a cemetery?" she asked.

Robinson looked around, then shook his head. "There's no one here to see."

"How about we drive home to a place that isn't quite as exposed to spirits."

She watched Robinson's expression change from sensual speculation to worry. "What's wrong?" she asked.

"I just remembered."

"What?"

Robinson took her hands in his. "Toinette, the police called while I was at the center. Your assistant Dawn told me to tell you that a Captain Thriven said charges would be brought against you. Police were on their way to the center."

CHAPTER 35

"We can work this out together, Toinette," Robinson said.

Toinette looked at the man she loved. "Maybe you meeting Judi was a good thing. It looks like I'm going to jail."

"Toinette . . ."

"No, listen to me. We're going to go back to the Quad-A center, and I'm going to get arrested for a crime I didn't commit. I didn't take any money from the program, Robinson."

He wrapped his arm around her shoulders. "I know that, Toinette. I believe you."

"But it sure looks like I did. I'm not rich, Robinson. I have a child in college, a child who is going to law school soon. I don't struggle to make ends meet, but it gets tight now and then. Like when Aaron needed that chunk of money to keep from being evicted. Those types of financial problems would be easy for someone investigating to discover, put two and two together, and come up with a guilty verdict. And the books, God, I just wasn't thinking. I had work at home with me but had forgotten about the ledger. It was an innocent enough thing to just work in another one. But now, it makes me look like I was keeping two sets of books. Then there's the payroll. That just defies explanation. I could claim it was an accounting error, but that, coupled with all the other little things, makes me look guilty as sin. And damage to the program has been done. Forever and ever people will look at Quad-A and say, 'Oh, I wonder if she really took that money?' " She looked away.

Robinson turned her so they faced each other. "Toinette, a lot of people who care about you and your work are in your corner. You have John MacAfree, one of the city's most successful businessmen, and Ben Trammer, a nationally recognized corporate CEO, flanking you on the evening news. That's what people remember. As for the other things, you and I both know that I gave you the money for Aaron. If it came down to it, I'd have my checking account records submitted as evidence for you. What you're forgetting is that just about everything in C.J.'s nasty little article can be explained. The one thing that can't we'll work on *together* until we find the answer."

Toinette cupped his face in her hand. "Thank you for bailing me out with Aaron. I felt badly about asking you for the money. I'm always teaching and counseling my Quad-A mothers to be independent, to stop looking for a handout, to learn to solve their own problems without turning to a boyfriend or lover. Aaron needed money fast, and the first thing I did was pick up the telephone and call you."

"Everything I have is yours, Toinette. I will continue to be a resource, a friend, a confidant." He smiled at her, and Toinette's heart turned over. "And a husband," he added.

Robinson pulled her to him for a tender kiss. Then, arm and arm, they walked to where Toinette had parked her car. She never looked back at Woody's grave.

About forty-five minutes later Toinette and Robinson arrived at the Quad-A center. Chaos reigned outside. Two police cruisers with blue lights silent but flashing were parked in front. Dawn stood outside frantically wringing her hands as she talked to a uniformed police officer and a man in a suit. Two other uniformed officers were trying to hold back the neighborhood curiosity seekers who had come out to see what the fuss was all about. Toinette could see the curious faces of children pressed against the center's front windows.

The media pack surrounded her before she could open her car door. But Robinson was there. He pushed an overzealous cameraman out of the way and took Toinette's hand as she stepped from the car. He wrapped an arm around Toinette's shoulders. The reporters yelled questions, but Toinette remained silent as she and Robinson walked the gantlet of reporters to the door of the center.

"Oh, Mrs. Blue. Thank God you're back," the senior aide said with more than a sigh of relief. "I kept telling them you'd left to run an errand and would be back soon."

Toinette smiled at Dawn. "Thank you, Dawn. I knew you could handle things." Toinette looked at the little faces she loved so much. She lifted a hand and waved when one of the children grinned and waved at her through the glass. "Dawn, why don't you go inside and get the kids started in some sort of group activity that takes them away from the windows. Tell them everything will be fine out here."

"Mrs. Toinette Blue? I'm Captain Thriven." The man in the suit stepped forward. "It's unfortunate that this is such a public spectacle," he said so quietly that only Toinette and Robinson heard.

The crowd gathered outside grew louder. Someone shouted out, "Mrs. Blue didn't do it." Mumblings of concurrence raced through the mob. Someone started a chant: "Quad-A is good! Quad-A is good!"

The police captain explained why he was there. Toinette nodded solemnly when he finished. The captain nodded to the uniformed officer who stood at his side. The officer pulled a small card from his pocket and began to read from it.

"You have the right to remain silent. . . ."

Robinson wrapped an arm about Toinette's waist. He could feel her tremble as the police officer read Toinette her rights. Robinson looked out at the reporters, who were furiously taking notes. Right in front, as if leading the pack, was C.J.

She looked up and their gazes met. Robinson saw his sister flinch as if she'd been hit. For a long time they stared at each other. The jangle of handcuffs drew Robinson's attention back to Toinette.

"Captain Thriven, is that really necessary?" he asked.

Photographers surged forward to capture the moment.

Toinette stood stoically before them. "Let them do their jobs, Robinson. I'll be okay." She turned so the officer could handcuff her.

"Wait! No!" someone in the crowd yelled out. "She's innocent. Mrs. Blue is innocent."

Jostling through the crowd Judi Christian pushed her way to the front. She was dragging another young woman with her. "Wait, officer!" she appealed. "You can't arrest her."

Toinette turned around when she heard her daughter's voice. "Judi! What in the world are you doing?"

"There's something you need to know," Judi told her mother and the police.

"Ma'am, please step aside. You're impeding a police procedure," the captain said.

Judi stood her ground. "No. Listen to me. My name is Judi Christian. She's my mother and she's not guilty."

"Ma'am . . ."

The woman with Judi looked up then. Toinette gasped, and the woman said, "Officer, Toinette Blue didn't do the things you're about to arrest her for. I did."

Reporters started asking questions. Captain Thriven threatened to have everyone arrested and charged with obstructing justice. The crowd grew quiet again.

"What in the world? What are you two doing?" Toinette said. "Have you lost your minds? I know you love me, but you don't have to go to this extreme to protect me."

Tears tracked down the young woman's face. She was dressed neatly but looked old and tired. "This isn't an extreme, Mom. It's the truth. I'm sorry that what I did hurt you this way."

"Miss, I don't know who you are . . ." the police captain began.

The woman pulled a piece of paper from her pocket. She turned and faced the television cameras, reading from the paper she held.

"My name is Angela Blue and I'm a drug addict."

Toinette cried out and reached for Angie. Robinson and the police captain held her back.

"My mother, Toinette Blue, is director of the Achieving Against All Adversities program," Angie continued, reading the prepared statement. "My mother is innocent of the charges made against her by the media and by city investigators. By profession I am a certified public accountant. For the last eight months, I have diverted money from my mother's personal checking accounts and from the Quad-A accounts to finance my cocaine addiction. Until this last time, I had been able to replace the missing funds before anyone noticed a discrepancy. I never meant to have my mother implicated in this. I apologize to the men and women of the Quad-A program. I apologize to the city. And most of all," she said, turning to Toinette, her voice breaking. "I apologize to my mother for all the pain and suffering I've caused."

Reporters surged toward Angie and Judi, and started yelling questions.

Toinette looked at her two daughters, then collapsed in Robinson's arms.

EPILOGUE

Toinette slipped the multijeweled earrings on. Tonight was the perfect night to wear the beautiful gift from Robinson. She took a final look at herself in the cheval glass in her bedroom, then picked up her small evening bag and went downstairs.

"God, you're beautiful," Robinson said as she held out her arms and pirouetted before him. The shimmering gown hugged her curves and then cascaded down her legs.

Toinette fingered the lapels of his tuxedo. "You're not so bad yourself, either."

Robinson held the door for her and they walked to the white limousine waiting at the curb. Once settled inside the plush interior of the car, Robinson turned to her.

"Are you sure this is all right with you, Toinette? Some woman is going to bid on me tonight and I'll be hers for some dismal date."

"It won't be dismal, Robinson. And remember, it's for a good cause. Quad-A is one of the benefactors of this bachelor auction tonight."

"I'm not long a bachelor," he pointed out.

Toinette took his hand in hers. She lifted it and kissed him. "It's okay, Robinson. Really. But are you going to be okay with me traveling around the country to administer the Foundation?"

"You bet. Because I plan to be by your side on most of those trips."

Toinette shook her head and smiled. "I'm glad you and C.J. made up."

"We had a long talk. Just the two of us. She explained about the anonymous sources and the tips she got. Sometimes reporters just don't get to find out who calls in a tip. They investigate the ones that sound plausible. It was a combination of unrelated things that first sent her in search of you."

"Well, I'm just glad you two are on speaking terms again," Toinette said.

"The newspaper is planning a series on white collar addicts," he said. "C.J. has asked to be transferred to another beat and won't have anything to do with that project. No more conflict of interest issues for her to deal with. And as far as the newspaper goes, the Page One story clearing you and announcing the foundation's work helped."

"We're having an independent audit done. The computer system Trammer and MacAfree are setting up will ensure that there are no more holes in recordkeeping. It was too easy for Angie or anyone else to get ahold of our account numbers. I was just too trusting."

Robinson looked around the limousine's interior. "It was nice of Trammer to send the car around."

"Yes. His support through the ordeal was unflagging. I worry about Angie, though. Robinson, how could one of my children be addicted to drugs and I not know it?"

He spied a bucket and pulled a bottle from it to read the label. "It's not unheard of, Toinette. You have to remember that you rarely saw her. And you trusted her with your personal finances. At least, unlike some addicts, she recognized her problem and sought help."

"Judi suspected all along and never said anything."

"She wasn't positive, Toinette. She just thought Angie was stressed from work. I'm sure she didn't want to unnecessarily upset you or anyone else without being one hundred percent sure. And she said she wasn't until she got the telephone call from Angie and picked her up at that bus stop. Judi was trying to help Angie by talking to her. No one can make an addict change. That has to come from within. Angie took the first and most difficult step in admitting she has a problem. She's in rehab now and is trying to get her life back together."

"She's going to have to go to jail," Toinette said sadly.

"That remains to be seen. She has the best legal representation in the city. We'll just have to wait and see what happens."

Toinette sighed. "Sort of like you and Russell."

Robinson rolled his eyes and put the champagne bottle back. "You understand, Toinette, that your son and I may never be friends."

"Russell is a grown man, Robinson. I'm a grown woman. He has to live his life and I have to live mine. It's going to take him some time to come to grips with what his father did. I never realized how deeply Russell had been affected by Woody's desertion. But those are issues he has to work out within himself. I love you, Robinson. My love and my loyalty are to you."

He kissed her deeply, then placed a hand over her flat stomach. "About kids . . ."

"Robinson, I'm forty-seven years old and . . ."

He talked over her. "I've been looking into some things. There's a children's home in the city that is looking for African-American couples to be adoptive parents."

Toinette smiled and wrapped her arms around his neck. "I love you, Robinson."

Robinson grinned through a short kiss. He reached for the bottle of champagne, then opened it and handed Toinette a delicate champagne flute.

Linking his arm around Toinette's, he offered, "A toast."

"To what?" she asked.

"To new beginnings and a lifetime of love."

"I'll drink to that, Robinson. I'm yours forever. Body and soul."

SEDUCTION

For Monica Harris
an editor with vision; an editor who believed
Thank you, Monica

Acknowledgments

Many, many thanks to the U.S. Marshals Service in Arlington, Va., and to David M. Branham, U.S. Marshals Service public affairs specialist, for assisting with this project; and to Michelle Fronheiser whose prodding "just give it fifteen minutes" helped get me to the end.

Special thanks also to Chris Steuart, Tracy Palmer Parris, Michael T. Jackson, MaryAnne Gleason, Mike Gleason, and Adrien Creecy for moral support and answering myriad questions.

In Memory of William L. Mason Jr.

PROLOGUE

C.J. Mayview stopped her car on the emergency pull off section of the bridge. She cut the engine, got out of the car, and stared back at the city. Twilight time. That half day, half night part of the day fell on the city with its purplish-blue hues.

C.J. soaked in the sight of the city before her. She loved the hushed pregnancy of twilight—the period as day ended and the quiet expectancy of night cast its shadows over the horizon. The night held secrets. Twilight, with the answers to those secrets, cast its warm glow through the sky: secret longings and secret dreams. The night held passion and crime. The cover of darkness that would come after twilight hid so much. C.J. watched twilight fold into night, long shadows chasing the hushed expectancy away.

Breathing in the scent, the fresh, free, freedom smell of saltwater and breeze, C.J. listened above the rush of traffic, listened to the water lapping against the bridge pilings. She listened and longed for the freedom of the waves.

Soon. Soon she would be free.

C.J. loved the water, and she loved the sight of the city coming to life in lights. Gazing out at the horizon she knew that any minute now a cop might come and ask if she was having car trouble, then chase her away. But right now, now it was just the twilight and the water.

She glanced at the car that held all the possessions she'd carry into her new life. It wasn't much, but that's the way she wanted it. The vehicle, a sturdy but unpretentious four-wheel drive, would get her where she wanted to go. It was a far cry from the preppy little BMWs she'd been driving for the last fifteen years of her life. She'd traded the latest Beamer in for the basic transportation that now held all the worldly possessions she'd deemed suitable for this new life. She had traded the old car in just as she was trading in that old lifestyle.

She again turned to contemplate the skyline. Night had fallen. Twilight, like the years of her life, had slipped away into something else; something dark, foreboding. As the night held its secrets, C.J. held her own. She was paying private retribution in the only way she knew how: by walking away from it all—from family, from friends, from a career she'd painstakingly built, from the addictions that threatened to consume her.

A solitary tear, one she couldn't even claim was of regret, fell as she said a quiet "Farewell" to all that remained familiar, all she knew and loved. Bending low to the ground, she felt around for a small reminder. Her fingers closed over a stone. The loose piece of granite she picked up wasn't smooth. That was appropriate, she thought. Nothing that she had done or become had been smooth, not in a lot of years. Maybe in the beginning she had been smooth, easy, laid back. But not now.

The stone, like C.J., was rugged, rough around the edges, as if it had had to toughen itself up to withstand the ravages of the elements. C.J. identified with the stone. She felt ravaged and ragged. A smooth edge peeked through but in no way dominated the texture of the rock. She liked that. The smoothness in the middle of the coarseness meant hope still existed. Over time, with steady care and constant polishing, the stone could be made smooth.

C.J. liked the analogy. With the stone in hand, she made her way back to the car. She strapped the seat belt around her and wiped away the single wet track on her face. She put the vehicle into drive and headed toward tomorrow.

CHAPTER 1

Wes Donovan needed a cigarette. He reached for the pack tucked in his shirt pocket. Then, with a mixture of disgust and irritation, he remembered he'd given up the smokes. Wes squinted through the dark lenses of his wraparound sunglasses. He stared at the brick masonry of the federal building and frowned. God, he hated coming here.

He looked around to see if he could bum a smoke from anyone. But all the suits walking around him looked as if the stench of tobacco would never be something they inhaled, let alone enjoyed.

The tie at Wes's neck choked him. He hated ties. The one he wore today was nothing more than a facade, just like the black pinstripe suit he'd had to have dry cleaned and pressed before he could put it on and come down here for this meeting. Wes didn't have anything against suits—as long as the jacket and pants could be thrown in a washing machine. The contraption he'd bundled himself into today had been worn just twice. Wes shied away from thoughts of those two funerals.

Wes knew that to anyone paying attention he looked like all the other pinstripe suits scurrying about. Except, that is, for the shades and the custom-made cowboy boots. Wes patted the place where his smokes should have been, just to convince himself he really didn't have any. Then, with a sigh of resignation, he took a deep breath and hurried into the big building.

"Donovan? That really you?"

Wes turned and smiled. He recognized the voice. "Scotty, what's up man?"

The two old friends clasped hands then headed to the elevator.

'"It's been a long time," Scotty said.

"Not long enough since I've been here," Wes answered as they got in the elevator.

"It's your attitude. You need to get it adjusted."

"Um hmm," Wes said, stepping aside to make room for a woman with a paper cup of coffee in her hands. Lips too small, chest too flat. Nice legs though, Wes thought.

"What you in for?" Scotty asked.

"Meeting."

"That would explain the suit," Scotty said dryly. "Almost didn't recognize you."

Wes smirked as the elevator lurched.

The woman with the coffee got off on three. Scotty stepped forward to depart on four.

"Gimme a call some time. Let's get together for a beer."

Noncommittal, Wes nodded as the elevator doors slid shut again. He wondered what time it was. He didn't wear watches. Despite the suits' preoccupation with time, Wes didn't think time was something to manage. It was to be spent, enjoyed, or in Wesley's case, a thing that was simply marked from one moment to the next, day in, day out, month after month. He wondered how many months it would take, how much time would have to pass, before he was able to forget . . . and forgive.

The doors swooshed open at the sixth floor. Wes stepped out and turned left. He reached in his jacket pocket for the magnetic ID badge that would allow him entrance. At a deceptively plain-looking door, Wes stuck the ID card in a slim gray hole, waited for the little green light to appear then punched in a short access code on the small keypad next to the slot.

The door popped open and Wes was inside.

He didn't recognize the woman who expectantly looked up at him from her receptionist's desk. Nice mouth, too much mascara and eye goop.

"May I help you, sir?"

Wes held out his identification badge. "Donovan. I'm in for a nine-thirty with Casey and Holloway."

The woman consulted some paperwork in front of her then smiled up at Wes. Nice smile, he thought.

"Right that way, Mr. Donovan," she said, pointing to her right. "They're expecting you."

A small, two-finger salute and an easy smile were his answers back to her. Wes headed toward Holloway's office, aware that the receptionist's gaze followed his progress.

"This job does have its assets."

Wes heard her mumbled comment and smiled to himself.

He found the door he was looking for and entered without knocking.

"Donovan, it must be that cold day in hell you mentioned the last time I saw you."

Wes smiled at Ann Marie Sinclair and fingered the lapel of his black suit. "That's the weather report I heard this morning."

He took a seat in the chair next to her desk and picked up a silver paperweight. "You're still the only reason coming down here is palatable."

Ann Marie shook her head and smiled. "Still a charmer." She stilled the hand that tumbled the paperweight. "Hey, Wes."

Slowly his eyes met hers. She waited until she had his full attention.

"Are you taking care of yourself?" she asked quietly.

Wes swallowed and looked away.

"Wes?"

He met her gaze this time. The gentleness in Ann Marie always soothed him. She knew more about him than a lot of people. And she understood far more than he found comfortable. "It still hurts," he said.

Ann Marie squeezed his hand. "I know, Wes. I know."

"Coming here doesn't help."

Ann Marie nodded then glanced at the telephone console on her desk. "Holloway's off the phone now."

"And Casey?"

"Not here yet," she said.

Wes rolled his eyes. "Probably off in a closet somewhere . . ."

"Watch your mouth, Donovan. You don't need to pick any fights today."

Wes looked at Ann Marie and smiled. "Forewarned," he said.

He stood up.

"Wes, anytime you need anything, you know I'm here for you."

Wes smiled at Ann Marie. He owed her a lot. They'd started working at the bureau the same day twelve years ago, Wes as a Deputy U.S. Marshal, Ann Marie as an office temp. She'd parlayed that temp assignment into a full-time position and had worked her way up the secretarial ranks. Few people knew how much power she actually wielded. Wes had always known.

Until just now, he'd had no idea why he'd been summoned to headquarters. The subtle warning she'd given him about the day was all he needed to prepare himself for this meeting. Wes steeled his back and rapped twice on Holloway's office door. Any trace of sensitive nineties guy, the type of man he could be only around Ann Marie and just a few others, disappeared completely as he took the first step into the office.

C.J. Mayview had come to the end of her endurance.

She'd survived far longer than she ever thought she would be able to manage. She congratulated herself on thirty whole days cold turkey.

Thirty days of freedom. Thirty long, cold endless days and nights of nothing.

Her hands trembled as she flipped pages in the thin telephone book. She sighed a huge sigh of relief when she found the listing she wanted. She punched the numbers out on her telephone keypad and impatiently waited for the connection.

"Hi," she said as soon as a voice came on the line. "I need you to come out here as soon as possible. I don't care how much it costs. I just need you this afternoon. *Now* would be even better."

C.J. rolled her eyes at the response. "You don't understand. This is an emergency. I'm really, really desperate. And I'm not too proud to beg. I'll pay cash."

She listened again, then glanced at the wall clock. She was absolutely, positively going to die if she had to wait another four hours. She was so jumpy that even her fingers itched.

"Okay. Look. Where can I go right now and get what I need?"

C.J. scrambled over a well-worn plaid sofa to grab an ink pen off one of the cushions. She wrote the address on the palm of her hand. "Is that near the fire station?" She nodded. "Okay. Okay. I know where that is. Fine. I still need you to come out here, though. If I'm not here just walk in and leave everything I need. And make sure I get the royal treatment here. I'm hurting bad."

She listened again to the voice on the other line, then answered. "That's right. Now my name is Jan Langley. That's L-A-N-G-L-E-Y. I'll leave the cash in an envelope on the sofa."

She completed the transaction and replaced the telephone receiver. Then she grabbed her wallet, pulled several bills out of it and stuffed them in an envelope. She tossed the envelope on the sofa.

C.J. Mayview was a junkie. Trying to give up her habit, at least this one, had been a noble gesture but she couldn't take it another day.

If the cable company didn't get her hooked up to CNN today she was going to die. She'd been thirty whole days without the hypnotizing bass of James Earl Jones declaring, "This is CNN." Thirty days without round-the-clock instant news.

C.J. was a die-hard news junkie. For a month she'd been without cable, without even a newspaper or newsmagazine. No *Wall Street Journal,* no *Washington Post,* no local news, no nothing. The rest of the world could have fallen off the edge of the earth and she'd have been clueless.

She glanced at the address she'd scribbled in her hand. She draped the long, thin strap of her wallet over her body and dashed out the front door. She didn't bother to lock the door. Serenity Falls, North Carolina, had a zero crime rate. At her picket fence that needed a coat of paint, she glanced at her hand again. The cable guy said the hardware store next to the fire station had a TV department. She could go stand in front of the display models and get the fix of national and world news she so desperately needed. Maybe they'd even let her use the remote control.

The feel of the room was off. Tension vibrated through every part of Wes as he watched Casey. The man would not meet his eyes. Not a good sign, Wes thought. Sweat trickled down the middle of his broad back but none of the discomfort he felt showed as he stoically stood facing Holloway's desk. With his feet braced and his arms folded across his chest, Wes knew his stance intimidated most men. Casey, while of the male gender, couldn't signify as a man. Weasel, turncoat, jellyfish, wuss, mama's boy, all came to mind; but not man. Holloway on the other hand was a different story.

Wes didn't like him but he could respect him. Holloway had made a career out of his bureau work. Shrewd, cunning, and ruthless were apt adjectives. Wes didn't doubt for a moment that every breath Holloway took was a calculated move to advance him a step on the chess board. Wes could respect him, but he always, always watched his back around Holloway.

"Why don't you both have a seat," Holloway offered.

Casey darted to a chair closest to Holloway. Wes snorted and rolled his eyes then took a seat in the straightback chair in front of Holloway's desk. He briefly wondered if he was about to get canned. After twelve years with the bureau, he'd be sorry to leave if that were the case. The only two bad things about the job were the times when he had to come in here and the wimp Casey. But he'd honed the skills necessary for the survival and sanity of every one of Casey's employees: how to work around and through the obstacle called Donald Casey. Long ago, Wes had stopped believing in a God, but he knew someone up there had been looking out for him. He could have been unlucky enough to be one of Casey's direct reports. It was bad enough being in his jurisdiction.

Wes did a quick mental inventory to see if there had been anything in the recent past to warrant this confab. He drew a blank. Not a good sign. He briefly wished that Ann Marie had given him some other clue.

Casey cleared his throat. Wes and Holloway both glanced at him.

"I know you're wondering why I called you in here today, Donovan," Holloway said.

"It had crossed my mind."

Holloway leveled a sharp glance at Wes. "Don't be wise, all right."

"That's right," Casey piped up from the safety of Holloway's desk. "One of these days, Donovan, your mouth is gonna write a check that your behind can't cash."

"Any day, Casey. You name the time and the place," Wes said quietly.

Casey paled beneath his splotchy tan.

"That's enough," Holloway said.

Holloway walked around the perimeter of his desk and sat in the large tobacco-colored leather chair. "I called you two in here today because there's a case I want to assign you. Donovan, it'll require that you relocate. Casey, it'll mean you pick up any loose ends left from Donovan's case load."

Both men jumped up at the same time. Sputtering his indignation, Casey objected to the notion.

"I'm not some flunky you have whose sole purpose is to pick up the leftovers and dregs from the likes of him."

"I have about three highly sensitive cases I'm working. To bail now would mean losing months of work. And competent research," Wes added, looking in Casey's direction.

"Are you implying that my background work is incompetent?" Casey huffed.

"If the shoe fits," Wes replied.

Holloway ignored the byplay between the Deputy Marshals. Each, in his own way, was the best at what he did. It was a shame their personalities and work styles clashed so violently. They would be a formidable pair working as a team. That would happen the same day polar bears took flight.

"So wrap up what you can do on your caseload in the next week, Donovan. Leave the rest for Casey. On Monday you're on the road to Serenity Falls, North Carolina."

"North Carolina? No thanks. I decline," Wes said.

Holloway looked from one man to the other. "It's not an option," Holloway answered. The glacial stare backed up the statement.

"And if I make an issue of it?" Wes asked.

Holloway picked up a folder from a short stack on the right side of his desk. He tossed the not thin file to Wes.

"That's not an option either," Holloway said.

Wes reached for the folder and saw his own name neatly typed across the flap: DONOVAN, WESLEY K. He didn't need to open the file to know what it contained: Details of every run-in he'd ever had with Casey and probably an eyewitness accounting and report of the brawl before Marc's funeral. Three Deputy U.S. Marshals had to be rushed to the hospital by the time Wes was subdued by five deputies.

Wes took a deep breath and tossed the folder, unopened, back on Holloway's desk. So, this was to be his punishment. A two-week suspension hadn't been enough.

"What's in Serenity Falls, North Carolina?" he asked.

Holloway's smile was cold, just like his soul. He knew he'd won. "Have a seat, gentlemen."

CHAPTER 2

Serenity Falls had been home for a month. Now that she had cable and once again felt connected to the outside world, C.J. didn't think the town too shabby. She still resisted the local newspaper and even the big national dailies that could be found at Manheim Brothers Drug Store and Grill.

C.J. liked the intimacy of the small town. She was even getting used to saying "Hello" and chatting a few moments with strangers on the street. Leaving the house unlocked was still taking some getting used to. The day the cable installation guy came by was really the first time she'd done it. No way would she have even contemplated leaving her doors open in Baltimore. The condo she'd sold before moving to Serenity Falls was in an exclusive, upscale building with twenty-four-hour security. C.J. would no more have thought to leave a door unlatched than she would have thought to stick her hand in the open flames of her brick fireplace back home.

She glanced around the small living room of the two-bedroom bungalow. It wouldn't be right to call this place shabby.

"You have character," she told the tiny living room. Only a couple of knickknacks, a vase here, an ottoman there, had made the trip with C.J. from Baltimore and that old life.

She'd spent much of the last month trying to figure out how to re-upholster chairs. C.J. cocked her head and took a critical look at the two chairs that flanked a knicked coffee table. She'd painstakingly chosen the floral chintz fabric. One of the chairs looked better than the other but it didn't matter.

C.J. grinned, proud of her handiwork. No one in Baltimore, including herself, would ever believe that C.J. Mayview, Pulitzer Prize-winning investigative journalist, Type A career woman, would be caught dead in small-town North Carolina. The nearest real department store was in Charlotte, a ways away. Most people here had never heard of espresso and thought cappuccino was the last name of some actor in Hollywood. Folks who wanted homemade bread kneaded it with their hands and let it rise on a kitchen counter. Bread machines and fancy coffee makers were for city folk.

C.J. couldn't wipe the grin from her face. Her biggest worry was not whether a crackhead would rob her in an alley or if a politician was lying to her. C.J.'s biggest dilemma rested in one monumental decision: whether to sand and refinish the coffee table next or to tackle the challenge of reupholstering the sofa.

She looked from the table to the sofa and chose neither.

"I'm going on to another project today. I'll get back to you guys soon."

With that she headed to the kitchen. From beneath the sink she pulled a pair of floral-print gardening gloves. She tugged them on and grabbed a small boom box from the counter. She kicked open the screen on the back door of her little two-bedroom bungalow. She'd fallen in love with the house on first sight, paid cash for it, and devoted part of her days into transforming a hard rock piece of soil in the backyard into a lush English garden—or at least her approximation of one. So far, she'd broken three nails and one shovel handle in the process, but C.J. didn't mind. As a matter of fact, she thrived on the hard work of gardening and the honest day's labor of learning to repair furniture. It made it easier for her to appreciate what she had. And more importantly, it made it easier for her to forget what she'd left behind.

Wes Donovan rolled into town in a beat-up pickup. Sometimes he thought he was getting too old for these games and masquerades. The truck needed new shocks. Wes needed a shave, a cigarette, and the feel of his '67 Mustang under him. He briefly thought of what else would feel good under him. But he knew he'd be getting that about as soon as he'd get his own sports car back—not until this bogus job was done, which might be three weeks after never.

Wes jounced about in the cab of the truck. His gear, including his bike, was in the flatbed. At least he got to take the Harley this time. Small comfort. It would probably rain every day he was stuck in North Carolina.

The oil light came on in the dash. Wes swore out loud. This heap of rust had been Casey's doing. Wes figured that in another life Donald Casey must have been a real prick. He probably hadn't gotten it right then and was sent to this time for the sole purpose of tormenting Wes.

Wes glanced down at the map open on the seat next to him. This would be Main Street. Aptly named, Wes figured as he took in a hardware store, a grocery, a bank with a green ATM machine sign. At least the twentieth century had arrived here in Mayberry RFD.

He had vowed to himself never to set foot in another place like this. His hometown was small enough for Wesley Donovan. Except for Mama Lo and her family, home was a place he'd just as soon forget ever existed. And now he found himself trapped in another tiny town. If this assignment could be likened to being shipped off to Siberia, Holloway couldn't have chosen a better punishment.

Making a right at a stop light, Wes turned onto Chauncey Street. He pulled into a service station just as steam started seeping from under the hood of the truck.

Wes hopped out of the cab and went around to the hood.

"Careful with that," a voice called out. "Looks like yur overheated."

"Yeah," Wes concurred as he raised the hood. The voice joined him at the truck. "Hey," Wes said, sticking a hand out. "You got a mechanic on duty?"

The man wiped one oily hand on his blue jean overalls before shaking Wes's outstretched one. "That'd be me. Name's Ray Bob."

"Hey, man. I'm Wes. Can you take a look at my truck and get it fixed?"

"Gotta let it cool down first. Maybe a couple hours."

Wes nodded. It figured as much. It would probably cost an arm and leg to get this clunker fixed. For the benefit of Ray Bob, Wes frowned. "Don't think it's gonna cost too much, do you?"

"Cain't say till I take a look at 'er."

Wes shielded his eyes from the sun. The profile on Serenity Falls, North Carolina, said blue collar. Real blue collar. "Got any jobs around here?" he asked Ray Bob.

"Hear tell the factory takin' on for second shift. They got a few midnight spots open, but those go real fast. You looking for work?"

"Low on cash. Gotta do something," Wes answered.

"Miss Clara Ann run a rooming house 'bout three blocks over. Lot of the single guys from the plant stay there."

"What's the name of it? I'll look it up."

"Ain't got a name. Just ask anybody for Miss Clara Ann's place. They point you in the right direction."

Wes tried to hide his sudden irritation. Any minute now he expected to see Andy and Aunt Bea walk up. Scotty had been right. Maybe what he needed more than a suspension, more than a vacation, more than this bogus assignment, was an attitude adjustment. And his hands around Casey's neck.

"Help me push this over there," Ray Bob said, indicating a spot near the service station's double repair bay. "It'll be outta the way and you can come back for it in a coupla days."

Wes got the Harley and strapped his two bags to the back. In minutes he was headed out of the service station and back toward town.

The first thing C.J. registered was that the man in black looked like he had been made for the motorcycle he was riding down the street. He had on a black T-shirt, black jeans, black boots and looked like he was out for blood. C.J. was immediately attracted to him.

She paused to stare after the man. She liked bad boys. And this one knew how to handle the bike. For a brief moment, before the sun's glare forced her to turn away, C.J. got a glimpse of dark hair and rich copper skin. Her own skin tingled with the thought of what it would be like to be pressed against the hard body of that dark warrior as they rode through the streets and back hills of Serenity Falls.

C.J. shook her head. "Umph. It's been a long time since you had some of that."

As the motorcycle figure continued down the street and out of view, C.J. resumed her walk. The guy in black represented yet another thing she had spent the last month trying to purge from her system. Just because it felt good was no reason to jump in bed with a man. In her past, the one she'd closed the book on when she pulled out of Baltimore, C.J. had hopped in bed for reasons not even as noble as that one. That was the old C.J. The next time she gave herself, it would be for love—or the closest thing to love she was capable of feeling.

She put the thought and the vision of the dark warrior on the motorcycle out of her mind. Today she was in search of herbs to start a small herb garden in a raised area near the back porch. The owner of one of the town's three lawn and garden stores had told her to come back when she was ready to plant. C.J. was now ready.

Wesley drove around for a while then found the rooming house. Serenity Falls was bigger than he'd first thought. The town had a Wal-Mart, a three-screen cinema, and what billed itself as an all-night skating rink/bowling alley. Wes couldn't remember the last time he'd been bowling.

He kicked the bike's stand down and swung a long leg over the seat. Taking the stairs to Miss Clara Ann's two at a time, he admired the pots of geraniums on the steps. Miss Clara Ann obviously liked flowers.

Wes rang the doorbell.

"Come on in. It's open," a voice from somewhere inside called out.

Wes gave the door a dubious look. These people left their doors unlocked? He really had landed himself in the middle of Mayberry.

Wes took the last step up and into a Florida room.

"Hi there, young man. How're you doing today? My you are a big one. If you're looking for a room, you're in luck. I got one with a bed big enough and long enough for the likes of you. Are you hungry, baby?"

Wes glanced down at the diminutive lady in front of him. He liked her on the spot. The top of her head, covered with a green scarf tied back, came just about to his navel. The dish cloth in her hand and the apron around her waist told him she'd probably been in the kitchen cooking or cleaning. She had to be seventy if she were a day.

"Are you Miss Clara Ann?"

She looked up at him and laughed. "Well, who else would I be? This is my house. I'm Clara Ann. What's your name, baby?"

"I'm Wesley, ma'am. Ray Bob over at the Texaco said you might have a room to rent. I'd just need it until I find myself an apartment."

"Shoot child, stay as long as you like. The room is seventy-five a week. That includes linens, a wake up call, and a bottomless cup of coffee. If you want meals it'll be another twenty-five."

"Don't you want to check my references or anything first?"

Clara Ann laughed out loud. "Whatever for? If you're in Serenity Falls and Ray Bob sent you this way, you don't need no other reference."

Wes shook his head then grinned. Small-town life sure had a different feel to it.

"Come on this way, Wesley. I'll give you the key to your room. You're from the city aren't ya? I can always tell. City folks the ones who want to know about references and damage deposits. The way I figure it, if you damage something, you pay. Folks who ain't decent enough to do that, well, the Lord'll make sure they get theirs."

Miss Clara Ann opened room number five and waved Wes in. "This is the big room. It has its own bathroom. I usually charge extra for that."

"How much?" Wes asked.

"Oh, don't worry about it. Right now there are only four other people staying here. One's a regular. I have eight rooms that I let out though."

Miss Clara Ann walked into the room and opened the three windows. "See, it's got a TV with the cable. The bathroom's that way. I leave fresh linen every other day. The door has a deadbolt lock. No cooking, no loud music, no parties, no drugs. What you do in your room is your own business, meaning I don't mind if you have company. Just don't disturb the other guests. There's a little parking lot in back. Long time ago that used to be my vegetable garden. Use the spot that's the same number as your room."

"What time are the meals?" Wes asked.

"Breakfast is from six to eight. Don't serve lunch. Dinner is six to eight. If you are working over at the plant and on midnight or four to twelve, I leave a plate."

Wes smiled. "I'll take it."

He slipped a hand in his back pocket and pulled out a well-worn leather wallet. He peeled out two hundred twenty-five dollars and handed the money to Miss Clara Ann.

"What's the extra twenty-five for?"

"The bathroom."

Miss Clara Ann took the money then tapped Wes on the forearm with it. "You and me gonna get along just fine."

After she left, Wes searched the room. It was unlikely that anything had been planted there. He'd chosen the place on the spot. But in his line of work, Wes learned early that you could never be too careful.

When he was sure both the room and adjoining bath were clean, he left the room, locking the door behind him. He'd grab his gear, park the bike, then get a feel for the town on foot before making his way over to the plant to fill out an employment application.

CJ., with her head stuck in the directions she'd been given on starting her herb garden, walked smack dab into the wall of a mountain. It took her a full minute to register that there weren't any mountains in Serenity Falls. She looked up into the face of the solid force in front of her. C.J. caught her breath and at the same time marveled that she'd finally figured out what it meant to get weak in the knees over a man.

"Dark warrior."

"I beg your pardon? Are you all right, miss?"

"Sorry about that. I wasn't paying attention." Only then, after speaking a few words, did she realize that he was supporting her arms. C.J. got her balance but didn't move out of his sheltering embrace. He smelled the way a man was supposed to smell, of time and sweat and hunger. And just beneath the surface, teasing her senses, C.J. picked up a faint scent of an earthy cologne or aftershave. Just from the smell of him she wanted to crawl in his arms and hold on tight.

In another time he would have been a king or a warrior. She knew that just like she knew that this man would belong to her. C.J. didn't question her instinct or the fact that people didn't belong to each other. This man, with his chiseled features and hard mouth, needed tenderness the way a flower needed rain.

CJ., fairly tall for a woman, didn't necessarily feel dwarfed in his presence. Her five-foot-eight frame was sheltered in his arms. The solid wall she'd walked into turned out to be a broad chest covered in thin black cotton. Without thinking, C.J. raised a hand and touched. Beneath the T-shirt, she could feel the strength of him flex.

She felt more than heard him draw in a breath.

She had eyes the color of dark chocolate, eyes in which he could see the dawn of civilization; from the pyramids of ancient Egypt to the longing dreams and desires of the special creature called woman. Wes looked into her eyes and felt something in him shift, reconfigure, and settle. Eyes, he'd always read, were the window to a person's soul. This woman's soul was old and proud and passionate.

At her full lips, she wore just a hint of color. The shade enhanced her cinnamon and sugar complexion. Wes held his breath. If that mouth, that gorgeous, gorgeous mouth parted any more, Wes wasn't going to be able to stand it.

Wes had definitely had his share of women but he couldn't remember the last time he'd been so attracted to a woman so fast. He wanted her now and hard and fast. Standing up right here in the street would do. But Wes also knew he couldn't have her. Not now, probably not ever. She'd called him Dark Warrior. She was the one he'd been sent here to protect.

With more will than he thought he possessed, Wes stepped away from her.

"You're the most beautiful man I've ever met."

What was almost a small smile curved his mouth. "Isn't that supposed to be my line?"

C.J. smiled. Before he could stop himself, Wes lifted a hand to caress those perfect lips. This woman's mouth was made for kissing. He wanted to see her lips swollen with the pressure of his own. His thumb, in a whisper of a caress, brushed the side of her mouth. When her lips parted, Wes lowered his head.

Closing his eyes, he sighed. Wes took one deep breath and moved away from her. This woman, no matter how kissable, was off limits to him. There were lines. And this was one he didn't believe in crossing. By law he couldn't cross it. Wes had never mixed business with pleasure and wasn't about to start now in the middle of Main Street in Serenity Falls, North Carolina.

C.J. watched the fleeting expressions cross his face before he dropped a concealing mask over himself. She wanted to know the man under the mask, not the one who now stood before her looking like an unforgiving rock of a mountain. C.J. was intrigued, as she always was by challenges. She liked chameleons because they adapted to their surroundings. C.J. got a feeling that the man standing before her had many of the characteristics of a chameleon.

"What changed your mind?" she asked, sure that he would know exactly what she meant. She didn't regret or apologize for the come on. What would be the point? They were both adults. Even consenting ones. She ignored the little voice in the back of her head reminding her that this constituted one of the things she was supposed to be purging from her system.

Wes took a step back and studied her. One of those string purses women liked so much was draped across her body. The strap divided her breasts. Wes took a deep breath and tried not to focus his attention there. "You called me Dark Warrior. Why?"

Her brows furrowed and she cocked her head. A tiny smile splayed at her mouth. Then with a deliberate sensuality that made Wes ache, she checked him out from the top of his head to his boot-enclosed feet. Her gaze lingered and assessed in some of the places along his body. Wes felt as if he'd been plugged into an electrical outlet. She hadn't touched him but his body felt like she'd run a thousand ostrich feathers over his naked skin.

She licked her lips then smiled coyly at him.

"No reason," she said. Then, with a look that belied her words, "Sorry I ran into you." She paused just long enough to make sure she had his undivided attention. She did.

"I wasn't watching where I was going. See you around."

With that she pulled a Houdini on him. By the time Wes found his way out of the sensual fog that enveloped him, she was nowhere in sight. He scanned the street and shop fronts. No one about even remotely resembled the woman. It was almost as if she'd never been standing in front of him. Wes could hardly be classified as a man given to delusion or illusion. And besides, more than anything else, more than the magic in her eyes, the challenge in her voice, or the sweet honey of her mouth, the very solid erection in his jeans let Wes know the woman had been real.

Now all he had to do was find her again. And make her his.

CHAPTER 3

Careful not to get stuck by the coil spring that had poked its way to the surface of the old plaid couch in her living room, C.J. sat on the edge of the sofa. Her herb garden forgotten, at least for now, she tried to assess her feelings. In addition to the physical work she'd been doing at the house in the last month, she'd been spending quite a bit of time getting in touch with her inner self, a being that had been suppressed for so long that sometimes the hard truths she'd unearthed had been painful lessons in self-identity.

One of the lessons she'd learned about the real C.J. was that "C.J. the reporter" did things so methodically and meticulously that "C.J. the woman" frequently—usually—took third place on the priority list.

C.J. closed her eyes and practiced the deep breathing exercise her older brother had taught her. With each exhale she drew closer to her true self as well as the feelings and emotions coursing through her being. Adrenaline was there. So was desire. No. Desire was too tame a word for what she felt toward the dark warrior. She felt primal and passionate. Primal passion.

She inhaled then exhaled, cleaning out and sorting through her feelings. There also existed an element of fear and danger. Not fear for her physical safety. No. Not that. The threat posed constituted an emotional one. It would be all or nothing with that man.

"Breathe, C.J. Don't forget to breathe."

Inhale, exhale. Desire, passion, fear . . . and peace? Peace? That was an odd addition but just thinking the word soothed her. It fit.

Deep inhale, slow exhale. C.J. slowly opened her eyes. She'd courted danger on the sidewalk today in Serenity Falls. The experience hadn't really diminished any of the progress she'd made so far on this mission to recovery. If she put the man with his solid good looks out of her mind and focused her attention in the right place, everything would be just fine.

"So why does the right place seem to be the backseat of a Harley?"

She didn't have an answer to that, but she did have a solution. Work. She went to her bedroom, changed out of the slacks and blouse she'd worn into town and slipped on a pair of jeans and a lightweight Fisk University sweatshirt. She grabbed all of her supplies, including the gloves that would protect her hands, and headed to the backyard.

Back in his room at Miss Clara Ann's boarding house, Wesley placed a call on a small flip telephone he pulled from his bag.

"Dark Warrior has landed at the desert rendezvous. Recon in progress."

He didn't wait for a reply. Wes flipped the phone off and tucked it back in a black leather backpack. From another satchel he pulled the few clothes he'd traveled with: clean shirts, briefs, socks, moccasins and loafers, two additional pairs of jeans, one blue, the other black like the ones he wore, and an easy wear suit that would need just a little pressing to be ready to roll. He placed a small toiletries kit on the vanity in the bathroom and eyed himself in the mirror.

He ran one large hand over his chin. "You're not losing your touch. This is probably what scared her away, old pal."

Wes pulled off the black T-shirt and reached for a white hand towel draped over a rack on the door. He tossed the towel over his shoulder and turned the faucet on. A quick shave would help him feel more human. Wes grinned at his reflection. Actually, nothing could make him feel more human than the honest male response he'd had to the woman on the street. He liked the fact that she didn't overdo it on the makeup. She wore enough to enhance her God-given assets, high cheekbones, a full mouth, and expressive eyes.

He lathered up his face with shaving cream then began the smooth strokes down his face that would clear away the shadow of the beard. He did, after all, want to make a good impression when he showed up to fill out an application for work at the plant.

Wes wondered what kind of impression he'd made on the woman. He didn't even know her name. After the stop at the factory, he would begin an earnest search for her. But Wes smiled as he cleared away more of the shaving cream from his face.

If she was who he thought she was, she'd be in search of him soon and would likely find him faster than he'd be able to locate her.

The smile became a grin. "Sometimes, you know, Wesley, this job is a whole lot of fun."

Later that day Wes arrived back at Miss Clara Ann's with the satisfaction that he'd secured a job at the recycling plant. He had been somewhat surprised to discover that the company had a human resources department. He'd fully expected to make application at a trailer stuck off to the side of the entrance. He'd anticipated a broken-down step, the stale smell of old coffee and cigarette smoke, and a general order of disarray. What he'd found instead was a coolly efficient and well-run HR office.

"You're going to have to cease with the preconceived notions about small towns, Wesley," he chided himself as he kicked the Harley's stand down in his parking space. "It makes you slack in your thinking."

If the recycling plant had been what he'd expected—like the coal mining companies he grew up with—workers were either hired or rejected on the spot in a rusted-out white trailer. As it stood now, he'd have to wait three days for the HR types to run a drug test, handwriting analysis, driving record, and criminal background check.

He had no doubt that everything would come back clear. It just meant he had some extra time and a weekend to kill. He could get a lot done under the guise of waiting for a job call back.

Wes smiled as he made his way around extensive flower beds to the front door of Miss Clara Ann's. He wondered what *she* did there. And he wondered what her name was. With her exotic eyes and arched brows, the woman he'd met on the street today could be an Eve or maybe a Zora. She'd have a strong feminine name. Of that he was sure. He wondered if she had one of the Afrocentric names that had been popular in the late sixties and early seventies. Maybe she was a Nia or an Ashanti.

He guessed her to be in her mid- to late twenties, five foot eight, one twenty five to one thirty, size 10, B cup that was doing its best to spill into C.

Wes grinned and took the steps two at a time.

"Share the humor," a light feminine voice said.

Wes turned. His mind had been so focused on the woman he'd met on the street that he'd almost run down a woman at the door who held an armful of books.

She tried to extend her hand but thought better of it. "Hi. My name's Margaret. Are you a resident here, too?"

"Yes. Let me get the door for you." Wes pulled open the door and picked up a bag near her feet. "Is this yours as well?"

Margaret looked over her shoulder. "Oh, yes. But don't pick it up. It's quite heavy."

Wes smiled and hefted the bag in his hand for her to see.

"Ooohh, so strong," she cooed.

The woman made her way to the front parlor. Wes rolled his eyes and followed her through the Florida room. Then he raised an eyebrow and reassessed. Her back side might be a bit broad for his tastes, but she sure knew how to work that walk and make a man take notice.

He followed her to the front parlor where Miss Clara Ann sat in a wooden rocker with a cup of tea.

"Oh. There you are, Margaret. I was sitting here figuring you wouldn't make it in tonight. Come here girl and let me take a look at ya."

Wes placed Margaret's bag at the foot of the stairs then found his arms filled with books.

"Would you hold these for a second? Thanks," Margaret called back to him, already on her way across the room to greet Miss Clara Ann. Wes raised both brows at the woman's familiarity with him. Did she think he was the hired help? There was nothing worse in Wes's book than bourgeois black folk. He'd had enough to deal with trying to cope with his mother's airs. Just the thought of Eileen, the woman who gave birth to him but could never be called a mother, made him frown. He stared after Margaret who was now kissing Miss Clara Ann on each cheek.

Wes unceremoniously dumped the books on the closest step then leaned back on the banister with one booted foot resting on a step behind him.

"Oh, good, I sees you done met Wesley. He joined us just today. Come on in baby and get a proper introduction. This here is my niece, Margaret. She come to stay here in Serenity Falls for a little spell."

When he hesitated, Miss Clara Ann prodded him. "Come on now, baby."

He didn't particularly want to be rude, at least not to Miss Clara Ann. Wes pushed himself away from the stairwell and sauntered across the room.

He stuck out a hand in greeting to Margaret even as his brows drew together. There was something vaguely familiar about this woman. "Nice to meet you."

"It's all my pleasure," she assured him.

"Margaret here hasn't managed to snag herself a husband yet," Miss Clara Ann said. "And she's almost thirty years old."

"Aunt Clara!"

"So I told her to come on down here. We got lots of eligible bachelors. What about you Wesley, you hitched up?"

Wes swallowed a smile at the blatant matchmaking but ignored the curious hopeful expression on Margaret's face. "No, ma'am. Can't say that I am. I like being footloose and fancy free."

Miss Clara Ann grunted. "Hmmph, that's what you say now. You just ain't found the right woman. The right one'll change that thinking in a flash."

"Aunt Clara, which room is mine?"

"Don't be trying to change the subject on me, girl. Ya'll two young folks, both of you single, standing here looking like you don't know which way is up. I tell you. You would think that after almost seventy-five years on this earth that I could find a little peace. But I can see that ain't to be yet. My work is still cut out for me."

"Aunt Clara, please."

Wes grinned. Miss Clara Ann had gumption. She'd obviously been a beauty in her day. Her hair was more white than gray, and her mahogany skin, while it had a few lines, still shone with youthful vigor. She'd probably spent her whole life meddling in other people's business. And he'd bet the Harley that she would have been a pistol in her prime.

Wes glanced at Margaret and actually felt sorry for the woman. With Miss Clara Ann as an aunt, Margaret would probably find herself marching down the aisle to a husband whether she wanted one or not. Wes knew one thing for sure, though: He wasn't the man for her.

With her pert nose and bow mouth, Margaret was attractive in her own right. Wes, however, had always been attracted to the sensual Earth Mothers over some of the more traditional standards of beauty. The face of the woman on the street came to him and Wesley smiled.

"You're embarrassing him and me," Margaret said, waving a hand in Wes's direction.

Miss Clara Ann sucked her teeth and pushed back to get the rocker going. "I think I'll put you right next door to young Wesley. Take room four, Margaret."

"Aunt Clara, that's really not necessary. I'll go up to the third floor."

"Cain't do that. I got an artist living up there. He's in residence. Says he gets his inspiration out on the widow's walk. I think he's been talking to the pigeons too much. Ain't seen a nary painting from him and he's been here four months. Pays on time though and don't cause no trouble, so he can talk to the pigeons all he wants."

Wes realized something, something that should have hit him when he first met Miss Clara Ann. Here was a woman who probably knew every person in town and all their relatives back to the day the ship arrived from the motherland. Maybe instead of courting Margaret as Miss Clara Ann seemed so intent on him doing, he'd court Miss Clara Ann herself.

He smiled. "If you two ladies would excuse me, I have a little work to do." With that, Wes bent low, kissed Miss Clara Ann on the cheek then headed out the parlor and up to his rented room.

From a pink plastic water pot with a sunflower emblazoned on its side, C.J. gently watered the peppermint sprigs she'd just planted. She patted the rich soil then sat back on her haunches to admire her work.

"It looks good, Jan."

C.J. looked up, responding more to a voice than to the name. She was still trying to get used to the fact that she'd told people her name was Jan. When she'd closed on the house deal and signed her name on the paperwork she'd almost written her full formal name, Cassandra Ja'Niece Mayview. Jan was totally foreign but it was the first thing that came to mind when someone had asked her name. Remembering her fake last name was a little easier. Langley had been her mother's maiden name. C.J. didn't really care who Jan Langley was. Her purpose for being in Serenity Falls was to discover who C.J. Mayview was.

Her new friend Amber Baldwin stood near the cracked bird fountain in CJ.'s backyard. The toddler on her hip gurgled and swatted at a butterfly.

"Hi, Amber," C.J. said, dusting her hands on her jeans. She tugged the gardening gloves off and got up to meet Amber.

"Hope you don't mind I came on back here. I didn't get an answer at the front door."

"Not a problem. It's good to see you and the baby."

C.J. wasn't real sure how to deal with little people, particularly ones this small. Children mystified her, always had. C.J. had never had a single maternal instinct in her. Maybe that's what her problem was. She reached a hand out and offered the baby a finger. The child tugged the finger to his mouth.

"Frank Jr. stop that," Amber scolded as she gently batted at the boy's hands.

C.J. took the opportunity to recapture her hand and finger, then surreptitiously wiped her finger on her jeans.

"Do you mind if we stopped over? I thought we'd take a short walk and get some air and when I looked up, we were on your street."

"I was just about to take a breather for a minute."

C.J. sat on the bottom step. Amber put the toddler down and watched as he stumbled across the grass to chase another butterfly.

Amber settled on a step where she could keep watch over the baby. "Do you mind if he runs around?"

"Amber, what I mind is you always asking 'Do you mind?' No, I don't mind. It's grass. Kids are supposed to play in it. Just say what's on your mind. You don't have to preface everything you say or do by getting someone else's permission. You're your own woman."

Amber looked away and then back at C.J. But when she spoke, she couldn't meet C.J.'s eyes.

"That's what I like so much about you, Jan. You're independent and free thinking. Me, well, all I've got is Frankie and Frank Jr." She glanced at her son who was busy inspecting the trunk of one of the two apple trees in the far corner of the backyard. "I was brought up to believe a woman's place was in her house, minding her man and her babies."

C.J. rolled her eyes. "Hmmph."

Amber smiled shyly. "See, that's what I mean. I don't know what you did before you came to Serenity Falls, but me, well, the only time I've ever seen any of that women's empowerment stuff is on TV and everybody knows those people aren't real."

As she'd done in every previous conversation with Amber and anyone else who'd asked, C.J. ignored the questions about her past. With Amber, it was simpler. The woman never asked a direct question. That alone nearly drove C.J. crazy. The woman's self-esteem was nonexistent. Amber was an attractive woman but you'd never know it by the way she carried herself.

The woman's thick dark hair was combed straight back and secured with a headband. She never wore any makeup, not even a hint of color on her mouth. C.J. was willing to grant that some of it had to do with having an eighteen-month-old on her hands. But still . . .

"Amber, a lot of women are out there with successful careers and family lives. Some of them are burned out now because for so long they've been burning the candle at both ends. But at least they can say they made the effort." That was about as close as C.J. would get to explaining her previous life.

The young woman shook her head. "Maybe there was a time when I thought I could be one of those women but now . . ." Amber shrugged. "Remember that old commercial about women bringing home the bacon and frying it up in a pan? Frankie and I saw that on one of those funniest video shows a little while back. He said that's what's wrong with America now: Too many women are out there trying to be men."

That did it. C.J. had never met Frankie Baldwin but she was sure she didn't like the man. He'd crushed all the potential out of Amber just like his son was about to crush a petunia C.J. had planted. C.J. frowned at the toddler. Then she inhaled and exhaled. Relax. It was just a flower. Definitely not the end of the world. She gave herself points for being calm—another of the lessons she'd been spending time on in the last month. If Frank Jr. crushed a flower, she could plant another. If Frank Sr. further crushed the spirit of his wife, that might not be as easy to replace.

C.J. looked at Amber and smiled.

"What? What're you up to, Jan?" Amber asked. "That smile looks devilish to me."

"Oh, nothing. I was just thinking about all the projects I have to do around the house." C.J. slapped both hands on her jeans-clad thighs. "How about we break for cookies and lemonade?"

"Sounds good to me."

C.J. held the screen door while Amber collected the baby from a half-planted flower bed at the foot of the back porch steps. She followed Amber and Frank Jr. into the house.

C.J. had added another item to her list of projects: Amber Baldwin.

* * *

The first thing C.J. noticed later that afternoon as she approached the grocery store was a black Harley-Davidson motorcycle in the lot. She wondered if it belonged to him. It looked like the one she'd seen earlier in the day. But before she had the chance to conjure an image of the dark warrior and match him with a motorcycle, a commotion near the entrance of the store got her attention.

Several people crowded around a person on the sidewalk. C.J.'s reporter instincts kicked in as she approached the throng. She scanned the crowd, getting a feel for place, time, and people, storing information as if she were taking a snapshot. A man in dark pants and an electric blue jacket with white racing stripes peeped around metal grocery carts lined up near the front of the store. He looked up, saw C.J. watching him, and ducked into the store. A little boy about seven or eight tugged on his mother's sleeve, pointing to the video store next to the supermarket. The mother ignored him, and like the rest of the crowd, hovered near to see what the fuss was all about.

"Give the man some air," someone said. "How can he breathe with all you folks in his face."

"Someone call 9-1-1," a woman called out.

"Hey, mister, is he gonna be okay?"

C.J. edged forward and around a heavyset woman who was trying to get a better view.

"What happened?" C.J. asked.

"Mr. Parker was standing there and then he just collapsed," the woman said. She turned to get a look at who she was talking to. "Oh, hi there, Miz Langley. Remember me, Bettina, from the bakery? You asked me about biscotti."

C.J. smiled and nodded. She'd remembered to remember that her name was Jan Langley. "Hi, yes. I'm going to stop by for more of those brownies of yours." She'd settled for a brownie with her coffee because biscotti, like bread machines and cappuccino, were foreign in this small town.

"Come on over. I always have brownies," the baker said before turning her attention back to the scene.

The shrill wail of an ambulance's siren parted the crowd. People moved aside as the emergency medical technicians leaped from the ambulance to tend to the fallen man.

When the crowd parted, C.J. got a good look at the victim and at the person on the ground administering CPR.

The dark warrior was saving a man's life.

CHAPTER 4

C.J. stepped aside to let the ambulance attendants wheel a gurney next to the fallen man but her fascinated gaze remained glued on the dark warrior who breathed the breath of life. She watched him breathe and push and count, one, two, three.

One of the emergency technicians got across from the man and picked up the rhythm of the cardiopulmonary resuscitation procedure.

"Breathe, dammit. Breathe," she heard the dark warrior command as he continued the maneuver. A few moments later, the man sputtered and coughed and the crowd sighed in relief.

In minutes, the attendants had the man secured on the gurney and headed into the ambulance. C.J. offered up a quick prayer as she watched the vehicle race down the street. When she turned back her heart beat faster than usual.

Used to the adrenaline rushes that came with the excitement of chasing a good news story, C.J. knew that the moment, watching a man's life being saved, could cause that adrenaline. Ever honest with herself though, she knew what she was feeling had little to do with the moment. It was the man.

He sat on the curb wiping his face with the tail of his T-shirt as people patted him on the back.

"Nice job there, mister," a man said. "Your quick thinking probably saved old Jesse Parker."

"I'm sure glad you knew how to do that," a woman with a yellow scarf tied over hair rollers told him. "I've seen it on those rescue programs on

TV, but now I'm gonna take a class to learn how to do what you did. You never know when you might need to do it. I sure hope Mr. Parker is gonna be okay."

"Hey, mister? That was really cool. Are you okay? You need some water or something?" a teen asked.

As other people jostled forward to congratulate the man on his heroic deed, C.J. saw a photographer snap a picture then drop the camera back on his chest. The photographer scribbled something in a notebook and asked a question. C.J. pegged the young man as somewhere in his mid- to late twenties, probably the local reporter working double-time as staff photographer.

A woman in an apron emblazoned with the store logo pressed something in her hand and nodded toward the man. C.J. looked down. Bottled water.

"Would you give that to the man, please," the woman asked.

C.J. looked from the plastic bottle in her hand to the dark warrior who was rising from the curb. A dark trail of perspiration dampened the blue T-shirt. C.J. wanted to trace that trail and lick up the moisture of his skin. He tugged the shirt down and tucked it into his pants. Her eyes followed the movement then dipped lower to assess. He was a man's man and C.J. liked every inch of what she was seeing. When she'd gotten to be so shallow she wasn't really sure. The outside wrapping didn't ensure that the inside was any good. But, Lord, the outside sure made her want to explore the rest. Besides, she figured, a biker who does CPR can't be all bad.

"Sir, hello. My name is Kenny Sheldon. I'm a reporter for the *Serenity Falls Gazette.* People are telling me you're a hero. What happened here?"

Wesley looked at the reporter and sighed. All he'd wanted was to get a quart of milk and some chips and stare at the packages of cigarettes. He hadn't bargained on this. And had this guy taken his photograph?

"Nothing really. I did what anyone would do."

The reporter chuckled. "Modest I see. What's your name?"

Wes eyed the camera. "I'd really rather not be in the paper if you don't mind."

"Oh, this. I just got a good scene shot of all the people talking to you."

Wesley sighed then looked to his left in the direction the ambulance had taken. His gaze connected with a serenely beautiful woman who stared back at him. It was her! She was standing right in front of him.

"Hi. Here's some water for you," C.J. said. "A store employee brought it out for you."

Wes accepted the bottle, twisted the cap, and took a deep swallow. His eyes never left hers. She was exquisite, just as beautiful as she'd seemed earlier in the day.

"Thank you."

"Anytime," she said.

"I'm Wes Donovan," he said, extending his hand to her.

The reporter jotted the information down.

"Nice to meet you. That was a great thing you did here. You probably saved that man's life."

"If it meant the opportunity to meet you, then that's two good things that will have come out of this. You pulled a disappearing act on me earlier."

She shrugged and smiled. Wes was lost. "Listen," he said. "I was just on my way into the store to grab a couple of things. How can I thank you?" he said, holding up the bottle of water.

"I told you, it was from the store."

"Then how can I get to know you better?"

"Why?"

"Why?" he asked back. "Well, lots of reasons." Smooth skin, pretty brown eyes. A mouth that begged to be kissed. Full breasts. And hips and thighs that promised a dance of delight.

She folded one arm over the other and rested her chin in her hand. "Well, I'm waiting," she said.

Wes loved a challenge. "For what?"

"One of those reasons."

Wes laughed out loud. "You have a beautiful smile."

She gave him a look that said You-could-have-come-up-with-something-better-than-that.

"Thank you," she said, acknowledging the compliment. "I'm here to pick up a couple of items. Yogurt and cottage cheese."

Wes couldn't keep the grimace from his face.

"Not your taste, huh?" she asked. "The grocery has lots of selections. There are other things you can eat."

Wes knew better than to mention where that comment took his thinking.

"Mr. Donovan, may I have a few minutes? I promise I won't take up much of your time."

Wes had forgotten about the reporter. "No, thanks. I decline Sheldon. These folks out here can tell you what happened."

With that, Wes took her elbow and guided her into the grocery store.

C.J. picked up a small basket. Wes did the same.

"Why didn't you talk to that reporter? He seemed like a nice enough guy."

"I like to keep a low profile."

C.J. wondered why but let the obvious follow-up question go. Her reporting days were over. She'd joined the ranks of regular citizens. They headed in the direction of the dairy products aisle. C.J. picked over the yogurt, checking expiration dates and frowning at the flavors offered.

"You know, that stuff'll kill you. Too healthy," Wes said.

C.J. selected several containers of strawberry, blueberry, and raspberry yogurt and put them in her basket. "Have you ever even eaten yogurt?"

Wes shook his head and regarded her. "Nope. Just like chitlins, don't like the smell of it. I'll stick to frozen yogurt. At least it looks like the ice cream it's pretending to be."

C.J. laughed. "Yogurt is not like chitlins."

"How would you know? You've probably never eaten a chitlin in your life."

He was right but she wasn't about to admit it. "What do you know?" She pulled a container of strawberry yogurt from the dairy shelf. "Here, try this," she said, putting it in his basket. "It's blended yogurt so it'll taste and look more like the frozen yogurt you're used to."

She moved a few steps down and picked up a container of cottage cheese. "Why'd you say that?"

Wes followed her. He placed his basket on top of the sour cream containers. "Say what?"

"That I'd probably never eaten chitlins."

"You were standing there grumbling because the store doesn't carry apricot yogurt. A woman who eats apricot yogurt just doesn't strike me a chitlins and cornbread type."

C.J. was insulted but she couldn't quite put her finger on the reason why. "And you are?"

"If they're cleaned and cooked right. Mama Lo makes the best. But it took her a long, long time to get me to taste 'em."

C.J. smiled, forgiving. "Then you should give yogurt a chance like you gave the chitlins. Who's Mama Lo?"

"She's my . . ." Wes paused for a moment. "She's my mother," he finished.

C.J. looked him over. She'd bet his parents were striking people. To produce a son who rivaled the Greek gods, they'd have to have some good genes. His bronzed skin was rich. She wondered if he'd gotten his height from his father, from Mama Lo, or from some other ancestor. He'd shaved since the morning. C.J. couldn't decide which she liked better, clean shaven or the touch of whiskers. Whisker burns came to mind and she smiled, feminine and mysterious as she engaged in just a touch of fantasy about this man and certain parts of her own body. He would lick slow and easy, like savoring in ever tightening swirls, a delicious ice cream cone.

"What're you thinking?"

"Uh, just a few errant thoughts."

C.J. looked in her basket. "It was nice chatting with you. I'd better run." She turned to go, but he captured her arm. White heat licked through her at the contact. C.J. sucked in her breath and looked at him.

"Pardon me," he said.

Before C.J. could ask why, his mouth closed over hers. She felt him take the small grocery cart from her hands and then his hands framed her face.

Desire rushed forward and reason scampered away. C.J., bold in her own yearning, stepped into his embrace. She opened her mouth and Wes accepted the gift. His lips, hard yet soft, teased her, filled her, claimed her.

A hot ache consumed her, and C.J. realized she'd never before been this hungry. Nor had she ever been as conscious of her own femininity as she was in Wes's arms. She felt small, delicate.

As Wes roused her passion, his own grew stronger. He pulled her closer to the erection that was filling his jeans. She swiveled her hips and Wes groaned. His mouth moved from hers, to her neck where he rained tiny kisses along her earlobes.

A polite clearing of the throat brought them back to the surface. C.J. blushed and stepped back. She fought for breath but failed when she realized his gaze was riveted on her breasts, her hard nipples telling him exactly what her body wanted.

"Mouth to mouth resuscitation is your forte I see," an amused male voice said. The man stuck out his hand to Wes. "Hi, I'm Rusty York, the store manager. I was in the back when the heroics were going on. My people told me what you did. Thank you."

"No problem," Wes said.

C.J. retrieved her basket from the sour cream display where Wes had put it. "I'll see you around." With that, she took off at a fast pace down the aisle.

"Hey, wait a minute," Wes called after C.J. "Be right back," he told the store manager.

With a few long strides he caught up with her. "Why are you running away from me?"

"I don't know you," she pointed out. "You could be a killer or a rapist for all I know."

Wes cocked his head. "I'm not and you don't believe any of those things. I'm a good guy. Ask my mom."

C.J. couldn't stop the smile. "I'm sure your Mama Lo would vouch for you."

"Have dinner with me."

"Excuse me?"

Wes lifted a hand, one gentle finger traced her lips. "After that wonderful dessert I thought we should follow it up with dinner."

C.J. laughed. The sound of her voice rushed through Wes like wildfire. He stifled a groan.

"That's the best pickup line I've heard in a while."

"What time would you like me to pick you up?" he asked.

"Seven-thirty." She gave him her address then left him standing in the aisle alone.

Wes shook his head as he watched her retreat. Mercy. The Lord knew what he was doing when he put that package together. Wes turned to head back to the store manager and the milk he needed to buy. He added condoms to the list of items to pick up.

It wasn't until later he realized he didn't even know her name—and that she just might be off limits to him.

CHAPTER 5

Amber Baldwin was frightened.

"Frankie, don't talk like that. You scare me when you talk like that."

Amber went to Frank Jr.'s playpen and lifted the toddler in her arms. She held the baby, shielding it from his father's ranting.

"Look at you," Frankie smirked. "You're gonna turn him into a pansy boy the way you smother the kid. Let 'im be. God, I tell you, Amber Faye, you are worse than your mama. No wonder that low-life brother of yours is a . . ."

"Frankie, you said you weren't gonna talk about that anymore." Amber hugged the baby closer to her. It pained her when he spoke ill of her family, a family he would no longer allow her to see or communicate with.

Frank glanced over his shoulder then quickly peeked out their open living room curtains. "Yeah, well, I'm not. I was just using that as an example."

He walked over to the telephone on the crate-style end table. Amber watched as he twisted open the two ends and looked under the speaking and listening apparatus. She was used to the obsessive ritual her husband had. He believed that "they" were listening in and trying to catch him. Who "they" were, she'd never been able to get out of Frank. But the one thing she'd learned and learned well, was fear. Fear and living on the run.

They'd lived in Serenity Falls the longest. Eight months. Long enough to put down a few roots, make a few friends. But Frank always cautioned her against friends. "Friends turn on you," he always said. Amber thought about Jan Langley. Jan wouldn't turn on her. She was too nice. Frank didn't know about Jan, and Amber intended to keep it that way. If she got too friendly with anyone, Frank would just pick them up to move again.

When they met in Las Vegas two years ago, Amber had been a cocktail waitress at a casino on the strip. Frank Baldwin was a regular with a wad of cash and a serious line of credit. Three months after meeting him, they were married in one of the classier wedding chapels. Frank treated her like a queen for the first few months. They lived on champagne and pâté and he lavished her and her family with expensive gifts. Then he said they would winter on the Florida coast.

Amber had never been to Florida and was excited about the trip. But when they arrived, they didn't stay at a fancy hotel or even a nice house. Frank drove up to a dilapidated trailer in a trailer park and said they would stay there for a while. When she'd questioned him about it, he said he wanted to "see how the other half lived."

That trailer had been the worst but not the last one they lived in. They'd been observing the other half for some time now, from roach-infested trailers to rundown apartments in not-so-good neighborhoods. Amber was more than ready to return to the lifestyle they'd known in Vegas.

Amber shifted Frank Jr. to her hip and followed Frankie into the kitchen of their apartment. "Frankie, what kind of trouble are you in? Let's talk about this together. Maybe together we can come up with a solution."

Frank turned from his inspection of the telephone on the kitchen counter. "I told you, princess. I'm not in any kind of trouble."

"Then why do you always check the phones? They're the same every day. Nobody comes in here."

Frank replaced the receiver and walked up to her. He pulled her chin in his hand and planted a quick kiss on her lips. "Hang tough with me, Amber Faye. One more month and we'll be home free."

"Da," the baby said.

"Hey, little man," Frank answered, lifting the baby from Amber's arms. "What say you and me watch a ball game while Momma fixes us up some supper?"

The baby grinned. Frank patted Amber on the behind as he left the kitchen. "Hurry it up, too, babe. I'm hungry."

Amber went to the sink to rinse off the chicken she was going to fry for dinner. She ran cold water on the poultry then turned to stare at the telephone so recently checked out by Frankie. One more month and they'd be home free.

At Miss Clara Ann's house, Margaret reviewed her strategy. First she'd lure her prey, then she'd reel him in with teasing promises and whispered entreaties. She knew she could count on Aunt Clara Ann to both wittingly and unwittingly assist her in her plan.

Margaret smiled into the bureau mirror in her room. She spritzed herself with a light, flirtatious cologne and freshened up her lipstick. She loved these games, loved the thrill of the hunt. And this time, her prize would be a big one.

Kenny Sheldon typed the last paragraph of his story, then sat back and smiled. He'd done a good job. And he hadn't had a lot to work with. The eyewitness accounts were good. He just wished that the hero of the day, Wes Donovan, had been more willing to talk.

Kenny picked up the telephone and called the nurse's station at County General.

"Hi there," he said when he got someone. "This is Kenny Sheldon over at the *Gazette.* I was just calling to check on Mr. Parker's condition one more time before I turn my story in." Kenny listened for a moment then, "Sure, I'll hold."

While waiting for the nurse's report, Kenny picked up the black and white print of the scene at the grocery store. He nodded, pleased with his work. He'd captured the moment: a weary rescuer sitting on the curb with his head down being comforted by townsfolk.

"That Donovan sure is a big one," he observed, not for the first time. For a moment earlier that day, Kenny had been almost certain the modest hero who had to be about six four, two twenty, was about to land him one in the face. Thank goodness that woman was there.

Kenny had seen her around town once or twice. She was pretty and for the most part seemed to stick to herself. If he himself had felt more comfortable around beautiful women, he may have asked her out on a date.

"It's not too late, Clark Kent," he said, then smiled to himself. "Oh, yes. I'm still here," he said into the receiver. "Guarded but stable. Got it. Thanks a bunch. You have a good evening."

Kenny replaced the receiver, pushed his horn-rimmed glasses up then updated his story, made a print out of it, and shipped it to his editor. The *Gazette* had finally joined the twentieth century with four computers. Kenny had one, the newspaper's features reporter had one, the editor had one, and the layout guy in the backroom used a Mac to do the page design.

Kenny Sheldon was biding his time. He'd been on staff at the *Serenity Falls Gazette* for a year and a half. He'd started as a correspondent writing up the county high school sports stories. Now he was a full-time sports and news reporter. He figured he'd stay one more year then make his break to the big time. What he needed was a big story that the editor could put out on the wires with the byline Kenneth J. Sheldon. But nothing big ever happened in Serenity Falls, North Carolina. Even though the town could boast more than twenty-five thousand residents, it remained small town U.S.A.

Kenny sighed. Maybe he'd give the *Gazette* only another six months instead of a year.

C.J. opened her front door to a smiling Yancey Yardley. If ever there were a made up name, Yancey had it. But time and again, he swore on his "dear departed mother's soul, bless her heart," that that was the name he'd been given at birth.

"Yancey, what brings you here, tonight?"

"Just passing through, so to speak," he said.

C.J. laughed. Yancey lived on the other side of town, in the opposite direction of the established little street C.J. lived on. "Um hmm," she said.

If Yancey was waiting for an invite in, he'd be disappointed tonight. He obviously was coming straight from work; he still wore the telltale blue shirt with the plant seal at the breast. The matching pants completed the uniform. Yancey, with his blue eyes, short afro, deep tan, and engaging smile, reminded her of singer Tom Jones in his prime. Normally she liked shooting the breeze with the truck driver. Yancey offered a perspective on the town that C.J. had been unable to get anywhere else.

But tonight she was keyed up and anxious about her date with Wes Donovan. C.J. had never been one to let grass grow under her feet when it came to a man she'd like to get to know better. She still hadn't decided what to wear. But before she could do that, she had to get rid of Yancey, no easy feat if he was in one of his usual talkative moods.

"Come on, now, Jan . . ."

C.J.'s smile faltered a bit at the name.

"You know I take this route home every night."

"Whatever you say, Yancey," she answered. "What's up though? I'm kind of in a hurry."

Yancey shifted his feet and stepped aside. He hefted up four cardboard boxes. "The rose bushes you special ordered came in. I was over at the lawn and garden shop picking up some crab grass killer. Mrs. Charleston was telling me about your pretty roses. I mentioned I was headed over this way and voila! Personal delivery."

"That was sweet of you. Why don't you bring them this way."

C.J. opened the door wider and followed Yancey.

"Where do you want them?"

"Kitchen counter will do. I want to read the directions first."

Yancey did as he was bid.

"Thanks so much," she told him.

Yancey eyed the cookie jar on the counter. He'd somehow gotten the notion that C.J. cooked. C.J.'s idea of cooking was nuking restaurant leftovers. "No cookies, Yancey. But I do have some brownies from Bettina's Bakery. Picked them up fresh this afternoon."

C.J. offered him the waxed bag.

"Don't mind if I do. Hey, did I ever tell you about the time—"

C.J. cut him off at the pass. "Yancey, I'm really running late. We can talk maybe tomorrow."

"Oh, yeah. You did say you were in a hurry. Where you headed?"

There were some things C.J. detested about small town life. This was one of them: why everybody assumed they should know everything about you.

"Out."

Yancey looked hurt. C.J. felt bad. She'd never been really good at subtleties. She left those things for people like her brother, Robinson, who both enjoyed and was good at the art of the nuance.

"Yancey, I'm sorry. I didn't mean to be rude. Thank you for bringing the rose bushes over. Have another brownie. Forgive me?"

Yancey grinned. His blue eyes sparkled. "No harm, no foul, Jan. I'd better be going." He stuck his hand in the waxed bag and pulled out another brownie. "Bettina makes the best," he said.

C.J. followed him to the front door. Yancey pushed the screen door open and stepped out on the porch. "Hey, did you hear about old man Jesse Parker? Had a heart attack or something right outside the grocery today. They said some guy on a motorcycle stopped and gave him CPR."

C.J. nodded. "Yeah, I was down there today."

"I sure hope Mr. Parker's gonna be okay. He's a nice old man. Well, you have a good night. Let me know when those pretty roses of yours bloom. I'd like to see them."

"I will. You have a good evening, too."

Finally he was gone. C.J. sighed. All of this good will and small talk was draining. People in the city just sort of ignored you. C.J. was discovering that perhaps that wasn't so bad after all.

She went to the kitchen to look at the clock on the stove. She had less than half an hour to get dressed for her dinner date with Wes Donovan.

C.J. looked at the rose bush boxes marked FRAGILE—LIVING. They could wait. Getting dressed couldn't.

Since she wasn't sure where they were going, she opted for an outfit that could pass for dressy or casual: a silky loose burnt orange shift with a black miniskirt. C.J. thought her legs were her best feature, not that anyone in her former life would know that. She'd never been a power suit type, preferring loose, casual clothing, usually slacks, designed for comfort rather than style.

She plucked from a jumbled pile of jewelry a cowrie shell necklace. She wrapped the necklace over her right wrist several times to form a five-layered bracelet. She found a pair of funky earrings designed from cowrie shells and put them in her ears.

Adeptly applying makeup so it looked like she wasn't wearing any, C.J. finished dressing just as the doorbell rang. She opted against a purse or bag. She slipped her driver's license, some "just-in-case" cash, and house key in a slim skirt pocket and went to the door.

Wes Donovan looked good enough to eat. The bad boy image personified, he wore a black shirt, black slacks, and black boots. If he didn't carry it so well she may have made a comment about being a Johnny Cash wanna-be. The black clothing is where the Johnny Cash resemblance stopped though. If she were to hazard a guess, she'd figure that in addition to the African influence, Wes Donovan had more than a little Native American and Mediterranean blood flowing in him. His dark skin was flawless, his facial features hard, like she suspected all the rest of him would be. His thick brows hooded eyes that seemed to undress her as she stood in the doorway.

"Hi. You look great," he said.

"You're not so shabby either."

"Hungry?" he asked.

C.J. looked him over. Wes took a step forward.

"Um hmm," she just about purred.

He chuckled, the sound a rumbling like thunder in the distance. "How about some more dessert before we go to dinner?"

He pulled her into his arms. His lips were hard and searching, hot and searing. But before C.J. could get her arms up and around his broad back, Wes stepped away.

"Let's go before I get some other ideas," he said.

Oddly disappointed, yet at the same time pleasantly surprised, C.J. locked her front door, a habit she couldn't quite break. When she turned to follow him she met the wall of his chest. He braced her so she didn't stumble.

"I don't even know your name," he pointed out.

C.J. had a choice. She could tell him the truth or she could lie the same way she'd been doing with everyone she met in Serenity Falls. For some reason, the simple lie didn't seem so simple and she couldn't quite roll it off her tongue as she'd learned to do in the last month. She looked into the face of this man and knew that to lie to him would be like lying to herself. Funny thing, though, she'd been lying to herself about so many things for so long that that no longer seemed like a sin; it was just more of the masquerade she'd perfected to a science.

In the end, caution won out. She'd come too far to blow it all now and just for a piece of a hard body.

"Jan Langley," she mumbled.

Wes looked at her oddly before heading down the walkway and to the gate. "You know, it's a funny thing about names. I would have bet money that you had a strong, Earth Mother name."

Affronted, C.J. fired back, "What's wrong with Jan?" It was, after all, her middle name . . . sort of.

Wes opened the gate and let her walk through it before him. "You could use a paint job on this," he absently observed. Then, answering her question, "Nothing. It just doesn't seem to fit. You're dark and mysterious. I guess I was expecting something like Eve or Zora."

C.J. smiled. "I love her stuff."

Wes lifted a brow. "Zora Neale Hurston? Yeah, I like the short stories better than some of the longer work. But the autobiography *Dust Tracks on a Road* is probably my favorite."

C.J. was surprised . . . and well, surprised: a bad boy biker who was familiar with the writing of a black feminist author who lived before her time. She half expected him to next tell her that he had a Ph.D. in anthropology and was fluent in Mandarin Chinese. She didn't bother to ask though. With her interviewing skills, honed over the years as a beat reporter, she knew she'd know everything she wanted to know about Wes Donovan by the end of the evening.

The Harley-Davidson was propped up at her curb.

Wes looked from the bike to C.J. in the short skirt and black pumps. "Hmm."

"Not a problem," she said stepping up to the bike.

"You want to drive your car?" he asked.

"Nope. I'll hang on to you real tight. I've always wanted to ride on the back of a Harley."

Wes grinned as he handed her his helmet. He hopped on the bike then turned to see that C.J. got settled. "I like tight," he said.

"I'll just bet you do."

With that, Wes took off.

CHAPTER 6

He felt a twinge of guilt. She was obviously someone with something to hide. Weren't they all? Every person in the government's Witness Protection Program had something to hide. He wondered what secrets Jan Langley held and who she'd been before being relocated to Serenity Falls.

Then again, Wes figured, maybe she was what she looked like, a woman living alone in a small town. But Wes had been a Deputy U.S. Marshal too long to believe that. He'd ruled out the possibility that she was his own contact. He was here to assess the alleged breach of security on a relocated witness. That didn't mean that there was just one protected and relocated witness in the town. For all he knew, Jan could be one of many. She acted like a woman with a lot of secrets.

The secrecy and need-to-know status of many of the Marshals Service's cases made it impossible for him to know the details of every file. And in this case, Holloway had been unnecessarily vague on just who Wes was to be meeting. Since the recycling plant was the largest employer in the area, it stood to reason that his guy worked there.

As for Jan Langley, he'd drop a few well-placed clues throughout the evening. She'd open up before the night was over and he'd know what he wanted to know. In the meantime, it was hard, pun intended, he thought to himself, to concentrate on guilt when her soft hands were wrapped around him and surreptitiously inching lower. If she kept that up, he was going to have to find a hotel in the town and take care of business. But then again, if her hands didn't do him in it would be those smooth thighs flush against him.

The bike was covering some ground. Behind him, Jan let fly a whoop and a holler.

Up front, Wes grinned. He turned back to take a quick look at her then put his attention back on the road. "Having fun?"

She pressed closer to him and held on tighter as he made a sharp left turn. "Awesome."

A few minutes later, they pulled into the parking lot of McCall's Restaurant. C.J. had heard good things about the food and had passed by the place several times but had never had a meal there. Wes cut the engine on the bike. C.J. got off then tugged at her skirt.

Wes didn't miss the motion or the fact that she'd done that with more grace than many women would have mustered. He settled the bike then joined Jan, following her with his hand at her waist. Maybe a beer would cool him off a bit.

At Miss Clara Ann's, Margaret made an entrance into the dining room. The low-cut blouse was provocative but not too daring. A man at the table with Aunt Clara stood up when she walked in.

"Good evening," he said.

"Hello. Hi Aunt Clara."

The man pulled a chair out at the table and helped her take her seat.

"Thank you."

Miss Clara Ann shook her head. "You're too late. He left 'bout half an hour ago," she said with no additional explanation. "Garrison, I'd like you to meet my niece, Margaret. Margaret, this is Garrison, the artist I was telling you about who's staying up on the third floor."

Margaret smiled and managed to hide her disappointment. She'd heard him come in his room and had timed her arrival in the dining room so he'd be about midway through his meal when she arrived. Instead, here was some artist who was just starting on a salad.

"Are you visiting?" he asked.

Margaret managed not to roll her eyes. Of course she was visiting. This guy had probably been breathing too many paint fumes. "Yes, I'll be here a few weeks," she said sweetly then helped herself to a small portion of salad from the large bowl on the table.

As usual, Aunt Clara had prepared a big spread. Ham and okra with mashed sweet potatoes, corn on the cob, and spoon bread. She'd have to make sure to go jogging in the morning, maybe tonight, too.

Maybe she'd catch Wesley at breakfast. With that thought, Margaret cheered up and asked the artist about his latest work.

Wes led C.J. to a table. McCall's was obviously having an identity crisis. It seemed the place couldn't decide if it wanted to be a country western theme joint, a sports bar, or a family restaurant. Wes hoped the menu wasn't too schizoid. He would have preferred cooking himself. But living in a rooming house didn't give him that luxury. He'd found this place while on his way to the job interview earlier in the day.

"This is nice," C.J. said as she settled in their booth. "I've never been here."

Wes held his comment and ordered a beer when the waitress placed menus before them.

"What can I get you to drink, ma'am?"

"Do you have herbal tea?"

"I'm sorry, no. We have iced tea. Would you like a glass of that?"

"Sure."

"Be right back to take your orders."

The waitress walked away. C.J. and Wes studied their menus for a minute.

"Steak and potatoes for me," Wes said.

A traditionalist, C.J. thought. A meat and potatoes kind of man appealed to her on lots of levels.

She pondered the choices a while longer. "I'm trying to decide between the grilled chicken and the Santa Fe salmon."

When the waitress returned with beer and iced tea, Wes looked at C.J. After a quick question to their server, she settled on the salmon. Wes then ordered his steak, medium rare.

"I'll get some bread and house salads to you just as soon as I place your order," the waitress said as she collected their menus.

Wes downed a considerable portion of the beer. C.J. watched him drink and licked her lips, imagining the cool refreshing taste of the imported brew. She added sugar to her tea, squeezed a lemon over the ice and stirred it, then sipped at the beverage.

Wes leaned back so his head rested on the high cushion padding of the booth. "So, tell me, why did you call me Dark Warrior?"

"When did I call you that?"

"Earlier today. On the street when you bumped into me."

C.J. smiled. "Oh. I didn't realize I'd said that out loud." She studied him for a moment. "Because you're dark, almost swarthy, like a pirate or a desert sheik. And when I walked into you today, sorry about that, you stood before me scowling and glaring like an ancient warrior king."

Wes smiled. "So, you're a fiction writer?"

C.J. watched him take another swallow of beer, she really would have preferred the brew over the tea. One step at a time, she told herself, one day at a time. She lifted the glass of iced tea to her mouth, pretended it was an icy cold one then answered his question with a question. "Why do you say that?"

"The imagery of your description."

She smiled. "That's not imagery. It's the truth through my eyes."

"And they are beautiful," he said.

"Flattery will, of course, get you . . ." she paused long enough to make him wait, "anything you want," she added softly.

Wes leaned forward. "Well, in that case, let me tell you about those legs you had wrapped around me. And your mouth . . ."

C.J. sat back, smiled and wagged a finger at him. "Unh uh. It has to be sincere flattery."

There was a faint glimmer of humor in his eyes, and then they darkened even more. C.J. felt as if she were standing on the edge of a two-thousand-year-old volcano that was about to blow its top for the first time. She smoldered under his intense gaze and knew like she knew her name that she'd be with this man. It no longer was a matter of *if*, if she could even claim she'd ever really doubted it, but a matter of *when* and where.

Without a word, he continued to stare at her. C.J. unable to tear her eyes away from him, met him unflinching, gaze for gaze.

"I want you," he said smoothly, with no expression on his face or inflection in his voice. He stated it as simple fact. C.J.'s breathing deepened and her eyes dilated.

She was spared an answer when the waitress arrived with a small loaf of fresh-baked bread and two generous green salads.

"Here you go, folks," she said. "Be careful with the bread, it's straight from the hearth. The butter spreads are honey maple, strawberry kiwi, and boysenberry. If you'd like some regular I can get some for you." She placed the bread on the table then put a salad in front of each of them. "Fresh ground pepper?"

"No thanks. I'm hot enough as it is," C.J. mumbled.

Wes smiled and shook his head no.

"Another beer for you, sir?"

"Yes, please. Jan, would you like a glass of wine?"

What C.J. really wanted was a double scotch on the rocks and a cold shower. "I'll take more tea, please. Thank you."

"Sounds good. Your meals will be up in a few minutes. I'll come back by to refill your drinks and bring you some more bread if you'd like it."

When the waitress left, Wes turned up the heat again. "Do I make you nervous?"

Her mouth quirked with humor. "That's not exactly the word I'd use."

"Then what word would you use?"

"Needy. Achy."

Wes smiled in masculine understanding. "Good," he said simply. Then he turned his attention to the salad before him.

C.J. watched him eat and wondered when he'd gotten the upper hand of the conversation. It was time he squirmed a bit.

"Do you come on quite so strong with every woman you meet?"

"No. It hasn't been necessary. I've never felt this way before."

"How do you feel?" she asked.

Wes paused, salad fork speared with a black olive, he looked at her. His gaze dipped to her breasts then meandered back to her face. "Needy. Achy."

C.J. downed the last of the iced tea in record haste.

By the time the waitress brought their entrees the conversation had shifted to more neutral ground.

"How did you come to be in Serenity Falls?" she asked.

"Mostly just passing through," he said. "It seemed like a nice enough place to pause for a while."

"Where are you from?"

"West Virginia. And you?"

"Originally from Maryland. But I've been around, here and there most of my life." She hoped the answer was vague enough for him to avoid a more specific follow-up question.

"I've been to Baltimore several times," he said. "I love the Inner Harbor and the aquarium. Have you ever been there?"

He was dancing awfully close to home, too close for comfort. C.J. nodded vaguely and then lobbed another question statement his way, one she hoped would steer him away from the subject of Maryland and her hometown Baltimore.

"So, tell me about yourself. You handled that CPR today like a pro."

Wes smiled. "I try to keep current. You never know when you'll need to know something. Or when you might be a contestant on 'Jeopardy.' "

"What other things do you know?" she asked with a teasing smile.

"A few foreign languages, mostly enough to get by, enough tae kwon do to have earned a black belt, how to rebuild the engine on a '67 Mustang, and which fork to use at a formal banquet."

"I'm suitably impressed."

"You should be," he grinned.

"Any of it true?" she asked.

Wes let loose with laughter that was deep, warm, and rich. C.J. fell in love with the sound.

He answered her in smooth French.

C.J. blinked. Her French skills were rusty. Practicing the language was not something she got a chance to do often while she reported stories from low-income areas of Baltimore.

It took her a moment but she managed to translate most of his statement. He'd said: "Only that which you choose to believe."

After another moment of thought, she answered back in French: "I'll grant you the benefit of the doubt for now and believe it all."

Wes smiled and held his glass up to her in salute.

"To the here and now," he said in English.

C.J. clinked her iced tea glass with his.

They ate in silence for a few minutes. The waitress replaced their bread round then slipped away.

"Your turn to impress me," he said.

The comment was simple and it was fair; they were getting to know each other. But C.J., for the second time that night, found herself debating about telling him the truth or telling him the vague tale she'd used to fend off the more curious of Serenity Falls's inhabitants.

Lying came moderately easy for C.J. But it felt wrong, as if she would be cheating not only herself but Wes if she told him less than the truth. Rare was the occasion when she even thought twice about bending or stretching the truth when it came to getting information she needed. She really hated the getting to know you part of relationships. It generally proved tedious beyond measure. And now, she not only had to contend with that part but the minefield of half-truths she'd so recently created. It was far easier to just acknowledge mutual lust, grab a couple of condoms and bid someone a fond but forever farewell in the morning.

"What do you want to know?" she finally asked him.

"What do you do for fun?"

C.J. could have wept in relief. If that was the toughest question she had to tap dance around, the rest of the night would be a breeze.

"I garden. I've spent the last few weekends trying to turn part of my backyard into an English garden. I'm also experimenting with an herb garden. My newest recreational activity is reupholstering and refinishing furniture—or at least trying to."

Wes's brow furrowed, he peered closer at C.J. She swallowed her last bite of salmon and laughed.

"What?" she said smiling. "Not exactly what you were expecting?"

"To be honest, no," he said. "I sort of figured you for an outdoors type but outdoor sports."

"That's just like a man to think something like that. I play a pretty mean game of tennis," she admitted. But she left out her better than average golf and lacrosse games. Telling him about the country club sports she'd grown up with would give too much away. She also didn't count the two grueling hours she put in in aerobics every morning. Well, every morning before moving to North Carolina. She'd ceased that obsessive activity as soon as she arrived and now contented herself with half an hour of step aerobics in her living room every morning.

"So, you have a green thumb?"

C.J. held her right thumb up and turned it one way and then the other. "Looks brown to me," she said, smiling. "Actually, no. That's why I decided to try my hand," she said, tipping her hand to him at the small pun, "at gardening."

Back in Baltimore, she'd had a service come in to take care of the few plants she did maintain. If left up to C.J., the ficus trees and houseplants scattered about would have died of neglect and dehydration. One of the reasons she'd decided to do the outdoor garden when she arrived in Serenity Falls was because if and when she tired of the notion of playing Miss Green Thumb, the natural rain and sunshine would take better care of the plants than C.J. ever would.

"What do you do, as in for a living?"

This one was easy, she thought. "Whatever I want to. I'm recuperating."

She waited for the inevitable next question. Most people assumed recuperating meant you'd been in an accident or had had an illness. C.J. let the good people of Serenity Falls believe what they wanted to. So half of the folks in town that she'd met thought she'd been sick and the other half thought she'd been in a car accident.

Wes smiled. "We all need to recuperate sometimes."

C.J. sat back, cocked her head to the side and regarded him. "You surprise me, Wes Donovan."

Wes took the last bite of the baked potato on his plate. He chewed and swallowed. "How so?"

"Oh, you just do," she said. "Do you come from a large family?"

Wes shook his head. "Immediate family, no. Extended family, yes. What about you?"

C.J. smiled. Obviously, the man was adept at not answering questions, even simple yes/no ones. She wondered how he got to be that way. "One older brother."

They sat back when the waitress arrived to clear their dinner plates. "Can I interest you folks in dessert? We have some really good ones."

"Dessert's my favorite," C.J. said with a wink at Wes.

"Mine, too," he said.

"Well, then, I'll be right back with the menu and dessert tray. Would you like coffee?"

"Yes, please," Wes said. C.J. asked for hot tea.

A few minutes later, Wes was putting serious dents in a generous helping of apple pie à la mode while C.J. worked on strawberry cream pie.

"You said you were just passing through Serenity Falls," she said. "What do *you* do for a living?"

"Well, right now I'm hoping to get on at the plant and earn back the money I'm spending to get my truck fixed. Usually though I work on call as a troubleshooter for a government contractor. I show up where they send me, assess the situations, fix them if I can, call in for assistance if I can't. It's pretty good work."

"What have been some of the situations?"

C.J. could have sworn he looked surprised at the question. If he seemed to take a while thinking about the answer, she let it go as trying to come up with a suitable example to impress her.

"My juris . . . My work takes me lots of places. There was this guy in Silicon Valley who'd lost a whole lot of money for his company. I came in as a management consultant so to speak and got him squared away."

C.J. noted and stored the fact that he seemed about to say "My jurisdiction," and "management consultant," as she well knew from doing several stories about criminals, covered a wide spectrum. For all she knew this guy could be a cop or a bank robber. But seeing that he spoke several languages, or said he did, and claimed to be a black belt in martial arts, if he were indeed a criminal she decided he'd be a jewel thief. But he said he was a government contractor. Maybe he was an arms smuggler.

She smiled at her fancy. "It's been too long," she said.

"Too long what?"

"I was just thinking out loud. Too long since I've been in the company of an interesting man." She'd always been quick thinking on her feet. The real answer though was too long since she ever took what people said at face value, simply as the truth as they perceived it. Maybe it was time to stop looking for the next great story, the next conspiracy theory. It was past time to just relax, enjoy life, and take people at their word.

They finished up their dessert. Wes patted his shirt pocket. Then sighed.

C.J. smiled in understanding humor. She'd seen that gesture enough in the newsroom to interpret it. "How long has it been?"

A full brow lifted in question.

"Since you gave up smoking?"

"Not long enough."

C.J. leaned forward, rested both elbows on the table and her chin in the cradle of her hands. "So, what do we do now?"

"Sex sounds good to me," he said.

CHAPTER 7

"Let's do it," she said.

If Wes was surprised by her answer it didn't show. He signaled for their waitress, settled the bill, and within five minutes had C.J. on the back of the motorcycle. He handed her his helmet then bent low for a kiss. Hot and hungry, it promised heaven. Wes settled himself on the bike, and with C.J.'s arms wrapped about his waist they headed to her house.

Without a word spoken between them, C.J. led him through the dark bungalow and to her bedroom. Wes felt along the wall for a light switch but C.J. stilled him. She pressed her soft woman's body against him. Wes closed his arms around her and inhaled her scent.

Clasping her face in his large hands, he lowered his head and their mouths met. His covered hers hungrily, with the same gusto and enthusiasm with which he'd devoured the steak during their meal.

C.J. ran her hands up the hard wall of his chest then around to his back. She smoothed her palms along him until she grasped his buttocks. When she squeezed he whirled her around and braced her against the wall. C.J. wrapped her arms around his neck as his tongue left her mouth and staked a claim on her neck.

She gave herself up to the hot licks of fire that ran up and down her spine in concert with the movement of his mouth at her neck and nape.

C.J. moaned. Or was it him?

She pushed at his broad shoulders until he stepped away, a question in his eyes.

C.J. backed him up to her bed. When the back of his legs hit the mattress she reached up and pressed on his shoulders until he sat.

Wesley smiled.

She stepped away from him and lit several candles scattered about the room; well aware that his gaze followed her every movement. She returned to the bed a few minutes later. Leaning forward to brush his lips against hers, she kissed him slow and easy as if time and the moment existed solely for them to share the nectar of the gods.

When Wes lifted his arms to pull her closer to him, she took three steps back and shook her head.

Wes smiled and rested his arms behind him on the firm but soft mattress.

Slowly, with a deliberate taunting that made him sit up and lick his lips, C.J. came out of every piece of clothing. Her hips undulated as blouse, skirt, and bra pooled at her feet. A gentle kick, sent the clothing out of the way.

She stood before him in high-heeled black pumps and hose. The triangle of her white panties peeked through the hose. She parted her legs. Wes stood up.

With a taunting smile she wagged a finger at him. He got the message and sat back on the edge of the bed. The tension in the room was palpable. Swinging her hips with each slow step, C.J. came to him. She held her full breasts, one in each palm and offered the erect tips to him. When Wes opened his mouth to capture the treat, C.J. chuckled and shook her head. Starting with the button at his collar band, she undid each of the small black buttons on his shirt. When his skin was bare, she ran her hands over his chest, kissed each of his small male nipples, then pushed him backward on the bed. She climbed astride him and in no time found herself flat on her back with Wes's head buried in her breasts.

She allowed him that because to deny him would be to deny her own pleasure.

Except there was one thing wrong.

She watched as Wes suckled and nipped. He gave one more delicious swirl at her breasts and then sat up long enough to pull out of the rest of his shirt, kick off his boots and get out of his pants. He left his white boxer shorts on but there was no denying he filled them up—completely and then some. The soft candlelight cast him in flickering shadows that enhanced C.J.'s feeling that she was about to be loved by a god come to life.

But there was one thing wrong.

"May I break the silence?" he asked quietly.

C.J. nodded.

"I need to go."

"Go?"

"All the beer."

She smiled. "Oh. Then go. Over there," she said, pointing toward the door that led to her bathroom.

Wes seared her with a kiss. C.J. felt scorched all the way to her toenails.

"Hold that thought," he said huskily.

Wes swung across her and off the bed.

C.J. took the time his absence afforded to kick off her shoes and hose. When Wes returned a few minutes later, she was sitting up in bed, her back against the wooden headboard, her chest bare but a sheet pulled to her waist.

Wes sat on the edge of the bed facing her. He reached one hand out to fondle the ripe fruit of her breasts.

C.J. giggled.

"What?" he said, smiling.

Her giggle became a quiet reflective laugh. "We're not really going to do this are we?" she asked.

Wes pulled his hand away. He shook his head. "I don't think so." Then, with a slight frown, "Why not?"

C.J. scooted down on the mattress until they sat face to face. She kissed him lightly on the lips. "I'll make us some tea."

Wes nodded. He stood and assisted C.J. from the bed.

Unmindful of her nakedness, she walked to her closet, pulled out a long burgundy and pink robe and wrapped it about her body.

"We can sit out back," she said.

A few minutes later they sat on the steps of C.J.'s back porch quietly contemplating the stars visible in the night sky.

"I blew the candles out," he said. Then, after a short pause, "What was that all about?"

C.J. sipped from her mug then turned her head to look at him. "I don't know. Mutual lust."

"But definitely the wrong way to start a relationship?" he asked.

"Are we starting a relationship?"

"I don't know. You tell me."

"I don't know you. You don't know me."

Wes placed his mug on the step next to him then reached one bronzed hand into the folds of her robe. C.J.'s breast puckered in anticipation. He rubbed her until the relaxed nipple was again a hard pebble and warm heat flowed through her.

With his free hand he removed the mug from her hands and set it aside. Guiding her small hand to his lap he curled her fingers around the hard length of his erection.

Wes took a deep breath when her hand began a slow rhythm. "We have this in common," he said, as his own hand gently squeezed her breast.

"And this is gonna be good. But if we want something more, it can't be based on sex alone."

"I agree," she said.

"So, where do we go from here?"

"Maybe you should leave," she suggested.

"I'd rather cut off an ear."

C.J. smiled. "Then let's say we stop tormenting each other and take things as they progress." She removed her hand from him but was unable to halt the sigh of disappointment when his strong hand ceased its gentle kneading. She watched as he quietly adjusted the fold of her robe.

C.J. picked up his mug and handed it to him. She lifted her own and sipped from the warm tea. They sat quietly and watched the stillness of the night. A steady chirping of crickets and the occasional croak of a frog filled the air, a natural symphony that more than anything else, served as a quiet reminder to C.J. that the world didn't have to be a hectic, ugly place.

She wrapped her hands around her mug and stared into the darkness. "I moved to Serenity Falls to get away from this sort of destructive behavior. I figured I wouldn't get myself in trouble or be overly tempted in a serene North Carolina town so I relocated here. I'd thought I was doing okay," she said. Then quietly added, "Until I bumped into you."

Wes evaluated her words and sighed inwardly. Relocated. That was one of the specialties of his line of work. He had no business getting involved with this woman. He could probably get fired for what had happened so far. But still he wanted her. He wanted her like he'd wanted no other woman, ever.

In the quiet of the night, Wes figured that was a bonus punishment that Holloway hadn't figured on, one that would do more to break his spirit; even more than Marc's death had done. Jan Langley was beautiful and off limits. And still he wanted her.

He tried to guess what she had done or been in her past life. What she knew or had seen that had gotten her a new identity fully paid for by the U.S. government. Wes glanced at her. In profile, she looked like an African queen: proud, arrogant, confident. Her features, perfectly shaped, fit her face, the smooth brown skin beckoned his touch. An arched brow tapered off. Wes wanted to run one finger along the small waves in her hair.

Wesley's gaze next examined her ear and the place on her neck he wanted to again bury his head. She smelled of woman and of exotic nights. Wes smiled. She had two holes in her left ear visible above the big earrings she wore.

"What did you do before?" Even as he asked the question Wes knew it was inappropriate. If she were indeed a good witness, no matter what she told him, it would be a lie. She'd protect her old identity.

She turned to him and smiled, no longer a serene smile. "Let's not talk about that. Tell me about growing up in West Virginia."

Wes accepted her answer for what it was: the best truth she could offer him. He'd get the information he wanted to know another way. There was always another way. He sipped from his cup, frowned when he realized she really had made tea, then lowered the cup and silently watched the night.

"West Virginia was a long time ago," he said after awhile. "I haven't been home, what you'd probably call home, in more years than I care to remember. It doesn't necessarily bring back fond memories."

"What about Mama Lo?"

For a moment, Wesley looked surprised. Then he remembered he'd mentioned Mama Lo's cooking to Jan earlier in the day. He nodded and smiled. "Yeah. It would be nice to see Mama Lo."

He hadn't seen her since the funeral. She'd looked older then, old and tired. Wes hoped that healing had started for her by now. He couldn't say the same for himself but he wished healing and comfort for the woman who was like a mother to him.

"I've been thinking," he said.

"About what?" she asked.

"The sex thing."

"We are two consenting adults," she pointed out.

"I have condoms."

C.J. put her mug to the side and moved to the step in front of him. She settled between his legs and leaned back. She smiled when his legs opened wider and he draped his arms about her neck and shoulders. She turned her head back and they kissed, this time letting the need in them flower slowly.

Safe within the shelter of his embrace C.J. faced the night again and contemplated the moonlight between the trees in her backyard. The soft night and the gentle stroking of his hand along her neck soothed C.J. in a place where for too long she'd felt turmoil. This man's hungry kisses and gentle embraces fed a place in her that she didn't realize was lacking. She wanted him. She knew she'd have him. But she wondered if having him would make him just like all the others, a mountain once conquered, no longer a mystery or thing to be desired.

She sensed within him a power restrained, a harnessed energy waiting for the right moment. Given her own track record, C.J. knew that giving in with Wes Donovan would mean one of two things: destroying him like she did every man she'd ever had a sexual relationship with or so deeply losing herself that she'd be forever lost in a mire of dependency just like her new friend Amber. C.J. could see no balance, no middle ground anywhere between the two extremes. She'd bought hook, line, and sinker the spirit of the 1980s overachievers: work and play hard. She'd extended that notion to every aspect of her life and was now faced with a question that had never needed answering—what comes after you work hard and play hard?

"Why did we stop earlier?" Wes quietly asked.

She smiled to herself at the question. Then she felt him shift behind her. His head nuzzled her neck and his hands began a slow exploration. C.J. sank deeper into his embrace.

"I was just thinking about that," she said.

"And did you come up with an answer?"

"No. Not really," she said. She captured one of his hands and kissed the palm. "This is going to happen. But I don't think it should be tonight."

She surprised herself with that answer. Did that mean she was maturing? It had to be, she figured, because she'd never denied herself pleasure before, and the one thing she wanted most in the world right now was for Wes Donovan to keep doing all the things he was doing with his hands, with his mouth, with the erection she felt pressed into her back.

But even as she prided herself on her newfound restraint, a part of her was pissed off that it had to come now, with this man. Waiting, patiently waiting, was not one of her strong points unless it had to do with ferreting out a story. And what she was feeling now had not even a smidgen to do with newsgathering.

C.J. leaned forward out of his embrace and then stood up and faced him. Wes silently watched her. She pushed him back until his back lay on the wooden planks of her porch. C.J. crawled along his long body, pausing here and there to explore an interesting tidbit.

She heard Wes suck in his breath. "I thought you just said 'Not tonight.' "

"I'm not a tease," she said. "I've run hot and cold tonight. And that's not fair to you."

Her hand traced the now full erection in his jeans.

"Let me ease your pain," she said, as her hand slowly unfastened the top and worked at the zipper.

A shuddering sigh was Wesley's answer.

Back in his room at Miss Clara Ann's Wes thought about what had transpired this night. He had stopped her on the porch. At the time, he didn't know why. He wanted her with every fiber of his being. But he wanted her right, and right meant together and whole. Damned if he could figure out why it made any difference. It never had before. But he wanted the total woman, not the Jan who gave of herself while he lapped up all the sweetness and offered her little or nothing in return.

The lady had said no, then seemed to change her mind. He wondered at her choice of words. She'd distinctly said that she moved to Serenity Falls to cease "this sort of destructive behavior." Since the only behavior that had been going on was their foreplay, Wes concluded that maybe she'd been a high-level call girl. He did a mental inventory but came up blank in trying to remember if there had been a prostitution bust or case in the recent past that would warrant Witness Security and relocation. Maybe she was the girlfriend of a Mafia boss or a gang leader.

But that just didn't fit. "The woman speaks French for God's sake," he said.

Yeah, Wes, and think back to the most dazzling courtesans of old, he argued with himself. Lots of them were bi-, tri-, and quadlingual, just part of the package.

Wes pulled off his shirt and boots and padded into the bathroom. Grateful he'd gotten a room with a private bath, he turned the shower on. A strong steady stream of water poured forth. Wes stuck his hand in the spray to test the water temperature. He shook his head.

"That won't do." He adjusted the water.

He came out of the rest of his clothes, dropping the jeans and shorts over the commode. Wes gritted his teeth and stepped into the now icy stream. "This better work," he mumbled.

It didn't.

CHAPTER 8

Old habits die hard. Without the benefit of an alarm clock, Wes woke up at four in the morning. He pulled on a pair of running shorts, socks, and athletic shoes then dug out of his bag an old gray sweatshirt with the sleeves ripped off. Less than ten minutes after waking he was out the front door of Miss Clara Ann's and running the dark, deserted streets of Serenity Falls.

In the room next door to Wes's, Margaret swore out loud. She guessed that he might be a runner. He had to do some sort of regular intense physical activity to maintain the physique he had. Glancing at the digital travel alarm she'd placed on the night stand next to the bed, Margaret calculated how long he might be out. She jogged almost two miles every day but got started at the more civilized hour of five-thirty; she guessed Wesley might do a three- or four-mile run.

Aunt Clara had given him a room with an adjoining bath so she couldn't contrive to "accidentally" walk in on him while he showered. Breakfast might be her next best opportunity after this one. Margaret smiled in the dark as she tossed off the percale sheet that covered her. She had plenty of time to set her bait and lure in her prey.

"And what a fine specimen he is," she said while pulling on a bright pink running suit.

Running cleared Wes's mind. He generally spent the first two miles monitoring his breathing and clearing his head of all thoughts except the process of running, of putting one foot in front of the other. The second two miles he took in his surroundings, and the last two he always spent organizing his day—except for this morning when his thoughts were so very narrowly focused. When he got to the organizing his day part he tried to come up with a legit reason to stop by Jan Langley's. He failed to create one but didn't sweat it; he'd see her today by one means or another.

He'd check on the truck then scope out his guy. Orders from Holloway had been not to spook the witness just make contact and assess the situation. The witness's field inspector, whose job it was to remain in total contact with the witness, had landed himself in a cast from ankle to hip and would be out of commission for at least ten weeks. Wes smirked as he ran by the closed up stores of downtown Serenity Falls. Everything about this assignment smelled bogus. What kind of marshal tripped over a trash can, fell down a flight of steps, and wound up totally out of commission? There probably wasn't even a protected witness in Serenity Falls.

Except for Jan Langley.

He'd run a make on her. With any luck, the sort of luck that would keep him employed, she'd be just what she said she was, a woman recuperating in a small town. He hadn't bothered to ask recuperating from what. Wes wasn't really interested in whatever lie she needed to tell to maintain her former identity.

Wes sensed before he heard the other presence. Imperceptively he slowed his pace a bit. He let the other person draw near. Tense but loose Wes was ready for action.

"Geez, oh man. They told me you got up real early. This is crazy," the runner said from a few feet behind.

Wes glanced at the person trying to keep pace with him. He slowed up a bit more. "Good morning."

The runner grunted and caught up. "It was until I had to sit up all night waiting to see if you'd be out. I think somebody has made me."

"Made you what?"

The runner snorted. "You Marshals are the most cloak-and-dagger James Bond people I've ever met. Look, are you here to protect me or what?"

"What's the problem?"

"I think somebody knows who I am or rather who I was. Look, can you slow up a bit. I'm in fair shape, or thought I was. You're going to give me heart failure."

Wes came to a quick halt that threw his partner off guard. The runner stopped a few feet ahead and then walked back to where Wes stood stretching and limbering. Wesley took a good, long look at his contact. He'd need to be able to recognize this person under any circumstance, any time of day or night.

The jogger looked left and right and then leaned forward. "You know that accident that Jackson had? Messed up his leg."

Wes didn't give any indication that he knew one way or another.

The jogger leaned closer still then imitated the stretching exercise Wes had done. "I don't think it was an accident," the runner whispered. "I think that was a message to me. You know, 'You can run but you can't hide.' "

Wes began to jog in place. His shadow did the same. "What else can you tell me?" he asked.

"That's about it for now."

"What do you mean 'For now'?"

The witness shrugged. "How do I know I can trust you?"

"Sometimes in life you have to trust people."

"Yeah, right. The last time I did that I almost ended up dead." The witness again looked to the left and then to the right checking for eavesdroppers. "I'm outta here. This is making me crazy out here in the middle of the night. For all I know a sniper with night vision glasses is scoped on us right now."

To anyone who may have been observing so early in the morning, Wesley's run had been random. But he'd spent most of the time surveilling the area. With no backup security detail, he couldn't be 100 percent sure, but he was 80 percent sure there were no snipers on any of Serenity Falls's roofs. Wes had to admit, however, that those odds sucked. That 20 percent could have just as soon been 100 percent for all the difference it made.

"I'll be in touch," he told the witness. Wes watched the jogger nod and then duck around an industrial-size recycling bin and disappear.

Wes continued his run, eventually making his way back to Miss Clara Ann's. Well, he thought, it looked like there actually was a witness in town after all. He had some work to do.

A little more than an hour later Wes scowled over a cup of black coffee and the morning edition of the *Serenity Falls Gazette.* He sat by himself at Miss Clara Ann's guest dining room table. In the next room over, he could hear the early morning news on television as Miss Clara Ann prepared breakfast. The smell of frying bacon, more than hunger, kept him in his seat. Every now and then he'd hear her short bark of laughter or a sassy comeback to some of the morning anchors' witty repartee.

He read the first few paragraphs of the rescue story. Kenneth J. Sheldon obviously fancied himself as a grand journalist in the Woodward and Bernstein tradition. But stories about Little League and the county bake-off weren't going to win the guy any Pulitzers. The lead story in the paper was the so-called "miraculous rescue," for God's sake. The only good thing Wes could say about the story on the *Gazette*'s front page was that his name was spelled correctly and the photo didn't show his face.

Wes wasn't so much worried about working undercover, he rarely did that these days, but he was real concerned about keeping a low profile. He'd purposely come into town looking and acting like a regular Joe. It felt odd to travel without the heavy firepower though he had enough heat to get him out of basic types of trouble. And the claptrap truck Casey had set him up with couldn't even claim to be a fully outfitted armored government vehicle in disguise. It was exactly what it looked like, metal and rust that had seen better days.

Seeing his picture on the front page of the paper didn't serve any of his purposes for being in Serenity Falls. With luck, the paper didn't circulate anywhere out of the small northwestern North Carolina county. The way the media operated, Wes knew how futile that hope could be.

The scent teased him first. He didn't turn around or in any way acknowledge it. He smelled it above the bacon and eggs and coffee. It wasn't heavy but it wasn't light, the essence heady and straightforward and all woman. The scent had to have been formulated for the sole purpose of capturing a man's attention. It worked.

Margaret slid into the seat next to him at the table. Wes bit back a smile. A tigress was on the loose, he'd have to be careful. Knowing it would come quickly, he waited for her first move.

"Good morning," she said. "I heard you prowling around early this morning. Have a rough night sleeping?"

She had not just a nice voice, she had a great voice. It curled around him, reminding Wes of smooth, rich honey. He'd have to be careful not to be a fly stuck in that honey.

"No. I'm just an early riser."

"Me, too. Dawn is my favorite part of the day. You learn a lot when you're up and about early."

Wes glanced at Margaret. Her short, bobbed haircut flattered her face. She looked familiar in the way some black women did, like she'd stepped from the pages of *Essence* magazine, strong, black, and in charge. Her features, including the pert nose and the bow mouth, were attractive. But Wes didn't find himself responding to her obvious appeal.

"Morning's my favorite part of the day, too," he said.

Miss Clara Ann backed into the room carrying a platter heaped high with bacon and eggs. She settled it on the table. "Be right back with some biscuits hot from the oven. Mornin' Margaret, didn't think you got up this early," she said before heading back into the kitchen.

Wes bit the smile that threatened. Margaret said nothing.

The three ate breakfast with general conversation about the weather and the morning news.

"Wesley here is a hero," Miss Clara Ann said. "Helped save old Jesse Parker. Don't know why you bothered though, Jesse's nothing but an old rogue, chasing after some young thing is what probably give him a heart attack in the first place."

"What'd you do?" Margaret asked.

Wes buttered another flaky biscuit. "Nothing really."

"Shoot. Where's that paper, boy?"

Wes smiled in good humor and handed the newspaper to Miss Clara Ann who proceeded to pass it on to Margaret.

"I like that photograph. It captures your weariness," Margaret observed. "The mayor should give you a citation for bravery," she said after reading the story.

That was the last thing he needed. But Wes didn't say that. "I'm just glad the man's going to be okay."

After downing another cup of coffee and what he deemed a suitable amount of time, Wes excused himself from the table with the excuse that he wanted to go explore the town.

Margaret dabbed her mouth with a paper napkin. "Mind if I join you? It's been a while since I was here. I'm sure things have changed."

Miss Clara Ann saved Wes from having to respond.

"Margaret, stay back would you? There's a coupla family matters we need to discuss."

Wes caught Margaret's look of exasperation before she masked it and smiled sweetly at her aunt.

"Of course, Aunt Clara."

Wes beat a hasty retreat but did overhear Miss Clara Ann scold Margaret.

"If you want to capture that man, you needs to listen to me girl cause I ain't seen no moves on your part that would make him interested. What'd you do this morning, fall in a bottle of perfume?"

Wes grinned all the way to his room.

From a pay phone about an hour later he put in a call to headquarters and got his old buddy Scotty to agree to run a check on Jan Langley. Citing his need to know as an "integral part of the current operation," Wes secured an albeit reluctant Scotty to do what he could.

His next stop was to the service station to check on his truck.

"Be good as new in about two hours," Ray Bob assured him. "She needs a couple of hoses, some other parts, and some transmission fluid."

"How much is it gonna run?" Wes asked.

Ray Bob scratched his head and looked at the sky. "Don't rightly know yet. I'll leave a message for you at Miss Clara Ann's place. That's where you're puttin' up, right?"

Wes nodded. This guy was going to try to take him on this. Wes decided to let the mechanic know he knew cars. "If it'll save on the labor I'll just buy the parts. If I rebuilt my Mustang's engine I can handle a couple of hoses. I have time this weekend."

Ray Bob eyed him, obviously skeptical, but Wes figured, not willing to lose any work. Ray Bob studied the oil and dirt under his fingernails for a moment.

"Yeah, well, it won't likely be that much."

Wes smiled. "Thanks. Appreciate it."

"I heard 'bout what you did for Jesse Parker. Figure that counts for something."

Wes nodded, not quite sure how the man who collapsed equated with work he needed done on his truck. But he wasn't of a mind to figure it out. He had an important destination.

"I'll swing by later today. What time you close up?"

"Don't really," Ray Bob answered. "I live upstairs," he said, pointing to an above garage apartment. "If I'm not out here, just knock on the door and we'll settle up."

"Good enough." Wes put the dark glasses on and swung a muscled leg over the seat of the motorcycle. With a two-finger salute to Ray Bob, Wes pulled out of the station garage.

It took him less than fifteen minutes to make his way to Jan Langley's small house. He kicked the stand down on the bike and sat for a moment looking at her home. It was small, old and comfortable looking, one of the few houses on the street with a detached garage instead of a covered breezeway. A few bushes in the front could use a trim but the grass was cut. The gate definitely needed a coat of paint. He could grab a couple of gallons at the hardware store he'd seen and probably get the job done in a few hours.

Wes blinked. Where in the world did that come from? he asked while unfastening his helmet and getting off the bike. Being in this town less than forty-eight hours has you acting like a Mark Twain character.

The last time he'd done any painting he and Marcus had redone Mama Lo's dining room and kitchen. They'd gotten her instructions backward though and had painted the dining room walls yellow and the kitchen a pale blue. Wes smiled as he remembered Marc trying to sweet talk Mama Lo into leaving the walls the way they were.

"Blue gives the kitchen a soothing, restful feeling," Marc had pointed out.

"You won't be feeling too soothed or restful if you and Wesley don't do these walls the right way," she'd shot back.

It took them another eight hours after the paint dried to do the job right.

Wes was still smiling at the memory when C.J. opened the door.

He hadn't been a figment of her imagination. She'd been having a difficult time coming to grips with the fact that she and this man had been naked in bed together . . . and had done nothing. Not one blessed thing.

"Hi."

"I spent a little time trying to manufacture a reason to come and see you. Then I said what the hell. I'd just come."

"I'm glad you did," she said more candidly than she'd anticipated. "I didn't get much sleep last night."

Wes smiled. "Why is that?"

"I kept thinking about what we, what I, was missing out on."

Wes knew the feeling. But until he got the "all clear" from Scotty, Wes had to have a care about what he said with and did to this woman. Why did life have to be so complicated sometimes? He'd worked with liars and low-lifes so long that when he found a little ray of sunshine it seemed all the more bright and tempting to him. Jan was that sunshine. And right now, she was off limits. Sort of.

But off limits didn't mean they couldn't spend time together.

"Have you ever been fishing?" he asked.

"You mean like bait, hook, line, worms?"

"Those things generally define it."

She smiled, saucy and challenging. "Then no. I've never been fishing."

"Wanna go?"

"When?" she asked.

"How about now? I'm free."

C.J. cocked her head and stared up at him. "On one condition."

"Your wish is my command."

"Don't say that, dark warrior, we'd never leave the house if that were the case."

Her provocative words had an immediate masculine effect on him. The cold shower hadn't worked last night and Wes knew he couldn't count on any sort of relief by trying to psyche himself out now. What was it about this woman that was so hot? That made him so hot?

His voice was huskier than normal when he asked what her condition was.

"I need a couple of hours to finish up the project I'm working on."

"Granted. On one condition," he said.

A small smile tugged at her mouth. She folded her arms and leaned against the doorjamb. "What?"

"Let me kiss you."

The small smile slowly transformed into feminine awareness. The space around them crackled with sensual electricity. He had to feel it like she did. In one forward motion she was in his arms. She caught his breath, warm and moist against her face, a moment before his mouth closed over hers. The velvet warmth of his tongue aroused her further as they drank from each other. Her mouth burned with a fire she didn't want quenched, not now, not ever. Nothing and no one had ever made her feel this way: cherished and sexy and hot; achy and needy and wanting more. So much more.

As if sensing her need, Wes clasped her buttocks and lifted her up and closer to him, closer to the erection he didn't want to conceal. He claimed her with his mouth and knew an ecstasy he'd never imagined. God, he wanted to be inside this woman. Inside her so deep he forgot where he ended and she began.

C.J. ran her hands over his short cropped hair. Blood pounded in her veins and her heart swelled. This felt so right, so good.

A dog's barking drew them apart. C.J. opened her eyes and stared into Wesley's brown ones.

"Wow."

"Yeah, wow," he said. He slowly lowered her, the feel of her firm body cascading down his did nothing to lower his temperature.

C.J.'s breath came in short but deep gasps. She had to get oxygen to her brain. It couldn't be possible for one man to make her feel like this. She almost told him to bag the fishing date. She could think of far better things they could bait than fish.

"Give me two hours," she told him.

Wes leaned forward for another kiss, this one short and sweet. But if C.J. thought she'd gotten control of herself, she was mistaken. Wesley's hand caressed her from the bridge of her nose, slowly around her mouth and over the bottom of her full lips. That large, smooth hand curved around her chin and trailed down her neck in a maddeningly slow descent. When his palm closed over the fullness of her breast, it came as no surprise to C.J. that her nipple was hard and ripe, ready for him, aching for him. He squeezed the delicate flesh. C.J. moaned and turned into the embrace; closing her eyes giving herself to him in this small way.

"Open your eyes."

When she did, his mouth closed over hers, hot and hungry. Then he released her, all of her, by stepping back. "I'll pick you up at ten-thirty," he said.

C.J. nodded and leaned against the door. She watched his retreat down her walkway and out the wooden gate. C.J. swallowed. Wesley Donovan was an addiction she'd like to never give up.

Wes killed time by crisscrossing the town and outlying area. By the time he got back to Main Street people were out and about and the shops open. And Wes could get anywhere in a twenty-five mile radius practically with his eyes closed. He believed it important to know the lay of the land. That information could come in handy down the road.

He stopped in a convenience store and got a cup of coffee. Then, outside on the far edge of the store's parking lot, he pulled a flip telephone from a small pack on the bike.

Wes punched out a number on the cell phone and sipped at the coffee while waiting for the connection. Scotty, his old buddy from headquarters, picked up on the first ring. "Hey, man," Wes said. "Got anything for me?"

"Yeah and no, Donovan. I can tell you this. If she's one of ours she's deep, real deep. No paper anywhere."

"Keep looking." The request sounded more like a command.

"I can get into some deep shit about this, Donovan. You know the rules. Why do you need this woman made?"

"Part of the case," Wes lied. "I need to know what's going on down here. She may be part of it, might not be. Come on Scotty. I swear to God I won't bother you again if you can pull up some background on this woman."

"You're supposed to be down there working on an attitude adjustment. At least that's the word that's going around here," Scotty said. "It sure doesn't sound like you've made any progress. Still as insolent and demanding as ever."

Wes chuckled. "Part of my charm. Interesting spin on this assignment. Particularly since I was thinking the same thing. You start that rumor?"

He kept to himself the early morning encounter he'd had. If word was going around that he'd been sent to North Carolina to get his attitude adjusted, chances were that Holloway had kept a lid on what Wes was really up to. More and more, it was looking like his assignment wasn't bogus after all.

"You wound me, Donovan. You really do," Scotty said. "I'll see what else I can find out about your woman. Don't hold your breath though on this one."

Wes rang off with Scotty. He'd been in this business so long that he was suspicious of everyone he met—and with good reason. Most of the people, men and women alike, who crossed his path generally had criminal records or ties longer than his arm. For a moment, just a brief one, Wes longed for the old days when he served warrants for the Marshals Service. Busting down doors and arresting the bad guys, even if you'd been on a stakeout for weeks or months, had a certain satisfaction to it, certainly more appeal than his current assignment.

He stashed the phone in his gear bag and finished the coffee. Crumpling the cup, he tossed it in a trash can. It was time to go check on his truck and pick up Jan Langley for their fishing date.

"There is no conflict of interest," he said aloud.

Maybe if he kept telling himself that he'd believe it.

CHAPTER 9

When Wes arrived to pick her up, C.J. had a wicker basket waiting on the porch.

"Lunch?" he asked hopefully.

"Not exactly. Something to put lunch in. I found it in a closet in the house. I figured we'd pick up something to eat along the way."

He looked good enough to eat but C.J. kept that thought to herself. He'd traded the boots he'd worn the night before for a pair of scuffed moccasins. A long-sleeved plaid shirt worn open and on top of a white T-shirt tucked in well-worn jeans made him look rugged yet comfortable. C.J. in knee-length khaki shorts, a matching top, and loafers felt positively overdressed.

She locked her front door, tucked the key in a pocket, and picked up the basket.

"There's a bakery in town that has wonderful brownies. We can stop and get some for lunch."

"Are they chocolate?"

C.J. nodded and licked her lips. "Double chocolate. Some have white and dark chocolate with nuts and fudge icing. They're to die for."

Wes grimaced. "You can say that again. I'm allergic."

He held the gate open for her and she walked through before him.

"Really? That's too bad. Chocolate is wonderful. Sometimes better than sex."

"I doubt it," he mumbled, watching the sway of her hips as she walked.

C.J. laughed over her shoulder. "I heard that. Better Than Sex is an awesome cookie recipe. As a matter of fact, it's the only thing I know how to make besides tea."

"You don't cook?"

C.J. shook her head and eyed the truck. It had seen better days. "I thought we were going on the bike."

"You like the Harley, huh?"

She climbed into the cab of the truck and watched as he walked around to the other side and got in. "I liked the wind on my face and the hard body on my chest," she answered.

Wesley, about to turn the key in the truck's ignition, paused and looked at her. "We don't have to go. There are other ways we can . . ." he paused and let his gaze linger over her eyes, her mouth, her breasts, "get to know each other better."

C.J. smiled and faced forward. "Drive, Donovan, before I forget my resolve."

He continued to stare at her until she glanced at him and then, flushed and unaccountably shy, she looked away and out the passenger window. Wes cleared his throat, turned the ignition key, and pulled out.

"I figured we'd get outfitted at the Wal-Mart. They should have everything we need."

"Do I get a pair of those big rubber boots?" C.J. asked.

He had an idea about rubbers but they had nothing to do with boots or fishing. "Sure, if you want to. This isn't fly fishing though. We'll be on the bank of the river. I found a good spot for us this morning. It's shaded and it looked like the fish were jumping."

A few minutes later Wes pulled the truck into a parking spot at the local Wal-Mart. The lot, crowded with vehicles and folks pushing package-laden carts to their cars, had more people in it than C.J. had seen in her entire month in Serenity Falls.

"Are they having some sort of special sale today?" she asked.

Wes killed the engine. "There's always a sale at Wal-Mart."

"Must be a good one. The place is jammed. I've never been in one before."

Wes couldn't hide his incredulousness. "You've never been in a Wal-Mart?"

C.J. shook her head and pushed open her door. "Nope. I've seen their commercials though."

"Well, this should be interesting," Wes said, joining her.

Tires screeched.

Wes dashed into the road. Amid horn blowing and a woman's scream, he snatched a toddler up a moment before a station wagon hit the child.

Everything happened fast. Wes, with the child safe in his arms, dashed to the frantic woman. An infant in a carrier on the woman's shopping cart cried. The driver of the station wagon shook his head, then swearing about unattended kids, drove off.

"Oh, my God! Oh, my God! Are you okay, Jeremy?"

Wes handed the child to the mother.

"He's OK, ma'am. Just a little frightened about all the commotion."

The woman hugged the now crying toddler to her and then scolded. "Haven't I told you not to go wandering off. Stay here by me and you'll be safe."

Wes chucked the child under the chin. "You listen to your mom, champ. Okay?"

The child wiped his nose and nodded.

"Thank you," the mother said.

C.J. eyed Wes as he ruffled the kid's hair and said a few words to the frightened mother. Not very many people had reflexes that fast. She hadn't even seen the child in the street. Just who was Wes Donovan? So far he seemed to be a French-speaking Ninja-looking rescuer who favored cowboy boots and black. He seemed to have a knack for being where the action was. One thing she knew without any doubt, Wes Donovan was a man's man . . . and he belonged to her. For all she knew though, he could be married with a wife and kids.

His interaction with the small child in the parking lot sure looked fatherly. She'd have to find out. But she got distracted watching him walk back to her. He walked slow but with a moderated ease and purpose that reminded her not so much of a swagger but of a black panther slowly stalking its prey—modulated, easy, always ready to attack, to protect, to make slow, sweet love to her.

C.J.'s stomach tightened as heat engulfed her. She'd met this guy yesterday and had wanted him from the get-go.

He draped an arm about her shoulder. She slipped her own arm around his waist and hugged him. "You're awfully good at that," she said.

"What?"

Arm in arm, they walked to the store entrance. "Helping people out, responding quickly to emergencies. Take yesterday for example. You didn't have to stop to help that man."

Wes shrugged.

"Good morning. Welcome to Wal-Mart," called out a smiling greeter in a blue jacket.

"Hey," Wes said. "We're looking for fishing gear."

"Sporting goods department is right over there," the greeter said, pointing in a direction near the back of the store.

"Thanks."

C.J. accepted a shopping cart and Wes fell into step beside her. "This place is huge," she observed, looking around at the various departments.

As they wheeled by the intimate apparel department C.J. grinned when Wes slowed his pace and eyed the lacy teddies and camisoles. He looked from the silky lingerie to C.J. She stopped pushing the cart. "Yes?" she said, dragging the word out.

"Oh, nothing," he said, fingering the edge of a creamy vanilla camisole.

C.J. sucked in a breath. She felt as if his finger, slowly outlining the fabric on the hanger, were on her own flesh. Wes moved to another piece and then inspected some ultrafeminine bras in bold, bright colors. He selected one from a dainty hanger and turned to assess C.J.'s chest. Eyeing her full bosom he shook his head and picked another one with a considerably larger cup. He looked from her to the bra, her again then back to the bra and raised his eyebrows.

She folded her arms and bit back a grin. "I thought we were getting fishing rods."

"Yeah, we'll get some of those. I like being a careful shopper though. Don't want to miss any good deals."

He put the brassiere back in its spot then walked around a display of lace-edged, hi-cut teddies. Wes picked one off the display and returned to where C.J. stood at the shopping cart. He held the champagne-colored garment up to her.

"It complements your skin," he said.

C.J. swallowed. "I wear a ten/twelve."

"That a fact?" He looked at the size tag in the teddy, then took the piece back to the rack. He picked out one in the right size and put it in the basket. "Funny, you didn't offer up your bra size."

C.J. cleared her throat and looked away. Wes chuckled.

"Thirty-four B but spilling out of it. Spilling out of it big time," he added.

She didn't give him the satisfaction of an answer. How could she when he was right on the money. She glanced down into the basket. "We, uh, need a teddy to go fishing?"

"Is that what you call that, a teddy?"

She nodded.

Wes grinned. "Yeah. It distracts the fish and makes 'em rise to the bait."

C.J.'s eyes roamed over him. Things were definitely rising. She refrained from comment though and fell in step as Wes, chuckling to himself, pushed the cart away from lingerie and toward sporting goods.

She breathed a sigh of relief when they made it to the fishing section without any other distracting stops.

"Okay. We need rods, reels, line, lures, and a tackle box."

"It all looks the same to me," C.J. said. She picked out two rods from the display and stuck them in the basket.

"There are differences," Wes said from where he crouched, looking at lures on a low shelf. He selected what he wanted and tossed them in the basket. When he looked up, she was gone.

"Jan?"

"Over here. The next aisle," she called out.

Wes grinned. He liked the sound of her voice. Actually, he liked a lot of things about Jan Langley. Like how she stuck her tongue in the corner of her mouth and looked away when she was embarrassed. She'd done it twice today. He wondered if she was as aroused as he was. The episode at the lingerie department had cost him more than he cared to admit. He'd taken one look at the soft, sexy garments and imagined the soft, sexy woman wearing them.

Wes stood up and grabbed the first tackle box he saw. He dropped it in the cart then wheeled around to the next aisle.

Jan had a hunter green fishing hat on her head and was shrugging into a sleeveless net jacket.

She saw him and smiled. "Fishing guys on TV always have on these things. I need some of those feathers and what-not for the hat."

Wes smiled. Feathers and what-not. This woman called out and appealed to him on so many levels Wes couldn't even begin to comprehend the complexity of his feelings. He answered the call the best way he knew how. He bent his head and captured her mouth with his. His tongue explored the recesses of her mouth. The hat fell off her head. Wes took advantage of that and ran one large hand up over her nape. She was a heady sensation for him as she kissed back, just as hot and eager as he was.

Reluctantly Wes eased up. He nibbled at her lower lip, kissed her nose, her brow and then hugged her to him.

"You don't know what you do to me," he said.

"Yes, I do. It's the same thing you do to me."

"I want you."

She glanced around. "This isn't really a good place."

Wes looked left at a row of canoes and oars, then to the right at life vests and fishing jackets. "I guess you're right. We have everything we need. Let's head to checkout."

He picked up the hat and dropped it in the cart. The playfulness of their earlier encounter had disappeared, replaced by the restless humming of sexual need.

They wheeled the cart through the store. Wes paused at the linen department. "Did you put a blanket in that wicker basket?"

C.J. shook her head in the negative. Wes grabbed the first one he saw and tossed it in the basket. "For our lunch picnic," he said.

"Um hmm."

Wes looked at her, grinned, then shrugged. They made their way to a snack food section. "Grab what you like. I'm going to see if they have any Vienna sausage."

C.J. tried not to crinkle her nose. If this guy's idea of good eating was Vienna sausage, they were going to have some major compatibility problems. "Is that what you're eating for lunch?"

Wes laughed. "That's what the fish will eat for lunch. We'll use it as bait. We're gonna eat well. We can stop at the deli next to that bakery in town and pick up some sandwiches."

C.J. breathed a sigh of relief. While Wes searched the aisle for the canned meat, C.J. picked up potato chips, pickle slices, and M&M's. Their shopping cart was getting full. She shrugged out of the fishing jacket and added it to the other merchandise they'd selected.

"Got it," Wes called out. He returned bearing two of the small cans of meat.

"Wouldn't they prefer caviar or pâté?" C.J. asked.

"Caviar would be cruel and pâté's consistency isn't thick enough. Come on, city girl. Let's get this date started. The day's a wastin', as Mama Lo would say."

They headed to the checkout aisles. "You sure know your way around this store," C.J. observed. "I thought you'd just arrived in Serenity Falls."

"I do and I did. All Wal-Marts have basically the same layout no matter where you are in the country. This is my store. I get just about everything I need here."

C.J. looked around. The place did have a certain appeal. She thought about all the upscale malls and exclusive boutiques she normally shopped in. Once a year, C.J. and her mother flew to Paris to get undergarments. She had a feeling though that she was going to cherish the lacy teddy Wes picked for her more than any of her froufrou silks and satins.

Wes paid the bill with a credit card. C.J. watched him sign his name in bold but meticulous detail. She liked a detail man. Actually she liked everything about him. Including the way he handled himself in tough situations. Wes Donovan was the kind of person you'd want to watch your back. C.J. looked at Wesley's back as he accepted packages from the cashier and put them in the cart.

Without thinking she raised a hand and smoothed it over the broad expanse of his back. She flushed all over as she remembered exactly how his skin felt, how hot and hard and broad he was.

Wes turned, a tender smile playing at his mouth. "Ready?"

"More than you know," she mumbled.

They made a gas stop, picked up sandwiches, fruit, and bottled water at the deli then headed to the river.

"How'd you find this place?" C.J. asked as she followed Wes through a clearing and to a glade sheltered by tall trees.

"I was out running this morning and came up on the water. I checked down at the hardware store to see if the river is good for fishing. The man there directed me to several likely spots. And I picked up a couple of licenses."

"So this is a popular spot?"

Wes shrugged. "Don't know. I ignored all the ones he suggested and scoped this one out myself."

He put the fishing gear on the ground. C.J. did the same with the picnic basket. She looked around and found a relatively flat spot with a big rock. A frog sat atop the rock sunning itself.

"Mind if we share?" she asked the frog.

"What was that?"

She looked over her shoulder at Wes and smiled. "Nothing. Talking to myself." C.J. spread the blanket about a foot from the base of the boulder.

She went back to where she'd left the hamper and put it on the edge of the blanket. When she turned to see what Wes was doing she found him staring at her.

"What?"

"I don't think we're going to get a lot of fishing done."

C.J. met his intense gaze. "I think you're right but let's give it the old college try."

"Whatever you say." Wes reached into one of the bags for the line and lures. "Come on over here and I'll show you how to get everything set up."

He kicked off the moccasins and sank to the ground in a fluid motion. C.J. watched him in a quiet awe. "Do you dance?"

Wes looked up. "I beg your pardon?"

C.J. sat on the ground next to him in what she knew was not as naturally graceful a movement as he'd achieved. She crossed her legs and rested her arms on her knees.

"Have you danced professionally? Like ballet."

Wes chuckled. "No. What would make you ask that?"

"You're very light on your feet, and quite graceful for a man."

Wes laughed out loud. "There's an insult in there somewhere isn't there?"

C.J. smiled and shook her head. Maybe it was his martial arts training. "Okay, professor. Show me what to do."

Wes spent the next half hour teaching C.J. about hooking, baiting, and casting. When she was ready, they stood.

"Oh, wait. I can't do it without my hat and jacket."

Grinning, Wes pulled the garments from one of the bags and handed them to her. C.J. ripped off the price tags and tucked them in one of the mesh pockets on the jacket. When the hat wouldn't quite fit on her head, she removed the two combs that held her hair up and put them in another of the jacket pockets. She pushed the hat into place, and then, like Wes, kicked off her shoes.

Standing with legs spread and the fishing rod held in her hands like a flag pole, she announced, "Okay. I'm ready now."

Wes shook his head and smiled.

They moved a little closer to the water's edge. Wes cast his line and watched as C.J. did the same. She kept waiting for it to land in the water with a quiet plop like Wes's did. She turned to question him.

A rumbling like thunder in the distance made her scowl, particularly when she recognized the rumbling as his laughter. "What?"

"You're supposed to aim for the water."

"Where's the line?" she asked.

Wes pointed to a bush to the back and left of C.J., her hook and line tangled in the brush.

"Oh."

"Hold on to this," he said, handing her his own rod.

C.J. put hers on the ground and accepted his. Wes went to the bush to inspect and recapture C.J.'s line.

He untangled the mess.

"Uh, Wes. There's something tugging on this."

He ran back to where she stood at the shore, feet braced and pulling on the rod.

"Reel it in," he instructed.

"What do you . . . Oh, this." C.J. reeled the line in, taking steps backward as she did.

"Hold still. Just keep reeling."

A six-inch fish hung at the end of her line. Wes grabbed the line and swung it in. "Nice job."

"It's so little. It's gonna die."

Wes laughed. "That's the point, Jan."

C.J. frowned—at the fish, at Wes, and at the name. She watched him unhook the catch and drop it in a bucket he'd brought from the truck and filled with river water.

"Wes, it's not like we're hunters and gatherers. We don't need that fish to live. Can't we let it go?"

Wes smiled and gave in. "We'll let them all go when we're done. That make you feel better, city girl?"

"Don't call me that."

Wes came up behind her and circled one large arm around her waist. He leaned forward and nibbled on her ear. "Okay."

C.J. forgot what she'd been mildly miffed about. She sank into his embrace, loving the feel of him at her back.

"Okay. Time for another casting lesson," he said.

He positioned her hands around the rod she held. "Stand like this," he instructed as his muscular thighs shifted hers to the right position. "Now, when you cast off, keep your wrist steady, lean back just a bit." He guided her body in the proper motion. "Let it flow from you, steady, easy."

The line plopped into the water about twenty feet out.

"I did it!"

Both of Wes's hands snaked around her waist. She felt so right in his arms. "Yes, you did." He lowered his head and licked her neck.

C.J. arched into him and moaned.

"Look," he said, his hot breath at her right ear. "We can pretend that there isn't fire between us or we can dive right in, burn ourselves to ashes and then see if anything, like the phoenix, rises from those ashes."

In answer C.J. dropped the fishing rod and stepped out of his embrace. She didn't say a word as she turned to face him. She shrugged out of the jacket then crossed her arms at the edges of her khaki shirt and pulled the cotton top over her head.

Wes's mouth went dry. She wore no bra. The ripe fruit was his for the taking.

CHAPTER 10

She lifted her breasts to him in silent offering. With one step forward he stood before her then lowered his head. Capturing first one firm nipple in his mouth and then the other, Wes gently bit into her. C.J. cried out at the pleasure pain. Wes bent at the knees, suckling, nibbling, swirling his hot tongue over her until she swayed on her feet.

With one final lap at her breast he chucked out of his clothes then knelt before her.

"What, what are you doing?"

"Loving you," he murmured. His hands unfastened the belt at her waist. Unzipping the shorts she wore and skimming them over her thighs and legs came easy. The sight left for him made Wes glad he was already on his knees.

His hands revered her smooth brown skin. She stepped out of the shorts and kicked them aside. Wes buried his head in her navel, lapping and licking while murmuring words and sounds of extreme male delight.

C.J. thought she'd die of the pleasure. He moved too fast . . . and too slow. She crushed his head to her belly and cried out when his mouth rimmed the thin band of the string panties she wore. By the time he'd worked them down over her hips C.J. was ready for him like she'd never been ready for a man before.

She tugged at his shoulders, encouraging him to rise. But Wes grunted, pulled her hips closer to him and used one large hand to part her thighs. When he buried his head between her legs, C.J. almost doubled over his back. She cried out for mercy but he was relentless in the thorough examination of her core. She exploded in a million pieces and called his name over and over.

Before she thoroughly recovered, Wes reached into the pocket of his pants, found one of the condoms he had and put it on.

"Wes," she panted. "Wes?"

A slow finger meandering up her leg and then higher to her inner thigh was the answer she got. C.J. sighed and then gasped when she was lifted in his arms a moment later.

"Wrap your legs around my waist."

She did and was hefted higher. The blunt maleness of his erection pulsated hot and heavy at the place she wanted him most.

"Now, Wesley. Now!"

He thrust into her and they both cried out. C.J. threw her head forward and bit into his neck. The intensity of their desire and the rough play turned her on as much as the man who pounded himself into her like there was no tomorrow.

She felt her climax coming and tried to wait for him. She shivered and cried out his name. Wesley followed shortly after her.

He carried her to the blanket she'd spread out on the ground. Then, kissing her the whole time, he slowly let her languid body slide over his until she again stood on her feet. Wesley helped her to the blanket and they stretched out together.

She lay drowned in a floodtide of emotions, physically spent yet wanting him again . . . and again.

"I have never, ever . . ." her voice trailed off on a soft gasp when his palm circled a full breast. "Wow. You wow me, Wesley Donovan."

"I'm glad you think so because I delight in your body. You're strong and soft, tight and warm."

C.J. sat up and leaned on one elbow. Her other hand strayed to wander over his chest. Well-defined pecs captured her attention. She leaned over him and licked the small male nipples so alike, and yet so different from her own.

Wes shuddered and stilled her soft hand. "Rest."

"I'm not sleepy," she said. Her hand skimmed down his flat stomach and to his inner thigh. "And neither are you," she noted at a certain part of him.

"Where are the other condoms?" she asked.

"Pants pocket."

C.J. leaned over and kissed him on the mouth. "Be right back."

A while later they remembered the fishing. Wes sat up from his spot on the blanket. The rod she'd dropped was nowhere in sight. He grinned. With his luck, a twenty-five-pound catfish had probably swum off with the thing. Wes glanced down at a dozing Jan. A fish may have captured his fishing rod, but he'd gotten the better catch with his own.

He got up and went to the pile of clothes they'd shed at the shore. Pulling on his shorts and pants, he saw the rod submerged in shallow water. He grinned and retrieved it.

"Best fishing lesson you've ever given," he said. He dumped the bucket with Jan's small catch back into the river. Turning to look at the sleeping Jan, Wesley smiled. Then he came to a grim conclusion: If she was a protected witness he was screwed because he wanted her for his, for always. But he didn't want to think about that now.

After tidying up the fishing gear, Wes picked up his shirts and Jan's clothes and returned to her.

She watched him approach and wondered if what she felt meant she was falling in love. C.J. had had her share—and probably some other women's share—of relationships. But nothing and no one had ever left her wanting more. She knew how quickly she tired of new things and wondered if, now that she'd had the dark warrior, she'd be ready to move on to the next challenge, the next hard body.

But as she looked inside herself while watching him put his clothes on, the only answer she'd found was more. She wanted more of Wesley Donovan. Not just more sex, that had been hot and wild, just the way she liked it, but even with Wes the sex had been different. The why of the difference eluded her. And so she watched him.

"Hey, beautiful. You're awake."

"I've been awake since you left me. I wanted to watch that warrior king body of yours without you knowing I spied."

"You can spy on me anytime. But don't be alarmed if you see a marked physical reaction as a result."

C.J.'s smile contained a sensuous flame, one that needed little encouragement to grow into a larger conflagration.

He handed her her clothing. "If you don't put something on, I won't be responsible for my actions."

In response she leaned back on the blanket, opened her legs wide and lay spreadeagled before him. Wesley fell on her with a ravenous hunger that surprised neither of them.

About an hour later, after they'd both dressed they sat cross-legged on the blanket munching on the sandwiches and fruit they'd bought for lunch.

C.J. took a swig of the bottled water to wash her sandwich down then ripped open a package of M&M's.

"Have you always been allergic to chocolate?"

Wes reached for the half sandwich C.J. hadn't eaten. "As long as I can remember. Although in the beginning we didn't know it was chocolate that was causing me to break out. My mother just thought I'd been playing in the poison ivy."

"Didn't Mama Lo know the difference?"

Wes nodded. "Mama Lo did. My mother, Eileen, was too drunk to care or to investigate."

C.J. looked at him. She'd thought the Mama Lo he'd so lovingly referred to was his mother, or maybe his grandmother.

"You and your mother aren't close."

Wes looked up, surprised. "Eileen? Hell, no. The only thing she's ever been close to was her bottle of Thunderbird."

C.J. winced at the venom coming from him. She knew, well knew, what it was like to be close to a bottle. She'd counted almost fifty days of sobriety. She'd given up the bottles before leaving Baltimore. Every day was a struggle. Every day she took it one moment, one day at a time. She wondered if Eileen fought the same demons.

"It's an illness," she said. "Not everyone can control it."

"Eileen never wanted to control it. Why control something that brings you your greatest pleasure . . . and your worst nightmare."

"Is she still living?" C.J. asked.

Wes shrugged and bit into a pear. "Don't know. I haven't seen her in years. The last time I heard from her she wanted a thousand dollars. Said she was going to go clean and check herself into a detox center, start going to AA meetings. Stupid me, I sent the money."

"What happened?"

"She stockpiled liquor at her house and then crashed her car into a light pole coming home from a party. Unfortunately, only the light pole suffered."

C.J. hurt for Eileen, but mostly she hurt for Wes. Given her own loving relationship with her parents, she couldn't imagine not communicating with them. Genevieve and Robinson Mayview, for example, hadn't agreed with their daughter's decision to quit her job and leave Baltimore, but they understood her need to do so. What they didn't understand or know about was her alcoholism and the little white pills she used to keep her going.

C.J. had finally admitted she was powerless over the addictions. She'd busted every bottle in her house, flushed all the prescription pills down a toilet, and then sat in her dark living room crying. Afraid to ask for help, afraid she'd go out and buy a drink, she'd called the only person she knew she could trust to keep her secret. She called her older brother, Robinson.

It had been Rob's idea that she get away for a little while. "Take a vacation, go stay at the beach house in Rehobeth for a couple of weeks. You deserve a vacation. You haven't stopped running since you accepted that Pulitzer. Did I ever tell you how proud I am of you?"

She'd nodded and then cried in his arms. All the world thought she had it totally going on. What few people knew was how miserable she was. C.J. had taken Rob's advice; taken it to the extreme. She turned in a letter of resignation at the newspaper, sold her condo, sold her new BMW and all her furniture. She stuffed only the clothes and things she needed in a four-wheel drive Cherokee she bought used and headed southeast. She drove past Rehobeth. She drove past Virginia.

A detour on the road and a need to fill up the gas tank found her in Serenity Falls, North Carolina. She liked the name of the town. She liked its smallness. She stayed. She'd stayed and was slowly recuperating, finding the self she'd lost somewhere between her first job as a cop reporter and winning a Pulitzer Prize.

"Maybe she wonders about you," she told Wes as she made a mental note to call her own parents that night.

"Eileen doesn't wonder about anything except where her next drink is coming from. Look, why are we talking about this anyway?"

His gruffness hurt her but she understood the source of his anger just as she could understand some if not all the depth of his pain.

Suddenly no longer desiring the taste, C.J. put the chocolate candy away. She reached for an apple and bit into it.

Wes smiled a small smile. He leaned forward to catch the juice that ran down her chin. "I didn't mean to snap at you."

"I know."

"You want to fish some more?"

Her smile was radiant. "I'll never look at fishing in the same light again." She shook her head no. "If we try to do another fishing lesson, it'll be well past dark before we ever leave this spot."

Wes leaned forward to steal a kiss. "You're probably right. I want you again."

"I want you, too."

Wes took the fruit from her hand and cleared the remains of their lunch from the blanket by tossing it all in the wicker hamper. He then reached for her and slowly lowered her to the soft padding of the blanket on the ground.

This time when they made love, it was slow and tender, with a poignant sweetness that brought tears to C.J.'s eyes. She held him and loved him and gave to him all the gentleness that he'd never found in his mother's arms. She gave him hope and strength and something she'd never given before: 100 percent of herself.

CHAPTER 11

It was dusk when Wesley dropped her off at her house. At her door, he kissed her.

"Stay the night."

"I'd like to," he said. "But there are a couple of things I need to check on." Like what kind of job I can land after being fired for getting romantically involved with someone in the Witness Security Program. But with a clarity that rocked him, Wes realized he didn't care. Jan Langley was worth losing his job over. She was special.

"Tomorrow?" she asked.

Wes nodded. "Tomorrow. I'll call before I come over. What's your number?"

She gave it to him. He repeated it back to her and had it memorized.

Wesley pulled her into his arms and pressed her close to the part of him that still, amazingly, reacted to her closeness. He ran a hand down her back and cupped her firm rear. "Tomorrow can't get here fast enough."

With a reluctance they both felt, Wes let her go. He waited until she was safely inside and he heard the deadbolt click before leaving.

Halfway down the steps he thought of something. Jan Langley had city locks on her doors, the kind of protection someone with something to worry about might have even in the midst of wholesome small-town America. Wes sighed. The sooner he found out who she was the easier he'd stop feeling so conflicted.

You didn't feel too much of a conflict down by the river, his conscience pointed out.

"Shut up."

Not that he was particularly hungry, but Wes figured he'd better grab something to eat if he wanted dinner. He'd probably missed Miss Clara Ann's cutoff time for serving dinner. He climbed into the truck and pulled away from the curb.

The piece of junk Casey had supplied him with didn't have a cassette player in it. It barely had a radio. Good thing he wasn't a big music person. He liked to work out to classic rock but that was about it. Wes found one crackly AM station that played country music. He thought he recognized Patsy Cline's plaintive tone but it could have just as easily been the contemporary country artist k.d. lang who sometimes had a Patsy Cline sound.

The song reminded Wes of Eileen. He scowled and turned the radio off. His mother had always pretended she was white, using her light skin as a bargaining chip in the community. She never knew how people, black and white, laughed behind her back and called her a lush.

She'd sent her husband, Wesley's father, to an early grave with her false airs and nagging. People around town said Winton Donovan died of the black lung after working so many years below ground in the mines. But Wesley knew better. The coal dust may have contributed a bit, but his daddy had been nagged to death.

With Winton gone, yelling at Wes when he made friends with dark-skinned kids seemed to be one of Eileen's favorite pastimes. Sometimes, Wes admitted, he did it on purpose. Eileen had never forgiven herself for getting knocked up by a dark man. Her plan had been to marry white and eventually deny any black blood in her own veins. But too much to drink at a party one night put a halt to those plans. Winton Donovan had done the right thing and married Eileen. But through their entire marriage Eileen never let him or her son forget that they both had been bad mistakes.

Yelling at Wes was high up on Eileen's list of priorities, right after beating him for reasons as lame as daring to wake her up from a blackout to tell her he'd gotten an A on his geography test. But Wes had taken his last beating from Eileen more than twenty years ago. Once, just once, he'd struck back. Eileen tore into such a rage that he still bore a small scar in the place where the sharp edge of a kitchen utensil had sliced into his arm.

If she was sober enough to see, he knew Eileen would be appalled at how her son turned out. He was black and proud of it, glad that his father's darker genes were dominant in his skin, and secure in the knowledge that he didn't judge people on the hue of their skin. Wes was good at what he did and, for the most part, liked and respected among his colleagues. He'd dated women of all races, but none seriously. In his line of work, he wasn't willing to put a woman through the changes and the violence that were a necessary part of his job.

Jan Langley would be different. If she was indeed a protected witness she'd understand those things.

Wes pounded the steering wheel in frustration. He hoped Scotty had an answer for him.

He picked up dinner at a drive-through chicken place and made his way to Miss Clara Ann's.

A couple of residents were watching television in the parlor. Wes stopped in and met Garrison the artist and a quiet man who looked up from his book only long enough to grunt a brusque "Hello."

Miss Clara Ann sat in her rocker with an afghan thrown over her knees.

The tigress was nowhere to be found so Wesley decided to linger for a while. Maybe Miss Clara Ann could tell him something about Jan Langley. He sat on the couch opposite the artist.

"Have some anyone?" he asked as he opened the chicken box. Eileen hadn't bothered to teach her boy any manners but Mama Lo had seen to his proper raising.

Miss Clara Ann smiled. "You go on and enjoy, baby. We done finished up eating for the night. There's some pie on the counter though." She stopped rocking and sat up. "I can gets you a piece if you want."

"No, ma'am. You stay right there. I'll get it when I'm through here."

Miss Clara Ann continued her rocking. "Um hmm. Just like I thought. You got some home training. I told that Margaret you'd be a good catch."

"Your niece Margaret is a delightful woman, Miss Clara Ann. We engaged in a brief conversation just yesterday."

Miss Clara Ann rolled her eyes at Garrison. "You been watching too much of that public television, boy. You needs to learn how to talk right."

Wes glanced at Garrison and stifled a grin. The harumph from the wing chair could have been the other man's commentary on the conversation or his reaction to what he was reading. Wes really didn't care. He liked Miss Clara Ann. Sitting in her parlor reminded him of evenings in Mama Lo's kitchen. He and Marcus's brothers and sisters would sit around the table with cups of chickory coffee and talk about the big lives they'd have after escaping from the coal mining town.

As it turned out, only he and Marcus escaped. One of Marc's sisters left to go to college farther south but returned after she graduated to teach school at the town's only high school. Wes thought about Marc's brothers and sisters. He thought about Mama Lo. He hadn't seen her since the funeral.

Sitting in Miss Clara Ann's front parlor, Wes decided to go home again. He'd check on Mama Lo then come back to Serenity Falls.

His mind made up, Wes finished off the chicken.

"You awfully quiet tonight, Wesley. You thinkin' a man's troubling thoughts or you just enjoying our company?"

Wes smiled. "Just enjoying the company, Miss Clara Ann. I was wondering about the town though. Do you know a lot of people here?"

"Knows everybody who was born and raised here and even some who wasn't."

That's just what he was counting on.

"I met a young woman, Jan Langley, and a fellow by the name of Marshall." Wes tossed in the name of the deli owner so as not to draw undue attention to his interest in Jan.

Miss Clara Ann stopped rocking and her brow furrowed. "Jason Marshall opened up that little sandwich shop next to the bakery. That boy charge two-fifty for a piece of bread with some mustard on it. Gotta pay extra to get any meat. Spent too much time in the city and got too much education to have any common sense."

The old woman resettled the afghan about her legs then commenced rocking. "Now Jan Langley. Let me see, cain't rightly say I know that name. Oh, wait a minute. Langley. She be the pretty young thing what bought Mr. Tucker's old house. Girl paid cash money for it too from what I hear tell. Quiet thing. Keeps to herself. Miz Charleston over to the Garden Club been trying to get her to get active since she always in the lawn store buying dirt and flowers.

"Think I heard tell she'd been in some kind of accident and was laid up for a while. Word about town is she got herself a big insurance claim, too. That's how she bought Tucker's house for cash money. Folks say she just been taking it easy these days."

If Jan Langley had been injured in an accident recently, she'd had a remarkable recovery. Her flawless skin and athletic ability, not to mention her appetite for him, wore him out and gave not the least indication that she'd been laid up as Miss Clara Ann put it.

"You got a sweet on her, baby?" Miss Clara Ann asked.

That was one way to put it, Wes thought. He smiled. "Just wondering."

A loud guffaw was the elderly woman's answer. "I told you, boy. When you meets the right one you gon' be knocked over backwards and them footloose ways you was talking 'bout earlier gon' end. That Jan Langley's a pretty one for sure. Seen her at the grocery. She got old eyes though. Look like she done seen too much, more than a child her age ought to. Now my Margaret, she can be kind of bold for a woman, but sometimes that's okay. And her eyes ain't old," Miss Clara Ann added with a wink to Wes.

"I wouldn't call Margaret bold, Miss Clara Ann," Garrison piped in. "She has a refreshing outlook on issues of the day."

Wes looked over the slightly pudgy and definitely rumpled artist. His tan was even, that much Wes could give him. A pair of short, wire reading glasses balanced on his forehead. Wes wasn't sure if the man's bald pate was by choice or necessity. Whatever the case, he seemed to have an interest in Margaret. He could have her. The woman's voice was sweet honey, but that was about all that appealed to him. There was still something vaguely familiar about Margaret. It disturbed him that he couldn't put his finger on it. Maybe in some ways her airs reminded him of Eileen.

Wes grunted. He hadn't thought about Eileen this much in the past ten years. Jan had sure stirred up a hornet's nest with her innocent question about his allergy to chocolate. He'd noticed that she hadn't eaten any more of the M&M's after he'd told her.

He got up and dumped the trash left over from his dinner. He cut a slice of the pie Miss Clara Ann left out and poured himself a cup of coffee. Carrying the items back to the front parlor, he took his seat on the couch.

The small group chuckled through a half hour sitcom and then Miss Clara Ann got up. Wesley stood as she did.

"Well, children. I gots to be getting me some beauty sleep abouts now. It takes those beauty fairies a little longer to work they magic these days. I'll see ya'll in the morning."

She looked at Wesley. "Yeah, boy. I see your mama sure done raised you right. Sit down, child. I'm just an old woman making my way to bed. Save yo' jumpin' up energy for the pretty young things."

"You obviously give the beauty rest angels all the pointers they need to help out the less fortunate."

Miss Clara Ann's cackle of laughter filled the room. Even Garrison smiled. A grunt issued forth from the wing chair.

"Ooh, boy," she said, patting Wesley's back. "Margaret missed out on a good one when she didn't turn your eye. Ya'll have a good one now."

Miss Clara Ann made her way through the parlor. Wes figured her rooms were somewhere downstairs. All the upstairs rooms had discreet numbers on them.

"She's a pistol isn't she?" Garrison observed.

"Yeah. I like her," Wes answered as he took his seat again.

The lump in the chair offered no opinion. Garrison shrugged at the man then lowered his glasses and looked over the wire rim at Wesley.

"We didn't officially meet. I'm Garrison. I'm an artist letting out the third floor of Miss Clara Ann's residence as my working studio."

Wes shook hands with the man. "Nice to meet you. Name's Wesley."

"Do you have an interest in Miss Clara Ann's niece?"

"Oh, not at all," Wes answered, probably too fast to be polite. "Feel free." Something about Margaret told him she probably didn't do the interracial thing, but the artist could make a shot at it.

Garrison puffed his chest out. To Wes, he still looked like what he was, some wayward artistic type. Wes relaxed and folded his arms behind his head. He stretched out, his long legs crossed at the ankles.

"I will," Garrison declared, taking a critical look at Wes. "I plan to. Good to know you're not the active competition for her affections."

Wes was inclined to agree with Miss Clara Ann. This guy had been breathing too many paint fumes up on the third floor. They were starting to interfere with reality. Garrison needed to get in touch with the language patterns of the twentieth century. He talked like he just stepped out of some sappy historical novel.

Somewhere in the back of the house a telephone rang.

A few minutes later, they heard Miss Clara Ann holler out. Wes was through the door and down the hall in a flash with Garrison hot on his heels.

They found her sitting on the edge of her bed holding a phone to her ear.

"Lord, Jesus have mercy. Barbara Jean don't know 'bout this yet, do she? Lord, have mercy, Jesus. The news gon' send Barbara Jean into a heart attack. And poor Betty. Ain't she about seven months along. Lord, have mercy. What we gon' do?"

Wes and Garrison looked at each other. Whatever had happened, hadn't happened to Miss Clara Ann.

The old lady looked up and saw the two men standing, indecisive, in her doorway. "A tree done killed Jimmy Peterson," she told them then turned her attention back to the call. "Well, I be over to the house early in the morning. I bring some fresh made biscuits and my Mahalia albums. We gots to get prayed up cause dat family gon' need all the Jesus they can get."

Miss Clara Ann concluded her call and shook her head sadly. "Umph, umph, umph. Terrible thing. Terrible thing."

"Miss Clara Ann what happened?" Garrison asked.

"Are you all right?" Wes asked.

Still shaking her head, Miss Clara Ann pushed herself up from the bed. "Po, thing. Jimmy got killed. Ya'll come on with me to the kitchen. I gots to put out some extra for tomorrow to take over to the Peterson place."

Wes and Garrison looked at each other and shrugged. They let Miss Clara Ann pass between them then followed her to the kitchen.

"How does a tree kill a person?" Garrison whispered to Wes.

"I figure we'll find out in a minute."

Miss Clara Ann, still clucking about Jimmy's fate, poured each man a cup of coffee and pressed the mugs into their hands.

"Who is Jimmy Peterson?" Wes ventured.

"That poor child, bless his soul, is Barbara Jean Peterson's baby boy.

He own that car store lot round the way from the Wal-Mart. That boy been tinkering with cars and trucks since he was a little kid. Nobody was surprised when he grew up to be selling cars."

"What happened to him, Miss Clara Ann?" Garrison asked.

"He was testing out a new car he had. Sitting at a stoplight up off Route 18 when a big, old tree fell on him and the car."

"Freak accident," Garrison concluded.

Yeah, Wesley thought. Freak accident just like the one where a marshal tripped over a garbage can and resulted in his own arrival in Serenity Falls. "How long ago did this happen?" he asked.

"Etta Mae say just 'bout an hour ago. There still be police at the scene," she said, accenting the first syllable so police came out poe-lease.

"Are you going to be all right, Miss Clara Ann?" Wes inquired.

She waved him and Garrison out of the room. "I be's fine. I'm gon' lay out everything I needs to make a couple extra batches of biscuits then I'm gonna find them Mahalia Jackson albums to take over to the house. I'm worried 'bout Barbara Jean. Her heart ain't too good. And Jimmy's wife Betty, she be due soon with another young un. Lord, that girl gon' need some strength to see her through this."

Miss Clara Ann looked at the remaining piece of apple pie. She reached in a cabinet, pulled out a small plate and put the slice on the plate. Handing it to Garrison with a fork, she said, "Eat this boy. I'm gonna make ya'll some peach cobbler tomorrow."

Garrison patted his stomach. "Miss Clara Ann, I think I've already gained ten pounds since I moved in here."

"Ain't nothing wrong with that. Do some exercise and you burn that fat you carrying around right off. Eat the pie so I can wash the plate, boy."

"Yes, ma'am." Garrison took a bite of pie.

Wes made his excuses then left. He wanted to get to the scene of the so-called freak accident to take a look around. He quickly debated whether to take the truck or the bike. In the end, he strapped a black leather case to the back of the motorcycle and took off in the direction of Route 18. If need be, the bike could get him in and out of some places the truck couldn't go.

It was close to nine by the time Wes got to the accident scene. It had happened, like Miss Clara Ann said, off the busier thoroughfare so traffic wasn't a real problem. Gawkers, however, were. It looked like every resident of Serenity Falls had heard about the accident and showed up to take a look at what was left of Jimmy Peterson and his new show car.

Wes sat astride the motorcycle still wearing his helmet. He scanned the crowd looking for a nervous, anxious, or recognizable face. All he saw were curiosity seekers. And Kenny Sheldon from the *Gazette*. Wes frowned. Reporters were like vultures, always picking over the remains of the fallen while waving the banner of the First Amendment.

He scanned the crowd again, then froze. He zeroed in on one familiar face, the face of the person who had met him running early that morning. Wes unzipped the black leather bag attached to his bike. He might need the firepower handy if things got weird.

Gunning the bike, he circled closer until he was within ten feet of the witness.

CHAPTER 12

Amber Baldwin plucked Frank Jr. from the floor then picked up the ringing telephone on the kitchen counter.

"Hello?"

No one answered. "Hello? Is anyone there?"

After a pause a muffled voice came on the line. "Mrs. Baldwin? This is a friend. Tell your husband to watch his back. We'll be sending a sign." There was laughter and then the line went dead.

Amber, her eyes wide, stared at the telephone receiver. With shaking hands she returned the receiver to the cradle. Hugging Frank Jr. close to her, she made her way to the crate-style sofa.

"Frank, dear, God, Frankie. What kind of trouble are you in?" She hugged the baby so close to her that he began to fret. Amber put him on the floor and picked up a throw pillow. She squeezed it close and prayed for her husband.

Frankie had said he was working a double at the recycling plant. He said he worked a lot of double shifts, but Amber never saw any of the extra money he was supposedly making for them. She offered time and again to get a job, even a part-time job. But Frankie wouldn't hear of it. Now he was in some kind of trouble.

The man on the phone said they'd be sending a sign. What did that mean? A sign of what and to whom?

Amber rocked back and forth, bit her thumbnail and chewed on her lip. She glanced at the telephone on the end table. She looked around, then picked it up and punched out her mother's number. Her mama would tell her what to do. But before the line connected she slammed the telephone down. Frank Jr. jumped at the sound and started crying.

She handed him a pacifier from the table. "Shush, Frank Jr. I'm trying to think."

Frankie didn't allow her to call her mother. He'd said they had to cut all ties with the past, to forge their own way. Amber sighed and plopped back on the sofa. She didn't see how not talking to her mama helped them at all. She gnawed at her thumbnail and stared at the telephone.

If she just had somebody to talk to she'd feel better. Maybe the caller had been one of Frankie's buddies from work playing a joke on him.

Amber picked up the phone again. She had a friend she could call. She'd call Jan Langley.

Margaret Shelley touched up her lipstick and smoothed her hands over her full hips in the tight jeans. She'd gotten a lot done this night, more than she'd even anticipated. On the backseat of her car were several packages, her ammunition so to speak.

If that gorgeous Wesley Donovan thought he'd given her the slip, he had another thing coming. She'd get him to notice her this time. She'd even taken Aunt Clara's advice on the perfume and bought a lighter scent with earthy undertones.

Margaret smiled into her compact then snapped the case shut. Getting home had taken longer than necessary. She had to make a detour around an accident. She smiled again then dropped the compact in her handbag and opened the back door of her blue sedan to get her packages.

"It's best to get their attention with a big bang."

Amber got a busy signal when she tried Jan Langley's house. She briefly thought about taking Frank Jr. and just going over there. She glanced at her watch and thought better of that idea. If Frankie called and she wasn't home, he'd go nuts with worry. She couldn't do that to him. She'd try Jan again in a few minutes.

C.J. sat propped up in bed with a cup of chamomile tea in one hand and the telephone in the other. "What do you mean something or someone has obviously made you happy?"

"C.J. It's me, Rob. Remember, I know you. You sound positively giddy. It must be a man."

She chuckled at her brother's logistical arguments. "What if it is?"

"I can have a PI check him out. I need to make sure he's good enough for you."

"I thought you only had your wife's background checked out by private investigators."

"Ouch, C.J. That hurt," Robinson Mayview said. "She's talking about you," he said to someone in the background.

"That Nettie? Tell her I said hello."

"C.J. says 'Hello.' Toinette says get some rest and stop running up your long-distance bill."

C.J. smiled. Times hadn't always been as easy between her and the older woman her brother married. At one point, the lowest in her career, C.J. thought she'd lost her brother's love over Toinette and the center she ran for welfare mothers. That whole debacle had all been quite a while ago. Sometimes it still hurt like yesterday.

"Rob?"

"Yeah, sis?"

"I'm glad you and Nettie are happy."

"Me, too. Nice job at trying to change the subject. It didn't work though. Who's the guy, some southern gentleman with Old South charm?"

C.J. thought of the tall, powerfully built Wes Donovan, the black clothes, the easy French, the quick reflexes, the sexy motorcycle, his oh-so-slow hands. "Not exactly," she said. "This is new. So we'll see. I'll think about keeping you posted."

"You know you have a place when you're ready to come home again."

"I know."

"And what about the other part?"

She knew what he meant. "Fifty-three days and counting."

"Good girl. Be strong. You reading that material I gave you?"

C.J. leaned over the side of the bed and opened a small drawer on the night table. She pulled out the twelve-step handbook Rob had given her. "Every day. I'm working on that moral inventory part. Tough stuff."

"You need to go to the meetings, C.J."

She shook her head no. On that point she'd steadfastly refused. Sitting around with a bunch of people talking about their drinking problems wasn't her idea of recovery. Rob had repeatedly made his case and even volunteered to go with her. But C.J. wouldn't budge on that point. She'd go this alone. She'd created the mess of her life by herself. She figured she'd find her way out by herself.

"You still there?" he asked.

"I'm here."

"You call me if you need me, C.J. Any time, day or night."

"I will. Love you. Tell Toinette I said 'Goodnight.' "

A few minutes later she sat in the bed finishing up her tea. She opened the twelve-step book and looked at the inventory of steps. She'd never been a real Jesus person so the whole God and Higher Power concept had been difficult to comprehend. It wasn't until she'd been able to view God as a spirit power as opposed to some omnipotent being that she'd been able to make some progress.

God was the spirit who gave sunsets and rain, the spirit that made flowers grow and the one who'd brought Wes Donovan into her life.

Their day together had been beautiful. C.J. spied the fishing hat on the bed post where she'd put it. She grinned. Maybe they'd find some more nature to explore tomorrow.

She glanced at the clock on the night table. Now that she again allowed herself TV she restricted it to one hour each day, national news only. She hadn't seen any today. She still avoided the local channels and newspaper. That part of her life was over. The folks back at the paper wanted to believe she was just taking an extended leave of absence but C.J. knew better.

The book in her hand weighed heavy, not so much in her hands but on her heart. She hated lying to Wes Donovan. She cringed every time he called her Jan. Yes, it was technically her name but the spirit, if not the letter of truthfulness, was what mattered.

Would it hurt to tell him the truth?

The question that caused her greater pause was why was she going through changes over the man? She could honestly claim that the sex was the best she'd had, but sex didn't make a relationship. For a reason she couldn't fathom, if she wanted anything from Wes Donovan she wanted a relationship more than she wanted the sex. She wasn't about to give up the sex but she wanted more.

And that desire for more frightened her.

At the accident scene the protected witness spotted Wesley and gave a quick shake of the head to indicate everything was okay. Almost imperceptively Wesley nodded but left his leather case unzipped. The cops weren't letting people near the tree that was already being cut into pieces to clear the roadway.

With a smirk Wes noted that ace reporter Kenneth Sheldon was making a nuisance of himself. But people were talking to the guy while pointing to the tree, gesturing, and describing what they saw when they first arrived.

The whole thing looked like what it was supposed to be: an accident. Wes figured there was nothing wrong with erring on the side of caution though. He parked the bike, zipped up his bag and took his helmet off. As if he were just another gawker, he eased his way into the crowd and toward the witness.

"What happened?" he asked a man two people away from the witness.

"Jimmy Peterson was test driving a new car and that tree fell on him when he was sitting here at the light," the man volunteered.

Wes had to give it to Miss Clara Ann. Her communications network was good. She hadn't left her house and knew as many details as the people at the scene.

He edged forward as if to get a better view as workers used chain saws to cut through the big tree.

"Sure is a big one," he said conversationally.

"They say it's about a hundred years old. Must have rotted from the inside," the protected witness said.

Wes leaned forward and turned his head slightly. Anyone watching would think he, like everyone else, was jockeying for the best roadside view. "This involve you?" he asked quietly.

"No. An accident," the Marshals Service's witness responded just as quietly.

"Call me."

With that, Wes straightened and moved around the circle of people. When he looked back a minute later, the witness was gone.

For someone who was supposed to be on an assignment getting his attitude adjusted, Wes had to admit he hadn't done much in that department. He lay in bed wearing just white jockey shorts in his room at Miss Clara Ann's and thought about the day. Propped up on a couple of pillows, he tucked his hands under his head. It had been a long day and a lot had happened.

He thought about Jan Langley then swore out loud.

Wes swung his feet off the bed and turned the television on to see what time it was. Eleven-thirty-two. Damn. Too late to call Scotty at home on a nonessential check. He'd do that first thing in the morning. He d give Scotty her telephone number and see what, if anything, came up with that. Wes glanced at the pager he'd turned on and put on the night table. If the witness called, he'd get the message by pager.

He left the television on with the sound muted then got back on the bed.

Something Miss Clara Ann said came back to him. "She'd paid cash money for her house."

Not a lot of people could afford to do that. But the house was older and on the small side. Maybe Jan Langley had used savings. Wes frowned. "Yeah, right."

He had a savings account. The balance was healthy but not enough to buy a house and fully pay for it in cash. In the morning, he'd find the courthouse or treasurer's office and look up the deed for Jan Langley's property. If what Miss Clara Ann had said was true, and frankly, Wes doubted it, that accident settlement of Jan's must have been a big one.

With his plan for the next day in place, Wes pulled the sheet over him. With the remote, he turned the television off. When he closed his eyes, the vision of Jan's tight, firm body came to him. Fishing sure was a pleasure. In the dark room Wesley grinned. He lowered a hand and stroked himself. Maybe he'd take Jan Langley down by the riverside again.

A few hours later Wes sat up in bed, awakened by a noise that sounded like a car backfiring in the distance. He listened to the now quiet of the night. Nothing seemed to stir. Through his open bedroom window he heard crickets and nothing more.

And then the pager went off.

He flipped the sheet off and pulled his jeans and running shoes on. A check of the pager showed a local number.

For what was supposed to be a sleepy little Southern town there sure was a lot going on.

Wes thought about using the cell phone then changed his mind. He grabbed his wallet, keys, and black bag then left the house with little noise.

He bypassed the pay phone closest to Miss Clara Ann's house and used one two blocks over. He dialed the number.

"This is Donovan. What's wrong?"

"You said 'Call me.' "

Wes looked heavenward. "What's the situation? It's like three o'clock in the morning."

"You Deputy Marshals are early bird types. That's why you always get the worms."

If the witness had been in front of Wes, he would have strangled the person. "Tell me what's been going on."

"How do I know this line is secure?"

"You don't. You can talk to me now. Or meet me in ten minutes."

"You know where the IHOP is?"

"I'll find it." He flipped through a phone book at the booth and got the street address.

Wes went back to the house, got the truck, and picked the witness up under a lamppost.

Wes turned toward Route 18. "Okay. The truck is clean. It's just you and me. What's the story?"

"I like it here," the witness said. "The people are nice. I have a good job. I'm tired of moving."

"But?"

"But for the last couple of weeks, I've been feeling like someone is watching me. It's unnerving."

"Have you seen anyone you recognize? Any car or vehicle that looks familiar?"

"No. I know the drill though. Then, when Jackson got busted up, it seemed like, well it seemed like just the kind of thing they'd do to send me a message or a sign."

Wes turned onto the open highway and headed south. He, too, viewed the field inspector's accident as suspect but for a different reason. "Do you think you've been made or not?"

The witness sighed. "I don't know. Sometimes I just think my whole life is one paranoid move to another. Sometimes, you know, this really sucks."

"I know," Wes said quietly. Life for people in the Witness Security Program wasn't easy. That's why he wondered why Jan seemed so easy, so confident, and self-assured. Most of the folks he usually dealt with were paranoid, and with good reason. Most of the relocated witnesses had contracts out on them in their former lives.

"Do you want to relocate?"

The witness looked out the window and sighed again. "I don't know. Give me another week. Why are you staying at the old lady's boarding house?"

"Seemed easier. I applied for a job at the recycling plant, too."

The witness laughed. "What? You undercover or something? Your picture on the front page of the newspaper isn't any kind of undercover I ever heard of."

Wes had to admit to himself, he was wondering now why he'd applied at the plant. It had seemed like a good idea at the time. He needed a reason to just show up in a relatively small town. Looking for work seemed reasonable enough. He didn't expect it to be quite so easy to locate the witness. Usually they were real reluctant to open up to strangers, even strangers who were Deputy Marshals. It was that paranoia thing. And he sure could have done without that nosy reporter snapping pictures at the grocery store.

"Wanted to blend in," he told the witness. "This place is small."

"Not that small. There's more than twenty-five thousand people here."

Wes glanced at the witness and grinned. "What are you now, spokesperson for the Chamber of Commerce?"

The witness laughed. "I told you, I like it here. Would hate to have to leave."

"Your safety comes first."

"I know. Sometimes, here in Carolina, though, it's real easy to forget what life was like before."

Wes nodded. "You need anything?"

"No. I'm fine. The only thing I want is to be left alone. To live the rest of my life out in peace."

"It's my job to see that you do."

The witness nodded. Wes pulled into a roadside store got coffee and doughnuts for them both then headed back toward Serenity Falls.

By the time Wes got to Miss Clara Ann's place dawn was peeking over the horizon. He'd gotten all of three hours sleep. He shucked his jeans and shirt and got back in bed. Maybe, if he was lucky, he could get a another hour or two and cut his morning run short. He'd gotten a good workout with Jan Langley. Wes drifted off with a smile on his face.

* * *

Amber Baldwin tuned to the news on the radio as she fixed breakfast for herself. Frankie hadn't come home until real late, or real early in the morning. He'd been quiet when he got home, too. He didn't even kiss her, and he didn't look in on Frank Jr. like he always did.

What she heard on the radio made her worry more. She tuned the station in a bit more and adjusted the antenna.

". . . small explosion last night at the Woodsong Recycling Plant in Serenity Falls. Three people were slightly injured when a canister of what authorities believe was hazardous waste exploded about two-thirty this morning. Plant officials sent employees who work in the area near the accident home. Officials are investigating the incident. And in other news . . ."

Amber turned the volume down and looked at the bedroom door. Frankie lay sleeping behind that door. She glanced at the telephone on the counter and wondered if the explosion at the plant had been the sign the caller was talking about.

She'd been unable to reach Jan Langley. Her line was busy for a long time. Just as soon as Frankie left, she'd go to Jan's house. Jan was smart and confident. She'd know what to do.

CHAPTER 13

Mulling over coffee at Miss Clara Ann's breakfast table Wes thought about what the witness had said the night before. He also thought about Jan Langley. What a woman. God, what a woman. Instinctively, he'd known it would be good between them, but he hadn't bargained on the surge of protectiveness he was feeling. The only thing that bothered him was the lingering worry that she was living under the auspices of the U.S. Marshals Service Witness Security Program; not much else could explain her vagueness on some things. If she turned out to be a witness he'd have a rough time justifying his actions.

"Didya read 'bout that explosion last night over to the plant?"

Alert now, Wes sat up. "What explosion?"

"Paper said last night. 'Bout two in the morning." Miss Clara Ann handed Wesley the morning edition of the *Serenity Falls Gazette* then topped off his cup of coffee.

"Thanks," he said.

"Sure is a lot of bad stuff happening around here in the last couple a days. First old Jesse's heart, then the accident last night. Now this."

Wes scanned the front page. Battery acid from a drum full of discarded batteries had exploded. Three people were taken to the county hospital for minor lacerations. The lead story was short but promised more details in the next day's edition. Officials, according to Kenny Sheldon's story, were investigating the accident.

Wes filed the information as more small-town happenings. At least the reporter Sheldon had a decent topic to write about.

"Weekend starts today," Miss Clara Ann observed. "You got yourself some plans?"

Wes smiled. Not really up to Miss Clara Ann's matchmaking, he didn't want to sound too available. "Sort of," he lied. He had hoped to take a few hours off and drive up to see Mama Lo, but with the real threat of an antsy witness, he'd have to stay put for the weekend. As long as his plans included Jan Langley he'd be fine. Just fine.

"The Garden Club ladies having their annual picnic this weekend. Been telling Margaret about it. She got up and out early today. Said she had some thinking to do. Anyway, that picnic be tomorrow over at the town square. They always put on a nice show."

"That a fact," Wes said, noncommittal. "I'm not real big on flowers."

"But you likes to eat," Miss Clara Ann said while nodding toward Wesley's now empty plate. "The Garden Club always has a real nice spread. You put a hurtin' on them griddle cakes. You want some more? Garrison usually makes his way down 'bout this time. I'm gonna make up another batch."

"No, thank you. I'm full."

"Bet it takes a lot to fulfill a man like you," she said, clearing plates from the table.

Curious at her choice and tone of words, Wes looked up but Miss Clara Ann was already headed to the kitchen. "Now what did she mean by that?" Shaking his head in quiet bemusement, Wes flipped through the remaining pages of the newspaper.

A telephone rang in the kitchen. A few moments later, Miss Clara Ann popped her head through the door. "Call for you Wesley, baby. You can take it in the parlor. There's a telephone over next to my rocker."

"Thank you."

Curious as to who would be calling him, who knew he was at Miss Clara Ann's, Wes went to take the call.

"Did you see that story in the newspaper today?"

Wes immediately recognized the voice of his witness. "I saw it."

"That was a message to me. I just know it. There were a couple of, shall we say, interesting bangs in my former line of work."

"All right. Look, lay low. I'll get you out as soon as possible. You know the drill. It's going to take a little while to arrange things."

"No. I don't want to leave."

Wes shook his head and frowned. "You just said . . ."

"I know what I said. Maybe I'm just jumping at shadows. Look, I shouldn't even be on the phone with you. I think I'm just gonna disappear for the weekend. Maybe take a long drive, somewhere out of the way."

Wes got an idea. "I have a suggestion for you." He agreed to meet the witness in thirty minutes to go over the plan.

When he got off the telephone Wes smiled. If the witness went for it, he'd get to see Mama Lo after all.

Later that morning, confident that the witness was safe and secure and that his suggestion had been met with enthusiastic agreement, Wes made his way to Jan Langley's house. The information he'd dug up at the treasurer's office in town didn't make him happy and he really had no way to nonchalantly bring up the topic with Jan. But he was curious, real curious, about a woman who paid cash money for a house and two acres of land.

He found her in the backyard on her knees. A small boom box on the steps churned out Top 40 tunes from a local radio station. Faded denim curved across a tight rear end. Wes knew what that denim felt like, he'd been that close to her skin. And judging from what the sight of her was doing to him, he was going to need to get real close again, real soon.

From what he could see she was planting some kind of bush. But Wes had to be honest. He wasn't really paying that much attention to what she was doing in the front. That wiggling behind kept him riveted to the spot, mesmerized even. Jan was aggressive in bed—not that they'd actually had sex in a bed. Maybe she'd go for a few alternate positions. That thought brought a slow, knowing smile. He'd seen a hammock between a couple of trees out here and wondered if it would support their weight. She stretched forward and patted something on the ground then sat back and pulled out of her shirt. Wes completely lost his train of thought.

"Mercy." Wes gritted his teeth. He wanted her. Now.

The smooth brown skin of her bare back glistened with a fine light sheen of sweat. She wiped her brow with the faded white cotton shirt she'd taken off then spread her arms wide in a deep stretch. She leaned to one side and then the other, then with her hands at her waist she twisted around in a limbering motion.

"Wes! I didn't hear you come up." She rocked back on her heels and pushed herself up.

Wes swallowed, hard. Heat shot through his entire body and he could focus on just one thing: the way this woman filled out a halter top. He hadn't seen one of those things in years. Didn't even know women still wore them. Marc's sisters had pranced about in them back in the '70s, but they were girls then, just barely able to fill their training bras. There was nothing, not one thing, girlish about Jan Langley's halter top. The crisscross design in a blue-jean-looking material separated and lifted and proudly showed off those fabulous wanna-be C cups.

He licked his lips and stared.

She dusted her hands off on her jean-clad thighs. The movement caught his eye. He couldn't claim to have ever been jealous of a pair of pants but Wes was jealous of those jeans. They hugged her thighs the way he wanted to. Those tight jeans and that halter made him want to howl. Wes knew exactly why a cave man would throw his woman over his shoulder and haul her off into a cave. Everything he was feeling now was positively primitive.

"Hey, Wes. You okay?"

Wesley licked his lips again and tried to swallow, tried to breathe. Down boy. Down boy. Keep your hands to yourself, Donovan.

"Hey," he finally got out, more grunt than greeting.

He reached up and took off the dark shades. C.J. gasped and took a step back. His eyes, his stare, everything about this man pulsated. She'd never seen that much desire in a man. Heat suddenly swirled through her, clenching her abdomen, making her knees weak. She would have stepped back again, more in self-preservation than anything else. But she couldn't move. She was rooted to the spot just like the rose bushes she'd been putting down would root in the ground.

His burning eyes held her still.

C.J. wondered at and marveled over the sheer, unleashed power of this man. His gaze held her captive and she wondered at the fates that brought her to this time, to this place, to this man. Had she been told a mere two months ago that she'd find herself in North Carolina, in a backyard that belonged to her, staring into the intense brown eyes of the man she loved, she'd have laughed out loud.

Her eyes widened, and this time she did take a step backward. Love? Impossible. Where that errant thought came from she couldn't imagine. Lust. She'd meant lust, deep, soul-wrenching, all-consuming lust.

She swallowed and licked suddenly dry lips.

"I didn't hear you come up. Hi. Have you, uh, been standing there long?"

Wes slipped the handle of his sunglasses down the neckline of his white ribbed shirt. "I wanted to see you."

She answered with a small smile. "I wanted to see you, too."

"I've been thinking about what we talked about last night. I'm going to drive home for the day, probably stay overnight and then get back here sometime Saturday afternoon or evening. Would you like to come with me?"

"To West Virginia?"

Wes nodded. "To meet Mama Lo and maybe Elizabeth, Hannah, Christopher, and Curtis."

"Who are they?"

Wes hooked one finger through a belt loop on his jeans. "They're like my sisters and brothers."

"And Eileen?"

The immediate scowl on his face made C.J. wish she hadn't mentioned the woman's name. The sensual tension in him suddenly replaced by an uglier tension wasn't difficult to see.

"What about her?"

With a shrug, she let it go. She wanted the other awareness back. Eileen wasn't important right now. C.J. advanced toward him until she stood right in front of him. She unhooked the finger at his jeans and placed his hand at her throat.

He needed no additional encouragement. He wrapped his other arm about her waist and pulled her to him. With one slow finger he caressed the smooth skin of her neck. That tantalizingly slow finger meandered its way down. C.J. closed her eyes and lost herself in sensation: Hot, like being too dangerously close to an out-of-control bonfire; cold, like the shivery coolness of a double chocolate milkshake on a parched throat. She moaned.

The soft touch of his hand at her neck and the hard length of his erection at her abdomen made her think of the rough smooth stone she'd plucked off the ground the night she left Baltimore. And then she didn't think about anything—except the soft rustle of fabric as Wes untied the straps of her halter top and bared her breasts to his gaze.

She opened her eyes and watched his own darken. The straps of her halter fell away. Wes took half a step back. Her breasts jutted out, full and proud.

He wet his two index fingers on the tip of his tongue then brought each finger to the tip of her breasts. Instantly her nipples puckered and turned into hard pebbles.

C.J.'s breathing came quickly.

Their eyes met. Wes smiled, slowly, knowingly.

He ran each finger over each nipple, around the areolae of her breasts. And then he fully cupped her, weighing and assessing the lushness of her breasts.

When his mouth finally closed over one, C.J. cried out and arched into him. "Wes!"

The sound from his throat could have been "Hmm?" It could have been "Umm," as in "Umm, this is good." But C.J. didn't really care. She pulled his head closer and stroked the corded strength of his neck as he suckled her.

She looked down at him. With his eyes closed and all his concentration seemingly centered on nothing but giving her pleasure, C.J. wondered how it would feel if he were suckling her breasts full to bursting with mother's milk to nourish their child.

Startled, she gasped and quickly stepped back. Open-mouthed, C.J. stared at Wes. He blinked several times, clearly not sure what had happened.

"Huh? What? What's wrong, Jan?"

"My name's not Jan," she blurted out.

Damn, that wasn't what she meant to say. He'd gotten her so confused that she'd forgotten herself. But her name wasn't as important as the thought she'd had about her breasts. For her to have mother's milk, she'd need to be pregnant—with his child. C.J. didn't want any kids. She didn't even think she particularly liked kids. The thought of being both pregnant and pregnant with Wesley's child was enough to cool her down and clear her head. Big time. Why was she thinking these things?

Focusing on Wes again, C.J. realized that something about him had changed. He no longer looked at her with passion-glazed eyes. He stood tall and strong, with his arms folded at his chest.

"Cover yourself."

C.J. glanced down. Her bare chest looked incongruous in the now harsh light of day. She looked wanton and felt cheap.

Turning her back to him she tied the halter straps around her neck then picked up and pulled on the white oxford shirt she'd been wearing. She buttoned it all the way to her neck then tucked the flaps in her jeans. Fully clothed again, she turned back to him.

His expression was hard, unforgiving, even cold. With his arms crossed and his feet braced, he looked like a cop assessing a particularly gruesome sight. And the fact that he'd put those sunglasses back on bolstered the image.

"What's your name if it isn't Jan?"

C.J. hadn't liked lying to him but she definitely didn't care for the superior attitude he was taking now. She'd heard cops interrogate witnesses with friendlier tones.

"Jan isn't the name I usually go by. It's a shortened version of my middle name."

"So, what's your name?"

It was difficult to believe that the man standing before her was the same one who had just moments ago been lapping at her breasts like a sex-starved maniac. If he was going to cop such a cold attitude, he didn't deserve to know the truth.

"My name is Ja'Niece." She then spelled it for him.

Stoic, he stood before her, as if assessing the truth of it. "What's with the apostrophe?"

C.J. smiled then, for a moment. "My parents expressing their creativity."

"And Langley?"

C.J. blinked. "What about it?"

"That your real last name?"

"What is this, twenty questions? Do you normally meet people who run around giving you fake last names?" She hoped the question would startle him and get him off this path. She wouldn't be lying, exactly. Langley was on her birth certificate—as her mother's maiden name.

"As a matter of fact, I do."

C.J. reached for the gloves she'd dropped. "What is it you do, exactly?"

"I'm an Inspector for the U.S. Marshals Service."

Great, just great, she thought. She stared up at him. It fit though. It also explained his quick reaction at the store parking lot yesterday and his vague description about being a government troubleshooter. He'd looked, smelled, and reacted like a cop, especially in the last few minutes. Of course, it had to be too good to be true to meet a man like Wes in a small town like this one.

She didn't like cops; she didn't particularly dislike them either. Federal ones though were a pain. She'd dealt with enough overly cocky FBI and DEA types to know she didn't want to get mixed up with one personally. A good roll in the hay was another thing entirely. She and Wes had had that. It was time to move on.

"Are you here in Serenity Falls working a case or vacationing?"

"Does it matter?"

C.J. looked him over from the top of his head to the tips of his feet. The ribbed shirt was some sort of cotton material. His jeans fit him the way jeans were supposed to fit a man. Boy, was this ever a setback in her personal recovery program.

She reached for the watering bucket and sprinkled water over the four rose bushes she'd planted.

Then, turning to face him again, she said, "No. It doesn't matter. Not in the long run. It wouldn't be a good idea for us to continue this."

"Conflict of interest?" he asked.

C.J. smiled a small, sad smile. "Something like that you could say. I told you I was here recuperating. One of the things I'm recuperating from is men like you."

"What does that mean?"

"It doesn't matter."

C.J. gathered up the boxes the rose bushes had arrived in. Wes picked up the other two and followed her to the area on the side of the house where her garbage cans were. She broke down her boxes and tucked them between the cans. Wesley did the same.

"Jan? Ja'Niece?"

When she ignored him, he grabbed her arm and pulled her toward him.

She tugged at him but to no avail. "What do you want, Wesley?"

"You," he said right before his mouth closed over hers.

This kiss was rough and ragged and punishing. He didn't want to want her. But he wanted her . . . and he needed her. His hard lips slanted over hers and his tongue boldly stroked the tender inside of her mouth. No gentle or even exploratory kiss was this.

For C.J. his hunger and his anger came through. She got the message as clearly as if he'd been shouting. She understood the hunger, wondered about the anger, and matched him stroke for stroke in aggressiveness. She kissed him back with pent up longing and heartfelt regret. If this was their last kiss, they'd both burn with the memory of it for some time to come.

When he finally pulled away from her mouth, C.J. touched her lips with a tentative finger. She knew they'd be swollen with his brand. She watched him pull off the wraparound shades. When she turned to leave he stopped her.

"Come to West Virginia with me."

CHAPTER 14

When she didn't answer him, Wes caught her chin in his hand and turned her face toward him. His touch gentle, his eyes pleading, he asked another question. "Who are you running from, Jan? Tell me. I'll protect you."

Like images captured on film, Wes watched emotions move across her face: desire, pain, resignation, confusion, and this last one, the one that hurt him the most, anger. She had reason to be angry with him. He'd suspected all along that she was a protected witness. She didn't even blink when he'd told her he was a Deputy Marshal. Most people asked what it meant to be a Deputy Marshal—was the job like the ones shown in the movies. But not Jan, or rather, Ja'Niece. The nickname Jay seemed like it would suit her more than Jan, he thought as an aside.

Not only had she not asked him more about his job, she seemed resigned to the fact that he was a federal law enforcement agent. She asked if he was in town working a case. Not many people would have that as their first question to someone who'd just introduced himself as a Deputy Marshal. But witnesses would think to ask that question.

Wes didn't like feeling out of control of any situation. But that was the only way to describe what he felt right now. He lost control of himself when he was around her. All he could think about was holding her, being deep inside her, loving her and protecting her from the demons that haunted her physically and emotionally.

She jerked free of him and stalked back to the watering can. Lifting the can, she made her way to the raised platform near the back steps and then watered little sprigs of green in rich brown soil.

"What makes you think I'm running from someone? And why do you want me to go to West Virginia?"

Wes sat on the top step and watched her. She bent to pluck some offending item from the soil then flicked it away with her fingers. Patting the soil around the small plants, she steadfastly ignored him while waiting for his answers.

"I'm a Deputy Marshal, Jan," he said, putting emphasis on her name in a way that made her turn and face him. The look she gave him challenged him. Wes let it go—for now. "My specialty is Witness Security, WITSEC. I've been protecting federal witnesses for the last six years."

"And?" she said.

He ignored her caustic tone. "I can help you."

"The only thing I need from you, Wesley Donovan, is to be left alone. I think we've done enough damage already. If I need any help, I'll call a Boy Scout."

"You can't deny what's between us," he said quietly.

"Yes, I can. You're a step I thought I'd conquered. I can see now that I'm going to have to go back and work on it some more."

"What are you talking about?"

"I'm talking about addictions, Wesley. Pretty boys are a particular weakness of mine." She put a hand on her hip and assessed him. Wesley tried to keep still under the close scrutiny. When she walked toward him, he wasn't sure if he was going to be able to not touch her. But she solved his dilemma by reaching out to him.

Her small, smooth hand caressed his temple then soothed down the side of his face around his ear then over his neck. Wesley closed his eyes and shuddered.

"You see, Wes. All my life I've never denied myself pleasure. I believe in working hard . . ." she said, as her index finger traced the contours of his mouth. When he would have captured her finger in his mouth, she moved her hand and cupped his chin then eased her palm along his neck and to the rim of his shirt.

"And playing hard," she continued. "The pursuit of a hard body was as equally enjoyable to me as pursuing . . ." she paused. She'd almost said a story for the front page. "As pursuing other pleasures," she said after a moment. "I've had more men, more ways than I can remember." She ceased the teasing caresses and stepped back from him.

With her hands now folded in front of her and her eyes cast down, she looked like a small sorrowful child, about to do penance for a real or imagined wrong.

"More ways and more men than I'm proud of or could ever be sorry for," she said. She sighed then looked him in the eye. "I came here to get away. You asked who I was running from. I'm running from people like you, Wesley. You can't protect me. You can't protect me from me."

"Come with me to West Virginia."

She shook her head. "Have you been listening to anything I've been saying? What does West Virginia have to do with anything?"

Wes was hard put for an answer, particularly one that wouldn't make him look stupid. The only answer he had for her was that he didn't want to lose her, that her past didn't matter to him, that the connection he felt with her and for her was too strong to ignore.

He couldn't think of a suitable lie so he told her the truth.

"I don't want to lose you, Jan," he said. "I know this is new. It's likely to get me fired and you in trouble but that's the way it is. For too long now, I've lived on gut and instinct. Both are telling me right now that we're supposed to be together. I don't know for how long or how it'll work out in the end, but I figure a day and a half together will help tell us what's what."

She looked at him. In her brown eyes he could see her assessing and weighing the validity of his words. Wes held his breath as he waited for her answer.

C.J. looked deep inside herself for the answer to give him. Afraid to admit she felt the same way, she balanced the pros and the cons. All her life she'd been confident and competitive, a classic overachiever. If she targeted something as a goal, she went after it with a single-minded determination that won her many reporting and writing awards. She'd never looked a challenge in the face and said no. Except now.

It mattered now. Everything in her told her that if she turned her back on this man, she'd be saying goodbye to her future, farewell to any chance at permanent happiness. She was still shaken by the two earlier thoughts she'd had: love and babies. C.J. didn't think herself capable of handling either one. Love was for people like her brother, Robinson, and his wife, Toinette. And babies were for people who had patience.

Far outweighing any reasons to go with him, however, was the primary reason she had to say no, to take what they'd had together and live on sweet memories. She'd told him more of the truth than she'd ever admitted to her secret self: she thrived on sex with gorgeous men. She loved the chase and getting captured. She liked the feel and the smell and the weight of a man on her body.

And with each new encounter, she hated herself more.

She was always, always responsible. Safe sex was too important to leave to chance. But being protected did nothing for the way she usually felt the morning after. She hadn't felt that lonely, desolate feeling with Wes. But Wes Donovan would have to be the last of her one-night or one-weekend stands. Her life and sanity depended on it. The masquerade of her life had finally fallen away. She didn't like the person she saw clearly when the façade no longer shielded her. Her recovery from all the addictions that threatened to consume her back home was riding on this. She'd come too far, one day at a time, to blow it now.

A slow ballad on the radio caught her attention. C.J. stared at the boom box.

Wes followed her gaze and listened to the soulful crooner ask his lady for one more chance at love. Wes didn't know about love but he knew a whole lot about chances and gambles. He was taking a big one with this woman. He didn't know the why of it, but he easily recognized the how come—because his very life depended on it.

"Ja'Niece? What's your answer? Will you come with me?"

C.J. looked at him. She had to say no.

"Yes."

C.J. tossed a toothbrush and styling gel into a small floral-designed overnight bag. A black sheath that needed little ironing and just a strand of pearls to make it dressy was followed by the black high-heeled pumps she'd worn to dinner with Wes.

"It's not too late to tell him no. You don't have to do this," she told herself.

The chime of her doorbell halted the internal argument. She glanced at the digital clock radio on her night table then dropped a package of pantyhose in the bag. A small pile of items that needed to go were scattered on the bed.

"You said we'd leave at one, Wes. It's just twelve-twenty now."

But when she opened her front door, Amber Baldwin with Frank Jr. on her hip greeted her.

"Hi, Amber. Come on in."

Amber smiled a trembly smile and hugged the toddler close to her. "Are you sure you don't mind?"

C.J. leveled an exasperated look at her friend. "What did I tell you about that?"

"Oh. Yeah. I forgot."

C.J. shook her head and followed Amber into the living room. She eyed the baby and looked around the room. Had this been her condo in Baltimore, no way would an infant be permitted to scramble about. But here, in the cottage she'd bought fully furnished, she didn't mind.

"Frank can play on the floor. I'll get a blanket to put down for him. Can I get you something to drink?"

"Some of your herbal tea would be great. Don't worry about a blanket though. He's used to going about without one on our linoleum floor."

C.J. shrugged and went to the kitchen to put water on for tea. "I don't have a lot of time. I'm headed out of town at one o'clock."

When the water boiled, C.J. made two cups of chamomile tea. She handed one to Amber and then followed her friend to the living room. C.J. sat in one of the chairs and Amber settled herself on the edge of the sofa.

"Watch that spring," C.J. warned. "I haven't reupholstered the sofa yet."

Amber grinned. "I remembered."

C.J. sipped from her tea cup and waited for Amber to meander into whatever it was she wanted to say. C.J. had learned soon after meeting Amber that you got more out of her if you waited and let Amber get her thoughts together.

Amber looked at Frank Jr., stirred her tea then looked at C.J. She put the cup on the coffee table and clasped her hands together.

"Jan, I need to confide in you about something. You're the only real friend I have here. Frankie and I have only been here a few months. I don't know who else to turn to."

"What's wrong, Amber?"

Amber glanced at C.J.'s front door as if checking to see if it were indeed closed. She leaned forward and whispered. "I think Frankie is mixed up with the Mafia."

"The Mafia? Why would you think that?"

Amber told C.J. about her life in Las Vegas, about the moves from city to city, about Frankie's strange behavior.

"Maybe he just owes someone some money," C.J. offered after listening to Amber's concerns.

Amber shook her head, then smoothed her straight hair held in place by a thin hair band. "I thought of that, too. Particularly since we never seem to have enough to get by on. And I know the recycling plant pays good. I'm the one who saw the ad in the paper and told Frankie he should try to get on over there."

"So what makes you think it's the Mob?" C.J. asked. "I mean, the Mafia," she amended. She hadn't seen any signs of organized crime in Serenity Falls but you never knew. Still waters run deep, she thought. For all C.J. knew, Serenity Falls could be the southeast headquarters. But she'd bet her grandmother's best pearls that that wasn't the case.

"The telephone call is what made me think that. A man called and threatened us. I didn't tell Frankie about it yet though. I didn't want to upset him. He already jumps at shadows and checks our apartment for hidden microphones every night."

C.J. sipped from her tea and nodded for Amber to do the same. "What did the caller say?"

"He had one of those scratchy voices like you hear on TV, you know, a gangster voice," she said, demonstrating. "And he said Frankie would be getting a sign soon." Amber reached into Frank Jr.'s diaper bag and pulled out a folded up newspaper. On her knees, she smoothed out the *Serenity Falls Gazette* then handed the paper to C.J.

"Is this the local paper?"

Amber nodded. "Don't you get it?"

"No. I'm allergic to news," C.J. said. She caught Amber's puzzled expression and waved the comment away. "Not important right now. What did you want me to see?"

Amber pointed to the top story. It was barely eight inches long. C.J. quickly read it then looked up at Amber.

"Okay. So there was a small explosion at the recycling plant. No one was seriously injured."

"Frankie was supposed to be there. That's the section where he works."

"So, where was he? What did he say about the explosion?"

Amber shook her head. "I don't know. He came home really late. Normally he always checks in on Frank Jr. You know, kisses him goodnight even though he's asleep. Then he always takes a shower and gets in bed and pulls me close. This morning though, he didn't do any of that. He just came home and fell in the bed."

"That's it?"

Amber nodded.

"Amber, I think you're the one jumping at shadows. Maybe Frankie just has a paranoid streak in him. Some people are like that. The call could have been one of his buddies playing a joke on him."

Amber chewed on her bottom lip. "I don't think so. Frankie doesn't have any friends. He doesn't even have any family but me and Frank Jr. All of my family is in Nevada. They don't know we're here in North Carolina so it's not them."

"What time do you have?"

"It's a quarter to one. Oh, I'm sorry. You said you were about to leave. We can go."

"No, no. Just come with me so I can finish packing. We have a little more time before my friend picks me up."

In her bedroom, C.J. added a few remaining items to her bag: perfume, panties, and the champagne-colored teddy from Wal-Mart. On second thought, she pulled that out of the bag.

"Ooh, that's pretty, Jan," Amber said while bouncing Frank Jr. on her knee. "I wish I had pretty underthings like that."

C.J. looked from Amber to the teddy. Lost for a minute in the moment when Wes had picked it out, she didn't immediately answer Amber.

"No, Frank. You can't play with that."

Amber plucked from the baby's hands a box of condoms. Blushing, she handed the box to C.J.

"I'm thinking that maybe I won't need either of these things with me."

Then she thought about how quickly she and Wes fell into each other's arms. "Better safe than sorry," she said, dropping both the condoms and the teddy in the bag. She added a T-shirt and a pair of jeans then snapped the bag closed.

"We're going to have to have a girl's day out when I get back. When was the last time you had a manicure and a pedicure?"

Amber looked at her hands and smiled. Frank Jr. took the gesture as an invite to play patty-cake. Amber obliged the baby, then, laughing, answered C.J.

"Not since before I got married. There hasn't been the time or the money for that sort of thing since we left Vegas."

"Well, it'll be my treat. We'll find a sitter for Frank Jr. and spend the afternoon doing girl stuff."

Amber's smile transformed her face. C.J. saw all the possibilities in Amber and was glad she'd made the commitment to help her.

When the doorbell rang, the two women looked up.

"One o'clock. He's right on time."

Amber lifted the baby in her arms and followed C.J. from the bedroom.

"I'll call you when I get back and we'll make a date for next week to do our girls' day out. Okay?"

Amber smiled. "Okay."

"And, Amber, don't worry too much about your husband. If there was a real threat to you or to the baby, I think he'd let you know about it." Even as she said the words though, C.J. hoped they were true. She knew from countless stories about lying boyfriends, cheating husbands, and domestic violence that men could be liars.

Amber went to the sofa to get her diaper bag while C.J. opened the door to Wes. He grinned at her. They were dressed practically identically: blue jeans, white oxford, tan jacket. C.J.'s upturned shirt collar and jewelry, an intricate concentric metal pin and matching earrings, added a touch of femininity to her outfit.

Wes pulled off the shades and stepped into the house.

Holding the baby's hand, Amber walked to the door. She looked up at Wes and blinked.

"Amber Baldwin, this is my friend Wes Donovan. Wes, Amber."

Amber squinted up at Wes. "You look familiar. Have we met before?"

"I don't believe so. Pleased to meet you," he told Amber. Wes squatted down. "Hey, what's up little man?" he asked the baby.

Frank Jr. grinned. "Da."

Wes laughed. "No, I don't think so little buddy."

Amber smiled down at her son. "That's the only word he knows besides 'Ma' and 'moo' which means milk."

"He's a great looking kid, Ms. Baldwin."

Amber lifted Frank Jr. in her arms. "It's Mrs. and thanks. Well, I'm going to be leaving. Have a nice trip, Jan. Nice to meet you, Wes." She shifted the boy and looked up at Wes. "Oh, now I know why you look familiar. You remind me of a croupier back in Las Vegas."

All of a sudden, Wes knew exactly what his protected witness must be feeling. To have someone from the past recognize you, particularly when the past was thought long buried, could be scary. This Amber had a sharp memory. But he wasn't about to tell her that several years back he'd been working undercover as a croupier at a Vegas casino. Amber must have worked there, too.

Amber took her leave. Wes followed C.J. to the kitchen where she made sure everything was turned off.

"Who is she?" he asked.

"Who Amber? She's a friend. We met shortly after I arrived in town. Her husband works over at the plant. Why?"

"Just asking."

But he filed the information away in his head as another so-called coincidence and definitely a reason to be even more on guard than he had been before.

C.J. turned off the lights and locked her front door.

At her curb sat a white Crown Victoria, the classic cop car. "What'd you do? Go out and buy a car for this trip?"

"It's a rental."

C.J. eyed the car then looked at Wes. "Yeah, right." He was already headed down the walk with her bag. "An armor-plated rental from Feds-Are-Us," she murmured to herself.

"We should get there about five."

"Can we stop at Bettina's Bakery. I'd like to get some croissants or something to munch on."

"First stop, Bettina's. Second stop, Interstate 40 East."

They walked into the bakery shop looking like identical twins. Yancey Yardley was at the counter chatting with Bettina. Her soft, round face was flushed with pleasure. She looked up when the bell twinkled signaling incoming customers.

"Miz Langley. Nice to see you again."

Yancey turned around, doughnut in hand. "Hey there, Jan. Good to see you." He nodded at Wes, said "Hello" then turned back to Bettina.

C.J. hurried to the counter to peer in at the sweet treats. "We came for croissants."

"Ah, then you're in luck," the baker said. "I have chocolate, lemon, and regular today."

C.J's eyes widened and she smiled. "Chocolate?" Then she remembered Wesley's allergy. She turned to look at him. "Is lemon okay for you?"

"Don't worry about me. Get the chocolate ones."

C.J. shook her head. "Bettina, I'd like three of the plain and three lemon."

"Coming right up. Ya'll sure look cute dressed like that."

"It was an accident," C.J. said. Then to Yancey, "I got those rose bushes in the ground this morning. I let them sit in water overnight like the directions said then grounded them this morning."

"I can't wait to see the results. About how long will it take for them to bloom?"

"I don't know. The box said a few weeks. We'll see. I'll let you know though."

"Here you go," Bettina said, handing C.J. the waxed bag with the baked goods. "That'll be nine sixty-five."

C.J. reached in her pocket for the money but Wes stepped forward with a ten.

"Did you all hear about the explosion over at the plant? Yancey was just telling me that his delivery truck was right nearby where it happened."

"Yeah, I read about that in the newspaper," Wes added. "You were lucky. Maybe you should be more careful where you park your truck next time."

"Yancey, I'm glad you're okay," C.J. said.

"Me, too," Bettina added from the other side of the counter.

C.J. looked from Yancey to Bettina. She should have suspected that the talkative truck driver liked black women. He'd spent enough time chatting her up. Bettina looked happy and the soft glances in Yancey's direction confirmed for C.J. that there had been more going on before she and Wes walked in than talk about a plant accident. Since she genuinely liked both Bettina and Yancey, she silently wished them the best of luck.

"Jan, we'd better get going," Wes prodded.

"Okay. Thanks for the croissants. See you both later."

Wes nodded at Bettina and Yancey then held the door open for C.J.

She walked out of the bake shop before him. When they were settled in the car, Wes started the engine and C.J. dug into the pastry bag.

"That's really sweet," she said, as Wes pulled into the street.

"What?"

"Yancey and Bettina. They make a cute little couple."

Wes glanced at C.J. and looked back at the bakery but kept his comments on the matter to himself.

CHAPTER 15

A little more than four hours later, Wes pulled into an already crowded driveway of a small gray house.

The house reminded C.J. of ones in working-class neighborhoods of Baltimore.

To Wesley, this house represented home, security, and most of all, love.

"Looks like everyone's home," he said. Wanting to surprise Mama Lo, he hadn't called ahead. But it looked like she already had a ton of company. For a Friday night, that was odd. But it didn't matter because Wes wasn't company. He was family.

C.J. opened her string purse and pulled out a tube of lipstick. She applied the color to her mouth then blotted her lips on a tissue. Wes came around and opened her door for her. He watched her step out of the car then tuck her shirt in her jeans and tug at her collar.

"Do I look okay?"

Wes leaned down and planted a small kiss on her mouth. "You look fabulous. Ready?"

She nodded then lifted a finger to smooth lipstick off his mouth. Wes grinned and kissed her again.

C.J. smiled and shrugged. "Well, some men do wear makeup."

Hand in hand they climbed the steps to the front porch. Wes ran a hand over his mouth, opened the screen door then rapped three times on the front portal before turning the knob. The door was unlocked, as he knew it would be.

"Anybody here! I'm home," he called into the house as he and C.J. stood in the doorway.

"Lord have mercy that sounds like Wesley," someone called from somewhere in the house.

C.J. looked up at him and grinned. And then they were overrun by people swooping into the room from all corners.

C.J. took a step back and watched as a small child literally leaped into Wesley's arms. He caught her and hugged her hard as another set of small arms wrapped around his legs. And then there were adults hugging him and slapping him on the back and grinning from ear to ear.

"Uncle Wes! Uncle Wes!"

"Hey, little man. I see ya down there. Let me give your sister a big fat kiss."

With loud kissing noises that made the girl giggle, Wes planted a big, sloppy wet one on her cheek.

"Are you my boyfriend now, Uncle Wes?"

Wes grinned. "Angelique, you know you stole my heart the day you were born."

"You weren't there the day I was born."

Wes rubbed noses with the little girl. "Was, too. You just don't remember."

He kissed her on the cheek again then put the girl down and squatted with open arms to the little boy. He hugged the boy hard.

Feeling somewhat like an intruder, C.J. took another small step back. She couldn't hear what Wes whispered to the boy. She smiled as she watched Wes interact with his family. Obviously a favorite son, he was welcomed with loving open arms and tears of joy. A pretty young woman with a bob haircut was in his arms hugging him, then a man about Wes's height and weight, then another woman.

It was odd seeing him this way. She'd never really thought of him as being connected to family, to people. It was as if their time in Serenity Falls was make believe . . . and this was real. This was what mattered.

C.J. watched the homecoming and wondered if she'd ever lay claim to one of these reunions. Her own family was small. Her brother Robinson and her sister-in-law Toinette weren't likely to be having any children but they were planning to adopt another child. Any of these joyful gatherings at her own parents' home would depend on her. She touched her flat stomach and wondered how it would be to feel a life growing there.

For the first time in her life, C.J. didn't shudder with just the thought.

She looked at Wes. He was tall and strong and committed. His was the best loving she'd ever had. When Wesley wrapped himself around her and in her she felt whole and complete. Just like she did right now—and he wasn't even touching her. That made her pause. She cocked her head to study him, to analyze what she was feeling.

At that moment, Wes turned and smiled at her. Something in C.J. flowered even as heat encompassed her. Not, she realized, sexual heat, but warmth and joy . . . and peace? She belonged here.

She'd been searching for peace for a while now. To find it in a living room in West Virginia seemed incongruous.

She smiled back at him and reached out to touch him, to connect with him in some small way.

"All right now. You all done seen enough of him. Let me take a good look at my boy."

The crowd in front of Wes parted. C.J. took a small step to the left, closer to the open door, so she could see who spoke with such a commanding voice.

Mama Lo.

The tall, big-boned woman was the color of sweet chocolate fudge. The green and white checked housedress cloaking her large frame was covered with a cream-colored bib apron. Her hair, flecked with more gray than black was plaited on each side and coiled around the top of her head in a coronet.

She opened her arms. Wes closed the distance between them then wrapped his arms around the woman. It was difficult to see who leaned on whom. They hugged long and hard. When they finally broke apart, she reached into her apron pocket and pulled out a white handkerchief. But she didn't try to stem the flow of tears from her own eyes. She reached up to dry Wesley's.

"Wesley, child, dry your eyes."

He smiled down at her. "You're crying too, Mama Lo."

"That's because I've missed you. And I love you."

Wes hugged her tight again. "God, I've missed you, too. And especially Marc."

She rocked him in her arms. "Shush, now. We'll talk about that later. Introduce me to your pretty lady friend you left over by the door."

"Yeah, Wes. I've been waiting for that," one of the men said.

"I just bet you have, Curtis," Wes said.

"Don't pay him any mind, Wesley. He's been right steady these last couple of months with the new waitress over at the Lounge."

"I'm always looking out for, what do they call it, new opportunities," Curtis said as his gaze wandered over Wesley's guest.

With one arm still around Mama Lo's waist Wes reached a hand out to Jan. She clasped her hand in his and Wes made the introductions.

"Mama Lo, I'd like you to meet Jan," he glanced at her, "Ja'Niece Langley, a friend of mine. Jan, this is Mama Lo who at one point in her life was known as Loretta Kensington."

C.J. extended a hand in greeting. "It's a pleasure to meet you, Mrs. Kensington."

The adults in the room chuckled.

"Who is Mrs. Kensington," the four-year-old Angelique asked.

The question brought more laughter from the adults.

"That's Mama Lo's other name," somebody answered her.

Mama Lo pulled C.J. to her bosom for a hug. "If you're a friend of Wesley's and he brings you to my house, that means you're family. And family calls me Mama Lo."

She smiled. "Yes, ma'am."

Mama Lo pulled back then situated C.J. next to Wes. Taking a careful step backward, she sized up the two. Then she nodded and smiled. "That's good. That's real good."

C.J. wasn't certain but she could have sworn Wes actually blushed before he turned to introduce her to the rest of the family. The fraternal twins, Christopher and Curtis, and Christopher's girlfriend Sheila; the children, Angelique and James; and the other adults, Hannah with the short bob haircut and Elizabeth who looked to be late into a pregnancy. C.J. quickly attached names to faces.

"You all hungry?" Hannah asked. "We were just finishing up dinner and was going to have some dessert. I can fix you up some plates, Star Gazer."

"Sounds good to me," Wes said.

C.J. turned a questioning look up to Wes at the nickname but he, with her hand clasped in his, had already turned to follow the others into the dining room.

In no time, C.J. and Wes were seated next to each other at the table. Brimming plates of collards, honey-glazed ham, sweet potatoes, and stewed tomatoes were put before them. Wes dipped a piece of cornbread in a small honey pot and popped it in his mouth.

"I didn't see you say grace, Wesley," Mama Lo said. "You have to remember to thank the Lord for what He provides."

Before bowing her own head, C.J. glanced at Wes who looked mildly chagrined. But he bowed his head, muttered what had to have been the fastest prayer she'd ever heard then dug into the food with gusto. As C.J. picked up her knife to cut into the ham, she realized she couldn't remember the last time she said grace before a meal. She'd strayed far from her own upbringing.

"What you doing up this way, Wesley? Didn't figure we'd see you again for a while," Curtis asked.

The question may have been directed to Wes, but C.J. felt Curtis's eyes on her, assessing and evaluating. She looked up and stared him straight in the eye. With a half smile, he nodded his head and turned his full attention to Wes.

"I was thinking about Mama Lo and decided to drive up for the day."

"Drive up for the day? Shoot, it takes about ten hours to get from here to D.C. I hope you wasn't planning on driving back tonight."

"We came up from North Carolina," Wes said.

Hannah and Elizabeth shared a glance then looked quickly at Mama Lo.

"Marshals Service transfer you to North Carolina, Wes?" Elizabeth asked.

Wes chewed and swallowed a piece of sweet potato. "No. I'm still based in Washington." He looked at Mama Lo. "But I don't know for how much longer."

"Uncle Wes, you catching the bad guys like my daddy did?" James wanted to know.

An awkward silence fell over the room.

Mama Lo closed her eyes and shook her head. "Lord, Jesus, give me strength," she mumbled.

Hannah got up and put her arms around her mother's shoulders. "It's gonna be all right, Mama. It's gonna be all right." She pressed a paper napkin in her mother's hands.

"Yeah, Jimmy, I'm still catching the bad guys."

"When I grow up I'm gonna be a cop like you and my daddy," James proclaimed proudly.

"Lord, Jesus!" Mama Lo cried out.

"Hey, come on you two. Let's go see what's on TV." Sheila whisked the two children away from the table.

"What about our cake?" Angelique asked on the way out the door.

"Elizabeth will bring some to us in the front room."

Elizabeth glanced at C.J. then took the cue from Sheila and got up to cut cake to take in to the children.

"Mama, Jimmy didn't mean any harm," Christopher said.

"I know. I know that," she said, dabbing at her eye with the napkin. "Lord, you'd think after these few months I'd have gotten myself together a little better. But it's just so hard, so hard. The thought of that baby growing up and being a policeman just scares me."

Hannah hugged her mother then returned to her seat at the table. "There are worse things he could grow up to be, Mama."

"Yeah," Curtis said. "He could wind up being like one of them low-lifes that got Marcus killed."

"I know," Mama Lo said. She clutched her fist to her chest. "But that can't stop or lessen a mother's pain. He was my oldest child, my first born."

Elizabeth walked through with cake on paper plates for the children.

Hannah glanced at her mother who sat at the head of the table with her head bowed.

C.J. had a hundred questions she wanted to ask. Now, however, wasn't the appropriate time. Given what had transpired in the last few minutes, she wasn't sure when the right time might be.

She took a sip of iced tea from the tall glass in front of her. "This is wonderful, Mama Lo. I haven't had ham this good since I left my own mother's house," she said.

Mama Lo looked up and beamed at her. "Well, I can see that just like Wesley you like to eat. I can't stand people who pick at their food. I always say eat what you want, you can work it off later, right Wesley?"

Wes grinned at Mama Lo. "Yes, ma'am."

"Pardon my outburst, Jan," Mama Lo said. "I, we, lost a son not quite six months ago. It's still hard for me to believe. My grandbaby James is the spitting image of his daddy, Marcus, who was killed. He was a police officer."

C.J. tried to remember the stories about cops being killed in the last few months. There had been a few so she couldn't pinpoint the case.

"I'm very sorry," she said.

Mama Lo nodded. "Thank you, child. I can see you mean that. Now, tell us where your people are from. You been in North Carolina a long time? We have some second cousins down there near Raleigh."

"I'm on the other side of the state. Between Asheville and Winston-Salem," C.J. said. "But I've only lived there for a month or so. I'm originally from Maryland."

Christopher asked about the baseball team and the conversation steered away from the painful topic of death.

C.J. and Wes finished up their cake. Curtis got up and returned from the kitchen with three beers. He handed one to Wes and offered the other to C.J.

"No thank you," she said while looking at the can. "I have a tea bag. If I could get some hot water that would be great."

"I'll zap some in the microwave for you," Elizabeth offered.

Wes nudged Hannah. "She's always drinking that nasty tea. Stuff's too healthy for me."

C.J. stuck her tongue out at Wes then got up to help clear the table.

"Sit down, Jan. You're company," Mama Lo said.

"But I'll just help with the dishes."

"You can help the next time. For tonight, you're a guest."

C.J. sat back in her chair. Wes leaned over and draped an arm around her shoulders. "You better bask in it while you can. The next time she sees you she'll put you to work cleaning the oven or the bathrooms."

The folks around the table laughed.

"Wesley, quit telling tales out of turn," Mama Lo said, chuckling herself.

"I'm not telling tales. That's what you did with me. Second time I was over here I had to scrub the front porch."

Mama Lo's laughter filled the room. "Lord, I forgot about that. Well, you sure enough are right about that. Jan, I won't make you scrub the porch when you come again."

"No. She'll probably make you clean the grout out of the bathtub."

Mama Lo chuckled as Elizabeth returned with a mug of hot water. "You all stop that before you send Wesley's lady running out the front door."

Elizabeth put the cup in front of C.J. who pulled a tea bag from her jacket pocket and put it in the water to steep.

"I'm glad Wes found himself a good sister. It's about time."

"Liz," Wes said in warning.

She ignored him. "Star Gazer was always so quiet I wasn't sure if he even knew how to talk to girls."

Wes laughed and playfully punched Elizabeth in the arm. "Yeah, well, you know what they say about still waters."

She rolled her eyes and laughed. "Um hmm. You trying to tell us something, Star Gazer?"

"Why do you call him Star Gazer?" C.J. asked.

Mama Lo grinned at C.J. from her chair. "When he was a boy, Wesley would sit on the porch step and just ponder the heavens. The kids took to calling him Star Gazer and teased him about it all the time. I always told my child to keep reaching for his stars."

"I did, Mama Lo," Wes said quietly.

"I know that." She nodded toward C.J. "And looks like you've captured yourself an angel."

Embarrassed, C.J. looked away. Wes took her hand in his and squeezed it.

"Mama, it's six o'clock. Want me to turn the news on?" Christopher asked.

Mama Lo shook her head. "Ain't interested in them lies those media people always telling. Go find me that new *Jet* magazine so I can look at the wedding pictures." She looked at Wes. "Maybe there'll be another one in there soon that I'll want to clip for my scrapbook."

C.J. pretended not to notice but couldn't miss the sly, smiling glances thrown her way by Wesley's sisters and brothers. But Curtis's look was a tad more predatory.

They sat around the table talking for another two hours before someone suggested going to a movie. Mama Lo begged off saying she was going to watch a little television. Someone found the movie listings in the paper. The group decided on an action-adventure film.

C.J. asked where the bathroom was and went to freshen up her lipstick. On the way out, Curtis cornered her in the hallway near a bedroom.

A nice looking dark-skinned man just a few inches taller than C.J., Curtis missed the mark of downright sexy. The arrogance stamped on him outshined everything else. C.J. met his gaze when he finally lifted it from the study of her breasts.

"Excuse me, please," she said.

Her attempt to move past him in the narrow shotgun hall was thwarted by one thickly corded arm across the expanse.

"That's not what I'd like to do to you, baby." Curtis licked his lips and nodded. "Wesley is kind of backward and what do they call it, anal, about some things. But he's a good judge of woman flesh."

C.J. folded her arms. "Is there a point to this?"

"You're wasting your time with Wesley." He lifted his other arm to caress her cheek. "I can show you what a real man is like."

C.J. slapped his hand away from her. "Don't touch me, Curtis. You don't know me and I don't want to know you."

He smiled. "I like a woman who plays hard to get. Heightens the, what do they call it, sexual tension."

He wrapped an arm about her waist and pulled her to him. C.J. twisted to the side.

"Lay off pal or you're gonna get hurt," she said.

Curtis chuckled and reached for her again. "I'm not afraid of Wesley." He lowered his mouth to capture hers.

In a flash, C.J.'s knee connected with the sensitive part of him below the waist. Curtis swore and doubled over.

"It's not Wesley you need to be worried about," she said. C.J. stepped around Curtis and left him in the hall moaning and holding his crotch.

C.J. was worked up and turned on. Action films just had a way of doing that to her. She squirmed in her seat then took a chance. No one would see in the dark theater. Everyone's attention was riveted on the large screen while the squeals and sirens of a high-speed chase zipped by. As the film built to its final climactic end, C.J.'s hand edged into Wesley's lap. She stroked him and felt his entire body tense.

People in the movie audience yelled for the on-screen hero to watch out. Wesley grunted. C.J.'s hand grew bolder. She felt him grow hard and she smiled. Her hand worked him over.

He slid down a bit in his seat and C.J. angled herself. It looked as if she were getting a better view as a warehouse exploded and a car crashed through a line of orange construction barrels. She caressed him, toying with the inside of his thigh and the hard outline of his erection.

The action hero jumped from the car moments before it crashed into an ammunition supply shed. The car burst into flames. The movie theater audience yelled and applauded.

"Yes!" Wes cried out.

He and C.J. were the first up and out of the theater before the credits rolled.

Wes barely got to the car before pulling C.J. into his arms. With her back against the Crown Victoria's rear door, Wesley trapped her between his thighs. Grinding himself against her, his mouth slashed across hers in a kiss just as hot as the action on the film. He was full, aching, hard as a rock, and wanting her.

People from the theater began to spill out into the parking lot. Wesley's hand squeezed a full breast then smoothed its way down her body. C.J. moaned.

"Get in the car."

She fumbled with the door while Wesley went to the driver's side. She ignored the seat belt and slid as close to him as possible. When her hand inched its way to his lap Wes halted her.

"Don't touch me, Jan. I don't know if I'm going to be able to get out of this parking lot as it is."

She ignored his words and stroked him. Leaning into his arm, her breast a brand on his skin, she bit his ear.

Wesley swore out loud then pealed out of the theater parking lot.

In less than ten minutes Wesley had them checked into a roadside motel.

Wes locked the door behind him. C.J. was already coming out of her clothes. "I hope the sheets are clean," he said.

She knelt before him and unzipped his jeans.

"Who needs sheets."

CHAPTER 16

Late the next morning they sat across from each other at a pancake house waiting for their breakfast orders to arrive.

"We should have gone to Mama Lo's for breakfast," Wes observed. "The food would be better and the company more to my liking."

C.J. looked around. Animated conversation, the clink of coffee mugs, and the smell of short-order food filled the air. "As late as it is, if we got to her house now they'd know what we spent most of the morning doing."

Wes grinned at her. "They're gonna know that already. The way we hauled out of the movie last night was a definite clue."

C.J. narrowed her eyes at him and then smiled. "Besides, there's nothing wrong with this place. It's clean. The waitress is nice. And look," she said, indicating the almost-to-capacity breakfast crowd, "it's a popular restaurant with the locals."

Wes looked around. The place was jammed with the faces of what he would have been had he stayed here. Men who lived life to the fullest while the black dust slowly killed them from the inside out. Wes had worked below ground one summer. He'd wanted to meet and greet the mistress who stole his father from him. What he'd found every morning when he emerged and squinted from the harsh glare of daylight, was a renewed sense that he had to escape.

In Marcus and Mama Lo he'd confided his dreams. Mama Lo told him to look beyond the stars he gazed at every night before going below ground and to reach for his dreams. Marc decided to follow him East to college and the big city.

Coal mining was an honorable profession. Generations of men in this community and others like it toiled day in and day out to earn keep for their families. But Wes had rebelled from the idea. His father's lot didn't have to be his own. And so he'd fled. And except for Mama Lo, he'd never looked back.

He didn't regret it. Until now. As he watched the faces of the miners, some off today and having breakfast with their families, Wes wondered what his life would have been like had he stayed and endured.

The soft touch of Jan's hand on his pulled him back.

"Hey, are you okay?"

Wes smiled at her. Had he stayed, he never would have met this incredibly special woman. "This place is okay."

The waitress brought their food and they dug in. After finishing the meal, they lingered over coffee and hot tea.

Wes leaned back in his chair. If he inhaled deep enough he'd be able to catch some of the sweet acrid smoke he missed so much. Someone a couple of tables away in the smoking section was puffing on his brand. He tried to remember why he'd given up the smokes. Oh, yeah. A promise to Marc.

"So, what would you like to do today?" she asked.

"I was thinking we ought to rent a couple of action-adventure films and see what develops."

C.J. balled up a paper napkin and threw it at him.

Wes caught the missile and chuckled. He leaned forward. "Tell me something," he said in a conspiratorial whisper. "Do those kinds of movies always make you that hot? I wasn't sure if I was going to be able to walk today."

C.J. folded her arms and stuck her tongue in her cheek. "I just wanted to make sure you were paying attention."

"If you mean to the film I was trying to watch last night, I can assure you this, I'm going to have to go back, by myself, to see what it was about. At a certain point, I just sort of lost track of the plot line."

"That a fact?"

He grinned at her then leaned back when the waitress refilled his coffee cup and left more hot water for Jan.

"I was thinking about driving you around to see the sights. There's not much here but I can show you where I used to hang out as a kid."

"I was hoping you'd take me to your mother's house."

"I did. We were there last . . ." He looked at her, his mouth became a thin, hard line. "You mean Eileen?"

She nodded.

"Why would you want me to do that?"

C.J., for all her skill with words on paper, was having a difficult time coming up with the right words now. Family was so very important. Yes,

Wes had a good relationship with the Kensington family. But blood was important, too. She just didn't want to see him live to regret not mending his relationship with his mother. C.J. knew from first-hand experience how important it was to mend fences. She'd almost lost her brother for a front-page byline.

"I don't want you to regret not having made peace with her. From someone whose been there"—in more ways than you can guess, she added to herself—"I know how important it is to make amends with family. Sometimes, when everything else falls away, family is all you have to depend on."

"Why do you care about this so much?" he asked.

C.J. chose her words carefully. "A while back, my brother and I had a falling out. His girlfriend at the time, now his wife, came between us because I did what I thought was the right thing to do. To make a long, painful story short, we came to realize that the dispute wasn't worth what we'd both lose in the long run. For us, forgiveness didn't come overnight. We had to work at it and work at it."

Wes was quiet for a long time. She desperately wanted to know what he was thinking and feeling.

Finally, he pulled out his wallet and dropped a twenty on the table. "Let's go."

C.J. didn't question him as she followed Wes to the door.

The neighborhood, old with a slightly run down feel to it, reminded C.J. of some of Baltimore's neighborhoods. Wes stopped the car in front of a house typical of its surroundings. What there was of grass in the matchbook-size front yard was cut low. A row of trimly cut box shrubs defined the yard on either side. The house, with its black shutters, could have used a coat of paint, but then, so could her own house in North Carolina.

C.J. glanced at Wes. He hadn't said a word to her since leaving the restaurant; he'd twisted and turned the large car through the streets until they arrived at this place. She knew, without being told, that this was Eileen's home. His mother, whom he said he hadn't seen in years, lived in this house.

His expression was stony, and again, she wanted to know what he was thinking.

"When were you last here?"

Wesley's hands gripped the steering wheel and he stared straight ahead. "Here? On this street and in that house? Nine years ago."

C.J. hurt for him.

"The last time I talked to Eileen was about six years ago when I sent her money and she drank it up."

"Six years is a long time, Wes. Maybe she's changed," she said quietly.

Over the rim of his wraparound sunglasses he looked at her. His expression spoke volumes. "Don't bet anything important on it."

They got out of the car and walked hand in hand up to the door. At the foot of the steps were two tires that at one time may have held flowers. Specks of white paint about the tires looked like someone had tried to pretty the place up—a long time ago.

Wesley knocked on the door.

When after three seconds passed and no one answered, he turned to leave.

"Wes, come on. At least give it a try."

C.J. knocked on the door.

A few moments later a light-skinned man with a day's growth on his face answered the door. He was tugging a white T-shirt over a pot belly that hung below the waistband of his pants.

He opened the door wider and squinted through the storm door at Wesley and C.J. He pushed the storm door open. "Oh, hey, thanks anyway but we don't need no Bible tracts. We got all the religion we need."

C.J. smiled to herself. She'd never been mistaken for a holy roller. "We're not evangelists," she told the man.

"I'm looking for Eileen Donovan," Wesley said.

The man opened the door a bit wider and shielded his eyes from the sun's glare—except it was overcast outside.

"Hey, you Eileen's boy? She got a picture round here somewhere that looks like you."

When Wes nodded, C.J. wondered what it cost him to admit he was his mother's son.

The man waved them in. "Come on in. We had a little party last night so the place is kind of a mess. I was just getting ready to run down to the store to grab a coupla things. Eileen! Hey, Eileen! Get yourself out here. You got some company."

C.J. and Wes followed the man then came to a halt. The place looked like lots of parties had been hosted in the room and no one had bothered to clean up between the occasions. Beer cans and bottles overflowed from several small trash cans as if someone had tried to straighten up a bit but then tired of the notion. A couple of half empty bowls of pretzels and cheese doodles were on top of the television and coffee table. The stained carpet may have once been beige. A matching sofa, loveseat, and chair all carried myriad cigarette burn holes visible from where they stood near the door. The room reeked of stale cigarettes, cheap wine, and old sex.

Wesley gripped C.J.'s hand in a vise. She glanced up at him but said nothing.

"Eddie, didn't I tell you to get rid of 'em. My head hurts and I don't feel like talkin' to nobody. Hurry up and go get the aspirin."

The man grinned at C.J. and Wes. "Guess you figured. My name's Eddie. Me and Eileen sort of stay together." He sized Wesley up and took a respectful step backward. "Uh, that all right with you?"

"You don't need my permission," Wes said dryly. "You're both adults."

C.J. squeezed his hand in warning. He didn't need to pick a fight with this man.

Eddie looked unsure for a moment. He scratched his stomach through the T-shirt that barely covered his gut, then hollered for Eileen again. "You all find a seat. I'll go get Eileen."

Wes looked around the room. "No thanks. We'll stand."

Eddie, already on his way to the bedroom, cleared off the edge of the loveseat and tossed the debris into a trash can. Then, looking back at C.J. and Wes, he grinned. "Go on, make yourselves comfortable."

When he disappeared, Wesley took off the sunglasses and looked around the room.

"If you're wondering," he said, "yes, the place still looks the same. The furniture is new though. But it's taking the same kind of beating that all Eileen's furniture gets. Sometimes, after my father died, I'd lay awake at night afraid to go to sleep because I was afraid she'd fall asleep on the couch with a cigarette and burn the house down. First my father looked after her. When he died, the job fell to me. Eileen always was one for appearances, outside that is. At home, she didn't give a damn."

A few minutes later, Eddie came back out into the living room. He hadn't shaved but he'd put a shirt on over the T-shirt.

"I'm gonna go get some beer and cigarettes. And some aspirin for Eileen. You all want me to bring you anything back?"

C.J. smiled at Eddie. "No, thank you. We're fine. But thanks for asking."

Eddie glanced up at Wes, whose expression remained stony. "It's a pleasure meeting you, Wesley. Your mama's told me some nice things about you."

"That a fact?"

C.J. elbowed Wes in the side.

Clearly not sure what to make of the chilly reception, Eddie shrugged. "Well, I'll be back. Don't want to intrude on your homecoming. Eileen'll be out in a minute."

Eddie left them standing in the living room.

"You don't have to be rude," C.J. hissed at Wes. "He was being nice."

Wes said nothing. He stared at the woman who stood framed in the doorway between the living room and the kitchen.

C.J. turned and followed his gaze.

Eileen wore a pair of leopard print leggings with high-heeled mules. A short-sleeved cream-colored blouse with ruffles around the collar completed the ensemble. Her face, however, stopped C.J. cold.

Time and hard living had taken its toll. A long time ago this woman was a beauty. C.J. could clearly see where Wesley picked up his Mediterranean features. But there the resemblance ended. Where Wesley's short hair was thick with a high gloss and healthy sheen, Eileen's hung long and dank. Wesley was a dark, golden brown to Eileen's light complexion.

With lipstick smeared outside the outline of her mouth, Eileen had obviously put her makeup on in a rush and without the benefit of a mirror. Or maybe, C.J. thought, what she was looking at was the remnant of last night's face. The woman, thin as an anorexic, teetered forward, careful to keep a steadying hand on a chair here, the sofa back there.

"Well, well, well. Look who's here. The prodigal son returns."

Wes stood tall and stoic in front of Eileen but C.J. was almost knocked backward by the woman's alcohol-laced breath. The party may have been last night, but Eileen and Eddie clearly had started up again early today.

"Hello, Eileen."

"Call me Mama, Wesley. Show some respect. I'm your mama."

Wes stared at her. C.J. squeezed his hand in hers, silently encouraging him to do as Eileen bid.

Wes looked at her then at Eileen. "This is my friend, Jan."

C.J. extended her hand to Eileen. "It's a pleasure to meet you, Mrs. Donovan."

Eileen laughed, the sound harsh and bitter. "It might be for you. But I can see here that Wesley disagrees. He's still as talkative as he was as a boy."

She turned and carefully walked into the kitchen. "You all come in here. I need to make myself a cup of coffee. Where are my cigarettes?"

Wes stood stock still in the living room. C.J. tugged on his arm until he followed her.

In the small kitchen, Eileen tossed a couple of pizza boxes in the general direction of what looked to be a large green garbage bag. She then rummaged through a drawer until she found a half crushed pack of cigarettes. Tapping one out, she turned on a burner at the stove and leaned into the gas flame.

C.J. gasped, half expecting at worst for the place to explode, at least for Eileen to catch her hair or face on fire. But neither thing happened; the woman apparently was proficient at lighting her cigarettes in this manner.

Eileen turned off the burner and took a deep drag on the cigarette. She then exhaled the smoke in Wesley's face. She chuckled when he merely waved the smoke away.

"You still running around pretending to be a cop?" she asked.

"Couldn't get on at a real police department like your old friend, huh? I heard about him getting himself killed. It was in the paper and on the news here. Saw you on TV at the grave, too. You was in town for that black boy's funeral but you didn't come by to see your mama."

When Wes didn't respond, C.J. glanced up at him and tried to fill the awkward silence.

"I'm sure he would have stopped by if he'd had the opportunity, Mrs. Donovan."

Eileen laughed then turned and reached into a cabinet for a jar of instant coffee. "That a fact, you say, Jan. Wesley ain't never been too busy for them Kensingtons. But his own flesh and blood he treats like dirt."

C.J. looked at the stoic Wes. He seemed nonplussed by any of his mother's words.

Eileen poured instant coffee straight from the jar into a mug. She ran hot water at the sink, stuck her finger in the stream to test the temperature, then filled the cup. "You want some coffee, Jan?"

"Uh, no thank you, ma'am."

"Ain't no need in me offering any to Wesley. If it don't come from his precious Mama Lo's kitchen, he don't want it."

Eileen opened another well-stocked cabinet. She pulled down a fifth of whiskey and poured two fingers' worth into her coffee. She stirred the concoction with a pink plastic drink swizzle stick.

With two hands she brought the mug to her mouth and greedily drank. She topped the cup off with more whiskey then screwed the cap on and put the bottle away. After her third long sip from the cup she seemed calmer—and more caustic.

"You ain't sent your mama any money in a long time, Wesley. This place needs some fixing up. Your daddy's check from the mine company don't go as far as it used to. Eddie and me don't have the resources to do this place up right."

Wes stood near the table with his arms folded, C.J. at his side. "I'm not giving you any money, Eileen."

She slammed the mug on the counter top and tottered toward him. C.J. reached a steadying hand out to Eileen when it looked like the woman would fall over.

"I bet you send lots of money to that cow Loretta Kensington. You been trying to pretend I wasn't your mama for too many years now Wesley. I'm sick and tired of it."

Eileen saddled up to his side and reached a bony hand to his face. He turned away from her.

"Look at you, you even trying to look different than me." She held a thin arm next to his. "You used to be just a shade or so darker than me. Now you look nearly black as your daddy."

Sorry she'd instigated this meeting, C.J. looked from mother to son. From the stillness in Wes, she guessed he held onto his temper with iron control.

Eileen stepped around and got in his face.

"You too good to answer me, boy? You just like all them nigra Kensingtons you used to run with. That's where you picked up such a uppity attitude."

C.J.'s eyes widened at the slur. She never would have expected to hear anything like that. She moved closer to Wes.

"Answer me, dammit. You been sending money to Loretta Kensington?"

C.J. looked at Wes. He refused to be baited. Eileen lifted a hand as if to slap him but Wes caught her wrist in his fist.

Eileen tried to twist free. "Ow, dammit. You're hurting me, Wesley."

"Wes . . ." C.J. said.

He looked at C.J.

"Let her go," she said quietly.

Wes opened his hand and released Eileen. She shook her wrist and then slapped Wes across the right cheek with all the force she could muster.

C.J. jumped between them and pushed at Wes before he did something he might regret. His eyes darkened. She recognized the rage in him and feared for Eileen.

"Don't you ignore me, Wesley Donovan," Eileen railed. "I brought you into this world. I'm your mama. You ought to be taking care of me."

Eileen's shrill screams about neglect became louder and uglier as C.J. continued to move with Wes through the kitchen and living room.

"Don't you turn your back on me, you ungrateful bastard," Eileen screamed. "What'd you come here for anyway!"

Eileen chased them to the front door. "You found yourself a little ethnic piece did you, Wesley? You always did have something about them dark-skinned Negroes. When I see that old Kensington woman in town every now and then she looks at me as if I wasn't even there. Bunch of uppity nigras, that whole family. Never did understand why you ran with them. You're no good just like the lot of them."

C.J. wanted to get as far from the house and Eileen Donovan as fast as she could but Wesley's steps were measured and slow as he walked to the car.

Eileen stood at the front door screaming obscenities at them.

Wes opened C.J.'s door for her. She hopped in the car and wanted to scream in frustration when he took his time walking around to the driver's side. When he finally got in the car and started the engine, C.J. was crying.

"I'm sorry, Wes. I never should have insisted we come here. I'm so sorry."

Wesley, silent, pulled away from the curb. He drove to Mama Lo's house, the only home he'd ever really known.

C.J. gave up trying to talk to him. His one word answers to every comment made her feel even worse for putting him through such an ordeal. She hurt for Wesley, for the pain he must have suffered growing up with Eileen. She glanced at him as he put the car in park in Mama Lo's driveway. She reached a hand out to touch him then pulled away, not sure if he'd welcome her touch.

He seemed unfazed—almost as if he'd been in a trance the entire time they were at Eileen's.

"Wesley, talk to me please," she pleaded.

He looked at her. "There's nothing to say. You wanted to meet Eileen. You met Eileen."

He opened his door. C.J. scrambled out of the car. "Wes, I'm sorry. I didn't know."

"There was no way for you to have known. Besides, I gave her the benefit of the doubt like you wanted."

Wes climbed the steps to Mama Lo's front porch then walked into the house without knocking.

Hannah sat in the living room watching a religious program on television.

"Hey, we looked for you but you two pulled a disappearing act after the movie last night. Mama asked where you were at breakfast this morning."

Hannah got a good look at C.J. She pressed the mute button on the remote control and got up. "Jan, what's wrong? You look like you've been crying."

C.J. shook her head and wiped at her eyes.

Mama Lo walked into the room then.

"Wesley, Jan. There you are. I was expecting you to come for breakfast this morning."

Wes turned and looked at Mama Lo. "I'm sorry. We went to the pancake house."

His dull, flat voice made Mama Lo look at him closer, and then at his girlfriend. Hannah had her arms around the shoulders of Wesley's lady. Mama Lo's gaze made its way back to Wesley. She sighed and came to him.

"You went to see your mama didn't you?"

Wesley closed his eyes.

She folded him in her arms and hugged him close. "Come on, baby. We'll go talk. Hannah, make some tea for Jan. Jan, sweetheart, I'm gonna go have a talk with Wesley. You going to be all right?"

C.J. looked at Wes. He refused to meet her eyes. Her mouth trembled but she nodded.

"Okay then," Mama Lo said. "Hannah, stop standing there and go get the tea."

"Yes, ma'am. I'll be right back, Jan. Here, take the remote."

C.J. watched Mama Lo lead Wesley from the room. The old woman seemed to be supporting the virile young man.

C.J. prayed Wes would forgive her for forcing him to face Eileen.

CHAPTER 17

"She told me some little story about having a falling out with her brother. They eventually kissed and made up. I guess I was supposed to take that and apply a fairy tale mist to my own relationship with Eileen."

Wes sat on the edge of a wing chair in Mama Lo's bedroom. She sat from her bed watching him and listening.

He got up and paced the area between the chair and Mama Lo's big sleigh bed. "It was worse than I imagined and exactly as I expected it to be. Eileen was sloppy. It's barely noon. She had on some leopard costume and looked like a Las Vegas show girl on crack. She's hooked up with some guy named Eddie."

"That would be Eddie Galatian. He's an above ground supervisor over at the mine."

"I wish them much happiness," Wes said caustically.

Mama Lo caught his hand when he walked by again. He stopped and stared down at her.

"Why'd you go, Wes?"

He ran his free hand over his face then looked heavenward. Swallowing hard, he then looked away. Get a grip, Donovan, he told himself.

"I don't know."

"Wesley, it's me, Mama Lo, you're talking to."

He sank to his knees on the floor next to her. With his hands folded on the coverlet of her bed, he faced away from her as he spoke.

"Listening to Jan, I guess. I don't know. When she talked, it was as if I owed it to myself, to my daddy, even to Eileen to give it one more try. Jan pointed out that a lot could have changed in the six years since I last talked to Eileen. The only thing that's changed is that she looks worse than before and she's shacking up with a slob."

Mama Lo ran a soothing hand over Wesley's head and then his back. "In her own twisted way she probably loves you."

Wes looked up at her. "Spare me."

She smiled sadly. "Well, maybe that is pushing it for Eileen. Tell me how you feel about her."

"Who? Eileen or Jan?"

"I meant your mother but you can tell me about Jan, too."

"You're my mother."

Wes put his head in Mama Lo's lap. She held him and comforted him like she'd done so many times when he was a child. She wondered at the miracle that had brought this boy, this man, into her family.

When she heard him sob, she closed her eyes and hugged him closer. It took a lot to make a man cry. It took even more than that to make Wesley cry. He had so much bottled up inside him. She knew Marc's death still weighed heavy on his heart. And to add Eileen to the mix . . . she felt his pain to the marrow in her bones. She rocked him and held him close and prayed that her love—and the love of a good woman—would be enough to heal him, to make him whole again.

"I hate her. I despise her. I loathe her. I'm sorry I even carry the same name she does."

"Hush, Wes. Don't let Eileen's poison eat at you. Most of the time with her it's that bottle talking, not Eileen the real woman."

Wesley looked up. "Don't you understand, Mama Lo. They are one in the same."

He got up, wiped at his eyes and resumed pacing. "Eileen's been living in liquor for so long, to tell you the truth, I was surprised to see her still alive."

"What are you going to do now that you've seen her?"

Wes shook his head. "Try to forget I did."

"Your lady is going to want to know details."

"She won't get them. The past is dead and buried." He paused and then looked at her. "Just like Marc is."

Mama Lo pressed her lips together.

"Just like there's nothing I can do to help him now, there's nothing I can do for Eileen. But unlike Marc, with Eileen, there's nothing I'd rather do more than dance on her grave."

"Hush up, Wesley. I've been telling you for the last twenty some years that each person on this earth is responsible for his own destiny. You got good genes in you and your daddy's work ethic. That's carried you too far to let this setback knock you down. You've been fighting too long."

"Sometimes you have to concede defeat."

"Is that what you're doing? Are you going to turn into an alcoholic now and let yourself go like Eileen and Eddie Galatian?"

Wesley whirled around. "I'm not an alcoholic. I drink a couple of beers now and then but I know when to say when. There's only one thing I hate more than alcoholics."

Since Mama Lo knew what that one thing was, she didn't question him on it.

"I didn't say you were, Wesley," she responded quietly. She rose from the bed and went to him. "I'm asking you if you're giving up on life and living. If you are, you need to take that woman out in the living room back to wherever you found her. She represents life and living, Wesley. She looks like she's already more than half in love with you. If you feel the same, you need to do something about it. If you don't, I can give you the papers to your spot over in the Kensington family plot at the cemetery. You can just climb right on in next to Marcus and call it quits right now."

Wesley looked at her. A small smile slowly turned into a wide grin. "Must you always be so dramatic?"

Her answering smile was just as broad. "Come give an old woman a hug, Wesley."

In the living room, C.J. anxiously watched the arched doorway Mama Lo and Wesley disappeared beyond. They'd been gone a long time. Try as she might, she wasn't able to follow the conversation Hannah tried to have with her. Eventually, the other woman lapsed into silence and waited with C.J. for the two to reappear.

"He might take a walk," Hannah said. "Star Gazer used to do that sometimes when he came over from his mother's house. He and Mama would talk for a long time and then he'd go for a walk. Usually it was nighttime though. We'd eventually find him on the porch looking at the stars."

Now this was a line of conversation C.J. found interesting. "What was Wes like as a boy?"

Hannah shrugged. "A lot like he is now. Quiet, reflective, intense. When he feels, he feels deeply."

She paused for a moment then peered closely at C.J.

"Jan, do you mind if I tell you something. I don't want you to take offense or anything."

After surviving Eileen Donovan's tirade, C.J. didn't think she'd take offense at much else.

"What is it?" she asked.

"Well, we, meaning me, Christopher, and Elizabeth, and Curtis, too, we were all kind of surprised when Wes showed up with you yesterday. We talked about it after the movie last night."

"Why?"

Hannah paused, clearly embarrassed.

"I won't be upset by whatever you say," C.J. assured the woman.

"We've never seen Wes date anybody as light as you."

"Excuse me?" Was everybody in this town color struck? C.J. looked at her skin. It was far from being light.

"Wesley's mother, Miss Eileen, well, she always had this thing about light skin and dark skin. She used to run around pretending she was white. Wesley kind of took the opposite tack and he only went out with real dark girls. Like even darker than me. You know, 'the blacker the berry . . .' "

" 'The sweeter the juice,' " C.J. finished the old saying.

"What do you mean?"

Hannah frowned. "Well, it's difficult to say. It wasn't a secret around town Miss Eileen had a preference for lighter skin tones. Now why and how she got hooked up with Star Gazer's father I don't know. But Wes, well, since he just talked to dark-skinned girls, I always figured it was his way of getting back at Miss Eileen. You know what I mean?"

C.J. nodded. "I suppose so. It seems awfully calculated though."

"He may not have even been aware he was doing it. Don't get me wrong. Wes is a good judge of character. He doesn't like people who are phony or who put on airs." Hannah laughed. "Maybe that's why he's fit in so well with our family."

C.J. looked at the beautiful brown woman Wesley considered his sister. Her flawless dark skin glowed with reddish-orange undertones. C.J. didn't consider herself dark, but she wasn't what some people called high-yellow either. In actuality, she and Wes were about the same complexion.

"He's been gone from home for a long time though," Hannah continued. "He and my brother Marcus went east as soon as they graduated from high school. I don't know what Wesley did or who he dated over there but here, well, he was always real clear on where his allegiance was, in terms of color I mean."

"Color shouldn't matter," C.J. said.

"Yeah, I know. But if you grew up in Eileen Donovan's house, you'd probably have a color complex too, one way or the other."

C.J. didn't have anything to add to that. She'd heard enough of Eileen's invective to agree with Hannah.

The one thing she planned to do as soon as she got back home though was find out all she could about the death of Marcus Kensington. Everyone talked around it and about it as if she knew all the details. Wes hadn't shared many details of that part of his life with her. But C.J. knew an easy way to get all the information she needed.

Mama Lo appeared in the arched doorway.

"Jan, Wesley went for a short walk. He'll be back in a little bit. Can I get you something to eat?"

C.J. looked at Hannah.

"Told you," she said. "Some things just don't change."

Wes was glad that some things didn't change—like the woods out beyond the end of Mama Lo's street. He'd expected that developers would have built it up by now like some other parts of the mining town. His woods were still the same, yet somehow smaller than he'd remembered. Half-hidden trails through the underbrush told him that other people, probably little boys looking for adventure, made their way through here from time to time.

He breathed in the fresh scent of the early summer day. He let the chatter of birds and scampering squirrels surround him.

When he looked within himself, he was both surprised and upset to see that Eileen still had the power to hurt him. He'd been angry and embarrassed that Jan had seen and been subjected to Eileen's rages. More years ago than he could remember he'd learned to turn inward, to block out the rage and the pain and find shelter in a calm place deep in the core of himself. He'd gone there today while at Eileen's, but part of him remained on the surface to protect Jan. In doing that, he'd laid himself open to actually absorbing what Eileen said. He'd taken each barb like a physical beating.

As a child, on more than one occasion he'd gone to Mama Lo battered or beaten with little recollection of what had happened. She'd tended his physical wounds and loved him past the emotional ones.

He came to a small clearing, paused, and took off his shoes. Taking a deep breath, he relaxed all of his physical being. Blocking out all sound and all thought, he concentrated on breathing, then slowly worked through the graceful meditative tai chi he'd taken up in college.

When he finished, he stood in the clearing and let the sounds of the woods and his surroundings come to him one at a time. He breathed deeply and heard birds. He exhaled and recognized the rustle of a small creature, of a dog barking in the far distance, someone cutting grass. Slowly, he opened his eyes. Blinking twice he took in all that was around him. The green of leaves, poison ivy growing near the base of a tree. He took it all in then looked within himself and found he was whole.

Only then did he make his way back to Mama Lo's house—back to Jan.

Hannah had told her to wait on the back porch. If Wes followed the habits of his childhood, he'd come back to the house and pause on the porch.

C.J. saw him approach and wanted to run to him and throw her arms around him. But something stopped her. Maybe it was the purpose of his step or the set of his shoulders. She was too far away to see his eyes, and besides, he had again donned the wraparound sunglasses. Maybe he wore them to shield himself from the harsh realities of both the sun and life. She rose from the caneback chair and stood at the top of the steps waiting for him.

She watched him and then she knew. Someway, somehow she'd fallen in love with this man. He was hard and unforgiving; gentle and loving. C.J. gripped the banister for support. She'd never been in love before. She'd never had time for anything as mundane as an emotional attachment to a man. Relationships, she'd always believed, were simply for achieving a means or an end to something. She'd collected and discarded men as easily as she did panty hose. But Wes Donovan broke that mold.

Asking herself the tough question, she wondered if what she felt was pity, not love. After all, through the years she'd written about a lot of families just as dysfunctional as Wesley's. She wrote their stories and felt a gamut of emotions, sometimes sorrow, sometimes pity, at other times empathy or sympathy. But it was never personal.

Never had she felt like this. Grounded. Sure. Anxious about tomorrow and the day after that. She wanted to hold him and love him, and not a single one of the things she felt had anything to do with his mother.

He reached the bottom of the steps. "Hi."

"Hello." She reached out a hand to him. He climbed the three steps then sat down with her on the top one. He pulled the sunglasses off and tucked them down the front of his shirt.

C.J. wrapped her arms about his waist and hugged him to her. "You okay?"

He nodded.

"Mama Lo told me you went for a walk."

He nodded again. "I needed to clear my head."

She rested her head on his shoulder. "I'm sorry, Wes. Had I known what a bad scene it would be at Eileen's I never would have harped on you."

He looked down at her then kissed her head. "You didn't harp, and you have nothing to apologize for. If anything, I should apologize to you for even exposing you to that. Eileen is . . . Eileen. She'll never change."

For a long time they sat together on the steps enjoying the silence of the warm afternoon.

Wes held out his right arm and indicated a faint but visible inch-long scar on his arm. "I'd gotten an A+ on my geography test. Geography was hard for me. I don't know why since I spent a great deal of time thinking of all the places I could escape to. I was so excited about the grade on the test that I forgot one of the cardinal rules at our house: Don't wake Mom up out of a drunk. She was slumped over at the kitchen table and I woke her up to tell her about my class and the test. She grabbed the first metal object she could get her hands on and sliced me with it. Blood spurted out everywhere, all over me, the table, my bookbag and my test. I grabbed my arm and ran to Mama Lo's house."

C.J. hugged him tight as he spoke.

"It wasn't the first time," he said.

He placed both palms behind him and leaned back. C.J. let him go, tucked one leg under the other and faced him.

Nodding back to the door, he said, "This house, with this family is where I found out that not all people lived like we did. Things weren't so bad when my father still lived. But after he got sick and died, it was like my mother had no self-control. My guess is that he controlled her as much as was possible when he was living. But all I remember is their fights and her nagging, constant nagging and yelling."

He smiled a small, bittersweet smile. "There was a deaf kid at our school. I always wanted to be like him. He talked with his hands. If he didn't feel like being bothered with you, he turned his back. If you yelled at him, he couldn't hear. Every night when I went home, I wanted to be deaf like that kid at school."

"How did you meet Mama Lo?"

Wes smiled then, a real, honest to goodness feel good smile.

"Mama Lo was an angel God sent down to watch over me. I was seven, maybe eight years old. At this point, I can't remember what I'd done or said that set Eileen off. It was pretty bad though. All I remember is that everything hurt, I mean everything. I ran away and was hiding in some bushes in those woods out there," he said, indicating with a nod of his head the direction in which he'd just recently come.

"I don't know how long I was there but it had gotten dark. I wanted to go to sleep but it hurt too bad every time I tried to lay down in the grass and brush. Then I heard somebody coming. I started crying because I thought it was Eileen. I thought she'd found me. My ribs hurt from where she'd been kicking me. My arm hurt where she'd tried to put a cigarette out on me but I tried to ball myself up as small as possible to hide."

He sat up and dropped his hands between his knees. "It was Marcus Kensington who found me huddled up like an animal. He helped me up and half carried and half dragged me to his mother's house. The last thing I remember was him hollering for his mama and then strong arms lifting me up. Those strong arms, I later found out, belonged to Mr. Kensington. He died a few years back."

C.J. put a hand on his thigh. Wes closed his own hand around hers and brought it to his mouth. He kissed her hand then entwined his fingers with hers.

"It didn't take them long to figure out what was happening. There'd been talk all over town for years about my mother's drinking and her temper. I didn't know about that until later though," he added. "Marc and I were inseparable after that. He never told a soul about what he'd found in the woods. I'd come here as often as I could and stay as long as I wanted. By the time I got too big for Eileen to beat me, I was part of this family."

Wes turned and looked at C.J. She offered him a trembly smile. He leaned forward, wiped the single tear from her face, and pressed his lips to hers in a soft, quiet kiss. Then he pulled back and stared into the space that was the Kensington family's backyard.

"My father and Eileen gave me the middle name Lamont when I was born. When we were fourteen, Marcus and I took this blood oath that we'd be brothers forever. When I turned eighteen, I legally changed my middle name to Kensington. We were blood brothers as well as brothers in name."

C.J. wrapped her arm through his. "Thank you for sharing that with me."

Wes shrugged. "I wanted you to know."

They sat on the step holding each other.

His pager going off broke the quiet between them. Wes pulled the pager from the waistband of his jeans and looked at the number. No digital message came after it.

"I need to go answer this."

C.J. nodded as he got up.

When the back door shut behind him, C.J. wrapped her arms around her legs and rested her head on top of her knees. In all her own months of darkness, she hoped and prayed that she'd never sunk as low as Eileen Donovan. C.J. knew that when she was drinking she drank to numb the pain, she drank in a fruitless attempt to forget what she'd allowed herself to become.

Sobriety was sobering. There were few things she could think of that supported sobriety as much as the sickly, vindictive and drunk sight of Wesley's mother. C.J. shuddered and thanked the God she didn't necessarily believe in for one more day of being clean and sober.

A few minutes later, Wesley popped his head out the back screen door. "We need to hit the road."

"Okay."

They said their goodbyes to Hannah and Mama Lo.

Mama Lo hugged C.J. tight and whispered in her ear. "That boy needs some good loving, Jan. You're the one to give it to him."

"I'm trying my best," C.J. answered back.

Hannah and Mama Lo saw them to the car. The older woman tucked a cooler on the backseat.

"That's lunch for you," she said. "Wesley, you two call and let me know you got home safely."

"We will," he answered. He hugged her again. Then held the door for C.J.

They waved to the two women and Wes backed out of the drive. Before he got to the street, his pager went off again.

He muttered an expletive. C.J. looked at him then pulled her seat belt on. "Uh, have you been working or on-duty or whatever you Deputy Marshal types call it, while we were here?"

He looked at her. "What do you think?"

C.J. was thinking maybe she needed to go get a rental and drive herself back to North Carolina.

Wes pulled the pager from his waist and read the message. This one wasn't a telephone number.

Watch your back. These are strange days with bad blood flowing. 007.

Wes frowned. The cryptic message was from Ann Marie Sinclair at headquarters. The joke that had started between them twelve years ago as they filled out paperwork on their mutual first day with the service remained.

Ann Marie had said she really wanted to be James Bond but the only listed opening was for a temp so she settled for that. He'd called her 007. In the years since, as they both rose through their respective ranks, Ann Marie had paged him just twice. Both times she'd signed the message as 007. Both times, his life had depended on heeding her warnings.

CHAPTER 18

"Wes, are things about to get weird?"

"Not any weirder than normal," he answered with a grin.

"That's so very reassuring," she said.

Wes reached for her hand and kissed it. "I'd never put you in any physical danger."

C.J. stared at this man she knew she loved and wondered at his choice of words. She was already deeply entrenched in the emotional danger zone.

She took a look at their hands, joined on the seat, then glanced at the dash of the car. If the Crown Victoria was a cop car like she'd first suspected, the car was working undercover. It looked like your basic vehicle—except she'd never met a real person who drove one.

"Is this a cop car?"

Wes looked at her but didn't answer.

To C.J.'s relief, they arrived back in North Carolina without any high-speed chases or any defensive driving. Her relief was short-lived though. About twenty miles outside of town, blue and white lights flashed from several police squad cars. Flares along the road and the red flashing lights of two ambulances heralded an accident. Wes slowed as they approached the scene.

He carefully watched a blue sedan in front of them ease its way beyond the two officers working traffic detail. Wes followed the sedan and the cop's hand signal directions. He slowed up some more and rolled his window down.

"What happened, officer?"

"Wrong way, driver. Had a head-on collision here. Keep it moving, pal."

Wes eased around the accident scene but kept a close eye on the progress of the sedan in front of him.

"Oh, my God. That's terrible," C.J. said. She'd turned around in her seat to rubberneck and get a good look at the scene.

The twisted metal and scrunched car bodies left little to hope for in the way of survivors. The roof of the smaller car lay in the middle of the roadway and a child's car seat dangled from the popped open rear door of the other vehicle. Glass was everywhere.

In her earlier days of reporting she'd done the cop stuff and had worked many an accident scene. This was one of the worst she'd ever seen.

As Wes cleared the scene, the siren from one of the ambulances fired up. The emergency vehicle sped past them. C.J. faced forward again.

"That makes you wonder why and how we so readily put our trust in these tons of steel and plastic that hurtle so recklessly down these paved over horse and buggy trails."

"Stagecoaches with actual horses and buggies were just as dangerous in their day."

"I know," she said quietly.

"What do you drive?" he nonchalantly asked.

"Just your basic transportation. I walk most places I need to go."

Wesley sighed inwardly. So much for trying to get some answers out of her. Now that they were back in Serenity Falls, the reality of their situation hit him. He knew his job was on the line with this woman. And unless Scotty had had any better luck at pulling up her background, he could think of just one way to find out if she was a protected witness. If she was, he'd need to start looking for a new job.

He thought about how much of himself he'd revealed to her in the past twenty-four hours. It was more than people he'd known for the last twelve years knew about him, more than he would have thought just last week, that he'd ever want a woman to know about him.

He turned onto her street and pulled up in front of her house.

"Jan, there's something I need to ask you."

C.J. unbuckled her seat belt and leaned over the back seat to grab her string purse.

"What?"

Wesley's eyes narrowed at the sight of her behind pushed up in the air. He reached up a hand to pat that sweet temptation then caught himself.

"Are you in the U.S. Marshals Witness Security Program?"

C.J., clutching her small bag, sat back down with a plop. She looked at him and grinned. "You mean like wiseguys and gangsters using the feds to hide out from their buddies they informed on?"

Wiseguys? Feds? Either she watched a lot of television or she knew exactly what he was talking about. Regular people weren't quite that familiar with the lingo.

Wes nodded.

C.J. chuckled and patted his cheek. "What do you think?"

Wes grabbed her arm and pulled her body against his so she was half kneeling and half laying on him.

"I think you're an addiction I need to give up cold turkey," he said right before his lips covered hers.

The hot embrace fast turned into something more. Their breathing was erratic, their heartbeats accelerated when Wes finally let her come up for air. But he didn't let her go. Not yet. He wanted her too much.

"Do you want to come inside?"

"More than you know, Jan Langley."

She smiled when she caught his meaning then rubbed one smooth palm over his chest. "I meant into the house, my bedroom."

Wes twisted his hips and brought her hand down to feel his erection. "Actually, what I'd really like is to do you on the backseat." If he was going to lose his job over this woman, he might as well make it memorable.

"Well, that certainly is a retro idea. But there's one problem."

When he raised his eyebrows in question, C.J. sat up and tugged her shirt down. "It's still broad daylight outside. Someone, like a little kid, would walk by and see us."

"Where's your sense of adventure? Don't you like to flirt with danger?"

"I've been hanging out with you for the last couple of days. I'm getting a good dose of it." She paused and looked him over. "Along with some of the hottest sex I've ever had in my life."

"I want to make love to you," he said.

C.J. looked up quickly. She'd been thinking the same thing. It surprised her that he'd distinguished between the two. After their first wild coupling at the river, they'd made love . . . on the ground. A part of C.J. wanted to be seduced, the old-fashioned way. No quickies in the car, standing up, or in cheap motels. For once, she wanted to make love with and be loved by a man. There was only one man for her. But she knew she wasn't worthy of love, particularly not the love of a man like Wes. She'd seen and done too much to be worthy of a pure love.

She leaned toward him and kissed him on the cheek. "Thank you for inviting me to day trip with you. I enjoyed meeting your family. Mama Lo is a terrific lady."

"I'm glad you liked her. She definitely liked you."

"I better go," she said quietly.

"Okay. I'll get your bag from the trunk."

C.J. let herself out her door, glad that Wes understood what she'd meant about meeting his family, the Kensingtons. Eileen Donovan didn't merit counting as family.

He carried her bag to her front door.

"When can I see you again?" he asked.

She caught herself before she answered "Never."

"Want to come over for dinner tomorrow? I can't promise to make you a meal like Mama Lo's, but I'm sure I can find a box of something to feed you."

Wes frowned. "A box of something? Tell you what. I'll come over. I'll bring the groceries. I'll cook."

She grinned. "Sounds like a plan to me."

"And what are you going to provide?"

"Dessert."

Wesley's head lowered to hers. "I do love a good dessert."

She watched him walk back to the car and drive off. C.J. dropped her bag in a chair and went to the telephone. It had been more than a month since she'd dialed any numbers at her old newspaper but she remembered the extension.

"Hey David, it's C.J. Mayview," she replied when she got an old friend on the line.

She small talked with the reporter and then got to the point of the call.

"David, I need a favor, an overnight mail or FedEx type favor."

"Whatever you need, C.J."

"Would you go to the library and pull all the clips you can find on these two names: Marcus Kensington and Wesley K. Donovan." She spelled the names to make sure he got them down correctly.

"Don't stop at our clips, do the entire region. D.C., Virginia, Maryland, even West Virginia. I want anything and everything you can find. Copies of any photographs, too, if you can swing it."

"How fast you need this stuff?"

"Like yesterday."

The reporter chuckled. "You always were a demanding diva. Can I ask a question?"

"That's what they pay you the big bucks to do," she answered, smiling.

"Are you really on leave of absence or are you working some top secret investigative assignment like the rumors around here have it?"

C.J.'s eyes widened. Top secret investigative assignment? Why didn't anyone believe she'd just tired of doing what she'd been doing for the last ten years of her life?

"You're a reporter, David. Figure it out."

C.J. grinned. She knew the answer was oblique and would only add fuel to whatever rumors were already making the rounds in the newsroom. But it was better than revealing why she really wanted the clips.

She gave him the address to send the material then rang off after he caught her up on some of the latest newsroom gossip.

C.J. took her overnight bag to her bedroom, changed into a pair of shorts and a tank top then went to the kitchen to brew a cup of tea. The telephone rang just as the tea kettle whistled.

"This is C... Uh, Langley residence," she amended. She still wasn't used to answering the telephone. Years of responding to ringing phones by stating her name was hard to alter overnight. Besides, no one ever called her here in North Carolina. Few people even knew where she was. David might be a problem but she'd worry about that later.

"Jan, this is Amber. Please, you've got to help me. I think Frankie is trying to kill me."

"Amber calm down," C.J. said. Her friend sounded on the verge of hysteria. "Where are you? Where is Frank Jr.?"

Amber had started crying. "I'm at the pay phone outside the apartment building. Please, help me. Tell me what to do."

"Amber, where's the baby?"

"He's right here. I have him. Frankie's got a gun, Jan. He's going to kill me."

"Okay. Listen to me, Amber. Are you listening?"

"Uh huh," she sniffled. "Please hurry."

"Does Frankie know me? Do you think he's ever seen me?"

"No. He doesn't allow me to have any friends. I've never told him about you."

"Okay, listen. I'll be at your place in about five minutes. Can you hold on that long?"

"Uh huh. We'll hide in the bushes."

"Amber, I'll be driving a blue and silver Cherokee with Maryland tags, okay. Don't get in the car until you're sure it's me."

"Okay. Please hurry."

C.J. rang off, turned the burner off under the kettle and grabbed her string purse.

The stuck garage door took several pulls and tugs before it lifted. She hadn't used the four-wheel drive since she'd arrived in town. C.J. turned the ignition and prayed the vehicle would start. When it kicked over, she breathed a sigh of relief and backed out of the garage.

As she took off down the street, a blue sedan followed her. "Well, well. This is an interesting turn of events," the driver said. The driver passing by noted the house number and the open garage door then stepped on the gas so as not to lose the woman in the Cherokee.

CHAPTER 19

Less than half an hour later, C.J. whisked Amber and the baby into her house. She locked up the Cherokee and pulled the garage door down and locked it.

Amber was a wreck. For the first time in a long time, C.J. wished she had some alcohol in the house. Amber needed something to calm her down. As it was, all C.J. could do was offer herbal tea.

Frank Jr. was irritable and agitated, probably more a response to his mother's mood than what he was really feeling. Amber had run out of the house without her diaper bag. C.J. had made a fast dash into a convenience store for milk and disposable diapers. She didn't have any baby bottles in her possession. She poured milk into a paper cup and set it on the table. Amber could figure the rest out.

Except she was in no shape to do any creative thinking. The woman's hands shook and her eyes constantly darted to the two doors of the small cottage.

C.J. got her to sit down on the sofa. Frank Jr. started crying. C.J. looked at the kid.

Scrunching up her face she lifted the boy under his arms. She didn't do kids and wasn't sure how to deal with this crying one. Carrying him well away from her body, like a sack of foul smelling garbage, she handed him to Amber who clutched the child to her breast and rocked.

C.J. brought the tea into the living room and sat in the chair closest to the sofa. She sat fascinated as Amber quieted the child with soft coos and comforting.

"Okay Amber. Start at the beginning. What happened? What did Frankie do?"

"I, I told you yesterday how he came home from work and just went straight to bed."

C.J. nodded. "You said he didn't look in on Frank Jr. or follow his usual routine."

Amber sniffled and wiped her nose. The baby settled in her arms and dozed off. "That's right. Then the explosion over at the plant I told you about. Well, when he finally got up, and he didn't sleep as long as he normally does, he said he had some business to attend to and left. That's when I came over here."

C.J. nodded and sipped from her tea, anxious for Amber to hurry it up and get to the point. "So what happened that made you think he's trying to kill you?"

"He came home with a gun and pointed it at me and Frank Jr."

C.J. sat up. "Tell me more, what happened, exactly."

"I was fixing lunch when he came tearing into the house. He told me he needed me to keep alert, that 'they' were close and watching."

"Who is 'they'?"

Amber shook her head. "I don't know. He won't ever say. Whenever I ask him about it, he just says the less I know, the safer I'll be."

"The gun," C.J. prompted.

"Frank Jr. was in his high chair while I was mixing up some tuna salad. Frankie came out of the bedroom with this big steel gun. He aimed it at me and Frank Jr. I said, 'Frankie, what are you doing with that thing? You might hurt somebody.'"

Amber shifted the baby in her arms and held him close. "Then he told me to shut up and sit down. I sat on the sofa just like here and he was in the chair about where you are."

Amber started crying again. C.J. handed her a tissue. "What happened then, Amber?"

"He was going on and on about no place being safe and he had to think. I don't know what all else he said because I just kept my eyes glued to that gun he was waving around. Frank Jr. started crying and he told me to shut the kid up. I gave Frank Jr. a bottle and put him in bed. Frankie told me to hurry it up and get back in the living room."

Amber looked down at her son and kissed his forehead. "I was so scared I didn't know what to do. My hands were shaking, my legs were shaking. I didn't want to do anything that would set Frankie off, not as long as he had that gun in his hand. When I got back to the sofa, he pushed me down and put the gun to my head. I heard it click like he was getting ready to shoot me. I was crying and begging him not to kill me. He told me not to move, not to even breathe and that when he got back I better be there."

"What'd he do then?"

"He picked up a small bag and left. I didn't see him again until a few minutes ago. He came in and was acting like nothing had happened. His clothes were rumpled up and he hadn't shaved. I was still sitting on the sofa. I had Frank Jr. in my arms. I didn't move, just like he told me, except to get Frank Jr. when he woke up and started crying. I sat there all night scared out of my mind that Frankie was gonna come back and kill me."

"You should have called the police, Amber."

The young mother shook her head. "No police. Frankie says the police lie and can't protect you."

"Yeah, well, someone needs to protect you from Frankie." C.J. got up and pulled out a telephone book. "Amber, I'm going to try to find some help for you, a safe house." She flipped to the blue pages in the directory. "There ought to be a shelter around here somewhere. If not, I can get you to Winston-Salem. Or maybe Charlotte. That's a bigger city and . . ."

"Jan, I can't leave him," Amber said.

C.J. looked up from the directory. "What do you mean?"

"He's my husband. I can't leave him."

"You just sat here and told me he's threatened you. What do you mean you won't leave?"

"He needs my help," Amber whispered.

"*You* need help, Amber. What makes you think that the next time he won't kill you?"

The tears started down her face again. "I can't leave him, Jan. He needs me."

Frustrated with Amber, C.J. decided to forgo working in her garden for a walk. Maybe she could get her head cleared. She slipped her housekey and a few dollars in the pocket of her jeans then slipped out her front door. Still light out, the summer evening was perfect for a stroll. She shut her gate and decided to head toward town.

Amber had refused to go anywhere except back home to Frankie. C.J. had hated covering domestic violence stories back at the newspaper because what many women did was the same thing Amber did—rationalized away the sick behavior of the men who assaulted them. Amber, just like so many other women, needed counseling and a safe haven, not a return for more punishment.

C.J.'s pace was slow, meandering. She waved as she passed people on their front porches, kids playing in the street. She wasn't out to exercise and had no real purpose except to enjoy the evening. Except her thoughts wouldn't let her. She worried about Amber.

Then it hit her. Wesley! Frankie Baldwin. She paused and thought about the two men. It all fit. Amber's husband was probably in the

Marshals Protected Witness Security Program. Amber had described constant moves. The couple had crisscrossed the country, and, according to Amber, the Mafia was after Frankie. From the little she knew about the U.S. Marshals Service, dealing with people hiding from the Mob was one of their specialties. Wes had to be in this small town on some sort of assignment. Serenity Falls was too off the map to justify anything else. She'd just met his family and they all lived in West Virginia. Could there be some other reason for his presence here?

She started walking again, layering the pieces of the puzzle over each other just like she did with the news stories she used to write. One action led to reaction, which led to action, and so forth. When woven together the pieces created a tapestry that, depending on the merits of the case, would land her on the front page, on a section front, or as one story did, on a platform accepting a Pulitzer Prize.

One part didn't fit though, the puzzle piece at an odd angle. People in the witness protection program got new identities, new names, and from what C.J. knew, they weren't supposed to talk about the past. Amber had never given any indication that she or Frankie had had other names. And she knew their background, at least their background according to Amber: They'd met in Las Vegas, then moved to Florida and now North Carolina. Maybe the pressure of the constant moves was getting to Amber and she needed to unload on someone.

C.J. filed the information away. Just because the puzzle piece didn't fit right now, it didn't mean the odd piece was something to discard.

When she looked up she was in the center of town. It just took about five minutes to get there from her house. Main Street bustled with activity, as far as small-town bustling went. Traffic was pretty heavy and all going in the same direction—toward the old armory for Saturday night bingo. C.J. thought about going, then discarded the idea. A room full of cigarette smoke, conversations, and people yelling didn't quite appeal to her now. But a chocolate croissant did. She hoped Bettina's Bakery was still open.

She stopped at a corner then stepped into the street to get to the side where the bakery was. She waved to someone who waved to her in one of the slow-moving cars.

Tires screeched.

C.J. whirled around and instinctively jumped toward the center of the street. A blue sedan whizzed by in the opposite direction of the traffic.

Her breathing came hard and fast. She clutched her chest and stared at the place where she had been standing. A second or two longer and she'd have been hit by that careless driver.

"Hey, lady, you okay?"

C.J. turned and looked at the man who called to her from his car window.

She nodded. "It just scared me."

The man shook his head. "I tell you. These young kids get their driver's licenses and act like they own the road."

He waved for her to safely finish crossing the street.

She did, then waved at him as he slowly made his way down the street in the bingo traffic. C.J. looked in the direction the blue car had gone then shook her head. "You'd think this was Baltimore."

Another block put her at Bettina's. C.J.'s mouth dropped open. The façade of the bakery was completely knocked in. Small bits of concrete and glass littered the sidewalk. Orange construction cones and yellow tape cordoned off the area.

C.J. peered through the front door that remained in tact. Bettina saw her and waved her in.

With one more look at the front of the store, C.J. went into the bakery.

"Bettina, what in the world happened? We were just here yesterday."

The chubby baker shook her head. "It wasn't too long after you left. I was in the back fixing to decorate a couple of cakes for the Garden Club's annual picnic when there was a crash. The building shook. I heard glass breaking. I thought we were having an earthquake or something. I came out to see what had happened and there was a car, big as day, sitting in the place where my front window used to be."

C.J. followed Bettina to take a closer look at the mess. C.J. picked up what used to be the plastic top tier of an elaborate wedding cake. The groom was missing a leg and his top hat.

"Don't even bother with that mess, Miz Langley. The insurance man just left. It's gonna cost a pretty penny to get this fixed up."

"What happened?"

"Well, that's the darnedest thing. It didn't take me but a minute to get out here from the workshop in back but by the time I did, whoever was in the car that crashed through the window was gone. The place was a wreck, the car was still running with the driver's side open."

"Do you know whose car it was?"

Bettina shook her head. "Police are checking but so far they've come up empty."

C.J. didn't believe in coincidences. Everything in life happened for a reason and all events were in some way connected. Did this constitute two more pieces to the same puzzle or a separate but interlocking, interrelated puzzle? She thought about the car that had almost run her down a few minutes ago. Could this have something to do with Frankie and Amber Baldwin? It seemed farfetched, but stranger things had happened.

"Do you know Amber Baldwin?"

Bettina looked up from her perusal of the damage. "Scared looking woman with a toddler?"

C.J. nodded.

"She comes in here for one-eighth of a pound of chocolate-covered strawberries every now and then. I usually slip an extra one or two in her bag. She always looks so pitiful. I just want to help her. What put you in mind of Miz Baldwin?"

"The hard pretzels on the counter looked like something the baby would like." The lie out of C.J.'s mouth came easy. Too easy.

She blinked back sudden tears. After carefully guarding herself and her actions, how could she so easily slip back into the persona of the person she wanted to forget?

It's only been a month, C.J., the voice of her conscious told her. *It'll take longer than that to break habits and behavior that you've cultivated over more than a decade.*

But C.J. didn't pay attention to that voice because she knew who and what the real culprit was. Wesley Donovan.

"Miz Langley, you all right?"

C.J. looked up. She'd just about forgotten where she was. She nodded to Bettina. "I'm fine. Do you need any help around here? Is there something I can do for you?"

Bettina shook her head. "Nope. I'm just here trying to go about my regular business. The contractor can't come until Monday. Mr. Anderson over at the hardware store is gonna secure a tarp over this in," she glanced at her watch, " 'bout half an hour or so. Thanks for offering, though. Can I get you anything?"

C.J. grinned. "I came for a chocolate croissant."

"You're in luck."

Bettina went to fetch the pastry. C.J. turned to assess the damage again.

It reminded her of her life. She'd taken a wrecking ball to her own façade and was starting over. Except Wesley Donovan had stepped onto the stripped canvas and was wreaking havoc on the carefully plotted and meticulously serene landscape she'd created.

He didn't leave her feeling cheap or emotionally shattered like all the other half-developed relationships she'd had over the years. He left her wanting more, always more.

Like an addict.

"Here you go," Bettina said, coming up with a pastry bag.

C.J. pulled money from her blue jeans pocket and handed it to the baker.

Bettina shook her head. "No charge."

C.J. tried to hand her money again but Bettina folded her arms over her ample bosom and shook her head. "Everything's free today to friends."

C.J. laughed. "Okay. If you need me to help with anything just let me know."

After leaving the bakery, C.J. picked pieces off a croissant—Bettina had put two in the bag—and thought about Wesley. She thought about him being an addiction and came to a conclusion as she slowly walked down Main Street.

She could yield as she'd always done in the past, capitulate to the desires and demands of her body. Or she could be strong, stay focused on her recovery goals. The only way to do that would be to get away from the temptation. Her willpower was nil. She recognized that character fault for what it was and just went on with her life. She was the spoiled baby girl in a very well-to-do family. As far back as she could remember she'd always gotten what she wanted. If her parents said no to something she wanted, she just worked harder and longer to attain it. That's how she'd gotten her first BMW at seventeen years old.

All of her friends thought that rich, little C.J. Mayview had asked her parents for a Beamer and had gotten the car lickety split. But Genevieve and Robinson Mayview had said no sixteen-year-old with a fresh driver's license *needed* a BMW. If she wanted a car to drive, her parents said, she could drive the station wagon that sat unused in the garage. C.J. had turned her nose up at the car then gave up Friday, Saturday, and even some Sunday night dates in favor of extra baby-sitting and housesitting jobs. With the extra work and the money she already had in her savings account, within a year she had enough to buy the used Beamer she wanted.

Proud of her accomplishment, she'd taken snapshots of the car and sent them to her brother who was in college at the time. Robinson sent her a card telling her that he was proud of her. She still had the card. And even though she was now a grown woman, she still wanted her big brother to be proud of her.

C.J. wanted to be proud of herself. Then she thought about how easily she'd shed her convictions and joined Wes for his quick trip to West Virginia. She couldn't ditch all her hard work, all the soul-searching she'd done so she could be the person she'd been three months ago.

When she looked up, she found herself at the end of the sidewalk. In front of her, just across the street, the armory's parking lot was jammed with the cars and trucks of Saturday night bingo players. To her right was the last store on the block.

She put the remaining bit of the chocolate croissant in her mouth and stepped up to the store window. She swallowed the pastry and scrunched the top of the bag in her hand. Her mouth watered, but she knew it had nothing to do with the sweet treat she'd consumed or the remaining one.

The business at the end of the street was a liquor store.

Fifty-five days. She'd been clean and sober for fifty-five days. As she stared in the window, she got a mental image of Eileen Donovan. C.J. had never been a sloppy drunk. Like a lot of journalists, she drank too much.

Her favorite after-work hangout was a sports bar most folks from her newsroom congregated to after hours. She'd never gotten a DUI. No one had ever had to drive her home or call a cab for her, but C.J. knew she'd been dependent on the liquid courage, the sharp smooth edge of the liquid fire to soothe her at the end of a rough day. She'd had a lot of rough days.

Like a child longing after a mountain of toys in a Christmas store window display, C.J. stared in the window of the liquor store. For just a moment she thought to move on, away from the temptation.

"You can run but liquor will always be in your face," she said aloud. What better way to prove she was capable of handling alcohol than to have it readily available and still say no?

"You're strong," she said. "You can do this."

Determined to prove to herself that she was indeed strong and that she could overcome and pass this test, she pushed the door open. Minutes later she departed with a small brown bag. It held a bottle of her favorite smooth Kentucky bourbon.

CHAPTER 20

Margaret Shelley tired of the cat and mouse game. It was time to stop dallying around and get down to business. Her ploy hadn't worked quite as effectively as she'd planned. That sexy Wesley slipped out of town on her. But he was back now. And Margaret was ready. She sashayed into the dining room, the open splits on her car wash style dress showing flashes of shapely leg. Her makeup, expertly applied, was flawless.

Margaret frowned. The place where Wesley sat at the table was empty.

Miss Clara Ann harumped. Garrison glanced up, then scrambled from his seat to assist Margaret.

"Girl, you gots the most awful timing I done ever seen in my life," Miss Clara Ann said. "If you all prettied up for that there Wesley, you done missed him again. He come in, got himself a quick bite, cleaned up, and headed back on out the door."

Margaret stomped her foot in exasperation.

"Miss Margaret, may I have the singular honor of seating you next to me?"

She rolled her eyes.

"How long ago, Aunt Clara?"

"Oh, 'bout ten, fifteen minutes."

Margaret's shoulders slumped. Garrison held out a chair for her. She gave him a weak smile.

"I'll be right back," she said.

There was no need in chancing that she'd spill something on the expensive dress. Margaret dashed back upstairs to her room, took off the dress, scrubbed her face clean, and pulled on a pair of baggy gray sweatpants. She tugged on a raggedy T-shirt and slipped her feet into a pair of rubber flip-flops. Figuring that her bad timing served her right for not focusing on business, she stomped downstairs.

When she arrived back in the dining room, Miss Clara Ann took one look at her and laughed out loud. "Margaret, you are something else. You trying too hard, baby."

Margaret tried not to let her exasperation and frustration show as the artist Garrison helped her into her seat. Then he passed her a platter of meat loaf. Margaret sighed as she selected a slice for herself.

Half an hour later, the small group at the dinner table greeted Wesley when he poked his head in the door. Margaret's mouth dropped open. Miss Clara Ann's bark of laughter filled the room. Even Garrison grinned.

"What's the joke?" Wes asked.

"Missed opportunities," Garrison replied.

Wes shrugged, bid the group "Good night" and went to his room.

"Don't either of you say a word," Margaret threatened.

Garrison and Miss Clara Ann shared a look and smiled.

C.J. unpacked the overnight bag she'd dropped in her bedroom earlier in the day. The champagne teddy caught her eye and made her pause. Lifting the delicate garment from the bag, she took it to the mirror over her bureau.

She held the lingerie up to her chest and imagined how Wesley would respond if he saw her in it. Reflective now, she went to her bathroom, teddy still in hand, and started drawing a bath. Sprinkling lavender and rose bath salts in the water, she watched the tub fill and the water swirl. She ran the silky smooth material of the teddy over her cheek and wondered what it would be like to live on memories.

She'd never wondered what love felt like. It was, in C.J.'s opinion, an emotion for fools. But now she knew what it felt like. And she knew love was something she couldn't afford to feel.

"Telling him goodbye is going to be the hardest thing you've ever done," she said out loud.

But you'll have good memories, glorious memories, she reminded herself. And besides, he never has to know how you really feel.

Turning to face the mirror in the bathroom, C.J. stroked the piece of lingerie then folded it and placed it on the vanity. With both hands on the vanity she leaned forward and critically studied her face.

"You look old and tired, C.J. Mayview, not young and in love." She thought about the fake name she'd been running around with. Jan Langley. Ja'Niece Langley. No one had ever called her Jan or Ja'Niece. No one had even ever called her by her first name, Cassandra.

"You're supposed to be in love and the man you love doesn't even know your name." C.J. shook her head in disgust, at herself more than anything else.

She brushed her teeth then turned off the running water in the tub. Coming out of her clothes, she left them in a pile on the floor then slipped into the soothing bath. It had been a long, emotionally exhausting day. She thought about Eileen Donovan. She thought about Mama Lo Kensington. She thought about Amber and about Bettina, about Wesley and his brother Marcus Kensington, about children forced to grow up before their time, about violence and fear and about love that was so often intricately woven into the fabric of destructive behavior.

C.J. sighed, closed her eyes and sank deeper into the water. Sometime later, she woke with a start. She shivered from the cold water. With her toes she unstopped the tub then got out, dried herself off and moisturized and powdered her body. The teddy went into the top drawer, the dirty clothes she dropped in a hamper then fell into the bed. Her sleep was fitful and troubled.

In his own room at Miss Clara Ann's place, Wesley stared at the ceiling for a long time. Hours later, he closed his eyes and eventually slept.

C.J. slept late, much later than usual. But when she woke up Sunday morning, she felt like a new person. After dressing and grabbing a bite to eat, she called Amber. The young mother assured her that all was well even though she couldn't stay on the telephone to chat. Refusing to let the frustration of Amber's situation ruin her day, C.J. counted the hours until she'd see Wes for dinner.

With about eight hours to kill she figured she could get the sofa reupholstering project underway. But instead she opted to putter in her garden. It was too beautiful a day to stay cooped up in the house. The rich soil and the process of helping something grow had a soothing effect on her psyche. Four short days ago she'd met Wesley Donovan. He'd managed to wreak havoc on her senses and turned her carefully orchestrated world upside down. She would be able to put things into perspective while she gardened.

She made a pitcher of herbal iced tea then picked up her gardening gloves and the boom box. She tuned the radio to a cool jazz station then went to inspect and try to resurrect the petunias the toddler Frank Jr. had trampled.

Humming along with the jazzy tunes on the radio, she worked all afternoon on the living things that grounded her. After heaving fifty-pound bags of mulch and ringing every tree in the backyard with the stuff, she drank long and deep from the pitcher of tea. Then, deciding to rest for a while, she sank into the sturdy hammock hoisted between two of the older trees. Before long, she drifted to sleep.

That's how and where Wesley found her.

He looked at the sleeping woman and smiled. He didn't know what her yard looked like before but she obviously spent a lot of time out here. Protected witnesses were strongly encouraged to steer clear of their previous occupations once they secured their new identities. So he doubted that Jan Langley had been a gardener or florist in her former life. He had a pretty good inkling of what she'd been though.

He'd spent the better part of the previous night analyzing everything he knew about her, everything she'd said and had not said. She'd admitted, bluntly, that she had been with men, lots of men. He couldn't particularly hold that against her, not when he himself had been with lots of women. The last thing he needed or wanted in his life was a naive virgin who would have to be schooled every little step of the way.

The only lessons Jan needed were in how to cast a fishing rod. Wes grinned.

She shifted in the hammock. He watched her move, sensuous even in slumber. His smile faded as the reality of his situation hit him. In a worst case scenario, he was falling for a former prostitute or the ex-girlfriend of a drug lord or Mafia boss. They'd eventually stop using condoms and would have to have regular HIV and AIDS testing done. She could very well be on the run for the rest of her life, constantly hiding, always looking over her shoulder. While most people in the Witness Security Program followed the rules and lived out their lives with just one new identity, some, like the other one he was working with here in Serenity Falls, had to constantly move. Sometimes through no fault of their own.

Wes thought about that life and wondered if he'd be able to deal with it. He'd finish up this case, turn in his resignation, and then get to live out his life with Jan.

Was it worth it?

He studied her. Jan was a beautiful woman. But beauty faded over time. Would he love her when she was old, if she got sick, if she put on fifty pounds, if an old lover tried to claim her?

"Yes."

Wes blinked, momentarily surprised by his answer. Then, it settled in him, warm and tender, a realization he'd never thought he'd have.

"Hmmm?"

He'd awakened her but her eyes weren't open. Jan turned again in the hammock and almost rolled out of the netting. Wes was there though, to catch her, support her; like he wanted to do for a long, long time to come.

"Wes?"

"It's me, sweetheart."

Sweetheart? He had never called anyone that. If falling in love meant turning mushy, he'd have to guard against that part. There were few things as disgusting as watching two adults cooing at each other.

Jan rubbed her eyes and swung her legs over the edge of the hammock. He held her around the waist as she rose.

"Hi. You're early. I think. I fell asleep."

"Hi, yourself, beautiful."

Jan ran a hand over her face and grubby clothes. "I'm more a mess than anything else. I got everything done though. For now."

Wes held her about the waist with one hand and with the other he smoothed a knuckle down her cheek.

"You're beautiful to me." His mouth lowered to hers.

But Jan turned her head and twisted away from him. "No, Wes."

He let her go.

"What do you mean 'no'?"

She stepped away. "No as in we shouldn't do this."

"Have dinner?"

Jan huffed then folded her arms. "This, this sex thing between us. I let you talk me into . . . no, I ignored my own better judgment and went with you to West Virginia but that doesn't mean I've changed my mind about us. I can't afford to be with you, Wesley. Can't you understand that?"

He could. She was probably having the same doubts and worries he harbored himself. But he also knew how to overcome those problems. Every relationship wasn't like the one between his mother and father. Mama Lo and Mr. Kensington had shown him how a loving couple interacted. They'd had problems but every couple did.

Then he paused as a thought hit him.

"It's Eileen isn't it?"

C.J. turned from picking up her gloves. "Eileen? What does she have to do with this?"

"Nothing. That's my point," he said.

She shook her head. "Wes, let's just have a nice dinner and then we can go our separate ways. Okay?"

No. It wasn't okay. But he wasn't going to argue the matter. He had a better plan. He'd show her that she was wrong. He'd prove to her that they could overcome their pasts and make a future together. And he would start right now.

He smiled. "I'm going to impress you in that kitchen."

She grinned. "Oh, really? Well, I'm going to go get cleaned up so I don't smell like soil and mulch at the table. This better be good, too. I'm hungry."

Wes helped her carry gardening tools to the porch, then hefted up the brown paper bags of groceries and supplies he'd left there and followed her in the house.

She didn't know it but he even had a necktie to change into for dinner. If she knew how much he hated ties, she'd know how serious he was about her. Before this night was over, he planned to make sure she knew exactly how he felt.

C.J. closed the door to her bedroom and leaned against it. Her resolve had a tendency to melt whenever Wes Donovan was near. She couldn't think straight, half the time she could barely get her well-reasoned thoughts out in a semi-articulate manner.

Wesley was just the latest in a long string of headed-no-where, for-a-good-time-call-me relationships.

Stop lying to yourself, her conscience scolded.

She pushed herself from the door and stripped off her grubby sneakers and grass-stained jeans. By the time she made it to her tiny closet, she was naked except for the panties she wore. She looked in the closet and for the first time since moving to North Carolina, she wished she hadn't been so rash in giving away all her nice clothes. She'd carted off boxes upon boxes of things to the Salvation Army and a women's shelter.

With her new life, she knew she'd never have need for the sequined dresses and matching high-heeled slings she had needed to attend country club events with her parents. All that frivolous stuff that her mother insisted she own got shipped to the needy. She wasn't going to report another story from City Hall and had no need for suits and blouses. She'd held onto her jeans, all of her expensive lingerie, and one or two semi-dressy outfits.

The black sheath would have to do. She quickly pressed the dress she'd taken to West Virginia but hadn't worn. A pair of sheer black hose and the black high-heeled pumps would have to be it. She then studied what she'd kept of her jewelry and selected a jazzy brooch that she would wear just off her shoulder. Her dinner outfit selected, C.J. made her way to the shower. With the water on as hot as she could stand it, she put a shower cap on and got under the spray. She let the hot water cascade over her and she rehearsed what she'd tell Wes at dinner.

Basically, she needed a relationship about as much as she needed a hole in the head. She'd tell him about her addictions to stress and to work. She'd tell him about winning the Pulitzer, about her years of reporting and living by her wits and her love of journalism, of the writing prizes she'd won and things in her life she was proud of.

He'd have to understand why this sojourn, this period of self-discovery and healing was so important to her—so very vital to her existence and her peace of mind.

All she'd ever wanted was peace.

C.J. held her face in the water and let it beat her up. The hot stings of water hit her like so many pin pricks. She took it until she winced, then turned around and let the soothing stream massage her back.

Wes had been rude to that reporter the other day, she thought. But she remembered as she reached for a loofah sponge and lathered it up with scented body wash, he was after all a Deputy Marshal, a cop. Cops and reporters had a love/hate relationship when it came to information. Wes had implied but hadn't confirmed that he was working on a case, so being in the local newspaper, small as it apparently was, was probably the last thing he wanted.

C.J. could tell him about notoriety and dealing with the press. It could hurt sometimes—a lot. She knew that firsthand when she inadvertently found herself in the news. Someone had implied that she got a great front page story about a welfare program when her brother leaked her the information. The charge had been ludicrous, of course, but the damage to her credibility and to her relationship with her brother had already been done by the time everything was cleared up.

She sighed as she lathered her legs. Then she frowned and reached for her razor. She quickly shaved her legs and arms then proceeded with her shower.

One bad experience with the media was all some people needed to forever bad mouth the entire profession. Look at what Mama Lo Kensington had said at the dinner table Friday: "Ain't interested in them lies those media people always telling."

C.J. turned so the shower spray would rinse her body. She then moisturized herself with her favorite body moisturizer. When she stepped out of the shower and dried off, she was surprised to discover how much time had passed.

"Better hurry or he'll be in here knocking the door down."

She waved her hair up. C.J. had never been one for a lot of makeup. A touch of color at her cheeks and a bit at her lips finished off her face.

At the bureau, one of the pieces of furniture that had come with the house, she reached for a pair of silky panties and matching bra. She paused when her gaze fell on the champagne-colored teddy Wes had bought at Wal-Mart. She turned and glanced at her closed bedroom door.

"He'll never know."

Smiling to herself, she donned the teddy then opted for sheer black thigh-high stockings instead of the pantyhose.

Her mother's advice came to her as she secured the hose at her thigh: "You can look good and feel good about yourself even if you're facing a bad situation. No one has to know what you have on under your clothes." C.J. smiled as she thought of her mother.

She reached for a bottle of cologne in the same earthy scent as her bath moisturizer, then, at the last minute, changed her mind, opting instead for the perfume of the same essence. After putting on her dress and shoes, C.J. stood in front of the bureau mirror wishing the house had a full-length mirror. She smoothed her hands over her hips. The form-fitting sheath hugged her shape. It was one of her favorites because of its versatility. Tonight, she'd dressed it up.

And tonight, she'd tell Wes Donovan goodbye. She'd worry about getting through tomorrow later on. One day at a time would be the way she'd deal with this.

Funny, the prospect of goodbye had never hurt before, she thought. She had embraced just about every previous farewell with a joyful relief, not this unforgiving ache.

She sighed.

"You can't have him, C.J. Not that way. Be grateful for the pleasure you've found in his arms and let it go."

She sighed again. "Just let it go, girl."

With that advice to herself, she turned the light off in her bedroom and went to see what Wes had cooked up.

"I hope whatever you made is good because . . ."

C.J.'s voice faded away to nothing and her mouth fell open. Wes had transformed her tiny dining area into a romantic setting for two.

The beat up table she wanted to strip down and refinish was covered with a pristine white lace tablecloth. A low arrangement of fragrant yellow and red tulips served as centerpiece. C.J. knew she hadn't brought any china with her to North Carolina, yet two beautiful place settings adorned the table.

"Where? How?" she got out.

From the kitchen with his back turned to her Wes answered. "Did I forget to tell you that magic is also one of my specialties?"

C.J. smiled. "Yes. You forgot that part."

He pulled something from the oven and placed it on the counter on top of folded dishcloths. When he stepped around the counter, C.J. looked at him and her mouth dropped open for the second time. He wore a crisp white shirt with a blue and gray tie. Her gaze traveled down the rest of him and took in the dress slacks and shoes. Either he'd had the clothes tucked in one of those bags or she'd been so busy staring at his face earlier that she'd missed the rest of him.

He cleaned up real well, but with a bit of wonder that actually surprised her, she realized she liked him better dressed in bad boy black. With the way he looked now, like a newspaper editor or publisher about to meet with stockholders, it would be too easy for her to forget that the man standing in front of her was the very one who threatened the foundation of her existence.

He lifted a suit jacket from the back of a chair at the table and shrugged into it. "You look fabulous."

C.J. swallowed. "Thank you. So do you."

Wes advanced a step. C.J. retreated two steps.

"Actually," he said, "you look better than fabulous. You outshine the stars in the heavens."

Oh, boy. "Wes . . . there's something we need to get clear about. Something I need to tell you."

Wes reached for her arm and pulled her into his embrace. "Save the serious talk for later. Right now, I just want you to relax and enjoy the evening."

He hummed a slow tuneless melody and slowly twirled her about in the small space. C.J. thought he was bending to kiss her but he instead smoothed one large hand across and down her hairline. His touch light, his voice low, C.J. felt her resolve melting away. He slow danced her to her chair then helped her into it. Brushing a light kiss on her cheek, he left her and went to the kitchen.

C.J. took a deep breath.

"The table is beautiful, Wes."

She was dying to know where and how he'd come about this stuff: crystal stemware, white china rimmed in a gold leaf motif, linen napkins. While all were staples in her former life, she'd abandoned most of the evidence of conspicuous consumption for the less complicated, healthier lifestyle she'd adopted in Serenity Falls.

He smiled and held up a bottle of wine. "Would you like a glass?"

"No, thank you," she said, and meant it. She thought about the bourbon she'd bought and made a mental note to throw it out. She was strong, but she realized now that she didn't have to have temptation in the house to prove that she was strong.

Wes simply nodded. "I've already put water on for your tea. Dinner will be ready in about five minutes."

A few minutes later he placed before her marinated chicken breasts, almond glazed baby carrots, and au gratin potatoes. C.J. opened her mouth in question.

Wes leaned over her, placed a quick kiss on her lips. "Before you even ask the question, the answer is Mama Lo. She made sure all her boys knew how to fend for themselves in the kitchen. There's one thing I haven't quite mastered though. I hope you don't mind my substitute."

"What's that?"

"I never quite got the hang of rolls and biscuits. I make a mean pan bread though."

C.J. got up and went to the kitchen. It wasn't trashed, but there was evidence that real cooking had been going on, an open box of cornmeal, brown sugar, an opened package of almonds. She looked in the waste can for the tell-tale red and white box of a Kentucky Fried Chicken restaurant or foam takeout trays from a restaurant.

Wes chuckled.

C.J. looked up at him and grinned. "You amaze me."

Wes grabbed a potholder and overturned the pan bread from a small cast iron skillet onto a small napkin-covered plate.

"Dinner is served."

C.J. looked at him and shook her head. "You're really something else."

"So are you.

They shared a quiet meal together, talking about inconsequential things, getting to know each other's likes and dislikes. As each minute ticked by, C.J. found it more and more difficult to bring up her concerns about their relationship. How could she tell him she couldn't see him again when she felt she was being slowly, deliberately and delicately seduced into submission. She'd never seen this side of Wes, gentle, loving, ever considerate of her every wish and need. There was no way he could know she'd actually been missing some of the trappings of her other life. She hadn't even dared admit that to herself.

When they finished dinner, Wes cleared their plates.

"Dessert's coming right up."

"You're spoiling me, Donovan," she said.

"That's what I'd like to do for a long time to come," he answered quietly.

C.J. looked up and caught her breath. He was there, so close she could see the whiskers from his sexy five o'clock shadow, so close she could pick up the faint citrus scent of his aftershave. So close she could feel his breath mingle with her own. Heat swirled in her abdomen as desire snaked through her. But she had to be strong.

She kept telling herself there was nothing special about this man, nothing out of the ordinary that made him different from any other man she'd been with.

Nothing except the way he makes you feel, the warmth he brings to you, and the fire you share, her heart's voice challenged.

C.J. closed her eyes. His kiss, light, easy, and flirtatious as it was, held an undercurrent of barely leashed passion. She knew he wanted her just as much as she wanted him. He pulled away then, and when she heard a soft rustle she knew he'd stepped away. She sighed. "Wesley, there are some things I need to tell you."

"Not now," he murmured. "Open your eyes."

She obeyed the husky command. The sight before her was a treat to behold. Wes sat close by holding the tip of a strawberry dipped in chocolate at her lips. Not sure which she wanted to nibble on more, the man or the chocolate, she eyed both with equal amounts of desire. Each promised to be sinfully delicious. Without thinking, she captured his hand in hers then opened her mouth and bit into the sweet delicacy.

She licked first her lips then his fingers. Wesley cleared his throat.

"I cheated on dessert. I stopped by Bettina's. She said that next to her brownies, your favorite is chocolate swirl cheesecake."

C.J. followed his gaze and noticed the slice of cheesecake garnished with sliced strawberries on a small plate with a small bowl of uncut strawberries beside it.

She smiled and ran his finger over the contour of her lips.

"Jan, I'm trying to be a gentleman tonight."

"No you're not," she said. "You're trying to seduce me."

It was his turn to smile. "Is it working?"

CHAPTER 21

"I think you know the answer to that question."

He fed her the rest of the juicy fruit. "I want to hear your answer."

C.J. swallowed the strawberry. "I think you're a man who knows what he wants and goes after it."

He smiled. "You're right about that." His gaze dipped to the scoop neckline of her bodice. "Did I tell you you're putting a hurtin' on that dress?"

"Not in those words."

He cut a small piece of cheesecake with the tines of a fork and held it to her mouth. Accepting the morsel and the fork with a smile and an "Mmmm," C.J. released his hand long enough to slice off a bit of the creamy dessert and offer him a taste.

He shook his head, took the fork from her and fed her the cheesecake.

"But . . ." she protested. Her eyes widened when she remembered. Wes was allergic to chocolate. That explained the bowl of plain strawberries. She took the fork, dropped it on the table and wrapped her arms around his neck. "Oh, Wes."

The man cared enough about her wants and desires to buy and then feed her chocolate, the one thing that he had to deny himself.

She rained tiny kisses along his face then plucked a piece of fruit from the bowl. She put the wide end in her mouth and offered to him the juicy tip. They nibbled until their lips met.

A small giggle escaped when a tiny trail of juice from the succulent fruit escaped her mouth. Wes caught it with one well-defined finger then brought that finger to her mouth.

Fire raced through C.J. Wes moaned.

And then they were standing, holding each other, slender arms draped around broad shoulders, her soft woman's body pressed close to his tall, hard one. Their dessert forgotten, Wes first kissed the tip of her nose, then her eyes. When his mouth finally slanted over hers, C.J. pulled him closer and moaned the satisfaction she found.

His tongue danced over hers first lightly, then with a passion that made her knees buckle. Wes supported her.

He tore his mouth from hers long enough to bury himself in her neck. "God, woman, you make me burn."

Too dazed to speak, too involved with the way she was feeling, light and airy, explosive, hot, hungry, C.J. simply threw her head back to give him better access, then slid her hands over his back. She loved the muscular strength of him, the honed physique that let her know he cared about his own physical well being.

And then she stopped thinking at all.

Wesley's tongue rimmed her ear and she let out a shuddering exclamation . . . of need, of fire and desire.

Wes moved and she followed. When he made to sit on the sofa she stopped him.

"Not there. Bad spring."

"Um hmm."

She wasn't sure if he comprehended what she meant to say but he shifted and settled in one of the chairs. With an "Oomph!" she landed in his lap.

C.J. grinned. "Hope I didn't break anything."

She felt his deep chuckle before the sound issued forth. He ran a hand down her thigh. "It'll take more than that . . ." his voice trailed off.

His hand paused then inched back up her thigh over the sheer hose. He eased the short hem of her dress up a bit.

"Mercy." It was a curse and an exultation.

C.J.'s breath came in short gasps. "Wes?"

His hand eased up her thigh exposing the lacy edges of her stockings. "No garter belt?"

She shook her head. "They stay up by themselves."

"Not if I can help it."

His large hand left the exploration of her thighs and legs just long enough to turn her face to his. Their lips met in a fierce battle of need. She wrapped her arms around his neck.

A crash, almost like an explosion ripped through C.J.

Then the lights went out.

"What the . . . ?"

She sat up. "It sounded like something crashed in the yard." If the lights hadn't shut off at the same time, C.J. would have sworn the earth moved when Wes kissed her.

He stood her up. Wes went to the back door while C.J. headed to the front door.

"I don't see anything," he said.

"Oh, my God. Oh, my God."

She snatched the door open and Wes dashed to where she stood. Street lights were out all up and down the street, but clearly visible in the early evening light was a small plane and the path of destruction leading to where the plane precariously balanced on its nose in the front lawn of a house three doors down.

In a sprint, Wes shot out the door. C.J. ran back in the house kicking off her high heels. She called 911, changed into some flats, and looked for a slim reporter's notebook. Adrenaline pumped through her. She quick-scanned the counter, the coffee table. She knew there were at least a dozen of the things around, she always kept some at home just in case she needed to hit the street from home.

Then she stopped. Who she was, what she was, and where she was hit her with a staggering force. She sighed. It would take longer than a month to break habits ingrained for so long that they were reflexive actions. "You're not a reporter any more, C.J.," she said aloud. "You don't carry press credentials and don't have to call news in to the city desk. You don't have any reporters' notebooks around here, either. You live in North Carolina, not Baltimore."

She glanced around her house, taking in the small kitchen, the tiny dining area, the sofa that needed to be repaired. "Definitely not Baltimore."

The pretty table with the cheesecake and strawberries reminded her of the other important thing. "You have to let him go."

The shrill cry of a siren startled her. C.J. ran to the front door, and like the rest of the neighborhood, gathered at the crash scene.

The small-engine plane rested in a front lawn less than three feet from the side of a house twice the size of C.J.'s. Sod kicked up and whacked off shrubbery gave testimony to the plane's path. Downed power lines trailed behind it.

Mothers held back curious children. Two police cruisers rolled up and officers shooed people away from the power lines. From where she stood with the gathering crowd, C.J. could see Wes and another man helping the man in the plane.

A fire truck, ambulance, and hazmat van all screeched to a stop at the same time. Red, blue, and white flashing lights backlit the crash scene.

Someone knocked into C.J.'s side. "Ow!"

When she turned, she saw someone shoving through the crowd and toward the street. C.J. frowned. The guy had either elbowed her or hit her with something. Shaking her head, she put a hand over her side where pain still throbbed and turned her attention back to the crash.

A shadow of memory made her turn back to the fleeing man but the crush of people all clamoring for a better view was all she saw.

First someone tried to run her over, now this. Serenity Falls, North Carolina, was more dangerous than Baltimore.

And there sure was a lot of weird stuff going on for such a small place. But then she had to admit, cars crashed and people had heart attacks all the time.

Almost an hour later, the crowd began to disperse. Tile ambulance, long gone, had taken off for the hospital. Wes found C.J.

"Hey."

She wrapped an arm around his waist. "Hey, yourself. You sure you weren't a dragon slayer or a knight of the realm in a former life?"

Wes chuckled. "Why do you say that?"

"Always on the scene to rescue the distressed. Maybe that's why you're a Deputy Marshal. Sort of like the Old West, huh?"

"That pilot kept his cool the whole time. That saved his life and his wife's. She's a little banged up and has some scratches. He walked away though."

"What did he say happened?"

They followed hangers-on around a police cruiser. Power crews were already working on the downed lines strewn across the sidewalk and yards. C.J. saw the town reporter interviewing someone and smiled.

Wes waited for a woman with a stroller to pass by them, then steered C.J. to the middle of the street for the short walk back to her house.

"He said the engine just quit on him. He was trying to aim for a field about three hundred yards away but when he realized he wasn't going to make it, he said he was aiming for the middle of the street."

C.J. shook her head. "That was really close. Someone could have been killed."

Tires screeched. The woman with the stroller shrieked and frantically pushed to get out of the way. Wesley's pager went off at the same moment the car gunned toward them.

He whirled around. The mother frantically worked at the straps to free her baby. Wes grabbed the stroller and the woman's arm, dragging them to safety. When he turned to look after Jan his heart stopped beating.

The car was going to hit her.

The woman with the stroller screamed. Wes sprinted and dived. Tackling Jan about the waist he dropped and rolled, his own body shielding hers as the car sped by.

He held her close, not sure if the trembling he felt came from her or from him. A moment later and he'd have been too late. A moment later and she'd have been hit, injured, maybe killed.

His heart beat frantically. But as Wes held her close he realized with a start that he loved her. Right or wrong he was in love with Jan Langley. The prospect of losing her shook him to the core. He'd never imagined loving someone, feeling this way—particularly about one woman. But in the moment he thought he'd lost her, he knew. She was his destiny.

The siren from a police car squawked.

Wes hugged Jan close then helped her up.

With her baby tucked securely in her arms, the woman who'd been pushing the stroller ran over to them. "Oh, my God. Are you all right? That guy must have been nuts. He tried to run you down."

With Wesley's steadying hands at her waist, C.J. dusted off her knees then her rear end. "I'm fine. I'm fine, really."

Wes looked her over, then, with his hands scanned her body in a modified frisk. Her eyes were wide with shock probably setting in. Her elbow was scraped but otherwise she looked okay.

"Does anything feel broken, Jan?"

She shook her head. "I'm okay. Really. I just . . ." Her voice trailed off and she looked at him.

Wesley folded her in his arms. She shuddered and then pushed him away. "I, I need to go home. I've got a run in my hose."

"Jan, you're in shock. It'll take a little while for your heartbeat to settle. Why don't you stay right here? I need to go talk to that cop."

C.J. shook her head. "I need to go home," she mumbled.

"One of them took off after that driver," the woman with the baby said. "I can't believe he tried to run us all down. People are just crazy today."

Wes looked in the direction the blue car had taken. He hadn't had time to make the plates. All that registered with him before he dived for Jan was North Carolina tags with a T and a 2. The nondescript blue sedan looked like a hundred other cars he'd seen in the same make and model. Jimmy Peterson must have had a fire sale on the model before he got killed by that tree.

Wes looked the woman and baby over. "Are you all right, ma'am?"

The woman cuddled the now fretting infant then kissed the baby's forehead.

"Yes. Thanks to you," she said. "I don't think we'd have made it if you hadn't jumped and snatched the stroller up. I owe you my life and my baby's life. How can I thank you?"

"Did you happen to get a look at that driver or get the license plate on that car?"

The woman shook her head. "I'm sorry. I wasn't thinking about that. Maybe those policemen over there saw something."

"Yeah," Wes said.

He turned to check on Jan. But she wasn't there. He saw her walking through her front gate. She was home. She'd be okay for a few minutes. He wanted to talk to the cops.

In a daze, C.J made it to her front door. Was someone trying to kill her, injure her? She would bet cash money that the driver had been the same one who almost ran her over on Main Street yesterday.

She shut the door and without purpose or reason went to the kitchen.

She had no enemies in North Carolina. For God's sake, she didn't even know anyone here. She made it to the sink and turned the water on, surprised to see that her hands were shaking. She ran cold water over a cloth then pressed it to her elbow. Wincing at the sudden sting, she stared at the still running water.

Was someone trying to kill her? Injure her? Send some sort of obscure message?

She dropped the cloth in the sink and reached up to open a cabinet. What she needed was there, there right next to the few glasses she had. With trembling hands she broke the seal on the bottle of Jim Beam and shakily poured a generous amount in a juice glass. She twisted the bottle's cap back in place.

Someone had tried to run her down. Twice.

She stared at the rich amber bourbon. She liked her liquor neat. No chaser. Someone in a blue car in North Carolina wanted her dead or injured.

She raised the glass. Closing her eyes, she took a shuddering breath and wondered who had a grudge against her. Maybe it had all been an accident. Maybe it was just a coincidence.

C.J. didn't believe in coincidences and hadn't for some time. Everything that happened in life happened for a reason. She could smell the pungent whiskey. Kentucky produced the best there was. Her mouth watered.

She opened her eyes and stared at the glass. Then she brought it to her mouth, anticipating the warming fire and the calming effect the drink would have on her. Maybe the car had something to do with Wes, maybe the case he was working on.

The thought of Wes brought Eileen Donovan to mind.

C.J. shuddered. She lowered the glass and looked at it, then looked at the bottle on the counter.

Eileen Donovan was a drunk, an alcoholic.

So are you, the voice of her conscience taunted.

C.J. raised the glass to her mouth again. One taste wouldn't hurt. One sip wouldn't make any difference. Jesus, she'd just narrowly escaped being run over by a car. She needed something to calm her nerves. Paralyzed with fear that the woman pushing the stroller was going to be hit, she'd paid no attention to her own safety. Wes had knocked her to the ground seconds before the car would have struck her.

Her hand shook. Drops of the bourbon sloshed over the rim of the glass. She breathed in the smell of it, rich, pungent, welcoming. She'd been dry a long time. One drink wouldn't kill her.

She closed her eyes. Eileen Donovan's face swam before her. The skewed lipstick, the liquor breath, the morning coffee more alcohol than java.

C.J. slowly lowered the glass from her mouth then turned it upside down. The amber liquid hit the metal sink and trailed down the drain. She turned the faucet on and let the clear water wash away the bourbon and the corner in the glass. Unscrewing the bottle, she poured the remaining contents down the drain, then carefully rinsed the bottle.

Her hands continued to shake.

"That took a lot of courage."

C.J. whirled around. The Jim Beam bottle fell from her hands and crashed at her feet. Running water, her heavy breathing and the sound of shattering glass echoed through the kitchen.

"I'm proud of you," he said quietly.

She turned away from him. "I didn't hear you come in."

Wrapping her arms about herself, she leaned forward toward the sink and rocked. "Somebody tried to kill me, Wes."

"I know, baby. I know."

She heard the crunch of glass and knew he'd come up behind her. Leaning over her, Wes turned off the faucet.

She turned, staring up at him. He enveloped her in his open arms.

C.J.'s mouth trembled once, and then she wept.

CHAPTER 22

When she woke a while later, C.J. was in her bed and naked except for the teddy. Normally she slept in the nude. A sheet and a lightweight blanket covered her. She opened her eyes to glance at the alarm clock on her bedside table. A single lamp cast warm shadows in the room.

Her gaze locked with Wesley's.

For a few moments neither of them said anything. They simply stared at each other, the silence a communion of spirits rather than an awkward space.

"How did you know it was a problem for me?" she quietly asked.

Wes unfolded his long, athletic frame from the chair he'd brought in from the living room. Sitting up, with his hands dropped between his knees, he watched her.

"I didn't really. Not until just now. There were signs though. Signs I should have recognized. At Mama Lo's your eyes tracked the beer I had from the moment Curtis brought them in to the time I belted the first one back. You asked for water for tea but you watched me. Tea, that's all I'd ever seen you drink. You watched me and it just seemed too intense, almost sexual."

C.J. closed her eyes and sighed. "My whole life has been too intense."

"Do you want to tell me about it?"

Opening her eyes again, she looked at him. "Yes."

The first thing she had to tell him was her name. The next thing would be why she'd run to North Carolina. The one thing she couldn't tell him, not now, not ever, was that she'd fallen in love with him, fallen in love with the one addiction she couldn't afford to deal with.

C.J. sat up. When his eyes tracked to her chest, she unconsciously tugged the sheet up. She scooted over a bit on the bed, silently offering him the space next to her.

Without a word, Wesley accepted the invitation, settling himself on top of the blanket. C.J. propped pillows at her back and braced herself against the bed's headboard and took in the picture they made: she, barely dressed, looking wanton with her hair flying in a hundred directions, yet modestly clinging to a sheet that shielded what he'd already seen and had. He, a bronzed dark warrior come to life from another age, indolently stretched out on his paramour's bed. He'd ditched the tie and slipped his shoes off.

With his feet crossed at the ankles and his arms folded behind his head, he looked as if he didn't have a care in the world. He was a hard, lean warrior who had mapped out a seduction for the evening that had been spoiled by a plane crash, a crazy driver, and her insecurities.

C.J. sighed as she tried to smooth her hair down with one hand. He'd still managed to get what he came for, he was in her bed. She knew, just like she knew that she'd always fight the temptation of "just one drink," that they'd have sex before this night was done. Then it would be over, done, and finished like every other relationship she'd had. In the morning she'd hate herself, but she'd still love him.

First she folded her hands together, then she drew up her knees and wrapped her arms around her legs. She rested her head on the top of her knees and looked at him.

Wesley's heart constricted. She was his sun, his moon, his stars. Mama Lo had been right about him catching an angel. With an inward smile Wes thought his Kensington brothers and sisters had had some sort of psychic vision when they nicknamed him Star Gazer. This beautiful, strong woman could only have been sent to him from some heavenly being.

He loved the small waves in her. While she slept, he'd run his hands through the softness. He'd watched her sleep and yet again marveled at her capacity to touch him so deeply in such a short span of time.

Yeah, he was curious about her past. But its importance paled when compared to their future together. She sat in bed staring at him. He wanted her, but more than desire he felt a surge of protectiveness that overpowered every other longing. She looked so fragile, so beautiful. Her eyes held secrets though. Miss Clara Ann said she had old eyes. Jan's eyes held the secret longings and secret dreams of strong black women through the ages.

He brought his arms down then reached out to her, unable to resist not touching her. One well-defined finger traced her hairline, smoothed its way to her full mouth.

The light touch sent ripples of heat through C.J. Desire welled within her. She sat up and blinked back sudden tears. She couldn't control anything, not even her body's willful reaction to this man.

"Tell me, Jan," he said quietly. He sought her hand then laced his fingers through hers.

"People call me C.J. That's my name. Not Jan.

He squeezed her hand encouragingly.

"As a matter of fact, until I moved here, that's the only name I've ever answered to. I came here to get away. Too many things in my life were pressing in on me. My job, my personal life. Stress was killing me. Even the stress caused by good things happening to me."

She looked at him, and then at their hands clasped together. She tried to pull away, but Wes just held her hand tighter, stronger. Like an anchor in a storm.

"I can't remember the first time I needed, really *needed* something to help me cope. My doctor was accommodating. He'd known me and my family for years. Pretty soon I was depending on those little white pills to get me to sleep at night, the blue ones to calm me down during the day when the assignments got to me."

She shrugged and glanced at Wes. "When the family doctor became suspicious about my need for refills, I simply went to another physician. It was easy. I pushed myself, more and more. I wanted to be the best, the absolute best. Long hours, bad food, and a bag full of legal drugs to keep me going. As for the alcohol, well, that's legal, too. Sometimes I couldn't wait to call it quits for the day so I could stop by a bar and get a drink."

Wes lifted their clasped hands and pressed a kiss on the top of her hand. C.J.'s answering smile was sad.

"I told you about my brother. His name is Rob. After the falling out we had I lost three days in a drunken haze. The only reason I know for a fact that I drank nonstop was because of the credit card bill."

"The what?"

"Apparently I was calling the liquor store and having them deliver straight to my apartment. I don't remember going out. I may have. God, I hope not. I just don't remember. When I got that charge card bill and realized I hadn't had a big party or anything at my place, not one that I remembered at least, I got scared. I couldn't physically or financially afford drunken binges like that."

C.J. shuddered. That time remained a blank spot in her memory. The only thing she could figure was that the housekeeper who took care of her place had cleaned up after her. She'd been too embarrassed to ask.

She'd simply enclosed an extra one hundred dollars in the woman's pay envelope and prayed that she never again lost control that way.

"I cut back on the liquor. I had to be able to keep my head together to do my job. I attacked it with a vengeance. My boss and coworkers thought I was possessed. I figured if I kept myself busy I'd be too busy to drink or to rely on pills, that when I finally fell into the bed at night it would be in pure exhaustion and not supplemented by a little pill."

A little laugh, of derision and of wonder, escaped her. "I did some of my best work then. It's amazing, here I was living the total dream, racking up praise, getting big raises and bonuses. Hell, I was employee of the month six out of eighteen months. And on the inside, I was falling apart. I was a shell. I'd even lost about twenty pounds. One day I woke up and I knew. I couldn't keep at that pace any longer. So I left. Just walked away from it all and came here to lick my wounds, to heal myself."

Wes shook his head. "Wait a minute. So you're not in the federal Witness Security Program?"

C.J.'s face scrunched up. "What? I told you the other day I wasn't. Why did you think that?"

He ignored the question and asked one of his own. "Then what do you do?"

C.J. looked up at him. Her radiant smile dazzled him.

"I garden. It's peaceful."

An eighty-pound weight fell away from Wes. She wasn't a potential felony or a firing offense! He could keep his job, keep her. They'd be able to find a place to settle, if not in this little town, maybe someplace near D.C. or Baltimore. They could always go to West Virginia. Working the coal mine was no longer his only employment option. He'd put in for a permanent transfer. He'd turn his whole world upside down to make this woman happy. She needed peace and he needed an anchor.

He wrapped his arm around her and snuggled her close. Her soft curves pressed into his chest, his midsection, his thigh. He felt himself harden, lengthen, for her, only for her. She had to feel it, too. He couldn't hide—didn't want to hide—his physical reaction to her.

Wes buried his head in her neck and kissed her in the tender place behind her ear. C.J. moaned then snaked a hand around to stroke his leg.

"Kiss me, Wes."

She sighed when their lips met. Lingering, she savored each moment, each not so gentle swipe of his tongue against hers. She loved the taste of him, the feel of him. Quivering at the sweet, hot tenderness, she turned. She wanted to feel her breasts, aching for his touch, against the hard strength of his chest.

In a moment, she found herself on her back. Wesley's gaze burned into hers. Like a moth attracted by the dazzling flame that would consume it, she came to him, reaching for the buttons on his dress shirt.

"Make love to me, Wes."

He stilled her hands. "Jan . . . C.J., I want to make sure you understand something."

The edge to and command in his voice shamed her. She lowered her hands and lay back, ready for him to throw her past in her face. She lay still, waiting for the conditions he'd set. She'd willingly given him weapons with which to hurt her.

Maybe, after all she'd told him, he no longer wanted her for anything except what she had so freely and carelessly given to so many others. How could she convince him that this time it was real? She closed her eyes against the pain. How could she explain to him something she couldn't quite grasp herself?

With his voice calm and his gaze steady, he studied her. "Open your eyes, C.J."

The lace edge of the—what did she call it?—a teddy, beckoned him. The rush of desire that hit him when he'd undressed her and seen the scandalous bit of clothing now assaulted him even stronger than before. His fingers shook as he reached for her.

Like he did in the store when they'd bought the silky piece, his finger rimmed the lacy edge. This time, however, her soft, radiant skin, not a hanger, filled the garment. She arched into his touch and a soft moan escaped her. That small sound almost broke him.

"What I want you to understand," he said, "is that I want to make love to you and with you."

"I . . ."

With a flick of his thumb over her nipple he silenced her. She cried out and again arched toward him. The bud hardened under his hand. Through the fabric of the teddy, he gently fondled her breast, tracing small curliques, teasing her, and, he hoped, making her as hot for him as he was for her.

"I want to make love to you. Not sex. Not screwing or bumpin' and grindin' or doing the nasty. I want to make slow, sweet love to you."

He lowered his head to her breast. His intense gaze never left hers while his tongue lapped over the fabric to scorch her skin.

C.J. sank into the mattress. "Yes."

She stretched her lithe body, giving him access. He caught her hands and held them over her head, then continued the exquisite sampling, soft skin here, a full breast there. The feast before him promised an endless buffet of delight. And he had all night long.

His mouth closed over her breast.

"Oh, God. Yes, Wesley, yes!" She pulled his head in a vain attempt to get closer, closer.

He had all night to show her with his actions and tell her with his words how much he cared, how very much he loved her. This night, her pleasure constituted his solitary goal.

He lifted his head then slowly stripped the tangled sheet and blanket from her body. He kissed every bit of skin exposed along the trail of the sheet. C.J. His woman. Wes worshipped her with his mouth, with the slow stroke of his hands, with everything in him he had to give her.

C.J. shuddered and sighed when his mouth kissed her knee. Her other leg lifted and stroked his. The cloth of his trousers frustrated her, she wanted to feel his hot skin next to hers. She'd been holding back her feelings for so long, so very long. Tonight, she'd give to him. She wanted to tell him but she couldn't speak to form the words. Every part of her was focused on what he did, how he made her feel. Cherished, lost in a sea of sensation.

He lifted her leg and flicked his tongue over the tender flesh at the back of her knee.

C.J. cried out.

Wes smiled. "Do you like that?"

Incapable of speech, she merely shook her head back and forth on the pillow.

"What? No, you don't like that? Well how about this?"

His big hand stroked down her leg and then slowly back up. He bent low to again lick the area behind her knee, then he moved up and over to kiss her inner thigh.

"Don't want any part to feel neglected now."

Had anything been funny C.J. would have laughed. As it was she merely moaned his name. Then his hand covered the core of her. Opening her legs to him, she knew she'd died and gone to a place where only pleasure existed.

"These snaps are awfully convenient," he observed while undoing them. He unfastened the last one and lifted the lacy edge of the fabric away from her. C.J. lifted her hips to him.

"Thank you," he murmured. "How'd you know that was one of my favorite things in the whole world?"

His head lowered and she lifted her legs. He positioned them over his shoulders and loved her with a maddening slowness. C.J. writhed beneath him. A storm raged in her, heat and flame and a desire she never suspected even existed.

The first trembling spasms shook her.

"Wesley!"

"Let it come," he murmured.

Wes lapped her sweetness then made his way up her body. Stradling her with a knee braced on either side, he stared into her eyes as his hands closed over her breasts.

His breathing came ragged, uneven, as if he'd run the 100-yard dash.

"Let me love you, Wes."

He smiled. "Tonight is for you."

C.J. reached for the erection in his pants. She stroked him. "I want you deep inside me."

His tormented groan spurred her. With her free hand she brought his head to hers. The kiss, deep and powerful, promised more rapture, if either of them could stand it.

Wesley's weight settled on her. C.J. wrapped her arms around his neck. He rolled over so she was on top of him.

She could feel the blunt hardness of his erection through his trousers. C.J. rocked back and forth, savoring the feel of him, loving the way his eyes had darkened. He gripped her thighs and thrust upward, seeking the release they both wanted.

While kissing him in short, greedy spurts, she worked at the buttons on his shirt. Finally exposing his rippled chest, she broke away from his mouth and kissed each of the taut male nipples. He groaned again then crushed her to him, his mouth slashing over hers. But she wasn't finished with him. Unbuckling the slim leather belt at his waist, she glanced down at him, a wicked suggestion in her eyes.

"Jesus." Wes pushed her hands away and in short order came out of his pants and briefs. Then he pulled the lacy teddy over her head. "Wal-Mart is always going to have a fond place in my heart."

She did laugh then. On her knees in the middle of the bed she stretched languidly and watched his eyes track her every movement, then, like radar, settle on her full breasts. "There are other places to be fond of," she said.

His mouth curved in an unconscious smile. C.J.'s heart flipped even as she watched him draw near.

"I can see a few worth endless exploration," he said. He pulled her to him. They fell together on the firm mattress.

"Show me."

He did.

CHAPTER 23

She woke with a start. It was light out and she knew she was alone in the bed. They'd made slow sweet love before dawn. The last thing she remembered before drifting into a well-satiated sleep was being snuggled spoon fashion next to his big, warm body. His large hand covered and caressed her breast even in sleep. She'd felt secure, loved.

But his warmth no longer comforted her. He'd left without saying goodbye.

She waited for the guilt to kick in, for the self-recriminations to do their usual number on her. But nothing happened. Except for the pounding on the door.

Realizing what had awakened her, she flung the sheet to the side and dashed to the closet for her robe.

A quick glance at the clock told her it was . . . she couldn't see the clock. A piece of paper propped against it obscured the face. She smiled. He'd left a note.

The knocking on her front door continued.

"Coming."

When she opened the door, a Federal Express driver thrust a clipboard at her.

"Good morning," she cheerily greeted him.

The man smiled. "It's afternoon, ma'am. Sorry to disturb you."

"Not a problem. I'm expecting this." She accepted the package sent from her reporter friend. David had really done a scramble to get this to her so quickly.

The driver turned to leave.

"What time do you have?" she asked.

"One-thirty-three, ma'am. You have a good day."

C.J.'s mouth dropped open. It couldn't be that late.

She closed the door and ripped open the package as she made her way to the kitchen. She put water on for tea then remembered what had almost transpired in her kitchen last night.

"First things, first," she said, reaching for the telephone book on top of the refrigerator. She looked up the listing for Alcoholics Anonymous and dialed the number.

"Hi. My name is Jan Lang . . ." She paused and took a deep breath. "My name is C.J. Mayview and I'd like to know where I can go to an AA meeting." She wrote the time and day down then got directions. Robinson had been right. She needed to attend the meetings. She could try to go it alone, but would her will be strong enough to overcome the next temptation and crisis? Not likely.

She looked around the kitchen and in the trash but couldn't find either the shattered pieces of the bourbon bottle or the bottle of wine Wesley had brought with their dinner. As a matter of fact, her kitchen was spotless, cleaner even than it had been before Wes had arrived the night before. He must have cleaned while she'd slept.

In a crashing wave, she remembered why she'd thought she needed a drink, why she'd cried in Wesley's arms, why he'd put her in bed. Someone had deliberately tried to run her down. There were no ifs, ands, or buts about it. And she'd be willing to bet it was the same driver as the one on Main Street.

The kettle whistled. C.J. poured hot water over a tea bag of her favorite, chamomile. While the tea steeped she finished opening the FedEx packet. Then she remembered the note in her bedroom. She pulled a file folder from the packet then left it on the counter and went to her bedroom.

Sitting on the edge of her bed she plucked up the note Wes had left propped against her alarm clock.

> You are my life, my sun and moon and stars. Thank you for giving to me the wondrous gift of yourself. There are some things I need to do today, but I'm counting each moment until we can be together again.
>
> Yours,
> W. Donovan

C.J.'s mouth trembled. The man was sheer poetry and she loved him beyond reason. She clutched the short note to her breast and closed her eyes. His bronzed image came to her. The strength in his face, the power in his hands, the undiluted maleness of every part of him. He'd opened his heart to her in West Virginia. C.J. knew that the experience of seeing his birth mother had taken its toll on him. But he'd been willing to give the woman the benefit of the doubt.

She thought about his niece and nephew then spread her hand over her stomach. She glanced back at the rumpled sheets on the bed. They'd forgotten about protection last night. She had never, *ever* done that before. They'd loved through the long, dark hours and into the dawn of the new day. She could be pregnant even now.

C.J.'s mouth blossomed into a smile and then a huge grin. Pregnant. Not only did she fail to cringe at the thought, she embraced the possibility.

When she'd awakened, she hadn't been beset with doubt, anger, or self-directed loathing. Maybe, just as she'd come to the realization that she needed to accept Alcoholics Anonymous, maybe, just maybe, she also needed to accept that Wes was different from the other men. Different in ways that mattered. For the first time, her heart was involved. She loved him. It was just that simple.

She reread the note from Wes then carried it to the kitchen. She added a touch of sugar to the tea then picked up the packet from David and carried the tea, the folder, and Wesley's note to the living room. Smiling, she read Wesley's note again then put it aside. Sipping from the cup of tea, she pulled off a yellow sticky note from David: "Here's what you asked for C.J. I want research credit in the tagline of your story. David."

C.J. shook her head. Apparently, she was the only person who believed she left journalism for good.

Mindful of the bad spring in the sofa, she settled on the edge, opened the file and quickly scanned through it. It was pretty thick, some of the stories dating back more than ten years. David had found a lot of clips on Wesley Donovan. Clipped together at the end were black and white photocopies of pictures and one color photocopy of an official-looking mugshot.

"Marcus Kensington." She recognized him even though she'd never met him. He looked just like his brothers. In his eyes she saw compassion, and she wondered what kind of man he'd been. He'd left behind two small children, and, C.J. presumed, a wife. His family still grieved for him. Wesley still grieved for him.

Not sure where to begin, C.J. spread the clips out on the coffee table. The photograph of one in particular caught her eye. The somber picture was at a gravesite. Black umbrellas and dark suits dominated the photo. She read the outline: "Law enforcement officials from eight states gathered Friday for the funeral service of slain police officer Marcus Kensington."

C.J. took a sip of tea then settled back to read the funeral story. What she read made her uncomfortable. About an hour later she finished reading everything in the file. She tossed the clips on the coffee table.

She pinched the bridge of her nose and rubbed her eyes. "Oh, God. Now what?"

Mama Lo's words came back to her, the meaning now painfully clear. *Ain't interested in them lies those media people always telling.*

Just like Mama Lo, Wesley probably wasn't interested either. So many things made sense now. Wes Donovan probably didn't just dislike the Serenity Falls reporter as a person, most likely he despised all journalists in general.

From beneath the stack of newspaper clips about him and Marcus Kensington, she pulled out the note Wes had left for her. Would he feel the same way about her when he found out what she did for a living?

Wes made two telephone calls. The first to his pal Scotty at headquarters to thank him for running the make on Jan, or rather C.J. He didn't know what she'd done for a living before arriving in Serenity Falls but it didn't make any difference. The important thing was she wasn't in the Marshals Service's Witness Security Program.

The Serenity Falls witness who was, however, was in trouble. Wes had put the witness in a safe house, one secured by Scotty and signed off on by Casey and Holloway. The page that had come while a car was trying to run him and C.J. over had been from the witness who swore up and down that a maid at the motel looked a whole lot like a contract killer. The witness had slipped out a back window and run hard and fast to the first phone.

Wesley's second call had been for backup. In less than two hours he'd have the witness tucked safely on a plane headed for a new identity, a new life on the run.

A lot could happen in two hours. Wes didn't like the odds. Too many weird things went down in this town for him to feel secure about anything. He shifted, the weight of the Kevlar vest he wore under a lightweight jacket reminding him that danger lurked everywhere, even in little Southern towns like Serenity Falls. The witness had gone to ground, as safe as could be under the circumstances.

Ace reporter Kenneth Sheldon's big story of the morning had been heralded by a huge headline: "Town under siege by calamities." The reporter's main story was about the plane crash on C.J.'s street. Then every little blip and sneeze that had happened up to that day was recounted: first the old man who collapsed at the grocery store; then Jimmy Peterson, the car dealer, got snuffed out by a falling tree; and battery acid caused a small explosion at the local plant. According to Sheldon's story, a car had crashed through the front window of the little bakery he and C.J. had stopped in before leaving for West Virginia Friday. A head-on collision on the interstate right outside town came next, followed by a plane crash.

Wesley added an incident the reporter didn't have in his story: the car trying to run C.J. down.

Wes didn't care for Sheldon but he couldn't ignore the fact that all the town's bad luck had started the day he rolled into Serenity Falls. Coincidences were rare. He sorted through each incident looking for a common link, any common denominator. In some fashion or another he'd managed to get himself embroiled in a couple of the incidents. But he hadn't been around for the plant explosion, and Jimmy Peterson's accident with the tree didn't seem to have any link to anything. But Wes didn't discount those things.

Mentally, he carefully reviewed his protected witness's lengthy dossier.

He rubbed his chin in frustration. "God, it could be anything, it could be nothing."

He had just one priority: Keep the witness alive and safe. He'd left a lot open with C.J. but he felt secure that what they had was real. They'd been on fire for each other the previous night. She'd shared her past with him, and he'd loved her beyond it.

Then he remembered something, something important. *Dark Warrior.* She'd called him that when they first met. In the midst of passion she whispered it just last night. He'd let his guard down and had been too caught up in the silken feel of her to make a deal out of it then. But he remembered now. He remembered and he wondered if somehow, someway he'd been played for a fool.

Amber Baldwin threw clothes into a small particleboard suitcase. Frankie had called and said they had to move again. This time they had to leave everything except what she could fit in one bag. Amber started crying as she stuffed Frank Jr.'s favorite rag doll in the bag. She was tired of this life, tired of running. Maybe she'd just leave him and go home to Las Vegas. Her legs still looked good. She could easily get work.

She slammed the suitcase closed and pressed the latch down. A sudden pounding on her front door made her squeal. She snatched the baby from the couch where he dozed and stared at the door.

She didn't know who or what was on the other side of that door. She glanced at the phone, picked it up to call 911 then remembered Frankie's warning. "Don't use the phones. They're all bugged." With wide eyes she backed away from the door.

"Please don't kill me. Please."

"Amber! Amber are you in there?"

A voice penetrated Amber's fear. She recognized the voice.

"Amber, come on now. If you're in there, please open up."

Jan! It was Jan Langley, not some hired killer or Frankie gone completely crazy.

Amber ran to the door and unlatched the four locks Frankie installed when they'd moved in.

"Oh, Jan. Thank God it's you. I was so frightened."

C.J. walked into the small apartment and looked around. The toddler fretted in Amber's arms until she placed him on the sofa. Amber then turned and quickly locked the door again.

C.J.'s eyebrows lifted. "I haven't seen that since I left Baltimore," she said, nodding toward the multiple dead bolts and chains securing the door.

"Frankie . . ."

C.J. waved her hand. "Yeah, yeah. Frankie. By the way, where is he?"

"I don't know," Amber responded. "He called about thirty minutes ago and told me to pack. We have to leave again. We're going to Texas this time."

C.J. eyed the suitcase on the crate coffee table. "How long are you going to run and how many times are you going to let him threaten you before you leave?"

Amber looked at the floor. "He's my husband, Jan." Her gaze lifted to C.J.'s. "We'll be okay. *I'll* be okay. I'll send you my address when we get wherever it is we're going in Texas."

There was little use in arguing with Amber. C.J. well knew the statistical chances of Amber leaving Frankie. She also knew how many women eventually found themselves in emergency shelters and safe houses after running for their lives with just the clothes on their backs and their children in tow.

She sighed.

"Here," she said, handing Amber a white business-size envelope.

"What is it?"

Amber peered into the envelope. "Jan, I can't take this. It's money." Her eyes widened as she took in just how many crisp fifties were in the envelope.

"Look, you never know what might happen down the road. Take it. There's also a telephone number on a card in there. It's for a national hotline. If you ever need someone to come get you, if you're ever in trouble and think you have no way out, someone at that number can get help for you. Understand?"

Amber nodded, then stepped forward and hugged C.J.

Uncomfortable with the show of affection or gratitude, whatever it was, C.J. patted Amber's back then stepped away. Amber wiped her eyes.

"I'm sorry I didn't get right back to you," C.J. said. "I had company yesterday and I'd turned the ringers off and the answering machine down. I didn't get your message until about an hour ago."

Amber picked up the baby and bounced him in her arms. "I don't know where we're going to be in Texas. Frankie never tells me anymore. I was surprised he told me that much. We just get in the car or whatever and wind up some place. I've been thinking about what you said though. I've been thinking maybe I should just go home. My mama can take care of Frank Jr. while I work. People talk about Vegas and sometimes it gets a bad rap but Las Vegas is home for me."

C.J. kept her opinions about the city to herself. "Maybe home will be good for you. Can I help you finish packing?"

Amber shook her head. Her straight hair, as always held back with a head band, barely moved. "That's all I can take. Frankie said just one bag. He wants to start fresh. I'm taking a big purse though. I can fit lots of extra stuff in there.

C.J. didn't know what else to say or if anything else could be said. "May I hold him for a moment?"

Amber blinked, obviously surprised by the request. Then she smiled and handed the toddler to C.J. "I didn't think you liked kids."

So, it was that evident, C.J. thought. Frank Jr. reached for the spiral triangle earring dangling at her ear. "I used to think the same thing. Now, well, let's just say, I'm re-evaluating my position."

Cooing at the baby, she captured his little hand when he tugged on the earring. "This one is mine. Maybe when you grow up a little more your Mom'll let you get your own earring."

Amber laughed. "Frankie would have a fit if any son of his came home with a hole in his ear. He says that's a mark of fairy boys and sissies."

"That's not true," C.J. said. "Some of the most sexy straight guys I know have earrings, a couple of them even have holes in both ears."

C.J. sat on the sofa and played patty cake with Frank Jr. who laughed and gurgled at her.

"I know," Amber replied. "Frankie can be so traditional sometimes."

There wasn't anything traditional about a man physically and emotionally threatening his wife, but C.J. again kept her thoughts to herself. Amber didn't need a sermon, she needed a solution—and a divorce. But that decision would have to spring from Amber, not from C.J.

Hugging the baby to her one last time, C.J. kissed his forehead. "You take care of your mom now, okay?"

"Ma!"

C.J. laughed then hugged him close again before handing him back up to Amber.

"Well, I better leave. If there's anything else I can do for you, you know where to find me."

Amber smiled. "In your garden."

"I'll plant petunias for Frank Jr. and a rose bush for you," C.J. said with an answering smile.

Amber quickly hugged her again. This time, C.J. didn't recoil from the embrace.

"Jan, don't worry about me. I was just overly emotional the other day.

I'll be fine. We'll all be fine. Thank you for the gift of your friendship. It's meant a lot to me."

C.J.'s smile was sad when they stepped apart. Then, a moment later, standing outside the door, C.J. heard Amber redo all the locks on the apartment door.

The only thing Margaret Shelley disliked was lying to Aunt Clara. She'd outdone herself this time though. In a blind stroke of luck mixed with providence, her quarry had landed in little Serenity Falls, North Carolina.

Margaret could kill a man, woman, or child without flinching, had done so many times. Her work generally took her far, far from her North Carolina roots. This time, however, she couldn't do the job. She'd let a personal issue distract her from her main purpose. She'd managed to spook her quarry while enjoying a cat-and-mouse flirtation with the man sent to protect her prey.

Everything in her protested the necessary act of returning part of her substantial fee. As a professional, she prided herself on a clean, quality hit. If she got a little playacting in at the same time, so much the better. Margaret had always wanted to be an actress. Contract killing paid better.

But a job undone remained a job undone. She couldn't put Aunt Clara in danger. So far she'd managed to remain a peripheral shadow for her quarry, just enough to make anybody nervous, edgy, and looking over the shoulder at every turn.

She could take out the witness but didn't like the odds. He may have talked and given that Wes Donovan enough information to actually work with. How Donovan had ended up at Aunt Clara's remained a troubling mystery—just the sort of loose end coincidence that always caused trouble.

Margaret packed her last bag. She'd come up with a plausible story for Aunt Clara, an out-of-the-blue work assignment she couldn't possibly turn down.

She laughed. Twice now, Donovan had looked at her as if they'd met before. Funny what losing fifty pounds, changing hair and eye color, and having a little nip and tuck done on a face could do to alter appearance. She'd even gone so far as to use her real name on this job. That had been a mistake.

It wouldn't take Donovan or his buddies in D.C. long to figure out what was what if she took out the witness and left all the peripherals walking around. Following him had been a stroke of genius. Calling in an associate to take care of the rest had been a necessity, even if he was an incompetent idiot, failing twice now to do an easy hit-and-run.

She'd like nothing better than finishing up this job and giving herself the added bonus of striking out at Wes Donovan through the little piece he'd gotten himself in this town. But she couldn't risk any harm or the notion of guilt by association to Aunt Clara. Besides, her original prey could be stalked to another town, another day.

"Ah, well. It was fun while it lasted."

CHAPTER 24

Wes gunned his bike toward Miss Clara Ann's house. He saw Margaret hug Miss Clara Ann then wave, get in her rental, and drive off. By the time Wes parked the Harley around back and made his way to the front parlor, Miss Clara Ann was coming in the door.

"Wesley, baby, there you are. You just missed Margaret. She got called back to the city for her job." Miss Clara Ann shook her head. "Never did understand just what that girl does for a paycheck. That ain't important though. You done missed lunch again. I gots some leftovers if you hungry. You hungry, baby?"

"No, ma'am. I was just coming in to gather my gear. I'll be on my way soon and I wanted to say goodbye."

"Goodbye? Boy, you just got here the other day. I'm gonna have to give you a refund on your money."

Wes smiled. "No, you keep it. I've enjoyed my stay with you."

"I tell you, all you young folks pulling out at the same time. First Margaret, now you. And that Garrison, I ain't seen hide nor hair of him in a while. All his artist stuff still upstairs though so I reckon he'll be back for it. You younguns keep some busy lives."

Wes kissed Miss Clara Ann on the cheek.

"I'm gonna make you up a bag. I knows you said you ain't hungry now but that don't mean you won't be later."

Wes smiled. "Yes, ma'am."

"Well, you get on up there and get your stuff together."

He did. It took less than five minutes for Wes to toss his gear in his bags. His immediate problem consisted of too many vehicles on hand. The truck Casey secured for him was just a truck. Maybe Ray Bob over at the service station would buy it. Wes grinned, wondering if he'd get any brownie points with Holloway if he turned a profit for the Marshals Service.

"Not if your witness winds up dead," he reminded himself.

He looked at the ceiling in the room he'd called home for the last few days. "Never did get to see the artist's studio set up up there."

He thought about taking a peek now but discarded the idea. It didn't matter now.

The pager at his waist beeped. Wes pulled it off the waistband of his jeans and stared at the number. Two exclamation marks followed ten-digits. Wes recognized the long-distance number and swore. The simple code at the end meant call ASAP and don't worry about a secure phone line.

He checked the bathroom then glanced around the room one last time. He clipped the black pager back on his jeans then checked the gun he shouldered and grabbed his bags.

In the hallway a moment later, had he not been looking down at the pager that was going off again he would have missed the book of matches on the floor near a table leg at the top of the stairs. Wes bent low, snatched up the matches and checked the pager display. He then got a good look at the matchbook cover.

"Son of a bitch!" He took the stairs three at a time.

"Miss Clara Ann!" he called out.

"In the kitchen, baby."

Wesley burst through the door and confronted the old woman. Her puzzled expression tempered his anger a bit, but not much.

"Where is she?"

Miss Clara Ann wrapped a chicken leg in foil. "Where's who?"

"Your niece," he said, stressing the word niece.

"Margaret? I done told you. She got a call from her fancy job up north. Said they told her she had to cut her vacation short and get back up there."

Vacation my ass, he thought. The matches were from the same motel he'd tucked the witness in. And the witness swore up and down he'd seen a maid he recognized. The hazy description of the woman, prompted more by fear than true recollection, fit Margaret.

Miss Clara Ann handed him a brown paper bag. Wes stared at it like it was a dangerous explosive.

"What's this?"

"That's your lunch, child." She smiled up at him. "You sure been some good company to this old lady."

Wes looked at her. She was either a first-rate actress or completely in the dark. His gut gave him the answer.

"You don't know, do you?"

"Know what, baby?"

Wes smiled and shook his head. "Never mind. May I use your phone?"

He answered the page.

"There's trouble headed your way," Holloway said when he got on the line. "Robbi Langston busted out today while being taken to a medical appointment. He has people in the Charlotte area. The all points bulletin says he's armed, dangerous, and may have a hostage with him."

Wes swore. Then looked at Miss Clara Ann and mouthed "Sorry."

Langston was a bank robber who'd killed three people. He'd been serving life in a federal facility. "That's just what I need. Any reason to believe he's in this area?"

"You're in the path to Charlotte."

Wes rang off with Holloway. He'd wanted to ask about Margaret but couldn't, not with Miss Clara Ann standing there. Bending low, he kissed Miss Clara Ann, wished her well, then hightailed it to the Crown Victoria.

If Margaret was who and what he suspected she was, he might already be too late.

Curious about all the commotion a few blocks away, C.J. headed in the direction of the flashing lights after leaving Amber's apartment.

"This sure is a bustling little place," she said aloud as she drew nearer to what turned out to be a police road block.

Saddling up to an officer, she couldn't resist the who, what, when, where, why, and how that constituted a second nature for her.

"Ma'am, I'm going to have to ask you to step back. Going home and locking your windows and doors would be even better."

Itching for a notebook in her hands, she asked, "Why?"

"Bank robber and killer escaped from prison earlier today. Indication is he might be headed this way."

"What's his name?"

The cop eyed her with a look of part irritation, part male interest. "Why? You know some bank robbers or something?"

C.J. laughed then backed off. News gathering was no longer her job. The curiosity, she figured, would be with her until she drew her last breath.

"Can't say that I do."

"You'd be better off in the security of your own home, ma'am. There's no telling what might happen if he comes this way."

C.J. waved as she left, then did what reporters always do, inched her way around to another vantage point.

About to ask another officer the same questions, her peripheral vision picked up an all-too-familiar sight. A satellite news truck rolled up the street and stopped less than three yards from where she stood.

"Excuse me officer . . ."

Her voice trailed off as she watched the television crew set up. What in the world was going on?

"Ma'am," the officer said. "You shouldn't be here. I'm going to have to ask you to leave."

"What's going on?" she asked.

"Escaped convict. A killer and bank robber is headed this way. We're searching every vehicle."

She was about to ask another question when the Crown Victoria rolled up. When Wes got out of the car and strode to where she stood, C.J. found herself struck by two truths: first, she loved this man beyond reason; second, she had to tell him what she did for a living before coming to Serenity Falls. Opening her mouth to just blurt it out and have done with it, she paused. The wraparound sunglasses obscured his eyes, but every inch of him screamed *cop*, from the snug Levi's right on down to the toe of his cowboy boots. She wondered how she'd missed it before.

An image of Marshals of old came to mind: rugged men, ready to lay down their lives for the law. Wes Donovan fit that mold. All he was missing was a shiny tin star at his breast pocket, a horse, and a six-shooter at his hip. Six-shooters remained a relic of the past though, she thought. Under that jacket he probably had a semi-automatic in a shoulder holster.

"C.J., what in the world are you doing out here? You need to be at home where I don't have to worry about you, too."

C.J. picked up on the inconsistency. "Too? Who else are you worrying about?"

Wes smiled as he tucked the glasses in his jacket pocket. Lifting his hand, he softly ran his thumb over her cheek and down her chin. With his thumb, he lightly rimmed the contours of her mouth then bent for a quick kiss. "I have some business to attend to but I hope to see you tonight or tomorrow."

C.J. nodded. "Okay. But there's something I need to tell you." She glanced at the uniformed cop then back at Wes. "Do you have a minute?"

"Not really. I'm serious though. I'll be less distracted if I know you're safe at home." He pulled out a badge and addressed the cop. "Who's the on-scene commander?"

"That would be Captain Parker. He's over there."

Wes turned to look in the direction the cop pointed and bumped into a man who'd approached him from behind.

"Sorry about that," he said.

"Not a problem. Hi. I'm Reuben Black with Action News. Are you in charge here?"

Wes stepped aside. "No."

The reporter shrugged at the curt tone and looked around Wes to the cop.

"C.J. Mayview! Is that you? I should have known this was something hot. How long have you been down here reporting this story?"

C.J.'s eyes widened. She shook her head to deny the words.

Wes whirled around. "What did you say?"

Unaware of the sudden tension, the reporter continued addressing C.J. He grabbed her hand and pumped it. "It truly is a pleasure to meet you. I'd recognize you anywhere after all those pictures and the award. I always read your stuff. Well, I used to that is before I took this job in Charlotte a couple of month ago. What's it like winning a Pulitzer? That has got to be one awesome feeling."

C.J., ignoring the TV reporter, only had eyes for Wes. What she saw made her wince. The warmth shining in his eyes just a moment ago was gone, replaced by a dull flat glare, the sensuous mouth that had so recently danced across hers was now a tightly compressed line. "Wesley, I can explain. I've been trying to tell . . ."

"You're a reporter?" he asked.

"It's not what you think, Wesley."

"I have work to do." Glancing at the notebook the TV reporter held he looked at her again, "I suppose you do, too." Disdain dripped from his voice.

With a look that in no uncertain terms was reserved for the scum of the earth, Wesley's gaze flicked over C.J. and the TV reporter. Then he turned his back on her and strode to where the on-scene commander stood talking with some cops.

"What's his problem?"

Tears filled C.J.'s eyes. "Excuse me," she mumbled to the reporter then chased after Wes. "Wesley! Let me explain. It's not at all what you think. I'm no longer . . ."

Wes whirled around. C.J. paused in mid-step, mid-sentence. The fury in him radiated across the few feet separating them. His curt voice lashed at her. "Save it, Jan, C.J., Ja'Niece, whatever the hell your real name is. Go write your story."

"That's what I'm trying to tell you. I'm not writing a story."

"Ma'am, this is now a restricted area," the original cop said. "I'm going to have to ask you to leave."

Wes turned his back on her and went to the officer identified as Captain Parker.

"Wesley!"

The cop blocked her way then took her arm. "Ma'am, I don't think you want a citation."

C.J. sighed as her shoulders slumped. She watched Wes and the cop get in a car. Pulling her arm free of the restraining officer's light hold, she muttered, "I'm leaving."

With one last lingering look in Wesley's direction, C.J. turned away.

Less than ten minutes later, with everything set up to his satisfaction, Wes looked for C.J. She was nowhere in sight. But that other parasite was. Wes wanted some answers. Quickly.

"Excuse me," he butted into the conversation the TV reporter was having with a cop. "The woman you were talking to. Who did you say she is?"

"Oh, don't you know? That's C.J. Mayview. She won a Pulitzer Prize for investigative reporting a little while ago. It was for a dynamite story package on corruption in the day care system. Then she just sort of dropped out of the scene." The reporter grinned, displaying perfect pearly white teeth. "Boy am I glad I got this assignment. If C.J. Mayview is here, it must be something big. Now what was your name again?"

Wes grunted and walked away. He had all the information he needed. A reporter! She was a reporter. No wonder she'd defended that little weasely punk Kenny Sheldon. Wes shook his head in disgust. Of all the people for him to get involved with.

But he didn't have time to indulge in justifiable anger right now. The cops would see to it that he got through the roadblocks without any hassles. It was time to whisk his witness to safety.

Margaret Shelley was about to head out of town and toward the interstate when she got a deliciously wicked idea. Glancing at the digital clock in her dash, she figured she'd have enough time for one last dig at Wesley Donovan.

It still grated on her that the job was undone and that she'd let her personal conflict with Wes Donovan get in the way. But it was a reaction she found herself unable to control; the one part of her that refused to be a professional. It was like her brain shut down and her body kicked into overdrive where Donovan was concerned.

Margaret checked her hair in the rearview mirror then laughed. She loved this stalking game even more than the final victory of bringing down her prey.

With a sharp left, she wheeled the mid-size sedan around in a U-turn.

Wes took care of business.

The witness whined and moaned but eventually boarded the small charter flight at the municipal airport.

"You know where to find me if you need me."

The witness grinned. "Unfortunately, the answer to that is yes. Hey, thanks for your help, man. I really hate leaving here. More than you'll ever know."

"You gotta do . . ." Wes said.

"What you gotta do," the witness finished. "But I'm gonna pay you back on account of this outfit. Don't you know this priest get up is a cliche? They do it in all the movies."

Wes took in the cleric's robes and wire-rimmed glasses the witness had donned. It was his turn to grin. "We all must carry our burdens."

"Yeah, right," the witness said. "There's saints turning over in their graves right now. I can't even remember the last time I celebrated Mass or went to confession."

"Then you're way overdue. You can practice what you'll say on the way."

A nun with a 9-mm Sig Sauer poked her head out the single door. "Mr. Yardley, we gotta get a move on before we get made."

Wes and the man known as Yancey Yardley shook hands. "Take care. Hope I don't have to see you again."

"Yeah, me too. And thanks . . . for everything."

The Deputy Marshal in the nun's outfit pulled the stairway up. Wes hopped back and watched the small plane taxi to its takeoff spot.

Wes stared after the plane until all that remained was a speck in the sky.

His job was done in Serenity Falls.

He thought about C.J. Mayview also known as Jan Langley. Lightning quick anger bubbled to the surface. He'd opened his heart and his soul to that woman, told her things a reporter had no business knowing. Wes swore. Striding back to the Crown Victoria, he kicked the rear tire so hard that he found some small satisfaction in the pain shooting up his leg.

His witness was safe and secure now. By the time he finished with C.J. Mayview she was gonna need a safe and secure place to hide.

CHAPTER 25

Serenity Falls, North Carolina, had lost its appeal. C.J.'s quest for peace of mind had been interrupted by a bronzed dark warrior. She would live through the heartache. She'd survive just like she did at every other turn.

Grateful that she'd packed light when she'd left Baltimore, she stuffed the meager contents of the bottom bureau drawer into an oversized duffel bag she'd picked up at an Army-Navy store. Everything else, and it wasn't much, was already in the Cherokee.

She could sell this little house anytime. Right now, she had one priority: run to a hiding place to lick her wounds. C.J. didn't know where she'd go. She just couldn't stay here. Not in a place that in every corner reminded her of Wesley. Even though what happened achieved the very end she'd wanted, she had hoped they could part amicably, maybe even as friends. She'd wanted the memories to be sweet, not bitter.

"Your good intentions were overcome by events, C.J.," she said, walking into the bathroom to cram toiletries in her bag.

Alcohol, she knew, wasn't the answer. Neither were the small pills that used to help her sleep. She'd go this alone, clean, sober, and ever mindful that each day would present a new mountain, a new struggle. Eventually, with time and with care, the heartache would fade, Wesley's memory would dim and she'd look back on this week and laugh.

There was no laughing now though. She'd finally fallen in love and her own desperate need for self-preservation had ruined that love. Her sin had been one of omission; not so terribly wrong when compared to other sins. But she could think of no penance Wesley might accept, not with what she knew about Marcus Kensington's death.

The newspaper stories David sent had spelled it all out: Marcus had been working undercover on the vice squad. An overzealous young police reporter at a small newspaper who was eager to make a good impression on his new editors had chased down a good lead about a prostitution drug ring. With a camera and notebook in hand, the reporter had slipped unnoticed into a warehouse where undercover cops were doing deals.

According to the clips, including one that had been written up in a media journal, repeated pleas to the newspaper not to run the pictures had been made by police officials all the way up to the chief of police. The reporter and his newspaper editors maintained that while the quality of the photos weren't the best, they captured the mood and essence of street life and that no one in the photos could be clearly identified.

The story and pictures ran on the front page of the reporter's small-circulation newspaper and were picked up by the wire services. Marcus Kensington's bullet-riddled body was dumped outside a police precinct the next day and found by officers changing shifts.

The reporter had had the gall to show up at a memorial service. Wesley would have killed the reporter if deputy marshals and cops hadn't subdued him.

So many things made sense now. The perfect vision of hindsight painted a picture she at any time could have altered, if only she'd known beforehand.

She wiped at tears that obscured her view.

"South Carolina. South Carolina has nice little towns in it." Her mind made up, C.J. dragged the duffel bag to the door.

Heavy pounding on the door rattled the front windows. Startled, she gasped and jumped back. C.J. swallowed. She didn't have to look to know it was Wesley.

With a degree of well-deserved trepidation she opened the door.

For a moment he looked surprised to see her. Then a scowl like thunder crossed his face.

"You must be fast at your muckraking."

His self-righteous, accusing tone ticked her off. "If you didn't go flying off the handle and let me explain—"

"What's there to explain?" he interrupted. "You lied to me. Here I was all this time thinking you were a well-protected witness in my agency's Witness Security Program. But no, you're just another parasite sweating for a byline."

He brushed by her and walked in the house.

"I don't remember inviting you in."

Wes turned and leveled a look at her. "Tough. I'm in."

"Now you wait just one minute, Mr. U.S. Deputy Marshal. You come sweeping in here like some avenging angel. Who the hell are you to pass judgment on me and what I do? You don't know me. You don't really know anything about me."

"You're right. I don't, *Jan.*"

His derisiveness on that point was well-deserved. "I told everyone here that my name is Jan. Not just you. And besides, I told you I came here to get myself together."

He smirked. "Yeah right. That TV reporter friend of yours told me all about your big Pulitzer Prize. You want me to believe you just walked away from that life and now hang out in small-town North Carolina. Well, pardon me if I just can't swallow that bull."

Wes strode into the room and stopped near the coffee table. Folding his arms he stared her down. "So, tell me, what's your big undercover expose?"

Before she could answer, the telephone rang. C.J. ignored it and advanced toward him.

"Do you know what I made the mistake of doing?"

He lifted one eyebrow and looked at her.

"I made the mistake of falling in love with you." C.J.'s laugh was filled with irony. "I guess it serves me right, though. The first time I fall in love, head over heels, and it's with somebody who doesn't have an ounce of compassion in him."

"Compassion!" he thundered. "You're accusing me of not having compassion. You belong to a profession that not only doesn't know the meaning of the word, but makes sure that any ounce of it that might accidentally slip by and get in a newspaper or television report, gets suitably trounced in short order."

She continued as if he hadn't spoken. "For so many years, people would ask me how could I pour so much emotion and compassion in my stories. The answer was simple. I stole all of it from my own life and breathed it into the words that eventually landed me the top prize."

"C.J., this is Max." They both stopped talking and turned toward the answering machine on C.J.'s kitchen counter. "Listen, I know what you said. I know what we agreed to. But David Woods told me about the story you're working on and gave me this number. C.J., please, don't take it to the *Post.* Give me a call, okay. You know the number."

C.J. winced. Of all the times for her old editor to call. She should have known David would take tall tales back but this wasn't something she'd bargained on. Especially not at this moment.

She turned to look at Wesley. Then she got a good look at what he held in his hand: the newspaper clips about him and Marcus Kensington.

She shook her head to deny the cold accusation in his eyes, to refute the damning evidence right before her eyes.

"It's not what you think, Wesley," she whispered.

"What is it you think I think?"

She had no words for him. She could tell him the truth, that she'd been curious. But he would spin that to his own way of thinking and make her honest curiosity about the Kensington case a bad thing. The circumstantial evidence was stacked against her. She *looked* guilty. The silence between them grew then became unbearable.

"Well, I guess that answers that," he said.

Flinging the papers toward her, he stalked her. His smile was cold. "It was all a game to you, wasn't it? Were you betting that I'd invite you home?" Wes swore in such a rage that C.J. did back up two steps.

"I took you to Mama Lo's house. I exposed my family to you. You had a hidden microphone on you the whole time, didn't you? What's the story you're working on? Is your big investigative piece on the grieving family six months after the tragedy? Is that the kind of story that won you the Pulitzer? Do you specialize in human suffering and grief?"

C.J. called on all the reserve she'd built within herself during her time in Serenity Falls. She'd chosen the town because she had been in search of serenity. There was a time in the not too distant past when she'd have been in his face matching him temper for temper, cuss word for cuss word. But what was the point? He would believe what he wanted to believe. Like so many others before it, this storm would pass if she kept her wits about her, if she looked for the serenity that dwelled within her.

Bracing her back, she stood before him. "Wesley, I know you're angry and I know it feeds your anger to feel like a victim now. I have never done anything to hurt you."

Wesley walked around her as if he were inspecting a prime cut of beef at a butcher auction. "You know, you've got a body and a half on you. I'm glad I got myself a taste." His almost jovial tone belied the cruel words. "It isn't often a man gets to meet a woman who prostitutes herself for a byline. You come awfully cheap. You need to tell those newspaper editors of yours to pay you more money. Or do you do your buddy Max like you did me down by the riverside?"

C.J. clinched her eyes shut. Every word felt like a physical blow on her already emotionally beaten body. She'd hate him if she could, but his vicious words echoed too loudly in her ears the same thoughts she'd had about herself. C.J. wrapped her arms around her body to keep within her the scream that threatened to erupt. She turned away from him.

"And to think, I was ready to turn my life upside down for you. I thought you were a hooker or a gang leader's girlfriend." Then, a question, "You know what?"

C.J. didn't bother to answer.

He grabbed her arm and turned her to face him. His mouth crushed hers, the kiss a cruel punishment. Standing stoically under him, she refused to open her mouth. He sought to dominate her. C.J. couldn't deny his superior physical strength. She'd seen how effortlessly he'd grabbed and twisted Eileen's wrist.

When he finally released her, C.J. knew her mouth was swollen and bruised.

"I wish you had been a whore," he said. "At least then I'd know there was a chance of you having a heart."

Unblinking, she stared at him, the heaviness of her heart reflected in the sadness in her eyes.

She wanted to cry but wouldn't give him the satisfaction of her tears. She knew she'd gotten exactly what she deserved. If not for her perceived sin and infraction in Wesley's eyes, for the countless times when she had been in the wrong and flaunted either herself or the First Amendment to get a story. Chickens come home to roost, her mother always said. C.J. understood the statement—now, when it was too late to repair the damage already done.

Humiliated and defeated, C.J. soundlessly turned away from him. She didn't have the energy or the desire to fight him. All she wanted to do was get away. She left him standing in her living room. From a small bowl on a bookshelf she plucked up the stone she'd taken as a souvenir the night she left Baltimore. Hoisting the duffel bag over her shoulder, she walked out her front door without looking back.

Wes stood in the middle of the floor wondering why the sense of euphoria and self-righteous vindication he should have felt was nowhere to be found. As a matter of fact, he was actually feeling kind of sick to his stomach. He looked down and saw his brother's smiling face look up at him from a police department studio photo. He picked the picture up and stared at it.

"Why Marc? Why?"

But the photocopied picture did not have an answer to the why that held so many questions.

She hadn't railed, she hadn't screamed. She'd simply said it wasn't what he thought . . . and that she loved him.

Wesley's lip turned up. "Yeah, right. She probably doesn't know the meaning of the word. The only thing she loves is her name on top of a story."

Even as he said the words, Wes could hear and feel the hollowness in the charge. He wasn't about to back down, though. She'd lied to him over and over again. Jesus, she'd even slept with him to get a story. How low would these reporters go?

He conveniently ignored the fact that he was the one who initially pursued her. He was the one who had insisted she go to West Virginia. But, he argued to himself, she'd known he was a man and would be incapable of resisting what she willingly threw at him or what she withheld.

Wes frowned, not quite buying his own rationalizing.

When he heard a vehicle gun up and peel away down the street, he went to the door. He'd parked behind a Cherokee with Maryland tags. It was gone. C.J. was gone.

Wes searched himself trying to see if he cared. He didn't.

C.J. Mayview who ran around with the arias Jan Langley didn't deserve his care or his love.

C.J., crying so hard she could barely see, made her way downtown. There were a couple of people she needed to say goodbye to: Mrs. Charleston at the lawn and garden store and Bettina at the bakery. Both had been incredibly kind to her during her brief sojourn in Serenity Falls.

"You never did find out if there's actually a falls that this place is named after." C.J. wiped her eyes when she realized it didn't matter how the town got its name. She was no longer a resident.

She put on a dab of lipstick to cover the bruise at her mouth. Wesley had kissed her so hard and in such anger that he'd drawn blood.

The garden store was her first stop but Mrs. Charleston was in Charlotte for the day a clerk told her. C.J. bought a small peace lily even though she felt more like the unlucky fly caught inside a venus fly trap. The peace lily would give her courage. Just like the plant, she'd grow and maybe flourish in her new home—wherever it might be.

She pulled the Cherokee to a stop in front of the bakery and got out. Contractors, busy clearing the rubble of the facade, said hello. She returned the greeting.

A closed sign hung in the door. C.J. peered through the glass panes. She knocked and a moment later, the chubby baker appeared dabbing her eyes with a paper tissue.

"Bettina, what's wrong?"

"Oh, hi, Miz Langley." She waved the tissue. "Nothing's wrong. Nothing at any rate that can be fixed."

C.J. looked dubious. "Are you sure?"

Bettina nodded. "I'm sure. I just got some sad news on the phone about a friend. I'll be all right. What can I do for you?"

"Well, I was just coming to say farewell. I'm leaving Serenity Falls."

"Leaving? You just moved here."

C.J.'s smile was sad. "I know. But it's time for me to put down somewhere else."

"I'd give you some of those chocolate brownies you like so much but I don't have anything left. I'm officially closed until the repairs are done." Bettina smiled. "Did you enjoy that chocolate swirl cheesecake your fellow brought for you?"

C.J.'s lower lip trembled. Had that just been yesterday? It seemed a lifetime ago. "Yes," she managed to get out. "It was wonderful like everything you make here."

"I wish you happiness wherever you go next. You write or call, okay?"

"Okay." C.J. and the baker hugged. Then C.J. left the store and climbed back into the Cherokee.

When she pulled from the curb, she didn't notice. the car following her.

CHAPTER 26

Margaret Shelley could afford to bide her time. They had to get through the police road blocks. This whole escaped prisoner thing was a drag. But then she smiled, realizing the bright side of it: All the cops would be focused on the escaped killer instead of the one who could do even greater damage.

Following two cars behind the Cherokee, Margaret hummed a little ditty. The prospect of doing someone bodily harm always put her in a good mood.

She glanced at her nails, done in a bright fuchsia polish. "Sure is going to be a shame to mess up this manicure though."

C.J. spread a map out over the steering wheel and dash. She could stay on the main roads, picking up Interstate 40 and then Interstate 77 South. Or she could meander her way through the little back roads and state highways.

Given her shattered emotional state, she figured it might be better to stick to the big roads where she wouldn't have to pay so much attention.

Inching through a roadblock, she thought about the encounter with the cops at the other one, and of Wesley's reaction when that TV reporter announced her identity. C.J. sighed.

An officer checked her license and registration, peered in the windows then waved her through.

Folding the map with one hand, she tucked it away and reached for her worry stone. A tiny bit of the surface had been worn smooth by her constant rubbing, particularly her first weeks alone in North Carolina. It would take a long, long time for the entire stone to be smooth.

"Just like it's going to take a long, long time for your heart to heal," she said.

Sighing again, she leaned forward and turned the radio on. Tuning beyond the all-talk news station, she settled on a country music station, the closest thing she could find to blues. After a few minutes, the somebody done me wrong songs got to her and she tuned the knob to mindless Top 40 music.

She drove for about twenty miles without thinking or feeling. Then she noticed a car that was following her too closely.

Impatiently, Wes waited while Scotty's computer did its thing. He would have killed for a cigarette.

"Bingo, Donovan," Scotty exclaimed on the other end of the line. "But you're not gonna like this."

"Just give it to me straight."

"I ran lots of combinations on the name. Your Margaret Shelley at one time was Margaret Shelton. She was also Peggy Shellaberg and Meg Shelton. And get this, when she worked for us she was Shelley Ann Grayson."

"What do you mean 'when she worked for us'?"

"Shelley Ann Grayson worked a year as a Deputy Marshal. Then she got kicked following a substantiated charge of excessive force and abuse of privilege."

"What?"

"I'm just reading you what NCIC spit out. You want it or not?"

"Keep reading," Wes said. The National Crime Information Center's incredible database had helped a lot of cops locate and then put a lot of scum bags behind bars.

"Lost her job, was put on probation for six months, and was never heard from again."

"Shelley Ann Grayson. I could swear that rings a bell. So what's with the aliases?"

"Fingerprints. Some small-time criminal stuff with vague links to organized crime, and a manslaughter conviction. Did her time on that, then poof! disappeared again."

"Grayson. Average height, fat, brown hair?" Jesus, if it was the same woman, he remembered her. They'd worked together once and she'd come on to him. He'd let her know he wasn't interested. Shortly after that, she was transferred. Or fired as it may have been.

He could hear Scotty keypunch.

"Um, not a bad looking woman. The agency pic is just head and shoulders though and it's several years old."

"Anything else from NCIC?"

"Has relatives in North Carolina," Scotty reported.

That was all Wes needed. "Scotty, man, I owe you one."

"Whatever happened with the other name you had me run? That Langley woman."

"It's a short, ugly story. I'll tell you about it over a beer."

Wes rang off with Scotty. Could Shelley Ann Grayson still be holding a grudge because he wouldn't sleep with her? The idea seemed ludicrous. Until he stopped to think about how many times he'd rebuffed Margaret at Miss Clara Ann's house. If Shelley Ann and Margaret were the same person, and deep inside Wes knew that to be the case, she'd have more reason now to want to strike out at him. She'd looked vaguely familiar but he never would have made this connection. The woman had lost a lot of weight, and done something to her hair and face. Margaret was an attractive woman in her own right, but she just didn't inspire the lust Jan Langley could stir up in him with just a look.

Jan. C.J.

Margaret. Shelley. Shelley Ann Grayson.

Wes swore out loud. His witness was safe, well on his way to a new place and a new identity. But Margaret was still on the loose. She'd apparently killed before. Was being spurned by him enough to make her kill again?

He didn't like the answer to his own question: Yes. Particularly if it was personal. He'd snubbed her again. A woman spurned could be a dangerous entity. Someone had already deliberately tried to run C.J. over. Had Margaret been driving that car?

Wes didn't know where to look first. C.J. was in danger and it was all his fault.

Then he remembered the roadblocks police had set up as a precaution in case the escaped con rolled through. Officers were checking every vehicle. C.J. was driving and would have passed through one of them at some point.

In her rearview mirror C.J. could see a woman with a bob haircut following her way too close for comfort. If she had to stop suddenly or even brake the other car would collide with hers.

"These nondrivers really get on my nerves," she said as she accelerated a bit to get some distance between her Cherokee and the woman's car.

But the woman stayed on her tail. C.J. frowned. Then gasped. That nut was going to hit her. The sedan ran so close up on her back bumper that C.J. swore out loud. Then, at the last moment, the car swerved to the left and came up alongside her. C.J. powered her window down to yell at the other driver.

The woman smiled, grinned, then pointed her index finger and thumb like a child pretending to shoot a gun.

Too late, C.J. remembered she was supposed to be searching for peace. Letting rude drivers get to her was something she was to have left in Baltimore. She powered the window back up, shook her head and watched as the other driver proceeded ahead of her in the left lane. The North Carolina license tags and a bumper sticker advertising the company proclaimed the car a rental.

Five minutes later though, C.J. swore. That same driver had drifted back and was at her side again. And once again the woman grinned and did the finger pointing thing.

Had C.J. been in her own car, the one she'd sold before moving south, she'd have used her cellular phone to call the cops on this nut case. As it was, all she could do was speed up and hope to lose the woman. It went against her grain though. C.J. had few idiosyncrasies. Driving the speed limit was one of them. While most drivers took posted speed limits as a suggestion instead of a rule, C.J. believed posted speed limits were there for safety reasons. In her early days as a reporter, she'd covered too many accidents involving high speeds to take lightly the damage cars could do to each other on the road.

Accelerating a bit, she eased ahead of the woman. She looked to the left and breathed a sigh of relief. The other car was gone. The relief was short-lived though. Right up on her back bumper was the woman in the blue sedan.

Wesley's hunch had played out. An officer remembered seeing both C.J. and Margaret pass through less than twenty minutes before.

With a Serenity Falls cop in a squad car backing him up, Wesley wheeled the Crown Victoria to the interstate. As he slapped a single blue flashing light on his dash, he prayed he wasn't already too late.

The speedometer hit sixty-five, then shot past seventy-five and eighty-five as Wes raced to catch C.J.

If his own pigheadedness caused her harm, he'd never forgive himself. When he stopped being angry at her and thought things through he realized she had already been in Serenity Falls when he arrived. Even if she had been a working journalist, no way would she have known he would be headed there. He hadn't even known until the last minute.

Wes swore out loud. With the squad car close behind, the Crown Victoria ate up the miles separating Wes from the woman he loved.

And love her he did. With everything in his being. She personally had not had anything to do with Marc's death. Every journalist wasn't like the one who'd gotten Marc killed. He had no right to judge C.J. the same way he judged that other scum.

"But she lied," argued the still angry part of him.

And you didn't let her explain, he shot back. How many times had she tried to tell you something, something she said was important only to have you cut her off with a kiss? If C.J. was guilty, he shared in that guilt.

The two police cars whizzed by the little traffic there was on a Monday afternoon. Wes glanced at the speedometer in his dash, the red bar beyond ninety now. He was driving way too fast but he could no more slow down than he could stop breathing or stop loving C.J. She was in danger and it was his fault for not recognizing Margaret.

C.J. looked at the plate of glass in front of her. The used Cherokee she'd bought didn't have an air bag. If she crashed or that woman ran her off the road and into something, there was going to be a lot of shattered glass.

She gripped the steering wheel and glanced in the rearview mirror.

A gun! The woman had a gun.

About five or six miles back she could see the flashing lights from police cars.

C.J., who didn't necessarily believe in God, hoped and prayed those cops were coming to rescue her.

She jerked forward at the sedan's first impact on her rear. She swerved to the left but the car stayed with her.

They passed a white Volkswagen. That driver ran off the side of the road when he saw the gun and the two cars practically attached to each other.

C.J. swerved to the right again but was quickly coming up on a tractor-trailer. A school bus chugged along in the left lane.

"Hurry up. Hurry up." She begged the driver as well as the police.

The sedan crashed into her bumper again. Then the woman pulled up alongside the Cherokee and hit the driver's side. The school bus pulled into the median and the trucker blew his horn.

C.J. chanced a quick glance out her side window. The woman aimed the gun at her. C.J. ducked, cussed, and slammed her foot on the accelerator. A bullet shattered the back passenger window.

"Oh, Jesus. Help me, please."

She leaned on the horn in a vain attempt to get the van driver ahead of her out of the way. She could hear the sirens from the cop cars now but a glance out her window told her the help had come too late. The Cherokee wouldn't go any faster and the woman, driving with one hand, had the gun pointed straight at her.

Wes swore and floored the Crown Victoria. The cop behind him must have radioed for backup because two state police cars were crossing the grassy median to join the chase.

He saw the first shot fired and helplessly watched the Cherokee swerve to the left and then the right.

"Hold on, baby. Don't lose your cool. I'm coming."

Seconds later he rammed into the back of the sedan. Margaret's gun went off. He knew the moment she recognized him behind her. She took her eyes off the road to aim at him. Her back window exploded from a hail of gunfire. Wes swerved to the right.

Too late, Margaret turned her attention back to the road. Rubber burned and tires screeched, but her last-second attempt to slow the impact was a failure. Margaret's car crashed into a guardrail and flipped over twice.

Wes looked for the Cherokee in front of him, but saw it in his rearview mirror. The state cops could take care of Margaret. He whipped the car in a U-turn and drove along the shoulder back to C.J.

Margaret's last wild shot had taken out C.J.'s left rear tire. Skids on the road surface were evidence that she tried not to hit the airport limousine van. But the van driver had either moved in the same direction or not been fast enough. The van sat in the middle of the roadway with a smashed in rear. The Cherokee's front end was crushed. The battered and bent Cherokee sat disabled and turned in the wrong direction in the road. Steam poured from under the hood.

Wes barely brought his car to a stop before he dashed out and ran to C.J.

He ripped the door open.

"No, God! Please no!"

The first thing he noticed was the blood. The second was that his heart had stopped beating.

CHAPTER 27

C.J. sat in the bed at Serenity Falls General Hospital and picked at the bandage on her forehead. The doctors said she'd have a headache for a while. This pain thing was getting old. Another bandage over her shoulder and left arm concealed the place where she'd been grazed by a bullet and cut by flying glass.

The last thing she'd remembered was pain shooting everywhere and crashing into that van. C.J. closed her eyes and prayed those people were all right.

At the knock on her hospital room door she opened her eyes. "Come in."

Wesley poked his head in. "Hi. Up for company?"

He was the last person she wanted to see. She turned her head away.

Ignoring the rebuff, Wesley came forward.

He thrust a bunch of flowers, red and yellow roses with baby's breath, at her. "I brought these for you."

She turned to face him, looked at the flowers and ignored them. "Why are you here? You made it perfectly clear what you thought of me. Just go away and leave me the hell alone."

"C.J., please. Hear me out. I'm sorry for the things I said. I know I hurt you. I'm sorry."

"And you think some flowers will make it all better?"

The ice and the hurt in her voice cut through Wesley. He deserved it though. She'd almost died because of him. It wasn't until he'd lost her that he realized how terribly wrong and unfair he'd been. Now it was looking like she had no forgiveness in her. Frankly, Wes didn't blame her.

"Please, C.J., take the flowers. I'm sorry."

"Oh, so now it's C.J. I distinctly remember being called let's see, a parasite, a muckraker, and a whore. I think you covered all the bases. Get lost Donovan."

She reached for a pillow to prop behind her back but Wes was there, fretting, assisting. She flinched away from him.

"Are you comfortable now? Do you want a drink of water? Should I call a nurse?"

"I'm going to call security if you don't leave me alone. I don't have anything else to say to you."

"Well, fine," he fired back. "Just shut up and listen to me then."

C.J. glared at him. She looked away for a moment then forced herself to look him in the eye. Why *was* he here? He'd made it painfully clear exactly where they stood and what he thought of her as a person. Somehow, someway, someday she'd get over the pain of loving him and losing him.

Realizing that harsh words and anger weren't going to carry him very far, Wesley changed his approach. He couldn't afford to mess this up.

He handed the flowers to her again. "Would you please accept these as a token of my regret for what I said in anger?"

C.J. accepted the flowers and inhaled their rich scent.

"Thank you," she said.

Taking that as encouragement, he pulled up a chair and sat close. Taking her hand in his large one, he pressed a kiss to the back of her hand. C.J. pulled her hand away and tucked it under the hospital blanket.

Wes winced at the rejection. "C.J., please forgive me. Can you find it in your heart to forgive me? I said some things to you and did some things I regret. I know I no longer deserve your love and I won't blame you one bit if you hate me. But do you think you could, maybe with some time, find it in your heart to forgive me? Please."

C.J. smiled sadly. "You told the truth as you see it. I'm the one who should be asking for forgiveness, Wes. I wasn't totally honest with you, or for that matter, with anyone in Serenity Falls. What I told you was true. I quit my job at the newspaper because I no longer wanted to do what I'd been doing."

She picked at a yellow rose petal. "The why and wherefore's of that aren't really important now. Just suffice it to say journalism had stopped being fun for me long before I won the Pulitzer. I sold my condo, my furniture, and my car and gave most of my clothes away and came down here to find myself. I was in search of peace and serenity and was on my way to South Carolina to try to find it when that woman started shooting at me."

"About that woman . . .

She silenced him with a finger over his lips "Shhh. Let me finish then you can explain." When Wes nodded and looked down, she continued.

"What I discovered in those last minutes when I knew it was all over for me on that highway was that you can't run to peace. You have to find it within yourself wherever you happen to be. And you can't control who you fall in love with. You just have to deal with the cards you're dealt."

"And of love?"

"What about it? Love is for fools and people who can afford the luxury of a foolish emotion."

Wes watched her. "I don't believe you. And I don't think you believe that either."

C.J.'s answering smile was tentative. "Well, there's this sexy dark warrior I bumped into on the street the other day. I've been wondering if he's available."

Wes smiled and relaxed. "He is. About that name. How did you know?"

"Know what?" she asked.

"That Dark Warrior is my code name"

"Code name? You people really use those things?" At his hesitant nod she smiled indulgently. "The first time I saw you on that motorcycle, all I could think of was you in a sheik's outfit or in the ceremonial robes of an ancient Saharan warrior king. Dark Warrior."

"That's what made me think you were in the Witness Security Program."

"Who was shooting at me, Wes?"

"Her name's Margaret Shelley. She used to be a Deputy U.S. Marshal but got kicked out. She's in custody now, charged with an arm's length of things including attempted capital murder. The man she hired to run you down sang like a bird to cut a deal."

"I don't even know the woman. Why was she after me?"

Wes smiled to himself. Holloway did his best work as a spin doctor. He'd already put the appropriate and plausible explanations out to the media. Margaret was going to be in prison for a long, long time. Only she, Wesley, and Holloway would ever know that Margaret had been behind the explosion at the recycling plant, and that the car crashing through the bakery window had been to scare the witness. In her few days in the town, Margaret had picked up on Yancey's habits and favorite hangouts. Stalking him had been part of her game plan.

As far as the service and Wesley was concerned, everything else that had happened could be chalked up to a woman spurned . . . or just plain coincidence in small-town North Carolina.

"She had a grudge against me and that's why she went after you. She figured out how much you meant to me."

"What are you saying?"

He took the flowers from her lap, placed them on the bed then took her free hand in his.

"I'm saying I love you no matter what your name is, no matter how you earn a living."

"What about your brother's death? I'm not now and I was never working on any story, Wes. I was simply curious about the little you and your family said about Marcus. I might be retired from daily journalism but I'm still a reporter."

"When I saw you unconscious at that steering wheel with blood all over the place I was able to put things in perspective. Marcus is gone. I can better serve his memory by thinking about the good times we shared growing up rather than how he died. That doesn't mean I'm going to instantly declare a love fest with reporters. I'm just going to judge each person on his or her own merits. Marc left behind two beautiful children. I'm the godfather," he said proudly.

"Those kids need to grow up without the bitterness the rest of the family has. It's going to take some time." He paused, then looked into her eyes. "I have a journalist in mind who might teach me the error of my ways."

"Oh, really? What's his name?"

Wes grinned. "I love you, C.J. . . . Jan . . . Ja'Niece. Now what exactly is your name?"

C.J. hit him with a pillow then sank into the mattress when his welcoming weight settled over her. Their kiss held promise and hope for tomorrow.

"Hey, C.J.?" Wes murmured as his lips feathered across hers.

"Hmm?"

"Let's go fishing just as soon as they spring you from this joint."

C.J.'s laughter echoed through the room then swiftly changed to a soft moan when Wes buried his head in her neck and demonstrated how he planned to love her forever.